RED RAIN

www.**transworldbooks**.co.uk

For more information on R.L. Stine and his books,
see his website at www.rlstine.com

RED RAIN

R.L. Stine

Doubleday

LONDON · TORONTO · SYDNEY · AUCKLAND · JOHANNESBURG

TRANSWORLD PUBLISHERS
61–63 Uxbridge Road, London W5 5SA
A Random House Group Company
www.transworldbooks.co.uk

Originally published in the United States of America in 2012
by Touchstone, a division of Simon & Schuster, Inc.

First published in Great Britain in 2012
by Doubleday, an imprint of Transworld Publishers

A CIP catalogue record for this book
is available from the British Library.

ISBN 9780857521392 (cased)
9780857521378 (tpb)

Add   UK

The Random   ncil (FSC®),
the leading in   ying the FSC
label are pri   ion scheme
endorsed by tl   e. Our paper
procure   onment

MIX
Paper from
responsible sources
FSC
www.fsc.org   FSC® C016897

Typeset in Sabon Lt Std Roman, 11.5/15.25

Printed and bound in Great Britain by Clays Ltd, St Ives plc

2 4 6 8 10 9 7 5 3 1

For Jane

But Zeus sent from heaven a show'r of blood stain'd rain.
In sign of many a warrior's coming doom
—The Iliad

Prologue

By morning, the hurricane had passed. But not before destroying every home, every building, every life on the island.

Lea lowered her hand from her eyes and waited for them to adjust to the yellow-gray glare. The light reminded her of a sickroom, a hospital room, that chilling light that carries no warmth at all.

No clouds in the sky, but the sun was hidden, lost behind the swirling dust and mist and chunks of dirt that clogged the air.

The light feels dirty.

Now, two dogs began to wail. Not in pain. Howling a mournful song. Sharing the horror of what they saw.

Lea took one step, then another, concentrating on keeping her balance.

Stay on solid ground. Don't stumble and fall off the edge of the earth, into the ragged piles of death. Keep moving and you won't be buried here.

Lea's thoughts were a jumble. No way to straighten them out, not with the dogs howling and the children crying, and the corpses all witnesses, all of them, lying so still and watching the living in silent accusation.

Her sandals sank into a deep puddle of cold water. She kept walking. Ahead of her, she could hear the rush and roar of the waves. She was walking to the beach without realizing it.

The winds and thundering rains had burrowed deep trenches in the sand. Lea stumbled and slogged through them, not seeing them, paying no attention to the mud and wet sand that invaded the bottoms of her jeans and clung like wet plaster to her legs.

The sweaty mist carried by the wind off the raging waves didn't revive her. It seemed to blind her even more, as if she were stepping into a whirling, warm cloud, swallowed by it, vanishing. The roar drowned out the howls of the dogs. Drowned out everything, even its own sound. A kind of noisy hollow silence Lea never knew existed.

The beach was soaked and soft, *soft as quicksand,* she thought. And as her sandals sank deep into the muck, she pictured herself sinking down . . . down . . . until she disappeared forever into a dark, quiet world.

In the water, a canoe bobbed crazily, upside-down. Something pale and flimsy tossed on the waves. Was it a sail? A bedsheet?

Something crunched beneath Lea's sandal. She stopped with a gasp. She pictured a human hand. "Oh no."

She lowered her eyes to the sand. Tentacles. A pile of wriggling creatures. She jumped back. Struggled to keep her balance. No. They weren't moving.

Salt air off the ocean made her eyes water. When she could finally focus, she recognized them. Starfish. Dozens of them. Stiff and already dry. A pile of a hundred dead starfish, trailed by hundreds more, a long line all down the shore. They must have been washed from the sea by the storm.

Lea bent to examine them. She had never seen so many starfish. Never imagined so many would travel together. Travel together to their deaths.

She picked one up. Prickly. Nearly as hard as a seashell. She turned it over in her hand. The arms so stiff. As if it had never been alive. She dropped it onto the pile.

This has to be a symbol of bad luck.

But how can the luck get any worse?

She was still leaning down, her eyes trailing the long line of starfish corpses, when she felt the first warm drop on the back of her neck. She brushed it away with the palm of her hand and stood up.

A high wave crashed onto the beach, more violent than the others, sending up a spray of white foam before retreating. Lea felt another warm drop, this time on her forehead.

She took a step back from the ocean, shoes squishing on the mucky sand. A soft patter made her gaze around.

It had started to rain. She felt a few warm taps on the top of her head, another on her forehead. She raised a palm and felt warm raindrops on her skin.

Gazing up, she saw only white glare. No rain clouds. But the raindrops made a *pit-pit-pit* sound on the sand all around her. And the shoulders of her sweater were already wet. And her hair—

She uttered a soft cry and squinted into the falling rain. Something strange. Something not right. Like the dead starfish all gathered in a line on the shore.

Something wrong with this rain. The brightness of the sky and the darkness of the raindrops . . .

Very wrong.

Lea began to shiver. So unnatural. The darkness of the raindrops . . .

As the storm grew stronger, it became easier to see that the raindrops were red. A shimmering deep scarlet.

"Holy shit," she murmured. "It's raining *blood*!"

She raised both palms and watched the red raindrops bounce onto her skin. Fascinated and horrified, she didn't move. Stared at her hands as the red drops trickled down her palm. She lifted her eyes to the raindrops falling all around her.

Red . . . As if the blood of all who had died here last night was raining down on her. The blood of all the victims pouring doom over the island, a final terrifying drenching good-bye.

It soaked her hair and poured down her face. Bloodred raindrops pattering down from a cloudless sky. *A blood rain.*

Where had she heard that phrase before?

Yes. She had read about a blood rain in southern India several years ago. For real. The sky had opened up and red rain poured down on a village. And the people were terrified. Lea remembered.

They were frightened that the red rain was the onset of the world's end.

Now sheets of rain fell, driven by the gusting winds off the ocean. *Like red curtains, blowing and parting and closing again.*

Yes. Red curtains of rain all around her.

So wrong. So unnatural and wrong.

And as the billowing blood curtains appeared to part, two boys came stepping out. Two blond-haired boys with bright blue eyes, walking solemnly side by side.

Identical blond boys, wavy hair brushed straight back off their broad, gleaming foreheads, bare-chested and barefoot, wearing only ragged, torn white shorts stained by the red raindrops.

Their faces glowed pink. Not a healthy pink but a reflection of the red rain falling around them. They gazed straight ahead at Lea, unblinking, faces drawn, their expressions stern, wooden, unreadable.

Angels, she thought, unable to move, forced to stare back at them. *Like blond angels.*

Two angels floating out from a curtain of blood and horror.

How strange to see these two rays of light appear from all this darkness. Strange even for this island of mystery.

Pale chests and arms, white as angel feathers. Hands tucked into the pockets of their stained shorts.

Glowing figures, they moved in unison, walking together lightly over the soaked sand. Blue eyes locked on Lea. Closer.

Until Lea was forced to cut the spell. She blinked a few times. Then, squinting harder at them, she called out, shouting over the roar of the dark rain, "Can I help you?"

PART ONE

Two Days Earlier

1

BLOG POST
BY LEA HARMON SUTTER
Travel_Adventures.com

(April 10) Well, here I am on this island everyone calls mysterious and frightening, and I hope you are as curious as I am to find out if any of the stories are true. I tend to be skeptical. I have a bunch of older brothers who loved making up stories to terrify me, and I quickly learned not to believe any scary story anyone ever told me.

I suppose it's odd to begin a travel blog by saying that no one comes here. But before I can begin to describe the unique charms and dark mystique of Cape Le Chat Noir, I really have to start with that fact.

No one comes here.

Of course, no one really believes the island is cursed. But there are too many frightening stories from its past to ignore. The dozens of Spanish ships that mysteriously sank off the island shores in the 1600s? The rumors of dark-magic rituals? The stories—that many believe to this day—of the living dead walking the island in broad daylight?

If you are an adventure traveler like me, those all seem like *good* things!

But the fact is, no one has paid much attention to this island of whitewashed shacks, tall pine forests, fishing villages, and eccentric islanders—despite the fact that you can almost reach out and touch the place from the Outer Banks beaches of South Carolina.

Located a hop, skip, and a splash from the Cape Hatteras National Seashore, vacationers have avoided Cape Le Chat Noir like—shall I say it?—a black cat crossing their path.

For you history nerds, here's the 411: The island was annexed by the English sometime around 1650. They had little interest in it. Too small and too far from the mainland. Most English settlers chose the Roanoke Colony to the north (and we all know how that worked out).

Small groups of nomadic American Indians found their way to the island. Spanish pirates arrived later, sometimes unhappily, because they watched their ships go down just offshore.

Yes, this part of the ocean is known as the Graveyard of the Atlantic. You can Google it. Don't bother to look for a *reason* why all the ships sank. No one can tell you. But this was the beginning of the island's bad reputation.

When French traders arrived and heard the stories, they gave the island its unlucky name. I haven't been able to find out what they were trading. Most likely rum or some concoction like it. The islanders I've met seem to drink from morning till night. And if that's your idea of travel adventure, go ahead—pack your bags.

I've saved the best (or worst) for last. Here's the most interesting historical detail—and it's definitely creepy. Especially with frightening forecasts of a big hurricane heading this way.

I don't want to talk about the hurricane now. I'm pretending it's not going to happen.

You see, Le Chat Noir was devastated by one of the most powerful storms in hurricane history. It was the Labor Day Hurricane of 1935. And I have every finger crossed that history is not going to repeat itself now.

I heard the story of that dreadful hurricane shortly after arriving at Cape Le Chat Noir and stepping off the bouncing, wooden dock. Believe me, folks—it did not exactly make me feel as if a welcome mat had been put out for me.

The jeep-taxi to take me to my hotel was late. Squinting in the bright sunshine, I glanced around. The dock area seemed to be deserted, except for two ragged-looking fishermen setting off in a tiny flat-bottomed skiff. Definitely no official tourist greeter waiting with a rum punch or even a friendly smile.

I spotted a tiny brown shack across the dirt road with the sign *Tea Shop*. So, with suitcase, laptop case, and camera in hand, I made my way there to wait for my ride.

Inside, the room was dimly lit, with red neon lights over the mirror at a bar and small gas lamps on each table. The tables were round cylinders, like conga drums. Wall posters from tea companies provided the only cheeriness. I liked a poster that showed a grinning Chinese child holding a big steaming cup, and the words *How Long Since You OOLONG?*

The place was totally empty. I took a seat at a table near the bar. I coughed, hoping it might summon someone from in back. A wooden overhead fan squeaked as it slowly made its rounds.

An old woman emerged—white bristly hair under a black bandanna, pale skin tight over her cheekbones, silvery gray eyes, a little hunched over. She wore a long black dress, not exactly island wear. Without asking, she set a cup of dark tea down on my table with quavering hands.

"Thank you." My voice sounded muffled in the heavy air of the tiny room. The squeaking fan seemed to grow louder.

"Why have you come?" Her voice was velvety smooth, much younger than her looks. Not exactly a friendly hello, huh, folks?

I stammered an answer about writing a travel story about Le Chat Noir.

"There's a big storm on the way," she said. "Hurricane Ernesto. Didn't you hear about it?" She had no accent at all. Her eyes were so glassy, I thought she might be blind. But then I remembered she had set the teacup down on the little table with ease.

"Yes. My husband warned me not to come here in hurricane season," I said, inhaling the bitter steam from the cup.

Mark is so sweet. He always wants me to stay home. But exploring my backyard would make for a dull travel blog, don't you agree?

Well, to cut to the chase, the woman told me her name was Marguerite. She procured her own cup of tea, sat down across from me, stared unblinkingly into my eyes, and began to talk in her smooth whisper of a voice.

"The hurricane of 1935 didn't have a name. They didn't name them then. But it didn't need a name to be remembered."

I blew on the cup, then sipped the tea. "You mean it was a bad one?"

She nodded. Her throat made a rattling sound. I pretended not to notice.

"The storm showed no mercy. It swept over the Outer Banks, up to Chincoteague Island and the Virginia coast, flattening everything in its path. Nothing was left standing on this island. Not a house, not a shack, not a bait shop, not a teahouse. All shattered. All ruined. Even the lighthouse on the south shore was toppled over, into the ocean."

I tsk-tsked. "That's horrible."

"My friends . . . people I knew, members of my family . . . Many were crushed, buried, drowned. I was a child. I saw the corpses. They were floating in lakes and rivulets caused by the storm. Even at my age, I knew the horror. I knew the pain, the suffering. No one could decide where to pile the bodies. They lay sprawled in the sand and sea grass and on piles of wreckage. The corpses . . . They were feasted on for days by seagulls and starving dogs."

She took a long sip of tea. Her throat rattled as she swallowed. She gripped the cup with both hands, I guess, because her hands were so shaky.

I felt a shiver go down my back. The story was terrifying and sad, but her whispered voice made it even more frightening. I had to remind myself that this took place in 1935.

"I was a child but the pictures never faded from my eyes. The island was devastated. Turned to rubble. But it took only *weeks* to rebuild Le Chat Noir. Why? Because of a miracle. You might not call it a miracle, dear. You might call it a *nightmare*."

She waited for me to react. Her silvery eyes still hadn't blinked.

I set down the cup. "What do you mean? What kind of nightmare?"

She swallowed. She leaned closer, close enough for me to see the thick layer of powder on her tight cheeks. "Le Chat Noir returned to normal in weeks. Because the *old* dead—the dead from centuries past—came back to life. All the dead of the island returned to help rebuild it. No eyes, flesh rotting, bones yellowed and broken, they floated up from their flooded graves and went to work. They joined the survivors to bury the recent dead and restore and rebuild Le Chat Noir.

"When the job was done, did they return to their graves? No. The dead were proud of their handiwork. And they enjoyed the sunlight. It healed them and made them look almost normal, so normal most of them could blend in with the living. They decided to stay."

I squinted at her. "The dead? The dead people stayed?"

She nodded, her expression solemn. She reached across the table and squeezed my hand. Her hand was dry and hard, like solid bone. "That's what makes Le Chat Noir special, dear. It's the only place on earth where the living share their space with the living dead."

I glanced down at my empty teacup. The tea leaves on the bottom appeared to form an X. Of course I didn't believe Marguerite's story. But it left me feeling strange, kind of cold and tingly.

She smiled for the first time. Her smile cracked the powder on her cheeks. Placing both hands on the table, she pushed herself to her feet. "I see you are thinking about my story."

I nodded. "Yes. It's . . . frightening."

Her smile faded. "Not that frightening, dear. I died ten years ago, but I'm doing pretty well. Can I bring you another cup of tea?"

My mouth dropped open.

A dry laugh, more like a cough, escaped her throat. "I'm only teasing you. I see your ride is outside. Enjoy your stay on our beautiful island."

2

Lea sat on the edge of the bed, smoothing her hands over the tropical-colored, flowery quilt, letting the warm sea breezes tickle her face. The lace curtains fluttered at the open window of the rooming house. White and yellow daisies floated in a glass bowl of water on the bed table beside her.

The small, second-floor room was bright with afternoon sunlight spreading across the blond-wood floor, and spotlessly crisp and clean with a vague aroma of coconut in the air. Red and blue starfish dotted the wallpapered walls, appropriate since the place was called Starfish House.

The two-story, shingled house with a sloping red-tile roof stood on a low, grassy dune overlooking the Eastern shore beach and a row of white fishing huts along the water.

Is this the calm before the storm? Lea wondered. *Or has Hurricane Ernesto changed its course?*

She didn't want to check. She didn't want to spoil her first day.

She could hear the hushed voices of her hosts drift upstairs from the front desk. An hour before, when the jeep-taxi dropped her off at the front door, they had both come bursting out, clapping their hands and speaking rapidly and excitedly in French, almost dancing around Lea and her two bags.

Maybe they are just warm, excitable people, she thought. *But they're really acting as if I'm their first guest.*

Macaw Henders and her husband, Pierre. They owned the six-room inn. She was a big woman, Spanish-looking, with cocoa skin, round, black eyes and straight black bangs across a broad forehead.

She wore an expansive red-and-fuchsia housedress with feathery sleeves and collar and a red bandanna over her hair. Lea had to suppress a laugh since it really did look like bird plumage.

In contrast, Pierre was as thin as a pencil, balding, with brown eyes deep-set in a serious face. One of those people who always looks worried, Lea figured. No way to determine how old he was. He could be thirty or fifty.

A soft knock at the doorway startled Lea from her thoughts. She stood up as Macaw appeared, holding a tray with a white china cup. She handed the cup to Lea. Lea gazed down at a foamy, dark brown drink. She expected the cup to be hot, but it was cold.

Macaw smiled, revealing a gold cap on one front tooth. "Go ahead, Madame Sutter. A welcome drink. Take a small sip to start." She spoke in a lilting singsong.

Lea took a small sip, then another. Coffee with vodka? No. But definitely potent and sour. She could feel the warmth slide down her throat, into her chest.

"Macaw, what is this drink called?"

The woman hesitated. She ruffled her feathery housedress, much like a preening macaw. "Kill-Devil," she said finally, lowering her eyes.

Lea laughed and gazed into the cup. "Kill-Devil? Do you know why?"

"Because it's powerful enough to kill the Devil?"

Lea took another sip. She was starting to like the bitter taste. "This is a lovely room," she said, gesturing with her free hand. And then blurted out without really thinking about it, "Am I the only one staying here?"

The woman nodded.

"But, why?"

Macaw's smile faded. She pretended to be interested in something on the tray. "I guess they have their reasons, Madame Sutter."

3

(April 11) The bad news is that Ernesto still has its sights on Le Chat Noir. The hurricane is slow-moving, about fourteen miles per hour, which is even more bad news, because the longer it stays in one place, the more damage it does.

The only good news is that it gives me a little time to find some kind of adventure to write about before I have to duck and hide.

I'm writing this post on my iPad. I can feel the emergency vibes. People are boarding up their windows and pulling their boats on-shore. The sky has turned an ugly lead color, and the wind feels heavy and damp.

My hosts, Macaw and Pierre, were reluctant to let me leave the house. I'm not sure they understood that my job is to go out and do risky things so I can write about them.

I'd been in touch (by email) with a woman who lives on Le Chat Noir, named Martha Swann. Martha told me about an island ceremony called *Revenir*, which is French for "to come back." She explained that the *Revenir* ritual is part of a practice called *Mains*

Magiques—Magic Hands. She believed the French traders picked it up somewhere and brought it here with them. Martha wrote that it is a must-see.

I told my hosts I wanted to attend a *Revenir* ceremony, and they reacted not with horror but with definite disapproval. They both started shaking their heads, as if it would persuade me to drop the idea.

"It's all a fake," Macaw insisted. "They put on a show. The priest—he performs it every week."

"It's bad for the island," Pierre agreed. His eyes took on a sadness. "These magic rituals, they make us look foolish. Primitive."

"Why scare the people away?" Macaw said. "Why not talk about the beauty here? The natural beauty. Not the *unnatural*."

"I know it isn't real," I said. "I'm not going to write that it's real. But I think my readers will find it interesting. You know. It's all about life and death, right? It's been practiced for hundreds of years. It's so . . . colorful."

"We don't want to be colorful," Macaw said in her red-and-fuchsia dress.

After a lot of begging and pleading and explaining, they finally agreed to find a guide to take me to the ceremony.

He turned out to be a sandy-haired, boyish, tanned young man in khaki cargo shorts and safari jacket, who seemed so shy and spoke so softly I never did figure out what language he was using. I believe his name was Jean-Carl. He always looked away when he spoke to me, as if he was ashamed of his job or where he was taking me.

He drove me in an open jeep over the one single-lane paved road that leads to the center of the island. The road was lined on both sides by amazing cabbage palmettos. Their clusters of long leaves gleamed, even in the darkening light of the sky. Talk about magic! The trees were flowering, the yellow-white blossoms flashing by like tiny lights.

I didn't see any other car traffic. Jean-Carl parked the jeep in the shade of a clump of palms at the edge of a sandy path, and we began to walk, the soft sand tickling my feet as it flowed over my open sandals.

I tried to ask Jean-Carl questions about what I could expect to see. But again, he seemed embarrassed or else just painfully unsuited to his job. He kept repeating the word *scary* and shaking his head.

Of course, that only heightened my anticipation. And when we reached a small crowd of people—men and women of indeterminate age in colorful beach caftans and robes—I was ready for my *Mains Magiques* adventure.

4

Lea estimated twenty people in the crowd, mostly men. They stood at the edge of the thick rain forest, inside a circle of the strangest palm trees she'd ever seen. "What are those trees called?" she asked Jean-Carl.

He gazed at them, blinking a few times. He didn't answer.

What a great guide. I don't think he speaks English.

A well-dressed, middle-aged woman with pink cheeks, short blond hair, and pale blue eyes turned to Lea. "They are called jelly palms, dear."

Lea studied the very fat trunks topped by long, delicate leaves that looked like feathers. "Y'all can make jelly from the dates," the woman said. She had a definite Southern accent. "The dates are big and juicy and very sweet." Then her eyes went wide. "Are you Lea? From Long Island? I'm Martha Swann."

Lea gasped. "Martha? Really? Hi. How did you recognize me?"

"From your Facebook photo. I feel like we're old friends."

"Wow! I mean, wow. How nice to meet you. See? I took your advice. I'm here. I always think these rituals are a hoot, don't you? They're almost always like from a bad horror movie. Hope I don't burst out laughing."

Martha pursed her lips. "I don't think y'all will laugh at this one." She glanced around. "My husband, James, and I come often. It's . . . really miraculous. We've even gotten to know the priest." She raised a finger to her lips. "Look. I think it's starting."

Lea turned and stepped forward, into the circle of people. They had gathered around a fallen log, smooth-barked, about ten feet long. A sun-bleached skull was placed in the center. *A human skull. No. It's an animal head. A goat, maybe.*

She turned to Jean-Carl to ask, but he had moved away to the other end of the log. She mopped her forehead with the back of one hand. The center of the island felt much steamier than the outer beach areas. She suddenly found it hard to breathe.

These weird ceremonies make me giddy.

She listened to the buzz of quiet conversations. Two older men in white robes and sandals appeared to be having an argument. A woman in a blue chiffon caftan stepped between them.

The crowd grew larger. Now there were maybe forty people standing in the circle around the log. Lea hadn't seen them approaching. They seemed to have emerged from the trees.

She turned and saw five people striding quickly on the path. Four of them were obviously American tourists. The two men were paunchy and pale and wore blue-and-red Chicago Cubs baseball caps. One wore a Budweiser T-shirt with a beer can emblazoned across the front.

The two women with them were slender and dressed in shorts and flowery tank tops. They had cameras hanging around their necks and were being led by a tall, serious-looking guide, dressed in khaki cargo shorts and safari jacket, like Jean-Carl.

Lea was startled. Actual tourists on Cape Le Chat Noir! She had the urge to say hello. To interview them and ask how they came to be on the island and if they knew what this ritual was about. But their guide led them to the other side of the circle.

People talked quietly, but the conversations ended when the priest—a tall, bald man wearing a long red robe tied with a yellow sash—stepped out from behind a fat-trunked jelly palm. He had a red face and shocking white-blond eyebrows that moved up and down on his broad forehead like furry caterpillars. His eyes were silvery gray, metallic. He had a tattoo of a blue five-cornered star on the crown of his bald head, almost big enough to be a skullcap.

Weird-looking dude.

He stepped into the circle, carrying a long wooden tray. On the tray were coconut halves, flat side up. Without uttering a word, he stepped up to people and raised the tray to them, offering a coconut half. Lea quickly realized that he was approaching only the men in the circle.

He handed coconut halves to six men. She could see that the insides had been carved to form a cup, and each cup contained a dark liquid. It looked a lot like the Kill-Devil drink Macaw had given her when she arrived the day before.

Lea felt a chill as the priest eyed her for a long moment. She couldn't read his expression. He flashed her an almost imperceptible smile. Then he moved to the center of the circle and gazed at the men holding the coconut cups.

"It's the Black Drink," Martha murmured in her ear. She leaned close and whispered surreptitiously, as if she was breaking a rule. "The Black Drink. Be grateful, dear. In the ceremony, the priest gives it only to the men."

"Why?" Lea whispered back.

Again, Martha raised a finger to her lips. Her eyes flashed in the gray afternoon light. She returned her gaze to the priest.

Lea glanced down the line to the tourists. All four of them were busily snapping photos with their cameras and phones.

The red-robed priest gave a signal, and the six men raised their coconut cups high above their heads, as if offering them to the sun. They all chanted something . . . in French?

Lea struggled to understand. She had studied French for two years at Northwestern. But this didn't sound like any French she'd ever heard.

When the six men finished, the priest chanted for a long time, mumbling to himself and moving his hands slowly in a strange sign language. The sleeves of his robe swayed beneath his bone-slender arms.

Lea kept her eyes on his hands. They appeared to take on a life of their own, like small, pale animals floating in the air.

Birds uttered harsh cries in the rainforest behind them. A gust of hot wind made the feathery palm leaves slap and scrape.

We need pounding drums here. Ominous background music.

She scolded herself for being so cynical.

The skin on her arms tingled. She wiped sweat off the back of her neck.

The air is so heavy and wet. Perhaps we are feeling the first winds of the hurricane.

She crossed her arms tightly on her chest to steady her heartbeat. *I certainly don't want to be out here in the middle of the island if the damned hurricane hits.*

The priest finally finished his low chant. He nodded. The six men lowered the cups to their mouths and drank the dark liquid down.

Lea heard soft cries in the crowd. Muttered words.

The men stood silently, swallowing even after lowering the cups to their sides. Palm leaves slapped loudly above their heads, as if clapping.

The sky darkened from pale gray to charcoal. The wind picked up, fluttering robes and skirts, lifting Lea's hair behind her head, making a howling moan as it swirled through the shivering trees.

Special effects, Lea thought. *The priest chants and the wind starts to howl. Very dramatic.*

But she wasn't prepared for what happened next.

As she squinted into the fading light, the six men all began to groan. They coughed and rolled their eyes. Their faces reddened. They bent their knees and knelt.

Bending low, faces purple, they uttered hideous choking sounds. Then rasping moans from deep in their throats. Their stomachs bubbled and heaved.

And they all began to vomit at once.

5

Groaning, moaning, bleating like sick sheep, all six men heaved together. At first they spewed a dark liquid and then the chunky orange and yellow of their undigested lunches.

Hands on their knees, heads bowed as if praying, they puked their guts out in a chorus of animal groans and splashing liquid.

Lea grabbed her throat. She felt her breakfast rise. Her stomach churned. She held her breath, swallowing hard, swallowing, struggling not to heave along with them.

This was no act. They weren't faking it. No one could fake those ugly sounds, those horrified expressions. She covered her ears from their choked gasps and bleats and retching moans.

The sour smell rose into the humid air and swept over her. She stared at the thick piles of yellow-green vomit, spreading puddles on the sand. Still holding her breath, Lea started to turn away.

But Martha held her by the shoulders. "It isn't over. It just started."

Just started?

A shudder ran down Lea's body. Her legs suddenly felt rubbery, weak. She forced herself to watch. The six men bleated and choked. They grabbed their throats. Their eyes bulged in panic. Their faces darkened from red to purple to a sick blue.

She cried out as the men collapsed to the ground. One by one, they folded up, coiling into themselves. Uttering strangled sighs, they dropped facedown into their own vomit. They sprawled awkwardly on the ground, eyes bulging, gazing blankly. Their arms and legs twitched, as if they were getting electrical shocks; twitched like grotesque puppets that had lost their strings. Then stopped.

No one moved.

Swaying in the gusting wind, the feathery palm trees slapped and applauded. The birds had stopped their shrill symphony.

The red-robed priest knelt beside one of the fallen men. The star tattoo on his scalp appeared to wriggle, alive, like a blue octopus. He placed two fingers on the man's throat. Minutes went by.

"*Il est mort.*" Announced in a whisper.

"Oh my God," Lea murmured. She suddenly realized she had been hugging herself tightly for some time. Down by the tight circle of onlookers, she heard the startled cries of the four tourists. No one else made a sound.

The priest moved to the next victim sprawled facedown on the sand, a young man with short red hair and a boyish, freckled face. He rolled the man onto his back. After a brief examination, the priest repeated the words. "*Il est mort.*" Flat. No emotion at all.

Lea turned and saw the two men tourists snapping photos with their phones. The women had their hands over their faces, blocking out the death scene.

"Is this for real?" the man in the Budweiser shirt boomed. "Hey—are they really dead?"

No one replied. All eyes were on the tall, bald priest until he knelt over the last of the six victims.

"*Tous sont morts.*"

Lea forced herself to breathe. She suddenly felt dizzy, the blood pulsing at her temples. She had hoped to write about travel adventures people would find exciting. But *no way* she wanted to watch six men drink poison and vomit themselves to death.

Squinting into the graying light, she could see clearly that the six men weren't breathing. Their chests showed no movement. No rise and fall. No movement at all. Their eyes bulged, gazing blankly like glass doll eyes. Their mouths hung open, frozen in their final gasps for breath.

Still, no one on the island moved or made a sound. She glimpsed Jean-Carl across from her in the circle. He had his head down, hands jammed into the pockets of his cargo shorts.

The tourists had stopped their picture-taking. One of the women was crying. Budweiser Man wrapped her in an awkward hug.

The priest, still expressionless, turned to face the crowd. His blond caterpillar eyebrows had gone stiff and still.

He clasped both hands in front of him. Lea noticed for the first time that his fingernails were painted black. He began to chant: "*Revenir . . . Revenir . . . Revenir . . .*" Softly at first, then louder, urging the audience to join in.

"*Revenir . . . Revenir . . . Revenir . . .*"

The chanting voices echoed off the trees of the rain forest. The chant continued for two minutes . . . three . . .

Lea screamed when she saw a hand move. On the ground. Fingers twitched.

"*Revenir . . . Revenir . . . Revenir . . .*"

The chant continued, no longer a word, just a low, breathy sound.

Another dead man blinked his eyes. Another raised his head an inch off the ground. A short groan escaped his throat. More hands twitched. Like crabs testing the sand.

"*Revenir . . . Revenir . . . Revenir . . .*"

As Lea stared in disbelief, the six dead men sat up. They blinked rapidly and shook their heads, tested their jaws, squinted at the chanting crowd.

The chant ended suddenly. People rushed forward to help the men to their feet. In seconds, they were all standing, taking small steps, still looking dazed, wiping chunks of vomit off their shirts and shorts and robes.

The priest raised his hands high above his tattooed head. "*Les hommes sont revenus,*" he announced. "The men have returned."

The six men were walking steadily now, making their way to the path. The circle of onlookers broke up, people heading in all directions. Lea listened to the excited conversations. Some people were laughing. The ceremony was over.

Lea shut her eyes. Again she pictured those men bent over, their streams of vomit splashing onto the grass. Their gasping, terrified faces. Their bodies coiled lifelessly on the ground in front of her.

And as rain began to patter down, she thought of the 1935 hurricane and the story of the dead returning to life to repair the devastating damage. The living sharing their space with the unliving.

Huge raindrops rattled on the palm leaves, like assault rifles. Loud as thunder. The wind swirled around Lea, pushed her right, then left. She planted her feet, determined not to be blown over. A suffocating wind rushed over her face, made her gasp for breath.

It came on so suddenly. I thought we had time.

Hugging herself again, she ducked her head and searched for Jean-Carl. Nowhere in sight. Perhaps he had run to the jeep.

A strong blast of wind bent the palm trees till they were nearly horizontal. Lea's shoes sank into the mud as she stepped onto the path.

She felt a hand on her shoulder. Gasping in surprise, she spun around. "Martha?"

Martha had a canvas tennis hat pulled down tight over her hair. Her sweater was already soaked through, matted to her body. "Better come home with me." She had to scream over the roar of the wind.

Lea blinked through the sheets of rain that swept over her. "No. My stuff—"

"Better come with me, Lea. This is going to be bad. It's going to be real bad."

6

As Hurricane Ernesto slowly made its way north, Mark Sutter was ending his book tour close to home at HamptonBooks in Easthampton, Long Island.

The store occupied a gray shingle building near one end of the long row of shops on Main Street, a few doors down from the Ralph Lauren store, a country antiques store, an old-fashioned toy store, and the Hamptons' branch of Tiffany's, all closed and deserted on this rain-tossed April night, before the summer people had arrived.

Mark arrived early, shaking out his umbrella and squirming out of the Burberry trench coat that no longer seemed to be waterproof. He liked to watch his audience come in, liked to size up the crowd before he spoke to them.

Crowd. Would there be a crowd on a night like this? He saw a few rain-bedraggled people in one of the long, narrow store aisles. A good sign.

A smiling, middle-aged woman hurried out from behind the front counter to greet him. "Hi, Mr. Sutter. I'm Jo-Ann, the manager. Welcome. You're early."

She was a mouse of a woman, small and gray, with lips the same color as her skin. She was probably forty, but she looked ten years older. She wore a loose-fitting gray turtleneck over black corduroy slacks.

"I like to come early and hang out a bit," Mark said. "You know. Chat with people. Kind of size up the crowd."

"Well, make yourself at home. We've already sold several books, and we got a lot of phone calls. I think there'll be a crowd." She squinted at him. "How does it feel to be controversial?"

Mark laughed. "I'm enjoying it, actually."

She nodded solemnly. "Of course you are."

Mark wondered exactly what she meant.

"Sometimes it's good to stir people up," she said. And then quickly changed gears: "Can I get you a bottle of water?"

"No. I'm fine."

"Sure? I have plenty of water."

"No. Really. I saw enough water driving here."

His joke fell flat. He knew it wasn't much of a joke. He shouldn't try to be funny. No one expected it of him. But what was this obsession with water? In every city at every bookstore, they tried to shove bottle after bottle of water at him.

"The rain is from the hurricane," she said, "but we're lucky. I have the radio on. They said it's veering out into the ocean. We'll just get the rain."

"Hurricane?"

She squinted at him. "You didn't hear? It's a big one. Down South."

Mark felt his throat tighten. "My wife is down South. On an island. I didn't know. I had my iPod in the car. I—"

"Maybe you should try to call her." She turned and saw the line of customers at the front counter. "I'd better get back." She gave his wrist a quick squeeze. Like saying *Good luck*. Then she turned and made her way back to the other two clerks at the counter.

She stepped behind one of the cash registers and pulled on a pair of tight white rubber gloves. *To protect herself from money germs?*

Mark slid his BlackBerry from the pocket of his jeans, raised it to push Lea's number. Then stopped. No bars.

I'm sure she's okay. I'll phone her after the book signing.

He stepped toward the back and leaned against a bookshelf where he could watch customers enter. He could see a gauzy reflection of himself in the front window, floating over the pyramid of display copies of his book. A gust of wind rattled the window and sent rivulets of rainwater streaking down the glass.

"Where do I put this?" A man in a brown rain slicker and canvas tennis hat shook his umbrella in a red-haired store clerk's face, sending a spray of rainwater over the front counter. The young man pointed to the tall can by the door, already jammed with wet umbrellas.

The store was small, narrow and deep with two aisles leading back through tall wooden bookshelves. Rows of low-hanging fluorescent lights sent down a pale glare, making everyone look a little green. At the back, a steep stairway led upstairs to the author event area.

Mark felt his skin prickle. He rubbed his stubbled cheeks. The air in the store felt hot and damp despite the cold blasts every time the door opened. He could smell the ocean.

In a few hours I'll be home.

He could hear a low mumble of voices from upstairs. A respectable crowd on a stormy Wednesday night in Easthampton. *Please— let there be fifty people.* That's all an author cares about. A crowd big enough not to be embarrassing. Please—not four people who all choose to sit in the back row.

To his relief, he saw several couples lined up at the cash register. They all had his book in their hands. Did they look happy? No.

They've all come for a fight.

He turned back toward the front door and felt his stomach rumble. Not from stage fright. He looked forward to another confrontation. If only he could keep them from shouting this time.

He suddenly pictured the young woman in Boston who turned purple and started to tremble. That was *awkward*. And the angry couple who followed him to the parking lot and refused to let him get into the car until they had their say.

His stomach churned again from the bacon cheeseburger he had eaten too fast at Rowdy Hall, the noisy, crowded hamburger joint across the street. He always ate too fast when he was alone.

I'll be home tonight.

His house in Sag Harbor was twenty minutes away, maybe a little longer if the storm continued. He had driven to the bookstore directly from MacArthur Airport in Ronkonkoma. He hadn't had even two seconds to stop at home and say hi.

Ira and Elena. When did he see them last? Two weeks ago? He talked to them on the phone every night, and he Skyped them when he could. But the conversations were always forced and hurried.

Elena was okay. Even at the gawky age of fourteen, she bobbed merrily through life like a kite in a strong wind. Ira was the sensitive one, always overthinking everything, so shy and serious. Poor guy. Sixth grade. His first year in middle school.

Mark should have been there to help him get through it. Or Lea. But she was away, too. He hated it when they were both away at the same time.

"When you write a travel blog, you kind of have to travel," Lea had said.

"I'm not accusing you of anything," he had countered. "I'm just saying . . ."

"That one of us should stay home."

"No. I'm just saying it's a *shame* that one of us isn't staying home."

That made her laugh. "I love your subtle distinctions. I wasn't a psych major like you, darling, but I know when I'm being guilted."

Guilted?

No way he could convince her to stay home till he got back. *Travel & Leisure* had let her go. Budget cutbacks. The usual thing. Now Lea was determined to produce the best adventure-travel blog in the universe, build a huge audience, collect millions in advertising, and show her old bosses what a mistake they had made.

She was ambitious. And she was a fighter. The youngest of seven, with four brothers and two sisters, Lea was used to fighting for what she wanted.

And so . . . they went their separate ways, and Mark's sister, Roz, stayed with the kids.

Mark had to admit, the ten-city book tour was not as glamorous as he had imagined. And he was taken by surprise by all the anger waiting for him at every bookstore. After all, he'd only written a book. He hadn't *murdered* anyone.

He wasn't naïve. He knew his book would spark controversy. But he never dreamed that parents would react with such alarm, as if he were threatening parenthood itself.

Which maybe he was.

Because of all the controversy, *Kids Will Be Kids* was at the top of the nonfiction bestseller list. Exactly what he had strived for. He wanted to reach as many parents as possible.

He wasn't trying to become famous by stirring things up. He believed his studies of his young patients validated his parenting theories.

He glanced at the clock, then watched more rain-soaked stragglers push into the bookstore. Someone tapped his shoulder. The red-haired store clerk—*Adam,* it said on his ID badge. "Mr. Sutter, can I get you some water?"

"No thanks. I'm good."

"You sure?"

He turned to the steep wooden staircase. He could hear the crowd up there shifting, folding chairs squeaking, the mumble of voices. Someone laughed loudly.

Showtime.

7

Not quite ready. He made his way toward the bathroom behind the office in back. A large man in a gray hoodie and faded jeans blocked the aisle. He was scanning a shelf of fiction, but turned as Mark approached.

"Hi. Are you here for my book talk?"

The man shook his head. "No. I'm not much of a reader. I'm here for my wife."

"Your wife?"

"Yeah. She heard there's a new James Patterson." He swung back to the bookshelf. "You're not him, are you?"

"No. No, I'm not. Sorry."

Sorry? Why did I say sorry?

Mark edged past him into the phone-booth-size bathroom and checked the mirror. Brought his face close and grinned. He rubbed his front teeth with one finger. No hamburger or lettuce there. Nothing hanging from his nose.

He smoothed a hand over the stubble on his cheeks and brushed back his short hair, his hazel eyes dark in the dim light from the ceiling. He wasn't admiring himself. He was *preparing* himself.

Lea called him Gyllenhaal. She said he was a dead ringer for the actor. Flattering? Yes. A two-day stubble, short, dark hair and big eyes, and he was Jake Gyllenhaal to her.

I love you, Lea.

Only thirty-nine but even in this bad light, he could see patches of gray spreading over the sides of his hair. No problem. A psychologist doesn't want to be *too* good-looking. He needs some maturity. Some authority.

He wore a trim black suit jacket over dark, straight-legged denim jeans. His white shirt was open at the collar. Not too formal. He wanted to appear open and friendly. They would see he wasn't a stuffed shirt. He was a young father. A child psychologist with a serious point of view. But casual. Even likable?

He grinned. He should wear a suit of armor. The lions were waiting upstairs to rip him to shreds and devour the remains.

His stomach churned again. Maybe it wasn't the cheeseburger. Maybe it was the two Heinekens.

Up the stairs, Mark. Go get 'em.

He used the wooden banister to pull himself. The steps creaked beneath him. He practiced a smile. It didn't feel right. Tried a smaller one. Above the mumbling of the crowd, he could hear rain pattering against the sloped skylight window in the ceiling.

The stage area came into view as he reached the top. A good crowd. The folding chairs were all filled. And a row of people stood behind them. Some leaned against the bookshelf walls. Two young women had made cushions of their coats and sat cross-legged on the floor to the side of the podium.

At least a hundred people. No. More like one fifty.

So far, a success. Jo-Ann flashed him a smile from beside the podium. Good. The store manager was pleased.

He surveyed the crowd. Mostly couples. Parents. Some gripped his book in their laps. To have it signed or to throw at him? They watched him warily as he moved toward the podium.

"He's young," someone whispered, just loudly enough to be heard.

"Does he have kids?"

"If he does, can you imagine what they're like?"

A cell phone erupted and was quickly cut off. He saw three very old people, frail, hunkered in the front row, still in their raincoats, shopping bags on the floor in front of them. Regulars, probably. Lonely people who come to every bookstore event.

Jo-Ann started to introduce him. There were hurried footsteps on the stairs. More arrivals. She wrapped her hand around the microphone as she talked, and it made an annoying scraping sound.

"—already seem to be familiar with our guest author and his book, so I expect a lively discussion tonight."

Mark heard a few people snicker at that.

"Some things you may not know about Mark Sutter," Jo-Ann continued. "He's a Sag Harbor resident, not a summer person. He and his wife live here year-round with their two children."

She read from a handwritten index card. One hand held the card. The other squeezed the microphone as if trying to get juice from it.

"Mr. Sutter was born on Long Island in 1973. He grew up in Great Neck. He has a BS in Child Psychology from the University of Wisconsin. Mr. Sutter has a national reputation. He has contributed to many major psychology and science journals. *Kids Will Be Kids* is his first book, based on studies he made over the past five years observing his own juvenile patients and their parents."

She finally let go of the microphone and motioned to Mark with a tight smile. "Let's all welcome tonight's author, Mark Sutter."

Tepid applause. Mark forced the practiced smile to his face and took two steps toward the podium.

Jo-Ann turned and wrapped her hand around the microphone again. The applause died quickly. She waved Mark back. "Oh, I almost forgot," she said, "while I have you all here. Such a nice crowd. It's so wonderful to see people come out on a rainy night to discuss books."

Mark shoved his hands into his jeans pockets and waited. He studied the crowd. A twentysomething couple in the second row had their heads down, tapping away on their phones. Behind them, a large man in a Yankees cap and blue-and-white Yankees jacket had the *Daily News* open in front of him.

Rain pattered the skylight window. Mark glimpsed a flicker of lightning high in the green-black sky. He blinked—and saw someone he recognized in the third row. A young woman in a short blue skirt over black tights and a white tube top.

His eyes took in the gleaming white-blond hair. Blue eyes. High cheekbones. Red-lipped smile.

She didn't register at first. Mainly because she didn't tell him she'd be there. The improbably named Autumn Holliday, his assistant. She realized he had finally spotted her. She smiled and her eyes went wide. She gave him an excited wave.

Why did she get all dolled up for this?

Autumn always showed up at his office in jeans and oversize rock-band T-shirts, her hair tied carelessly back in a ponytail. Now he couldn't help but stare. She looked like one of those stunning Nordic ice-queen fashion models.

"Autumn? What are you doing here?" He mouthed the words silently.

"—Thriller Night here at HamptonBooks," Jo-Ann was saying. "I think you'll all want to be here. Our guest author will be Harlan Coben, and if you were here last year, I'm sure you will remember how funny and charming Mr. Coben can be. So . . . don't forget next Saturday night."

Mark forced himself to turn away from Autumn. Jo-Ann was waving him back. This time there was no applause. He could feel the tension in the room.

Lightning flickered in the skylight above. People shifted their weight, sat up straighter, squeezed the books in their laps. The couple in the second row tucked their phones away.

Somewhere in the back, a baby cried. Mark suddenly realized there were several babies on laps, swaddled like tiny mummies.

Mark placed his hands on the sides of the podium. The microphone was a little too low. He leaned into it. "Good evening, everyone. Thanks for coming out on such a lovely night. Instead of a reading tonight, I know you all probably have a lot of questions. And I thought we could begin by discussing—"

Several hands shot up. They were too eager.

Here we go again.

"Are you Dr. Sutter or Mr. Sutter?" From a chubby, coppery-haired man standing behind the seats, wearing an ugly chartreuse turtleneck and gray sweatpants.

"I'm Mr. Sutter. I have a BS degree in child psychology. You can call me Mark."

"So you're not a doctor?" Accusing.

Before Mark could answer, a woman in the front row, her arm cradling a swaddled baby. "Why do you think children don't need parents? Why do you think they should grow up wild and undisciplined and untrained?"

Mark forced his smile to grow wider. He had learned a lot at the other bookstore appearances. The trick was not to get flustered. Remain calm. Be quieter and saner than the audience.

He glimpsed Autumn, her brightly lipsticked lips pursed, eyes narrowed with concern.

"Have you read my book?" he asked the woman in the front row.

She nodded. "Some of it."

A few people snickered.

"Well, I think you are misrepresenting what I wrote. I believe children need parents," he said. "My problem is with *too much* parenting."

"There can't be too much!" a man yelled from somewhere in back. The outburst drew some short applause.

Mark ignored it. "Basically, what I have found is that children thrive and grow happier and more creative with *less* parental supervision. I'm not saying we should ignore our responsibility to teach them the basics of what's right and wrong. We all must instill a good moral sense. But we all know about helicopter parents these days, who hover over their kids wherever they go. These control-freak parents hinder the natural creative growth—"

"Kids *need* to be controlled," the same man shouted.

"Kids *want* to be controlled," the woman with the baby contributed. "They don't *want* the kind of freedom you are talking about."

The audience seemed to erupt. Mark kept his smile, waited for them to settle down, tapping his hands on the sides of the podium.

"I appreciate your point of view," he said finally. "But for my book, I studied my patients and their parents for five years. My observations led me to believe what I wrote here. I believe parents should act like guides—but not like cops. Children need their parents to be warm and loving. But they also need to be independent from them."

The woman with the baby spoke up again. "You mean parents should act like friends—not like parents?"

"Friends love and support you," Mark replied. "What's wrong with that?"

Another eruption of angry voices.

Autumn was shaking her head, her hair shimmering like a silver helmet in the light. She stared at him wide-eyed, concentrating, as if sending him a psychic message of support. His one fan.

She has nice tits. How come I've never noticed? Because she's twenty-three?

"Let me give you an example from the book, the boy named Sammy. Sammy is ten. His parents treat him as an equal. They let him decide what to eat. They let Sammy decide when to go to bed and when to wake up. They let him decide how much time to spend playing video games or watching TV.

"As a result, Sammy is not only happy but well behaved. Mature. He has a confidence that I don't see in most ten-year-olds. You see, the extra freedom given Sammy by his parents has allowed him to—"

A vibration against his leg stunned him, and he stopped in midsentence. It took him until the second buzzing tingle to realize it was the phone in his jeans pocket.

Probably his sister, Roz, wanting to know when he'd be home.

He ignored it. It buzzed three more times before it shut off.

"A lot of doctors don't agree with you," a woman against the wall spoke up in a raspy smoker's voice. "I read a review by a psychologist in the *Times* who said your ideas are dangerous."

The phone buzzed again. The vibration sent a tingle up and down his leg. Roz wouldn't call back. Someone was being insistent.

"Excuse me," he said, grabbing the phone from his pocket. He squinted at the screen. *Lea?*

"I'm really sorry. I have to take this." He backed away from the podium. "My wife—she's on an island. . . ."

He turned away from the audience. Behind him, mumbled voices and grumbling. He raised the phone to his ear. "Lea? Are you okay?"

A deafening howl made him jerk the phone away. Then he heard her voice, high, shrill. "Mark—the hurricane . . ."

He could barely hear her over the static and whistling. "What? What did you say?"

"Ernesto . . . It . . . It's *horrible*, Mark."

She was screaming over the roar. She sounded frantic.

"The hurricane? Are you okay?"

The howling stopped.

A jarring silence.

He pressed the phone to his ear, so hard it hurt. "Lea? Are you there? Lea?"

8

Mark's hand trembled as he set the phone down on the podium. His whole body tensed. He tried to swallow, but his throat had closed up.

She sounded terrified.

He kept his eyes on the phone.

Call back. Call back. Call back, Lea.

The baby in the front row started to cry. The woman shifted it in her lap and stuck a plastic pacifier in its mouth. The crowd had grown quiet. Maybe they could sense that he was shaken. He found a bottle of water on the shelf inside the podium, twisted it open, and took a long drink.

"Sorry about the interruption." He stared at the phone. "My wife is on a tiny island off the Carolinas. I think she's in the hurricane. We were cut off."

He raised his eyes to the skylight. Waves of rain rolled over the glass. Jo-Ann leaned against the bookshelf on the wall, arms crossed tightly in front of her sweater. Her eyes were closed.

"Where were we?" Mark tried to start again.

They slumped in their seats now. The tension had gone out of the room. It was as if he had absorbed it all. His mouth felt dry.

He tasted half-digested cheeseburger in his throat. He took another swig of water to wash it back down, spilled some on his shirt.

Call back. Call back.

"I know what people call me. They say I'm the opposite of the Tiger Mom. They call me the Teddy Bear Dad."

That got a few snickers. The crowd seemed to relax just a little.

"But I'm not talking about *no* parenting. My idea is *less parenting*. The examples in my book show that children can be nurtured without being bossed, guided without realizing they are being guided. My theory is that parents who are *friends* to their children will be friends for life and will not encounter—"

An explosion of thunder, close enough to rattle the skylight window, ended that thought. The lights flickered. A few people gasped and cried out.

This was a problem of living on Long Island's East End. The power lines were all strung through the trees. He wondered if Route 114 was flooded. The drive home could be longer than he had hoped.

He was talking without really hearing himself, wishing he could wrap it up, sign their books, go home and try to reach Lea. But they had come with questions and he couldn't cheat them of a chance to spout their disapproval.

Do you raise your own children this way? Are you always their friend and not their father?

Can you tell us some firsthand examples of parents who tried your way? Didn't some of the kids become spoiled brats? Total monsters?

You really think kids should be raised like wild animals? Were you raised by wolves?

That question was greeted by laughter. It made Jo-Ann open her eyes and seemed to break the tension. Mark let out a long breath. A good place to end.

He thanked everyone for their opinions and for coming out on such a dreadful night. He could sense disappointment. They had come for the kill, but he was too distracted to do battle. They hadn't even wounded him.

About half the crowd left, funneling down the creaking stairway without having a book signed. Those who lined up for his autograph were quiet and polite, except for a small, frail-looking woman in a ragged gray trench coat, who glared at him through square spectacles and said, "You could do a lot of harm with this book." She then asked him to sign the book "To Megan."

By his count, he sold thirty or forty books. When the last customer, the man in the Yankees gear, made his way to the exit, Jo-Ann patted his shoulder. "Good job, Mark. That wasn't easy."

He sighed. "This is my last stop on the tour. Now I'm going to stay home for a while."

The phone, secured in his jeans pocket, remained a silent hunk of metal and plastic. Scenes of Cape Le Chat Noir rushed through his mind, fragments of photographs Lea had emailed him. He saw the wide yellow beach. Fishing boats bobbing in the calm water offshore. Small, square white cabins with red clay roofs . . .

"Your raincoat is in the office. I'll get it for you." Jo-Ann made her way to the stairs.

Mark stood up, then froze for a second, surprised to see Autumn lingering near the back row of seats. She had a shiny violet-colored slicker folded over one arm. She smiled and hurried toward the podium.

"I . . . didn't expect to see you here," Mark said.

She giggled. "I wanted to surprise you." The blue eyes flashed. The smile suddenly became teasing. "Did I surprise you?"

"Well . . . yes."

She swept her hair back with a quick toss of her head. "You were very brave." She squeezed his hand.

Just a light squeeze, but it seemed strange to him. Like a rehearsed gesture.

"Brave?"

"Well, yeah. I mean, when I proofread your book, I didn't really know it was, uh, so controversial. I couldn't *believe* tonight. It totally made people angry. But you handled every question. I was—wow—so *impressed*."

"Thanks, Autumn. Nice of you to come tonight." She lived in

Hampton Bays with her sister, he knew, nearly an hour's drive from the bookstore in Easthampton.

He started to the stairwell. "Are you coming to work tomorrow? There's mail to answer. And a few things . . ."

She shifted the raincoat. The white tube top had slid down, revealing the tops of creamy-white breasts. "Mark? Would you maybe . . . um . . . like to get a coffee? Or a drink?"

She's flirting with me.

He felt a flash of heat in his cheeks. "N-no. I mean, I really can't, Autumn. I haven't been home in so long. And I have to call Lea. We were cut off and . . ."

She nodded. He couldn't read her expression. Her face went blank, revealing nothing, except that the light faded from those deep blue eyes.

She nodded. "Just wanted you to know I'm here for you. You know. If you need anything?" Her pale cheeks turned pink. "See you tomorrow morning." She spun away, swinging the violet slicker onto her shoulders, and hurried to the stairs.

Mark watched her go. The coltish legs in the black tights. The silver-blond hair disappearing under the shiny rain hood.

She was definitely coming on to me. If I had gone for that drink with her . . .

Don't even think about it.

He tried phoning Lea from the car. Rain pelted the windshield. He let the engine run, waiting for the cold air from the heater to turn warm. The long row of stores were mostly dark. The street was empty.

The call went right to her voice mail. He left a short message. "Call me back. Where are you? Love you."

Why didn't she answer? Why did she sound so frantic when she called?

Maybe Roz would know. Maybe Roz had heard from her too.

The wipers set a tense rhythm. He pulled away from the curb and guided the car down Main Street through the torrents of rain. In the mirror, he glimpsed three or four people, huddled under black umbrellas, stepping out of the movie theater across the street.

In front of him, the Ralph Lauren store windows were brightly lit. Cruise wear on display.

He made the right onto 114. His tires sent up waves of rainwater on both sides of the car.

Maybe Roz will know what's up with Lea.

His poor sister. Five years older than Mark, she had shown up on his doorstep nearly a year ago with the one-year-old kid in tow and nowhere to go.

Talk about bad luck with men. Only it wasn't bad luck. It was poor choices. You didn't need a psychologist to see Roz had a problem in that area.

Mark could see the black eye she had tried to cover up with makeup. And the nervous tic with her eyes . . . that was something new.

"I'm giving up men," she had said as he and Lea helped carry her bags into the house. "Maybe I'll try women."

"What does that mean?" Ira had asked.

"She's making a joke," Mark told him.

Her son, Axl, with the bush of curly brown hair and the pudgy cheeks and freckles, started to cry.

"Naming your son Axl is looking for trouble." Yes, Mark had really said that to her over the phone the day after Axl was born.

Of course, Roz had laughed. She always laughed at Mark when he was too earnest. "If Axl has problems, I'll send him to you, Doc," she said.

They had a strange relationship, he thought. She was the older sister but in many ways he played the older brother. Not the older, *wiser* brother. Her razor-sharp sense of humor would never allow him to be that. She always cut him down to size even when he was helping her.

It worked. They had always been close. Their parents had been so absent, they had to cling together from the time they were little, and that habit stuck. Now here she was with the black eye and the trembling chin, holding back her tears with all her strength.

Her boyfriend, Axl's father, had left and taken her car and her savings.

Lea said, "The guesthouse in back is empty. Why don't you live there for a while, Roz, while you're getting yourself together? Ira and Elena will love having Axl around."

"Only if I can do something to earn my rent." From Roz. "You know. If I can help out somehow?"

Which is how she got to be the nanny. And damned good timing, too, since Lea and Mark were traveling so much lately. The kids didn't take long at all to adjust to little cousin Axl. Now age two, he was so cute and so preposterously curious. How could anyone resist him?

"What that mean?"

"Why?"

"What you doing? Why you doing that?"

It was so interesting to see the little guy's brain churning away. Ira and Elena didn't question much. They seemed to accept everything as it was. They had always seemed too into themselves to be explorers.

Roz seemed happy in the little guesthouse with its single bedroom and bath. In fact, Mark had never seen her so consistently cheerful. She had her straight black hair cut short and bought some young-looking clothes.

She found a part-time job doing office work for some real estate lawyers in Sag Harbor. And she proved to be an efficient and loving nanny. The kids quickly learned to laugh at her sarcasm and sharp insults. They ate all their meals together at the long wooden table in the kitchen. One big happy family.

Of course, Mark was wary. He always began to feel wary whenever things began to go right for his sister. He knew that a new boyfriend on the scene could change it all.

He wanted Roz to have a real life of her own. Actually, he felt the house was a little crowded with the two of them always there, and it was harder to spend quiet time with Lea or with Ira and Elena. He didn't want to keep her there forever as a kind of indentured servant. But he knew Roz needed time to heal before heading off to the next chapter of her life.

All these thoughts while sailing his small BMW through the

dark waves of Route 114, squinting through the rain-washed wind-shield. The rapid *smack-smack-smack* of the wipers the only sound except for the splash of rain waves off the sides of the car.

No phone. No phone ringing.

Lea, where are you?

And then a sharp turn through the opening in the low brick wall. The crunch of the gravel driveway beneath the tires. Mark eased the car to the side door. Cut the lights. Turned off the engine. Watched the wipers settle down into place.

Then he pulled the raincoat over his head and burst out of the car. To the door on the run. Shoes skidding on the wet gravel.

He reached for the knob but the door swung open. A sliding rectangle of light revealed Roz in jeans and a long, baggy brown sweater. Her eyes were red-rimmed. He smelled alcohol on her breath.

"Oh, Mark."

"Roz, hi. Have you heard from Lea? Has she called here?"

Roz gazed at him for a long moment. "I don't think she can," she said finally, her voice a whisper.

9

With the winds rattling the windows, Lea stood with her phone pressed to her ear. "The connection is lost." She turned to the Swanns, Martha and James. "I heard Mark, but I don't think he could hear me."

An explosion of thunder made all three of them jump.

The lights flickered and went out. "I have plenty of candles," Martha said. "And a kerosene lantern."

She had more in common with Martha Stewart than just her first name, Lea thought. She seemed to be a perfect host and home-maker, calm and competent, despite the howling winds that made Lea want to scream.

James was soft-spoken and low-key, too. "No phones, no inter-net," he said calmly, like checking off items on a grocery list. "We probably won't have power for long. We won't be able to communi-cate with anyone for days."

"How can you be so calm about it?" Lea's voice came out shrill, tight.

James's slender, lined face flickered into view as Martha got one of the candles glowing. His eyeglasses reflected the orange light. "Martha and I have seen a lot of storms since we moved here."

"Maybe none like this," Martha murmured. Another candle flared.

The Swanns had lived in Charlotte, North Carolina, all their lives. James owned three pharmacies there, two of them inherited from his father. But he never really enjoyed running a business. When Walgreens made him an offer he couldn't refuse, he sold them his stores and retired.

Martha, a photo researcher, freelanced for Reuters and other news agencies. The internet meant that she could work anywhere, so it was no problem for her to move. Ten years ago, the two of them had picked up and moved to Cape Le Chat Noir, just because it seemed the wildest, most unpredictable thing they could do.

A crash outside—shattering metal and glass—made the candle-light flicker.

"Whoa. That sounded like a car. Think this wind is strong enough to pick up cars?" James shook his head.

The oil lamp sent an orange glow over the Swanns' front room. Long blue-black shadows crept over the floor and walls.

The room had an arching, dark wood cathedral ceiling. Two rows of track lights beamed down on the living room area, all wicker and blue and green aquatic colors, in the front facing the road. A long dining room table, covered in a flowery tablecloth, divided the living room from the kitchen.

Sliding glass doors and an enormous kitchen window revealed a panorama of the beach and ocean inlet out back. James had boarded up the window against the approaching storm. But the glass doors showed the tossing, battling waves, an eerie, unnatural green against the charcoal sky.

The shifting shadows on the walls made Lea think of Halloween. She realized she was still gripping the cell phone and tucked it into a pocket, surprised at how hard her hand was trembling.

She stared through the glass doors at the dark ocean waves raging high, foaming angrily.

"People are going to die," she said.

The Swanns nodded but didn't reply. James fiddled with the neck of his black turtleneck sweater. Martha carried a flickering oil lamp to the window ledge in the kitchen.

"Why are you taking that back there?" James called.

"It might light someone's path," Martha said.

"I'm worried about Macaw and Pierre at the rooming house," Lea murmured. "It seems so rickety and frail."

Martha nodded. "You're much safer with us, on the west beach. The inlet is protected, Lea. And our house is solid. Not wood. It's thick Virginia fieldstone. We had it shipped from Charlotte when we built the house. We knew it could withstand hurricanes."

Lea shivered. "You're both so nice to take me in tonight. I mean, a total stranger—"

Martha laughed. "I feel like we're old friends. So many emails."

"Well, you're both very sweet," Lea said. "I don't know what I would have done. . . ." Her voice trailed off. She suddenly pictured Ira and Elena, so far away.

Earlier, Martha had prepared a magnificent dinner. Conch salad and salt oysters fresh from the ocean that morning, followed by a spicy-hot gumbo of rock shrimp, scallops, and lobster. A true feast. Along with a very dry Chardonnay from a winery on Hilton Head Island.

It should have been a delightful, relaxing time. But Lea kept glancing out the back doors at the flocks of birds flying frantically back and forth in the darkening sky, chattering and squawking in a panic, as if they didn't know where to light.

James was talking about Carolina wineries and how they had to import their grapes from all over. Lea tried to concentrate. He spoke so softly, she had to struggle to hear.

After coffee, they watched the progress of the storm on the Weather Channel until the power went out with a startling *pop*. Then, in the candlelit darkness, they talked loudly over the roaring winds, straining to pretend all was normal.

"I'm worried about my kids," Lea said. "And my husband, of course. They won't know if I'm okay."

"They'll get things up and running soon after the storm," James said. "You'll be surprised. The army will be here. The national guard. Hurricanes on the Carolina coast . . . people have experience with them."

"Do you have kids?" Lea realized she hardly knew a thing about her two hosts. Her emails with Martha had been all about life on Le Chat Noir.

"We have a son. In Phoenix," Martha said. "He's thirty. Not quite a kid."

Lea squinted at her in the candlelight. "You don't look old enough to have a thirty-year-old."

Martha's dark eyes flashed. "Flattery like that will get you a friend for life."

"He's still 'finding himself,'" James added, making quote marks with his fingers. "A lot of thirty-year-olds are still teenagers these days. He—"

"*We're* the teenagers," Martha interrupted. "Running away from home to a tiny island?"

"I wanted more kids," Lea said. "I come from a big family. Four brothers and two sisters. I really wanted a houseful of kids. But after Ira was born, the doctor said we couldn't have any more. I was so disappointed. Heartbroken, really."

Her words were greeted by silence. Martha and James stared at her, their faces appearing and disappearing in the flickering light.

Too much information.

Rain pounded the house, as loud as thunder. The wind howled like a wild animal. But the house was solid as promised. The ferocious winds tried but couldn't collapse it. James praised the strength of Virginia fieldstone. Martha spoke calmly about going down to the beach after the last hurricane and watching the incredible waves.

Lea could hear things breaking outside. Cracks and heavy thuds. She fought to hold down a rising feeling of panic. She held her breath, as if she could will it away. Held her breath until her chest ached.

It will be over soon. I think the winds are already slowing.

She screamed at the cracking sound above her head. Plaster snowed down on the three of them from the high cathedral ceiling.

"It's trying to take the roof," James said. His eyes were wide behind his glasses. Even in the shadowy light, Lea could see his calm was broken.

Lea pressed herself against the living room wall, praying for the roof to hold, for the winds to stop raging. She shut her eyes tight and thought about Mark. And Ira. And Elena.

Were they thinking of her? Were they horribly scared?

She shuddered again. It could be *days* before I can reach them and tell them I'm okay. *Will I be okay?*

Another cracking sound above their heads. Another stream of powdery plaster came floating down. James staggered forward, eyes wide. His mouth dropped open. His knees folded. He started to fall.

Martha grabbed him by the shoulders, struggling to keep him on his feet.

"The roof . . ." he breathed. "It's . . . coming down."

A terrifying *craaack*. A rumble like approaching thunder. A shower of powdery plaster.

Everything shaking. Everything.

Lea screamed as the world came crashing down on her.

10

Lea struggled to pull herself up from the ringing darkness. Her head throbbed as if about to explode. Waves of pain rolled down her back, her arms and legs. Blinking in the gray light, still unable to focus, she gazed up.

"Oh my God!"

The sky appeared so close, glaring through the jagged hole in the ceiling. She raised her head, feeling dizzy. Underwater, her clothing soaked and the couch beneath her like a furry wet animal. She brushed shingles off the couch. Still struggling to focus, she saw jagged pieces of the ceiling strewn over the room.

Martha and James bent over her. Their faces were tight with concern, ghostly pale in the heavy gray light washing down from above.

"Lea? You're coming to? Are you okay?" Martha looked twenty years older. Her hair hung in damp tangles over her forehead. Her eyes were red-rimmed and wet.

Lea pulled herself to a sitting position. The room spun around her. She tried to swallow, but her mouth was too dry.

She squinted at the shards of wood and broken shingles scattered crazily around the couch. Piles of wet plaster on the carpet. Like cake flour. A snowstorm blanketing the furniture.

"The roof—"

Martha gripped her hand. "Take it slow, Lea. Just breathe. Don't try to get up yet."

"What happened?" Martha and James slid in and out of focus. Lea smoothed a hand over her hair, trying to rub away the pain.

"Part of the roof fell in," James said, gazing up at the sky. "You got hit by some slate shingles. It knocked you out."

"We were so worried." Martha squeezed Lea's hand. "It just came crashing down on you. We put you on the couch and—"

Lea shuddered. "I . . . think I'm okay. Just a headache. The dizziness is going away."

"Oh, thank God," Martha said.

"We all got soaked," James said, his voice hoarse, croaky. "But we were lucky." He glanced away, as if trying to force down some heavy emotion. Despite his attempt, a sob escaped his throat.

Martha held on to Lea's hand. "So glad y'all are okay. We were scared. You were totally out. Look. You might have a bump on your head, but it didn't even break the skin."

Lea brushed back her dark hair with both hands. "Wow. Guess I'm lucky. I feel okay. Really."

"It's morning. The rain stopped a few hours ago," Martha said. "The winds—"

James motioned toward the broken ceiling. "The rain. It soaked everything. The house will never dry out."

"But it's still standing." Martha turned to her husband. "I think we may be the fortunate ones. I . . . I'm afraid to look outside."

James shivered. "I need dry clothes." He started toward the bedroom. His shoes squished on the carpet.

Martha followed him. She turned back to Lea, her face almost apologetic. "We've been up all night. Maybe James and I should catch a few hours sleep. Before . . . before we face what's out there."

"Yes. Don't worry about me." Lea shook off another wave of dizziness. "You two are so kind. I'll never forget this. I'll be okay. Get some rest."

"Help yourself to anything in the fridge. We have to finish it before it spoils. There won't be any power for a long time." Martha uttered a long sigh.

They disappeared down the hall to their room.

Lea watched streams of water run down the wall. Stretching her arms above her head, she stood up. Suddenly alert.

Beyond the glass doors in back, tall waves continued to battle, crashing against each other, tossing off islands of foam. The water's roar seemed to be inside her head.

I have to go outside.

She had to see what the storm had left behind. She stepped unsteadily to the door, shoes sliding on the wet surface.

I'm a journalist. I have to document this for my blog. Maybe I can sell the photos to a news network.

But she wasn't prepared for the horrors a few steps from the house. The fallen trees and flattened houses. Everything crumbled and broken and down.

The people covered in plaster dust and mud, scrambling over the wreckage, searching house to house for survivors to rescue, finding only bodies.

She wasn't prepared for the howls and cries. The half-naked man who ran over the debris on the street, screaming as blood flowed down his back like a scarlet cape. The pale white baby feet poking out from under the collapsed wall of a house.

I'm a journalist.

She raised her phone to her eye. Steadied it. Focused on a man carrying two corpses over his shoulder. And . . .

Oh no. She studied the phone. Out of power. Dead. She stared at it. Shook it. No way to charge it. No way.

So now she wasn't a journalist covering the tragedy. Now she was just another victim.

Men were already piling bodies where the little white post office had stood.

Lea saw arms and legs dangling from beneath crushed, collapsed walls.

She shivered. Each breath she took burned her nostrils and made her throat ache. The air was choked with dust and dirt that hadn't settled.

I'm alive.

The island had been flattened. She squinted into the billowing gray light. The houses and shops were piles of trash. Splintered boards strewn everywhere. Fallen walls fanned out on the rain-soaked ground like playing cards.

Fifty-two Pickup.

She thought of the cruel card game her brothers used to tease her with when she was little.

"Want to play a card game, Lea?"

"Sure."

"Let's play *Fifty-two Pickup.*" Then they'd raise the deck high and let all the cards tumble to the floor. "Okay. Go ahead, Lea. Pick them up."

That's what it looked like here. Playing cards tossed and scattered over the earth.

Is that how she would write it? Could that be the lead to her story?

I can't write it.

She slumped onto the trunk of a fallen palm tree and wrapped her arms around herself. *I can't write it because I don't believe it yet. And I don't want to write about such nightmare and heartbreak. Where would I begin? How would I ever describe an entire island crushed and flattened as if stomped on by a fairy-tale giant?*

Fairy tales and childhood card games were flashing through her mind. Obviously, because she wanted to escape. She wanted to go back to somewhere safe and clean and nice. It didn't take a genius to figure that out.

She suddenly pictured her father sitting in his Barcalounger in the tiny living room back in Rockford, holding the newspaper in front of him, folded down the middle the way he always read it, and shaking his head. Reading and shaking his head, his face twisted in disapproval.

You'd be shaking your head today, Dad.

How could she write about the corpses they were pulling out from under the debris? Dead faces, locked in startled expressions. She watched the mud-covered workers stack the bodies like trash bags in the town dump.

The smell . . . Already. The sour smell of death.

And the sounds. Moans and shrieks and anguished cries rang out in the dust-choked morning air like a horror-movie soundtrack. The pleas of the injured waiting to be rescued. The survivors discovering their dead. The sweating, cursing men digging, pawing, shoveling into the rubbled houses. The groans of the men hoisting more corpses onto the pile.

It seemed to Lea that everyone left alive was howling in protest. Everyone who could move and make a sound was screaming or crying or wailing their disbelief and anger.

I should be helping.

She jumped to her feet and started to walk toward mountains of debris where the road had been. "Oh!" She stumbled over something soft.

A corpse!

No. Clothing. A tangled pile of soaked shirts and shorts strewn over the grass.

What about my *clothing?*

Were her belongings scattered with the wind? Was Starfish House still standing? Had Macaw and Pierre survived?

Lea shuddered. The rooming house was on the other side of Le Chat Noir, the eastern side, the exposed side where the ocean could show its storm fury. Starfish House felt fragile even in calm weather, she thought. The Swanns' stone house had barely survived intact.

She felt a stab of dread in the pit of her stomach. Suddenly, it was a struggle to breathe. No way Starfish House could still be standing. But Macaw and Pierre?

She couldn't phone, of course. She remembered she had been talking to Mark—or *trying* to—last night when the service crashed.

Mark. What was he thinking right now? What was he doing? What had he told the kids? He had to be in his own nightmare . . . not knowing . . .

And no way to tell him.

My poor Ira and Elena.

Ahead of her, she saw an upended SUV, windows all blown out, sitting on the flattened roof where a little food store had stood. The SUV looked like an animal on its hind legs, standing straight up on its back bumper. Lea shook her head. Hard to imagine a wind strong enough to lift an SUV off the road, onto its back end, and drop it onto a building.

She spun away from it. But there was nowhere to turn to escape the horror.

The man lumbering toward her caught her by surprise. He was tall and broad and drenched in sweat, thinning brown hair matted to his red forehead. His T-shirt was torn and stained with brown streaks. His shorts were rags.

His eyes were wild and his mouth was moving rapidly although Lea couldn't hear his words. His arms were outstretched, his mud-smeared hands open to grab her.

He's crazy. He's out of his head.

Move!

But there wasn't time.

With a menacing groan, he grabbed her by the shoulders. He pulled with surprising force, nearly dragging her off her feet. She inhaled the rank odor of his body and his mud-caked clothes.

He groaned again. She wasn't strong enough to resist. He was pulling her away from the others, dragging her out of view, grunting and groaning like an animal.

"Let go! Let *go* of me! Please! What are you going to do? Please—let *go*!"

11

The radio squealed. Andy Pavano nearly lost his grip on the wheel.

"Vince, turn it down or something. Sounds like you stepped on a cat."

"Hey, I'm always kind to animals. Can you hear me now?"

"The rain is messing with the radio." Andy slowed the patrol car around a curve but still sent a tidal wave of rainwater washing over the narrow shoulder.

"It's these old Motorolas, man. They're not even digital." Vince said something else but the signal broke up.

"Vince, what did you say?"

"I said maybe you could talk to your uncle about springing for a new radio system."

"The chief isn't my uncle," Andy snapped. "He went to school with my cousin, that's all."

"Okay, okay. You're both Pavano. So it's an honest mistake, right?"

Headlights from an oncoming car blazed over the windshield. Andy tried to squint through it, but he couldn't see a thing. *Turn off your brights, bastard.*

He opened his mouth in a loud burp. The meatball hero from

that Italian place on Main Street . . . What was it called? Conca d'Oro? . . . it hadn't gone down yet.

He swerved to avoid a lake of rainwater that glimmered darkly over the right half of the road. He could feel the wind push the car sideways. "Vince, this rain is killing me."

"There's a hurricane, Pavano. Down South. A big one. It pushed out into the ocean, but we're getting the sloppy seconds."

Andy snickered. "Vince, you're a poet. Sloppy seconds? That doesn't even make sense."

"Hey, what makes sense?"

Andy joined the Sag Harbor Police Force three weeks before, but it was long enough to know that *what makes sense?* was the height of Vince's philosophy.

"The wind is trying to blow this fucking Ford off the road."

The radio squealed again. Then Vince's distorted voice: "Language, dude. Remember? People listen in. Civilians. Shut-ins. Keep it clean."

"Okay, Mom."

"You city guys don't know how to drive. How long were you a New York City cop?"

"I was a Housing Authority cop."

"Ooh, I'm wetting myself. I'm so impressed. How long?"

"None of your business, Vince. What's up with the chitchat? You just lonely?"

"I've got a wife, an ex-wife, and four kids, man. How do you get to be lonely? Tell me."

Andy didn't have an answer for that. He had an ex-wife, too. The lovely Susannah. One of the reasons he moved to Sag Harbor.

All My Exes Live in Texas.

Someone should write one like it about New York.

All of Andy's philosophy could be found in country songs.

He thought about Sari. Her dark hair falling over her forehead. Those beautiful eyes, oval and green like cat eyes. He should turn around and maybe drop by her house.

That first visit was awkward. No. Worse than awkward. *She was ice. She tried to freeze me.* All that talk about how she was in love, how she was going to get married. To a guy who owns the tennis shop in Southampton?

No. That's crap. No way that was going to happen.

Now she'd had time to think about him, get warmed up to the idea of Andy being around again.

Sure, he blew it the first time with Sari. Maybe this time . . .

"Pavano, what's your ten-twenty?"

"I'm east on Noyac. Am I going in the right direction?"

"Maybe you need a GPS. Like the summer people. You're still a tourist, Pavano. Why don't you talk to your uncle about getting a—"

"You're going to keep calling him my uncle, aren't you."

"Yeah, probably. My sense of humor, you know. Riding this desk you need a sense of humor."

"Riding this desk? You been watching *Cops* again?"

The car rumbled past the turn at Long Beach. The rain formed a heavy curtain. He couldn't see the bay. No cars in either direction. Who would be out driving in this?

"So tell me again where this house is, Vince."

"It's a left on Brick Kiln, then a left on Jesse Halsey. Go to the end. Take a right on Bluff Point Road."

Andy sighed and shifted his weight in the seat. "Got it. You know, I didn't sign on for shit like this. I came out here for peace and quiet. Maybe a domestic or two. A deer down on the road, someone steals a stop sign or takes a leak in a supermarket parking lot."

"That sounds a lot like whining, Pavano."

"Left on Brick Kiln, right? Okay. I'm here. I'm not whining, Vince. But, look—you're riding a desk, as you so colorfully put it. And I'm—"

"Got another call. I'm out. You're not the only cop out tonight, Sergeant."

"Just about."

The Sag Harbor Police wasn't exactly a big force. Vince on the desk nights, the chief, and how many patrol guys? Four? Andy ran through their names in his head. Three Italian, one Irish. He made the left, then the right.

"Vince? You still there? I can't do this. It's making me sick. Really. I'm going to lose my supper."

"Not in the car, please. If you're going to blow chunks, stick your head out the window."

"I have a weak stomach. Really. It's in my physical report. You can check it."

"Please don't make me cry. My mascara will run."

"I can't see a thing, Vince. It's total darkness here, and the rain—"

"You can do it. Just follow the regulations. Go to the house. Show them your ID. Say what you have to say. Then go throw up."

"Why did I get this, Vince? I don't even know where I'm going."

"No one else would do it, Andy. That's a ten-four."

The radio made a loud click. Silence.

Bluff Point Road curved around the south side of a part of the bay known as Upper Sag Harbor Cove. The houses were far back from the road, hidden behind trees and tall hedges. Ahead of the clicking wipers and the splashing currents of rain, they rose up in the windshield like dark walls, blacker than the sky.

How'd they expect him to find the house? Oh. There. On the right, near the end of the street.

He made a sharp right, and the tires spun over the wet gravel drive. *Slow down. You're not in a hurry for this.*

Behind a low brick wall, the house stretched across a wide lawn. A big modern house, gray shingles, with a terrace between the house and the garage. Small windows on this side. The side facing the bay was probably mostly glass. A single light cast a faint glow over the front door. Two well-trimmed evergreen bushes rose on both sides of the entrance.

Andy stopped the car near the front walk and cut the wipers and the headlights. He sat motionless for a while, staring at the rainwater rolling in waves down the windshield. Thunder crackled somewhere far in the distance.

He realized he had his hands balled into tight fists. The meatball hero weighed heavily in his stomach. *You're forty, Pavano. Maybe you need a better diet.*

It wasn't age. It was tension. Sure, he was tense. Who wouldn't be?

Who on earth would want to do this job?

He glanced into the mirror. Saw his eyes gazing accusingly back at him.

Get it over with.

He picked his cap up from the passenger seat and pulled it down over his thinning hair. He had an umbrella, but it was in the trunk. He pushed open the door, slid his legs around, and climbed out of the car. He was drenched before he got the trunk lid open.

Perfect.

The umbrella caught and refused to open.

Even more perfect.

He spun away from the car, slipped on the flagstone walk, caught his balance, and jogged to the safety of the overhang above the front door. Lights were on, but no sign of any movement in the front window.

Water rolled down the brim of his cap. He shook his head hard, then pressed the bell. He could hear it chime inside.

Footsteps. Then a man pulled open the door and stared out at him in a pool of bright light. "Yes?"

Andy gazed at the man's startled face. He was dark and had a stubble of beard on his cheeks. He reminded Andy of . . . reminded him of that actor . . . He had just watched *Brokeback Mountain* a few weeks before. Not his kind of thing, although the scenery was pretty.

And, yes. This guy looked just like that actor with the funny name. He wore designer jeans and a white dress shirt. He held a can of beer in one hand.

"Can I help you, Officer?"

Andy nodded solemnly. "Perhaps I should come in?"

A woman appeared behind the man. She had short black hair and a drawn face, kind of weary-looking. She had a baggy brown sweater pulled down over black leggings. "Who is it, Mark?"

"A police officer. I don't understand—"

Andy felt his throat tighten. Gusts of wind blew the rain under the overhang.

Just get it over with. No way you can make it any better.

What was he supposed to say first? What was he supposed to ask them? He couldn't think straight.

"Sir," he started, raising his voice over the wind, "I'm sorry. I'm afraid I have bad news."

The man and woman both gasped. Her mouth dropped open. The beer can slid out of the man's hand and hit the floor.

"I'm really sorry, sir," Andy said, suddenly breathless. "But they sent me to tell you that your wife has been killed."

12

The woman let out a cry and grabbed the banister beside her, struggling to hold herself up.

The man made a choking sound. He blinked several times. He turned and grabbed the woman's hand.

"I'm sorry, sir," Andy said, lowering his eyes. Rain pelted the back of his uniform shirt.

"How—" the man started. He made the choking sound again. The woman started to sob, burying her face behind the man's shoulder.

"It was a traffic accident." Andy kept his eyes down, partly not to see their grief. He had to force his voice to stay steady. "On Stephen Hands. Near 114. The Easthampton police—they didn't want to tell you on the phone. They asked me—"

The man's expression changed. His eyes went wide. He raised a hand to say halt. The woman lifted her head and squinted at Andy. Tears glistened on her pale cheeks.

"That can't be," the woman choked out. "You're wrong."

"My wife . . . she is away," the man said, staring hard into Andy's eyes. "She's on an island off South Carolina. She isn't in Easthampton."

Andy's throat tightened again. He swallowed hard. "Mr. Hamlin, I was told—"

"He's not Mr. Hamlin, you idiot!" the woman screamed. Her hands balled into tight fists. "He's not Mr. Hamlin. Oh, I don't believe it. I don't fucking believe it." She pounded the banister.

"I'm Mark Sutter," the man said. He slid an arm around the woman's trembling shoulders. "Roz, please—"

But she pulled away and flung herself toward Andy, furiously shaking her head. "How could you *do* that? How could you *be* so stupid? Why didn't you ask our names first?"

"I . . . was nervous," Andy said. "I should have done that. Really. I didn't mean—"

Could I just dive headfirst into the bay and drown myself now?

"I think you want Bluff Point," Sutter said softly. "This is John Street."

"Oh my God." The words tumbled out of Andy's mouth. "I am so totally sorry. I hope . . . I mean . . . The rain. It's so dark. . . ."

What could he say? "I'm sick about this, sir. Ma'am." He really did feel sick.

They glared at him, both breathing hard. Sutter reached for the doorknob.

"I can only apologize," Andy repeated. "I'm new out here, and, well . . . I'm so sorry. If you'd like to report me to my chief, I can give you my ID."

Roz spun away. She disappeared into the house. Sutter shook his head. "You should get out of the rain, Officer."

Andy nodded.

The door closed. He heard the lock click.

He stood there for a moment, letting the rain batter him.

Perhaps I'll laugh about this in a few weeks. Tell it like a funny joke.

He suddenly found himself thinking of the *Police Academy* movies. The cops were all total idiots.

I should join them.

He sighed and strode slowly to the car. No reason to run. He couldn't get any wetter. He slid behind the wheel. A cold shudder ran down his back.

The radio squealed. "Pavano, you there?" Vince's distorted voice.

"Yeah, I'm here."

"How'd it go?"

13

"Let go of me! Please! Don't *hurt* me!" Lea cried.

Mumbling crazily to himself, the man dragged her to a pile of boards and stones. His eyes were wild, bulging wide, his gaze darting from side to side. He didn't seem to hear her cries.

He's gone crazy from the storm.

What does he plan to do to me?

Then she saw the bare-chested boy, a stream of long hair hanging down over his face. His mud-drenched shorts clung to his hips as he bent over a pile of rubble. He appeared to be struggling with something in the pile.

As the man pulled her nearer, Lea heard the shrill screams. And saw the openmouthed, terrified face of a woman peering up from below a ragged crisscross of boards.

The boy had her by the hands and was tugging with all his strength, crying and tugging, trying to free her from beneath the caved-in house. The woman tossed her black hair wildly, her head tilted back in pain, and she shrieked in agony.

"Help," the man grunted, letting go of Lea. He motioned toward the screaming woman. "Help me."

He lifted the boy out of the way. He gave Lea a gentle push and motioned for her to take one of the woman's flailing hands.

I must have been the first person he saw. He's obviously in a total panic.

She gripped the woman's hand tightly. It felt cold and damp, like a small drowned animal. She gave the hand a gentle squeeze—and the woman screamed.

Startled, Lea dropped the hand and jumped back. Her heart was pounding in her throat. She had to open her mouth to breathe.

Don't panic. You can do this.

The man motioned Lea to grab one corner of a slab of drywall. Lea grabbed it. They tugged in unison and managed to slide it a few inches off the woman's chest.

The woman shrieked and wailed, batting her head from side to side.

Lea pulled up on a broken two-by-four. The man grabbed it from her and heaved it aside.

Then he turned back to the woman and wrapped his big hand around hers. The woman screamed again. Lea knew she'd hear these screams in her nightmares. Screams that seemed to have no end.

The man gave Lea a signal with his eyes. Working in unison, they forced the woman nearly to a sitting position. Then the man reached behind her back. Lea took her hands and gave a hard pull. With a moan of pain, the woman rose up, rose up in Lea's hands. Rose up . . .

Lea heard a wrenching sound. Like fabric tearing.

She gasped as the woman came stumbling out, falling toward her. Her face showed no relief. In fact, it twisted into a knot of agony. She pulled her hands free from Lea and shrieked in an inhuman animal wail: "My leg! My leg! My leg! My leg!"

Lea gasped. The woman was balanced on one leg. Blood poured from an open tear in her other side.

"Oh my God!" Lowering her gaze, Lea saw the ragged flesh of the woman's other leg trapped beneath the pile of debris. A white bone poked up from the torn skin.

No. Oh no.

The other leg. We left it behind.

It's torn off. I pulled it off. I pulled her leg off!

Blood showered the ground from the open tear in the woman's body.

"My leg! My leg! My leg! My leg! My leg!"

The man stood hulking in openmouthed shock. Fat tears rolled down the boy's red, swollen cheeks.

Heart pounding so hard her chest ached, Lea searched frantically for help. No one. No one around.

What could even a doctor do?

She and the boy and the weeping man took the woman by her writhing shoulders and lowered her gently into her own pool of blood. They stretched her out on the dirt, and the man dropped down beside her, soothing her, holding her hand, cradling her head till she grew too weak to scream.

Lea staggered away. She knew she couldn't help. She stumbled away, holding her stomach with both hands, gasping shallow breaths of the heavy, salted air. She wandered aimlessly into the wails and screams, the moans, the howls of disbelief, the symphony of pain she knew she would hear in her nightmares.

I'm not here. I'm asleep in our bed at home. I have to get Ira and Elena to school. Mark, give me a shove and wake me up. Mark?

"My babies! My babies!"

The woman's shrill howls shook Lea from her thoughts. She turned and saw a grim-faced worker holding two tiny lifeless figures, cradling one in each arm, as if they were alive. But their heads slumped back, eyes stared glassily without seeing, arms and legs dangled limply, lifelessly.

The shrieking woman, tripping over the jutting wreckage of her fallen house, followed after them, waving her arms above her head. "My babies! My babies!"

Lea lowered her eyes as they passed by. *I'm in Hell.*

Suddenly, she pictured Starfish House. Was the little rooming house still standing? And what of Macaw and Pierre? Were they okay? Had they survived? Her laptop was there. Her clothes. All of her belongings.

How to get across the island? James's truck was useless. The road would be impassable. She could walk, but it would be a walk of endless horrors.

A steady drone, growing louder, wormed its way into her consciousness. A hum quickly becoming a roar.

"Help is already on the way."

Lea turned to see James behind her. He had changed into baggy gray sweats. His eyeglasses had a layer of white powder over the lenses. Behind them, his eyes were bloodshot and weary.

She followed his gaze to the sky and saw the helicopters, five or six of them, pale green army helicopters, hovering low, moving along the shoreline.

"They probably can't believe what they're seeing down here, either," she murmured. She shivered.

James lowered his hands to her shoulders. "Are you okay, Lea?"

She nodded. "I guess."

His eyes locked on her, studying her. "No, I mean, really. Are you okay?"

"I . . . I'm upset. No. I'm horrified. But I'm okay, James. I was just thinking about Macaw and Pierre. . . ."

"Martha and I will walk you to your rooming house. It won't take long. Maybe half an hour."

"But—"

"If there's a problem there, you can come back and stay with us." He kept staring at her, as if searching for something she wasn't telling him.

Lea pictured the little white building with its bright yellow shutters and the sign over the entryway: *Starfish House*. She saw Macaw in her bright red-and-fuchsia plumage; Pierre, bored, hunched over the front desk, thumbing through a magazine, humming to himself.

"Yes. I hope there's no problem," she said.

But there was a problem. A sad and sickening problem.

14

Staring at the wreckage, Lea hoped she had made a mistake. *Maybe I'm in the wrong place.* But the sign still stood, crooked on its pole: *Starfish House.* The two-story house had toppled forward. The walls had collapsed on themselves, folded like an accordion on its side. And now the whole house lay in a broken, ragged heap, a low mountain of soaked and cracked boards and crumbled shards of drywall.

"No. Oh no." Lea covered her face with her hands. She turned to James and Martha, expecting them to be close, but she saw them across the road, helping to pull someone out from under an over-turned car.

"No. No. No."

She stepped onto the fallen front door. It sank into the wet ground. She caught her balance and started to shout. "Macaw? Pierre? Are you here? Can you hear me?"

Boards cracked and settled. A window casing toppled onto its side. Lea screamed and jumped back, thinking the house might fall on her.

"Macaw? Pierre?"

No answer. They must have gotten out safely before the house fell in.

But what was that splash of red from under a fallen slab of wall? A scarf?

Stepping carefully, Lea made her way onto the pile of debris and climbed closer. She stopped with a gasp when she saw the hand lying so flat . . . the hand, smeared with dark blood, reaching out from under a wall board . . . the hand open as if waving . . . waving good-bye?

Lea's stomach churned. She fought the sour taste rising to her mouth. "Macaw?"

She stumbled forward, grabbed the side of a wall, and hoisted herself higher on the pile. "Oh no. No." The splash of red was the sleeve of a dress.

Forgetting safety, Lea dove toward it. She slipped on a broken board. Banged her knee on something sharp. Ignoring the pain, she climbed to the red sleeve. She could see more of the dress beneath the edge of the wall board.

"Macaw?" Her voice trembling and tiny. "No. Oh no. Macaw?"

She stared at the pale hand, on its back, like a dead bird.

Macaw was trapped beneath a slab of wall board. Lea's stomach lurched again. She could feel the cold fear prickling her skin. She didn't think. She grabbed the top corner of the slab—and pulled. Hoisted it up.

It slid more easily than she had imagined. She almost toppled over backward.

She raised the wall board. Gazed down. Down at Macaw's lifeless face. At the puncture . . . the puncture . . . the blood-smeared puncture in her eye.

Lea gasped. She opened her mouth to scream, but couldn't make a sound.

The nail at the corner of the board—the rusted eight-inch nail, fatter than a pencil . . . Lea stared at the nail, then down to the blood-caked puncture in the dead woman's eye socket.

And she knew. She knew that when the wall fell in, the nail had been driven into Macaw's eye . . . eight inches . . . driven through her eye and into her brain.

15

Lea felt a sharp stab of pain in her right eye. She uttered a cry and pressed a hand over both eyes. Sympathy pain. It happened every time Ira or Elena hurt themselves.

The wall board fell from her hand and smacked the tumble of boards at her feet. The pile rumbled and slid beneath her. Eyes still covered, she struggled to keep her balance. Waited for the pain to fade.

A dog howled. She heard shrill, alarmed voices behind her.

"*Mes enfants? Avez-vous vu mes enfants?*"

"Do you live in the village?"

"The village is no more."

Dazed, Lea wandered away from the voices. No way to escape. She could go only as far as the beach. And even there, the moans and howls of stricken people mingled with the crash of the waves. The beach was littered with death, a long line of dead starfish.

As if the stars of heaven had fallen to the sand.

And then the red raindrops came down, soft at first, then in curtains like a waterfall of blood. The blood of the hurricane victims raining down, although there were no clouds in the sky.

And the twin angels emerged from the red rain. Two identical blond boys, so frail and thin, with glowing blue eyes, sad eyes.

They walked over the rain-spattered sand toward Lea, seemingly oblivious of the red drops falling around them.

"Can I help you?" she called. *They're so beautiful. So beautiful and sad.*

They didn't answer. They stopped and lowered their heads. They stood there perfectly still, blond hair gleaming so brightly as if the rain hadn't touched it. Their thin bodies appeared to tremble.

She took a step toward them, sandals sinking in the sand. "Are you cold? The rain. Where are your shirts?"

"It's all gone, mum," one of them said. He raised his blue eyes to her.

"Gone?"

The rain pattered more gently. The red curtains dissolved into raindrops. The world brightened to a yellow-gray glare. She wiped rain off her forehead.

"Our house is gone, mum," the boy said. He had a high-pitched voice, more like a five-year-old. *They have to be ten or twelve,* Lea thought.

"Where do you live?"

He shrugged his slender shoulders. "Nowhere now."

His twin let out a sigh. He kicked a wet clump of sand with a bare foot.

"You mean—?"

"It's all gone, mum. All of it."

Lea was staring at them so intently, she hadn't realized the rain had stopped. She swept her hands back, squeezing red water from her hair. Behind her, she could hear excited voices. Alarmed voices. People shouting about the blood rain.

"What's your name?"

"Daniel, mum. This is my bruvver Samuel."

Samuel nodded but didn't speak.

Lea wanted to hug them. Wrap them both in her arms. Tell them everything would be okay. *My heart is breaking for them. I don't think I've ever felt this strange emotion.*

"Can I help you? I mean, are you lost? Can I take you to your house?"

Daniel shook his head. "We don't have a house anymore," he said in an even tinier voice.

His brother sighed again. His blue eyes were watery, but his face revealed no emotion at all.

Is he in shock? she wondered.

"Where are your parents?"

"Gone, mum."

"Gone? Do you mean—?"

"Dead, mum. In the storm, don't you know. We lost them."

"Oh my God."

We lost them. What a grown-up way to say it. Not childlike at all.

What could she say? Trembling in their baggy little shorts, they looked so small and frail and frightened. Again, she felt the powerful urge to wrap her arms around them and hug them. Protect them from this whole nightmare.

But of course that was impossible. She couldn't protect *herself* from the nightmare. Once again she saw Macaw's dead face with the nail puncture through her splattered eyeball.

"Is there someone else in your family? Aunts and uncles? Your grandparents?"

They shook their heads.

"No one," Daniel said. His twin still hadn't spoken. "It's just us now, mum."

Lea spun around. Where were James and Martha? She couldn't see them from the beach.

Waves crashed against the shore. An upside-down canoe was carried onto the sand and tumbled to a stop against a steep sand hill. Seagulls soared low, chattering loudly.

"I'll take you to your house. You can get some clothes," Lea said.

"It was washed away," Daniel said, lowering his eyes. "All of it. Everything. Washed away. Samuel and I, we watched it go."

Samuel nodded.

"And you have no one? You're all alone?" Lea realized she was repeating herself. She didn't want to believe it.

"Just our friend." Samuel spoke up for the first time. He had a high, little boy's voice like Daniel.

"Friend?"

Daniel stepped in front of his twin. "He means me, mum. I'm his only friend." He gave Samuel a scowl. "His brain right now is kind of like shepherd's pie. You know. Everything all mixed together like."

Lea waited for Samuel to reply. But he lowered his eyes again and remained silent.

These two beautiful boys—what will happen to them now?

Ira and Elena flashed into her mind. She pictured them getting ready for school. The gulped-down breakfast. The yawns and groans and protests. The lost homework. The wrestling with Axl, Roz's funny child. Axl liked to jump on their backs and ride them around the room, especially when they were in a hurry and had no time for him.

Was Roz worried about Lea? Thinking about her right now?

Mark should be home from his book tour by now. Would he drive the kids to school or leave it to Roz? Or did he keep them home to watch the hurricane news on TV? Were they suffering? Not knowing if she'd survived . . .

Were they trying to reach her online? Her laptop was buried somewhere in the wreckage of the rooming house. Wreckage.

"Can you help us, mum?"

Daniel's tiny voice broke into her thoughts. He stepped forward and took her hand. His hand felt soft and cold in hers. He gazed up at her with pleading, wide eyes.

They're so adorable. Angels. Really.

"Can you help my brother and me?"

Lea squeezed his tiny cat's paw of a hand. And she felt something.

She didn't know what it was at first. She was trying hard not to think about what had happened here and what she saw all around her. But holding the boy's soft hand, she felt a strong connection.

It was so sad. So sad and overwhelming. She didn't want to

think at all. She wanted to push it all away. Yesterday. Today. This dreadful morning. Push it away forever.

But she felt a powerful attraction to this boy and his nearly silent brother. Something warm and soft and real. Two creatures who really needed her. And this crazy feeling that *she* needed *them*.

"Yes. Yes, I think I can help you."

16

Later, Martha warned her that she was being too hasty. "You don't know anything about these boys. You are acting on pure emotion. You need to wait till you can think about it clearly. Do some research. Try to find out something about them."

"They're so sad and alone, Martha. They break my heart. Really."

"All the more reason to take it slow," Martha insisted. "I know you said you feel a connection, but—"

"Not just a connection. I can't describe it. It's something like love, I guess. I mean, love at first sight. No. That's crazy. But I just feel. I don't know what I feel. I just feel I could be a good mother to them and—"

"Look how mixed up you are, Lea. At least let me do some research. That's what I do, you know. Let me see what I can find out before you take them home with you."

But Lea, not persuaded, couldn't wait to talk to Mark.

"Mark, it's what we wanted."

"You're breaking up, Lea. Are you on your cell?"

"No. The national guard set up some special lines. I had to wait in line an hour. No one has phones or internet or anything."

"I read online they're working on it. They've got the coast guard and the national guard and—"

"I only have a few minutes, darling. We don't have time to discuss the news. These two boys—"

"You can't just snatch them away from their home. I don't understand—"

"I'm not snatching them. They don't have a home. They lost everything here. Their family. Everything. They're adorable, Mark. They will fit in fine in Sag Harbor. They—"

"I know you want a big family. You always said it. And we talked about adopting. But this is different, Lea. This is too weird. I mean, to come home with two strange boys. I don't like it. I really don't."

"They're not strange. They're frightened and confused. But they're so sweet, Mark. They—"

"There are laws, Lea. The authorities there in Le Chat Noir—"

"What authorities? There aren't any. The island governor was killed in the hurricane. They found his body a few hours ago. There's no government here. There's no police. No offices. Nothing left."

"Lea, I'm sorry, but I really think this is insane. I think—"

"Mark, I'm taking them to safety. You can't imagine what it's like here. It's Hell. It's really Hell. I've got to make sure these boys are safe. We can search for relatives after I bring them home. But I feel something for them, Mark. It was this instant thing. I can't leave them here to die."

"I suppose we could talk to people here. Immigration people? What country are they from?"

"Country? They're from here. This island. They're American. We don't need immigration people."

"I don't want to do this, Lea. You're upset. You've had a terrible scare. You're not thinking clearly. You sound to me like you might be in a little bit of shock."

"Stop it, Mark. I'm not in shock. These two boys need us. They—"

"But we don't know anything about them."

"Mark, what do you want to know? They're adorable little twelve-year-old twins. Blond and blue-eyed. I'm not bringing home two-headed aliens from another planet. What are you afraid of? Think they have some kind of flesh-eating island disease? They lost their family. They're orphans. Someone has to adopt them. So—"

"It's going to be a hell of a shock for Ira and Elena. And Roz. And—"

"They all know we want a big family."

"But it's so sudden, Lea."

"So you're agreeing? I can bring them home?"

"No. I'm really opposed here. Bringing two island boys to Sag Harbor and expecting them to fit in with our family? No, Lea. Really. Think about it. Wait till your mind is clearer. You know. Calmer. Sleep on it."

"Sleep on it? You're joking. Don't you want me to come home? I have to get off the island. Today is the last day for the rescue boats. Tomorrow will be too late."

"But Lea—"

"Listen, honey, it could be your next book. Really. Two orphaned boys from a tiny island are taken to live with a middle-class family in Sag Harbor. Think of the possibilities, Mark. A study by you of how the boys adapt. What challenges them and what changes them and how they fit in with a family of strangers—and how they change the family. It could be a terrific follow-up book. And don't tell me you already have an idea, because I know you don't."

Silence.

"Well? You know it's a good idea, don't you, Mark? Think of the wonderful anecdotes—"

"Anecdotes? It's our *life*, Lea. It's not anecdotes. What if these boys—"

"They're sweet and sad, Mark. It's so tragic. They saw their parents carried away by the floodwaters. They lost everything. But they're adorable. I'm not exaggerating. When you see them, you'll fall in love with them, too. They're going to change our lives. You'll see."

———

"Daniel, you have to tell the woman about Ikey." Samuel stood at the open doorway of the fisherman's shack, white boards planked together to form a one-room shelter with a flat roof low overhead.

"She's not a woman. She's our new mum." Daniel lay on his back on the flat cot against the wall, hands behind his head.

"Ikey is fishing on the dock," Samuel said, pointing toward the water. "I can see him from here. You have to tell Mum—"

Daniel shook his head. He had a strange, smug smile on his face. As if the conversation was funny. "Ikey can't come. Mum won't take three of us. She only wants two."

"You don't know that. Did you ask her?" Samuel's voice rose with emotion. He wanted to wipe the smile off his brother's face. He stepped into the shack, ducking his head under the thick web of fishing nets hanging from the already low ceiling. "Did you ask her?"

Daniel pulled a segment of rope net down to him and twirled it around his hand. "Ikey isn't pretty like us. Mum doesn't want him."

"But she has to know—"

"No, she doesn't!" Daniel sat up quickly, blue eyes flaring angrily. A snort escaped his throat. Like an animal show of anger.

Samuel took a step back. He knew his brother's temper well. It taught him caution at an early age. Arguing with Daniel was such a waste of time. But he had to try. Someone had to look out for their little friend. Samuel had protected Ikey before. From others.

How could he protect him against Daniel?

"We will have a swimming pool," Daniel said, lying back down, twirling the fishing rope again. "Our own swimming pool, Sammy. And lobster to eat every night. And we'll wear new jeans and rule the school. That's what we always wanted, right, boyo? To rule the school?"

Daniel giggled, as if he'd said something hilarious. His head swung from side to side on the cot as he giggled some more.

Samuel felt his throat clench. Daniel was being Daniel again.

He took a deep breath. "I want to bring Ikey. Ikey is like our brother. He's our only friend. He's like family, Daniel."

"Family? Are you joking with me, lad?"

"No, it's not a joke."

Samuel scratched his chest. The new mum had found them jeans and T-shirts. But the clothes were stiff and scratchy. Samuel had sensitive skin. He needed soft fabrics or he'd break into a rash all over.

"We are starting a new family," Daniel insisted. "You. Me. The new mum. The new dad. A new bruvver and sister. A new family, Sammy. We'll swim all day in our own pool. We'll go fishing in the bay. That's what Mum says. And we'll rule the school. Like heaven. You want to go to heaven, don't you, Sammy? We're moving to Heaven."

Samuel made two fists. "I hate it when you talk stupid like that. You think it's cool, but it isn't. It's sick."

Daniel tossed the rope at the wall. He snorted again.

"I'm going to tell the new mum about Ikey," Samuel said, showing unusual courage. He knew he'd soon back down.

"Then she won't take us." Daniel swung around and leaped to his feet in a quick, graceful motion. He flashed Samuel a grin as he pushed past him and strode out of the little shack, onto the grassy approach to the beach.

"Where are you going?" Samuel turned to follow him.

"I'm going to explain to Ikey," Daniel replied without turning back.

"Explain to him? But—wait!"

Daniel trotted to the sand. Samuel could see Ikey sitting hunched at the end of the short dock in a beam of sunlight. Feet hanging over the side, fishing pole dangling beside him. Ikey smiled and waved as Daniel approached.

"Wait, Daniel."

Samuel sighed. He walked inside the shack and slumped to the damp floor. He scratched the sleeve of the starchy T-shirt. Mum seemed nice. She was pretty with that straight black hair and the shiny dark eyes. Almost like a movie star. But if all the T-shirts were this scratchy, it wouldn't be heaven.

At least their new home was near water. The ocean and the bay,

Mum had said. The place was called Long Island. That was good. Samuel had always lived on an island. Maybe it would feel like home right away.

What did that mean—feel like home? He'd never had a home. He'd never had parents. At least, not parents he could remember. Daniel was kind of his parent. Even though they were the same age.

Thinking this gave Samuel a bad feeling in his stomach. What kind of parent was Daniel? Very bad.

Samuel heard a short cry and a splash outside.

Oh no. Please, no.

A few seconds passed. Samuel sat up as Daniel strode back into the shack. He ducked his head under the fishing nets and dropped onto the cot. His face was a total blank. Eyes dull and lips pressed tightly together.

"What about Ikey?" Samuel's voice came out shrill and tight. "Did you explain? What did you tell him?"

"Don't worry about it," Daniel said without any emotion.

"But what did you say? What did you tell him?"

Daniel shrugged. That strange smile played over his face again. "No more Ikey," he said. His mouth did a strange quiver. Like a tic.

"Huh? No more Ikey? What do you mean?"

Daniel's smile grew wider. "No worries."

"But, Daniel—" Samuel couldn't find the words.

"No more Ikey," Daniel repeated in a singsong.

Samuel peered out the doorway to the dock. The dock was empty now. No boy sitting at the end. No fishing pole.

"No more Ikey," Daniel said. "So, no worries. Come on, bruvver." He jumped up and, putting a hand on Samuel's shoulder, guided him outside. "Big smiles now. Come on. Sweet smiles. Sweet. Be excited, lad. Let's go tell our new mum how excited we are."

PART TWO

17

Here he was at the Bay Street Theatre, just across from the bay in Sag Harbor, Andy Pavano and Vince's cousin Cora, in town from Bath, a little town in Maine, where she waitressed at a barbecue restaurant and took classes at Bowdoin, studying for a degree in social work.

Andy got all that info in the first five minutes when he picked her up at Vince's house and drove into town on a foggy, drizzly Saturday night. She talked quickly, with a slight Maine accent he hadn't heard much before, and kept tapping his shoulder as she talked, as if trying to keep his attention.

Cora wasn't bad-looking. She had sort of a bird-beak nose, but her eyes were round and pretty. She had the kind of smile that showed her gums, a toothy smile Andy liked. She was small and girlish—*except for her truck-driver laugh,* he thought. But maybe she just laughed like that because she was nervous. She said she'd never been out with a cop before.

"It's not really a date," he said. "Vince just thought we'd have fun together." Then he felt like a total dork for saying that. He could feel his face grow hot, but she didn't seem to notice.

She had to be five or ten years younger than him. Thirty maybe. She dressed young, like a college girl, in black tights and a purple square-necked top that gathered at her waist and came down low like a skirt. She didn't have much on top, he noticed. Her dark hair was short and layered.

Andy parked on the pier and they walked past a little lobster shack, closed for the night, and B. Smith's, a large, bustling restaurant overlooking the bay. A crowd stood at the entrance, waiting for the outdoor tables. Enormous white yachts lined the pier along the side of the restaurant.

The aroma of barbecued chicken floated out from B. Smith's kitchen, and Cora made a face. "Don't take me near a barbecue place. Sometimes after I've been at work in the restaurant, I have to shampoo three times to get the smoke out of my hair. Dogs follow me home because I smell like pulled pork."

Andy laughed. She had a good sense of humor about herself.

"You and Cora should hit it off," Vince had said the night before. "You're both in-tell-ect-u-als." That's how he said it, pronouncing every syllable. Was he being sarcastic? Probably.

Andy had told him he liked to read mystery novels and police procedurals, and Vince had teased him ever since, calling him Sherlock and telling him he should smoke a pipe.

Vince wasn't a Neanderthal, but he pretended to be. He thought it was part of his role as a small-town desk cop.

Cora seemed to think she had to tell everything there was to know about her before they got to the theater. Maybe she just had a thing about silences. Andy knew he wasn't keeping up his end, but it was hard to get a word in, and he was getting to like her soft schoolgirl voice.

She'd had a long affair with a guy in Bath she met at the barbecue restaurant. He said he was in the music business and seemed to know a lot about music clubs and new acts. But it turned out he sold jukeboxes and pinball machines, and he was married.

After she broke it off with him, he stalked her for a while, sitting outside the restaurant in his car and phoning her again and again, leaving threatening messages and muttering obscenities. When she changed her phone number, he finally went away.

"Did you call the police on him?"

She shook her head. "I didn't think they'd do anything. Usually, the police don't do anything in stalker cases till the woman is raped or stabbed in the chest."

"Usually," Andy agreed. "But sometimes a couple of cops can go to the guy's house and—you know—reason with him a little." Andy waved a fist.

Cora stopped outside the theater. "Have you ever done that?"

Andy stared at her. "Well, no. But I saw it on *Law & Order*."

They both laughed.

The play was called *Whodunnit?* Cora accused him of only having one interest in life. "Do you only go to plays about cops and crime?"

"I don't go to many plays."

The play wasn't great. It was supposed to be a comedy, but people weren't laughing. The mystery was impossible to solve. The murderer could have been any one of the six people onstage.

Andy hated stories like that where you didn't stand a chance of figuring it out. The culprit could even be the nearsighted police inspector hamming it up on the old-fashioned living room set.

Cora seemed to be enjoying it more than he was. She kept squeezing his arm every time something surprising took place. She laughed when the police inspector stepped on his eyeglasses and stumbled blindly over the tea cozy.

At intermission, Andy led Cora through the chattering crowd, out the doors to the walled terrace in front of the theater. Horns honked as traffic rolled by. The air smelled tangy, salty as the sea. He was about to ask if she wanted to skip the second act and go get a bite to eat when he saw Sari walk out of the theater.

Something pinged in his chest. A real physical feeling. Like a hard heart thump. Or an alarm going off.

Cora was saying something, tapping his shoulder, but he didn't hear her. He heard a rushing sound in his ears like water washing over a steep waterfall. How could Sari still have this effect on him?

She wore a short, white tank dress that clung to her body, showing off her long legs and her trim waist. Her black hair fell loosely behind her shoulders.

And who was the guy she was arm-in-arm with? Was he *the guy*?

That shrimp. He was at least a head shorter than Sari. Wearing a geeky black-and-white wide-striped shirt like a referee wears and white chinos torn at one knee, and a rope belt. Some kind of gold necklace hanging in front of his chest. And a tennis hat. The fucking guy wore a tennis hat with the name of his store on the front to the theater!

Andy lurched toward them. He saw Cora reach for him with both hands, startled by his sudden escape. But he wasn't moving on brainpower. This was some kind of weird primitive force propelling him, the rushing waterfall in his ears sweeping him away.

"Andy?" Sari let go of the shrimpy guy, her dark eyes flashing surprise.

Andy nearly knocked over the tall sign announcing *Whodunnit?* with photos of the cast. He caught his balance and took her by the elbow.

The shrimp peered out from under his tennis cap, eyes wide with surprise. He had freckles and a wide, innocent face. Reminded Andy of someone from an Archie comic book.

"I need to speak to Sari," Andy explained to him.

He expected more of a reaction. But the guy just shrugged and flicked his eyes toward Sari.

She didn't resist as Andy pulled her away, to the side of the theater. A few people turned to watch. He glimpsed Cora behind him, arms crossed now, following him with her eyes till he disappeared around the corner.

Sari giggled. "Are you crazy? We have to go back."

He backed her against the wall. Her skin felt soft and warm. Her eyes glowed even in the darkness here. He felt a rush of feeling, so powerful he had to take a deep breath.

She had hurt him so much the first time. Caused him so many feelings he didn't know he had.

And now here they were again. Here he was, feeling this insane rush of emotion, leading him . . . where?

"Andy, you look funny. What is your problem? You don't have anything to say to me—do you? We have to—"

"I'm back," he said.

And then he was kissing her. Kissing her. And she was kissing him back. And he felt the electric tingle of her fingers on the back of his neck. Just that light touch could make his head explode, he realized.

He kissed her harder. She wasn't resisting.

When the kiss ended, they stared dumbly at each other. Her hands slid off his neck. With a shiver of her shoulders, she slithered out from between him and the wall.

A long silence. Yes, his heart was pounding, and yes, the blood was throbbing, pulsing in his temples. But he didn't hear it now.

Silence. Silence.

And then she shook her head, sending her hair flying loose. She slowly rubbed a finger over her lips, as if wiping off the kiss. "That didn't mean anything," she murmured. "Hear me?"

Then she grabbed his head, pulled his face close, and kissed him again.

18

Andy didn't hear much of the second act. He was aware of Cora squeezing his arm a few times. Was she trying to snap him back to reality? He didn't want to go back. He could still smell Sari's perfume, like oranges, sweet oranges. He could still feel the silvery touch of her fingers on the back of his neck. The whisper of her hair falling over his cheeks.

Cora turned slightly away from him, eyes straight ahead, her lips pursed. She clasped her hands tightly in her lap. She was giving up. The characters moved across the stage, making broad hand gestures, shouting accusations at each other.

After the second kiss, Sari had repeated her warning. "That didn't mean anything, Andy. Please believe me." Then she turned away with a funny, short sigh and went running back to the shrimp.

When he saw her grab the guy's hands and lean down to kiss him on the cheek, Andy had some evil thoughts. Maybe arrest him for being unsightly. Then beat the guy to death with one of those new titanium tennis rackets.

It wasn't the first time he had thought of using his profession to settle a score or right a personal wrong. But of course he had never done anything like that. He was a good person and a good cop. A few free counter lunches were the only perks he had ever allowed himself.

He couldn't help it if his brain got overheated every once in a while. You can control your actions but not your thoughts. And yes, he had violent thoughts.

But the most violent moment of his life? It was back in the living room of the little two-family house in Forest Hills when his father, after too many Budweisers (for a change), settled an argument by punching his mother in the jaw. And Andy, maybe seventeen at the time, had grabbed the old man by the shoulders and shoved him hard, sent him staggering headfirst into the stone mantel. He could still hear the *smack* of his dad's bald head, the gasp of surprise, see the darkening line of blood on his forehead.

He'd expected the old man to spin around and come snarling back at him. But instead, he coiled his body, curled into a cowering position against the flowered wallpaper. To his shock, Andy realized his father was afraid of him.

It should have changed everything. But it didn't. Anthony Pavano was a bully. His son Andy wasn't.

Then Andy did twelve years as a New York City cop. Nothing as violent as that impulsive moment.

And why was he thinking of it now in this theater with people laughing all around him? Onstage, the nearsighted inspector was interviewing a coatrack. Andy glanced around, searching for Sari. But he couldn't locate her in the dark.

He really needed a smoke. He could feel the pack of Camels in his jacket pocket. Cora probably wouldn't approve. Who was Cora? He had to remind himself.

The play ended finally. Yes, the nearsighted inspector had committed the murder. But he was too nearsighted to realize it. At the end, he arrested himself.

Andy climbed to his feet and started to follow Cora across the aisle toward the exit.

"Very clever," a woman said behind him.

"Too clever," the man with her said.

"Did you guess the ending?"

"Yes. About an hour ago. But I still enjoyed it."

"It's one of his lesser works."

"All of his plays are lesser works."

Into the cool night air. A chatter of voices as people hurried to their cars. Cora walked along the sidewalk toward the pier till they were away from the crowd, then turned back to him. "It wasn't very good, was it." Said with a shrug and a sad smile.

"I don't think I laughed," he said. His eyes were over her shoulder, searching for Sari. How had she disappeared? He just wanted a glimpse of her.

"It was supposed to be sophisticated," she said. "But the actors camped it up too much, don't you think? If they'd played it sincere . . ."

He didn't want to discuss the play. He wanted to catch one more look at Sari and have a slow, soothing smoke. He wanted to burn his throat and let the smoke make his eyes water.

No. He didn't know what he wanted.

But when he heard the shrill shouts, he suddenly snapped alert. He turned toward the cries. From the pier? He spun away from Cora and took off running.

19

He heard shouts for help. Shrill cries. And, in the circle of light from a tall streetlamp, saw a small group of people wrestling against the side of the darkened lobster shack. He didn't realize they were children until he was a few feet from them.

"Stop! Police!" he boomed.

He stepped in something soft. Glancing down, he saw a smashed ice cream cone on the pavement beneath his shoe. Another cone lay near it, ice cream still round at the top.

"You dumb shit! You dumb shit! You pay me back!" a blond-haired boy in a blue Southampton sweatshirt was screeching.

A big dark-haired kid, nearly twice his size, had him by the front of the sweatshirt and swung a meaty fist above the boy's face. "Shut up! Shut the fuck up, liar!"

Two or three other kids stood back a few feet and watched. They were all shouting angrily at the big guy.

Not even teenagers, Andy realized. Their voices hadn't changed.

"You fuck! You pay me for that cone!"

"You want a cone? I'll shove it up your ass! You think I can't? You want to dare me?"

Kids!

The big kid started to lower his fist to the smaller boy's midsection. Andy stepped between them and absorbed most of the blow on his side. The kid had a pretty good punch.

"Break it up. Police."

He grabbed the big kid by the shoulders of his gray hoodie and pushed him backward.

"Get off me, asshole. You don't look like no police."

"Sag Harbor Police," Andy said, as if that would convince the kid. "What's the fight about?"

The blond-haired boy pointed to the asphalt. "My ice cream cone. He tried to take it."

"Liar!" the big kid screamed. He lunged at the smaller guy again. Andy caught him and stood him up.

"Ethan is telling the truth!" a girl cried. The others joined in agreement.

"You're Ethan?" Andy asked.

The blond kid nodded. He had tears in his eyes. He brushed back his straight blond hair with one hand. His whole body was trembling. Andy saw he was struggling with all his might not to burst out sobbing.

"And what's your name?" Andy asked the other kid.

No reply. Instead, a sullen stare.

"Derek Saltzman," the girl said. "He knocked down my cone, too."

"I'll knock *you* down, too," Derek told her.

"You're not going to knock anyone down," Andy growled. "What's your problem?"

"Derek is mean," the girl said. "He's always picking fights."

"He's always stealing our stuff," Ethan said in a trembling voice.

"Fucking liars," Derek muttered.

"Nice language," Andy said. "How old are you?"

"Old enough," the kid muttered, still offering up the surly glare.

He has a face like a bulldog, Andy thought. *And a personality to match.*

"He's twelve," the girl offered.

"And how old are you?" Andy asked Ethan.

Ethan took a step back. He didn't take his eyes off Derek. "I'm twelve, too."

Cora stepped up beside Andy. "What's going on?"

"Kids fighting," he told her. "Over ice cream."

"I didn't take their ice cream," Derek snarled. His fat cheeks puffed in and out like a blowfish. "They're total liars."

Andy noticed he cleaned up his language with a woman present.

"Then how did the cones end up on the pavement?" Andy asked.

Derek shrugged. "They dropped them."

"Liar!"

Cora squinted at them. "Why are you kids all alone out here? It's ten o'clock at night."

Before anyone could answer, hurried footsteps clicked over the asphalt. Andy turned to see a red-haired woman running awkwardly toward them on high, spiked heels. She was tall and lean and had a white jacket tied around her shoulders, which flared behind her like a cape as she ran. Gold bracelets jangled up and down one arm.

"Derek?" she called breathlessly. "What's going on?"

She stopped a few feet from Andy and Cora and eyed him suspiciously. "Who are you? Is there a problem?"

"I'm a police officer," Andy started. "I—"

"Police? What did he do? Who are these kids?" Her voice was throaty, hoarse, a smoker's voice. It rose with each question. Her chest heaved up and down beneath her violet sweater. The bracelets matched a gold chain with a jeweled heart that hung from her neck.

"I didn't do anything," Derek said, jutting his fleshy jaw out defiantly.

"Is he your son?" Andy asked.

She nodded. Then she brushed a strand of coppery hair off her forehead. "Yes. Derek Saltzman. He's my son. I'm Elaine Saltzman. I left him for ten minutes by the ice cream store." She pointed toward the end of the pier.

"These kids say your son tried to take away their ice cream. I think there was some kind of scuffle."

"Liars!" Derek shouted.

"We're not lying!"

Mrs. Saltzman squinted at Ethan, seeing him for the first time. "I know you. You're Ethan, right?" She turned back to Andy. "He's in my son's class. What happened, Ethan?"

Derek lurched forward. He raised both hands as if to give his mother a shove. "Why do you ask *him*? Why don't you ask *me*?" In a whining voice that made Andy want to cover his ears.

He glanced at Cora. Her eyes were on one of the tall, white yachts at pierside. Three people had come onto the deck to watch the confrontation.

Bet Cora is impressed seeing a cop in action, Andy thought wryly. *Spilled ice cream is a felony in this town. Ha. Wait till I slip the cuffs on the kid. She'll be all over me.*

"Derek tried to take our cones," Ethan reported. "When we said no, he knocked them to the ground."

"Stupid liar! They knocked *my* ice cream to the ground!"

Mrs. Saltzman stared down at her red-faced son. "Are you telling the truth?"

She didn't wait for him to answer. She wrapped her hand around Andy's arm and led him across the pier. She waited for an SUV to pass, then pulled him to the side of a parked car, out of her son's hearing.

"Derek has problems," she murmured, fingers still tight around Andy's sleeve. She leaned against him and brought her face close to his. He could smell her flowery perfume and a whiff of alcohol on her breath. "Ever since his father left, he's been angry, very troubled."

This was definitely more than Andy wanted to hear.

"Mrs. Saltzman, I really have to be going. Why don't you just solve this thing by buying cones for all three kids?"

She blinked. Did she expect him to get tough or something? She was still holding onto him. A strong breeze off the bay fluttered her hair.

"Good. Okay," she said. "I just wanted to explain. I mean, these days sometimes Derek acts out. But he's basically a good boy. He has a good head on his shoulders. A good head. Really."

Of course, neither Andy nor Elaine Saltzman, nor anyone on the pier that night, had any idea of what would happen to Derek's head a few weeks later.

20

"My parents say we'll have a house in Malibu. That's where they are right now. In L.A., buying it. It's right on the ocean. See, you go out the back door and you're on the beach."

"That's awesome, Ruth-Ann. Can I come live with you? I mean really."

"It's like being on vacation all the time. Only you live there. And there are celebrities all over the beach. You know. Movie stars. And TV. And you just hang out with them."

"You think Johnny Depp could be your neighbor?"

"No way. He's too old. They don't let old people in Malibu."

The girls both laughed. They sat almost side by side on Ruth-Ann's bed, talking and texting each other at the same time.

"Dylan Sprouse?"

"You like him? I like the other one."

"They could be your neighbors. You could hang with them and they'd ask you to be on TV. And you'd be a star."

"No way, Elena. I'm only fourteen. I don't want to be a star till I'm sixteen."

That made them both laugh again.

Elena Sutter and Ruth-Ann Glazer had been friends since third grade, and best-best friends for two years since sixth grade, mainly since they shared the same sense of humor, although Ruth-Ann was the real wit, sharp and sarcastic. And because they lived two houses down from each other and were in the same eighth-grade class at Sag Harbor Middle School, and because they looked so much alike, they could be sisters.

They agreed that Ruth-Ann looked like the older sister, because she was at least four inches taller than Elena, and already had the beginnings of a woman's body, meaning she had breasts, and wore her hair in a more sophisticated, layered look, which she acquired during one of her many trips with her parents to L.A.

They were both pretty and smart and popular. They both had an easy way of getting along with other kids, and of not getting in their own way when it came to success at school. They were both spoiled but not in an obnoxious way. They knew how to get whatever they wanted from their parents and still allow their parents to think *they* were the ones in charge.

Elena was a miniature fourteen-year-old version of Lea, her mother. Creamy-white skin framed by straight, black hair, serious dark eyes, a delicate face and a wiry body, perfect for the gymnastics classes that she was becoming more serious about.

They tapped on their phones for a few minutes without speaking. Elena's phone bleeped. She squinted at the screen. "Ethan."

Ruth-Ann lowered her phone. "Ira's friend Ethan? What's he want?"

Elena shrugged. "Nothing. Just said 'sup." She thumbed the keys rapidly.

Another bleep. "He wants to come over. His PlayStation broke."

"Tell him no way. Tell him your brother Ira isn't here. He's at your house. Ethan pretends he wants to hang with Ira. Then he just stares at you. Like a sad puppy dog."

Elena laughed. "He *does* look like a puppy dog." The light from her phone gave her face a pale tint. "Hey, I'm not kidding about Malibu. Your parents would let me come with you, right? Just for the summer, I mean."

Ruth-Ann studied her friend. "You're joking. You're getting two new brothers, and you want to come live with me?"

Elena scrunched up her face. "Why do I want two new brothers?"

"Because they're hot? Show me that photo again." She grabbed Elena's phone and began shuffling through photo screens. She stopped at the twins' photo and brought it close to her face.

Elena grabbed it away from her. "You think they're cute? I think they're blond freaks."

"You're messed up, Elena. They are totally hot. I mean, for twelve-year-olds. Check out those smiles. Those dimples on this one's cheeks. What's his name? Danny? Adorable. They could be on TV. Really."

Elena stuck her finger down her throat and made a gagging sound.

She squinted at the photo. Daniel and Samuel. Wavy blond hair, almost white. And those big blue eyes. Wearing red T-shirts way too big for them. And those sick, sweet smiles.

"Like they're posing as angels," Elena said. *Where did that thought come from? Weird!*

"Where are they going to stay?" Ruth-Ann studied the photo. "Are you changing rooms? They're not moving into the playroom downstairs, are they?"

"No way. Dad fixed up the attic. He made it really awesome. He bought them a laptop and a TV, and he got them a Wii. He said they've had a tough life. He wants to make things nice for them."

"Tough life? No kidding. They lost both their parents, didn't they? And their house? And all their stuff?"

Elena nodded. "I think Dad wants to write a book about them."

Ruth-Ann handed the phone back to Elena. "For real? You know, my parents were talking about your dad's book. Did you read it?"

"Not really. Just kinda looked at it."

"Mom said the book says parents should let kids do whatever

they want. Just let them be free. My parents made jokes about it. They said it would make a great sitcom."

"Is that all your parents think about? Sitcoms?"

"Well, yeah. Their show was picked up for another year. All they talk about are jokes and scripts and stuff."

"Ruth-Ann, do you watch it?"

"Of course not. No way."

They both laughed.

Elena twisted the phone in her hand. "My dad's book isn't true. He is stricter than your parents. I mean, he doesn't let Ira and me do what we want. I always have to trick Mom into letting me go places. Or Roz. Roz is the easiest because she's busy worrying about Axl."

"I forgot about Axl. It's gonna be crowded in your house, Elena. I mean, a mob."

"That's why I want to come to Malibu with you guys."

"How is Ira taking the new brothers thing? Is he freaking?"

"Of *course* he's freaking. Ira freaks when his shoelace comes untied."

"Now you sound like my parents. They'd like that joke. They'd type it into their BlackBerries right away."

"It's no joke. The poor kid is totally stressed already. I mean, he thinks sixth grade is really hard."

Ruth-Ann snickered. "Wait till he gets to eighth."

"He hates his teacher. Miss Montgomery. Did you have Montgomery?"

"No. I had Price, remember?"

"Montgomery acts real nice. She's real pretty and she's very sweet, but she gives hours and hours of homework every night. And then she doesn't even collect it or go over it or anything. Ira says she just makes you do it."

Ruth-Ann snickered. "Tell Ira to suck it up."

Elena sighed. "I think he really misses Mom and Dad when they're both away. Roz is great. But . . . you know."

Elena's phone rang, startling her. She stared at the screen, but she didn't have to. She recognized her dad's ringtone.

"Hi, Dad. Oh. Okay. Okay. I'm coming. Bye."

She clicked the phone shut. "It's my new brothers. They're here. I gotta go." She jumped to her feet and strode out of the room. She was making her way down the stairs when she heard Ruth-Ann's shout.

"Hey, Elena—good luck."

21

At LaGuardia Airport, Mark hugged Lea and held her close, wrapped her up like a prize that had almost been lost. He wanted to plant a hundred kisses on her face. The strong emotion welled in him, taking him by surprise. He was usually so level, no tidal waves of feeling rocking his calm.

But he let her go when he saw the two blond creatures gazing at him. *My new sons?*

Yes, they were beautiful boys. Their deep blue eyes were almost unreal. And Lea's description—angels—came pretty close to describing the sweetness, the innocence on their pale faces.

So why didn't he feel some kind of immediate connection with them? The wave of emotion seemed to pull back, leaving him with an empty feeling as he stared at the boys over Lea's shoulder.

He didn't want them here. He had argued with Lea almost until their plane had taken off. But he hoped that when he saw them . . . when he actually saw the two angels, he would fall for them the way Lea had, and his doubts and objections would fade away.

What a disappointment that their hopeful blue-eyed stares only aroused a feeling of dread.

And now, after the long drive to Sag Harbor, here they were in his house. About to meet his kids. About to join his family.

Just like that. Two strangers to take care of and worry about. And love.

The boys seem really happy to be here, Mark thought. *They haven't stopped smiling.*

Guiding them to the living room, Lea stood behind them, as if backing them up, or maybe blocking any retreat. Her expression was tense. Mark noticed her eyes were bloodshot. She had one hand lightly on Samuel's slender shoulder.

Ira stood halfway up the stairs, his chin on the wooden banister. He stared down warily at the two boys, gripping the banister tightly with both hands as if holding on for dear life.

He's staring at them like they were circus freaks. I told Ira to give them a friendly welcome. Did he forget?

"Ira, come down and say hi to your new brothers." Mark motioned him down.

"Hi," he said, without budging from his perch.

"Ira, come down." Lea's voice sounded tight, shriller than usual. "Can't you shake hands?"

"Kids don't shake hands." Ira's reply.

The twins gazed up at him with those sweet smiles on their faces. Their blue eyes appeared to glow. *Like jewels,* Mark thought. *They are extraordinary-looking.* He thought of beautifully crafted dolls.

Except they were so skinny, so gaunt. The red T-shirts and long white shorts hung on them like scarecrow clothes. Their flat white sneakers were as long as clown shoes.

We've got to buy them clothes. Then see about putting some meat on their bones.

The twins stepped forward, almost in unison, and gazed around the living room. "How nice is this?" Samuel said. "We never had a couch." He put a hand on the back of the green leather couch and squeezed it. Mark saw that when he removed his hand, he left a sweat stain on the leather.

Daniel turned back to Ira on the stairs. "Do you like to swim?"

Ira scrunched up his face, as if he had to think about it. "Not if the water's cold."

Is he going to say anything friendly or positive?
Guess it'll take time.

"Where do you like to swim?" Daniel asked Ira. He was definitely trying to break the ice. "In the bay or in the ocean?"

"My friend Ethan has a pool," Ira said, chin on the banister. He didn't move from behind the bars of the banister, safe in his cage up there.

Roz came bursting into the room from the kitchen, holding Axl by one hand as the chubby, dark-haired boy toddled beside her. She wore a long blue denim sleeveless dress and was barefoot, as usual. Axl had a little sunburn on his arms. She had taken him to the bay beach this morning.

"Welcome! Welcome!" Roz threw her arms around Daniel and hugged him, then pulled his brother into a hug, as if they had known each other for years. Roz wasn't usually this demonstrative, but she had told Mark she planned to do all she could to welcome the boys into a warm home.

Axl stuck out his stubby arms toward the twins, as if he wanted a hug, too. To everyone's surprise, including Axl's, Samuel picked the two-year-old up in his arms and hugged him. Axl grabbed a fistful of the boy's blond hair and tugged it hard. Samuel laughed and spun Axl around.

His twin watched the whole thing with a dimpled smile. When Samuel returned Axl to the floor, Daniel pointed at the toddler. "He's funny-looking."

Roz's happy expression changed. "What did you say?"

"He's funny-looking. His face makes me laugh."

Roz moved toward Axl as if she had to protect him. "He has a perfectly nice face. And his hair is coming in nice and curly."

"He's funny-looking," Daniel repeated. "No lie."

Lea stepped toward him and spoke up. "Sometimes it's better to say something nice," she said.

"Sometimes." Daniel's smile returned. He exchanged a quick glance with his brother. "But the laddy looks like a chimpanzee, don't you know?"

"Panzee," Axl repeated. He giggled. He seemed to like the word. "Panzee."

Roz started to say something but restrained herself. "Well, I hope you boys like it here. Welcome to our family."

"We like it already," Samuel said. "We never had a couch."

"Mark, show them their room," Lea said.

But before Mark could move, the front door swung open, letting in a burst of warm sunshine, followed by Elena. She stopped at the door and called to the new arrivals. "Hey, guys! You're here!"

They turned and studied her.

She swept into the room and shook hands with both of them at once. "Oh, wow. How do I tell you apart?"

"I'm the smart one," Daniel said.

"He's the weird one," Samuel told her.

"You can tell them by the dimples," Lea offered. "See? Daniel has those dimples on his cheeks and Samuel doesn't."

"Weird," Elena said. She squinted at them. "Do you always dress alike?"

"Your mum bought us this," Daniel said, tugging at the baggy red T-shirt. "We lost our clothes. We lost everything." His voice cracked on the last word. He lowered his eyes.

"Don't worry." Lea stepped up behind them and put a hand on each one's shoulder. "That's the first thing on my list. We'll go shopping and buy you all the clothes you need."

They turned their heads and smiled up at her.

Lea sighed. "Oh, I'm just so happy you are both here. Look at me. I have tears in my eyes." She walked over to Mark and pressed her face against the front of his shirt. "*Thank you*," she whispered.

"Panzee," Axl offered.

Daniel reached down and picked Axl up again. Axl poked his nose against Daniel's nose. "Chimpanzee," Daniel said.

"Panzee." Axl repeated the word.

Daniel lifted his eyes to Roz. "Do you feed him lots and lots of bananas?"

Roz squinted at him. "Excuse me?"

"You know. Chimpanzee food?"

Again, Mark saw Roz restrain herself. "I guess I'll have to get used to your sense of humor, Daniel."

Samuel snickered. "Daniel doesn't have a sense of humor. He's just strange, don't you know."

"Chimpanzee," Daniel and Axl said in unison. Then they both giggled.

Daniel turned back to Roz. "He's my new pet."

Roz's mouth dropped open.

Daniel twirled Axl above his head. Axl laughed. "Yes, boyo. You're my new pet. Gonna slip you lots and lots of peanuts."

"Panzee," Axl repeated and tossed back his head and giggled.

"Look how sweet they are," Lea whispered, leaning her head against Mark's shoulder and squeezing his arm. "They're being so nice to Axl. Isn't that the sweetest?"

"I'm not sure Roz would agree with you," Mark whispered back, watching Daniel twirl Axl faster and faster. "She looks upset."

"They're just being playful," Lea said, tears glistening in her eyes. "They don't know they insulted Roz. They're not trying to be mean."

The twins appeared to like their attic room. Mark had hired some local carpenters to add walls and finish the ceiling and carpet the floor and paint the room a comforting pastel blue-green.

The eaves were low, so they all had to duck their heads. He and Roz had gone to Hildreth's, the old department store in Southampton, and bought soft-looking, comfortable, homey furniture for the room. And twin beds, which Mark placed side by side at the end of the attic, with the window looking down to the backyard.

Now they were bouncing on their beds, giggling and raising their hands to the low ceiling. Watching them, Lea clapped her hands and let out a gleeful cheer. "They like the room, Mark." She kissed his cheek. Her face was wet from her tears.

Mark playfully tugged her hair. "I'm glad you're so happy."

"I *am* happy. I just know we're doing the right thing. I have such a strong feeling. . . ."

Elena stood behind them at the top of the attic stairs. She appeared to be studying the twins as if they were zoo specimens. Ira had chosen not to join them up here.

Earlier in the week, when Mark broke the news to Elena that Lea was coming home with two orphaned boys, he was prepared for some kind of strong reaction. He didn't expect the shrug he received and the muttered "Whatever."

Then she quickly added, "As long as they stay out of my room and don't annoy my friends."

That broke the tension. "They're going to be a little strange at first," he warned her. "They grew up on a tiny island. And they've been through a lot of tragedy."

Elena rolled her eyes. "Dad, they're twelve, right? *Of course* they're going to be strange."

They both laughed.

He knew Elena would take it in stride, as she did everything. There would definitely be problems with her along the way. A teenager with *three* younger brothers in the house? No way there wouldn't be conflicts and fights and tears. But Elena could always be counted on to ride out any emotional wave.

Ira was a different story. Take him to town for lunch and talk to him again? Tell him he had to pitch in and make this work? Tell him the family really needed his help?

Mark knew he'd just roll his eyes and say, "Tell me something I don't know."

Or worse: "Shut up, Dad. You're a jerk."

The twins were on their backs now, sprawled on the beds, luxuriating, sinking their heads into the pale green pillows. The room was pale blue and green, water colors, soothing and perhaps, a reminder of their island home.

Roz and Mark had put a lot of thought into all this while Lea was working to bring them off the island.

"Let's show the boys the rest of the house," Lea said. "Come on, get up, guys. We'll give you the grand tour."

Elena led the way downstairs. Her room was at the near end of the hall. She pushed the door open so the boys could take a glimpse. Above her bed, she had a framed poster of a girl gymnast, arms outstretched, flying high in the air. The closet door was covered with cutout photos of actors from the teen-trauma TV shows she watched on her computer. Skirts and jeans and colorful tops were strewn all over the floor. Elena had a lot of good qualities, but she wasn't neat.

"Nice room," Daniel said. He pushed Samuel out of the doorway to get a better look. He pointed to the gymnast poster. "Is that you?"

Elena rolled her eyes. "I wish."

Daniel started into the room, but Elena pushed a hand against his chest. "Two words to remember about my room, guys," she said.

They trained their blue eyes on her. "Two words?" Daniel asked.

"Keep out," she said.

They both burst out laughing. As if she had made a hilarious joke. They laughed and shook their heads. Daniel raised his hand for Elena to slap him a high five.

"You're funny, Elena," he said. Samuel nodded agreement.

"I'm serious," Elena insisted.

"Let's move on with the tour," Mark said. He guided the boys to the next room. His office. He pointed out the desktop PC and his shelves of psychology books, and the piece of moon rock on his desk. They took a quick glance but didn't seem at all interested.

At the end of the hall, Elena said, "This is Ira's room."

The boys shoved each other as they eagerly trotted down the hall. Their too-big sneakers made floppy sounds on the thick, white carpet. They all burst into Ira's room.

He lay sprawled on the bed, white earplugs in his ears, tapping away on a handheld game player. He didn't stop or look up as everyone invaded his room.

"Ira?" Mark called. "Earth calling Ira. You have visitors."

Ira tapped away, eyes on the game player.

The twins walked around the room. Daniel strode to the two windows, pushed back the gray curtains, and gazed down at the front yard and the street. Afternoon sunlight poured in, making his blond hair glow.

Ira's room was bare and undecorated. The walls were plain white. On the narrow strip of wall between the windows, he had a small, framed photograph of himself shaking hands with New York's governor, after Ira had won a state citizenship essay contest.

No other art or decoration in the room except for a small black stenciled octopus on the wall over his headboard. Mark didn't understand the octopus. Ira wasn't into sea life at all. In fact, he was timid and frightened around the ocean.

A low bookshelf stood beside the long white counter that served as his desk. The closet door was closed. No dirty clothing on the floor.

Ira didn't like clutter. He said keeping his room white and bare helped him concentrate on his homework. Nothing to distract him. And he said it helped him sleep at night because there were no scary shadows.

Samuel studied Ira's laptop. Photos of Ira and his friends on a class trip shuffled on the screen, Ira's screensaver. Daniel moved to the bed and sat down on the edge of the white quilt.

Lea tugged the earplugs from Ira's ears. He sat up straight, blinking in surprise. "Hey—"

"We're showing Daniel and Samuel the house," Lea said. "Do you want to tell them anything about your room?"

Ira shook his head. "Not really."

"Awesome room," Samuel said. "Sunny. Like an island morning, you know?"

Lea leaned toward Mark. "Don't you love their accent? Sometimes the way they talk . . . it's like poetry."

Daniel stepped up to Ira. His face turned serious. "Can I have your room?"

A short laugh burst from Ira's throat. "Huh? I don't think so."

Lea took a step toward Daniel. "You like Ira's room, sweetheart? It's kind of bare, don't you think?"

Daniel didn't respond. He wrapped a hand around Ira's upper arm. His eyes locked intently on Ira's startled face.

"No. Really," Daniel said, lowering his voice. "Can I have your room?"

Ira raised his eyes to Mark. A pleading glance. Mark felt too stunned to react.

"I'll have your room," Daniel repeated, patting Ira's shoulder. "Okay?"

22

"Mark, be reasonable. It's a perfect solution. I can't believe you're the one being the hard-ass about this." Lea's hands were clenched into tight fists over the kitchen table.

Mark reached across the table to take her hand, but she snapped it out of his reach. "I think I'm being the reasonable one," he said.

"I think *I* am," Roz insisted. She had put Axl down for his nap and joined them in the kitchen for what had started out as a quiet discussion and, much to Mark's dismay, quickly elevated into a shouting match.

Ira was sulking in his room. Elena had taken the twins on a walking tour of the neighborhood to show them the bay. The boys were hopping up and down with excitement and had no idea of the conflict they had caused among the three adults.

Lea took a breath and started another attempt to persuade Mark. "You saw the look on Ira's face when the boys wanted his room. He was *sick*. He was about to have a fit."

"Of course he was," Mark started. "He had every right—"

"So then they saw the guesthouse and totally fell in love with it," Roz interrupted. Mark gazed at the dark stains on the front of her sweater. Axl was constantly using her sweater as a napkin.

"They don't know *what* they want," Mark said, turning to Lea. "How could they? It's like they stepped onto another planet."

"They know they want to live in the guesthouse," Lea said, jaw clenched, eyes about to tear up again. "And Roz has agreed to move up to the attic."

"It's better for me anyway," Roz said. "I can keep a closer watch on everyone if I'm staying inside the house. And the attic is even roomier—"

"And that way, Ira will keep his room," Lea said. "That's so important. I wouldn't do anything to hurt Ira's equilibrium."

"No! No way!" Mark jumped to his feet, nearly knocking over his chair. "I built the attic room for the boys. They should be in the house. We don't know anything about them. We have to take special care of them. We can't have them living by themselves in their own house, even if it's in the backyard. That's *crazy*."

Lea motioned with both hands for him to calm down. "We want to make them happy, Mark."

Mark felt his throat tighten. "So you'll do *anything* they want? Is that your idea?"

"Mark, stop shouting. Can't we sit here and have a calm discussion? Roz and I agree—"

"Leave Roz out of this. We're the ones adopting these . . . these . . ."

"Leave me out of it? I thought I was part of this family. God knows, I'm the one spending most of the time with the kids."

Mark patted her hand. "Sorry, Roz." He turned to Lea. "I'm not trying to be difficult. I see how happy you are. I see you already have strong feelings for these boys. You know I didn't want them here, but I'm going to try, Lea. I'm going to do everything I can. But you can't just give in to them. You can't give them everything they want. They don't know—"

"You saw them pleading and pleading to live in the guesthouse. You saw how excited they were."

"I just think it's too soon to have them living on their own. We don't know how they're going to adapt. We don't know if we can trust them. We don't know—"

"They won't be living on their own. No way. They'll be with us all the time. We'll—" Lea gasped. Her eyes were over Mark's shoulders. "Oh no."

Mark spun around and saw the twins huddled in the kitchen doorway. He felt his heart skip a beat. "How long have you two been standing there?"

They both shrugged. Mark realized their eyes were on him. They were studying him. Had they overheard his true feelings?

An awkward silence in the room. Then Lea stood up and flashed them a broad smile. "Good news, boys. We had a vote here. And we voted two to one. Roz and Axl are going to move to the attic—and you two get to stay in the guesthouse."

She turned to Mark as if challenging him. But he knew when he was defeated.

The twins cheered and did a funny, awkward tap dance of celebration. But their smiles faded quickly. "Only one thing," Daniel said softly. "Samuel and I will take the guesthouse only if you promise us one thing."

Mark narrowed his eyes at them. *Now what? What is their next demand?*

"Only if Ira will come have sleepovers with us," Daniel said.

He saw Lea's chin quiver. The tears were about to flow again.

"Are they angels?" she whispered. "Is that the sweetest thing?"

23

Lea grabbed the car keys and stuffed them in her jacket pocket. She herded the twins toward the back door. "Where's Ira? Ira's coming with us? Did you see him?"

Before they could answer, Elena burst into the kitchen. "Have you seen my necklace? Did you see it anywhere?"

Lea blinked. "Necklace?"

"The one with the amethyst. You know. Grandma's necklace? It was on my dresser. I know I left it on top of my dresser. Now I can't find it anywhere."

"Maybe it fell off, sweetie," Lea suggested. "Did you look underneath?"

"Duh. Like of course. Like I'm not stupid." Elena turned to the twins. "Did you see a necklace anywhere?"

They both shook their heads. "Not me," Daniel said.

"We'll all search for it when we get back," Lea said. "It didn't fly away. We'll find it. Get Ira for me, will you? I'm taking the twins shopping."

Lea drove the twins to the mall at Bridgehampton to buy them clothes. Ira had protested vehemently, but she forced him to accompany them and help select what kids at his school were wearing. The twins had been with them for two days, and he hadn't made a single attempt to be friendly. Now he sat glumly in the front seat beside her, his arms crossed, staring straight ahead through the windshield.

In the Camry's backseat, the twins strained at their seat belts, leaning out the windows to see the passing scenery.

"I don't think they've ever been in a car before," she told Ira.

No response.

"Come on, Ira. Shape up."

"Look at that truck!" Daniel exclaimed. "Couldn't you fit a whole house in that truck!"

Lea found it so touching. These twelve-year-old boys seeing the world for the first time.

She turned into a long parking aisle and stopped while a blue pickup backed out of a spot. "Be nice to them," she whispered to Ira. "Be a help, okay? I'll buy you something special right now. To cheer you up. What would you like? What can I buy you?"

"A candy bar?"

Lea bought all three of them big Milky Way bars. The twins ate them slowly, taking small bites, savoring them, dopey smiles on their faces as if they were drunk from the chocolate.

"You had candy bars on the island, didn't you?" Lea asked.

They both nodded. "I got a Snickers bar for my tenth birthday," Samuel said.

"It was my birthday, too," Daniel said. "We had to share it, don't you know."

Ira stared at them. Lea thought she caught a moment of empathy on his face. Having to share a candy bar was something Ira could feel strongly about.

Still chewing on their giant candy bars, they followed Lea into T.J.Maxx.

"We need to get you boys at least three or four pairs of jeans to wear to school," Lea said. "Ira, what kind of jeans are the kids wearing these days?"

Ira licked caramel off his lips. "I don't know."

"Come on, Ira," Lea snapped. "Help out here. What kind of jeans?"

He shrugged. "I'll know it when I see it."

"Okay. Follow me. Boys' jeans are over there."

She led them to the tables stacked high with jeans. Only a few brands but several styles and colors of denim. Did kids still wear cargo jeans? Most of the jeans in Ira's closet had a dozen pockets up and down the legs.

She picked up a pair of straight-legged, faded denims and held it against Samuel. "This looks about your size. Ira, do kids wear these?"

Ira shrugged. "Maybe."

Lea searched through the pile and pulled out the same size. "You boys will have to go try these on. But wait. Let's find a few more."

Daniel had a smear of chocolate on his chin. "Only one of us has to try them on," he said. "We're the same size."

"But don't you want to pick the ones you like?" Lea asked.

Samuel gazed up at her. "Do we really get more than one? We don't have to share?"

"Yes. You can each pick two or three."

The twins clapped their hands, careful not to drop their candy bars. They let out squeaks of joy.

It takes so little to make them happy, Lea thought. *My kids take everything for granted.*

She had a sudden memory flash: the twins stepping out of the red rain, looking so lost and forlorn. All around them, the devastation, everything down and destroyed. The mournful wails. The heavy, sour smell of death with each breath she took.

She forced the images from her mind. "Here. Go try this smaller size. Take these and try them all on." She watched them race to the dressing room against the back wall. They were so small for their age. Ira towered over them.

Ira hunched beside her, doing his best to look bored and unhappy. "What am I supposed to do?"

"Help me pick out some shorts for Axl."

"Big whoop."

A short while later, success. Jeans were selected. T-shirts added to the pile. A couple of sweaters and long-sleeved shirts. It was April and the weather was still cool and damp.

"Thank you, Mum. Thank you." From Daniel.

Then Samuel: "Thank you, Mum. I'm so happy. I never had new clothes, don't you know."

"Do we love our new mum? Yes!" Daniel exclaimed.

They both hugged her so tight she could barely breathe. Lea was almost overcome by their innocent, joyful gratitude. She carried the pile of clothing to the registers up front.

She dumped everything on the counter. The three boys had wandered off. Where were they? She spotted them near the back wall. They were talking to another boy. A big hulk of a boy with a hard, bulldog face. Lea recognized him from Ira's class.

And there was his mother. Elaine Saltzman. Ahead of Lea in the line. Elaine turned as if she knew Lea was thinking about her. "Lea?"

"Hi, Elaine. How are you?"

Elaine swept her coppery hair behind one shoulder. She motioned toward the boys. "Do you have nephews visiting?"

"No. They're mine. I mean—"

"Yours?"

"I'm adopting them. They grew up on that island off the Carolinas. Cape Le Chat Noir? They lost their families in the hurricane. And I—"

"That's so wonderful of you, Lea. You just brought them here? You're adopting both of them? Do you know anything about them?"

"Not really. But look. They're sharing their candy bars with your son. Look how sweet they are."

Samuel thought the boy was funny-looking. *He looks like a big mean dog. Is he really only twelve?*

The boy's head was enormous, his black hair uncombed, falling wildly over his square forehead. He had such a mean scowl on his face. And those little bulldog eyes.

It didn't take long to see that Ira was afraid of him.

"This is Derek," Ira whispered as the boy lumbered up to them. "Be careful. He's really mean. Be nice to him."

Daniel chuckled. Samuel gave him a look, a warning, to be cool. *Don't be yourself, Daniel,* he thought.

"Hey," the big kid said. He had his eyes on Samuel's candy bar. "What's up?"

"These are my new brothers," Ira told him. His voice was suddenly trembly. *Like a warbling bird,* Samuel thought.

Derek sneered. It made him look more like a pig than a bulldog. "Brothers? Since when?"

"My parents are adopting them," Ira said. "They live with us now."

Derek eyed the twins up and down, sizing them up. "How old are you?"

"Twelve," Daniel answered.

"You don't look twelve. You look six."

Samuel felt a tremor of fear. *Please don't be yourself, Daniel.*

Derek leaned over them, trying to be intimidating. "What are your names? Babyface One and Babyface Two?"

"I'm Daniel and he's Samuel. Or maybe I'm Samuel and he's Daniel. Sometimes I forget."

Derek sneered again. "You're a funny guy." He eyed them slowly. "No. I got a better name for you. You're Shrimp One and you're Shrimp Two."

"I want to be Shrimp Two," Daniel said. "Can I be Shrimp Two?" He had the sweetest smile on his face. Samuel had seen that crazy smile before. It meant he wasn't thinking sweet thoughts.

Derek stretched out a porky hand to Daniel. "I'll finish your candy bar for you."

Samuel saw a hard jolt freeze Daniel's face. And then he caught the warning glance from Ira. Ira took a step back. He had his eyes on Daniel. "Just give it to him," Ira whispered.

"Give it," Derek ordered. He waved his hand in Daniel's face. "I'll finish it." He turned to Samuel. "I'll finish yours, too. You've had enough, right?"

"Right." Samuel had his eyes on poor, frightened Ira. He handed his chocolate bar to Derek. Then he waited to see what Daniel would do.

Daniel kept that sweet smile on his face, but his cheeks were kind of red. Samuel knew that look, too. He knew everything about Daniel. After all, he was almost him. Almost, but a little different.

To Samuel's relief, Daniel stuffed his candy bar into the big porker's hand. "Enjoy it, Derek," he said. "It's all yours."

Derek snickered. "I *will* enjoy it, dude." He took a big bite and chewed with his mouth open so they could see the chocolate chunks smearing over his teeth.

"Aren't you going to say thank you?" Daniel sounded hurt.

Derek chewed noisily. Some chocolate juice ran down his chin. He swallowed. "Funny," he told Daniel. "You're fucking funny. Next time, I'll want a *whole* bar."

Daniel's smile grew tighter. Like a mask.

Samuel felt his heart skip a beat. *Uh-oh.*

He saw the new mum by the front windows waving two big shopping bags at them. He tugged Daniel's arm. "We have to go. The new mum wants to leave."

Daniel nodded. He turned slowly and followed Samuel and Ira. Derek stood in place, a candy bar in each hand, stuffing his face.

Ira pushed between them, his face all sweaty. "You have to be nice to Derek. He's a bad dude. He likes to hurt people. Really. He beat up my friend Ethan behind the playground at school and al- most broke his arm."

"Doesn't he ever get caught?" Daniel asked.

"I think the teachers are afraid of him, too," Ira said.

They caught up with Lea. The twins thanked her again. All the way home, they kept thanking her and discussing which shirts and jeans to wear on their first day of school.

"That was so nice of you to share your candy with Derek," Lea said.

"We like to share things, don't you know," Daniel told her.

"On the island, people have to share," Samuel added. "Because there isn't enough to go around."

He saw a sad smile form on Lea's face as she made the turn onto their block.

As soon as they were home, the twins carried the shopping bags to their room in the guesthouse. Daniel closed the door behind them, making sure it clicked. Then he pushed the lock on the handle.

He tossed the shopping bags onto the floor and turned to his twin. "What did you get?"

Samuel pulled the red leather wallet from his back pocket. He handed it to Daniel.

He could see the surprise on Daniel's face. "You got a woman's wallet? What's in it?"

"Didn't have time to look. Someone dropped it on the dressing room floor."

Eyes flashing with excitement, Daniel poked through the wallet and pulled out a bunch of bills. "Yes. Yes. These are fifties, Sammy. Three hundred dollars. You did good." He gave his brother a congratulatory face slap.

Samuel giggled. He liked it when Daniel was pleased with him. "What did you get, Daniel?"

Daniel reached deep into both of his pockets and began to pull out shiny things. Chains. Chains with sparkly things attached.

"Necklaces," Samuel said. "Good boyo. So many sparkly necklaces. How did you get them?"

"Easy as salt clam pie, Sammy. The display case wasn't locked."

He swung the necklaces over his head, round and around, and did his funny Daniel dance. "I like sparkly things," he said. "I'll put these with the necklace we found in Sister's room."

24

Lea stirred the soup in the pot with a long wooden spoon. Behind her, the twins were already seated at the table, eager for their lunch. She smiled. So far they had devoured everything she gave them. They seemed to like any food you put in front of them. Ira was such a picky eater. These boys were a pleasure.

"Is it soup yet?" Mark entered the kitchen, scratching his stubbly face. "What a morning. The guy from the grant committee is coming here."

Lea turned from the stove. "Really? Did he tell you how much they're giving you?"

Mark snickered. He stepped up behind Lea and kissed the back of her neck. "You're such an optimist."

She frowned. "Well, they have to give you at least part of the grant, right? They wouldn't turn you down flat."

Mark shrugged. "Who knows? It's hard times. I know you don't read the newspaper—"

"I read it online. The guy's coming all the way out from the city?"

"He said he has a house out here."

"Why didn't he tell you over the phone? He likes to give good news in person?"

"Your guess is as good as mine. He wouldn't even give me a hint."

The soup made a sizzling sound. Lea spun around. She snapped the burner off before it boiled over the side of the pot. "Sit down. We're all having tomato soup. Homemade. I sliced the tomatoes and everything this morning."

"What a homemaker." Mark tried to kiss her again but she ducked her head as she lifted the soup pot from the stove. "Too bad you're going away again. Who will make us homemade soup?"

"Huh? Going away? Mark, I'm going to the city tomorrow morning for one night. I'll be back late the following day. You're not going to make me feel guilty about a day and a half in the city, are you?"

He backed away, raising both hands in surrender. "Just teasing. You know I'll miss you even if it's only one night. Every minute is precious to me."

"Shut up. You're not funny."

Ira and Elena were away at friends' houses. She ladled the thick tomato soup into bowls, then joined Mark and the twins at the table.

Daniel leaned his face to the bowl and took a long whiff. "Smells so good, Mum. Tangy as sea grass drying on the beach."

"My bruvver is a poet," Samuel said.

"I like the way you boys speak," Lea said, stirring her soup, watching the steam rise from the red liquid. "You have good vocabularies."

"There's no school on the island, Mum," Daniel said. "But our parents, bless their souls, taught us well."

Bless their souls? He sounds like an old man.

An old man, but a charming old man.

She wished Ira could pick up some of their charm and politeness. Maybe it would rub off on him. If only he would spend some time with his new brothers . . .

"Wonderful soup," Mark said, across the table from her. He raised the pepper mill and ground a load of pepper into it. He always added pepper, no matter what the food was.

If I gave him a bowl of pepper, he'd add pepper.

Lea had learned not to be insulted when he reseasoned her food that way.

She raised a spoon of soup and blew on it. "Careful. It's very hot."

The soup bubbled on the spoon. Red. So bright and red. Where had she seen that color before?

She flicked the spoon hard and sent the soup flying over Mark's shoulder. It made a soft splash on the wall.

The rain had come down so hard. Sheets of it. All bloodred. Red as the tomato soup.

Lea raised another spoonful, whipped her hand up, and sent the soup flying across the table onto the wall.

"Hey—Lea?" Mark's startled cry.

The twins laughed. Did they think it was *funny?*

The red rain. The bloodred rain. The rain of all the victims' blood. The dead crying their red tears down on everyone.

The dead. The raining dead. Their red tears steaming in her soup bowl.

Lea flung another spoon of the red rain, the bloodred rain, spoon after spoon splashing on the white kitchen wall. Tears rolling down her face. Sobs wrenching her throat and chest.

The red rain splashed on the wall. Splashed. Splashed again. Till Mark wrapped his arms around her from behind. Wrapped his arms around her so tight the spoon fell from her trembling hand.

"Hold on to me, Mark. Hold on to me." Where did those words come from? "Hold on to me. Don't let me go back there."

25

"When will Mom be back?" Elena lifted the whole toaster waffle to her mouth and bit off an end.

Mark took a long sip of coffee from the white mug in his hand. "She just left an hour ago. She was taking the first jitney. You already want her back?"

Elena gave him the eye-roll. "Just asking, that's all."

"She has meetings today. She's staying with her sister in the Village tonight. She'll be back sometime tomorrow afternoon. Okay?"

"Okay. Why are you such a grouch?"

"Sorry. Just tense, I guess. I didn't want her to go. She seems so shaky. She can't seem to leave that damned island behind her."

"Da-ad. Language." Elena motioned toward the twins having their breakfast at the table.

"Maybe some meetings in the city will do her good. Give her something else to think about," Roz chimed in from the other end of the table, Axl on her lap with an egg-stained face.

Elena swallowed a chunk of waffle. "Does Mom's cell work? I need to talk to her. You're being totally stupid and unfair."

Mark shrugged. "Yes. Everyone tells me I'm stupid. And unfair."

Across from Elena, Samuel and Daniel giggled. Daniel leaned toward Axl. "How's my monkey boy?"

Axl stuck his tongue out, pleased with the attention. But Roz snapped at Daniel, "I wish you wouldn't call him that."

"He likes it."

"I'm fourteen," Elena told Mark, dropping the waffle onto the plate. "All my friends go into the city on their own."

Mark sighed. He spun the coffee mug between his hands. The cuckoo clock above the sink chirped eight times. They were going to be late.

"You know my feeling on this. Why bring it up now?"

Elena's dark eyebrows formed arched Vs over her eyes, the sign that she was angry. "You're a total phony, Dad."

The twins giggled again. That made Axl giggle, too. Roz tried to wipe the caked egg off his cheeks with a paper napkin. Ira kept his head down, concentrating on his Cheerios, keeping out of it.

"Me? A phony?"

"You wrote a book saying parents should let their kids do what they want. But you—"

"That didn't include letting a bunch of fourteen-year-old girls go traipsing around New York City with no plan or idea of what they're going to do."

Elena balled her hands into fists and let out an angry growl. "We . . . don't . . . traipse." Said through gritted teeth.

"Let's table this for later. We're going to be late." He balled up his paper napkin and threw it onto the table. "And stop tossing my book back at me. I know you haven't read it. The book is a piece of research. It doesn't mean I can't make decisions as your father."

"Phony, Dad." The eye-roll again. "You're a phony and a grouch."

Mark watched the twins gobble down the last syrupy pieces of their toaster waffles. "How are you boys doing in the guesthouse? You like it back there?" He had to change the subject.

"We love it," Samuel said. "Our own house. We never had our own house."

"Our house was always crowded with a lot of strangers, don't you know," Daniel added.

"Really? Well, it was nice of Roz to give up her place for you, wasn't it?"

"Mark, they've already thanked me a hundred times," Roz said, obviously pleased. "And they were so sweet. They both helped me carry my stuff up to the attic. They're very hard workers."

Grinning, the twins raised their skinny arms, doing muscle poses, showing off nonexistent biceps.

"Well, I didn't think it was a good idea," Mark said. "But I'm glad if it works out. Your own secret hideout." He glanced at the wall clock. "Come on, guys. Get your backpacks. I'm driving today because Mrs. Maloney wants to meet the twins. Tomorrow you go back to the school bus."

Ira groaned. "I *hate* the bus. I get bus sick every day."

"Get over it," Elena said helpfully. She bumped him from behind. They bumped each other up the stairs to get their backpacks.

Roz stretched and smiled. "It's going to be so quiet here in just a few seconds." That was Axl's cue to start crying. "What are you doing today?" she asked Mark.

"Autumn and I are going over some foreign contracts and some mail. Then I have a meeting. A guy from the Blakeman Institute is coming here at four."

"Weird. He's coming all the way out to Sag Harbor? Is he bringing you a fat check?"

Mark laughed. "You and my wife are a lot alike. She asked the same question."

"Well?"

"I hope so. I'm counting on this grant. I won't get any book royalties for another five months."

"YAAAAAY." The twins came bursting into the kitchen with their brand-new blue canvas backpacks bouncing on their backs.

"Let's go, guys!" Mark said. "The principal wants to meet you two."

"Rule the school!" Daniel cried, pumping a fist above his head. "We're going to rule the school!"

"Rule the school! Rule the school!"

Mrs. Maloney was a solid woman, with short salt-and-pepper hair over a square, no-nonsense face. She wore no makeup. Her green-gray eyes were the most colorful parts of her face. They radiated humor and intelligence and were enough to make people find her attractive.

Her silky tan blouse pulled tightly over her bulge of a stomach, and even from the other side of her cluttered desk, Mark could see that she was straining her stretch-type brown pants. A tube of Pringles and a can of Pepsi on the edge of the desk revealed that she didn't care much about her weight.

She greeted the twins warmly as Mark ushered them into her small office. Daniel took the chair beside the desk. Samuel sat across from the desk. Mark watched from the doorway.

The principal showed them she already knew how to tell one from the other (thanks to a previous visit from Lea). And she gave them school maps and copies of last year's yearbook, which the twins seemed quite pleased with.

Mark knew quite a lot about Mrs. Maloney. She had first been principal at the Sag Harbor elementary school next door before moving to the middle school last year.

Sag Harbor had a large Irish community. They were the carpenters and landscapers and housekeepers, waitresses and pub owners.

Some said they came here because the weather so near the ocean was close to the weather in Ireland. But more likely, they came because they had relatives here. Mrs. Maloney and her husband had emigrated nearly twenty years ago from a town named Wicklow when they couldn't find teaching jobs in the local schools.

She still had her Irish accent, which made her sound as if she were singing instead of talking, and added to her warmth. She joked with the twins, and they seemed delighted with her.

"There's less than two months left of school, lads," she told them, turning serious. "But it should be enough time for you to learn your way around and make some new friends."

"We want to rule the school!" Daniel cried suddenly. That startled her into a laugh.

"Rule the school!" Samuel repeated, as if it was a chant.

"I like that," Mrs. Maloney said, gray eyes flashing. "Miss Montgomery will like that, too." Then she added, "She's your teacher. Normally, I would split you two up. But since it's so late in the school year . . ."

She raised her eyes to Mark, who was still leaning in the doorway. "I know we don't have any school records for these boys. Is there any chance of locating them?"

Mark frowned. "We're trying. But we haven't been able to find *any* records for them. No birth certificate. No family ID or anything. It's such chaos down there."

Mrs. Maloney tsk-tsked, shaking her head.

"The records were all blown away or underwater," Mark continued. "But we have someone looking for us. A woman Lea met down there named Martha Swann is trying to find whatever she can find."

She nodded, then glanced at the wall clock above Mark's head. "I guess that does it. Welcome to Sag Harbor, boys. We're very happy to have you. Mark, will you help them find room 204? It's the second door upstairs."

"No problem," Mark said.

Mrs. Maloney was fumbling her hand over her desktop. She raised her eyes to him. "Did you see my watch? I'm pretty sure I had it right here on the desk."

Mark shook his head. "Sorry. I didn't see it."

She peered under the desk. Pulled open the middle drawer and gazed inside. Then moved a stack of papers. "That's odd. Did you boys see a silver watch here on the desk?"

"No, mum," Daniel answered, eyes lowered to the desktop. "I didn't see it."

"I didn't see it, either, mum. Can we go to class now?" Samuel said.

26

Autumn came to work after her classes. Mark was glad to see her. After his book tour, there was a lot of work to catch up on. But at three o'clock she was suddenly sitting in his lap and his life went out of control.

She showed up a little after one, breezed into his office down the hall from the living room, and dropped a brown paper bag on his desk. "Cheese Danish? I stopped at the Golden Pear."

Mark turned from his keyboard and swung the black leather desk chair around to face her. He made a grab for the bag. "You're the best."

She smiled. Her eyes glowed. "I try to be," she said in a sultry whisper that surprised him. She tugged off her red hoodie and tossed it on his office couch.

Autumn wore a yellow scoop-neck T-shirt over a short, brown pleated skirt. He couldn't help but stare at her bare legs, lowering his eyes to the yellow sandals on her feet.

Her white-blond hair fell loosely over her shoulders. He didn't remember her wearing lip gloss to work before. And that citrus-like scent was new, too.

She grinned at him as if she had a secret she was keeping. He suddenly had the idea she was posing, standing in place so he could admire her.

She glanced back to the door. "No one home?"

He opened the brown bag and tugged off a piece of the Danish. "No. Lea's in the city. I took the boys to school for the first time. And Roz and Axl are doing the grocery shopping."

She leaned toward him. The lemony scent intensified. The low-cut T-shirt revealed more perfect, creamy cleavage. "And what are we doing today?"

"Mostly mail. And I have a number of requests to answer. Appearances. Some radio things."

She sent a strand of hair off her forehead with a toss of her head.

Mark took another bite of the cheese Danish. "I shouldn't eat this. Wish I had more willpower."

Her eyes flashed. "You? No willpower? Really?" She tossed her hair back again. "Are you going to travel more?"

"No. The book tour is over. I've done everything I can. Now it's up to the publisher." He swallowed another chunk. Tried not to stare at her boobs, which were at eye level. She stood so close. "Besides, I should stay around home for a while. You know. Because of the twins."

She turned suddenly and walked to the window. She pushed back the dark drapes and peered out. A gloomy day, storm clouds filling the sky. The mostly bare trees shaking. April rains.

"Mark, how are the boys doing?"

"Okay, I guess. They seemed excited about school. They kept chanting, 'Rule the school! We're gonna rule the school!'"

"Cute. They really are adorable."

"Yes. Lea is totally over the moon over them. Roz thinks they're *too* adorable. She says all twelve-year-olds are monsters. She's waiting for them to pull off their angel masks and reveal their hideous monster selves."

Autumn snickered. "Your sister is weird."

"She's a cynic. True, she's had a tough life. But she was a cynic *before* she had a tough life. When we were kids, I was always shocked because she had something terrible to say about everyone. But, Jesus, she sure could make me laugh. Still can."

He motioned to the narrow, chrome-armed chair beside his desk. "Sit down. I'm going to hand you things." He patted a stack of folders on the desktop.

She lowered herself gracefully into the chair. Smoothed the pleats of her short skirt. Then she reached her hand out and gently flicked a crumb of Danish off the side of his mouth.

His startled look made her laugh.

Should I talk to her about dressing less provocatively?

Well . . . actually, I like it.

He pushed the brown paper bag to the edge of the desk. Then he pulled the stack of folders in front of him, opened the top one, and started going through the varied requests—for autographs, for appearances, for charitable contributions . . . and a few for apologies.

There were several lengthy letters, some of them from other child psychologists, refuting his findings. One particularly venomous letter from a woman in Los Angeles accused him of demeaning the whole profession and "holding all psychologists up to ridicule by espousing this crackpot philosophy designed only to arouse controversy and sell books."

Mark shook his head. "She must have been speaking to my father."

"Your father?"

"He wrote almost exactly the same letter. I told you. He found my book a total embarrassment."

"Your father wrote to you? He didn't call you?"

"We don't speak."

"You're serious? He's a shrink, right?"

"He's not just a shrink. He's a big deal in the New York Psychoanalytic Society. And he's got his Park Avenue office with his celebrity patients and—"

"He *wrote* to you?"

Mark nodded. "He needed to tell me just how much I had embarrassed him. I think my whole career embarrasses him. You know. I didn't match up to his expectations right from the start. I mean, he went to Harvard and I went to Wisconsin."

Autumn chewed her bottom lip. "How do you want me to handle that letter?"

Mark flipped through it. Three pages single-spaced. "My psych advisor at Wisconsin gave me very good advice. She said, 'Never defend yourself.' She said you never can convince anyone, and if you try to defend yourself, you just sound weak. She said to always be positive, never defensive."

Autumn scratched her knee with her long red nails. "So what should I say?"

"Say thank you for your thoughtful letter. I really appreciate your taking the time to write."

That phony reply made them both laugh. Autumn was gazing at him with such total admiration, Mark had to look away.

Such a beautiful girl. He suddenly wondered about her social life. Did she have a boyfriend? He shared a lot with her about his private life. But he didn't dare ask her personal questions. It might seem like prying. It might seem offensive. And she never offered much.

Today she seemed different to him. Not just the sexy clothes. The secret smiles and the long gazes, as if she had some kind of plan, some kind of surprise.

They went through the files. Then she set the stack on the floor beside her chair and stood up. She stepped close to him. "You're a psychologist, right? Can you read my mind?"

He chuckled. "I'm not a mind reader, I'm a psychologist. But yes, I can read your mind. You wish you'd saved that cheese Danish for yourself. Right?"

"Wrong." She took his hand. Tenderly. "You really can't read my mind?" Her blue eyes caught the light. "You really don't know what I've been thinking for the longest time?"

"Autumn. Really, I—"

And then she was in his lap, squeezing his hand, pressing her hot face against his.

"Autumn—no. Come on."

She kissed his ear. Her breath tickled the side of his face.

"No. We can't. I can't. I mean—" He tried to stand up. But he couldn't move.

She turned his head and pressed her mouth against his. He could taste the creamy, sweet flavor of the lip gloss. And then she was opening her mouth, and his tongue moved despite himself.

"No—"

She held the back of his head and kept his mouth pressed to hers. He couldn't speak.

"No. This is wrong. Please—"

Kissing him. She took his hand and moved it between her legs. Kissing him so passionately. Beneath the short skirt her panties were wet. She pressed his hand into her.

"No, Autumn. Stop. We can't."

She uttered low gasps in his ear. "Oh, yes. Yes. Oh, yes."

Like a porno video.

He felt his erection grow. "I don't want this."

But suddenly he did.

She stood up and pulled him to his feet. Then she reached under the skirt and lowered lacy black panties to her ankles. She flipped the short skirt up as she leaned over the desk.

That creamy white ass. So beautiful. She grabbed the far end of the desk with both hands. "Mark—hurry."

Oh, God. Over the desk. From behind.

His khakis were down. And he was inside her.

This isn't happening. How can it be?

Sprawled over the desk, she moaned, rhythmic soft cries. He buried his face in her soft hair. He lost himself in her.

He lost himself.

Lost.

And came inside her. It didn't matter. All the doctors said he could never have more children.

He stayed on top of her for a long moment, breathing hard, gripping the shoulders of her T-shirt, the creamy ass still moving beneath him. Then, heart pounding, he pushed himself to his feet.

She climbed up slowly. Turned to him. Grabbed his shirt, brought her face close, and licked the side of his face. "Am I your best assistant?" A whisper that tingled his skin. "I want to be the best. Am I the best?"

A door slammed.

They both gasped. She squeezed his shoulders, eyes wide in alarm.

Mark heard the twins' voices. Footsteps.

Autumn bent down, grabbed her underpants and tugged them on. She straightened her skirt. Brushed back her damp, tangled hair with both hands. "Oh, wow. Oh, wow."

The footsteps louder in the hall.

He was scrambling to fasten his khakis. Still fumbling with the fly as the twins tumbled into his office, bumping each other, both talking at once.

Zipper stuck, Mark dropped into the desk chair. Crossed his arms over his lap. Forced a smile. "Hey, guys—how was your day?"

27

The twins had their eyes on Autumn, who leaned against the side of the desk, her skirt still crooked, her cheeks bright pink.

"How was school?" she asked them, sounding breathless.

"Good," Samuel said.

"Yeah. Good," his twin added.

"What did you do today?" Mark asked.

"Stuff," Samuel replied.

"Just some stuff," Daniel added.

Mark tried a third question. "Did you like Miss Montgomery?"

"She's nice, don't you know," Samuel said, eyes on Autumn.

"Nice," Daniel echoed.

Mark laughed. "You guys were talking your heads off till you got in here. Now we get only one-word grunts from you. What happened?"

They both shrugged in reply. Daniel giggled.

Mark studied them. They looked too clean, their new jeans and T-shirts stiff, not broken in. Their blond hair lay perfectly in place, like doll heads.

"Did you suddenly get shy?" Autumn asked. She was working on untangling a thick strand of blond hair.

Mark didn't give them a chance to answer. "Where's Ira? Was he on the bus with you?"

"The lad is taking the late bus," Samuel said. "He was doing a project with Ethan."

Mark smiled, pleased to get so many words from him. "So did you boys rule the school today?"

"Not yet," Samuel said with surprising gravity.

"Soon," his twin offered.

Their school day had gone very well, Samuel thought. Miss Montgomery split them up, seating Daniel in the front and Samuel in the back. But they didn't care about that.

Samuel sat next to an open window. The April air smelled fresh and salty. He liked that. He spent a lot of time watching two squirrels collecting and devouring acorns at the base of the old tree across from the school.

Daniel sat next to Ira in the front row. They didn't talk much. They weren't really friends yet. In fact, Ira seemed very uncomfortable around Daniel.

Maybe he was still angry about Daniel trying to take his room from him. Maybe he just didn't want new bruvvers.

He'll get over it, Samuel thought, watching Daniel and Ira ignore each other. *Daniel will win him over—one way or the other. He'll be true blue, that boyo.*

And Derek? Samuel looked for him, but Derek had a doctor appointment and didn't come to school till lunchtime.

Samuel and Daniel ran into him on their way out of the lunchroom. Derek wore baggy cargo jeans and a red-and-white New York Rangers sweatshirt. His eyes went wide, and his mouth opened in surprise when he recognized them.

"How'd you get into this school?" He managed to find his usual bluster. "This used to be a good school."

"It's our first day," Samuel said. "We're in your class."

Derek bumped Samuel's shoulder with a pudgy hand. "You got any money? Mom forgot to give me my lunch money."

"We don't have any," Samuel replied. "We already had our lunch."

"Let's see," Derek said. He grabbed Samuel by the pants, spun him around with surprising strength, and began to dig into his pockets.

Samuel squirmed. "Boyo, stop!"

Daniel moved quickly. He stepped up behind Derek and, with a powerful tug, hoisted Derek's heavy backpack off his shoulders.

Derek let go of Samuel and spun around furiously. "Hey, jerk! You almost ripped my arms off."

"Sorry, boyo." Daniel held the backpack above his head. "You want it? Jump for it."

Derek uttered a low growl. He narrowed his bulldog eyes and glared at Daniel. "*You* jump for it." He lowered his shoulder and bulled into Daniel, sending him crashing against a metal locker.

Daniel giggled. Holding the backpack high, he quickly regained his balance.

Derek rushed at Daniel, both hands outstretched. He grabbed for the backpack—just as Daniel let go of it. Derek couldn't stop his momentum and slammed headfirst into the wall.

The collision didn't faze him. His big belly heaving up and down beneath the Rangers sweatshirt, he grabbed the backpack off the floor and grinned in triumph. Slowly, he slid it onto his back. "You dudes should be careful. I can mess you up totally."

Samuel felt a tremor of fear. *Please, Daniel. Don't be Daniel. Let it ride.*

Daniel raised both hands as if in surrender. "Truce?"

Samuel took a step back.

"Okay, truce." Derek's reply after thinking about it for a while. "You're both new here, so you don't know what's up. I'll give you a break today."

"Truce," Daniel repeated. He stuck his hand out for Derek to shake.

Weird, thought Samuel. *What's up with the handshake routine?*

"Truce," Derek said. He stomped away without shaking hands.

The bell clanged above their heads. Lunchtime was over.

Samuel turned to find Ira, Ethan, and several other kids watching the whole confrontation. "What was *that* about?" Ira asked Daniel.

Daniel's smile made his dimples appear to grow deeper. "You'll see, boyo. You'll see."

Samuel wasn't in on his brother's secret, either. But all was revealed just before the final bell that afternoon. Miss Montgomery dismissed the class. And as the kids all gathered their books, stuffed their backpacks, and scurried from the room, Mrs. Maloney came charging into the classroom.

Her gray eyes gazed around the room and came to a stop on Derek, who was standing in the front. Arguing with a short, red-haired girl. "Derek, could I see you for a moment?" she called.

The girl hurried away. Derek eyed the principal warily as she approached. The classroom was nearly emptied. Samuel and Daniel watched from the doorway.

"Yes, Mrs. Maloney?" Derek suddenly being very polite.

She frowned at him. Rubbed her short salt-and-pepper hair. "Derek, I received a disturbing note this afternoon. About you."

His mouth dropped open. "Huh? Me? Who sent it?"

Miss Montgomery stood up behind her desk and looked on.

Mrs. Maloney's eyes locked on Derek, studying him. "It wasn't signed. But it said I would find something interesting in your back-pack."

Samuel glanced at his twin. He recognized the eagerness on Daniel's face. The anticipation. He'd seen it before.

Derek's blue backpack was on his desk. He stared hard at it as if it would reveal some secret.

"Is there something interesting in your backpack, Derek?" Mrs. Maloney asked softly, almost in a whisper.

Derek shook his head. "No way. Just my stuff."

"Nothing in there I should know about?"

"No. No way. Unless you mean a Snickers bar and some Starburst?"

Mrs. Maloney let out a long whoosh of air. "I'm sure you're telling the truth. But why would someone send me that note?"

Derek shrugged.

"Why don't we just empty out the backpack and settle the whole thing." Mrs. Maloney kept her voice low and friendly.

"No problem." Derek lifted the pack and started to unzip it. "I don't get it. I totally don't."

Holding the pack by the sides, he upended it and shook it hard, spilling the contents onto the desk. Books. Folders. A pencil box. An iPod. A cell phone. A Snickers bar.

Samuel squinted across the room, studying the contents. As soon as he saw the silvery watch slide onto the cover of a textbook, he understood.

Mrs. Maloney raised her hands to her cheeks. "Well, my faith. That *is* interesting," she said softly. She picked up the watch and slid the shiny band through her fingers. "Derek? How did my watch get into your backpack?"

Derek's face had gone pale. His mouth was working up and down, but he didn't make a sound. He shrugged. "I don't know."

"Do you want to think about it?" Mrs. Maloney remained calm. No sign of anger or even surprise.

"I . . . never saw it. Really." Derek's eyes down, shoulders slumped. Looking guilty as hell. "I don't know how it got there. Really."

"But it did tumble out from the bottom of your backpack, right?"

"Yes. But—"

"Derek, why don't you gather up your belongings here and follow me to my office for a talk. Do we need to call your mother? What do you think?"

She raised her eyes to the door and saw Samuel and Daniel standing, watching the scene intently. "What are you two lads lingering there for? This is no business of yours. Go on now. Don't miss the bus on your first day."

"Okay. Bye," Samuel said, turning to leave.

"See you tomorrow," Daniel said, then quickly added, "Good luck, Derek."

28

"We have work to do, Sammy." Daniel pressed his forehead against the window glass as the school bus bounced along Noyac Road, the tall trees along the side making the shadows dance in his eyes.

Samuel shifted the blue canvas backpack in his lap. He knew how impatient Daniel could be. He hoped maybe he would take his time, get to know the terrain, enjoy their new family, their new home at least a few weeks before setting things in motion.

"You gave that lug Derek a good lesson, Daniel."

Daniel tapped Samuel's knee with his fist. "Derek is dead in the pasture. The flies are already circling him."

Samuel laughed. But he could see the growing intensity on his twin's face.

"Work to do, Sammy."

"What's your hurry, Daniel? Haven't we got it made here?"

"We've waited a long time," Daniel murmured, gazing at a deer chewing tall weeds by the roadside. "A long time, boyo."

"But look at us now. We're in Heaven."

Daniel turned away from the window. He shook his head. "Sammy, it may be heaven but there's a devil on our cloud."

Samuel felt a chill, muscles tightening at the back of his neck. "Who is the devil?" He knew the answer.

"The new pa."

"Maybe he didn't mean those things we heard him say."

Daniel narrowed his eyes at Samuel. "He meant them. He said he didn't want us to come. He didn't want Mum to bring us here. And he didn't want us to live in the little house in the backyard. Why? Because he didn't know if he could trust us."

That made Samuel giggle. "He *can't* trust us, boyo."

Daniel didn't smile. His normally pale cheeks had turned rosy pink. "Pa doesn't like us, Sammy. He doesn't want us here. And he shouted at Mum. You saw him shout at Mum because she wants to make us happy and give us everything we want."

"But, Daniel—"

"He doesn't want us to be happy. Pa doesn't want to give us the things we want. You heard him. You heard every word. We have work to do. We have plans, boyo. We cannot let the new pa stand in our way."

Samuel felt the chill again. "What are you thinking, Daniel? Why are you saying all this? We can't *kill* the new pa. We can't. It would make Mum so sad."

"He's a devil, Sammy. A devil in our heaven."

Samuel grabbed his brother's wrist. "Don't think it. We can't do that to Mum."

"You're right. You're the sensible guy, Sammy. As sensible as potatoes in chowder. We don't want to kill Pa. We just have to keep him busy."

Samuel shook his head. The backpack suddenly felt heavy in his lap. He let it slide to the bus floor. "Keep him busy?"

Daniel nodded. He had that thoughtful look in his eyes that Samuel knew well.

"How do we keep him busy? What do you mean?"

A thin smile played over Daniel's lips. "I have some ideas. We can keep him real busy, Sammy. Maybe with the coppers."

29

Mark watched from the front window as the dark blue Audi pulled up the driveway. A young man with a thick head of wavy brown hair and a seriously tanned face climbed out. He leaned into the car to retrieve a slender laptop case, then walked crisply to the front door, straightening his red necktie and buttoning his dark suit jacket as he walked.

Autumn had left ten minutes earlier, weighed down by a tall stack of folders. She offered Mark several meaningful glances as she left. In return, he gave her a comic wave and a goofy grin, keeping it light. *Nothing serious happened here, Autumn. Did it?*

If only he could move back the clock. Would he move it? Maybe not. Moments before, he had kept his eyes on her long, slim legs under the short skirt as she bent to pick up the folders, and felt himself start to get erect again.

Am I crazy? What am I thinking?

Lea, I love you. Why didn't you stay and watch out for me?

Oh, what kind of juvenile thinking is that?

Roz had returned with a trunk load of grocery bags and a screaming, hungry Axl. Mark emptied the car for her. He saw the twins tossing a tennis ball back and forth in the backyard. He thought about joining them. But it was time for his meeting with this man from the institute.

What was his name? Hulenberger? Something like that.

Mark had suggested they meet and have tea at the American Hotel on Main Street in town. That way there wouldn't be kids underfoot, running in and out, demanding his immediate attention. Elena was already angry that he didn't have time for a long discussion about the sleepover she wanted to have with Ruth-Ann.

But Hulenberger insisted on coming to the house. And here he was at the front door, all tanned and prosperous-looking in a designer suit that fit his slender shoulders perfectly and a crisp white shirt that contrasted his tan.

"Mr. Hulenberger? Come in."

"It's Dr. Hulenberger. But call me Richard. Everyone does. Even my kids." A brief, hard handshake.

"Well, call me Mark. Come in. Welcome."

Mark led him down the hall to his office. He could hear Roz in the kitchen, pleading with Axl to sit still. The back door slammed, and he heard Ira calling, "Anyone home? Roz?"

"Nice day," Hulenberger said. "I enjoyed the drive. My wife and I have a house in Sagaponack, but we haven't opened it yet. It's almost May, but it still feels like October, doesn't it? All the rain. Incredible. We probably won't open up till Memorial Day. My wife hates the country. She always says she'd rather be on Madison Avenue. Ha."

Was he talking so much out of nervousness? Or was he just a chatty guy?

Mark stopped at the office doorway and pictured Autumn bending over the desk again. Her short skirt tossed up onto her back, black underpants around her ankles, and that smooth little ass . . .

Oh, God.

Would he see her there every time he walked into the office?

The whole left side of the desktop was empty. The papers and folders had all been swept aside. He wondered if Hulenberger noticed that something was odd.

He led him to the green leather couch against the wall. Hulenberger dropped onto the edge and sat up very straight, lowering his laptop case to the floor. Good posture. He slid a hand down his tie a few times. Nervous habit?

"Nice room, Mark. I like that photo behind your desk. I think I know those trees. From Brisbane, right? Australia? I walked in that very spot and admired those twisty roots all around the tree trunks."

Mark nodded. "My wife is a travel writer. A good photographer, too. She writes about adventure travel. Seems a lot of people are into it."

"Hannah and I were on a food and wine tour. We weren't impressed with the food in Queensland at all. Dreadful. In fact, we didn't have anything good to eat till we got to Sydney. Were you there with your wife?"

"No. She was on assignment. I had my patients. You know. And my book."

Chitchat, chitchat.

Mark suddenly had a heavy feeling in the pit of his stomach. He rolled his desk chair in front of the couch and dropped into it. The room still smelled of Autumn's lemony scent.

"Nice of you to drive out, Richard."

Richard cleared his throat loudly. Adjusted his tie. "Well, I wanted to tell you in person. I didn't think it was right to do it over the phone or by email. Too impersonal."

"You mean—about the grant?" His voice suddenly tight.

"Yes. Should I come right to the point? I think I should. We're not going to give you the grant, Mark."

Can silence be loud?

To Mark the silence in the room seemed deafening. Without realizing it, he slammed his head back against the leather seatback, like someone showing shock in a cartoon.

"You mean . . . you're not giving the whole amount? Only part?"

Richard sat even more erect. Mark saw a single bead of sweat appear above one brown eyebrow. "No. I came to offer our regrets. We can't give you any of the grant money at this time."

"But my studies . . ." *Why can't I finish a sentence?* His hands left wet marks on the leather chair arms.

"We approve of your work. Wholeheartedly. That's why we made the initial offer. We felt that your studies with juveniles would add considerably to the literature."

Mark was distracted by movement at the office doorway. He turned and saw Samuel and Daniel standing there, hands in their jeans pockets, serious expressions on their pale faces.

"How long have you two been standing there?" He didn't mean to sound so irritated. His mind was churning from the news of the grant money turndown. He should shout at Hulenberger, not the boys.

They didn't reply. Both had their eyes on Hulenberger. Staring at him hard, as if giving him the evil eye. Then, without a word, they turned and vanished down the hall, bouncing a tennis ball on the floor.

He turned back to Hulenberger, who was defiantly gazing at him, not backing down, not avoiding his eyes after bringing this devastating news. Macho guy.

"So, Richard . . . Can you explain? If it isn't my study . . ."

"It's your book. Can I speak plainly? It's the book. We understand why you wrote such an inflammatory thing. But that's the problem in a word, see. It's inflammatory."

"But it's a sincere study. It wasn't skeptical in any way. I wasn't just trying to make a buck with a piece of crappy pop psychology. I did my homework, Richard. I did years of research in addition to my own studies."

Whoa. Blowing it. He's sitting there coolly, and your voice is rising to soprano.

Richard kept his green-gray eyes on Mark, his face a blank. No emotion.

This man is a fish. I've seen eyes like that on a cod. He thinks he's terrific. But he didn't just fuck a beautiful twenty-three-year-old girl.

What am I thinking? Am I losing my mind?

"How can I say this, Mark? The book has attached a certain notoriety to you. I'm sure you won't disagree with that."

Mark didn't reply.

"And the grant committee . . . well, we feel we can't risk backing someone in your position, someone with that kind of controversy following him."

Mark remained silent.

Richard sighed and shook his head. "The institute has such limited funds now. You know how much the government has cut our funding. They're almost not subsidizing us at all. It's a crime. This country will pay for the shortsightedness in Washington. In the meantime, we have to be very judicious about where we spend what little we have. And I'm afraid—"

Mark jumped to his feet, visibly startling his guest. "Okay. I get it. Thanks for coming out, Richard."

Richard gazed up at him, swallowing hard. Mark realized he'd frightened the man. Richard thought Mark was about to get violent.

Maybe I should. Beat the crap out of him. What kind of notoriety would that bring me?

But he'd never been in a fight in his life. Not even on the playground. He'd never thrown a punch or wrestled another kid on the grass or come home with a black eye.

Mark was the good kid. The smart kid. The talker. The kid who was interested in how everything works. He always talked himself out of fights. He used *psychology*.

Richard finally climbed to his feet. He grabbed up his laptop case.

Why did he bring it? Did he just feel insecure without it?

He pulled out his phone and checked the screen. Then he tucked it back into his suit jacket. "I'm really sorry, Mark. I can see you are disappointed."

"Yeah. That's the word for it."

"My only suggestion—if you want any advice from me—is to apply again in a few years."

"A few years?"

"Yeah. Wait for the notoriety to die down. In a few years, people will forget your book, right?"

A smile crossed Mark's face. "That isn't exactly a compliment."

Richard blushed. "You know what I mean. Wait for the controversy to fade. People have short attention spans. You know that, right? Apply again. I'm not guaranteeing anything, but—"

Mark led him to the door. "Do you believe in freedom of speech, Richard?"

"Well, yes. Of course."

"But you don't think I should put my findings and theories in a book?"

"I didn't say that. The committee has to be careful. I know you understand that. You have a bestseller, Mark. No one begrudges you that. Some psychologists would *kill* for a bestseller like yours. This grant money—"

"Would have paid my mortgage for the next two years," Mark interrupted. "And would have paid for my *next* book, which I hope will have the same notoriety."

He pulled open the front door. He could see the twins playing catch at the side of Richard's car.

"I'm sorry. I mean that sincerely." Hulenberger stuck out his hand to shake. "I'm just the messenger here, you know. No hard feelings, I hope."

Mark shook his hand. This time it was cold and damp. He watched him walk down the gravel drive to his car. He deposited the laptop in the passenger seat, glanced briefly back at Mark, then climbed behind the wheel.

One of the twins fumbled the tennis ball and went running down the driveway after it. "Be careful!" Mark shouted to them. "Get out of the way, boys. He's going to back out!"

He didn't watch Hulenberger drive away. Mark turned and walked into the house, feeling heavy, a headache forming just behind his forehead. He sighed. *I need a glass of wine.*

He found Roz in the kitchen, stirring a pot of tomato sauce.

She had a gray long-sleeved T-shirt, torn at the neck, pulled down over the baggy denim cutoff shorts she wore nearly every day. She turned when he entered and read his expression. "Bad news?"

"You were listening?"

"No. The twins told me something bad was happening. That guy looked like the kind who'd bring bad news."

Mark opened the refrigerator and pulled out an already opened bottle of Chablis. "Yeah, well. Bad news is right. I'm not getting the grant."

She stopped stirring. "Because?"

"Because I'm too controversial." He found a wineglass in the cabinet and poured it full. "Mainly, I think, because I'm too successful."

"Yes. That's your problem. You're too successful and too rich."

"I wish." He took a long sip. "Guess I'm going to have to fill up my patient list. Put aside the next book for a while."

The tennis ball bounced hard against the kitchen window. The thud made them both jump.

Roz smiled. "The twins are having fun."

Mark took another drink. The wine wasn't helping his headache. "Think they're doing okay?"

"Yes. I think they're happy. I know you don't approve, but they love their little house back there. I'm surprised they've adjusted so well. Aren't you?"

"I guess. I'd like to see a little more interaction between them and Ira and Elena. Of course, twins often keep to themselves." He refilled his glass. The Chablis tasted a little sour. Or was that just his mood?

He thought about Hulenberger. The guy wasn't actually smug, but he was totally unlikable.

"Can I change the subject?" Roz broke into his thoughts. "I've been thinking I need a night off. You know?"

"A night off? You have a date?"

"Is that *your* business? I just need a night off. Think you could hold down the fort? Watch Axl for me? You know. Take care of him for a few hours without killing him?"

Mark grinned. "Axl and I get along fine. I stuff him full of Oreos and tortilla chips and he's a good boy."

"That's what makes you a good psychologist."

"Lea gets home tomorrow night. Maybe she and I will have a special playdate with Axl."

"Sounds like a plan. Go tell our four boarders it's dinnertime, okay?"

Carrying his wineglass, Mark walked to the stairs and shouted up to Ira and Elena. "Dinner. Come down. Now. Okay?"

He opened the front door and shouted to the twins. "Dinner!" But they had disappeared, probably to their house in back. The tennis ball lay in the driveway in front of Hulenberger's car.

Huh?

The wineglass nearly slipped from his hand. Something was wrong. Hulenberger's Audi was still in the drive.

Mark stepped out onto the stoop and squinted into the evening light. Yes. Hulenberger sat behind the wheel. Not moving. And his head . . . it was tilted back, way back.

Wrong. All wrong.

Something was terribly wrong.

"Richard? Hey! Richard?" he shouted.

Hulenberger didn't move.

"Richard! Hey—what's wrong? Are you okay?" He shouted louder with his hands cupped around his mouth.

No. The man didn't move.

Mark started to jog toward the car. But he stopped halfway. Hulenberger's head . . . it wasn't right.

He spun away, his mind whirling. From the wine. From the headache. So hard to think clearly.

Oh my God. Oh my God.

What has happened here?

"Richard? Can you answer me?"

A tightness gripped Mark's chest. A wave of cold washed over his body, a cold he'd never felt before.

He lurched to the car. What was splattered over the windshield? "Richard? Richard?" Breathing hard, he gazed into the open window. Grabbed the bottom of the window with both hands. Leaned toward the wheel.

And screamed. A long, shrill scream of horror from somewhere deep in his throat.

"No! Fucking no! Oh my God! Oh, shit. Oh my God!"

Dark blood splattered the windshield, as if someone had heaved a can of paint over the glass. And Hulenberger . . . Hulenberger . . . The blood had run down his shirt, his suit . . .

Like a sweater. A sweater of blood.

His head tilted back. His throat . . . it had been torn open. Ripped open?

"Oh my God. Oh my God. Fucking no!"

Fighting the tide of nausea, the drumming of his heart that made the blood pulse at his temples, Mark pushed himself back, away from the car. He turned to the house. He saw the twins standing at the top of the driveway.

"Get back! Go back! Don't come down here! Go back!" He waved them away with both hands. They turned and ran.

Had they seen anything?

His hands felt wet. He raised them to his face. They were covered in blood. Hulenberger's blood. He shook them hard as if trying to toss the blood away. Then he staggered into the house. Through the living room, to the kitchen where Roz was tilting the tomato sauce pan over a big bowl of spaghetti.

"Roz! Call the police." So breathless she didn't hear him.

He grabbed her shoulder, startling her. Her eyes locked on his hands. "Mark? Oh my God! Is that blood?"

"Roz—call the police! Hurry! Call the police! Call the police!"

30

"It's a ten-eighty-four, Vince. We're on the scene."

"I gotta learn those numbers, Chaz. I never know what Vince is talking about."

"Forgetaboutit, Andy. No one knows what Vince is talking about."

Pavano peered out the window as his partner, Chaz Pinto, eased the car up the gravel driveway. "Where are we? Why does this look familiar?"

"John Street, dude. You took the call ten minutes ago, remember?"

A dark Audi stood in the drive. Chaz stopped the black-and-white a few feet behind it.

"It's taking me awhile to get oriented, you know. We're by the water, aren't we?"

"Yeah. The bay is over there." Pinto pointed out the side door. They both gazed at the car in front of them.

"The caller was a woman. She didn't say what the problem was. Something about a car in the driveway. The driver . . ."

"I see him. The back of his head. Not moving."

"Heart attack?"

"Hope so. That would make it easy." Pinto leaned toward the radio. "We're going to check out the car, Vince. You there?"

"Of course I'm here. Where else would I be, Pinto? Don't sit there holding hands, you two. Get out and take a look."

"The driver appears to be in the car."

The front door to the house swung open, and a dark-haired man in jeans and a white polo shirt stepped out.

Pavano's eyes went wide. "Hey, I know that dude." His breath caught in his throat. "Oh, wow. Oh no. I don't believe this."

"What's your problem, Andy?"

Pavano pushed the car door open, flipped his half-smoked Camel to the driveway, and lowered his feet to the ground. "I've been here. That night. Remember? The rain? I had the wrong house. I told him his wife was dead!"

Pinto let out a hoarse wheeze of a laugh. "We're still talking about that one. Behind your back, you know. It's classic. We'll be talking about that asshole move for a long time."

"Thanks, partner." Pavano stretched his lanky body, adjusted his black uniform cap lower over his eyes. *Maybe the guy won't remember me.*

Yeah, sure. What are the chances?

Pinto was approaching the driver's side of the Audi. Pavano followed, boots crunching on the gravel driveway, eyes on the man inside the car.

"Hello, sir? Sir? Are you all right?"

The man from inside the house came running down the driveway. "I'm Mark Sutter," he shouted. "This is my house."

Pavano waved him back. "Please stay there."

The driver's side window was down. "Hey, sir!" Pinto shouted loudly into the car even though he was just a few feet away. "Sir? Are you okay?"

"He's not okay. He's fucking dead!" Sutter cried. He didn't heed Pavano's instruction. He ran up beside them, breathing hard. "He's dead. I saw him. It . . . it's horrible."

Pinto and Pavano both stooped and leaned into the window at the same time.

"Oh, my God!"

"Oh, fuck no! Fuck no!"

"I . . . can't believe it," Sutter stammered.

Pavano frantically waved him back. "Please stay back, sir. Let us do our job."

A pair of blond boys were watching from the front door. "Get the kids away, sir. Please!"

The boys stepped out onto the stoop. "Is he sick?"

"Please, Mr. Sutter. Get those boys inside."

"Oh, fuck. This is impossible!" Pinto gasped. "His whole throat . . ."

"It . . . it's open. Opened up. Like ripped open."

"No. It's burned. Totally burned. See the black skin around the hole? The skin is charred. It's flaking off."

Pavano turned away, his stomach tightening into a knot. The man's throat had been cut or ripped open. He shut his eyes and still pictured the dark red flesh inside, blackened. A hole, a gaping hole in the man's neck. Thick, dark blood caked down the front of the man's suit, puddled in his lap.

Someone opened his throat and let him bleed out.

"How did this happen? How *could* it happen? Here in my driveway," Sutter said, shaking his head.

"Mr. Sutter, please go in your house. Wait for us. And keep those boys away from the window. You don't want them to see this."

Sutter started to turn away, then stopped. "Hey, I remember you!"

Pavano ignored him and turned back to his partner. Pinto reached for the door handle, then thought better of it. "Fingerprints. Look. There's blood smeared on the door here. Might be good fingerprints. We need backup here. We need an ME. We need the crime scene guys."

Pavano raced back to the patrol car, flung the door open, and grabbed the radio. "Vince, we have a homicide here. We need backup. We need someone with a strong stomach."

"I take it you don't need an ambulance?"

"No. We don't need an ambulance. This is a murder scene. We need CS guys. We have a man with a giant hole in his neck and—"

"Save the details, Andy. I'm eating my dinner. Ten-four."

"Just hurry, Vince. I've never seen anything like this."

"You haven't seen much—have you, Andy?"

Who told him he always has to have the last word? And who told him he couldn't be serious even for a crime this horrible?

Pavano slammed the patrol car door and made his way back to Pinto. The big, older cop leaned with his hands on his waist, peering into the victim's window. Finally he turned, removed his cap, and scratched his thinning flattop.

"It's like a horror movie, Andy. The skin is all scorched. The hole is as big as a grapefruit. And it looks empty inside. Just burned skin." He swallowed. His teeth clicked.

Never realized he has false teeth, Pavano thought. *And then, why am I thinking about Chaz's teeth when I'm staring at a guy with a giant knothole in his neck?*

Pinto pulled Pavano back from the car. "Stop looking at him. Your face is green. No shit."

Pavano nodded and turned his back on the Audi. It didn't make him feel any better.

I came out to Sag Harbor to take it easy, get away from all the fucking crime in the city, maybe get back with Sari. What the hell happened here?

"We can't do anything," Pinto said. "Not till the crime scene guys get here. Let's go inside and talk to that Sutter guy."

Pavano nodded. "He acted totally innocent. That's the first sign he did it, right?"

Pinto patted him on the back. "Too much TV, Andy."

The sun had almost disappeared behind the house. The sky darkened to gray, and a cool breeze rattled the still-bare trees.

They stepped onto the front stoop. Pinto leaned close. "Andy, tell Sutter *this* time you got it right—the victim really is dead."

"Shut the fuck up, will you?" Pavano could feel his face turn hot. That rainy night on this doorstep had to be the worst moment of his life. And now here he was, ringing the doorbell again.

It took only a few seconds for Sutter to pull open the door. He had a glass of white wine in his right hand. Pavano saw the hand tremble. A few drips of wine spilled to the floor. "How did someone do that to him? Can you tell me?"

"Hard to say," Pinto replied softly, eyes narrowed on Sutter.

Pavano didn't see the blond boys, but he saw another boy, dark-haired, small, peering down from the top of the stairs.

"Dad, is everything okay? Why are the police here?"

"It's okay, Ira. Go back to your room, all right?"

"But aren't we going to finish dinner? My spaghetti's getting cold."

"We'll finish dinner in a short while. Please—get up to your room. And tell Elena to stay up there, too."

Sutter can't hide how tense he is. Tense because he murdered the guy?

"Sir, I'm Officer Pinto. He's Officer Pavano. As you can see, we're from the Sag Harbor Police Department."

Sutter gazed hard at Pavano. "We've met," he said quietly.

"Sir, can we go somewhere more private?" Pinto had Sutter by the elbow.

"Sure. Come into my office. I can't tell you much about Richard, but—"

"Is that his name? Richard? Do you know his full name?"

They stepped into the book-lined office. Pavano admired the dark wood, the big desk, the floor-to-ceiling bookshelves.

"Well, yes. His name is Richard Hulenberger."

Pavano pulled out his phone. He brought up the memo app and typed in *Richard Hulenberger*. The phone had replaced the little black notebook that cops used to carry in their shirt pockets. Pavano missed his notebook. But he was grateful. He could never find a pencil to write with.

"Is he a friend of yours?" Pinto asked.

Sutter motioned for them to sit on the green leather couch. "A friend? No. First time I ever met him." Hand still trembling, he set the wineglass down near the edge of the desktop.

The two cops remained standing. Pavano typed *Not a friend* into his phone.

Pinto shifted his weight. He gazed around the room. "Mr. Sutter, before we talk about anything else, I need to ask you one question."

Pavano watched as Sutter jammed his hands into his jeans pocket.

"Yes. What?"

Pinto took a breath. For dramatic effect? "Mr. Sutter, do you own a blowtorch?"

Sutter blinked. "Why, yes. Yes, I do."

31

A heavy silence for a moment.

Sutter lowered himself to the edge of the desk, hands still stuffed in his pockets. "I . . . don't understand. Why are you asking me about a blowtorch?"

"What kind of blowtorch do you have?" Pinto crossed his arms over his chest. Pavano noted on his phone: *Blowtorch*.

"Um . . . let me think. It's a fifteen-liter flame gun. I think that's what it's called. It's propane. Do you want to see it? It's in the garage."

Pinto motioned for Sutter to sit still. "The crime scene officers will want to see it. Thank you. But I'd like to ask a few more questions first." He rubbed his chin. "Fifteen-liter? That's a pretty big mother. Why do you have it?"

Sutter twisted his face. Was he confused? Struggling to figure out why he was being questioned about his blowtorch. Or was he pretending?

Pavano admired Pinto for thinking of a blowtorch. It was a good notion. That man's scorched neck wound could definitely be caused by a blowtorch.

"I use it for melting ice," Sutter said. "You know. In the winter. Ice covers the front stoop. It gets treacherous. I melt ice off the driveway with it, too. Why are you asking me—?"

"So tell us, who is Richard . . . whatsisname?" Pinto interrupted.

"Hulenberger. He's from the Blakeman Institute. In the city."

Pavano typed rapidly on the phone keyboard. He let Pinto ask the questions. Pinto was doing a good job. Pavano could see the Audi in the driveway from the office window. So far, the other cops hadn't shown up.

"And you never met him? He drove here from the city because . . . ?"

"He wanted to meet with me. I'd applied for quite a large grant."

"And he came to tell you . . . ?"

Sutter lowered his eyes to the floor. It took him a few seconds to answer. "He came to tell me they were turning me down. No grant."

The bitterness in Sutter's voice brought Pavano to attention. He felt his heart start to pound a little faster.

"He brought you bad news," Pinto said softly. "Very bad news."

Sutter nodded. He didn't raise his eyes.

"And how did that make you feel? Angry? Fucking angry?"

Sutter raised his eyes. His face showed a new intensity. He pulled out his hands and held them tensely at his sides. "Do I need a lawyer?"

"I'm just askin'," Pinto replied with a shrug. "Somebody brings me bad news, it makes me angry. You know? Kill the messenger? Know what I'm saying?"

"I'm a psychologist, Officer," he said heatedly. "I think I know how to control my anger so that I don't murder anyone who brings me disappointing news."

"You're a psychologist with a blowtorch?"

"I explained the blowtorch." He uttered a cry of frustration. "Is that what happened out there? Are you telling me Richard was murdered with a blowtorch? He left my house, sat down in his car, and someone took a blowtorch to him in my driveway?"

Pinto made a calming motion with both hands. Pavano could see this guy was strung tight. But the situation would make anyone a little tense. And, he didn't have much of a motive for killing Hulenberger. Not if he was telling the truth.

But was he hiding some things? Did he know Hulenberger better than he was letting on?

We should advise him to call his lawyer.

"It's definitely a homicide, Mr. Sutter," Pinto said, his hands still raised as if warding Sutter off. "The guy didn't take a blowtorch to himself. The crime scene guys will want to see your blowtorch. And they'll have a lot more questions. If you'd feel more comfortable with a lawyer present . . ."

"Yes. I'll call my lawyer. No. Wait. I didn't see anything. I don't know anything. Why do I need a lawyer?"

"Mr. Sutter, please take a deep breath," Pinto said softly.

Pavano could see the turmoil in Sutter's mind. His eyes were darting from side to side. He was thinking hard about something.

"I . . . have to tell you one thing," Sutter said, clasping his hands together in his lap. "There are fingerprints. I mean, I touched the car."

Pinto raised one eyebrow. "Fingerprints?"

"I grabbed the side of the car. You know. The window. I wasn't thinking. I didn't know. I . . . got blood on my hands. Blood from the side of the car. I was still washing it off when you drove up."

Pinto gave Pavano a quick glance. Pinto was suspicious of this guy. "Thanks for telling us," Pavano said, typing on his phone.

The doorbell rang. Pavano and Pinto followed Sutter into the hall. A woman carrying a little boy on her shoulder opened the front door. Pavano remembered her from the first time he was here.

A tall African-American man stepped into the entryway. He had a noticeably big, melon-shaped head, shaved bald, and a silver ring in one ear. He wore a baggy brown suit, wrinkled and frayed at the cuffs. He had a dark brown dress shirt underneath and a blue bow tie tilted under his chin.

"Can I help you?" Sutter motioned the woman away. "I'll take care of this, Roz."

The man ignored Sutter and approached Pavano and Pinto. "Are you the officers who discovered this?"

Both cops nodded.

"I'm Harrison. The ME."

Pinto squinted at him. "You're new?"

"I haven't been new for thirty years. I'm from Riverhead. You've heard of it?"

"You're an ME or a comedian?"

"I'm not as funny as your face. Let's start again. There are CS guys dusting the car right now. Then they'll sweep for fibers. You know. Stuff for the DNA lab guys. You're familiar with that, right? Or are you new?"

"Pavano's new," Pinto said, motioning with his eyes. "He's out here from the city."

Harrison had one brown eye and one blue eye. He focused the blue eye on Pinto. "Am I going to get his thrilling life story now, or are we investigating a goddamn homicide?"

"Sorry, Dr. Harrison," Pinto said. "We've been questioning Mr. Sutter here. He—"

"We'll get to you, Mr. Sutter," Harrison gave him a nod, then turned back to the officers. "Did you touch anything? Open the door? Roll down the window? Shake hands with the victim? Muss up his hair?"

Pinto squinted at Harrison. "Are you for real?"

"We didn't touch a thing," Pavano stepped in. "But Sutter did. He had his hands on the bottom of the window. Smeared the blood."

Harrison squinted at Sutter and tsk-tsked.

"Pinto and I looked into the car, but we stayed back. Then we called in right away," Pavano explained.

"Do you expect a Nobel Prize for that?"

Pinto exploded. "What the fuck, Harrison? What's your problem?"

Pavano just wanted to get out of the house. There were kids upstairs. They were probably listening to all this.

What happened to those two little blond boys?

"Have you examined the body at all, Doctor?" Pavano asked.

Harrison pulled a soiled handkerchief from his jacket and mopped his bald head. "Yeah. I did a cursory exam before the CS guys arrived." He tucked the handkerchief away and fiddled with his bow tie.

"And could you determine the cause of death?"

Sutter uttered a groan. Pavano turned and saw him gripping the bottom of the banister, his face pale. "Are you feeling okay?"

"Not really," Sutter uttered. "I mean, a murder in my driveway? I feel kinda sick."

"Why don't you go sit down. Get a glass of water," Pavano instructed. "We'll come back to you, okay?"

Sutter nodded but didn't reply. He made his way back toward his office.

"Cause of death?" Pavano repeated to Harrison when Sutter was out of hearing.

"Officer, you know I can't say till I do the whole goddamn exam." He motioned them outside. The cool evening air felt soothing on Pavano's hot face.

Harrison led the way to the Audi, where two uniformed officers were combing every inch of it. "You want to know a cause of death from my first cursory exam? Okay, I'd say it was asphyxiation."

Pinto and Pavano both uttered sounds of surprise. Pinto removed his cap and scratched his head. "Asphyxiation? What makes you say that?"

A grim smile formed on Harrison's face. "Here. I'll show you. You didn't eat dinner yet, right?"

"We didn't eat dinner. Why?"

"Because you probably wouldn't be able to keep it down."

"Another one of your jokes?"

The smile faded from the big man's face. "No joke."

He pulled open the back door. He pointed to something stretched across the backseat.

It looked like a wet pink snake to Pavano. No, wait. Some kind of long pasta noodle. Jagged on both ends. Dark streaks along the sides.

"What are you showing us?" Pinto demanded. "What is that?"

"The man's windpipe," Harrison said. "Whoever killed him ripped out his windpipe while he was still alive."

32

Pavano again let Pinto do the questioning while he studied Sutter's sister. Sitting across from them in Sutter's office, Roz kept her hands clasped tightly in her lap, squeezing her fingers. But it was the only sign of nervousness. She seemed like a straightforward woman, and Pavano believed what she told them.

Which was nothing useful.

She had come home from grocery shopping and was in the kitchen the whole time Hulenberger and Sutter were meeting in the office. She had heard voices, but she hadn't seen Hulenberger and definitely hadn't seen him leave the house. She hadn't heard anything unusual. Now she was worried about upsetting the kids.

"You certainly don't think the kids saw what happened?" she asked.

"We have to talk to them. You know. Be as thorough as possible," Pinto said, glancing at the notes on Pavano's phone. "It's possible they saw or heard something helpful."

"Elena and Ira were upstairs in their rooms," Roz told them. "I'm sure they didn't see a thing. And the twins . . . I'm not sure where they were. Probably in the guesthouse out back."

"Ma'am, could you bring them in one by one?" Pinto asked, speaking softly.

"A horrible murder like this could upset them terribly, Sergeant. Ira is very delicate. You might say he's troubled. And the twins just arrived here."

Pavano raised his eyes. "Arrived here?"

"Mark and Lea adopted them. She brought them home less than two weeks ago. It's hard enough for them to adjust. If you—"

"We'll do our best not to upset them, ma'am," Pinto said. "You and Mr. Sutter are welcome to stay in the room when we talk to them."

"Where *is* Mr. Sutter?" Pavano asked. Sutter had slipped away while they were questioning his sister.

Roz sighed. "I think he's trying to phone Lea. His wife. She's in the city."

Pinto shifted his weight on the desk chair. He suddenly looked old and weary. Pavano knew he was ten years older than he, but he looked even older than that. *Frayed*. That's the strange word that popped into Pavano's mind. The frayed life of a cop.

With another warning to be careful, the sister went to round up the four kids. Pavano picked up a pink paperweight from the desk and tossed it from hand to hand. It took him awhile to recognize it as a porcelain model of a human brain.

The color reminded him of the slender windpipe tossed on the backseat of the victim's car. He set the brain back down on the desk.

Elena, the fourteen-year-old, came downstairs first. She was a pretty girl with shiny black hair and lively dark eyes. She seemed confident and mature for her age. She spoke in full sentences, not in teenage grunts and fits and starts. She didn't seem at all hesitant to answer Pinto's questions, but she had nothing to tell them.

She had been in her room since getting home late from school, texting her friends and listening to music. She had glimpsed her father talking to a man in a suit but didn't hear what they were talking about and didn't see or hear the man leave.

Ira Sutter, the twelve-year-old, slunk down on the couch and pressed close to his aunt. He gripped the couch arm tightly with a slender hand. Before Pinto could ask a question, Ira demanded in a tiny voice, "Is Dad in trouble?"

"No, of course not." Roz answered for them.

"Then why is he so upset? Why are all these policemen here?"

"There was an accident. In your driveway." Pinto spoke up before the sister could answer. "We're just trying to find out what happened. No one in your family is in trouble. I swear."

"Ira, did you see that dark car in your driveway?" Pavano asked.

The boy had a slender, pale face. His natural expression appeared to be worry. "I saw it after the police came."

"But not before?"

He shook his head, then glanced at his aunt. Roz gave him a reassuring pat on the knee of his jeans.

"Did you see the man when he was talking to your dad?"

He shook his head again. "No. I was upstairs. Then Roz called us down to dinner but there was no man here."

A few more questions and they let him go.

"Do you want to see the twins together or one by one?" Roz asked.

Pinto sighed and rubbed the stubble on his jaw. "Together is fine. I know this seems like a waste of time. But we just have to do it. You know. So we can say our report is complete."

Somewhere a clock chimed. Was it seven o'clock or eight o'clock? Despite the horror of what they had seen, Pavano was starting to feel hungry.

The twins plopped down on the couch, all blond hair, wide eyes, and innocence. They were very cute, Pavano observed. They looked smaller than their twelve years. Their voices were little boys' voices.

The two cops chitchatted with them for a few minutes. The boys had funny accents, sort of English, sort of Irish. They didn't seem at all fazed by having to talk to policemen.

Their answers turned out to be a lot more interesting than those of the other two kids.

"Did you see the man talking to Mr. Sutter?"

"Yes, sir," the one with dimples seemed to be the one who liked to talk. "We saw him in the den with the new pa."

"The new pa?"

"That's what they call Mark," Roz interjected.

Pinto leaned forward in the big chair. "You saw them in here when you came home from school?"

Both boys nodded. "He was talking to the new pa, telling him bad things."

Pavano's breath caught in his throat. He squinted at the expressionless boy. "Bad things?"

"For sure. He said he had bad news. The new pa looked very sad."

Pinto and Pavano exchanged glances. Pinto cleared his throat. Roz suddenly looked troubled, her lips pursed tightly. She started to say something, but Pinto motioned for her to remain silent.

"So what did you do?" Pinto asked.

"Sammy and I took a ball and went outside to play."

"Did you hear the man have a fight with your dad?"

"No. They weren't fighting. Just talking, right, Sammy?"

Sammy nodded his head solemnly.

"Were they arguing? You know. Shouting."

"No. Just talking," Daniel insisted. "But I think Pa was a wee bit angry."

The quiet one spoke up. "Daniel and I went out to play catch. With a tennis ball."

"Where did you play?" Pavano asked.

"By the driveway. You know. Next to the garage."

"And so you saw the man's dark blue car?" Pinto asked.

They both nodded. "The ball bounced off it a couple of times, don't you know. But it didn't make a dent."

"And did you see the man leave the house?"

They nodded again.

"Did you see him get into his car?"

Daniel nodded. "He got in his big car. And the new pa shouted at us."

"He said get out of the way," his brother chimed in. "He said the man was backing up and we should get out of the way."

"So what did you do?"

"We went back to our house. In the garden."

"Your house?"

"Their room is in the guesthouse," Roz explained. "That's where they're staying."

"You went back to your room? And you didn't hear anything strange? Did you see anyone come to the driveway? Did you hear a shout or a fight or anything weird?"

The twins exchanged puzzled glances again. They shook their heads.

"We didn't hear anything. Not a peep, sir."

Pavano heard a baby crying somewhere.

Roz jumped to her feet. "That's Axl, my little boy. He's waking up from his nap. Officers, I have to go upstairs and get him. I'm afraid this interview session is over."

Pinto climbed up with a groan. Pavano's head suddenly felt like solid granite. *Too much. This is too much to think about.*

They followed Roz to the front. Before they could exit, the screen door swung open. A uniform cop, one of the crime scene guys, poked his head into the house.

"Sergeants, one more bit of info you can add to your report."

"What's that?" Pinto asked. Pavano pulled out his phone to write it down.

"That blowtorch in the garage? We went over it. Looks like it's been used recently."

33

"I wish I was there with you, Mark. I'm so sorry I'm not there to help you. Roz must be a mess, too."

"Lea, is it too late for the jitney? Can you get a train? I'll pick you up in Southampton."

"Mark, you're breaking up. I can't hear too well. Are the kids okay? Are they upset?"

"I don't know if they realize what happened. I think they're mainly confused. I'm going to talk to them later. After the police leave. You know. Try to see how they feel, what they know."

"How can you explain it to them? A murder right at our house?"

"I'll just be straight with them. I mean, I don't know how else to handle it. Just tell them what happened and be there for them."

"Oh, wow. I have the shakes just thinking about it. Right in front of our house. And you didn't hear anything? You didn't see anyone go up to his car?"

"None of us did. Listen, can you—"

"I'm worried about the kids, Mark. Poor Ira. Something like this . . . a horrible murder in our front yard . . . I mean, how much more traumatic can it be?"

"He was up in his room. I don't think he realizes . . . I'm going to sit down and talk to them all. Get their feelings out in the open."

"I can't hear you very well. You keep breaking up. I'll try to get back as fast as I can, darling. I'll cancel my meeting for tomorrow morning. I'll let you know what jitney I'm on. I'm so sorry I'm not there with you, sweetheart."

"Are you feeling okay? I really didn't think you were ready for the city. Those nightmares you were having. And . . . and the tomato soup thing . . ."

"You're breaking up, Mark. What did you say?"

"Do you feel okay?"

"Actually, no. Maybe you were right. Maybe this city visit was too soon. I feel weird. I can't really explain it. Kind of like I can't concentrate. I don't really feel I'm totally in control. It's nothing. I'm sure. Just tired, I guess."

"Please get home as fast as you can. We need you here. I . . . don't know what's going to happen. I mean, when word of this gets out. You know. I'm a public figure now. The publicity. 'Gruesome Murder in Bestselling Psychologist's Driveway.' It could get bad, Lea."

"But you had nothing to do with the murder."

"Don't be naïve, sweetheart. Does that matter? It happened in our fucking driveway. If the details are released . . . Can you see the front of the *Post*?"

"I'm so sorry, honey. I can't hear. I'll text you my jitney."

A soft click. Then silence. The connection was lost.

Mark headed to the bar against the den wall. *I need something stronger than wine.*

And then he felt a stab of anger: *How can she be away when I need her? When we all need her here?*

He knew what he was doing. It was obvious. He was angry at himself for what happened with Autumn. And he was transferring his anger to Lea. Embarrassing to be so obvious.

Autumn, you missed all the excitement.

He thought about kissing her. Fucking her on top of his desk. *Oh, Jesus.*

The two police officers left. He saw two other cops in the driveway, working over the car. They had set up halogen spotlights on poles to light their work. Yellow crime tape had been stretched across the bottom of the front yard. Cars moved slowly on the street. Gawkers wondering what had happened there.

Mark shook his head and took a long sip of his Cruzan Single Barrel rum. *The neighbors must have their binoculars out.*

Luckily, the houses were far apart, separated by tall, old oak and sassafras trees and high evergreen hedges. Mark had no idea who his neighbors were.

Richard Hulenberger's body had been removed. Wrapped and carried away in a silent ambulance. Now, gazing into the white halogen light, Mark saw that the car seats were on their backs on the lawn. One cop was leaning into the trunk, sweeping it with some kind of whirring device. A vacuum?

He gathered the four kids in the den while Roz went to feed and entertain Axl. The den had two brown, soft-leather couches at a ninety-degree angle against two walls, and a matching recliner chair, all facing a fifty-five-inch flat-screen TV mounted on the only wall without bookshelves.

A stack of glass shelves to the right of the TV screen held Lea's stuffed-monkey collection, dozens of specimens. Lea wasn't embarrassed to show off her monkeys. She told anyone who asked that growing up in a house jammed with so many kids, she never had room for any kind of collection. In a way, the mostly hideous monkeys were fulfilling a lifelong dream.

Samuel and Daniel sank into one couch and slumped down, looking uncomfortable, troubled. Elena took the recliner, sitting stiffly on the edge, not tilting back as she usually did. Ira perched next to her on one arm of the recliner.

Mark studied them for a few seconds. Elena wore freshly applied lip gloss. Ira had a tomato sauce stain on his chin.

"As you've probably figured out, something terrible happened in our driveway this afternoon. The man who was visiting me was murdered by someone."

Elena rolled her eyes. "Dad, please—tell us something we *don't* know."

Mark's impulse was to scold her for being so flip. But he quickly remembered that her attitude might be her way of dealing with something frightening.

"Elena, not appropriate."

"Sorry."

"I don't really know much about it," he confessed, standing awkwardly in front of them as if giving a lecture. He had set down his glass but found himself craving another few sips of rum. "But if I can answer any questions. I know you must be upset. And maybe confused."

Ira spoke up first. "Dad, did the killer mean to kill *you?*"

The question made him suck in a burst of air. Not a question he expected. "No. I . . . don't think so, Ira. The police didn't have anything to say about that. I don't think anyone wants to kill me."

Ira screwed up his face, thinking hard. "But will the killer come in the house?"

"No," Mark answered quickly, without wanting to think about that. "No one is coming in the house. We're all safe here. You don't have to be scared. We are all completely safe."

Elena shifted her weight on the edge of the recliner. "Does this mean that Ruth-Ann can't come for a sleepover Friday night?"

Mark blinked. *Is she totally self-involved? Doesn't she react at all to someone being murdered in front of her house? Maybe that's a good thing.*

"I don't see any reason why Ruth-Ann can't come Friday, Elena. But I think the news of what happened here will be out by then. We'll have to talk with her parents."

"Maybe she'll be too scared to come over," Ira suggested in a tiny voice.

Elena wrapped her hands over Ira's shoulders. "Well, you'll protect her—won't you, big guy?"

Ira squirmed out from under her hands. "Shut up."

"Don't tease Ira," Mark scolded.

"Sorry," Elena murmured. She gave Ira a bump with her shoulder. "It's just . . . I'll be so upset if we don't have our sleepover. We've planned it for weeks."

"Shouldn't be a problem," Mark said.

And suddenly both twins were on their feet. Both with the same forlorn expressions.

Daniel's eyes brimmed with tears. He took a tentative step toward Mark. "Can I have a hug?" In a tiny, high voice. He rushed into Mark's open arms.

"Me too," Samuel said. "Can I have a hug, please?"

Mark wrapped them both in a tight hug. He could feel their trembling bodies. They both made sniffling sounds.

Glancing over their heads, he caught Elena's trembling-chinned expression. She was near tears, too. Not as skeptical as he thought. Ira sat with his arms crossed tightly in front of him, staring into the distance.

Mark tried to pull his arms away, but the boys clung to him.

"Hug," Daniel said, burying his face in Mark's shirt.

"Hug," Samuel repeated.

34

Samuel closed the guesthouse door behind him, making sure it clicked shut. The two boys strode into their room. Each climbed onto one of the low twin beds, one against each wall. They stood up and bounced on the beds for a few moments, a gleeful trampoline act.

Bright lights set up by the police officers in the driveway broke the darkness outside their curtained window. The light swooped across the flowered wallpaper and caught the two boys as they leaped and bounced.

"Smoked meat," Daniel said when they finally slumped to their beds.

"Smoked meat," Samuel repeated. "There was Daniel being Daniel again."

Daniel stuck his chin out defiantly. "Smoked meat. Smoked meat. Smoked meat."

Samuel sighed. "Yes, the man was smoked meat. But—"

"This will keep Pa busy for a while."

"I know, Daniel. But, we just got here. Perhaps we need to go slow."

Daniel giggled. "You loved it, too, laddy. I saw your eyes shine. You wanted a taste of that smoked meat."

Samuel bounced lightly on the bed. "Don't be making a joke, Daniel. We don't eat smoked meat anymore—remember?"

Daniel giggled again. "Did you put the blowtorch back where we got it?"

Samuel nodded. "Sure, I did. But I don't really understand why we needed it, boyo."

"To keep Pa busy. To give the coppers something to puzzle about, don't you know."

Samuel's expression changed. He stood up and crossed to his brother. He put his hands on Daniel's shoulders and peered down at him. "I know you like a bit of fun—"

"You too."

"But if we get caught, it's all off. All. Off. And why did we adopt the new mum? Remember?"

Daniel grinned up at him. "To rule the school?"

"Yes. To rule the school. But if we go too fast . . ."

Daniel removed his twin's hands from his shoulders. His eyes flashed. Samuel knew that expression. Thoughtful. Devilishly thoughtful.

"Pa doesn't want us. He doesn't like us. So we have to keep him busy. Out of our hair, don't you know. And then, Sammy . . . And then . . . who will help us rule the school? Do you know? Can you guess? Who will be the first to help us?"

Samuel stuck out his jaw. "I can't read your mind now, can I? Especially not *your* mind."

"The bruvver and sister," Daniel said.

Samuel stared at him. "Who?"

"The bruvver and sister," his twin repeated. "You know. Ira and Elena."

"The two of them? Help us?"

Daniel nodded enthusiastically, eyes aglow. "The bruvver and sister know people, Sammy. They have friends, right? They know things. They will help us rule the school. They'll join us. And then more. And more."

Daniel jumped to his feet and pumped his fists above his head. "More and more and more. And when we own all the kids, we own the town. It will all be ours. All. And what does it take, Sammy? You know the answer. Teamwork, boyo. Teamwork wins the day."

"Daniel, listen to me. What if Ira and Elena don't *want* to join us? What if they tell Mum and Pa?"

Daniel giggled. His grin made his dimples flare. "We'll convince the bruvver and sister."

Samuel stared at him. "Convince them? Okay. But no smoked meat, Daniel. Okay? No smoked meat?"

Daniel nodded. "Total domination, Sammy. You'll see. Total domination."

A hard knock on the door ended the discussion. The door swung open, and Roz edged into the room, carrying a round tray with a bowl and glasses. "You boys didn't get much dinner, what with the police and all. I brought you some Cokes and a big bowl of popcorn."

Sweet smiles on both boys. "Oh, me goodness. Thank you, Aunty Roz," said Samuel.

Daniel's eyes lit up with glee, and his dimples flashed. "Thank you, Aunty. Who loves the popcorn? We do! Pop pop pop."

PART THREE

35

Mark wrapped his arms tightly around Lea's waist and pressed his face against her cheek. "I'm so glad you're here."

She stepped back, nearly stumbling over her overnight bag. Her dark eyes flashed. "It takes a murder to make you miss me so much?"

"Don't make jokes. Please. It's . . . been horrible for all of us."

"I'm so sorry I couldn't get back last night, honey. The jitney was booked. And I missed the last train. Then this morning there was an accident on the expressway, and—look at the clock. It's nearly two."

"It's okay, Lea. You're here now." He pulled her close again and kissed her.

"How are the kids? I worried about them all night. Are they—?"

"Roz and I got them off to school. They seem to be okay. A little quiet, maybe. Ira is glum, but I don't think more glum than usual."

"The morning papers could have been worse," she said, tugging off her red jacket and tossing it on a chair. She straightened her T-shirt and pulled it out from her jeans.

"For sure it could be worse. The police didn't reveal the details. Too sickening, I guess. If they had, it would have been on every front page."

Lea touched his face. "Poor baby. I feel so bad for you. Did you see the . . . uh . . . the body?"

"No. I—" He reached for her again. He had a sudden desire to pull up her T-shirt and kiss her all over.

The doorbell interrupted. Mark glanced over Lea's shoulder and saw two dark-uniformed men peering through the screen door. He recognized the two cops from the night before.

He groaned.

Lea turned to the door. "Hello?"

"It's Sergeant Pinto and Pavano," the big, older cop said. "Sorry to interrupt."

Lea pushed open the door, and they entered, both removing their dark caps. Pinto studied Lea. He had a toothpick riding up and down between his teeth. Mark smelled tobacco on the other one. Pavano held his arms tense at his sides, as if expecting trouble.

He always looks uncomfortable. Like he knows he's chosen the wrong line of work.

"This is my wife, Lea." Mark gestured to the suitcases. "She's just back. From the city."

The cops nodded at her. Pinto's eyes lingered longer than Mark thought they should. Pinto removed the toothpick and shoved it into his uniform shirt pocket. "Sorry for interrupting your afternoon, Mrs. Sutter. We need to speak to your husband for a few minutes."

"I've already answered all your questions," Mark snapped. "Do I need my lawyer?"

"If you prefer," Pinto said. "But then we'd have to have our talk at the station."

"But I've told you everything I know."

"We're making a report for the state guys now," Pinto said. "They're probably going to send their own cops down. They'll ask you the same questions. Then if the feds get into it . . ." His voice trailed off.

"It won't take long," Pavano said. "We have some test results."

"Results? You mean like fingerprints? You got them overnight?"

"The lab guys don't get cases like this very often," Pavano said.

"Perhaps if we could sit down." Pinto motioned toward Mark's office down the hall.

Mark sighed. Lea shrugged. She lifted the overnight bag. "I'll go unpack. Then maybe I'll make a nice dinner before the kids get home." She turned to Mark. "Unless you need me . . ."

He shook his head. "Go ahead, dear. No problem." He turned and led the two cops into his office.

Autumn had left a stack of mail on his chair. She arrived late that morning and didn't have work on her mind. Shining those beautiful eyes on him, she'd slid his hand over her breasts. Then she got all pouty when he told her Lea was coming home.

Autumn was young and beautiful and sexy, but seeing her made him feel sick now. How was he going to deal with her? If he told her yesterday morning was a onetime thing, would she go berserk? Tell Lea?

He couldn't fire her. That would be a definite lawsuit. And it would mean more hideously damaging newspaper stories.

And how did he feel about her? He hadn't had time to sort it out. He knew he didn't want to hurt her. But he also knew that Lea meant everything to him. He had done a stupid, impulsive thing. So unlike him. So totally unlike him.

He knew he needed to think about this all. But with the murder . . .

The two cops were staring at him. Trying to read his thoughts. Did he appear tense to them? Would they misinterpret it and decide he was guilty in some way?

He removed the stack of letters from his chair and sat down. Once again, they took their places on the green leather couch facing the desk.

Pinto dropped his cap onto the floor in front of him. Pavano pulled out his phone to take notes. He tapped a slow rhythm with the fingers of his other hand on the couch arm.

"One more time," Pinto said. "The victim brought you bad news, right? Very bad news."

"Well, yeah," Mark replied. "But I told you, he was just the messenger. It wasn't his fault I didn't get the grant. The board voted. They just sent him to tell me."

"And . . . I know you've already stated this. . . . Your feeling when he told you? Angry?"

"Disappointed," Mark corrected him.

Pavano tapped something into his phone. Then he raised his head and gazed intently at Mark. "The victim's car was in the driveway for how long before you noticed it?"

"Maybe fifteen minutes. Maybe twenty."

"You don't think it's strange that a car could sit in your driveway twenty minutes, and you didn't notice it?"

Mark shrugged. "What can I tell you? I didn't see it."

"And you never looked out the window and saw anyone approach the car?"

"No. No, I didn't. I told you."

"You never noticed another car drive by or stop?"

"No. I didn't look out the front. So I—"

"You saw no one in your front yard? No one walk up your driveway?"

"This is getting repetitious," Mark said.

Easy. Don't let them rattle you.

Pinto nodded. "I know. We have to do this." He glanced at the notes on his partner's phone. "Mr. Sutter, we have test results that show your blowtorch was recently used."

Mark blinked. His mind went blank for a moment. *What can I say? What can I tell them?* "Yes. Well, yes. I used it. Ira and I were doing a project."

"A project?"

"Yeah. Metalwork. We were building a robot, actually. I do these projects . . . Well . . . They're good for Ira. Help him build confidence."

"So if we ask your son about the blowtorch, he'll back up your story?"

"Well . . . hmmm . . . actually, no. He wasn't home. I used the blowtorch on the robot while he was in school." Mark could feel his face go hot.

Pinto shifted his weight. "Could you show us this robot that you used the blowtorch on? Is it here?"

"Ummm . . . I know this sounds bad, Sergeant. But the robot disappeared. Ira took it to school, and it disappeared from the art room."

They both squinted at him.

"I'm telling the truth. It must have been stolen." His face still felt blazing hot.

"The lab guys seem to think the blowtorch could have been used yesterday. As the murder weapon."

"I . . . don't know anything about that. The garage door was open. Anyone could have taken it out."

A long silence.

"Well, we have fingerprint results on the victim's car," Pavano said finally. He flipped through some screens on his phone.

Mark felt his throat tighten.

"The CS guys found only children's prints," Pinto said. "Children's prints on both front doors. And then there were three other prints. Round. Like a ball had hit the car."

They hadn't asked a question, but they waited for Mark to say something.

He leaned over the desk. He cleared his throat. "I'm not surprised by that," he said.

The two cops waited for him to continue.

"The twins," Mark said. "I believe you talked to them. And they told you they were playing with a tennis ball at the side of the driveway."

"And it's their prints on the car?" Pinto said.

"Pretty good bet," Mark said and then regretted sounding so sarcastic. "They were playing catch. They said the ball hit Hulenberger's car a few times."

The cops nodded. He could see they were studying him.

"And my prints . . . they must have been there," Mark said. "Remember? I gripped the side of the door? Under the window?"

"Actually, the crime scene guys couldn't get any good prints," Pinto said. "The blood was too smeared."

Pavano was flipping through his phone screens. Pinto licked at the side of his mouth. "So the twins saw Hulenberger get into his car. I recall that's what they said. But then they didn't see anyone come up the drive? They didn't see someone come up to the car?"

"I told them to get out of the way," Mark said. "I told them to watch out. He was backing up."

"And do they always obey you really quickly?" Pinto asked, leaning forward.

Mark pushed back from the desk. "I don't understand that question, Officer. What are you saying? That the boys stayed by the front? That they might have seen something?"

Pinto and Pavano exchanged glances. "They might have," Pinto said finally. "And maybe they're afraid to tell us?"

"They were there," Pavano added. "It's hard to believe they didn't see anything at all."

Mark rubbed his chin. The beard was getting long. He needed to trim it. "You may be right. Sometimes when kids are traumatized by something they've seen, they manage to lock it away, push it to a back burner, so to speak. Sometimes the fear is so powerful, they just force it from their memory. Stress-related memory loss is very common."

The cops nodded. Pavano clicked away on his phone.

Pinto climbed to his feet with a groan. His shirt had pulled out over his potbelly. "And sometimes do kids *lie* to stay out of trouble?" he asked.

Mark stood up, too. He didn't answer the question. He knew it wasn't really a question. He didn't know the twins well enough to know how truthful they were.

They seemed sweet and innocent. But, of course, kids can put on quite a show for grown-ups when they want to. If the boys saw something frightening, if they witnessed the murder, he felt terrible for them. What a welcome to their new home.

And then he had a memory flash: *I did see them at the side of the house. When I ran out to Hulenberger's car, the twins . . . were standing at the side of the house. They weren't in back. They were there.*

"We'll want to talk to the boys," Pinto said, studying Mark's face.

Mark returned his stare. "With me in the room?"

"No. But we'll have a psychologist in the room. We'll make sure they are comfortable. You can wait right outside. If you wish to have a lawyer present . . ."

That was a challenge. Mark felt a stab of anger. "Because you think if I'm not there, the boys are going to incriminate me? That isn't going to happen. You know the expression 'barking up the wrong tree,' I'm sure."

They both grunted in reply. Mark led them down the hall and held open the screen door for them.

After they had driven away, he found Lea in the kitchen, stirring an iced coffee. "That was weird." Lea poured in an envelope of Equal.

"You were listening?"

She nodded. She raised her eyes to him. "Mark, why did you lie to the police?"

He blinked. He could feel the blood pulse at his temples. "You mean . . . about the blowtorch thing?"

She nodded. "A robot project? You and Ira never built a robot. Why did you say that?"

"I needed an answer, Lea. I needed to tell them something. They said the blowtorch had been used. I guess I panicked a little. I mean, I couldn't explain it. I . . . thought it would be better to give them *something*."

She studied him. "But, Mark, it wasn't a good lie. They can check it easily. I don't understand—"

"Why are you looking at me like that? You don't think that I—"

"Of course not." She stepped around the counter and took his hand in hers. "But look at you. Your face is all red and—"

He let her hand slide away. "Forget about the blowtorch. That's not important. The twins were out front when Hulenberger left. The cops think they might have seen the murderer."

Lea gasped. "Oh, those poor boys! They must be so scared."

"Actually, they seem fine," Mark said, taking a sip of her iced coffee. "You need more ice."

"You know I don't like it too cold."

"The twins said they didn't see anything. They said they went back to the guesthouse when Hulenberger started to back down the drive."

"And you don't believe them?" Her voice rose a few octaves. She gripped the glass with both hands. "The way you said that, you think they were lying?"

"All honesty? I don't know what to think. I remember seeing them at the top of the driveway. When I discovered the murder . . ."

She shook her head. "Listen, Mark—I know you didn't want those boys to come here. But they are sweet, lovely boys. And accusing them of lying is—"

"We don't know what kind of boys they are, Lea. We don't know anything about them. Yes, I didn't want you to bring them here. But I'm giving them every chance. And I didn't accuse them of lying. If they saw something horrible, it's possible—"

He stopped. Spun around at the sound of a cough. The twins stood side by side in the kitchen doorway.

"How long have you been standing there?" It came out like an accusation.

They didn't answer. Instead, broad smiles crossed their faces. They dove across the room to wrap Lea in enthusiastic hugs.

"The new mum is home! Mum is home! Yaaaaaaay."

36

"Where are we going, Daniel?"

"To find the bruvver."

The twins wore their colorful surfer swimsuits, still crinkly and stiff, and white sleeveless T-shirts that came down nearly to their knees. Their plastic flip-flops clopped on the pavement. Daniel took long strides, eyes straight ahead. Samuel struggled to keep up.

A mail carrier in his tiny white truck waved as he putted past. Samuel returned the wave and watched a chipmunk dart under the truck's wheels. He waited for the bump and then the *squish*. But the little animal scampered out the other side.

"Close call," Samuel murmured.

Daniel didn't reply. He appeared lost in thought. The blue of his eyes had faded, as if all of his energy was retreating into his mind. Samuel had seen him disappear into himself before.

They turned onto Long Point Road, which snaked along the bay. Samuel's flip-flop snagged a clump of tall grass, and he had to stop to free himself. The afternoon sun beamed down on his face, making it feel more like July than May.

"Hey, Daniel—wait up! Do you mind telling me where we're headed, laddy?"

Daniel kicked pebbles into the tall grass along the side of

the street. Tall, leafy hedges hid the houses that lined the water. "Ethan's house," he said finally. He pointed. "Up there."

"Ira is swimming there with his friend," Samuel said. "That's why we're walking there? To swim?"

Daniel wheeled around, startling his twin. "Time to get in the swim, right, Sammy? Get in the swim. You know? Rule the pool?"

Samuel started to laugh but cut it short. He could see that his brother wasn't joking around. "You mean—"

"The new pa doesn't like us," Daniel said, a sneer making his features hard. His eyes suddenly ice instead of sky. "The new pa doesn't want us. The new pa is our enemy."

"Yes, I know that, boyo."

"The new mum will do anything for us. But Pa fights her. He shouts at her. He doesn't want to give us what we want. He is our enemy."

"Yes. So we keep him busy. I understand what you are saying. But what are you thinking? What does it mean, Daniel? Go ahead. Tell me."

Daniel stared so intently at his twin, Samuel had to turn away. "What it means is . . . What it means is . . . we don't have to take our time, Sammy lad. We can make our move now. It doesn't matter. We've no one to impress. We don't have to pretend anymore. That's good news—right? You want to rule the pool and rule the school?"

"But if we waited—" Samuel gazed at two fat yellow bees fighting over a tiny blossom tucked in the hedge beside them.

Even bees fight.

But not like Daniel.

The mailman waved again, moving the other direction in his stupid little cart-truck. This time, Samuel ignored the grinning jerk.

"Daniel, we already murdered someone to keep Pa busy. Maybe if we take our time . . . go a little slow . . ."

"Slow is no," Daniel sneered. He saw the bumblebees, too. He moved quickly, reached into the hedge, cupped them both in his hands, and flattened them between his palms. "Slow is no." He squeezed his hands together, grinding the bees flat.

"Mum deserves a better man," Daniel said, wiping his palms on the front of his T-shirt. "Mum deserves better. She'll want us to rule the school, Sammy. It will make Mum happy. You'll see."

Samuel shrugged. His face felt burning hot, not just from the sun. He knew he'd already lost the argument. "What do you plan to do?"

"Test the bruvver."

"What? Test Ira? You're going to start with Ira?"

"First Ira, then the sister. We have to show him. We have to dominate him—dominate him to win him over. Right, Sammy?"

Daniel didn't wait for Samuel to reply. He turned and started walking again, running his hand along the hedge, making bees fly and butterflies jump. "We have no choice. It's time to start. And we will start by dominating the bruvver."

They turned and Samuel followed his twin up a smoothly paved driveway that led to a wide three-car garage attached to a white frame house. He could hear the splash of water from behind the house and recognized Ira's laugh.

"Are we going to swim, Daniel? Can't we have a nice swim first?"

Daniel kept walking. "We need to test the bruvver."

"What are you going to do?" Samuel jogged to catch up. He grabbed his twin's shoulders and spun him to face him. "What are you going to do to Ira?"

A crooked smile crossed Daniel's face and his eyes regained their deep blue liveliness. "Maybe see how long he can stay underwater."

37

The lovemaking didn't seem the same.

Was it just his guilt?

No. Mark wasn't imagining it. They'd been married fourteen years. Long enough to know each other's every move.

Fourteen years and suddenly he decided to try another woman. No. Not a woman. A girl.

So, yes. Guilt had to play a part here.

Afterward, cradled in her arm, waiting for his heartbeats to slow and his breath to come easier, tapping one finger on his sweat-damp chest, he pictured the young Lea. Only twenty-two when they got married. What could she have been thinking?

He saw the diamond-sparkle of her dark eyes and remembered how sunlight shone in her hair, softer and flowing down past her shoulders then. What year was it? Yes, 1998. In another millennium. She smelled like lemons. Sweet lemons. When did she change her scent?

Once you start seeing the past, pictures fly at you as if falling out of an old album. *Does anyone still keep photo albums?*

He saw Lea's roommate, the lanky, toothy girl with the sexy laugh. Always pushing her coppery hair off her face, twisting it in her fingers, popping her chewing gum with that smile, as if it was some kind of clever joke.

Claire. Lea had moved from Rockford to New York with Claire. Their big adventure. Thank God Claire had a thing for the First Avenue bars, for that's where Mark met Lea. Very romantic. The two of them breathing beer fumes on each other.

Did she feel the instant connection he did? Of course, it was entirely physical. And what a jerk he must have been that night. Trying so hard to impress her with his stories about college life in Madison, and his studies in psychology. He even bragged about his father being such a hot-shit Park Avenue shrink.

Can you imagine? Using his father? Lying beside her, he cringed. Fourteen years later, he shut his eyes and tried to make the hideous memory go away.

Claire. Think about Claire. Claire Shiner. Yes. It took this long for her last name to reboot. Claire got pregnant. What did she expect, picking up men in the bars every weekend? Always so horny and obvious about it. She decided to go home to Rockford to have the baby.

If she hadn't gone home . . .

. . . Lea wouldn't have needed a roommate. Lea, he remembered, worked as an intern at the *New York Press,* a weekly give-away newspaper. She couldn't afford that East Side apartment she and Claire shared, tiny and sordid and odorous as it was. Would she and Mark have moved in together if Claire hadn't fucked her way back to Rockford?

All so romantic.

The breeze from the open window made him shiver. He wanted to slide under the covers, but he couldn't tell if Lea was awake. *Don't move. This is too nice.*

Too nice. In bed with Lea in the afternoon. A lovemaking matinee like young people. It seldom happened in this crowded house. He listened to the sweep of the curtains making the sunlight dance across their bed.

Silence everywhere else. Ira was swimming at Ethan's house. The twins had pulled on their swimsuits and hurried off to join him. Roz had dropped Elena and Ruth-Ann at the Bridgehampton mall. Roz and Axl were . . . He wasn't quite sure where they were. So hard to keep track of everyone.

So maybe the illicit nature of this rare chance increased his expectations.

No. That wasn't it. Sure, he was eager. He hadn't seen her in a week. And in a way, he wanted to reassure himself that they were okay. That he hadn't screwed up anything.

No. *You're thinking too hard, Mark.*

She had welcomed him with that little sigh from deep in her throat that she always made when he entered her. And he felt the same surge of joy as they began. But it didn't take long to realize that it was different.

Numb.

Such a strangely out-of-place word. But as he moved on top of her, the word invaded his thoughts.

Numb.

And he realized he was doing it all and she was just accepting. She had her arms around his neck and then his waist. But she didn't grasp him with the strength she always had.

And her eyes . . . gazing over his rolling shoulders. Yes, she seemed distant. Numb. She wasn't reacting, and she wasn't trying to hide it.

When he finished, she murmured, "Nice," and her eyes settled on him for a moment before losing their focus and settling back into what seemed to be a hazy world of her own thoughts.

"Lea? Is everything okay? You seem so . . . far away. I could see on your face." He took a breath. "You're still on that island, aren't you?"

It took her a long time to respond. And then she nodded her head, her gaze not on him but at the ceiling. "Yes. Still on the island." Whispered so that the words sent a chill down his neck. "Still on the island. Still back there."

A long sigh. "So many nightmares. Every night. Nightmares pulling me there, pulling me into all that death and horror. I can't get the wailing out of my ears. The wailing and the moaning and the crying. It's like I'm still there. Still there."

She squeezed his hand. "But . . . I want to come back, Mark. I really do."

And then an abrupt move. To break the sadness? Pushing him

aside, she stood up. "The kids will be home soon." It was still a thrill to watch her walk naked across the room. She vanished into the bathroom, and he thought of Autumn.

I can't keep her around. I don't want to ruin my life.

And what could he do to help Lea? The things she saw on that island. He felt as if he could see them, too, in her eyes.

Numb.

She had gone numb.

That will just take time.

He felt a heaviness lower over him, his eyelids suddenly heavy. What a luxury a Saturday-afternoon nap would be. He pulled the quilt up, shut his eyes, and sank into the pillow.

He drifted off. For how long? He didn't know. A gentle tapping sound woke him. He lifted his head to see Lea at her rosewood desk, her head a silhouette in the glow of her laptop monitor, leaning toward the screen and typing rapidly.

She moved her lips when she typed. So cute. It always made him smile. But her back was turned and he could see only the bobbing of her hair, pulled back in a loose ponytail, and the fingers of her right hand tap-dancing over the keys.

"Hi," he called. "How long did I sleep?"

"Not long." She didn't turn around. She was wearing a light green beach cover-up.

Mark pulled himself up. "It's a beautiful day. Feels like summer. Maybe we should round up the kids and drive to the beach. Sagg Main?"

She shook her head. "No. Think I need to get this written."

"The island? Are you getting your experience there in writing?"

She kept typing. Her head nodded toward the screen, then pulled back. "I'm not writing about that."

"What?" He stood up quickly. The breeze from the window tickled his skin. The short sleep had revived him. He did three or four knee bends just to show off to himself.

He walked to the dresser and pulled out a red Nike swimsuit. Tugging it on, he stepped up behind her. "What are you writing about?"

"Something different."

He chuckled and cupped his hands over her shoulders. "You're being secretive?"

"Yes."

He leaned over her shoulder to read what she had written. "You don't have secrets from your husband, do you?"

He thought of Autumn.

She lowered her hands to her lap. "I just . . . have some new ideas."

He squinted at the screen and his eyes scanned her last paragraph:

Tibet's inhuman climate and hard, stony ground makes burial nearly impossible. This is why Buddhists there choose a sky burial. Upon death, the body is chopped into small pieces which are mixed with flour. Then the remains are spread out over a tree to be eaten by scavenging birds.

Mark stood up and released her shoulders. "Lea, what is this? Dead Buddhists in Tibet? Sky burial?"

She turned and raised her face to him. The light from the laptop monitor bathed her in gray. "Death rituals," she said, just above a whisper. "I've been doing some research."

She hadn't said anything funny. Why did she have that strange, guilty smile on her face?

"Your blog," he said. "You're not going to write your travel blog?"

She shook her head. The strange smile remained. "I've kind of lost interest in that."

"But . . . you've put so much time and effort—"

She shrugged and turned her face away. "I can't write it anymore. It's just not interesting to me. You know. I have to write what I'm interested in. I've always been that way."

He blinked at the screen. "But, sweetheart—death rituals? Why death rituals?"

"It's all so fascinating. Did you know there's a province in Madagascar where people pull the dead out from their graves and dance with them? Every seven years, Mark. They dig up their relatives and dance with them. Isn't that sweet?"

Sweet?

He took a step back. He watched her type. She leaned toward the screen as if she wanted to dive in. Her eyes were narrowed in concentration.

As if I'm not here.

"Sky burials? Dancing with the dead? Lea? Should I be worried about you?"

38

"Hey, how'd you get here?" Ira raised his head from the fat blue inner tube and squinted at the twins as they pulled back the gate and stepped onto the deck.

"Walked," Daniel answered.

Samuel had never seen anything as beautiful as this pool. It was long and wide, nearly the length of the house. The pool walls were a light blue. Sky blue. The water sparkled with little patches of sunlight. *As if little chunks of the sun had fallen into the pool,* he thought. He wanted to dive in and scoop them up.

He just wanted to sink into the water, immerse himself in the clear, clean cold. Be clear and clean himself. But he knew Daniel had other plans.

"You guys know how to swim?" Ethan sat on the edge of the deep end, blond hair as bright as the sunlight, leaning down to fill a yellow-and-red plastic water blaster.

"We swim," Daniel said. "We lived on an island, remember, lad? Sammy and I swam before we could walk."

"That's cool," Ethan replied. Samuel had never seen a boy so pale, nearly as white as the fence surrounding the pool deck. He could see Ethan's rib cage poking out from his chest.

He's puny for twelve. The boy needs to pump up.

Maybe we can help him. If Daniel doesn't drown the lad today.

Ethan dipped the blaster under the water. Then he raised it and shot a lazy spray of water across the pool to Ira. Floating drowsily on his tube, luxuriating with his eyes closed, Ira didn't even notice.

"Is the water warm?" Samuel dropped to his knees and ran a hand through it. Under the surface, he could feel the spray of cold water shooting into the pool. "Nice."

Ethan aimed carefully and sent a long spray of water into Ira's face. Ira spluttered and dove off the tube. Ethan laughed. He had a dry cackle of a laugh. *Like an old witch,* Samuel thought.

Ira floated beneath the surface. He rose up in front of Ethan and spit a long stream of water onto his legs.

Daniel grabbed the chrome ladder and lowered himself into the water. He pushed himself away from the wall and paddled toward Ira. "How long can you stay underwater?" he asked, bobbing in a spill of gold sunlight.

Ira's head sank into the water again. He rose up and spit another mouthful onto Ethan's legs. Ethan gave him a blast between the eyes with the plastic squirt blaster.

"How long?" Daniel insisted, following Ira across the pool.

Samuel's body felt sticky and drenched with sweat from the walk to Ethan's house. He held his breath and leaped into the deep end. The shock of the cold water made him gasp, and he came up to the surface spluttering.

"Ira can stay underwater for a whole minute," he heard Ethan tell Daniel. "I've seen him."

Daniel eyed Ira. "A whole minute?"

Ira shrugged his skinny shoulders. "Yeah. I guess."

Samuel didn't want to listen. He knew the routine. He ducked underwater and swam the length of the pool. It felt so fresh and cold, and made his body tingle. *Alive. I feel alive.*

When he resurfaced, Daniel was continuing his act. "Do you have a timer?" he called to Ethan.

Ethan set down the water blaster. "There's a stopwatch on my dad's iPhone."

"Go get it," Daniel ordered. "You can time Ira and me." Ethan started to the house. His swimsuit hung on him, down to his knees. "Wait. Ethan, you want to be in the contest?" Daniel's voice made a ringing sound over the water.

Ethan turned back. "I don't want to swim. I have a scrape on my arm. From the cat. And the chlorine makes it hurt."

Ethan is not a superhero, Samuel thought, snickering. He made himself heavy and sank to the pool bottom, then kicked back up. *I could live in the water. Only place I feel alive.*

The kitchen door slammed behind Ethan. Samuel slid onto his back and floated, gazing up at the sun-streaked sky.

"I think I can stay under longer than a minute," Daniel told Ira. The two of them held sides of the tube, bobbing with it. Samuel spotted another inflated float leaning against a green chaise longue. Shaped like a big, gray whale.

That would be fun to ride. But Daniel has his own fun in mind.

"I can maybe do longer than a minute," Ira said without much conviction.

"Want to go first?"

Ira shook his head. "Why don't you go first?"

"Why don't you both go under at the same time?" Ethan said, reappearing on the deck with iPhone in hand.

Daniel slipped off the tube and swung himself around to face Ethan. "No. I want the Ira lad to hold me under."

Ira made a kind of squawking sound. *"What?"*

"Hold my hair," Daniel instructed. "Push me under. Hold me down, okay? You have to hold me or I'll float to the top, and you'll win."

Ira slid off the tube and pushed it toward the side of the pool. "You really want me to hold you under?"

Daniel nodded. "Just grab my hair and push down on my head."

"But how will I know when you want to come up?"

"No worries," Daniel told him. "I'll give a signal."

"You sure?"

Daniel grinned at him, dimples flashing. "Yes, I'm sure. Sure I'll win."

Samuel sighed. He dove under again. Peaceful down below. *Daniel should have been an actor.* Samuel surfaced, shaking water from his thick blond hair.

"Go!" Ethan cried from the deck, eyes on the phone in his hand.

Daniel let Ira push him under the surface. Ira gripped Daniel's hair and held his head down.

"Hold on tight," Samuel said, bobbing closer. "Don't let him come up."

"He . . . said he'd signal," Ira said, obviously not sure about this contest.

Samuel floated in a circle around Ira. Ira kept Daniel down with one hand, paddled the surface with the other.

"Push him," Samuel said. "Keep pushing."

"But—"

"One minute," Ethan called. He dropped onto the edge of a deck chair, concentrating on the phone. Samuel could see that Ethan's slender shoulders were already pink. Sunburned.

"It's kind of hard to keep him from floating up," Ira said.

"Keep pushing," Samuel told him. "He has big lungs. He can stay down a long time."

"He hasn't signaled," Ira said.

Samuel watched his brother float under the rippling water, his arms limp and relaxed at his sides, legs not moving.

"Two minutes," Ethan called.

"I . . . I think your brother wins," Ira said. "Two minutes. Wow. I can't—"

"Hold him under," Samuel said. "Don't ruin his turn. He gets angry if you ruin his turn."

"Did he just signal?" Ira very tense now. The strain showing on his face, pale, his features tight. "I thought I saw him signal." The muscle in the arm holding down Daniel quivered.

"Not yet," Samuel said.

Underwater, Daniel floated perfectly upright, arms limp and relaxed.

"Three minutes," Ethan called, jumping to his feet. "That's

enough, right?" He stepped to the edge of the pool, gazing down at Daniel's unmoving form. "People can't stay under this long—can they?"

"He . . . hasn't signaled," Ira said in a wavering voice.

Samuel and Ira both watched a string of bubbles float up from Daniel's mouth.

"Is that the signal? He said he'd signal."

"Four minutes. Are you sure he's okay?" Ethan lowered the phone. "I mean really. Is he okay? Four minutes?"

They all saw Daniel's head slump forward under the water. His head bent and one last bubble slid up to the surface. Then his legs suddenly splayed, and his arms floated limply to the top.

"Let go of him!" Samuel screamed. "Something's wrong, Ira. Let go of him—now!"

Ira gasped and swallowed a mouthful of water. His hand flew off Daniel's head.

Released, Daniel's body rose to the surface. His face appeared for only a moment, eyes closed, water spilling from his open jaw. Then his body tilted forward and he dropped facedown, arms outstretched and limp.

"Daniel! Daniel! Get up!" Samuel screamed. "Daniel! Daniel!"

Ira uttered another hoarse squawk. He gaped, eyes bulging at the floating, lifeless raft that was Daniel.

"Daniel! Daniel!"

Ira dove toward Daniel. Grabbed his arm. Tried to tug him up.

But he remained facedown, bobbing on the surface, arms and legs floating at such odd angles, as if they were all independent of each other.

"You *killed* him!" Samuel shrieked. He slapped the water angrily with both hands. Slapped it. Slapped it hard until it churned around him. "Ira—no! No! Ira—you *killed* him! You killed my bruvver!"

A hoarse cry escaped Ira's throat.

Ethan stood on the edge of the pool, his body trembling. He had left the phone on the deck. His hands were pressed against the sides of his face.

"Nooooooo." Ira wailed. "He didn't signal. It wasn't my *fault*!" He turned to Ethan. "Get help! Hurry!"

Ethan didn't move. "My parents—they're not home!"

Samuel splashed over to his brother. "Help me pull him out. Maybe we can get him breathing."

Another moan escaped Ira's open mouth. His eyes spun. His mouth twitched.

His face is going out of control. The poor kid is totally dazed.

Ira flailed across the water and grabbed Daniel's arm. And that's when Daniel lifted his head, shot straight up, turned grinning to Ira, and let out a loud laugh.

"Oh." Ira's hand slid off Daniel. The startled kid fell back, dipping underwater for a second before reappearing, his face showing his disbelief.

Daniel gave him a hard two-handed shove and laughed again, shaking water from his hair.

"You're okay? He's okay?" Ethan shouted from the side, his voice high and shrill. "Is he really okay?"

Ira still hadn't spoken. He bobbed in place, eyes on Daniel.

"Why'd you let me up?" Daniel pushed Ira again, more gently this time. "I didn't signal. I wasn't finished."

"But . . ." Ira struggled to find words. "It was five minutes."

Daniel laughed. "Did you forget? I *told* you Sammy and I were swimming before we could walk."

"But . . . that's impossible." Ira shook his head. "Five minutes?"

"I can't believe he's okay," Ethan called. "Hey, get out of the pool. Let's get some snacks or something. Come on. I can't stop shaking. Get out, guys."

Samuel could see that Ira would love to climb out of the water and catch his breath. But Daniel raised a hand. "Whoa. It's Ira's turn."

"Huh? No way." Ira slid back, rippling the water. "No way. I can't stay under for five minutes. You win."

Daniel grabbed Ira's shoulder. "You have to take your turn. Maybe you'll do better than a minute. That would be cool, right, lad?"

Ira didn't reply. "No. You win, Daniel. Let's get out."

Daniel grabbed Ira's hair. "Take your turn. Let's see how you do. Give me a signal. Just wave your arms when your chest starts to hurt. Okay?"

He didn't wait for Ira's reply. He gave him a hard push and sent him sinking. Ira's head disappeared under the water.

Samuel knew the smile on Daniel's face. He'd seen it before.

Behind him, he heard a splash. He turned to see that Ethan had dropped into the pool. He was wading toward them. "Ira can only do a minute. I've seen him."

Daniel gripped Ira's hair tightly. He kept his arm stiff, pushing the boy down. A few bubbles escaped Ira's mouth.

Daniel, still smiling, turned to Ethan. "What about keeping count? What are you doing here? You're supposed to time him."

Ethan peered down at Ira. "I told you. He can only do a minute."

A shadow swept over them as two large birds flapped overhead, squawking loudly. Samuel glanced up quickly. He lowered his eyes in time to see Daniel slide his other hand over Ira's head and push down with both hands.

Ira's legs kicked slowly. Distorted by the water, they reminded Samuel of pale, rubbery snakes. And then the boy's arms shot out. He began waving wildly.

Ethan stared at Daniel. "The signal. He wants to come up."

Daniel pushed down on Ira's head with both hands. The smile never left his face.

Ira kicked and thrashed. He tried to twist his head out from Daniel's grasp. But Daniel held on tight. A stream of bubbles rose up from Ira's mouth.

"Let him up!" Ethan shouted. "He's signaling. He's done."

Daniel held on tight, not moving. His jaw was clenched, nostrils flaring.

"Let him up! Come on, Daniel. Let him up!"

Ira shot his feet out. Twisted his head. Raised both fists above the surface. Beneath the water, his body flopped like a frantic fish caught on a hook.

Daniel scrunched up his face, his eyes shut, and pushed down on the struggling boy's hair, holding his head under the surface.

Samuel wanted to sink under the water and never emerge.

Please, Daniel, don't do it. Please don't do it this time.

Please stop now. Yes, I know why you are doing it. I know the new pa doesn't want us. I know you want to rule the pool. But, please, Daniel. It's too soon.

Please don't do it to Ira. Please.

39

"Why is Axl crying?"

Roz squinted at Mark. "Why does the sun come up every morning? You're the child shrink. You tell *me*."

Mark set down the book he'd been reading, a treatise about how sibling order determines your fate. *So interesting how often the oldest sibling is the achiever in the family.* He pulled off his reading glasses and folded them carefully. He grinned at his sister. "Maybe he's hungry."

"Oh, wow. Genius. I never would have thought of that." Roz rolled her eyes. She tossed the ball of dirty laundry she was carrying onto his lap.

He pulled a red pajama top off his head. "He's bored, that's all. Let's pick up the boys and take everyone to the ocean."

Roz started grabbing up the dirty clothes. "I thought doing the laundry might be more fun."

She turned as Axl came toddling into the room. "Beach! Beach! Beach!" He could always stop crying in a split second.

Mark chuckled. "He was listening to us."

"He listens to everything," Roz said. "He's a little spy."

"Beach! Beach! Beach!" He reached for his mom to pick him up, but her arms were full of laundry. So he wrapped his hands around her knees.

"Where are the boys?"

"At Ethan's house. All three of them. We'll have to pull them from the pool. I'll probably have to bribe them with ice cream to get them to come with us."

"They'll come. Axl, let go of me. I can't walk. Is Lea coming?"

"No. She's working. I'm not sure what's up with her. She's writing a piece about death rituals."

Roz squinted at him. "Odd."

"Yes. Odd."

"It's that island. The hurricane. She saw so much death. I think she's having trouble shaking it from her mind."

"We'll have to be very nice to her." Roz struggled across the room with Axl clinging to one leg. Giggling. He'd turned her into an amusement park ride. "The ocean will tire him out. That's good. Only thing I hate is that he eats the beach."

Mark nodded. "He's definitely a sand eater. I had to pry a huge glob of sand from his mouth last time, remember? Maybe he learned his lesson."

"Learned his lesson? Go ahead. Say something stupider than that. We'll just have to watch him like a hawk."

"Yes. Like a hawk. I'll start loading up the car. We'll take your SUV. More room."

"Do we need food?"

"No. Bring something for Axl. We're only going for an hour. No one will starve. And we can buy them ice cream from the truck in the parking lot."

"Let me just drop this laundry in the machine." She turned back to him. "This is the twins' stuff. It's so clean, you'd think they didn't wear it." She held up a white T-shirt. "But look at this. This ragged, dark spot on the sleeve? I think it's a burn mark."

"A burn mark?"

"Yes. The sleeve was definitely burned. Weird?"

"Weird." Mark stared at it. "Hope they're not playing with matches in their private hideaway back there."

"They love it back there, Mark."

"Really? Think they're happy here?"

"Well . . . I walked by the guesthouse last night after supper and I heard them in there giggling and giggling."

"Think they already feel at home?"

"They have funny jokes. One of them kept saying, 'smoked meat, smoked meat,' and then they'd laugh and laugh."

"I don't get the joke."

"They were being silly. I think they're doing a great job of fitting in. I mean, losing their family and all, moving from their home, it can't be easy."

Mark climbed to his feet. He glanced at his laptop monitor. No email. No one ever emailed him on Saturday. "Well, we'll see how they fit in. I mean, we haven't asked much of them. They live by themselves in the back. They don't share much about school with us. They don't—"

"Mark, there was a horrible murder right in our driveway. Maybe they even witnessed it. But they haven't seemed messed up by it. They haven't acted out or anything."

"I think it's good they went swimming with Ira. That's encouraging. They're the same age, so if they manage to bond with Ira, maybe . . ."

His voice drifted off. He still had major doubts about the whole thing.

He went upstairs to give Lea one more chance to come along with them, but she was captured in the glow of her laptop screen. Were her eyes glassy or just reflecting the light of the monitor?

"We're going to the ocean. I'm going to pick up Ira and the twins. Want to come with us?"

She mumbled something he couldn't hear and kept typing without turning her head. He couldn't help but be annoyed. "Sweetheart, don't you want to spend some time with the boys?"

Another mumbled reply.

He forced a laugh. "I'm going to have to pick you up and carry you away from that keyboard, aren't I."

She waved him away. "I need to get this all down, Mark."

He kissed the back of her neck, changed into a swimsuit and sleeveless T-shirt, found his Tevas, and hurried outside. Roz was struggling to fasten Axl in his car seat. "Just think. Only six more years of this. Lucky, huh?"

Mark laughed. "That's what I love about you, Roz. Always thinking on the bright side."

"Maybe I shouldn't have put the suntan lotion on him first. He keeps sliding out of the seat."

Mission accomplished with Axl, Roz climbed into the backseat beside him and they drove the few blocks to Ethan's house. The sun, still high in the afternoon sky, filtered through the trees, sending flickering light dancing over the windshield. On the side of the street, a dead squirrel had attracted the attention of several hungry blackbirds. The passing car didn't even make them flutter a wing or interrupt their feast.

Mark pulled the car to the bottom of the driveway. The three garage doors were open. No cars in view. Wasn't anyone home to watch the boys in the pool?

He left the air-conditioner running for Roz and Axl and climbed out of the car. It was a hot day, more like summer than May, a great beach day. Sunlight bounced off the front of the white frame house. He took a few steps up the smooth paved driveway. A chipmunk darted out of the garage, into the yard.

A few doors down he heard the low drone of a power mower. Across the street, two little girls rode pink and yellow tricycles up and down a driveway.

Nearly to the front of the house, Mark stopped to listen. The silence disturbed him. No splashing. No boys' voices. Usually they were decimating each other with water blasters, cannonballing into the pool and jumping out, shouting and wrestling and splashing.

Today silence.

They never went indoors when they could be in the pool.

A sudden feeling of dread made the back of his neck tingle. Too quiet. Too quiet. His legs felt heavy as lead as he started to jog toward the back.

Is something wrong back there?

What's going on?

He was breathing hard by the time he reached the white picket fence. Still silent back there. "Hey—where is everybody?"

He pulled the gate. When it didn't budge, he pushed it. He stumbled onto the deck and saw them immediately.

Oh my God.

Was that Ira? Yes. Ira flat on his back. Stretched out straight on the deck beside the pool. Daniel and Samuel on their knees, hovering over him, faces narrowed in concern.

Ira flat, his face pale white, head straight up, arms and legs so stiff at his sides. Not moving.

Not moving.

Ira. Not moving.

40

A few minutes earlier. Daniel pushed down on Ira's head. The boy kept thrashing and squirming under the churning water, but weakly now.

"Be careful," Samuel said, tugging his brother's arm. "Don't get carried away. You just want to scare him, Daniel. You don't want to drown him, do you? *Do* you?"

Daniel's eyes were wild and distant at the same time. Samuel always wondered what he was seeing at times like these. Samuel knew what *he* saw. An endless dark chasm stretching beyond them forever.

"Daniel, please—"

Daniel blinked, as if coming to consciousness. He lowered his hands around the struggling boy's waist and, with a grunt, hoisted him out of the water.

Ira emerged coughing and choking, eyes wide, water rolling off him, legs still churning. Daniel held him high, allowed him to spew up a stream of water, cough and groan and sputter.

Behind them, Ethan shrieked at the top of his voice: "Are you okay? Is he okay? Is he okay? Ira?"

Samuel thought he could see the heartbeats in the boy's bony white chest. Now Ira made hoarse vomiting sounds, dredging up only pool water.

Daniel held him up, his biceps round and hard, too developed for a twelve-year-old. But Samuel knew where his twin's strength came from.

Ira's hair was matted over his face like a clump of dark seaweed. His head was down, arms limp at his sides, legs finally still.

"Is he okay? Is he breathing? Is he going to be okay?"

Samuel gave Ethan a reassuring thumbs-up.

Ira grew quieter. His chest still heaved but the choking and vomiting had ceased. He raised his head slowly, groaning. He brushed the wet clump of hair off his eyes with one hand.

Daniel laughed. "You did it, laddy!" he cried exultantly.

Ira squinted at Daniel, struggling to focus. "Did it?" His voice a choked whisper.

"A minute-twenty!" Daniel declared. "You broke your old record. I knew you could do it!"

Ira just stared at him, his face vacant, obviously trying to decide Daniel's intent. Did Daniel just try to drown him? Was he playing a vicious game? Or was he really trying to help Ira break his underwater record?

Daniel kept the grin on his face. "Way to go, lad. Next time, a minute and a half." He lowered Ira gently into the water. Then he turned to Samuel. "Wasn't that amazing?"

"Amazing," Samuel echoed.

"But you *forced* him," Ethan protested. "Didn't you see he wanted to come up?"

"I knew he could break his record," Daniel insisted.

"C-cold," Ira stammered. "I'm . . . getting out." He started to paddle weakly toward the side, gliding as if in slow motion.

"Get him some more towels," Daniel ordered Ethan. "Maybe a sweatshirt or something."

Ethan splashed out of the pool. His bare feet thudded on the deck, leaving dark footprints as he disappeared into the house. As soon as he was gone, Daniel nodded to Samuel.

Samuel knew the routine.

Each taking an arm, they led Ira out of the pool. "Th-thanks," Ira stuttered. The poor kid was shaking.

"Here. Lie down in the sun," Daniel instructed in his most gentle voice. *Like a harmless little boy,* Samuel thought.

They helped Ira onto his back on the sun-hot deck boards. He stretched out flat, water running off him, still breathing hard, shuddering.

"Ssssh. Relax," Daniel whispered. He turned expectantly to Samuel.

Time for me to go to work.

It was so funny, actually. Daniel was the angry one. The bold one. Face it—the evil twin. Daniel was the one who wanted to act. Daniel wanted to rule the pool or rule the school or rule the fools.

Samuel knew he was different. He was shy. He was peace-loving and calm. No, *not* kind or sweet or feeling. But calm, at least. Not eager.

So funny, since Sammy was Death Man.

Sammy was the killer-man. Sammy had the beam, the ray, the whatever-you-want-to-call-it. Sammy had the heat. The burn. The furnace. Go ahead—say it: the fire of *Hell.*

Yes, together on the island where the dead met the living, they stepped out of a blood rain. Yes, the blood was on their shoulders and in their hearts. The blood splashed at their feet and puddled all around them, ran down their faces and stained their skin as well as their clothes.

Like a nightmare. I know we are nightmares.

And the strange part: Daniel brought the anger. But Sammy brought the death.

Now Daniel eyed him eagerly. Samuel leaned over Ira, brought his face close to the shivering boy's, and began to fire up his eyes.

Samuel's eyes clicked as if someone had bumped a switch. And they began to light instantly. The white around the pupils darkened to pink, and then the pupils disappeared into the growing red glow.

Like the coiled burners on an electric stove, Samuel's eyes reddened and the heat began to radiate. His eyes were bright fire now, hot neon, red and hypnotic.

So hypnotic, Ira made no attempt to move or look away.

"Easy," Daniel warned, bumping Samuel's arm. "Don't burn

him. Back off a bit. You'll blind him. We don't want to hurt him. We only want to open his mind. Easy. Easy. We don't want Mum to see that he is changed."

"Okay, boyo. I'm being careful," Samuel whispered. "Hurry. Ethan will be back." He could see the red-glare reflection of his eyes in Ira's eyes. "I'm just holding him. Not burning him. Go ahead. Tell his brain who is boss."

Samuel was always surprised that he couldn't feel the heat. Burning embers. No. Burning lasers. His eyes radiated blistering heat. But he couldn't feel a thing.

Daniel leaned over the prone figure. Ira was hypnotized in the red glow.

"Okay, bruvver, I helped you today," Daniel said, eyes on the glass doors of the house, watching warily for Ethan's return. "Now we will stick together, boyo. Stick together like bruvvers. Yes?"

Silence for a second. Samuel kept the light on Ira's face. "Yes," Ira answered. Robotlike. But he gave the correct answer.

"Bruvvers forever," Daniel murmured. "Even closer than bruvvers. And we'll all be together day and night, all together we'll rule the school."

"Yes," Ira said, this time without hesitating. He almost sounded enthusiastic.

Good boy.

Daniel gave Samuel the nod. The job had been done. Ira's mind had been fixed. Samuel shut his eyes. He could feel a little prickling heat on the backs of his eyelids. He kept his eyes shut until they cooled.

When he opened them, he saw the new pa burst through the gate and stride onto the deck, his chest heaving up and down. "What's wrong? Hey—what's wrong?" In a panic.

Daniel helped Ira to a sitting position. "Wave at your pa," he whispered.

Ira waved.

"Is Ira okay?" The new pa hurried up to them. Samuel saw the sweat stain on the front of his sleeveless tee.

"I'm fine, Dad. We were just taking a break," Ira said.

"We had an awesome swim, don't you know," Daniel said. "Then we did some tricks in the water. And had some contests."

"Ira can hold his breath a long time," Samuel told him.

Ira nodded. "I beat my old record, Dad."

The new pa studied Ira's face, as if he still thought something had gone wrong. "When I saw you lying on the deck like that . . ."

"Just relaxing," Ira said. "What's the big deal, Dad?"

"Where's Ethan?"

Ethan reappeared as if on cue, carrying a stack of towels. "What's up? Is Ira okay?"

"Of course I'm okay," Ira insisted.

Ethan squinted at Ira, confused.

"Ethan, want to come to the ocean with us?" the new pa asked, wiping sweat off his forehead with the front of his shirt. "We have room."

"No. Thanks. My mom said I had to stay home. She went to Cromer's to get dinner. She'll be back any minute."

"Okay. Next time. Let's hurry, guys. I left Roz and Axl in the car."

Daniel helped Ira to his feet. He kept his arm around Ira's shoulders as they made their way to the car. "I see you two are bonding," the new pa said.

No one replied to that.

At the gate, Samuel turned back to Ethan. "Can I borrow this towel?" He held up the ragged white towel.

"No problem," Ethan called. "Bring it back next time, okay?"

Samuel followed the others to the black SUV at the bottom of the drive. The boys greeted Roz and Axl. "Put beach towels down on the seats," she told them. "Don't get the car all wet."

"Roz, it's a beach car," Pa told her. "It's supposed to get wet."

"Wet," Axl repeated, and laughed.

Ira climbed into the passenger seat next to Pa. Samuel followed Daniel to the back. They climbed up next to the beach basket and supplies.

The car bumped off the driveway, onto the street. At the side of the road, Samuel saw big blackbirds feasting on the carcass of a stiff, dead squirrel.

After they had driven for a few minutes, Samuel poked his twin. Daniel turned from the window. Samuel grinned at him. "You win a prize," he whispered.

Daniel's eyebrows slid up. "What did you get?"

Samuel slowly unrolled the towel. Then, grinning, he revealed the prize inside. The iPhone Ethan had used to time the underwater contest.

Daniel started to giggle and soon Samuel was giggling too.

"What's so funny?" Roz asked.

"We're just happy lads," Daniel answered.

41

At police headquarters on Division Street in Sag Harbor, Andy Pavano didn't have his own office. There was a cubicle by the men's room that had been promised him. But it was filled nearly to the ceiling with junk, mainly old computer equipment and fax machines, and no one in the department seemed eager or even willing to clear it out for him.

Maybe they were waiting for him to do it himself, Andy thought. In the meantime, he was squatting in the office of Angie Donato, the one woman in the department, who was out on maternity leave. The only redecorating he had done to make it his own was to turn all her family photos to the wall because her four kids were really ugly. Beasts. No exaggeration.

Waiting for a meeting in which he knew he and Pinto were going to be bounced off the Hulenberger murder case, he sat on the edge of his (her) desk with the phone pressed to his ear, enjoying Sari's voice even though she wasn't saying anything promising to him.

The air-conditioning was on the fritz, so a large floor fan hummed and squeaked in the corner, making it hard to hear her. "What did you say? You what?"

"Rod and I are serious about each other, Andy. I mean, I don't know how serious. But—"

"Sari, please tell me his name isn't Rod. You're not going with a guy in a tennis hat named Rod."

"You're making jokes. He's a nice guy. He's nice to me. He—"

"You know you still feel something for me. At the theater the other night . . ."

"I told you that was nothing. Sure, there are leftover feelings. From before. Sure, we both have them. But come on. That's what they are. Leftovers."

Marie, the office secretary, began having a heated conversation with a lanky young cop in the hall outside his door. Andy turned his back and tried to drown out their voices.

He missed some of what Sari was saying. He just caught the name *Susannah.*

"Sari, what? What about Susannah?"

"How long were you married, Andy? Did you cheat on her, too?"

Ouch. That brought a physical pain, a sharp stab to the pit of his stomach.

"That's cold, Sari. That's not fair. You don't know anything about me and Susannah. And I didn't cheat on you. I—"

"You were a shit, Andy. You were a total shit."

"How about lunch?"

He heard her breath catch.

"Just a quick lunch at the Paradise. We won't be serious. No serious stuff. Just talk. Like old friends."

"You sound too desperate."

"Does that mean yes?"

She laughed. "Can Rod come, too?"

"Aaaaagggh." He let out a frustrated growl.

Pinto poked his big balding head into the doorway. "Are you having phone sex again?"

Andy tried to wave him away.

"Big Pavano is calling. Time to have our heads chopped," Pinto said, motioning for him to come to the chief's office.

Since Andy arrived on the force, the chief was always referred to as Big Pavano, which was a joke, since Andy was a head taller and had him by at least thirty pounds. But rank was everything, even on a police force of seven.

Andy waved Pinto away again and pressed his face against the phone. "Have to go. We'll set a date for lunch, okay?"

But Sari had already hung up.

Michael Pavano—as stated to anyone who commented, no relation to Andy Pavano—did not have the cliché looks of a local Long Island police chief. Yes, he had been a marine. Had a pretty good career, working his way up the ranks to master sergeant because he was smart and obedient and liked to follow the rules, felt more comfortable following the rules, liked a structured life and the sense of order the corps offered.

But when it was suggested he be moved to internal affairs, he balked and then resigned his commission. He had no interest in plotting investigations of men who had worked hard enough to become U.S. Marines.

The switch to a uniform in the Boston Police Department seemed natural, but he struggled to find the kind of structure he had as a marine. Of course, it didn't exist. So when a friend suggested the job opening in the Sag Harbor Department, it seemed like an escape and an opportunity at the same time.

To Andy's mind, Big Pavano didn't look like a marine or a cop. For one thing, he was short and slender. (He said he'd made the marine height requirement by standing on tiptoe, a rare joke for someone normally humorless.) He didn't have the beer pouch of an ex-soldier who had relaxed his standards. He had a full crop of straight black hair, streaked with gray at the sides, and a friendly face, warm blue-gray eyes that somehow always managed to look sympathetic.

There was a sadness about Big Pavano, Andy thought. Maybe because he'd always been married to his post, never had a wife or family.

He had three folding chairs waiting facing the desk in his small, nearly bare office, and motioned for Andy and Pinto to sit down.

As they did, a toweringly tall, light-skinned black man in a blue cop uniform ducked his head under the doorframe and stepped into the room.

"This is Captain Franks," Pavano said, "from the State Criminal Investigation Bureau. I called him in because . . . well . . . you know why."

"Morning, Sergeants." Franks nodded solemnly to them. He had short black hair receding on his broad forehead. His dark eyes studied them with interest, moving from Pinto and Andy. His broad nose had obviously been broken a few times. He had a long scar, old, across his chin.

Tough dude.

He was broad-chested, built like a heavyweight fighter, his uniform jacket stretched tight over his uniform shirt. His state cop badge caught the light from the ceiling fluorescents. Andy saw that he had a standard Glock .22—the policeman's favorite—in the black holster at his waist.

Chief Pavano dropped into the folding chair next to Andy, perching as erect as a marine. Franks stepped behind the desk and leaned his massive fists on top of the scattered papers on the desktop.

"So what do we have here?" he asked. He had a James Earl Jones voice, booming despite his attempt to speak softly. He wasn't asking a question, Andy knew. No one tried to answer.

"We have a man murdered in bizarre fashion inside a car in another man's driveway." Franks answered his own question. "The method of murder indicates that the killer had some strength and also used some sort of heat-producing weapon. Am I correct so far?"

Big Pavano coughed. "That's what we have, all right, Captain."

Andy scraped at some loose skin on the back of his thumb. He knew that he and Pinto were being removed from the case and Franks was taking charge. Why did Franks have to put on a show first?

"Now, we have blood all over the man's car," Franks continued, almost as if talking to himself. "The victim's windpipe is fucking tossed on the backseat, ripped from his throat. And his throat has been burned open. We have a gaping hole there, right, and the skin is scorched black. Like someone tried to fucking barbecue him."

Chief Pavano nodded grimly. Andy and Pinto stared straight ahead. Andy's stomach rumbled. He pictured the wet, blood-tipped pink noodle stretched on the backseat of the car. It made him sick every time he thought of it.

"With all that blood and ripped skin, we should have some evidence," Franks boomed. "The weapon. Fingerprints on the blowtorch? The killer had to reach in through the open window, yes? So how about a fingerprint or two on the side of the fucking car?"

"We took that car apart in the lab in Riverhead," Chief Pavano told him. "I mean, bolt by bolt, Captain. We dusted it and X-rayed it and lasered it and micro—whatever those guys can fucking do these days. We did everything but *taste* it. And we came up with nothing. Prints from a tennis ball. Kiddie prints."

Franks rubbed the scar on his chin, gazing at Chief Pavano thoughtfully. "Well, what *don't* we have here? We don't have a psycho serial killer, right? We don't have a Hannibal Lecter. At least the killer didn't *eat* the fucking windpipe. And God knows, we haven't had similar murders we can tie to this one."

"We don't have a lot of murders in Sag Harbor, Franks," Pinto murmured. "It's a quiet little village, you know."

Franks nodded. He pulled out a small key chain and twirled it in one hand. "So . . . we rule out serial killer. We have to look closer to home, don't we? I think I've gone over this story enough. Try this on for size. The psychologist, Sutter, writes a book that people don't like. He has a book tour. He gets booed and yelled at in one city, then another. Everywhere he fucking goes. City after city, people are angry at him. He comes home. Maybe he's upset. Maybe he's overwrought from all the abuse. Maybe the sonofabitch is about to lose it.

"So how does it go down? He needs money to pay the mortgage on his beautiful house by the bay. And he and his wife have just adopted two more kids. She doesn't work. The load is all on him. It's making him crazy. Nothing but stress and anger and abuse.

"He thinks he's going to get a big grant. He's *counting* on the fucking grant to keep him afloat. Then this guy Hulenberger arrives and tells him no way, José. Like a punch in the face, right? And Sutter fucking loses it. He runs outside, grabs his blowtorch from the garage, runs to the car in the driveway in a fucking insane rage and makes a mess of Hulenberger."

Silence for a long moment. Andy heard phones ringing down the hall. He heard Marie at the front desk laughing about something. A siren started up with a growl in a black-and-white out in the parking lot.

"Sutter seemed distressed by the murder in his driveway. But he didn't seem whacked-out or overly stressed," Pinto offered. "He seemed to have it together whenever Andy and I talked to him."

Franks frowned at Pinto. "So?"

"He had an excuse for the blowtorch. So we combed the house," Big Pavano said, shaking his head. "I mean, every inch. Tore up floors and everything, Captain. No other weapon."

Franks turned his glare on Pavano. "So?"

Silence again.

Franks turned to Andy. "Any thoughts?"

Andy realized he was tapping one shoe on the floor. He forced his leg to stop. "Maybe you're on the right track," he said, thinking hard. "It's just . . . no one saw anything. His two boys, the twins . . . they were playing ball in the front yard. They didn't see anything or anyone."

"Are they lying?" Franks demanded, leaning over the desk. "They're twelve, right? Twelve-year-olds can lie, yes? If they're frightened? If somebody scared them or threatened them?" He twirled the key chain. "Or if they want to protect their new father?"

Andy shuffled his feet. Did Franks want them to *disprove* his theory? Or was he the kind of cop who only wanted to be backed up in everything he said?

"We've talked to the twins twice with a psychologist in the room, Captain," Big Pavano said. "She found no evidence—"

"I think we have our suspect," Franks interrupted, slapping his hands together like cymbals. "There's a lot we don't know—yet. But we know it's Sutter. So let's get back to work and fucking nail him."

Chief Pavano jumped up and, adjusting his black uniform tie, stepped behind the desk to get to Franks. Leaning their heads together, they started to talk in low tones. Andy and Pinto remained seated, exchanging glances.

Finally, Andy spoke up. "You mean . . . Chaz and I . . . we're still working this murder?"

"We're sticking with you," Franks said. "You haven't screwed it up too badly so far. I'll be here. I'll be watching over everything. With your captain, of course. You go ahead and nail this sonofabitch. You'll be stars. You want to be fucking stars—don't you?"

Andy wasn't so sure. He nodded to the two captains and followed Pinto out of the room. When they were back in Andy's makeshift office, they both let out long whooshes of air, although there was no reason to feel relieved.

"You think Sutter did it?" Andy asked.

"I do now" was Pinto's reply.

PART FOUR

42

Breakfast Monday morning. Mark pulled on gray sweats. He thought maybe he'd run on the sand along Long Beach this morning. Downstairs, he was surprised to find Lea already in the kitchen, coffee made, a stack of frozen waffles ready for the toaster.

She wore a short, sheer green beach cover-up over a black one-piece swimsuit. Her hair was tied loosely back with a green hair scrunchie. She turned and smiled as he entered the kitchen. When he walked over and picked up a white coffee mug from beside the coffeemaker, she raised her face to him and kissed him tenderly behind the ear.

The kiss sent a tingle down his neck. He turned with a smile. He rubbed her cheek with two fingers. "What was that for?"

"An apology," she said. Her dark eyes stayed on his.

"Apology?"

"I've been . . . sort of distant since I got home. I'm sorry."

"I noticed," he said. "The island?"

She turned to the counter, lifted her mug, and took a long sip of black coffee. "I . . . I dream about it every night. Really. Every night."

He took her by the shoulders. "I'm really sorry."

"I hear those people screaming and crying. I see all those bodies.

Bodies piled up everywhere. *Parts* of bodies. Houses all broken and destroyed. Will I ever get over it?"

"Sure, you will," he said. Stupid, inadequate answer. He drew her close. He kissed her. Coffee breath, but he didn't mind. "Maybe you should see someone. I know some doctors in the city you might feel comfortable with."

She hesitated. "Maybe."

He kissed her again. Then he pulled his head back and studied her. "The twins. Daniel and Samuel. Do they keep reminding you of all the horror you saw? Are they keeping you from pushing it from your mind?"

She raised a hand to his mouth. "Stop. Don't even think it. You have to stop being so negative about them, Mark. I really care about them."

"Sorry. As long as—"

"I'm going to be better. I promise. I'm back. You'll see. It's just the shock of everything. Now that the travel blog is over, I—"

"Are you sure you want to end it? I know you're not a quitter. You came to New York with a goal and—"

She lowered her eyes. Her hair fell over her face. "I'm not quitting. I'm just changing."

"Well, at least you won't be traveling. Nice if you'll be home all the time." He raised his hands to her cheeks and started to kiss her again. But a cough interrupted.

Elena appeared in the doorway. "Yuck. Are you two kissing this early in the morning?"

"No." Mark lowered his hands from Lea's shoulders and took a step back. "Well, maybe yes. So what if we were?"

Elena didn't answer. She pulled open the fridge door. "Isn't there any cranberry juice? You know I hate orange juice. No one here drinks orange juice. It's too fattening. Why do you keep buying it?"

"So you'll have something to complain about," Mark said. "And hey, maybe I drink it? And maybe Axl drinks it too?"

She pulled out a yogurt container and closed the door. "Could you buy better juice? You know Ruth-Ann is coming for our sleepover Friday night. Do we have to have this grocery-store apple juice? Can't you at least buy Martinelli's?"

Mark laughed. "I had no idea juice was so important in your life."

"Dad, do you think you could stop laughing at me just for a few minutes?"

That caught him by surprise. Was he teasing her too much? Fourteen-year-olds were so sensitive.

"Where's your brother?" Lea said, pouring more coffee into her mug. "Is he getting dressed?"

"I don't know." Elena checked the date on the container bottom. Then she tugged off the top and started to stir the yogurt. "He wasn't in his room. I thought he was down here."

Lea blinked. "Not in his room? What do you mean?"

Elena stopped stirring. She scrunched up her face, as if concentrating. "You know, I think his bed was made. Like he hadn't slept in it."

"Huh?" Lea uttered a sharp cry. "Are you serious?"

"That's impossible," Mark said. "Go get him."

"Can't I finish my yogurt first?"

The kitchen door opened. Daniel and Samuel walked in. Mark squinted at them. They looked more disheveled than usual. Their hair hadn't been brushed and stood up in white-blond clumps over their heads. Daniel's jeans had a stain in front. Samuel's black T-shirt was wrinkled, tucked in in front but hanging over his jeans in back.

"Morning, Mum and Pa," Daniel murmured.

As they made their way toward the breakfast table, Mark and Lea gasped at the same time. "Whoa. What's on your faces?"

Mark nearly did a coffee spit. Each boy had a two-inch blue arrow, pointing up, on one cheek. "Hey, stop right there." He set down the coffee mug before he spilled it.

"Those aren't tattoos—are they?" Lea demanded.

The twins giggled. "No. Just the face paint, don't you know," Daniel answered.

Elena stood gawking with her yogurt spoon halfway to her mouth. "You painted arrows on your cheeks?"

The boys nodded. Daniel's wide grin made his dimples flare.

Mark reminded himself he needed to stay calm and not overreact. "But—why?" He kept his voice low and steady. "What do they mean?"

"We're going *up*," Daniel said, his grin not fading.

"We want to be cool," Samuel added. He popped two waffles into the toaster and pushed them down.

"That is *definitely* not cool," Mark said.

He stared at the arrows, so shiny and dark on the boys' pale skin.

"Definitely not cool," he repeated. "You have to go take them off. I can't let you go to school like that."

"But, Pa—" Daniel started.

"He's right. For once," Elena said. "Not cool, guys. Actually, we're talking freaky here."

The grin finally faded from Daniel's face and his blue eyes appeared to darken, as if a storm cloud had rolled over them. "We want to rule the school, Pa," spoken in a low voice just above a whisper.

"We want to rule the school," Samuel repeated.

Mark watched them both carefully. Daniel was always the leader. Samuel seemed to go along with everything Daniel said. He wondered about their birth order. Did Daniel come out first?

"I'm sorry, boys, but I can't let you go to school with arrows on your faces. Mrs. Maloney will just send you home. You don't want to get in trouble with her, do you?"

"She won't be sending us home," Daniel replied.

Such certainty, Mark thought. *They seem meek a lot of the time, but then they show tremendous confidence.*

His mind spun away from the issue at hand. *Maybe they will make an interesting book. I could do it as a diary of their development as they adapt to a whole new world.*

Lea had her arms wrapped tightly around the front of her beach wrap. She looked tense, but so far, she hadn't said a word of protest.

They stood defiantly, eyes locked on Mark. Stone statues.

Elena couldn't hide her surprise at their stubbornness. "You two are *weird*."

Lea pulled Mark to the back door. "You can't win this fight," she whispered. "Remember trying to get Ira to zip his coat in the freezing cold last winter? They get these ideas about what's cool and what isn't, and you can't ever win those fights. Kids are stronger and crazier than we are."

"Then what am I supposed to do?" he snapped, eyes on the twins. "Just do whatever they want? Is that really your policy? So far, you haven't said no to them once."

"Let them go to school. The other kids will let them know how dorky the arrows are. They'll learn soon enough. From their peers."

Mark shook his head unhappily. He shrugged. "Okay, I give up. I surrender." He turned to Elena. "Where's your brother? Go get him. He's going to be late."

Elena turned toward the hallway door and shouted. "Ira—get *down* here. You're going to be late!"

"Don't shout. Go get him," Mark snapped.

Elena groaned and pushed between the twins to get to the kitchen doorway. But the back door opened, and Ira came walking breezily in from outside. "Hey, what's up?"

Mark couldn't hide his surprise. "What were you doing in the backyard? Why weren't you in your—"

He stopped midsentence when he saw the blue arrow on Ira's right cheek. "What the hell—"

That made the twins giggle.

Mark rubbed his finger down Ira's cheek. "No, Ira. No. No way."

"I'm going to rule the school," Ira said brightly.

Mark shook his head. "No. No arrow. Please. Tell me I'm dreaming this."

"We're going to rule the school," Daniel repeated. He raised his palm, and Ira slapped him a high five.

"Go remove it. All three of you," Mark insisted.

"Why weren't you in your room?" Elena asked Ira.

He pointed to the twins. "I'm living with *them* now."

Mark's breath caught in his throat. "You're *what*? You're giving up your room?"

Lea: "When did you decide this?"

Ira shrugged. He seemed to have no idea of how poorly this was going over with the rest of his family. *Or maybe he doesn't care?* Mark thought.

But that didn't make sense. Timid, fearful Ira always needed the acceptance and support of Mark and Lea. He was desperate for their attention, their approval.

"It's cool," Ira said. "I moved some of my stuff out last night. The twins and I—we're going to stick together."

Mark took a long breath. "Isn't this something you should probably discuss with your mom and me? You can't just move out of the house without telling us. I mean, whose idea was this?"

He turned to the twins, who were spreading grape jelly onto their toaster waffles. "Was this *your* idea?"

Before they could answer, the phone rang.

Mark squinted at the ID screen. "I don't recognize the number." He picked up the phone from the kitchen counter and clicked it on. "Hello?"

"Hello, Mark? This is Ginny Margulies. Ethan's mother?"

"Oh, yes. Hi, Ginny. How—"

"Is Ethan there? Did he stay over there last night? I'm really worried. He wasn't in his room this morning and . . . and . . . is he there with you?"

43

Mark felt his throat tighten. He turned to Ira. "Did Ethan spend the night here last night?"

Ira nodded.

"Are you *kidding* me?" Mark exploded.

Ira grabbed a toaster waffle. The twins giggled.

"Ethan is here?" Mark demanded. He heard Ginny Margulies shout something in his ear. "Where is he?"

"Out back," Ira replied. He loaded the waffle into the toaster.

"Your mom and I were out. Didn't Roz check on you last night? She said she checks on the guesthouse every night."

Ira shrugged. "Axl was crying a lot. Roz didn't come."

Mark looked to Lea to say something. But she stood frozen, leaning against the refrigerator with her arms crossed. *Just watching. Why isn't she giving me a little support here?*

"You're not going to school till you explain this," Mark said to Ira. "And you are all going to remove those stupid arrows from your faces."

"I don't think so," Ira said softly.

"Is my family getting weird?" Elena chimed in.

"Ethan is here," Mark said into the phone.

"Oh, thank goodness." He heard a long sigh at the other end.

"But we didn't know—"

"You don't know who's staying in your own house?" Her worst fear over, the woman quickly turned angry. "I don't understand. Why didn't he call me and tell me where he was? Why didn't *you* call me? Somebody?"

"Please. Calm down. Ethan is fine. There was a mix-up, that's all. My sister was supposed to check on them."

Mark wanted to end the conversation. But he knew there was just more confrontation facing him after he hung up.

What is Ira's story? Why is he acting so un-Ira-like?

"Can I at least talk to him?" Mrs. Margulies's voice was tight and challenging.

"Well, no. I don't see him yet. He—" Mark realizing how feeble he sounded.

"Well, where *is* he?"

Mark lowered the phone. "Ira? Can you go get Ethan? His mother wants to speak with him."

Ira took a bite of toaster waffle. He stared back at Mark as if he didn't understand the question.

The twins giggled again.

Elena rolled her eyes. "What is your *problem* this morning?"

Lea finally uncrossed her arms. "We should have a family discussion later, don't you think?" She turned to the twins. "If you have guests back there—"

"We're not exactly guests," Ira interrupted. "We live there now."

"The school bus!" Daniel cried, pointing at the window that looked out on the driveway. "Let's go!"

"Not so fast!" Mark made a grab for Ira. But Ira dodged out of his hands and burst out the kitchen door.

The twins followed, shouting their morning chant, which was beginning to sound more and more unpleasant to Mark. "Rule the school! Rule the school!"

Maybe there's a meaning here I'm not getting.

Out the back window, he saw Ethan run out of the guesthouse and catch up with Ira and the twins. "Oh no," Mark groaned. "Is that a blue arrow on Ethan's face?"

Lea raked her hands through her hair, making it stick out in frazzled clumps. "I don't really understand. . . ."

Mark heard a chattering sound. He lowered his eyes to the phone. He forgot he was still holding it.

"Ginny? Ginny?" It took awhile to make her stop shouting. "Ethan just got on the school bus," he told her. "He's on his way to school."

"But what about his backpack? What was he wearing? What about his lunch? Did he have any breakfast?"

"I'm sorry. I really can't answer those questions. This is all a surprise to Lea and me, too. The boys slept in the guesthouse last night and . . . we didn't know."

"Excuse me? The guesthouse? You allow twelve-year-old boys to sleep by themselves in your guesthouse? And you don't even know who's there?"

"Normally, we check on them all the time. But I guess the boys had a sleepover together and forgot to tell us." *Lame.*

Silence at the other end.

Mark raised his eyes to Lea, who was pacing back and forth, hands in the pockets of her beach cover-up, hair still spiked like lawn divots.

"Ira is a nice boy," Mrs. Margulies said finally. "But I'm not so sure I want Ethan to come to your house."

"I'm sorry, Ginny. I feel as badly as you do."

"I read the papers, Mark. I know what happened at your house. The murder, I mean. You must be under a lot of pressure. I think Ethan should stay away."

"Well, if it makes you feel any better—" He realized she had clicked off.

He slammed the phone onto the counter. He turned to Lea. "Nice morning, huh? That was a warm family moment."

She narrowed her eyes at him. "Are you blaming the twins? You're going to berate me again for bringing them here?"

Elena backed away, hands raised. "I don't want to hear this."

"How are you getting to school?" Mark spun on her. He didn't intend to sound so angry.

She backed up against the kitchen table. "Ruth-Ann's dad. He's picking me up. You don't have to chew my head off. I didn't do anything."

Before Mark could apologize, he heard footsteps coming down the stairs. Roz stormed into the kitchen, still in her long blue flannel nightshirt and carrying Axl in her arms. Her hair was unbrushed. Her eyes darted around the kitchen.

"Roz—? Are you okay?" he started.

"Who did this?" she demanded. "Who was it?"

Elena squinted at Axl. She was the first to see it. "Oh my God."

"Who snuck up to the attic last night?" Roz shouted. "Who would do this to my baby?"

Mark took a staggering step toward her, then stopped short when he saw what Roz was talking about. The fat blue arrow, pointing up, on Axl's left cheek.

44

The halls at Sag Harbor Middle School smelled of some kind of strong disinfectant. The sharp odor made Samuel's eyes water and his nose burn. He had always been very sensitive to smells.

When he was younger, the pungent aroma of burning meat from the island's smoker pits always made him nauseous. But he had outgrown that a while ago.

The four of them walked past the principal's office and turned the corner into the long hall that led to Miss Montgomery's classroom. Daniel walked with an arm casually draped over Ira's shoulder.

Samuel kept close to Ethan, who still seemed reluctant to devote himself wholeheartedly to ruling the school. His assignment from Daniel was to keep close to Ethan and make sure his transition was smooth.

Samuel glimpsed a few kids turning from their lockers and staring at them as they passed. He wasn't surprised that the face arrows would draw some attention.

Two dark-haired sixth-grade girls, fresh from a morning basketball team practice in their blue-and-white team uniforms, noted the arrows and giggled. But they didn't stop to comment or ask what the arrows meant.

"You know those girls, boyo?" Daniel asked Ira. "They're pretty awesome."

Ira shrugged. "I know them, but they don't talk to me. I—I'm not really popular, you know."

Daniel chuckled. "You will be."

Samuel saw the big bulldog-faced kid, Derek Saltzman, bending over the water fountain on the wall. Derek raised his head as the four boys approached.

He narrowed his beady gaze on Ira. "Hey, Sutter. Did you have a shower this morning?"

"No. Why?" Ira said.

Derek filled his mouth with water, then turned and sprayed Ira's face and the front of his jacket. "There's a shower for you, dude." His laugh sounded more like hiccupping, a series of high whoops.

Ira wiped water off his cheeks with his hand.

Derek noticed the blue arrows for the first time. "What's up with that?" He took his thumb and smeared it over Ira's cheek. "Hey, it doesn't come off."

"Want one?" Daniel said.

"Yeah, boyo. Join the club," Samuel said.

Ethan hung back, almost using Samuel as a shield. Samuel knew Ethan was afraid of Derek.

"You look like fucking freaks," Derek snarled. "Here. Want to wash it off?" He spit another stream of water into Ira's face.

Daniel stepped in front of Ira to confront Derek. "You're a tough lad. Want to spit water in *my* face?" Daniel's features hardened, and he gave Derek an icy stare.

Oh, please, Daniel. It's early in the morning. Don't spoil the whole school day.

But Derek wasn't intimidated. "Fuck yes!" He sucked in a long drink and spit a stream of water in Daniel's face. Then he laughed his whooping laugh.

Daniel didn't move a muscle. Just let the cold water run down his cheeks and chin.

Daniel. Please.

"You forgot to add something to those arrows on your faces," Derek said, returning Daniel's unblinking stare. "You've got to put the words *I'm with Stupid*."

Some boys across the hall burst out laughing at that. Samuel spun around, surprised to find a small crowd watching the confrontation. He recognized the two girls from the basketball team and five or six other kids from his class.

Daniel and Derek continued their staring contest. Derek leaned his back against the porcelain fountain and crossed his beefy arms in front of him.

Samuel watched his twin clench and unclench his fists. Samuel's stomach tightened in dread. He knew this meant trouble. A lot of trouble.

But couldn't it wait till later? Couldn't they have a quiet school day first?

A hush fell over the hall as the two boys continued to glare at each other. No locker doors slammed. No footsteps on the tile floor. No voices.

And then heavy footsteps. And a ringing shout. And before anyone could move, Mrs. Maloney bulled her way through the crowd.

"What's going on here? What is the fuss and commotion, may I ask?"

Samuel took a step back. The principal wore a long gray crewneck sweater and a plaid skirt over black tights. Her beaded earrings jangled as she walked.

She pushed past Samuel, Ethan, and Ira, and strode up to Daniel and Derek, her eyes moving from one to the other. "Well, boys, I like shows. I like to be entertained. Can anyone explain to me what this show is about?"

They didn't answer.

"Well, there must be a show because I see you've got an audience." She motioned to the crowd of onlookers blocking the hall.

Neither boy spoke.

The principal narrowed her eyes at Derek. "Is there a problem here? I hope you haven't been giving our new students a bad idea of our school."

"He spit water on the new kid," a boy shouted from the back of the crowd.

"He spit on Ira, too," another boy chimed in.

Mrs. Maloney sighed and shook her head, making her earrings jangle. "Oh, Derek, Derek, Derek. After that nice long talk we had in my office the other day? You do remember that talk, don't you?"

Derek nodded his head and grunted.

"Well, we don't spit on people in this school. Lordy no. Do we need to have another long talk? Maybe call your mother in again?"

Derek's cheeks turned red.

Daniel tapped Mrs. Maloney on the arm, startling her. Samuel watched him turn on his sweetest, most angelic smile. "He didn't mean us any harm, mum," Daniel said in a tiny voice. "It was a joke, see."

Mrs. Maloney reacted with surprise. "A joke? Spitting on other kids is a joke?"

Daniel's dimples flashed. His blue eyes widened in innocence. "He meant it to be funny. He wasn't being mean."

"Yeah. It was a joke," Derek claimed. "I saw someone do it on TV."

Suddenly, Mrs. Maloney didn't seem to be interested in Derek. She was squinting at Daniel. Then her eyes moved to the other boys.

"Oh, good Lord in heaven!" she exclaimed, slapping her cheek with one hand. "I didn't even notice. My eyes must be going."

Samuel knew she had just seen the blue arrows on their faces.

This is not going to be a quiet morning.

"Well, goodness. Big blue arrows on your handsome faces. Ira, did you boys start a *gang*?"

Ira swallowed. "N-no."

"Do we allow gangs at Sag Harbor Middle School?" she asked, running a stubby finger down Ira's cheek. "I don't think so."

"It's not a gang." Daniel stepped in. "It's a club."

The bell clanged right above their heads. The sound made Samuel jump. The disinfectant smell had given him a headache. The tension in the hall wasn't helping. He thought about soft waves, frothy, clean, and cold, splashing on yellow sand.

"Everyone get to class." Mrs. Maloney waved them all away with both hands. "You too, Derek. Everyone but the Blue Arrow Gang."

Derek flashed Daniel a nod, as if to say thank you. He thought he'd escaped punishment this time. But Samuel knew he was mistaken.

Mrs. Maloney herded the four boys to her office. She brought in folding chairs and motioned for them to sit. Then she sat down heavily behind her desk and thumbed through a few pink phone-message slips.

She wasn't really reading them, Samuel thought. She was getting herself together, preparing what to say.

When she glanced up, her expression was stern. "Please explain these face tattoos to me."

"We want to rule the school," Daniel replied without hesitating.

She blinked. "I don't understand."

Daniel wore his most innocent face and spoke in his high, little-boy voice. "The arrows point *up,* see? It means we want to go *up.*"

"Up with Sag Harbor Middle School," Samuel added, always ready to help his twin. "Up with our school."

Mrs. Maloney rested her head in her hands. "So you lads are telling me you want to be cheerleaders?"

"Not really," Samuel answered. "We want to show that we are together, see."

"No, I don't see." She turned to Ira. "I know your father believes that kids should do whatever they want. But did he really approve of you painting arrows on your faces?"

"Not exactly," Ira replied in a whisper.

Mrs. Maloney sat up straight. She tapped one hand on the desktop. "Well, I'm glad you lads want to do well and show some pride in your school. But I think you've gone about it the wrong way. I'm afraid I can't allow it."

"Yes, you can," Daniel said in his little voice.

She blinked at him. "I want all four of you to go wash those arrows off right now."

"No, we won't be doing that, mum." Daniel's matter-of-fact reply.

She used the desktop to push herself to her feet. "Go to the boys' room now. Stay in there till the arrows are gone. Go!"

No one moved.

"We won't be doing that," Daniel said. He stood up and nodded to Samuel.

Okay. Heaven give me strength. Here we go.

Samuel concentrated. It took so much energy to heat up his eyes.

Mrs. Maloney crossed her arms over the front of her sweater. "Daniel, I don't understand. At your old school, did you talk back to your principal and disobey him or her?"

"We want to rule the school," Daniel said.

"Answer my question. Why are you acting like this? I know you are new here and things may be different for you. . . ."

Daniel turned to his twin.

Samuel saw only red now. A billowing sheet of red in front of him. His eyes made a sizzling sound, like bacon frying.

Burn time, Mrs. Maloney.

"Daniel, if you don't obey me, I have no choice—"

"You have no choice," Daniel said.

45

Mrs. Maloney uttered an alarmed cry. "Samuel? Your eyes! What's wrong with your eyes?"

"Are you going to burn her?" Samuel heard Ethan's voice behind him.

"Are you going to *kill* her?" From Ira, alarmed.

Samuel saw only shimmering sheets of red. But he could feel the excitement in the room.

"Ouch! Stop it! Are you *crazy*? What are you *doing*?"

I hate it when they scream like that.

Did we remember to close the office door?

Samuel felt his brother's hand on his arm. "Careful. Careful. Not too much," Daniel whispered. "Just enough to let me get inside her brain."

Mrs. Maloney was silent now. Samuel kept the fiery beam trained on her head.

Burn. Feel the burn.

Silence, except for the pop and sizzle of the red heat.

"Almost done," Daniel said calmly. "Ease up, boyo. I'm almost there. Ease up. Ease up. We don't want to leave burns. We don't want her to remember, do we?"

Samuel pulled the heat back. It was easier to harness it than to fire it up. He could feel his eyes cooling. His headache was gone. He gazed around the room and saw the principal slumped in her leather chair, a dazed smile on her face, arms dangling down the sides of the chair.

Ira and Ethan sat expressionless watching with silent awe.

Daniel still leaned over Mrs. Maloney, staring into her eyes. He patted her broad shoulder gently. He brushed a hand over her head, straightening her short hair. He lifted her hands and placed them in her lap.

"Did it work?" Samuel asked.

He grinned. "No doubt. No worries. Be happy."

He dropped back into the chair between Ira and Ethan.

Mrs. Maloney shook her head, as if waking up from a short nap. She squinted at the four boys for a long moment. Then she smiled.

"I'd better make that announcement now," she said.

She stepped around them to a table with a microphone and a stack of electronic equipment. She threw a switch. Cleared her throat. Leaned over till her mouth was a few inches from the microphone.

"Attention, everyone," she said.

Samuel could hear her voice echoing from classroom to classroom all down the hall.

"Attention, everyone. This is Mrs. Maloney. I have a special announcement this morning."

The speaker squealed. She jerked her head back. Then resumed:

"Our school has a new slogan I think you will all be proud of. It's *Up with Sag Harbor Middle School.* And we have a new school symbol. It's a wide blue arrow pointing up. Because we *all* want to move up, don't we?"

A pause. She turned and flashed Daniel a grin.

"So I'd like every student to stop by the art room at some point before you leave today, and we will have the school arrow painted on your face. I want you to wear it proudly. Don't forget. Everyone must stop in the art room and receive your school arrow *today.* Have a *special* day, everyone. Up with Sag Harbor Middle School."

46

"Lea, please come away from there. You're not even writing. You're just staring at the screen. Please—"

"I . . . can't, Mark. There's so much more to write. I'm sorry."

"I'm going to pull you away. You don't leave this room. We have to talk."

"Maybe when it's finished . . ." She turned on the desk chair to face him, her face pale, eyes tired.

"I'll take you to lunch in town. Where shall we go? We need to talk about the kids. The boys. How we're going to deal with this arrow thing."

She uttered a sigh. "The arrow thing. It's so silly, isn't it?"

"Well, yes and no. We need to figure out how we're going to handle the twins. I mean when there's conflict. You and I have been at each other's throats."

"No. We haven't. We—"

"Yes, we have. You're always the good guy, Lea, and I'm forced to be the bad guy."

"But you *are* the bad guy."

He stared at her. "Was that a joke? Are you *serious*? You're joking, right?"

She shrugged. "I can't do lunch today. I'm so sorry. I have to work."

"But you don't have a deadline, do you? You're not even writing it as an assignment for anyone."

She spun her chair back to face the laptop monitor.

"The kids are worried about you, Lea. Elena asked why you never talk to her anymore. The twins—well, you see they need some guidance, some care. You have to admit you've been neglecting them. And poor Ira—"

"Do you think he'll always be called Poor Ira?"

"That's not funny, Lea."

"I'm not neglecting the twins. The twins and I have a special bond. Even if we don't spend time together . . ."

"You're not making sense, sweetheart. Please get changed and come to lunch with me? It's a beautiful day and . . . and . . . I love you. I want to spend time with you."

She turned. Her eyes went wide. Her whole face constricted. He realized she was staring at the bed.

"Mark—why do we have black sheets? Black sheets mean *death*!"

"Huh? We've had those sheets for years. We—"

"No!" She jumped to her feet, face wide with alarm. "No! Black sheets are death! *Death!*"

"Lea—what are you doing?" He made a grab for her. Missed.

She dove to the bed. Grasped the end of the top sheet. Tugged it up. She gritted her teeth. Uttered an animal growl. And *ripped* the black sheet between her hands.

"Lea—stop!"

She ripped the sheet. Pulled hard. Ripped it some more.

"Lea—please." He ran over to her. Grabbed her arm. "Please stop."

She tore frantically at the sheets, growling and grunting. "Black sheets are *death. Death. Death. Death.*"

47

After school, Samuel could see how surprised Derek was when he and Daniel showed up at his front door. The twins knew Derek's house because it was one of the first school bus stops.

Derek had a stack of Oreos in one hand and a smear of chocolate on his front teeth. "Hey, you two weren't on the bus," he said, blocking the doorway.

"We walked," Daniel said. He eyed the Oreos. "After-school snack?"

Derek nodded. "Sorry. These are the last ones."

We didn't come for cookies, stupid.

"Nice house," Daniel said, peering into the front room.

It *is* a nice house, Samuel thought. Big, with lots of tall glass windows reflecting the afternoon sunlight, at the top of a gently sloping front lawn, surrounded by leafy old trees.

"You want to come in?" Derek couldn't hide his surprise at seeing them. The uncertainty seemed to change his personality. As if he'd momentarily forgotten to act tough.

He led them into the front room, all chrome and white-leather furniture, big glass tables, and a zebra rug on the light wood floor. Tall paintings of beach scenes, crowds in bright bathing suits, people swimming. High cathedral ceiling with a wide skylight.

Derek swallowed the last of the Oreos. He wiped his face with the back of a pudgy hand. "Hey, thanks." To Daniel.

The twins were gazing around the bright white sun-sparkling room. They'd never stood in such luxury.

Too bad. Too bad.

Along with the anticipation, Samuel actually felt a little trepidation.

We walk into this clean perfect sunlit house, and what do we do?

Daniel finally turned back to Derek, who stood awkwardly, leaning on the back of a low, white couch. "Thanks," Derek said again. "You know. For what you did this morning?"

Daniel gave the big kid a blank stare. Like he didn't remember what Derek was talking about.

"You saved my ass," Derek said. "With Mrs. Maloney. That was totally cool."

"Well, it was all a joke, right?" Daniel said, but he didn't say it in a friendly way. There was no smile in his voice. "When you spit the cold, cold water on me. All a joke, right?"

"Yeah, sure." Derek instantly saw the change in Daniel's face.

"You just lost your head, right, boyo?" Daniel definitely menacing now.

"Huh? I lost my head? Well, yeah. I guess."

Daniel gripped Derek's face by the chin and turned his head from side to side. "Hey, lad, you didn't get your school arrow."

Derek's cheeks turned pink. He pulled free from Daniel's grasp.

"I . . . forgot. You know. I didn't get to the art room. Maybe I'll go tomorrow."

"Probably not," Daniel said. He nodded to Samuel.

Samuel took a deep breath. Then he gritted his teeth and started to warm up his eyes.

Daniel wrapped a hand over Derek's beefy shoulder. "Can we see your room?"

48

Pavano wasn't fucking Sari. He was making love to her.

He wondered if she felt the same strong feelings he did. As she moved on top of him, he smoothed his hands over her ass and thought about how different this was. Sex with real feeling and not just sex.

How long had it been?

The last year with Susannah had been all the wrong feelings. After sex, he felt guilty. Sex with Susannah had been an assault. So much anger mixed in, anger that caught him by surprise. It was all too many feelings at once.

I'm a simple guy.

Why was he thinking of Susannah? *Damn it, go away, bitch.*

He wanted to be in the moment. But it seemed impossible to keep memories out of his mind. He remembered the birthmark on the back of Sari's knee. And her salty scent. And the way she cooed—like a dove—with each move.

He had been surprised when she agreed to lunch at the New Paradise Café in town. And then amazed when she led him back to her little cottage of a house off Noyac Road.

And then it seemed natural to find themselves in her bedroom. And comfortable. Yes. Natural and thrilling and comfortable at the same time.

Pavano shut his eyes and thought how smart he was to come back. How smart . . . how smart . . . how smart . . . Ohhhh, yes . . . how smart. Oh God.

When it was over, he reached to throw an arm over her waist. But she sat up quickly, reached down to the floor, and pulled on her red underpants. Her long black hair fell over her face. In the slanting afternoon light from the tiny bedroom window, her skin had a sheen of silvery sweat.

"Sari, come back. What's your hurry?"

She picked up her bra from the floor and slid it over her breasts, fastening it in back. Then she brushed back her hair with both hands. Her dark eyes locked on him for a moment, then turned away.

"Have to talk to you, Andy."

He patted the bed. The sheets felt damp and still warm. "Come back here. We can talk."

"No. I mean, we have to talk." She pulled on her jeans. Then she dropped into the small red armchair across from the bed. "Remember the other night at that theater?"

Why is she looking at the floor? Is she avoiding my eyes?

"Sure. Of course I remember."

"Remember I said it didn't mean anything? When I kissed you? Remember?"

"Yeah. So?"

"Well, today . . . this meant something." She finally raised her eyes. She spread her long fingers over the arms of the chair, then tightened her hands into fists.

"To me too," he said. He could feel himself getting hard, getting ready again. What the hell? He had time. He wasn't on duty till six.

"What it meant was good-bye." Sari was staring hard at him now.

"Huh?"

"I wanted to say good-bye, Andy."

"But . . . we just said hello."

She shook her head. A smile crossed her face. It seemed so out of place. "Andy, you're sweet."

"Sweet?"

"But you're such a jerk."

He blinked. He waited for her to continue.

"We had lunch, right? We sat across from each other? We talked. We ate. We even held hands for a few minutes?"

"Yeah. So?"

"So you didn't see the ring on my finger? You're supposed to be a cop, Andy. You're supposed to see everything?"

She waved her left hand in his face. The ring sparkled in the sunlight from the window.

He felt the muscles tighten on the back of his neck.

"I married Rod, see."

"What the fuck? You married the tennis hat guy? When?"

"Sunday. We got married last Sunday. So I wanted to tell you. You've been calling me and following me and trying to bring back the past and—"

"Only because I still have feelings for you."

Stop sounding like a girl.

"That's why I wanted to say good-bye." She stood up and searched for her T-shirt on the floor. "I have nice memories, too, Andy. So now we had another nice memory and a nice good-bye."

"Jesus, Sari."

His phone beeped. It took him a moment to remember it was in his uniform pants draped over the bench at the foot of the bed. He heard Chaz's voice: "Pavano? You there? Got an early call. Pavano?"

Andy lurched to the bottom of the bed and fumbled the phone from the pants pocket. "Chaz? What's up?"

"Where are you? Got to roll."

"Uh . . . Nowhere. I can meet you."

Sari, straightening her T-shirt, squinted at him. "Nowhere?"

Pinto gave him an address on Madison Street.

He clicked the phone off and stuffed it back in the pocket. He scrambled out of bed and grabbed up his clothes. "Hey, Sari—it's been real. Happy marriage. I enjoyed the honeymoon."

49

"I can't do this, Chaz. I admit it. I don't have the stomach for it."
Pavano hung in the doorway, unable to step into the small bedroom.

Pinto scowled at him. "Are you actually trembling? Pavano, how
long were you a cop in the city?"

Pavano swallowed. His Adam's apple rode up and down his
throat. "You know I was Housing Authority. I never . . . I never saw
anything like this. I . . . don't think we should fucking be here."

"We're fucking here, aren't we?"

"First the guy in the car. Now this. I'm having such a bad day.
This isn't working out for me."

"It didn't work out too good for this kid, either," Pinto muttered. "Actually, you're doing better than he is. That cheer you up?"

"You're a riot," Andy said, eyes on the window. Avoiding the
corner by the bed. Avoiding it.

*A few minutes ago, I was in bed with Sari. And now . . . a fuck-
ing horror show.*

Pinto softened his tone. "Look, we got the call. We'll do what
we can do. You saw me radio Vince. The crime scene guys are on
their way."

"Chaz, there's no one here. Who made the call?"

"A neighbor. Said she smelled something bad."

"Yeah. Smells bad, okay. Maybe we should wait for the CS to get here."

"Take a breath, Andy. You're not a fucking rookie. Be a pro."

"I . . . I never—" Pavano stopped himself. He forced himself not to look in the corner.

But what *was* that sick, sharp smell? It smelled like when Susannah burned a roast.

The bedroom was spotless. Not a thing out of place. A kid's room without even a dirty sock on the floor. No sign of a weapon. A row of track lights across the ceiling sent bright circles of white halogen light over the room. Brighter than daylight. Cheerful.

Posters of New York Rangers hockey players on one wall. A movie poster hanging a little crooked over the desk. Pavano recognized Buzz and Woody.

His eyes moved too far and he glimpsed the dark lake of blood on the carpet. And were those chunks of . . . burnt skin?

"He's burned up, Chaz. I mean, like someone took a torch to him. Like the guy in the car. It's fucking sick."

"You're babbling. Just shut up."

"But where are the parents? Where are the fucking parents? Why was he alone in the house?"

Pinto removed his cap, scratched his thinning flattop. Beads of sweat glistened on his broad forehead. His little bird eyes trained on Pavano. "Now you're starting to think like a cop."

Still eyeing Andy, Pinto slid the cap back on. Then he turned and took a few steps toward the corner.

"Saltzman. The mailbox said Saltzman, right? I think I met the kid's mother. On the pier one night. She's divorced. I remember she's divorced. She said the kid was troubled."

"He ain't troubled now. Come over here. Take notes."

"Wh-what are we looking for?"

"Are you stuttering now? Are you totally going to lose it?"

"I feel sick, Chaz. I mean really."

"Suck it up, man. We've got to look for clues. For anything. Till the ME gets here."

"Then what?"

"I don't fucking know."

Pinto leaned over the perfectly smooth white bedspread. Nothing to see. "You going to toss your dinner? Do it downstairs. Don't contaminate this room."

"The room—it's totally clean. It's almost like it's *sterile* or something. A kid's room without a piece of paper out of place. No dirty clothes. No backpack hanging over a chair. Nothing. But there *had* to be a fire or something. Right? It smells like there was a fire."

"Yeah. Smells like a barbecue."

Chaz bumped open the closet door with his hip, careful not to leave fingerprints.

He sighed. "No sign of a murder weapon."

"This is worse than the guy in the car. I've never seen anything like this."

Chaz whirled around. "Do you think I have?" His cigarette-hoarse voice went up two octaves. "It's a fucking nightmare."

Andy froze at the sound from the hall. Footsteps on the stairs.

"Vince radioed for CS backup," Chaz said. "Has to be the ME. And he had to tell Franks. Franks will probably bring some state guys. Now we got some kind of fucking serial killer creep, right?"

The red-haired woman burst into the room, eyes wide with fright, a raincoat flying behind her. "What are you doing here? This is my house. What are you doing here?"

Andy recognized her from that night on the pier. This was the same Saltzman, the victim's mother.

"Get her out!" Pinto waved to Andy with both hands. "Get out of here. Get her out!"

"I don't understand," the woman planted her feet and glared at Andy. "Why are you here? Where is my son? Where is Derek?"

"Get her out!" Pinto lurched toward Andy. "Out. Now. Out of here."

Andy felt in slow motion. Like coming out of a nightmare. Pulling himself awake slowly.

He took the woman by the shoulders. Too late.

"I don't understand!" Fear replacing anger. "I don't understand. Tell me—"

"Get her out! Get her out!"

Andy couldn't budge her. She saw. She saw the kid's body.

"My Derek! Is that my Derek? I don't understand. I don't under-stand. Do you hear me? Talk to me. Please. I don't understand."

"Come with me." Andy tried to turn her away. He held her shoulders and spoke softly. "Come with me. Please."

"I don't understand. I don't understand."

I've seen people go into shock before. But I'm not trained for this.

"Is that my son? Is that Derek?"

"Pavano—get her out of here. Don't stand there. Get her *out*!"

"Is that my Derek? But where is his head? Where is his *head*?"

Pavano managed to wrap his arm around her shoulders. She was screaming now, shrieking and sobbing. It took all his strength to force her into the hall.

Two uniformed cops were on the stairwell. Pavano motioned them up. "Take care of her. Call a doctor. This is her house. It's . . . her son."

He passed the screaming woman on to them. The two cops struggled with her on the stairs. She stumbled and they had to block her to keep her from tumbling down the stairs.

His stomach churning, Pavano returned to Pinto. He found him bending over, hands on his knees. "Pinto? You okay?"

"Not really."

"Huh? What?"

"Look under the bed, Andy. What's that thing under the bed?"

Andy sucked in his breath. He squatted down and peered at the round, dark object half hidden in shadow near the wall under the bed. "What the fuck?"

Pinto straightened up. He sighed. "Andy, I think we just found the kid's head."

50

Mark gripped Autumn around the waist of her white tennis shorts. He intended to lift her off his lap. But she took one of his hands and slid it between her legs. Then she lowered her face to his and began to kiss his neck. Slowly, she moved her lips to his cheek, then his mouth.

"No. Autumn."

She giggled and nibbled his ear.

"Lea is right upstairs. She could come down—"

"But she won't," Autumn whispered. "She never stops working up there."

She sat up straight, her white-blond hair falling over her eyes, holding his hand against the front of her shorts. "What is she writing?"

Mark glanced nervously to the office door. He could feel his erection pushing against his jeans. "I'm not even sure. A long piece. Something about death rituals. She used to share her work with me."

"And now?" Brushing her hair against his cheek.

"She stays up there day and night. I'm really worried about her. I can't even drag her away for meals. She's . . . not right."

"That's why I'm here for you, Mark." Whispered against his ear so that the skin tingled all down his body.

"No. Autumn—please." He worked his hand free and gripped her waist again. "Get up. Come on. Really. I'm serious."

She made a pouty face, her round blue eyes wide, mouth all satirical. "Don't you like me anymore?"

"We can't do this." Another glance to the door. Did he hear footsteps or just the house creaking? "Roz is home, too. And the boys are out back."

She nuzzled his neck. Her lips were hot and dry. "Doesn't that make it more exciting for you?"

"No. It just makes it more wrong."

"Wrong?" Her smile faded. "You don't really think it's wrong, do you?"

Is she delusional?

"Yes. Wrong. I mean, look. I have too much to deal with now. I'm so worried about Lea and stressed about the kids and . . . We can't do this. We—"

The front doorbell chimed.

Autumn scrambled to her feet. She frowned at him as she smoothed her short hair with both hands. Then she tugged down the legs of her shorts. "Wrong?"

"Of *course* it's wrong."

What's that song? "How Can It Be Wrong If It Feels So Right?"

"Mark. It's those two policemen again." Roz's shout from the front entryway. "Shall I send them back to your office?"

Mark stood up and straightened his blue polo shirt over his jeans. He squinted at Autumn. "What the fuck?"

She began straightening the stack of files on the desk. "Guess I'll go home. Say you'll miss me."

Mark didn't answer. He was trying to figure out why the police had returned. He heard their clomping footsteps, heard their voices as they made small talk with Roz.

Autumn slid out with her pouty face on. She glanced back as the two cops entered, then vanished down the hall.

Mark had a sudden fright. *Do I have lipstick on my face?*

Then he remembered Autumn wore only a clear lip gloss.

The two officers entered and apologized for disturbing him.

They sat down in their usual places on the couch. The one named Pavano looked tired, weary, as if he hadn't been getting much sleep. His partner didn't waste time getting to the point.

"Mr. Sutter, I'm sure you're aware that one of the students in your sons' class was murdered last Wednesday."

Mark nodded. "Yes. It's so horrible. So shocking. I spoke with our three boys—Ira and the twins—and tried to see if they needed counseling."

"Well, Officer Pavano and I think—"

"My wife and I—we know the Saltzmans. I mean, we knew them before the divorce. My wife was in a reading group with Elaine Saltzman. She . . . she must be beyond devastated."

The two cops nodded. Pavano tapped something into his phone.

"My son Ira wasn't friends with Derek. But they knew each other since fourth grade, I think. Ira is very sensitive. I think he had a nightmare last night. You know. About Derek."

"Sorry to hear that," Pavano said, glancing up from his phone. "They brought in grief counselors to the school."

Mark cleared his throat. "Yes. That's smart. I'm trying to work with Ira on my own."

"We went to the school yesterday," the big cop, Pinto, continued, keeping his small eyes steady on Mark, as if studying every reaction.

They couldn't think I had anything to do with the kid's murder. Why are they here?

"We spoke to Mrs. Maloney and to the teacher. What's her name?"

"Montgomery," his partner offered.

"You know. We're trying to cover every angle. Grasping at straws, really."

He and Mark stared at each other. Mark waited for him to continue. He could smell Autumn's lemony perfume. Was it on his cheek?

"We asked the principal to go over everything that happened on Wednesday," Pinto said. "We just asked if anything concerning the deceased stuck out in her mind that day. Anything at all."

"What were you looking for exactly?" Mark asked. He leaned forward and crossed his arms over the desk.

"We didn't know," Pinto said. "Just trying to get an idea of the boy's day."

"I don't understand," Mark said. "You talked to the principal. So . . . why did you come here?"

"Well . . ." Pinto removed his cap and tossed it onto the arm of the couch. "The principal remembered that Derek Saltzman had a fight with your boys that morning."

"Huh? A fight?"

"A spitting fight."

Mark felt his cheeks grow hot. "I don't think so. My son Ira would never spit on anyone."

"Mrs. Maloney recalled that Derek Saltzman spit water on your son Ira and on your twin boys as well."

Mark shook his head. "First I've heard of it. I do know that Derek has been in trouble before."

"Well, we thought your boys might have some kind of information or recollection from that day," Pavano chimed in. "Something that might give us a clue."

"That's pretty fucking desperate," Mark said, tapping the desktop with both hands.

"We agree," Pinto said quickly. "But there's one more detail." He turned to Pavano, as if asking for permission to continue.

Pavano gave an almost invisible shrug.

"This isn't being given out to anyone," Pinto said, playing with his cap, twirling it on one hand. "If you could keep it confidential. I mean, not spread it around to people in the community."

"Yes. Of course," Mark said.

"Well, you see," Pinto continued in a voice just above a whisper, "the boy's murder is very similar to the murder that occurred in your driveway."

Mark couldn't hide his surprise. "How do you mean?"

"The victim was burned," Pinto said. "Like with a blowtorch. Very similar. Only in the boy's case, his head was burned completely off. We found his skull—no skin on it or anything. We found his skull all scorched . . . under his bed."

Mark stood up. He took a deep breath and held it, fighting down his nausea.

"Horrible," he muttered. "Like a fucking horror movie."

The two cops nodded. Pinto spoke first. "So, since the murders were similar, and since your sons had the spitting fight with the victim on the morning of his death, we just thought it wouldn't hurt to talk to them for a few minutes. With your permission, of course."

"But tell me again. You certainly don't suspect—" Mark started.

Pinto waved a hand. "Of course not. No kid could do what we've seen in these murders. Pavano and I, we're just trying everything."

"You know, I've thought a lot about the murder in my driveway," Mark said, sitting up straight, leaning his head against the back of the desk chair. "I mean, it's hard to *stop* thinking about it."

"That's for sure," Pinto replied.

"I mean, it's not like you guys leave and I just turn it off. I think about it day and night."

"And?" Pinto said, showing a little impatience.

"Well, I just think you're looking in all the wrong places. I mean, coming here? That's a waste of your time. These murders . . . They're so violent. And nothing like this has happened in Sag Harbor before, right? So you need to check out new arrivals. Find someone who's moved here very recently, someone with a violent past. The summer people haven't arrived yet. That should make your job easier. I'm not a cop, but I'd be checking mental hospitals and—"

"Thanks for your advice. But you have to understand *you're* our number one suspect," Pavano blurted out.

Mark felt his face grow hot. He saw Pinto flash an annoyed scowl at his partner.

"A guy comes to your house with bad news," Pavano said, ignoring Pinto's displeasure, "he ends up dead in your driveway. A kid gets into a fight with your boys. The kid ends up dead in his room."

Mark wished they wouldn't concentrate their stares on him like that. Yes, he could feel he was blushing. But blushing could mean all kinds of things. He'd written a paper on it. Why was he thinking about that paper now?

"I can testify that Mark isn't a murderer."

The voice made Mark jump. Lea came floating barefoot into the office, in a sleeveless blue top and blue short shorts. Her hair fell loosely around her face.

Mark thought she looked beautiful, except for her eyes, which were red and tired from staring into the laptop screen all day.

The two officers climbed slowly to their feet. They all nodded at each other solemnly.

"Mark can't even kill a lobster," Lea said. "He's so squeamish, I have to drop them in the pot. He looks the other way. Really."

Pinto studied Mark. "I'm allergic to shellfish," he said.

"Too bad," Lea offered.

"Mrs. Sutton, you were away when the murder occurred in your driveway," Pavano said.

"I was in the city. I had some meetings. But I hurried home. I knew the kids would be upset."

"They've been very edgy and out of sorts," Mark added. "I've tried to get them to talk about it, but . . ."

Pinto turned back to Lea. "The twin boys were out in the front yard when the victim was murdered. Have they said anything to indicate—"

"That they saw anything?" Lea interrupted. "No. Not a word. Mark asked them directly more than once. They say they were in back. In the guesthouse, in their room. They didn't see a thing. And I believe them."

"The twins have had their lives turned upside-down," Mark said. "Losing their parents and their home on the island, moving to a very different place. I've been watching them very closely. I think I'd know if they were keeping something from me."

"Well, we appreciate all your help," Pavano said.

"We came to ask the three boys just a few questions. Do you think that would be okay now?"

Mark turned to Lea. "Roz was going to take them into town to buy dinner," Lea said. "But go ahead."

"I guess it would be okay," Mark said. "But if the talk begins to upset them—"

"We'll know when to stop," Pinto said, glancing at his partner.

"I'm happy to cooperate, even if you think I'm your number one suspect. But as I said, this is pretty ridiculous, a total waste of time," Mark muttered, walking to the office door.

"We have to do everything," Pinto said. "This isn't our usual kind of case."

"I'll go get the boys," Lea said. She turned to Mark. "I'm going back to my work. Roz will take the boys and get dinner when they're finished here."

Mark turned to the cops. "The boys are out back. In the guesthouse. They've been hanging out there. All three of them. My son is shy and difficult. But I think he's bonding with his new brothers."

"Nice," Pavano muttered.

Mark realized that was too much information.

I'm their top suspect. God. How stupid is that?

He heard the boys clomping down the hall.

I'll cooperate the best I can. But of course my main goal has to be to protect my kids.

51

A few minutes later, the three boys stepped in. They glimpsed the two police officers and lingered near the office door.

All three boys wore loose-fitting denim jeans and oversize dark T-shirts. Ira carried his game player in one hand. The twins had sweet smiles on their faces, which seemed strange to Mark. Why were they always so happy?

Pinto motioned for them to sit on the floor. He squinted from one to the other. "Those arrows on your faces."

"We saw them on kids at your school," Pavano offered. "The principal said—"

"It's our new school symbol," Daniel interrupted. He turned his face to show off his blue arrow.

"What does it mean?" Pinto asked.

"Up," Daniel replied. "Up with Sag Harbor Middle School."

"Nice," Pinto said. But he gave his partner a look that said it wasn't so nice. "Is everyone at your school wearing them?"

"They will be," Daniel answered. "It was the principal's idea."

"Different," Pavano commented.

"We just want to talk to you for a few minutes about your friend Derek Saltzman," Pinto said, leaning toward the boys with his hands on his knees. "Of course you heard about what happened to Derek."

The boys nodded somberly. "It's very sad," Daniel said softly.

"Is that how you feel? Sad?" Pinto asked.

The three of them nodded again.

"He wasn't very nice," Ira said, eyes down. "But he shouldn't be killed."

"Not very nice?" Pinto's eyes widened.

"He was mean to a lot of kids," Ira said, glancing at Mark.

Mark nodded, signaling him to be honest about Derek.

"Was he mean to you?" Pinto asked Ira.

Ira nodded. He stuffed his hands into his jeans. "Yeah. He took things from me. Candy and stuff. He did that to everyone. My friend Ethan, too. He took their stuff. He bossed kids around. A lot."

"It's . . . very scary," Samuel chimed in. "What happened to Derek." Mark saw a tear glisten on his cheek.

Daniel's shoulders trembled. "I'm scared," he said, eyes on Mark. "Why did a killer do that to Derek?"

Samuel and Daniel both sobbed. Tears tracked down their faces. Ira kept his head down. He kept picking at a scab on his thumb.

"I think that's enough for now," Mark told the two cops.

Pinto leaned closer to the boys. "Are you feeling too sad to answer a few more questions?"

Silence. Ira spoke first. "It's okay."

"You said Derek was mean. Is that why you got in a fight with him Wednesday morning?"

The question made Mark clench his jaw. But the boys didn't react at all.

"It wasn't a fight," Daniel said, raising his blue eyes to the cops. He wiped tears off his cheeks with both hands.

"It was just a joke, don't you know," Samuel told them. "That's all. A water-spit joke. We didn't have a fight."

Pavano tapped notes into his phone. Pinto studied their faces.

"You didn't get angry when Derek spit water on you?"

"Just a joke," Daniel muttered. "The boyo was joking us."

"Mark? Can you come here a minute? I need some help." Mark heard Roz call from the kitchen.

He jumped to his feet and motioned to the two cops. "Be right back." He hurried from the room.

Pinto scratched the side of his face. "Just one more thing. I need to ask you twins one more question."

They raised their eyes to him.

"You see, we talked to the school bus driver. He told us you two weren't on his bus Wednesday afternoon. Is that true?"

Daniel and Samuel exchanged glances. "Yes," Daniel answered. "We missed the bus, don't you see."

Pinto: "Where did you go?"

"To Derek's house."

Both officers leaned forward. Pinto studied the twins' faces. "You went to Derek's house after school? Why?"

"To tell him no hard feelings," Daniel said in a tiny voice. "We told him we weren't mad at him. You know. About the water spitting."

Pavano typed furiously on his phone. Then he stopped. "Does your father know you were at Derek's house?"

They both nodded. "He came to pick us up," Daniel said. His shoulders started to tremble again. His twin wiped tears from his eyes.

Pavano and Pinto exchanged glances again. "Funny. He didn't tell us about that."

"It was *so* scary," Daniel uttered. "Samuel and I—we were scared." Both twins looked to the doorway, checking to see if Mark was there.

"Why were you scared?"

"Pa yelled at Derek," Daniel replied, voice trembling. "Pa yelled at him. He was real mad. For spitting on us, I think. And Pa slapped Derek. He slapped Derek twice."

Both boys were sobbing now. "We were so scared," Samuel said.

"Pa made us promise not to tell," Daniel added, glancing to the door. "But it wasn't right. Pa shouldn't have done that. It made us scared."

52

"I need to talk to you boys." Mark burst into the guesthouse. "This is serious." His head was spinning. His muscles felt tight from . . . anger.

He wasn't expecting the scene confronting him. Ira and Ethan on the floor, backs against the wall of the small bedroom, books in their laps. Two lanky, dark-haired boys Mark didn't recognize, hunched on the twin's beds with video games in their hands. A boy and two blond girls in front of the TV on the dresser.

"Hey, what's going on?"

The twins appeared from the closet in back. They carried bed-sheets and pillows in their arms. Their eyes went wide when they saw Mark.

"Put those down," Mark snapped. "We need to talk." He gestured around the room. "If you two want to invite friends over, you have to tell us." He knew he should get his anger under control before he talked to them—but how could he?

"Sorry, Pa," Samuel said softly.

"Some friends from school, don't you know," his twin added. "It's Friday night, so—"

"I don't care what night it is. Come over here. I've been questioned by those two policemen for the past hour. Did you tell them that I was at Derek Saltzman's house?"

Mark felt himself lose it. He grabbed them both by the shoulders. Hard. "*Did* you? Don't lie to me. Tell the truth."

"Ouch." Daniel squirmed under his grip. The cry made Mark realize what he was doing. He let go and took a step back. The other kids were all watching him.

"Sorry. Tell me what you told the police. Did you lie about me to the police?"

"No," Daniel said. "Sammy and I wouldn't lie, Pa."

Mark stared at them both. He was breathing hard. His head throbbed. Daniel was lying to him. His face was as innocent as ever, but he was lying.

"Samuel, did *you* tell the police I was at Derek's house?"

"No, Pa. I didn't tell them anything. Why are you mad at us?"

"You're lying. You're both lying, aren't you?"

He saw the frightened faces on the other kids. Ira was watching him warily, chin trembling.

And then Mark saw something else.

Something sparkly in the open drawer of the bed table. He strode across the room, in front of the two boys he didn't know, reached into the drawer and pulled it out.

Holding it by its silver chain, he raised it to his face. Then he turned to the twins. "Isn't this Elena's necklace? The amethyst necklace? The one she is missing?"

The twins gazed at it as if they'd never seen it. They didn't speak.

"This is ridiculous," Mark said. "Are you two *thieves* as well as liars?"

For some reason, that made them giggle.

"It's not funny!" he exploded. "You all have to go home! Go on. Get out of here. All of you! I have to talk to these two."

"But we *are* home," one of the blond girls said. When she turned, he saw the fat blue arrow on her cheek. They *all* had the arrow, he realized.

Mark motioned to the twins. "Come with me. Now. We're going to get to the bottom—"

"Mark!" Through the open window, he heard Lea's shout from the house. "Mark? Are you out there? We're going to be late."

I should cancel tonight. I've got a serious problem with these boys.

I won't be good company, that's for sure.

But it's the first night I've been able to persuade Lea to go out—

"Mark? Where are you? We have to go."

He waved a finger at the twins. "Later. We're going to have a long talk later. When I get home. We have to get at the truth here, do you understand?"

They both nodded. Mark turned to Ira, on the floor against the wall, but Ira avoided his eyes. Mark spun away, clenched his fist over the amethyst necklace, and stomped to the door.

"Bye, Pa," Samuel called.

"Yes. Bye, Pa," Daniel echoed.

"Bye, Pa," they called in unison.

"Look. Look at this." Mark ran into the kitchen, waving the amethyst necklace in front of him. "Lea—"

Her head was tilted to one side as she adjusted a dangling red earring. "What's that?"

"It . . . It's Elena's necklace. The one that's missing. The twins had it. They stole it. They *stole* it, Lea."

She straightened up. Brushed back her hair with both hands. "Calm down, sweetheart. You sound like a crazy person."

He let out a long breath. "Are you listening to me? The twins stole this from Elena's room. They are thieves, Lea, and—"

She took the necklace from him and smoothed the chain through her fingers. "I'm sure there's a good explanation, Mark."

"No. No, there isn't." He didn't intend to sound so frantic, but he felt he might explode with anger. "And—and they lied, Lea. They lied to the police. Didn't you wonder why I was in there being grilled for an hour?"

"I was getting ready, dear. I thought you wanted to go out and have a good time. This is what you wanted, isn't it?"

"You're not even listening to me. Those boys you brought here—"

"I know how you feel about them." Her voice suddenly sharp. "You've made it perfectly clear."

"We've got a real problem, Lea. Can't you understand that?"

"I understand that your *attitude* is a real problem."

"No. No, that's not the problem. They are liars and thieves and . . . and God knows what else."

She startled him by grabbing the front of his shirt with both hands and tugging it hard. "They're *my boys*, Mark. Do you understand? *My boys. My boys. My boys.* And you're not going to ruin it for me. Understand?"

He pried her hands off him as gently as he could. Her eyes were wide with anger. Her shouts had been like animal growls. *I have to back down. She's losing control.*

"We'll talk about it later, okay, sweetheart? Okay? Let's go out and have fun and get drunk and enjoy ourselves. Okay?"

She nodded, but her glare didn't soften. "Okay. Let's go. Let's go have fun."

53

"I want that one." Elena stabbed a finger at the laptop screen. "Just a tiny black-and-red flower. Subtle, see?"

Ruth-Ann brought her face close to the screen. "Too subtle. It'll look like a birthmark or a mole or something."

Elena gave her friend a shove. "No, it won't. It will look like a perfect little flower."

"Where will you put it?" Ruth-Ann demanded. "On your butt?"

They both laughed.

"On my ankle," Elena said. "Right here." She touched her bare ankle with one magenta fingernail. Then she scrolled down the screen of tattoo designs. "Which one do *you* want?"

"I don't want color," Ruth-Ann said. "I don't like the colors. I just want black. There. Look. Those Chinese letters. What does that say?"

"I don't read Chinese," Elena said.

"There's a caption. Read the caption," Ruth-Ann leaned closer. "There. Yes. That's the one I want. In English it means *Sexy Beast*."

Both girls collapsed laughing. The laptop started to slide off Elena's lap. She caught it before it fell to the floor.

Ruth-Ann shifted her weight on the edge of the bed. "Can you imagine? All these people walking around with Chinese tattoos, and they think they say *Life* or *Hope* or *Peace* or something. But they really say *Kick Me*."

"No. *Eat me*."

They laughed some more.

Yes, they were a little giddy tonight. Elena felt more excited to see her friend than usual. Sure, they'd had sleepovers before. But not since the murder in the driveway.

Ruth-Ann's parents kept calling from L.A., telling Ruth-Ann she shouldn't spend the night at Elena's, "just to be on the safe side."

But Ruth-Ann persuaded Mrs. Ellison, the woman hired to take care of her, that Mark and Lea weren't ax murderers, and her parents were being extra strict only because they felt guilty about being away in L.A. for so long.

And so here they were, picking out tattoos online and texting boys in their class, and laughing a lot. They pretty much had the house to themselves on this Friday night. Roz had retired up to the attic with Axl. The boys were in their private house out back. Mark and Lea had gone to see friends in Sagaponack.

"How about a cute ladybug?" Elena asked, returning to the tattoo thumbnails.

"Lame," Ruth-Ann said. "Why do you want a bug crawling on you? Hey, Elena, think your parents would let you get that tiny flower tattoo? Your dad says kids should do whatever they want, right?"

Elena snickered. "That's total bullshit. No way they'd let me get a tattoo even if you needed a microscope to see it. We're fourteen, Ruth-Ann. You know what that means."

"No. What?"

"It means anything we want to do, we're not old enough yet."

Ruth-Ann thought about that, chewing her bottom lip. "Hey, you're right. You got it. That's exactly what fourteen means."

They tapped on their phones for a few minutes.

"Look at this." Elena shoved her phone into Ruth-Ann's face. "This photo Roshanna sent me. Roshanna kissing her dog. Look. With tongues."

"Eeuw." Ruth-Ann made a face. "Which one's Roshanna?"

That made them both laugh. "You're cruel," Elena said.

Ruth-Ann nodded. "It's my best quality."

Elena heard a sound. She glanced up to see Daniel and Samuel in her bedroom doorway. "Hey, guys."

"Hey, guys." Daniel mimicked her words like a parrot.

"You've met Ruth-Ann, right?"

"Hi. What's up?" Ruth-Ann poked Elena and whispered, "They're totally cute."

"What's up?" Daniel echoed. They stepped into the room, their blue eyes catching the ceiling light.

Like big cartoon eyes, Elena suddenly thought.

They wore matching denim cutoff shorts. Daniel had an orange T-shirt with a bright yellow sun on the front pulled down nearly to his knees. Samuel had a black sleeveless T-shirt that revealed his slender, pale shoulders.

Daniel held up something in his hand. A brown wallet. "Pa left his wallet on the floor in his office."

"Well, just put it back on his desk," Elena said.

Daniel nodded. "I'll do that." He tucked the wallet into the pocket of his shorts.

Elena clicked her laptop shut and set it beside her on the bed. "What's going on in your private little kingdom out back? You're not doing anything bad back there, are you?"

"You'll be wanting to come see," Daniel said. He kept his eyes on Elena, as if he was trying to tell her something.

"I don't think so," Elena replied. "Ruth-Ann and I are kind of busy here."

The boys stepped up to the bed, walking side by side, their faces blank.

Elena felt a tremor of misgiving. "What do you guys want?"

"Want to see our friend Roshanna tongue-kissing a dog?" Ruth-Ann offered. She reached behind Elena for the laptop.

"No. Don't show them that." Elena wrestled Ruth-Ann away. "They'll enjoy it too much."

She expected the boys to laugh or at least smile at that, but their stony expressions didn't change.

"You'll be wanting to come with us now," Daniel said, so earnest and innocent at the same time, she had an impulse to hug him.

"And why would we want to do that?" Elena demanded.

"Does your brother ever talk?" Ruth-Ann offered, her eyes on Samuel.

"I'm the quiet one, don't you know," Samuel said.

"I'm quiet, too," Ruth-Ann told him.

Elena poked her in the ribs. "Shut up. When are you ever quiet?"

Ruth-Ann laughed.

Daniel took Elena's hand and tried to tug her up off the bed.

She pulled back. "Hey, what's your problem?" She slapped his hand away.

He didn't seem to register the rebuke. "You'll be needing a bag or something. For the two of you."

"For what?" Elena jumped to her feet.

Ruth-Ann had a grin frozen on her face. "You dudes are weird tonight."

"You need to gather your things," Samuel said. "So you can join us and rule the school."

Elena frowned at him. "Does that make any sense at all?"

"Is this some kind of dare?" Ruth-Ann said, still enjoying it.

Elena felt on the verge of being creeped out. Her parents were away. And these boys were acting like . . . robots? Their eyes were icy, she thought. She couldn't see any joke in them.

I don't really know them at all. They've been part of my family for only a few weeks. And I don't really know what they are like.

"Do you have a bag to carry your things?" Daniel asked.

"You will come as well," Samuel said—very formally—to Ruth-Ann.

She leaned forward and placed her hands on Samuel's shoulders. She expected them to feel soft, but she could feel only hard bone. "What do you want to show us back in your little house? You're not explaining anything. What do you want?"

"To rule the school," Samuel replied. He didn't move. Didn't try to free himself from her hold on him.

"Yes. Rule the school," his twin echoed.

"I don't get it," Ruth-Ann said.

"I think that's why they've got those stupid arrows painted on their faces," Elena told her. She realized it was the first mean thing she'd said to them since they arrived. But they were starting to annoy her.

She had spent a lot of time telling Ruth-Ann how cute they were, how adorable they acted together. But they weren't being any fun tonight.

"If Ruth-Ann and I go down and see what you want to show us, will you leave us alone?"

"No." Daniel returned her stare.

Ruth-Ann laughed. "You *won't* leave us alone?"

"No." The two boys in unison.

"You will stay with us. You will help us rule the school."

"Stop saying that!" Elena snapped. "We're not going to stay with you, and we're not—"

Ruth-Ann grabbed her hand to silence her. She leaned over the boys, who were at least a foot shorter than her. "Why do you want Elena and me to stay with you? Are you frightened of something?"

That made them smile for the first time.

"We're not afraid," Daniel said. "We don't know fear of things, don't you know." His smile faded quickly. "You will both live with all of us. You will help us."

Elena squinted at him. "*All* of you? Don't you mean just you and Ira?"

"There are others," Samuel said. "We have others now who want to go *up*."

Elena and Ruth-Ann exchanged confused glances. "You have other kids living with you out there? Do Mom and Dad know about this?"

"They're joking," Ruth-Ann muttered.

"They don't look like they're joking."

Elena's phone chimed. A text message. She ignored it.

"Let's go," Daniel said, motioning with his eyes to the bedroom door.

"Bring your things. Hurry," Samuel said.

Both girls crossed their arms defiantly. "No way."

"Beat it, you two," Elena snapped. "You're annoying us. Get lost."

"You're my sister," Daniel said to Elena. "You will join us now. We are bruvvers and sisters."

"Sisters? Leave me out of this," Ruth-Ann insisted.

"Go away. I mean it," Elena insisted. "You're not allowed in my room, remember? Ruth-Ann and I want to be alone."

"This isn't your room, lassie," Daniel replied, his brogue suddenly growing thicker. "You will be living among your bruvvers now."

"Are you nuts?" Elena was a patient person, but they were pushing the limits here. She took a breath. *Don't lose it. Maybe this is some weird game they played on the island. Maybe it's a big tease.*

"Where's Ira? Why are you leaving him alone down there?"

"He isn't alone," Daniel replied. "I told you, there are others now. And they are waiting for you." He scraped a finger down her cheek. "I will be putting the arrow on right here. It will look so lovely."

"Get your hand off me. Hey—"

Her breath caught in her throat when she saw the change on Samuel's face. His eyes—those wet blue eyes—they were suddenly fiery red.

Ruth-Ann uttered a gasp. She bumped up against Elena.

Elena stared into the glowing red eyes. "Samuel? What's wrong with you? Are you okay? Your eyes—"

"We don't want to hurt you," Daniel said in a low voice just above a whisper. "But you cannot be insulting your bruvvers."

Elena heard a sizzling sound. Like something frying on the stove. It took her a long moment to realize the crackling and sizzling came from Samuel's glowing red eyes.

And then she felt the searing heat on her forehead, lowering over her face.

"Oww! That *burns*! Stop it! Stop it!"

And Ruth-Ann was screaming, too. The two of them screaming in pain as Samuel glared from one to the other, and the scorching heat pierced their skin.

"Stop! It hurts! Stop it! You're *burning* me!"

54

Lea yawned and dropped her bag on the blue granite kitchen counter. She shook out her hair. "God, I'm tired."

Mark tossed the car keys beside her bag. "It was an interesting group of people."

"Interesting makes me tired." She kicked off her shoes.

He brushed his lips against her cheek. She could smell the wine on his breath. "At least I got you away from that laptop for a few hours."

She made an ugly face. Then she pulled a bottle of Poland Spring water from the fridge and took a long drink.

Mark decided to change the subject. He didn't want to bring up the twins again. He'd been thinking about them all night. He knew he had to handle the problem on his own. It was so impossible to talk to her about them.

I'm still feeling the wine. Maybe I should wait till morning.

"Huntley had some good jokes." He started to unbutton his Hawaiian shirt. "The *Wall Street* guys always hear the best jokes. I always wonder where they come from."

"Where jokes come from?"

He nodded. "Yeah. They don't just spring up from nowhere."

"Boring," she murmured. She capped the water bottle and set it down on the counter.

He put on a fake pout. "Boring? You think I'm boring?"

"You're not boring, sweetheart. Jokes are boring. I mean, all you can do is laugh at them. That's not interesting." She pulled off her silver bracelet and shook her hand as if it had been too tight. "What I can't understand is why Nestor keeps all that African art in a summerhouse. I mean, really."

"I don't think that's strange, Lea. He just likes to have it around him. If you were into collecting African art, you'd want to be able to see it. Besides, he said his apartment in the city is filled up. He doesn't have any room left."

"But he's taking a hell of a risk, Mark. Anyone could break into his house when he's away in the city. It's all glass. And some of that art is valuable. The death masks—"

"Those are so interesting. Scary, really. The white carved ones. I wouldn't want them on the wall staring at me all day."

"They're not carved, actually. They're molded. Molded on the dead person's face after he dies."

"Oh, I forgot." Mark took the water bottle and twirled it between his hands. "You're the expert on death rituals now."

She slapped his wrist gently. "Don't make fun of me, sweetheart. You know, some tribes believed you could communicate with the dead person through the mask. The dead spirit was on the other side, but the mask was on *this* side, so you could talk through it. Sometimes, the mask was to protect the dead person from evil spirits. You know, disguise him so the evil spirits wouldn't recognize him. It's kind of how Halloween masks started."

"Lea, why are you doing all this research into death rituals? Tell me."

"It's what I'm interested in now. Can't you accept that?"

He rubbed his hand over his face. "Know any good jokes?" He dodged away so she couldn't slap him.

Lea yawned again and stretched her arms at her sides. "It's late. We should get to bed. I have a lot of writing to do tomorrow. I—"

Elena entered, carrying a balled-up bedsheet and pillow. Ruth-

Ann followed, arms loaded down with jeans and tops and other clothes.

Lea blinked as if she was seeing a mirage. The girls didn't offer a greeting. They moved past Lea and Mark on their way to the kitchen door.

"Where are you going?" Lea finally managed to say.

"Out back," Elena replied without turning around.

"Why?"

"Don't you say hello? Are we invisible or something?" Mark said.

"Hello," Elena offered. She shifted the bedclothes in her arms.

"Come back," Lea said. She shut her eyes. "Explain this to me." She opened them and squinted at her daughter. "You're taking all that stuff out back because—?"

"Moving in with our brothers."

"No, you're not," Mark said sharply. "You're definitely not."

"Both of you?" Lea squinted at them, confused.

"Are you crazy?" Mark's voice slid up a few octaves. Then he saw the blue arrows. "Huh? Oh my God! No! You too? I don't believe it. What is this about?"

Elena moved a hand up to the arrow on her cheek. "It's just a symbol. You know, *Dad*." *Dad* said as a word of disgust.

Mark shook his head. "No. I don't know." Through gritted teeth. "Tell me. Why did you let them put those arrows on your faces?"

Lea took another long drink from the water bottle.

"We want to move *up*," Ruth-Ann said. She tucked her chin over the ball of clothing she carried. "That's all. No big deal."

"No big deal?" Mark cried. "It *is* a big deal. Believe me. It's a big deal." He shook his finger at Elena. "You will *not* be moving back there with the boys. You will be staying in your room. Of all the stupid, crazy ideas. I thought you were the sensible one."

"I *am*!" Elena insisted with all the nastiness she could get into her voice.

"No arguing. No more talk. Take that stuff back upstairs to your room."

"Let's pretend this never happened," Lea said quietly.

Those words seemed to send a shock wave through the air. The girls froze, wide-eyed. Mark felt it, too.

Pretend it never happened?

But what was actually happening?

Don't we have to hear an explanation? We can't just pretend it didn't happen.

"Come back here. I mean it!" Mark cried.

But the girls were out the door. Mark could hear loud music and laughter from the guesthouse. The door slammed behind them, the window glass rattling.

The sound made Lea gasp. "Mark—what is going on?"

"It's . . . the twins."

"There you go again. The twins. The twins. How can you blame the twins if these two girls—"

"I could storm out there and yell and scream and send everyone home," he said. "But I'm kind of drunk, Lea. And I think maybe if we get calm first—"

"Get calm?"

"If we go screaming after Elena and Ruth-Ann and threaten to physically pull them back to the house, it's war. And we're the ones starting it. We need to be the adults here. I need to talk to the twins. But I need to go into the house and be the calm, reasonable one."

"Do you hear all the voices out there? It sounds like a mob. How can there be *room* for them all in that tiny guesthouse!" she said.

The kitchen phone rang. The sound made them both jump. Lea glanced at the clock above the sink. Nearly midnight. Who would be calling this late?

Mark made a move toward the phone but let her reach it first.

She recognized the voice of one of the class parents. Alecia Morgan. She sounded agitated. "Lea, is Justin over there? Is he with you?"

She hesitated. "I . . . don't think so. Was he—"

"He said he was going over to Ira's. He was supposed to call so we could pick him up. I've been calling him since nine-thirty, but I only get his voice mail."

"The boys are out back," Lea said, staring hard at Mark. He was mouthing something but she couldn't understand him. "In our guesthouse. They like having their own little hideaway."

The woman's voice turned cold. "I just want to know if he's there and why I haven't heard from him."

"I'll check. I—" A long beep. "Uh-oh. I'm getting another call. I'll get Justin and tell him to call you."

"Lea, wasn't anyone supervising them?"

Lea cut off the call without answering her.

"Mark, go see if Justin Morgan is out back with the boys."

He nodded and started to the door. But stopped to listen to the next conversation.

"Your daughter?" Lea made a shrugging motion to Mark. "Debra? No. I don't think so, Mrs. Robbins. Elena is having a sleepover with Ruth-Ann. But I don't think—"

"Would you check, please?" The woman's voice quavered. "I'm going out of my mind. She was supposed to be home three hours ago."

"Well, of course I'll check. Do you want to hold on? I'll—"

The doorbell chimed.

"I can't believe Roz can sleep through this," Mark muttered.

Lea waved him to the front door. She told Mrs. Morgan she'd call her back. When she stepped into the front hallway, Mark was talking with a smiling, middle-aged man in a gray running suit, a high forehead, square-shaped eyeglasses catching the entryway light.

"Oh, hi, Mrs. Sutter. I'm Steve Pearlmutter. Rex's father. Sorry I'm late picking him up. There was an accident on Noyac Road and the cars were backed up for over an hour. No way to turn around. Unbelievable."

Mark and Lea exchanged glances. *Rex Pearlmutter?*

Lea spoke up first. "Sorry you were stuck for so long. Let's go out back and find Rex." She turned and led the way to the kitchen. "It's been a crazy night. Our kids invited a lot of their friends over. I hope they haven't been too wild. Mark and I had to go out and—"

Pearlmutter's eyes grew large behind the square glasses. "You mean the kids aren't in the house?"

"They're right out back," Mark offered. "They love hanging out in the guesthouse."

Pearlmutter smiled. "We didn't have a guesthouse when I was a kid. My friends and I had to play in the basement."

"Is your son in Ira's class?" Lea asked, pulling open the back door.

Pearlmutter nodded. "Yes. And I think they know each other from tennis camp."

Mark shook his head. "Ira only lasted a few days at tennis camp. It was too rigorous for him. He got blisters."

"They worked them pretty hard," Pearlmutter agreed. "But Rex learned a lot. Really improved his technique." He laughed. "He's only twelve and he can pretty much keep up with me now."

They stepped outside. Low hedges clung to the back of the house. Rows of just-opened tiger lilies, bobbing in a light breeze, led the way along the path to the guesthouse.

Music blared from the guesthouse. Lea's bare feet sank in the dew-wet grass. The ground felt marshy even though it hadn't rained. She felt something brush over her feet. It scampered into the flowers, making them shake. A chipmunk? A mouse?

She raised her eyes to the guesthouse. The lights were all on. Two tall pine trees stood as sentinels on either side of the red wooden door. The light from the windows made their long shadows loom over the yard.

"Pretty loud in there," Mark murmured.

"They like their music loud," Pearlmutter offered. "We used to—right?"

"I guess you're right," Mark said.

"Rex is usually an early bird," his father said. "He uses up so much energy during the day, he's exhausted by eight-thirty or nine. Staying up past midnight is a special treat for him."

Lea stopped at the door. She had a heavy feeling in the pit of her stomach. She thought of Elena and Ruth-Ann. And who was the other girl? Debra Robbins?

Why would these snobby, sarcastic fourteen-year-old girls want to hang out with a bunch of immature twelve-year-old boys? Did that make any sense?

No.

And the blue arrows on their faces. Would fourteen-year-old girls really want to join a club for elementary school kids?

These thoughts made her hesitate with her hand on the brass doorknob. "Should we knock first?"

"Let's go in, see what they're up to," Mark said, motioning with his head.

Pearlmutter snickered. "Catch 'em in the act."

Lea pushed open the door. Music roared out. Bright yellow light spilled over them. The bedroom was in the front of the house. Behind it, a narrow hall had a bathroom and a long, thin dressing room on one side, a closet on the other.

"Oh, wow," Lea murmured, her eyes moving around the room. The bunk bed and the twin bed beside it had been stripped. Bare mattresses. No pillows. Nothing on the blue-green carpet. No clothes strewn about or tortilla chip bags or soda cans.

"Hello?" Mark called, squinting into the bright light. He moved quickly to the back of the room and swung open the hall door. "Hello?"

Lea's eyes went wide. She turned to Pearlmutter, whose knotted face revealed only confusion, and murmured in a voice that seemed to be coming from someone else, "There's no one here."

55

Saturday morning, Samuel followed Daniel onto a pale blue local Hamptons bus that took them on the old Montauk Highway to Hampton Bays. It was a warm, sunny morning, one of those beautiful May mornings with no humidity and the sweet fragrance of spring flowers in the air.

Samuel gazed out the window as they passed a green college campus. The sign said: Stonybrook Southampton. Trees were just sprouting leaves and the lilac bushes were spreading their violet flowers.

How good to be among the living, Samuel thought.

Living is so special.

Deep thoughts for a Saturday morning as the bus bumped along the narrow two-lane road, twisting past an inlet of the ocean now, sparkling waters under the clearest of blue skies.

What a shame. What a shame.

Samuel wished his brother could enjoy being among the living as much as he did. If only Daniel had the same appreciation for the spring air and the delightful aromas, the brightness of the morning, and that special vibrant green on the trees you see only in springtime.

But Daniel had a different agenda. And, of course, it had to be

Samuel's agenda as well. For he was the Burner, the Fire Man, the Punisher. And as sure as the lilacs opened every spring, Daniel had people to punish.

If Daniel could use his hypnotic powers without help, Samuel would be content to watch. And yes, enjoy. But wherever the power came from—Hell, most likely—it joined the two of them together the way no twins had ever been joined.

The bus bounced along the highway, past a model of an Indian teepee and a cigarette trading post. Some kind of Indian reservation, probably.

Samuel read somewhere that all this land had belonged to an Indian tribe. Now their territory seemed to be squashed down to a cigarette store on the old highway.

The road turned. They were rumbling through a suburban neighborhood of nice houses. The sun and the sky appeared brighter here.

Samuel and Daniel sat two seats from the back. No one else on the bus except for an elderly woman in the front seat, sound asleep with her head bobbing against the window.

Samuel thought about the big move. It had gone smoothly. And was very timely, since Mum and Pa had arrived home earlier than expected. Now they had room to spread out. And room to welcome the dozens of new kids flocking to them in order to move Up with Sag Harbor Middle School.

Monday will be the first hard day, Samuel knew.

We should rest up and enjoy our new home for the weekend. We should make sure that all the new minds are set. That the new followers are clear about the goal.

But no. Daniel had his other plans.

Pa had seen too much. Pa knew too much. Pa could ruin everything.

And so, it was important to keep Pa busy. Very busy.

And that's why it was so urgent and important to kill Autumn Holliday.

56

The twins found Autumn's house easily, on a street just off Dune Road near Hot Dog Beach. Set back on a small square of grass, it was a squat, two-story redbrick with white trim and white columns on either side of the front door.

The house was old and not very well kept up. One side had darkened, the bricks rutted and cracked. The paint was peeling from the two columns.

"Let's be quick, boyo," Daniel said. "We don't want to neglect the newbies, do we?"

They climbed onto the narrow stoop, up to the screen door. Samuel pushed the doorbell and they heard it buzz inside.

Footsteps. Then Autumn pulled open the door and stared through the screen at them.

"Huh? You two? Really?" Blue eyes wide with surprise.

"Hi," Daniel said shyly, smiling so his dimples would flash.

"Did you boys come all this way to see me? How did you find me? How did you get here?"

She pushed open the screen door before they could answer. Samuel followed Daniel into the small front room. He sniffed. The stale air smelled of coffee and cigarette smoke.

The brown leather couch on the back wall had a duct tape repair on one arm. He saw two folding chairs, a small flat-screen TV playing a cooking show. Fashion and gossip magazines were strewn over the low coffee table. A huge landscape painting of grassy sand dunes covered the wall over the couch.

"Not very fancy," Autumn said, as if reading his thoughts. "Not like *your* house. Oh, this stuff isn't ours." She gestured around the room. "My sister and I are renting the house just till we figure out what our lives are going to be about. Oh, wow. I wish Summer was here. I'd love for her to meet you guys. I've told her all about you. But she's in the city this weekend."

"Your sister's name is Summer?" Daniel asked.

She nodded. "Yeah. Autumn and Summer. Do you believe my parents? Good thing I don't have a brother. Spring is such a bad-news name for a guy." She giggled.

She's a beautiful girl. Too bad. Oh lordy, too bad.

Autumn's white-blond hair was like a smooth helmet, parted in the middle and cascading down to her shoulders. She wore a blue midriff top that matched her eyes and revealed several inches of creamy white skin, down to the red short shorts that showed off her long, slender legs.

Samuel's eyes stopped at the red shoes. They were velvety with red straps at the top, had tall spiked heels, at least four or five inches high, and thick platform soles.

"You're a giant!" Samuel blurted out.

She giggled again. "Are these *awesome*? I was just trying them on when you arrived." She pointed to the shoe box on the floor beside the coffee table. "They're sooo expensive."

She did some awkward strutting. The heels made tiny round imprints in the faded brown carpet. "This takes practice. It's like being in the circus. You know. A balancing act."

"They're pretty," Samuel murmured.

Daniel glared at him. They had a job to do.

"How did you boys get here?" She ruffled her hand through Daniel's hair as she made her way to the couch, tilting one way, then the other. Finally, she dropped onto the edge of the brown cushion.

"Bus," Daniel said, smoothing his hair back into place.

"Do your parents know you came all this way by yourselves?"

"I don't think so." Daniel's reply.

Autumn fiddled with the straps on one of the shoes. "So why did you come? Just to visit? For an adventure? That's so nice of you."

"No. We came to kill you."

Subtle, Daniel. Always the subtle lad.

Autumn let go of the red straps and raised her eyes to Daniel. "What did you say?"

Samuel clenched his jaw tight and started the fire in his eyes. He felt the warmth immediately. The light changed as if he were viewing the room through a filmy red filter. The warmth washed down his neck, his back, a rippling heat that swept over his whole body.

"We came to kill you," Daniel repeated, his face blank, eyes trained on hers.

Autumn giggled. "Why would you kill *me*? Is this a game? Something for school? No. A war game?"

"You did bad things with Pa," Daniel said, taking a step toward her. "We saw you."

Autumn didn't giggle this time. Her face creased as she narrowed her eyes at Daniel. She was beginning to realize he was serious.

"You—you two were watching us?" She stood up, awkwardly on the tall, spiked shoes. Grabbed the taped arm of the couch for support. "Really? You're serious? You were spying on us?"

Samuel blinked as the red before his eyes pulsed and began to sizzle.

"We saw you," Daniel said quietly. "You did a bad thing with Pa."

Autumn's mouth curled in anger. "That's none of your business. How is that your business? You're a kid. You don't know anything about grown-ups. Did you really come all the way here to tell me you were spying on me?"

"Now we have to do a bad thing to Pa," Daniel said.

"Listen, you don't know what you're saying," Autumn told him, hands on the waist of her shorts. "You're just a kid. You don't have to worry about any of this. You got yourself all stressed out over nothing."

She started to walk past him toward the front door. "I think you two have to leave now. And don't tell your parents—"

She stopped midsentence when she saw Samuel's eyes, and her mouth dropped open. Startled, she stumbled and backed into the wall.

"Samuel? What's wrong? Your eyes—"

"We have to do a bad thing to Pa," Daniel repeated. "It's important. You have to burn."

"No—wait! What's going on? What are you *doing*?" She pressed her back against the wall and raised her hands as if preparing to fight as Samuel moved close.

He raised his eyes to her and steadied his fiery gaze on her throat.

She uttered a cry. Grabbed her throat with both hands.

"Stop it! That *hurts*! Are you fucking *weird*?"

She pressed her hands around her throat. Samuel raised his eyes to her forehead. The heat crackled like electric current.

Still gripping her throat, she ducked her head. Slid down against the wall, struggling to avoid the painful attack.

"Stop! You fucking weirdo! Damn it! Damn!" She sank to the floor, covering her face.

Samuel aimed the red beam at the top of her head.

Beside him, Daniel watched, unblinking, his smile gleeful, hands balled into fists, thumping the air as if cheering his brother on at some kind of sports event.

"Damn! Damn! You're *hurting* me! Damn it! Stop! Fuck you!"

Samuel the Punisher, the Fire Man, Samuel the *Avenger* aimed the beam at the part in her hair. He saw a line on her scalp darken, saw the hair along the part blacken in the scorching heat. Saw the darkening skin start to peel open.

So sorry to make a big hole in such a pretty head.

Autumn, you are the prettiest one yet. So sorry it didn't help you survive.

You were so pretty and so bad.

Rolled into a tight ball, Autumn had stopped screaming. When she made her move, it was a blur of motion to Samuel. He stared down at her through the thick, pulsating curtain of red. He could see vague shapes and the direction of his heat beam. But he didn't see clearly enough when Autumn suddenly untucked herself.

Grunting like an animal, she made a wild grab at her foot, slapping at it, fumbling frantically. With a hoarse cry, she tugged off one of the red shoes.

Then she rose to her feet, her hair smoking, thrusting the shoe above her head.

"Look out, boyo!"

Daniel's warning came too late.

Samuel's vision was a blur of red.

Eyes wild, hair burning, Autumn lunged toward Samuel. She gripped the shoe by the toe with the spiked heel pointing out.

Like a sword blade. That was his thought as she swung it down on him. Plunged it down with all her strength, aiming for his eye.

He saw the long spike driving toward his face. And then felt Daniel push him, shove him back. He stumbled.

The heel missed his face—and she drove it deep into his chest.

Samuel saw it in slow motion. Saw it puncture his shirt. Felt it dig into the skin. Felt it. Felt it. Felt it slice into the tender spot just below his rib cage.

He dropped to his knees. The red curtain faded from his eyes. Everything went black for a moment, then his vision quickly returned.

The shoe hung tight to his chest. The spiked heel had been driven all the way in. He gripped it in one hand and watched Autumn stumble to the front door, staggering on one shoe.

Daniel made a grab for her. Missed. She hurtled through the screen door and dove screaming into the street.

The screen door slammed behind her.

Daniel started to the door, then thought better of it, and turned back to his brother, Samuel on his knees on the carpet. Daniel's eyes were wild. His whole body trembled.

"Sammy, what are we going to do? She got away."

57

"No, she didn't," Samuel told his brother. "No one escapes me. She's as good as dead, boyo."

He saw the panic on his brother's face. He knew he had to be brave, put on a good front. Daniel had never encountered failure. It frightened Samuel to think how his twin might handle such disappointment.

Samuel could still hear her screams out in the street. He motioned with his head to the shoe. "Help me."

Daniel hesitated for a moment, his face locked in horror. Then he wrapped his hands around the heel of the shoe—and pulled it out of his twin's chest.

It slid out easily, making a *sssllliick* sound like pulling a spoon out of a jelly jar.

Daniel tossed the shoe across the floor. Then he smoothed down the front of Samuel's T-shirt. "Afraid you've got a hole in your shirt, bruvver."

Samuel jumped to his feet. "Let's go."

"Whistle while we work," Daniel said. He whistled a short tune. *Daniel being Daniel.*

They burst out through the screen door together. Jumped off the stoop. Samuel saw Daniel remove something from his jeans pocket and drop it beside the steps.

The morning sun was high over the shingled roofs of the little houses that lined the street. Houses not much bigger than cottages. Each with a trimmed square lawn. An SUV parked in the driveway.

Not a fancy Hamptons neighborhood, Samuel thought as they took off running in the direction of the shrill screams. *This is where the workers live.*

Saturday morning and everyone must be sleeping in, for there was not a person in sight. Oh, yes. A man in khaki shorts watering his flower garden with a hose in the next block. A small brown dog sniffing around him.

Samuel saw Autumn pounding frantically on the front door of a small brick house down the block. No one answered. She leaped off the front stoop and, screaming all the way, fled into a sandy, pebbly alley lined by wooden fences that snaked behind the houses.

"Nice of Autumn to scream like that and let us know where she is going," said Daniel, trotting beside his brother, eyes straight ahead.

"She's a nice girl." Samuel's earnest reply.

They caught up with her behind a stack of blue and yellow boogie boards tilting against a wood picket fence. The boards formed a low tent. Autumn probably thought she would be hidden by them.

They found her huddled behind the boards, her body hunched and shaking, her breath coming in loud wheezes.

Panting like a dog. Like a cornered dog.

Samuel set his eyes to glowing. He felt anger now and new dedication to the task. No hesitation.

Did she really think she could wound the Avenger? The Heater? Punish the Punisher?

"Please . . . Oh, please . . . please . . ." She was begging now. Actually wringing her hands in front of her. She climbed to her feet. "Please?"

Samuel trained his gaze on the white skin of her tummy between the top and her low-riding shorts.

She shrieked in shock and agonizing pain as he cut a long line across the bottom of her stomach. Reflexively, Autumn grabbed at the deep opening in her skin and spread both hands over it.

But she couldn't keep her insides from spilling out.

The twins watched in intent silence, as if watching a medical demonstration, as her intestines came sliding out over her hands and poured like long pink sausage links to the ground.

She made a hoarse choking sound, grabbing frantically at the waterfall of shiny wet organs spilling out. Spilling out of the deep slit across her belly. A gusher of pink and yellow sausage oozing through her fingers.

She choked and gagged until her eyes rolled up and her knees folded and she slumped face forward with a loud *splaaat* into the still-throbbing puddle of her insides.

The twins gazed down at her in solemn silence.

Samuel waited for his eyes to cool. Then he stepped back, let out a sigh, and called down to her, "Oh, poor Autumn. Lassie, where are those beautiful new shoes now?"

Daniel laughed and gave him a shove. "You're a poet." He stared down at the young dead woman. His smile faded. "You know, bruvver, we don't have to worry about Pa now."

That made Samuel laugh. "I think Pa is deep in trouble," he said softly. "Come on, bruvver. Let's find our way back to the Harbor of Sag."

"A poet," Daniel murmured. "My bruvver is a poet."

It was a beautiful morning, just starting to warm up, the air so fragrant and fresh. White butterflies danced over a flowering hedge. A soft breeze tickled his skin and cooled Samuel's hot face.

It made him think of the island. The ocean breezes over Cape Le Chat Noir. The simple life. Waves splashing as he and Daniel and Ikey ran along the cool, wet sand.

"I think the bus stop is over here," he told Daniel. "It's such a pretty day. I know we're going to have a nice ride."

58

When Lea's Skype bell rang on Saturday morning, she was tempted not to answer it. But when she saw it was Martha calling from Cape Le Chat Noir, her curiosity won out over her weariness.

She clicked to take the call, and a second later, Martha's pale blue eyes gazed out at her from the laptop screen. Martha's short blond hair was wrapped in a colorful kerchief, but her face appeared pale and lined, and she wasn't smiling.

"Martha? What a surprise." Lea adjusted the laptop to get her face in the frame.

"How are you, Lea? Is this too early?"

"Well, no. Actually, I'm still up from last night. Look at me. I'm still dressed in yesterday's clothes. I . . . didn't get any sleep."

"Well, I'm sorry to call so early."

"That's okay. Really. It's nice to see you. We haven't been in touch for a few weeks."

"You look awful, Lea. What's going on there? Why were you up all night? Is everything okay?"

Martha's image froze on the screen. Her face didn't move but her voice continued. Then the screen popped, and her mouth caught up with her words.

Lea sighed. She rubbed her eyes with her finger and thumb. "It's a long story, Martha. What a horrible night."

"Why? What on earth happened?"

"The kids are gone. I mean, disappeared."

Martha's mouth dropped open. The screen stopped again with her face frozen in her startled expression.

"You mean the twins? You can't find them?"

"No. All the kids." The words tumbled out of Lea in a trembling voice. "The twins. Ira. Elena. Her friend. And a lot of other kids." She sucked in a deep breath. "Oh, Martha. I don't know what's happening!"

"I don't understand, Lea. You called the police?"

A bitter laugh escaped Lea's throat. "Oh, yes. The police have been here. Local police. State police. The FBI. They've been here all night, Martha. All night asking Mark and Roz and me questions. Questions. Like it's our fault. Like we're hiding something from them. Like we know something we're not telling."

"Oh, wow. It sounds like hell. Do you want me to get off? I could Skype you some other time. Or I could email—"

"No, it's fine. Actually, it's good to have a friend to talk to. I can't see straight I'm so frazzled and worn out. But it's good to have a friend."

"Well, where do they think your kids are? Do they think—"

"It's not just my kids. There are maybe seventy or eighty kids missing in Sag Harbor, Martha."

"Huh? That's *insane*."

Lea rolled her eyes. "Insane but true. At first the police thought it started here. You see, a bunch of kids were hanging out in our guesthouse in back."

"Seventy?"

"No, not seventy. A few. Several. I . . . don't know. Mark and I went out last night and—"

"Are you sure you want to tell me all this now? You look so tired and—"

"I don't understand it, Martha. They're just *gone*. Where would they go? How could they all sneak off together? It can't be a mass kidnapping. Whoever heard of that?"

"What do the police think? The FBI?"

"At first they didn't believe us. There's been some other trouble here. With Mark. And we had all these totally upset parents calling us and coming over. All night. Expecting Mark and me to know where their kids were. Angry at us. I mean, they blamed us for . . . for . . ."

"And no trace of any of them? No clues at all?"

"Not yet. The Sag Harbor police station—they started getting call after call. All from frantic parents reporting their kids were missing. So they finally caught on it wasn't just Mark and me. It was happening all over town."

"And so—"

"But that didn't stop them from searching our house. And tearing up the guesthouse. I don't know what kind of clues they expected to find. A map leading them to the kids? A ransom note for seventy kids? I—I—"

"Take a breath, dear. This must be so *horrible* for you. I can't believe what you are going through."

"No, you can't." Lea wrung her hands. "Elena is so sensible. I can't imagine . . ."

"Well, I'm sure they'll all be found soon. Such a big group of kids can't stay hidden for long, can they?" Martha leaned toward the camera. "Have the police considered this might be a big prank?"

"Huh? A prank?"

"You know. One of those mass jokes people dream up and spread over the internet?"

Lea shut her eyes. "No. No one is treating it as a joke," she said in a whisper.

"Well, I don't think I'm going to tell you why I Skyped," Martha said, rubbing her cheek. "Oh, wait. Maybe I'd better. Actually, as I think about it, what I called to show you might help."

Lea swallowed. Her throat felt dry as dust. "Help?"

Martha nodded. "I've been doing some photo research. You

know. That's what I do for a living. I promised you I'd do some checking."

Lea nodded. "I remember. Did you find something interesting?"

"Interesting, yes," Martha replied. "But not good news, Lea. In fact, it's totally disturbing."

Lea rolled her eyes. "Oh my God, Martha, what did you find out?"

"Let me email you the photos. I think you'll understand why I wanted you to see them right away."

"Okay. Send them to my gmail account, Martha. We can talk about them as I look at them. But what did you find? What is so disturbing?"

"Just wait. I'm sending them now. There are three JPEGs in all."

Lea watched Martha's fingers move over her keyboard. Her expression was tense, almost bitter.

"I'm really sorry to burden you with this, Lea. Especially with the hell you're going through. I hate being the messenger, really. James and I care about you. We think you did such a brave thing. I mean, adopting those boys. But you need to see these photos."

Martha blinked and typed some more. "Also, James and I . . . we kept something from you. We kept a big secret. We thought you'd be better off not knowing. We did it for your happiness, Lea. But the secret . . . I guess I just have to come out and say it. It's making us feel too guilty."

"What the hell, Martha? What are you talking about? Such a big fucking mystery? Maybe this isn't the best time. I—"

"Did you get the photos, Lea? You should have gotten them by now. Check your email. I'll just wait."

Lea slid the mouse and opened her in-box. Yes. There was the email from Martha.

Lea clicked twice to open the attachments. She waited for them to download, watching the little line slide across the screen. Her heart started to pound.

She clicked again, the Picasa program came to life, and a thumbnail photo appeared on the screen. She clicked it. And watched as it sprang up full-size.

A black-and-white photo. A beach scene? No. "Is it Cape Le Chat Noir?"

"Yes." Martha's reply in a soft voice.

"Oh, wow. I see. It's after the hurricane. All the houses are down. And the trees. I see."

She saw several forlorn people huddled in the background, fuzzy and out of focus. And near the camera . . . Standing together, one with his hand around the other's shoulder . . . Yes. The twins.

No mistaking them. Daniel and Samuel standing close together, surrounded by the hurricane's destruction.

"Martha, I see the twins."

"Take a good look, Lea."

"I *am* taking a good look. The twins are standing there together after the hurricane. They're holding on to each other and looking very alone and forlorn."

Her eyes scanned the photo. "I don't see anything else, Martha. Am I missing something? Why is this photo interesting?"

"Well, do you notice the photo is in black-and-white?"

"Yes. So?"

"It wasn't taken after the hurricane here last month, Lea."

"I don't understand."

"The photo was taken in 1935. The day after the hurricane of 1935."

59

The morning went by in a blur, and even two cups of strong black coffee at eleven didn't wake Mark's mind. Half an hour earlier, he had lifted his head, not recognizing where he was.

It took him a few seconds to remember he had fallen asleep after five in the morning on the couch in the den, the soft couch, his favorite napping couch, in the clothes he had worn to Nestor Bridger's house.

The police. The angry, frightened parents. They hadn't left till five. And then, his head throbbing, he had collapsed on the couch.

But who could sleep with Ira and Elena and the twins gone—missing—and at least seventy other children, and after an endless night of the phone ringing nonstop with frantic parents at the other end, and police and FBI and who-knows-what invading every corner of his house. And the questions . . . the accusing stares.

Could they possibly think he had kidnapped seventy kids? Where would he keep them? In the basement? In an upstairs closet?

Somewhere around three in the morning, they asked if he wanted a lawyer. He'd gone into a long rant—he should have held it in—but the wine and the exhaustion, not to mention the anxiety, made him open up and tell them how stupid they were to think he had any answers or anything helpful to say or anything to do with the disappearance of the kids.

Maybe his rant encouraged them to leave. No. Now he remembered. More angry, frightened parents showed up at the door, and the round of questions grew even more intense.

He pictured the two Sag Harbor officers he'd become very acquainted with, Pavano and Pinto. They'd been pushed to the back. Too low on the ladder to speak, they watched the whole thing, leaning against the living room wall, occasionally muttering among themselves as their superiors—who was that big guy, Franks, who paraded back and forth with his Glock hanging out of its holster?—asked all the questions.

The officers and agents didn't leave until after five. Mark sprawled fitfully on the worn-soft couch, the questions tumbling through his mind, struggling to think clearly about a theory of his own. It wasn't forthcoming. He didn't have a clue.

He was just as puzzled upon waking up. And where was Lea? A glance at the clock. Ten-thirty. *This is Saturday, right?*

She must be up in our room. Can she sleep? This is late for her not to be downstairs.

Rubbing the dark stubble on his cheeks, he shuffled into the kitchen for coffee, feeling stiff and not at all rested and in need of a shower. He squinted at a note in Roz's handwriting: *Axl upset by all the noise last night. Took him to the beach. Home after lunch. Have my phone. Call with any news.*

"No news, Roz."

He peered through the kitchen window at the guesthouse. Dark and silent.

His eyes burned. He suddenly craved a cigarette. Crazy. He hadn't smoked since college.

Don't be crazy. Don't give in. You have to be the sane one.

Lea printed out the three photos and sat at her desk gazing at them over and over. The first two—the twelve-year-old twins in 1935—came as a frightening shock.

The twins were twelve in 1935 and twelve today. Cape Le Chat

Noir . . . It's the island where the living coexist with the living dead.

"It can't be! Oh, shit. Oh, shit. Please. It can't be true!"

She sat in the glare of the monitor, gazing from one photo to the other, screaming at them without even hearing herself. Screaming at the beautiful twelve-year-old twins. Beautiful more than seventy-five years ago. Beautiful today.

"Oh, shit. Oh, shit. I brought them here. Martha warned me. Mark warned me. Oh, shit. It's all my fault." And then: "But I care about them. They *made* me care about them."

She slammed the two printouts onto the desk and gazed at the third one. This photo was *not* a surprise. She had suspected it. She prayed and prayed it wasn't true. But somehow, all along, Lea knew.

Martha had signed off, and her apologies reverberated in Lea's mind.

"So sorry. Really so sorry. I think I warned you not to rush into adopting those boys. I just had the feeling there was something *off* about them."

Not much of an apology, really. Of course, Martha was sorry for the way things turned out—*not* sorry for providing Lea with the truth.

And what did she mean by something *off* about them? Martha said she would send an email—immediately—with all the information she had been able to dig up about the boys. "It's not good news, Lea. I'm so sorry. I wish it weren't true. I'll send it right now."

And as for the third photo, Lea could see even on the grainy Skype image how uncomfortable it made Martha and how reluctant she was to discuss it at all.

"James and I hoped we were doing the right thing."

After that, Martha made an excuse to end the conversation. And repeated her apology, sounding a little more heartfelt this time. "I only wish . . ." No finish to that sentence. And then she was gone, and Lea sat in front of the screen, her eyes shut tight, but not tight enough to keep the pictures from her mind.

And things began to come clear, began to connect, starting with the twins, and moving to the murder in the driveway and the murder of Derek Saltzman and the disappearance of Ira and Elena and some seventy other kids.

Starting with the twins, who weren't really twelve. The twins, who had to be ungodly evil creatures she had brought home with her.

Was it coming clear? Did she have the connections right? It wasn't like she was blaming two innocent, adorable boys with such glowing blond hair and twinkling blue eyes. She wasn't condemning angels. She was starting to see demons.

But I care about them. I have such strong feelings for them.

And then Martha's email arrived, confirming her worst, most terrifying fears.

She couldn't read it all. Her eyes blurred the words. She didn't want to know the truth. Not *this* truth. She scanned through it, catching phrases that made her heart skip.

. . . Both died in the hurricane. The priest was summoned to perform the Revenir rite.

. . . The priest came too late. They'd been dead too long. He should never have revived them.

. . . They brought the evil of the grave back with them.

. . . They can kill. They can hypnotize. Like their bodies, their minds never advanced. They are still twelve.

. . . They lived in isolation on the island. People were afraid of them. They lived by stealing. No one was brave enough to stop them. They waited all these years for someone to take them away.

. . . They hate adults. They only care about controlling other children. They never got to be real children. So now they want to be leaders of children . . . To hold power over children . . . The only thing they care about . . .

Lea shut her eyes. "Oh, shit. Oh, shit. It's too much. It's all too horrifying. What will happen to Ira and Elena? How can I face Mark? How?"

Martha's words brought another revelation. The thought had been lurking in her mind. The email suddenly forced it to her consciousness. *The twins hypnotized me. They used their powers on me. They made me care about them. My connection to them . . .*

that feeling of love I thought I felt . . . it wasn't real. They used me. Used me to get here. No wonder I've agreed to their every wish. No wonder I never opposed them. . . .

She opened her eyes and shuffled through the three printouts again, as if hoping to see something she missed. Something redeeming. But there was no reassurance here. The past—and her future—held only horror.

Oh, poor Ira and Elena. Maybe there was time to rescue them. She *had* to try.

Carefully, she folded the three photos in half. She tucked them into the big pocket of her silky blue robe.

She heard a cough. Was that Mark stirring downstairs? The aroma of coffee made her stand up. She stretched her arms over her head.

Yes, she could feel her heart like a hummingbird in her chest. And the coffee aroma suddenly nauseated her.

Mark has to know.

She glanced at the clock on the bed table. Just past eleven. The morning had slipped past. But so what? What did a few hours matter when there was nothing to look forward to but more tears and grief and disbelief and anger and regret.

She moved to the dresser, adjusting the robe and tying it more securely, and picked up her hairbrush. She swept it back slowly through her straight black hair. It felt real. The touch of the bristles through her hair, the scrape against her scalp.

She brushed for a long time, leaning her head back, appreciating each stroke with a soft sigh. This was real. Nothing else in her life felt as real. Nothing else could be as real.

Oh, poor Elena. Poor Ira. What has Mommy done to you?

She forced herself to set the hairbrush down. Then she took a long, shuddering breath. She fingered the folded-up photos in her robe pocket and murmured out loud, "I'm going to tell Mark now."

Face the music, Lea.

Isn't that what her dad always said every time she had to be punished for some crime large or small?

You did the dance. Now face the music.

Did that make any sense at all?

The punishment was always the same: *Go to your room and stay there till I tell you to come out.*

She pictured her brothers smirking as she trudged off to her room, red-faced, fists swinging at her sides, ready to face the music.

Well, after all the years, now she was *really* facing the music.

She started to the stairs but stopped at the bedroom door when she heard the sirens. Approaching sirens, and there seemed to be a lot of them, a blaring concert of sirens, warring with each other.

Lea spun around and trotted to the bedroom window.

Several dark vehicles squealed up the gravel driveway. She saw the yellow letters *FBI* stenciled on one SUV. Two Sag Harbor black-and-whites, two unmarked SUVs, windows blackened, heavy like armored cars.

She gripped the windowsill and stared down at them all, her mouth hanging open, uttering small cries of shock.

Four or five dark-uniformed policemen lined up in front of the house, standing stiffly a few feet abreast of each other, weapons tensed in front of them. Were those automatic rifles?

She recognized the big black state police captain from the night before as he came roaring out of the backseat of an SUV. Was his name Franks? Yes. He had a pistol in one hand and motioned to the others leaping from their vehicles to follow him to the house.

They all had guns raised. All of them.

Do they plan to kill us?

"Mark?" Lea screamed, squeezing the wooden windowsill. "Mark! Do you hear them?"

Finally, she forced herself away from the window. She spun to the doorway, her robe tangling around her. And went running to the stairs.

"Mark! Can you hear me? Mark? What do they *want*?"

60

At first Mark thought people were screaming. The sound made him drop his coffee mug on the kitchen table. And as he hurried to the front of the house, he realized they were sirens.

And, strangely, the wailing cacophony made him angry. Because they had just been there, just invaded his house and his life, and he didn't want them back with their foolish accusations and misguided questions and insulting stares.

I'm sick of the bullshit. I just want my kids to be safe.

Why are they back here? What are they doing to find my kids?

Mark clenched his jaw tight and squeezed his fists until his fingernails dug into his palm. And then the pounding on the front door and the shouts shook him out of his anger.

He heard Lea calling his name. Turning, he saw her halfway down the stairs, her hand gripping the banister, her eyes wide with fright. "Mark?"

The pounding on the door drowned out the rest of her words.

"Mr. Sutter, police. Open the door." Barked. *Just like on TV.*

Mark pulled open the door. An army of men—it seemed like an army—led by Captain Franks, who came in with his shoulder low like an NFL blocking tackle, pushed into the house.

Mark stepped back, blinking at the force of it all. The sheer invasion. The anger. He saw the weapons raised. They forced him against the fireplace.

He heard Lea scream.

"Mark Sutter, you are under arrest for the murder of Autumn Holliday." Franks spitting the words in his face. Standing so close, Mark could smell the coffee on his breath.

"Huh? Autumn? What?"

Did the words make any sense?

Beside him, a wavy-haired cop was reading him his rights from the screen of an iPhone.

"Wait! Wait!" Mark raised his hands in the air.

The cops all tensed their weapons.

"What did you say?" His voice shrill, almost unrecognizable, shouting over the droning voice of the cop still reading off the phone screen.

"Did you say Autumn? Killed?"

He couldn't help it. He pictured her bent over his desk. Her hands gripping the edge of the desktop. That creamy white ass moving under him.

"Noooooooooo!" A howl of protest burst from deep inside.

Two cops stepped toward him menacingly, guns raised. He saw Pavano and Pinto holding back, still in the doorway, as if guarding against any escape attempt.

Were there cops outside in case he made a run for it?

What a joke. The child psychologist makes a run for it.

How could Autumn be dead? Why? Why Autumn? And why did they think he was the murderer?

"I—I can't . . . believe it." He felt sick. He grabbed his stomach. He felt the coffee rising up his throat. "Not Autumn."

He let out a long sigh, shut his eyes, and leaned back against the mantel.

"No. There's some mistake. Why are you arresting Mark?"

He heard Lea's trembling voice. Opened his eyes to see her step warily past Pavano and Pinto into the living room.

The officers ignored her and kept their eyes on Mark, weapons tensed.

"You don't have to answer any questions until you have a lawyer present," Franks said, the only calm voice in the room. "But you can help yourself by—"

"When was Autumn killed?" Mark interrupted, narrowing his eyes at Franks. "Last night? You know I was here all night. You were here with me."

"How was she killed?" Lea asked, moving up beside Mark, gripping his hand.

Her hand is ice cold. She's as terrified as I am.

"Our initial report says she was murdered this morning. Perhaps an hour or two ago." His dark eyes locked on Mark's, probing. "Mr. Sutter, if you'd care to cooperate. Could you tell us your whereabouts this morning?"

"Huh? My whereabouts?" The word didn't make sense to him. He knew he wasn't thinking clearly. The word didn't seem like English.

"Did you go out this morning?" Franks rephrased the question. This version sounded more like a threat.

"N-no. I was asleep. On the couch in the den. I woke up and made some coffee." Again he felt his stomach lurch. He held his breath, forcing it down.

"You didn't go out this morning?"

His answer came out in a sharp scream. "No. I fucking told you. I didn't go out. I've been in here all morning. Do I have to spell the fucking words for you?"

Franks didn't react. He turned his gaze on Lea, holding on tight to Mark's hand. "Mr. Sutter, can anyone vouch for your whereabouts? Can anyone confirm that you were here all morning?"

"Lea can."

Franks waited for Lea to speak up. Mark saw she was breathing hard. She'd gone very pale. "Actually, I was upstairs. In our bedroom. Mark was down here. But I know he didn't go anywhere this morning. You kept us up all night, remember?"

"So you were upstairs and didn't see him this morning?" Every question Franks asked sounded like an innuendo and a threat.

Mark gasped, startled by the anger that built up so instantly inside him.

You should be out finding my kids.

"I didn't see him," Lea started. "But—"

Behind Franks, a state cop dangled a pair of silvery handcuffs in front of him.

"You're wasting your time," Mark told him, unable to keep a trembling sneer from his face. "If someone murdered Autumn, the real killer is out there. And you're standing here arresting me, a child psychologist who's never even been in a fucking playground fight."

"Very eloquent," Franks commented drily. "Listen, Mr. Sutter, cooperate with us now and we can clear this up very quickly."

Mark blinked. "What are you talking about? What do I have to do?"

Lea let go of Mark's hand. "I'm going to go call Nestor." She turned to Franks. "He's our lawyer. He's in Sagaponack. I don't think Mark should say another word until he gets here."

"What do you want me to do?" Mark concentrated on Franks. "How do we clear this up? *Tell* me."

"Show us your wallet," Franks said. "That's all. Have you got your wallet, Mr. Sutter?"

"Of course I have my wallet."

Franks nodded. "Then will you be so kind as to show it to us?"

Mark thought hard. Where did he leave it? His brain was so churned up. His stomach rumbled with anger. He could feel every muscle in his body tensed and tight.

Where? Where?

"I left it on my desk last night." He started into the hall.

Two cops rushed forward and grabbed him roughly by the arms.

"We have to come with you," Franks said. "You're in our custody, remember?"

"I know I left it in my office." Mark let the two cops walk on either side of him. Franks followed right behind. "I can picture it next to the phone."

Into the office. A strong breeze rattling the blinds in front of the open window. Mark gazed at the desk.

Autumn, how can you be dead? Who would want you dead?

Autumn, you were so beautiful.

No wallet.

He fumbled his hand over the desktop. He shoved a stack of folders out of the way. He pulled open the desk drawer and shuffled through it.

Don't look frantic. Don't make them think you're frantic.

But he couldn't control his hands from shaking. Emotion had taken over. Rational thought always lost out to fear, to panic.

"I know I left it here yesterday. I was at my desk and I needed one of my credit cards to buy something over the phone and—"

"Do you want to search for it in any other room, Mr. Sutter?" Franks's deep voice, mellow and calm.

Sure, he's calm. What does he have to worry about? He's so pleased with himself, so pleased with his false arrest.

"Yes. Yes. Let me look for it upstairs. In the bedroom. Maybe I left it on the dresser. Sometimes I leave it there. I—"

"Can I save us some time?"

Franks's question made Mark spin away from the desk. He squinted at Franks. "Save time? What do you mean?"

One of the officers handed Franks a plastic bag. It looked like a food storage bag. Franks shoved it into Mark's face. Mark squinted at a wallet in the bag. "Is this yours?"

Mark reached for it, but Franks swiped it away from his hands. "No. No. Don't touch. It's evidence. Trust me. We saw your driver's license inside. Your AmEx card."

A dizziness fell over Mark. No. Not dizziness. Falling, a free fall. Like he was dropping down an endless black hole.

"Okay. That's my wallet."

Franks nodded to the cop at the office door. "Put the handcuffs on him." He turned back to Mark, shaking the wallet in front of Mark's face.

"Mr. Sutter, your wallet was found this morning in the grass next to Autumn Holliday's front stoop. My advice, sir: Don't say another word to me until your lawyer gets here."

61

As the solemn-faced cop moved forward raising the silvery hand-cuffs, Mark had one of those flashing-lifetime moments he had always believed to be only a staple of fiction.

The room grew dark and Franks and the other officers appeared to fade into the wallpaper. A white light formed like a glaring spot-light in his mind, and the images began to whir past—not of his childhood, not of the history of events that led him to this maddening moment.

In the two-second flash of bright light, the events of his *future* swept past him, a frenzied slide show of despair and ruin. He saw a clear picture of his office, now a closet piled high with cartons. His career over. The house empty. His family scattered. Bold newspaper headlines bannering his disgrace. He saw the sad faces of Ira and Elena, two hardened, disillusioned kids.

And Lea . . . Where was Lea? Gone? No picture of Lea?

And the last image of himself, handcuffed in a tiny gray prison cell, clanging the bars with the handcuffs, pounding out his anger, shouting, "But I'm innocent. I'm innocent!"

The light faded. The room came back into focus. And Mark, startled, found himself shouting, "But I'm innocent!"

"Wow. No one ever told us that before," Franks said.

Maybe it was Franks's sarcasm that set him off. Or maybe it was the frightening images of the future that flashed before him, almost like something in a science-fiction movie. Or maybe it was the burning outrage that was making it impossible for him to breathe.

This isn't right. I didn't murder anyone.

I couldn't murder anyone. I couldn't murder Hulenberger. I couldn't murder Autumn.

My kids are missing. My kids are in terrible danger.

Why are they arresting me? Why aren't they finding my kids?

Something clicked in his mind. He thought he heard the *snap.* It was too much. Too much. Without thinking, he started to move.

He saw Lea push her way past the cops in the doorway. And he heard her sharp cry: "It wasn't Mark! It was the *twins*!"

He heard her blame the twins. Yes, he heard her shout to the officers: "It was the twins." And he saw Lea pull some papers from her robe pocket.

But he couldn't stop himself to hear more. He was already moving. He already had the back of the desk chair gripped in both hands.

With an animal grunt, he gave the chair a hard shove. Thrust it forward on its metal wheels. Sent it skidding into the cop with the handcuffs.

He saw the seat cushion bounce into the cop's midsection. Heard the unsuspecting guy utter a startled groan and saw him toss his hands up, off-balance.

And then Mark dove to the open window. Both hands on the sill, he flung himself out, swung himself like some kind of circus acrobat.

Surprise, everyone!

He dropped onto his back on the hedge beneath the window. Scrambled like a turtle to right himself, arms and legs spiraling at once.

And yes, the element of surprise had helped him. No one was staring out of the window yet. As he forced himself to his feet, ignoring the bramble scratches on his back, his eyes gazed around the backyard. No cops back here. The idiots thought he would submit without any trouble to them.

He heard shouts and angry cries. Heard Franks's deep voice booming from the window. "Sutter—stop. Are you *crazy*? Stop or we'll shoot!"

But he was already around the side of the guesthouse, his sneakers pounding the hard ground, into the cluster of trees that bordered the yard. The ground sloped down, leading him into woods thick with ancient oak and sassafras trees, their fat trunks tilted and tangled and hugged by fat evergreen pines.

Every sense alert, his eyes darting to find a path through the thickening underbrush, Mark heard no shots. The shouts had faded far behind.

He couldn't think clearly. The rush of adrenaline and the blood pulsing so furiously at his temples kept his mind from focusing. He was an animal. An animal running to safety.

He leaped over a fallen trunk covered in green and yellow lichen. Pushed through two pine bushes, stumbled on the thick carpet of dead leaves under his shoes, caught his balance and kept running.

Small creatures scuttled out of his way. Chipmunks? Moles? Over the rushing in his ears, he heard the loud *caw* of birds high in the trees, and he imagined them calling to the police, reporting his location.

He realized he had never ventured into these woods behind his house. This was nature, the uncivilized world, and he was civilized. An author. A father. A husband.

But what was he now?

Running for his life, his freedom, what was he now?

And where was he going?

62

"I think we have a gang or something," Pavano said, chewing the end of his breakfast burrito. "I mean, something organized, don't you think?"

Pinto nodded. He drove past the middle school and turned the patrol car onto Ackerly Street, his eyes surveying the suburban-style houses, the neat lawns and paved driveways.

"Two burglaries on a Monday morning, and it isn't even eight yet," Pinto agreed. "I'd say it was the same guy."

"Couldn't be just one guy." Pavano wiped cheese off his chin with the back of his hand. His eyes were on the sidewalks. Perhaps they could catch them red-handed.

That would feel like an achievement. So far, my life here has been total frustration.

"Look at what they took, Pinto. Flat-screen TVs, desktop computers, phones, handheld video games. One guy by himself couldn't boost—"

"It's the food I don't get." Pinto burped loudly. He'd already finished his burrito. "I mean, emptying the fucking refrigerators? What kind of thief takes all the food, too?"

"A hungry one?"

"Ha-ha. Don't try to be funny, Pavano. You know what you are? You are antifunny."

"I'm not a fucking riot like you, Pinto. True. Let's try to think about this." He pushed a chunk of scrambled egg into his mouth. "This town has gone crazy, Pinto. Three fucking ugly murders. All those kids kidnapped. Now we got houses robbed and—"

The radio beeped. "Where are you girls?" Vince, able to sound harassed in only four words.

"We're on Ackerly near the school," Pinto answered.

"Good. I got another break-in for you. This one's on Clinton. Woman just got home. Thinks she saw the thieves running off. Maybe you can catch them. How fast can they run with computers and TVs?"

"Maybe they have a truck," Pavano offered.

"Maybe they have a flying saucer. Get over there."

The patrol car squealed like in the movies as Pinto made a high-speed U-turn, the car rolling over the curb, spinning up grass, then bumping back to the street.

"Vince, you sending backup?" Pinto, leaning over the wheel, eyes on both sides of the street at once.

"You're joking, right? Every other guy I got is with the feds and the state clowns, searching for Sutter. They're all over Sag Harbor yesterday and no one comes up with a footprint or a trace of the guy."

"You see the *Post* this morning?" Pinto slowed the car down as they approached the house on Clinton. "'Psycho Psychologist'?"

"Pretty good," Vince replied. "Hey, don't expect backup for anything. I got twenty more missing kids. The parents are out in front of the station banging on the door. Like a lynch mob or something. Where are you? You see any kids?"

"Of course I see kids," Pinto said. "We just passed the middle school. I see kids going in."

"School's gonna be a little weird," Vince said. "We got at least a hundred kids gone missing."

"Maybe there *is* a flying saucer," Pavano said.

Silence on Vince's end. The radio squealed, then cut off.

"There's the woman, waving to us on the porch," Pinto said. "Like we couldn't read her fucking address."

"People get upset when their house is robbed," Pavano murmured.

"Hey, you know what? You're a fucking genius."

"And how come you're in a total shit mood this morning?"

Pinto grunted. "I guess cuz everything is going so well in this town."

Pavano shoved the last chunk of burrito into his mouth. The car turned into the driveway. "You know, I don't think Sutter is guilty."

Pinto scowled at him. "Maybe I agree. But no one is asking us, Andy. Franks and the feds got their mind made up. They got the dude's wallet. They got the other two murders. And the fucking guy ran."

"It's not much when you think about it." Pavano reached for the door handle. The woman was running down the driveway toward them. "He just doesn't seem the type, you know."

"I don't know," Pinto said. "He seems pretty squirrely to me. That wallet thing. Does he ever look like he's telling the truth? No. And why did he run?"

"Just saying," Pavano murmured. "It's like a hunch, you know. Only stronger. I think he was totally shocked when he heard about his assistant being murdered."

Pinto grunted in reply. It was obvious he didn't agree. He cut off the engine. The two cops pulled themselves out of the car.

The woman was tiny, middle-aged, pretty. She was dressed in a white top and white leggings. She was screaming as she ran. "They cleaned me out! The little bastards cleaned me out."

Pinto stepped up to her. He was about a foot taller than she. Her streaked blond and brown hair was wild around her face. He squinted down at her. "Little bastards? You saw them?"

She nodded, breathing hard. "Yeah. Kids. A bunch of kids. I mean like little kids. Eight, nine. I screamed and they took off. Little bastards took my new iPad."

Pavano started up the driveway toward the house. "Can we come in? Look around?"

Behind him, he heard the radio in the patrol car squeal. He and Pinto both trotted to the car. Pavano got there first. "Vince?"

"Forget the burglary, Pavano. Get out of there."

"Why? What's up?"

"We're onto something. A neighbor spotted some of the missing kids. I need you over there now."

"Over there? Where?"

"They're in the school."

63

A buzzer rang and echoed in the line of classrooms down the hall. The signal to start class. But today no classes would be started.

Samuel knew the doors were locked, and the teachers had given up trying to enter the building. A group of seventh-graders had been given sentry duty, and they kept watch at all the entrances for any attempt to force open the doors.

Of course, the kitchen workers had been greeted warmly and ushered inside. They arrived first, just before seven, to begin preparing breakfast for the kids in the meal program. They soon got over their surprise at finding the new order, the new regime, as Samuel thought of it. The blue arrows were applied to their faces, and they immediately became pliable under Daniel's will.

Now they were in their white uniforms and aprons, preparing breakfast as usual, only this time for the new arrivals and for the robbery team who returned from their missions with great appetites.

The morning sunlight slanted into the classrooms as kids settled into their new rooms. Some of the light spilled in patches into the crowded, bustling hallway. The mood was cheerful and filled with anticipation for the adventures to come.

Of course, Daniel set the mood, sending his signals to anyone wearing the painted blue arrow, and he could alter the mood, change the emotions and feelings of the two hundred or so followers simply by changing the direction of his thoughts.

Now Samuel followed him down the line of kids who were showing off what they had stolen. He stopped in front of a frail, young-looking blond boy with a galaxy of freckles across his nose.

"What's your name?"

"David."

"How old are you, lad?"

"I'll be eleven next week."

"Well, I'm impressed, David. *Two* laptops. Good work! You're going to be on my special electronics team."

Samuel watched as a proud smile broke over the kid's face. Samuel patted the arrow on the boy's cheek, then pointed him toward the computer room, which had been a sixth-grade classroom but now was a storehouse for stolen computers.

Samuel gazed down the long hall, crowded with followers, some presenting their stolen items for inspection, a group of new arrivals seeking instructions, a girl who carried her brown short-haired dachshund with a blue arrow painted on the right side of its face, a sixth-grade boy with long stringy brown hair, leaning against one wall, softly playing a guitar, several kids hanging back, watching warily as the twins made their way through the patches of dull sunlight in the hall.

"Why did you take these sweaters?" Daniel asked a lanky redhaired girl with red-rimmed glasses.

"I liked the colors," she said. "And I think they're my size."

Daniel motioned with his head toward the girls' hall. "Go try them on. If they don't fit, put them in the clothing storeroom."

She nodded and hurried off with her armload of stolen sweaters.

"So much to organize, boyo," Daniel said, giving Samuel's face a gentle slap. "You know. Bright beginnings, right?"

"This school is *ours*!" Samuel declared. He pumped his twin a hard high five. His excitement actually made it hard to stand still. He wanted to hop and dance and bounce off the tile walls. What an amazing day! He hadn't felt this alive in many years.

Daniel may be the match, but I am the fire.

Samuel glanced through the window of the art room. He could see Ira standing at a table with several cans of blue and white paint. He was applying a blue arrow to the cheek of a chubby sixth-grade girl with braces.

"It's so simple. Once the arrow goes on, they're one of us," Daniel said, watching Ira work. "Better than hypnotizing them, my lad. They don't even know I'm putting thoughts in their brain."

"Ira is getting good with the paintbrush."

"Ira is a good bruvver." He flashed Ira a thumbs-up. "Feel like some breakfast, Sammy? We've worked hard this morning. But it feels like play, doesn't it, lad?"

Samuel nodded. "We rule, Daniel. It's what we always wanted. We waited so many years."

Daniel had a faraway gaze in his eyes. "It's a full school. And we rule. But we've only just started."

Samuel snickered. "I know your mind, Daniel. I know you want all the kids, all the kids . . . *all*."

"All." Daniel still had the dreamy look. "All. It's a start, right? Does it make you feel alive, Sammy? Does it now?"

Before Samuel could answer, someone stepped in front of them, someone large, blocking their path. Her appearance was so sudden and unexpected, it took Samuel a few seconds to realize he was staring at Mrs. Maloney, the principal.

She wasn't in her usual school outfit. She had an oversize man's white dress shirt pulled over sloppy, faded jeans. Her bird's-nest hair was matted in spots as if it hadn't been brushed. She kept blinking and gazing down the hall, as if trying to force away a bad dream.

"Well, what a surprise. To find so many of my lovely chickadees in school so early. What are you all doing here?" she shouted over the chatter of conversations. "Can any of you darlings explain this to me?"

Daniel stepped up to her. "How did you get into the building, mum?"

She lowered her gaze to him. "Daniel? Are you here, too? And your brother? What are you doing here? Why are the doors locked? Can you be telling me what's going on?"

"But how did you get in?" Daniel repeated.

The principal dangled a ring of keys in one hand. "I know some hidden entrances. This is my school, don't you know."

"No. You don't rule the school, mum." Daniel spoke softly, blue eyes probing hers. "We rule the school."

My bruvver looks calm but I can feel his agitation. We made a mistake last week. We forgot to paint an arrow on her cheek. We let her get away.

"Daniel, lad, you don't make any sense," she said. Her eyes were over his shoulder. Samuel could see her counting, taking a tally of the kids in the hall.

They had all grown silent. All eyes were on the confrontation between Daniel and the principal. And the tension was evident in the heavy, ringing hush over the hall.

"Who brought you all here?" She raised her head and shouted. "Did someone force you to come here?"

Silence. No one moved now.

"Somebody tell me what this is about. I don't want to punish you all. But you will give me no choice."

Daniel nodded as if he agreed with her. He signaled to Samuel with another nod of his head.

Samuel took a deep breath and started to heat up his eyes.

Mrs. Maloney seemed like a nice woman. She should have stayed home. Now she will be sizzling like Irish bacon.

"The police have been notified," the woman shouted. "They are on their way. I saw a crowd of people outside the building. Many of them are your parents, waiting to see you. How many of you would like to go out and see your parents right now?"

No hands went up. A boy giggled. That made several other kids laugh.

"What's funny, kiddos?" Mrs. Maloney demanded. "Someone tell me, what's funny?"

The red curtain had started to form over Samuel's vision. But he could see the uncertainty in her eyes, and he saw the uncertainty turn to fear.

She tried again. "Your parents will be so happy to see you. Come on, everyone. Follow me. Let's all go outside." She motioned toward the front doors and took a few steps. But no one made a move.

"You don't understand, mum," Daniel said almost in a whisper. "We rule the school."

Her eyes widened in surprise. "Daniel? You? You are behind this bizarre behavior? You and your brother? I . . . don't believe it. You are good lads, I know. What—?"

And then Samuel turned his eyes on her, aimed the full heat of his power at her forehead. He misjudged. Aimed a little too high, and her hair caught fire. That bristly steel-wool hair burst into red flames.

She screamed and grabbed at her head with both hands. And he lowered the beam to her forehead. The skin peeled open, blistered, and split apart.

Her head is opening up. Like a flower blooming.

She raised her hands and pressed them against her burning face. Dropped heavily to her knees. And Samuel sent the fire to the top of her head, a powerful blast that made him dizzy for a second, made him quake, his knees threatening to buckle.

Her head burned like a torch. Her eye sockets lay black and empty now. And her nose was gone, just a dangling flap of charred skin.

The eyes burn so quickly. How quickly a face melts.

The fire moved down her neck, crackling, popping, setting the shirt ablaze. She toppled forward. Her charred head hit the hard floor with a *smack*. Her big body a beached whale, a pile of kindling.

She ended her life as a bloody bonfire.

Samuel shut his eyes. Kept them closed, waiting for them to cool, listening to the sizzle of Irish bacon.

A hard pounding, a deafening *boom,* jarred him from the pleasure of the moment. He turned to Daniel as a deep voice on the other side of the front door bellowed: "Open up! Police! Open this door—*now*!"

64

Pinto and Pavano arrived at the middle school less than five minutes after they got the call. Pinto bumped the black-and-white onto the curb and muttered, "Oh, shit."

Pavano saw the crowd move toward them. Maybe twenty or thirty people. Parents? "How the fuck did they get here before we did?"

The two cops had no choice. They climbed out of the car. The shouted questions were like an attack.

"Are our kids in there?"

"What did you hear? Who brought them here?"

"Are they hostages? Is this a kidnapping?"

"What's going on? What are you going to do?"

A jumble of frightened voices.

Pavano spotted three people, two men and a woman, at the side of the building. It took him a few seconds to realize they were about to climb into an open classroom window.

"Hey! Stop!" Pavano took off, shouting as he ran. "Back away! Now! Back away from that window!"

A young man in gray sweats turned to face him. "We want to get our kids out."

"We'll get your kids," Pavano said, struggling to catch his

breath. "But we don't know who's in there. If this is a hostage situation, you could put your kids in even greater danger."

The three parents stared hard at him, a tense face-off.

"Step back. Let the police handle this. We have to figure out what is happening here."

The parents finally relented. Pavano led them back to the sidewalk.

The parents formed a circle around the two officers. The women were dressed in shorts and T-shirts, some in morning-run or workout sweats or tights. A few of the men appeared dressed for work. A very tanned man wore a black swimsuit and flip-flops and had a blue beach towel over his shoulder. A gray-haired couple held each other around the waists of their maroon sweats, tears rolling down their faces. *Must be grandparents.*

Pinto crossed his arms on his uniform shirt. He had a distant look in his eyes, as if he was willing himself away from this. Pavano raised his hands for quiet, but the shouts and frantic cries only grew louder.

"We know how worried you are. But don't do anything crazy. We're going to take care of this. Your kids will be safe." He told them what he thought they wanted to hear.

He glanced up the lawn at the school building. The red morning sunlight glowed in the long row of classroom windows. No sign of anyone near the school or at the double doors of the entrance.

Pavano let out a sigh of relief as, sirens blaring, a convoy of cars pulled onto the grass. He saw Franks in the first car, an old Ford Crown Victoria, black, with *New York State Police* emblazoned in yellow on the door. Followed by two more state cars and then the feds in three unmarked Escalades.

The state guys went to work, pushing back the crowd, herding them off the lawn and toward the street.

Jogging along the sidewalk, his brown suit jacket flapping around him, Franks waved both hands, motioning Pinto and Pavano toward the building. "Let 'em know we're here."

As if the sirens weren't a tip-off.

Pavano trotted after Pinto, up the long stone walk to the front entrance, past the bare flagpole, past an abandoned red backpack in the grass, the flap open, obviously empty.

"What's the plan here?" Pavano said, a heavy feeling rising in his stomach as they stepped into the shade of the three-story school. "We just knock on the door and they come out?"

"Beats the shit out of me." Pinto picked up the abandoned backpack, inspected it, and tossed it back onto the grass. "Do I know what the hell is going on? Kids go missing on Friday and Saturday. All found in school on Monday? Does that fucking make sense? Why would kidnappers take a hundred kids to school? It's fucking insane."

Pavano stared hard at his partner. Pinto was already red-faced and breathing hard, beads of sweat glistening on his broad forehead despite the coolness of the morning.

"You read the reports from yesterday. Just about every parent said the same fucking thing. Their kids vanished without a word. No sign of violence. No break-ins. The kids were just gone."

"I read 'em all," Pinto said, eyes on the entrance. "And what was that shit about blue arrows on their faces?"

"Just like Sutter's kids, remember? They said it was a school thing. The principal told them to do it."

Pinto grunted. "It's an alien thing, Andy. The kids were all abducted by aliens. They're slaves on another planet by now."

Pavano snickered. "Neighbors saw kids coming into the school this morning carrying laptops and TVs. No way they can be on another planet if they're robbing every house in the neighborhood."

"Just sayin'." Pinto didn't smile.

A shadow passed over them. Cawing birds swooping overhead made Pavano glance up. The clouds overhead were jagged and torn, as if a big cloud had been shredded into long pieces, the sky as frenzied and chaotic as everything down below.

Pinto took the front steps two at a time. He tried one door, then the next. "Locked." He raised both fists to the double doors and pounded against the wood. "Open up! Police! Open this door—*now*!"

Before they could detect any response, Franks stepped up behind them, badge dangling on his suit lapel, followed by four federal agents with *FBI* stenciled in red on their gray flak jackets.

Franks raised both hands in a halt signal. "Hold up. We've got to deal with these parents first. Make sure they're out of the way—in case there's trouble."

Trouble? Pavano wondered what the captain was expecting.

Franks rubbed the scar on his chin. "If this is a mass kidnapping or a hostage situation, we might face weapon fire. There could be explosives—"

The rest of his words were drowned out by the shouts of the parents. Ignoring the outnumbered state cops, they surged forward, stampeding to the bottom of the wide concrete steps.

"We want our kids."

"How are you going to get them out of there?"

"Who locked them in? Who brought them here?"

"What are you doing? You're just going to pound on the door?"

The parents glared up at the officers, their faces frantic, voices shrill. In their utter confusion and helplessness, they all shouted at once, anger rising over their fear.

Pavano saw one of the state cops hand Franks an electric megaphone and Franks began to plead for quiet. "I need you to step back. Quiet, everyone! Quiet! Everyone, please be quiet and step back."

His requests were unheeded. The shouts grew angrier and more desperate. Pavano saw more SUVs pull up and more frantic parents running to the steps. A young couple tossed their bikes to the grass and came jogging to join the others.

As Franks continued to plead, his voice washed back at him as if by a powerful wave. Two officers flanked him. They assumed a defensive position, their faces hard, and unholstered their revolvers.

That's what it took to quiet the crowd. Pavano let out a long whoosh of air. He hadn't realized he'd been holding his breath.

"What now? Their guns are drawn? They're going to fucking *shoot* the parents?" Pinto murmured, close to his ear.

Pavano shook his head. "Can't blame the parents for being in a panic. If it was your kid in there . . ."

Pinto spit in the grass. They stood just behind Franks. Pinto crossed his arms in front of him. Pavano stood stiffly, hands clenched into tight fists.

"We have no information at this time," Franks declared, his voice magnified like the voice of God, booming over the nearly silent crowd.

The exact wrong thing to say, Pavano thought. *What a fucking jerk.*

And yes, it ignited the parents again. Cries of alarm and a barrage of frantic questions.

When the cops finally restored quiet, Franks took a different tack. "We are going to get your children out of there. And we will get them out safe and sound."

Some muttering, but the reassurance seemed to calm them a little. Gazing down at the crowd from the steps, squinting into the spreading glow of sunlight, Pavano recognized Lea Sutter. She stood near the back of the crowd, dark hair down around her face, arms crossed, wearing a pale blue sweater.

Next to her, he spotted Sutter's sister. Roz. She stood with her hands on the shoulders of her squirming little boy, leaning over him, trying to get him to stand still. Lea Sutter stared straight up at the school building, frozen like a statue.

She has four kids in there. What must she be feeling? What horror is she going through? Four kids . . .

Pavano had read the report taken by a state cop late Saturday night. The Sutter kids were reportedly in the guesthouse out back with some friends. And all vanished, kids and guests, leaving no trace. He pictured the twin boys she and her husband had adopted from that hurricane-devastated island. What a tough introduction to American life those poor boys were getting.

He swallowed. *Especially if their new father is a murderer.*

And then he couldn't stop the gruesome images from playing through his mind. The young girl with her stomach burned open, lying facedown in a pile of her own intestines. If only he hadn't seen that. And the boy with his head completely burned off. And . . . and . . . the man in the car . . .

If only he hadn't seen the three victims. Then he wouldn't see them in his dreams. Or when he closed his eyes for a moment. Or when he woke up. Every day. He saw them every day.

I'll probably see them forever.

And if Mark Sutter was the murderer . . . Pavano wondered if Mark Sutter was haunted by the murders, too. He claimed he thought about the first murder night and day. Really? Did he think about the victims and think about how he had burned them . . . burned them open like some kind of monster from hell?

But Pavano knew Franks was wrong. He knew Mark Sutter wasn't the murderer. Sutter didn't have it in him. Pavano could read him. He didn't have the anger. He didn't have the insanity. He didn't have the *balls.*

And there stood Lea Sutter, on the edge of the crowd of frantic, shouting parents. Silent and still. Standing so stiffly beside her sister-in-law. No kids and no husband.

Your husband isn't a murderer. I know it.

So why did he decide to run?

Pavano knew the cops were no closer to finding the murderer of those three people than they were to knowing how a hundred or more kids disappeared from their homes and, presumably, were locked in this school building.

And thinking this, with Franks fading into the background of his mind, yammering on through his megaphone, Pavano suddenly felt the full weight of all his regret. It came so suddenly and as such a surprise, he felt his knees start to give as the heaviness swept down over him.

All the wrong choices he had made in his life suddenly confronted him, just as the crowd of parents confronted Franks. Such bad timing, but he couldn't shake it off. If only you could command your mind to think what it *should* be thinking.

But instead he thought of Sari and then back to Susannah, how he messed up his marriage. It could have worked if he had tried harder, if he hadn't been such a fucking jerk. And Sari . . . Again Sari. What the fuck? What made him think he could step into the past and just claim her as if he hadn't walked out on her before? Didn't he move to the Hamptons to step into his *future*? Well, she fucking showed him you can't go home again.

All the wrong choices. All wrong. Every decision of his life.

And now what?

What was happening? A young blond woman with a red polka-dot bandanna around her neck had stepped forward and was talking to Franks. Their conversation quieted the crowd as the parents strained to hear.

"You're a teacher here?" Franks said, lowering the megaphone.

"Yes. I'm Rhea Seltzer. I teach eighth-grade science. I arrived the usual time. A little before eight. With everyone else." She gestured to some other teachers, who stood apart from the parents. "The door was locked. We tried shouting for the custodians. We thought it was a mistake."

"Then what did you do?" Franks asked, brushing a fly from the broad shoulder of his jacket.

"We . . . didn't know what to do. We looked for Mrs. Maloney. The principal. She usually arrives about the same time we do."

"But you couldn't find her? Is she here?" Franks shouted into the megaphone. "Mrs. Maloney, are you here?"

"We saw her car. It's a white Camry. It's in the teachers' parking lot. But we couldn't find her." Seltzer pointed to a short man with a mane of curly black hair. "Mr. Munroe had her cell number. We tried it several times, but we only got her voice mail."

One of the cops leaned forward and said something in Franks's ear. "Are the teachers always the first to arrive?" Franks asked.

"No," the woman answered. "The cafeteria workers get here first. They have to make breakfast for the meal-plan kids. They arrive before seven-thirty."

"Where are the cafeteria workers?" Franks demanded, shouting as if at a rally. He raised the megaphone. "Are you here? Please step forward."

"Their cars are here. But they're not out here," the teacher Munroe called out.

"They must be inside," Seltzer suggested.

Pavano thought about it. The food workers arrive and are ushered in. Then the doors are locked. Are they hostages? Were they let in to cook for the kidnappers? For the kids?

Franks had to silence the chatter of the crowd again. Pavano turned to the building and gazed along the row of windows. The morning sun, yellow now and slowly rising over the trees, reflected in the glass. He couldn't see anyone inside the classrooms. The third window from the right was open, but no sound came out.

"My son has a cell phone but he's not picking up," a man in a dark blue running suit said.

"I found my daughter's phone in her room. She would never leave the house without it."

"I've been trying to call my daughter all morning. No answer. I don't understand it."

"My son is new in this school. Why did they take him?"

"Are you going to get them out or are you going to stand there asking questions?"

That shout made Franks's face twitch. He was a big, imposing man. He radiated strength, athletic prowess, and power. But his stance wasn't impressing this crowd of frightened parents.

They wanted action. Why weren't the police storming the building? Or at least trying to make contact with whoever was inside? It was obvious they thought Franks was stalling, that he had no clue what to do here.

And they were right.

Pavano's eyes surveyed the crowd. He stopped at Lea Sutter, still standing near the back, her arms crossed tightly over her chest. She hadn't moved.

Did she know where her husband was hiding? Sutter had eluded all three police departments for two days now.

A man in a white T-shirt and khaki shorts came along the sidewalk, walking his French bulldog on a leash. He stopped in surprise and stumbled over the fat dog when he saw the crowd. "Is this a school event?"

Some parents turned to set him straight on what was happening.

"Has anyone received a ransom demand?" Franks boomed, sweeping the megaphone from one side of the crowd to the other. "Has anyone received a communication from *anyone* inside the school building?"

The answer was a definite no.

One of the state cops said something to Franks, pointing to the school. Franks let the megaphone slide to the ground. He motioned Pavano, Pinto, and the other cops forward.

"Can't wait to hear his brilliant plan," Pinto muttered. "He probably wants to blow the fucking school up."

"That would get us home in time for lunch," Pavano replied, eyes straight ahead on Franks.

Pinto stopped him. "Whoa, partner. You're not developing a sense of humor, are you? Did you forget? I'm the sarcastic one?"

"Sorry," Pavano murmured. "The strategy just seems kind of obvious to me. I mean, there's an open window, right? So . . . we fucking go in and see what we find in there."

"And if the kidnappers start shooting?"

"Pinto, do you really think there are kidnappers? Kidnappers who grab a hundred kids, take them all to school, and make no demands?"

Pinto shrugged. "What else could it be, shitbrain?"

"We're going in," Franks announced. "Weapons in hand."

The weapons order drew loud howls of protest from the crowd. Franks motioned toward the open classroom window. "Ignore the crowd. If you see someone holding the children, shoot first. Just don't hit any kids. Shoot anything else that moves."

What movie did he get that line from?

Guns drawn, the feds in the FBI flak jackets strode to the open window. Pavano had to squint. The windows all gleamed as if the sunlight was coming from inside.

Pavano, Pinto, and three other local cops followed, almost as an afterthought. Pavano glanced back at the street and saw Big Pavano in his blue-black captain's uniform standing by himself. His cap was tilted over his head. His gun was holstered. He was shaking his head as if he disapproved of the whole thing.

"Where the hell has he been?" Pavano asked.

Pinto spit on the grass. "The captain likes a big breakfast."

"Franks probably hasn't kept him in the loop," Pavano suggested. "It's a miracle the feds are letting Franks run with this."

"Waiting for him to hang himself," Pinto muttered.

They were approaching the open window. Pavano still couldn't see any sign of life inside. He felt his chest tighten. Each step made him feel a little more tense and a little more alert.

What kind of madman kidnaps one hundred kids? What is he doing to them in there?

He pictured the boy with his head burned off.

Oh, God. What are we going to find?

"Here we go," he muttered without realizing it.

Pinto leaned close. "I've been in some tough situations," he said softly. "I always think of a line from a country song I heard." He poked Pavano. "You're a country music guy. You probably know it."

Pavano didn't reply. He waited for Pinto to tell him what song.

"'God is great, beer is good, and people are crazy.'"

Pavano grinned. "Yeah. I know that song, Pinto."

"It ain't a song, Andy. It's my Bible."

Pavano heard the French bulldog start to bark, as if warning them away from the window. Franks stepped up beside the feds. Cautiously, he raised his head to the window and shouted inside. "Can anyone hear me? We're coming in!"

Pavano and Pinto tensed their weapons.

"We're coming in!" Franks shouted again. "Police! We're coming in! Police!"

Pavano could see only the back of Franks's head. From his vantage point, the classroom was a sunlit blur. Was anyone in the room? Or even nearby?

Weapon in hand, Franks motioned for the feds to let him go in first. He started to raise himself over the window ledge.

Something caught Pavano's eye. He turned in time to see the front doors of the school building swing open. He heard parents gasp and shout in surprise.

"They're coming out! The kids are coming out!"

65

Lea leaned close to Roz, her hair brushing her sister-in-law's cheek. "It's all my fault," she whispered.

Axl let out a cry and tried to break free from Roz's grasp. But she had him securely by the shoulders, and he only succeeded in pitching himself off the grass, his tiny sneakers kicking air.

"Lea, what? I can't hear you." She lowered her arms around the little boy's waist and held him tight. "Take it easy, Axl. Be a good boy and I'll buy you some candy."

Lea wiped a tear from her eye. "I said it's my fault. All of this."

Roz narrowed her eyes at her. "What are you saying? I don't get it."

"Ira and Elena. I've put them in so much danger. I love them so much. I . . . couldn't bear for anything to happen to them. They're my children, Roz. My children."

"Lea, please—"

"Mark warned me but I didn't listen to him. I wanted those twins so badly. I mean, I *thought* I wanted them. And now, look what I've done, Roz. Look what I've done."

"Lea, you're not making sense. Of course you're upset. I'm upset. Look at everyone here. We're all going out of our minds with worry. But how can you blame yourself? You didn't—"

"I brought them home. I should have known. Why didn't I listen to Mark? To Martha? I can't believe it, Roz. I tried to tell the police it's the twins. I tried to show them the photos. But then Mark ran and they . . . they ran after him. They wouldn't have believed me, anyway." She couldn't hold back the tears any longer. Wrenching sobs escaped her throat.

Roz let go of Axl and wrapped Lea in a hug. "Stop. Stop it. You're saying crazy things. How can it be the twins? You know that can't be true. Lea, no one blames you. Mark doesn't blame you."

"He *should*. Don't you see? He *should* blame me. When he knows . . . Oh, Roz, when he knows . . ." Another uncontrollable round of racking sobs.

"Aunt Lea is sad?" Axl gazed up at Lea. He looked about to cry, too.

She forced herself in control for his sake.

"Yes, Aunt Lea is sad, but she'll be happy again soon. You wait and see, honey."

"Evil. So much evil. I have proof, Roz. I have the photos. I wanted to show the police. But they wouldn't look at them. I know you think I'm crazy. I know—"

"I don't think you're crazy, dear. I just know you haven't had time to recover from that horrifying hurricane."

"Recover?" Lea cried. *"Recover?"*

"Take it easy, please, Lea. You're frightening Axl." She wrapped him in another hug.

"Now here I am, I'm standing here helplessly while poor Ira and Elena are in there. My babies. They're in such danger, and there's nothing I can do. It's—it's too late!"

"Lea, the police are here. The FBI. Look at them all. They'll get the kids out. I know they will."

"No. You don't understand. They're helpless. They're completely helpless. They can't get them out. They can't save anyone against so much evil. Martha warned me. Martha emailed me again yesterday. All the details. All the horrible details."

Holding Axl between them, Roz pressed her cheek against Lea's. "Stop. Stop. It'll be okay. You'll see, dear."

They stood that way for a long moment. And then Lea pulled back when she heard cries and shouts of surprise from the crowd of parents.

"The front door is opening. Someone is coming out!"

66

A kid appeared in the doorway. Then two. Two blond boys.

It took Pavano a few seconds to recognize the Sutters' twins. He struggled to recall their first names. Old-fashioned names.

Everyone seemed to move at once. The feds and the cops stepped back from the window. The parents pushed toward the kids at the door. At first they cheered, but then a strange silence descended as the doors slammed shut behind the twins.

When the parents realized that no more kids were coming out, the shouts and confused cries rose up again.

The two boys stood rigidly side by side, hands balled into tight fists at their sides. They wore jeans and matching black T-shirts. The sunlight made the blue arrows on their right cheeks shimmer.

At the side of the building, Franks tossed down the megaphone and went running toward the twins. "I've got you! Come with me! You're safe!"

One of the twins raised both hands in a halt signal. "Stay back! Don't touch us!"

"Don't touch us!" his brother echoed.

Franks stopped short. "Why? Is there a bomb? What did they do to you? Did the kidnappers put explosives on you?"

"Stay back. Stay away." Both twins motioned Franks to retreat.

Pavano saw Lea Sutter push her way through the crowd. She stretched her arms out to the boys as she made her way toward them. "Daniel! Samuel! What are you doing?"

How totally fucking weird.

Pavano stared hard at Lea. She stopped at the edge of the crowd. She didn't run up to her two boys.

How totally fucking weird. She didn't ask if they were okay.

Instead, she asked what they were doing.

Wouldn't a mother want to know how her kids are being treated? If they are in danger?

"What are you doing?"

Pavano watched her as she repeated the question. Was that concern on her face? A mother's concern? No. The question seemed to be a challenge.

"Boys, can you get over here?" Franks called. "You're safe. We'll make sure you're safe."

The twins made no attempt to heed him.

"Who's in there?" Franks demanded, his voice amplified over the crowd, now hushed, tense faces watching the boys, watching the doors. "Were you kidnapped? How many are there? Is everyone okay in there?"

Pavano saw Lea Sutter take several steps toward her twins.

"Stay back, Mum," the one with dimples called. They both motioned Lea back. They were twelve, but their voices hadn't started to change yet. They had tiny angelic voices to match their faces.

Franks turned to the cops and agents behind him. "Careful. Those two aren't moving away from the school. I think someone planted bombs on these kids." That comment drew gasps and horrified cries from the crowd of parents.

"Get back, everyone!" Franks shouted. "Get back—*now*!"

"This is fucking weird," Pinto muttered. Pavano nodded in agreement. The twins didn't appear frightened at all. In fact, they had grins on their faces.

"We RULE!" the one named Daniel shouted. He thrust his fists above his head. "We rule the school!"

The other boy—Samuel—shook his fists in the air.

What the fuck are they saying?

"WE RULE THE SCHOOL!" they declared in unison.

Pavano saw Lea Sutter sink back into the crowd, her face pale with horror. Did she have tears streaming down her face? She turned away. Pavano couldn't see.

"We need you to step away from the building," Franks shouted. He moved toward the twins. The four feds followed him, hands on their holsters. "Put your hands down, boys, and come over to me. Slowly."

"We rule! We rule!" The twins screamed. "Bright beginnings! Bright beginnings, everyone!"

Franks tossed the megaphone to the grass. He motioned his officers forward. "Okay, boys. We're not going to hurt you. We're just going to take you to safety."

"I don't think so," Daniel replied. "We rule now. Bright beginnings!"

Pavano glimpsed something strange about the other twin. Samuel. What was he doing with his eyes? His face was turned away from the officers.

"Let's get them!" Franks cried. Flanked by the other lawmen, he took off, trotting toward the twins, arms outstretched.

Screams burst out as a blast of red light—like a solid flame—shot over the crowd of parents. Silent but blindingly bright, it bulleted over the cars, over the street, leaving a fiery trail against the pale blue sky.

Startled, Pavano ducked. By the time he overcame his shock and turned to follow the fiery beam, he heard what sounded like the crack of a lightning strike—the hiss and crackle of a powerful electrical charge.

He gasped along with others in the crowd as the dark-shingled roof of the house across the street burst into flames. The flames licked across the top of the roof, then spread quickly down the sides. A tall tree leaning over the right side of the house crackled as the top limbs caught fire.

Andy froze in confusion. He saw Big Pavano running to his car, most likely to call the fire departments. Franks squinted at the fire, revolver raised helplessly. He had taken a defensive stance, as if ready to do combat.

Screams rang out again as another beam of fiery light—like a laser rocket—soared high over the crowd. Seconds later, the next house on the block, a tall Tudor-style house rising high over a wall of green hedges, burst into flame. Windows shattered. Flames danced along the hedge tops.

Pavano heard horrified shrieks as the front door burst open and people came running out of the burning house. The front of the house was lost behind a wall of fire now. Trees burned. A flaming limb came crashing down on an open convertible in the driveway.

He saw Big Pavano, still on his radio, frantically waving people away from the burning car. The gas tank could explode at any moment.

Quickly, the hiss and roar of the fires threatened to drown out the horrified screams and cries. And a strong breeze brought choking black smoke sweeping over the crowd.

"They've got a *weapon*!"

The two blasts forced Franks to stop his pursuit. But it didn't take him long to recover. "The kid's got a weapon!" he bellowed. "Get 'em! Grab 'em! Get that weapon away from them!"

Ducking his head like a running back, Franks took off toward the twins.

"Oh my God. Oh shit. Oh my God!" Pinto cried. He grabbed Pavano by the arm as the red laser smacked Franks in the chest, sending him sprawling backward.

A *sploosh* sound escaped Franks, like someone diving into a swimming pool, and a gusher of bright scarlet blood gurgled straight up from his body. Pavano saw bright flames scorch a deep hole in Franks's chest, a hole at least as big as a cannonball. And before Pavano could move, the big cop was down on the grass, roaring and rolling and writhing in an agony of blood and fire.

67

Lea turned her eyes from the big black police captain. He had finally stopped writhing and moaning. At the end, he had flung his arms in the air, flung them up again and again, as if he wanted to take off and fly away from the burning pain.

Now he lay on his stomach in a lake of dark blood. The FBI agents were down on their knees beside him, shaking their heads.

Lea saw the twins—her twins—edge back into the school building. The doors slammed hard behind them.

Sirens squealed on the street as three hose-and-ladder fire engines, flashing bloodred lights, roared onto the block. Lea turned to see the wall of fire. She couldn't see the houses behind them. Trees burned, swaying under the weight of the roaring flames.

The whole block is on fire. Like hellfire. They're turning Sag Harbor into Hell.

"They killed a cop!" an old man in a gray sweatsuit was screaming, his eyes bulging, waving his arms like a madman. "They killed a cop! They killed a cop!"

Lea coughed and covered her face as waves of thick smoke rolled over the schoolyard. Two more fire trucks screamed onto the block. One bumped over the curb, nearly smashing the back of an SUV.

They must have called other towns, Lea knew. The Sag Harbor firefighters were mostly volunteer, not up to battling a fire this big.

"They killed a cop! They killed a cop!"

The police seemed in disarray now. Several dark-uniformed cops ran to the front doors of the school building and began to pound with their fists.

Lea spotted the two officers who had come to her house. They had moved to face the crowd of terrified parents. They were shouting something, but Lea couldn't hear them over the shrill squeal of the sirens and the shouts of firefighters as they leaped off their trucks into action.

Were the cops trying to get parents to leave the school grounds? They were shouting and motioning frantically as wave after wave of charcoal smoke, thick as cotton candy, rolled over everyone, turning the world dark and making people choke and gasp for air.

Like one of those black-and-white horror movies Mark likes so much.

"They killed a cop! They killed a cop!"

Couldn't anyone shut the poor guy up?

Lea turned and realized she'd lost Roz and Axl. *They were right beside me. Maybe Roz wanted to get Axl out of the smoke.*

Someone had covered the dead officer with a canvas tarp. The FBI agents were conferring in a circle with the uniformed cops.

As Lea watched, her panic swelled. She thought about Elena and Ira. A sob escaped her throat. She clenched her jaw. Bit her tongue, hoping the pain would force back her panic.

Without realizing it, she had moved up the lawn, toward the circle of law officers. She stopped when she heard the FBI agent's voice, raw and raspy: "They killed a cop. Prepare your weapons. We're going in."

Lea stifled another sob. She stumbled back.

Ira and Elena must be terrified.

She spun away, choking from the smoke, her throat burning as if *she* was on fire. She strode toward the street, toward the flames, the crackling trees trembling their limbs as if pleading for help, the frantic men hooking up long hoses, the flames, the flames, such a horrifying twitch and dance of the flames.

She walked quickly toward her car at the end of the block, fumbling in her pocket for the key.

All my fault. All my fault.

I have no choice. I have to find Mark.

I'll wait in the car, away from the choking smoke. As soon as the kids are safe, I'll find Mark.

And tell him everything.

68

Pavano joined the tight formation of agents and cops as they moved toward the open classroom window. Birds squawked, circling crazily overhead. He glanced back. The fire had spread to the next block. People ran screaming from burning houses.

Smoke and fire as far as he could see. The trees were being consumed by the roaring flames. On the street, five or six cars burned. People ducked and tried to cover their heads from the choking waves of black smoke, swirled by sharp gusts of hot wind from the fire.

The crowd of parents appeared to have been blown apart, people running frantically in twos and threes, in all directions. He saw some ducking low as they ran, covering their heads, making their way to the back of the school. Andy knew they might be in the way if the law enforcement people needed to use the back entrances, but there was no time to warn them or move them away. The FBI guys seemed determined to go in there and confront whatever awaited them without any further delay.

"Maybe we all get mowed down," Pinto said, sweat drenching his forehead. "That kid had a fucking laser blaster like in a movie. Did you see his eyes light up? Fucking weird."

Pavano struggled to hear him over the wail of sirens as more firefighters poured onto the block, adding to the snarl of the fire, the screams of the frenzied onlookers and the cries of terrified people fleeing their burning homes.

How could a quiet neighborhood erupt so quickly in such screaming terror?

"Did that blast really come from his eyes?" Pavano asked Pinto. "That's impossible, right?"

Pinto shrugged. "Beats the shit out of me. But I think we know how those three murder vics got burned. And it wasn't Mark Sutter."

They followed the backs of four FBI agents. The front row stopped under the window and ducked beneath the stone window ledge. Pavano could see their features tighten, their faces unable to hide their fear. He knew they were picturing Franks screaming and writhing on the ground as his body flamed and burned.

Suddenly, Pavano knew what he was going to do. He had known it for a while. It was there in the back of his mind, waiting . . . waiting for the moment he knew would come.

He pushed through the agents and cops to the window. He could see inside the classroom. It was empty and dark.

His heart suddenly beat so hard, he had spots flashing in his eyes. His mouth instantly became as dry as straw. He took a deep breath, willing himself to go ahead with this.

Because it was time to do something brave. Time to do something in his life that he wouldn't regret later no matter the outcome. Time to do *something*.

He couldn't remember which of the agents was in charge. Was it the good-looking guy with the steel-gray eyes and the short blond hair and the high movie-star cheekbones? Or the short, stern-looking older dude?

Pavano decided to try them both. "Let me go in."

They squinted at him as if he was speaking Martian. "Say again?"

"Let me go in first. Alone."

"Why?"

Because I've screwed up everything else in my life. Maybe I can be an actual hero today.

"I know those boys," Pavano said. "I've spoken to them before. They'll remember me. I can talk to them. I can reason with them. They'll listen to me."

They reacted with hard stares. Like he was totally mental.

"Maybe I can find out what's happening in there," he heard himself say. "Without any more casualties. If I go in by myself, maybe . . ."

The two agents exchanged glances. Behind them, Pavano glimpsed Pinto, casting him questioning looks, like, *What the hell are you doing?*

"Go ahead," the short bald one said. "One shout and we'll be there behind you."

Pavano blinked. "Really?"

The agent motioned to the window. "Better you than me, Sergeant. I hate the smell of burning meat."

69

It took Samuel a moment to realize that the gray-haired woman in the hairnet and crisp white uniform was a cafeteria worker. She carried in two plates heaped high with scrambled eggs, bacon, and hash brown potatoes, just as the twins had ordered. Like all the workers, she had a blue arrow stenciled on one cheek.

Daniel motioned for her to set them down on the teacher's desk, where the twins had settled after returning from their triumphant moment in front of the school.

Samuel lowered his face near the plate and inhaled. He loved the aroma of scrambled eggs. He could eat eggs all day long.

The cafeteria worker stopped to gaze at the poster hanging on the wall behind the twins. It was a portrait of the president of the United States, and someone had painted a blue arrow on his cheek.

"Go back and make eggs for everyone," Daniel told her.

She nodded obediently and turned to leave.

A window to a seventh-grade classroom Daniel had claimed as headquarters was open, and snakes of gray smoke billowed in, dissipating under the bright fluorescent ceiling lights.

Samuel leaned over the desk, dug his fork into the pile of eggs, and started to eat. The twins weren't alone in the classroom. Several boys sat at desks, playing handheld video games, reading books, joking with one another. Samuel knew they were restless, awaiting their next assignment. Were there more houses to break into? Some other mischief to perform to demonstrate who ruled the school?

Samuel knew what was coming next. Daniel would order them to round up more kids. More kids. More. Until all the kids of the town were together, and the helpless parents would go away, and Samuel and Daniel would rule forever.

He and his twin had waited all these years for someone to take them off the island. Sag Harbor was the perfect place for them. Small enough to be quickly conquered. Big enough to show how easy it was to take control.

The perfect place.

Samuel picked up a slice of bacon and bit off a big chunk. Crispy, the way he liked it. Chewing slowly, savoring it, he turned and saw that Daniel hadn't started his breakfast. He had a faraway look in his eyes that Samuel knew well.

The lad is going to spoil our breakfast.

"Ira"—Daniel waved to their brother, who sat at the back of the room talking with some friends—"Ira, come here. I need you to do something for me."

The other boys laughed at something Ira said. Then he climbed to his feet and shambled down the long aisle, hands in his jeans pockets. He stopped in front of the desk, eyeing the big breakfast plates. "When do I get breakfast, Daniel? I'm hungry."

"Don't be worrying about it, bruvver. I'm going to take care of you. First, I need you to do a tiny favor."

Ira tossed back his dark hair. "Favor?"

"Find our sister and bring her here. Do you know where Elena is?"

Ira nodded. "With Ruth-Ann and some other girls. In the eighth-grade room, I think."

"Tell Elena her bruvvers want to see her, all right, boyo?"

Ira nodded again, turned, and walked out the door.

Samuel took a big forkful of eggs. He watched his twin warily.

"When the bruvver and sister come back," Daniel murmured in his ear, "I'll need your help."

"Daniel, why? What do you want?"

"We don't want them anymore." Daniel's face hardened. His eyes appeared to freeze over.

"Don't want them?"

"We need to burn them, Sammy. It's important."

Samuel took a deep breath. He gazed down at the plate of food. He felt sick and knew he wouldn't be able to eat another bite. "Are you sure, Daniel? Both of them?"

Daniel nodded, then raised a finger to his lips. Ira was leading Elena into the room and down the aisle to the desk.

Samuel shooed the other boys out of the room. "Perhaps you lads would leave now." They hurried out, shoes clumping on the hardwood floor.

"Hi, guys," Elena said brightly. She wore a pink sleeveless shirt over white tennis shorts and pink flip-flops. Her hair fell loosely around her face. "What's up? Are we having breakfast?"

"No. Actually, we have to say good-bye," Daniel said, speaking matter-of-factly.

Ira squinted at the twins. "Good-bye?"

"Yes. We don't want you anymore," Daniel said. He stood up, hands pressed on the desktop.

Samuel saw the shock and confusion on their faces. Elena pressed her hands to her hips and strode up to the desk. "Daniel, what are you *talking* about?"

"We need to say good-bye to you now. We want Mum to ourselves, don't you see."

Samuel had his eyes shut. He concentrated and felt them begin to warm up.

"Whoa." Elena shook her head. "You're joking, right?"

"No joke. We want Mum to love us—not you. It leaves us no choice. We have to say good-bye."

Daniel turned to Samuel and gave a casual wave of his hand. "Go ahead, Sammy. Burn them both now."

Samuel opened his eyes, felt the heat, the incredible heat, and turned it on Elena first.

70

Pavano holstered his Glock and grabbed the window ledge with both hands. The granite ledge was shoulder high, and it didn't take much effort to hoist himself up onto his belly, turn, and lower himself into the classroom.

He waited for his eyes to adjust to the dim light. Smoke from the fires had drifted in through the open window, and he had to squint, as if peering through a heavy fog. The classroom, obviously a room for little kids, judging by the drawings hung on the walls, was empty and appeared untouched, in perfect order.

Pavano heard voices out in the hall. Kids' voices, he quickly determined. His legs suddenly felt heavy, his shoes rooted to the floor. He forced himself to move, stride silently to the door, where he stopped and listened for adult voices. For any clue as to who was giving the orders.

He realized he had grown used to his rapid heartbeats and the cold fear that prickled the back of his neck and made his hands so clammy and stiff.

Leaning against the doorframe, he peeked into the hall. No one in view, but the voices were nearby. Rectangles of light washed out from several classrooms. He stared down the row of gray metal lockers. Several of them had blue arrows painted on them, blue arrows facing up.

Pavano started to draw his weapon, then thought better of it.

I came in here to talk, not to shoot.

But it was impossible to force the ugly pictures of Franks's last moments from his mind. And impossible not to keep asking how that kid possessed the powerful and deadly weapon that had burned Franks to a crisp and made all the houses in sight erupt in flames.

His eyes darted from side to side, trying to take everything in as he stepped into the hall. Trying to act like a real cop who knew what he was doing in an insane, dangerous situation like this.

Pinto's country song flashed into his mind. *God is great, beer is good, and people are crazy.* No help. It might be Pinto's Bible but it was no help to Pavano now.

His eyes scanned the large blue-and-white banner that had been hung over a row of lockers. WE RULE THE SCHOOL.

That stupid phrase the twins had spouted when they emerged to face everyone at the school entrance. Was this really all about taking over the school? The twins weren't really the leaders, were they? Had they been hypnotized by their kidnappers? Had all the kids been victims of some kind of mass hypnotizing or mind control?

Pavano tried to force the questions from his mind as he moved slowly, step by step, toward the next room. After nearly tripping over a pair of white sneakers on the floor, he noticed a tall water bottle standing in front of an open locker. The locker was piled high with books and notebooks. Nothing unusual.

He kept his back against the tile wall, his hand poised over the holster. He edged up to the next room. A small sign on the wall read *Library*. He listened to the voices. Kids' voices. They spoke in normal tones. A girl laughed. A boy angrily told her to get away from him.

Pavano peered behind him, then to the end of the hall. So far, no one had noticed he had entered the school. He was about to reveal himself to the kids in the library. Would it send off some kind of alarm?

Does anyone else in here have that weapon, that incredible fire-breather?

He could no longer ignore his pounding heart. His chest ached, and he could feel the blood pulsing down his left arm. He sucked in a deep breath and held it, but it didn't help relieve the wave of panic swooping down on him.

He stepped into the rectangle of light at the library doorway.

"Hello. What are you kids doing?" His voice came out more shrill and menacing than he had planned.

He saw several kids sitting at low tables with books in their hands. Three girls were side by side in front of desktop computers. Bright games on the screens. A boy near the back of the room had his head down on the table, most likely napping.

All of the kids had blue arrows on their cheeks. Except for the napping guy, they all turned at the sound of Pavano's voice. "What are you doing?" he repeated, a little more softly. He took a few tentative steps into the brightly lit room.

Posters for children's books covered one wall. Four square columns that divided the room had book covers posted up and down them. One column had a long blue arrow pointing up on one side.

"Just doing library stuff," a red-haired girl said with her hands still on her computer keyboard.

"But . . . why are you here? Who brought you here? Are you being held against your will? Were you kidnapped? What's happening here?"

They stared at him. Made no attempt to answer his volley of questions.

"We rule the school," one of the boys said finally.

"Yes, we rule the school," the red-haired girl repeated.

"But who brought you here? Have you been kidnapped?"

They stared at him blankly. "Why did you leave your homes?"

Again, no one answered.

Pavano decided he'd better move on. He knew the FBI agents outside wouldn't give him much time. He wanted to solve this. He wanted to at least *learn* something before they came barging in. So little time, but he'd waited a lifetime to prove himself.

He edged back into the hall. Music echoed off the tile walls from a room somewhere in the distance. He could hear only the drums and the bass rhythm. Voices in the next room made him stop. Another locker stood open, this one with a photo of a white dog on the inside of the door. The locker was empty.

The small stenciled sign on the wall beside the next room read *7th Grade*. Pavano heard voices inside. He edged to the open doorway and listened.

"We don't need you anymore."

"We want Mum to ourselves."

"We need to say good-bye to you now."

Pavano recognized the high, little-boy voice of one of the twins.

He took a breath and stepped into the room. The twins stood stiffly behind the teacher's blond-wood desk. There were plates of food on the desk. On the wall behind them, a poster of the president with a blue arrow on one cheek.

He recognized Ira and Elena Sutter hunched in front of them, cowering together, hugging each other in terror.

"Remember me? Sergeant Pavano? I'm . . . a policeman." The words sounded wrong, as if he were speaking a foreign language. But he knew he had interrupted something.

Ira and Elena spun around, eyes pleading with him. "Help us. Don't let them burn us." They started to run up the aisle toward Pavano. But something . . . some kind of unseen force . . . stopped them halfway between him and the twins. Unable to move forward, they sank back against the chalkboard on the wall.

Daniel shook his head and stared at Pavano. "What a shame. What a shame. Don't you agree, Sammy?"

"What a shame," Samuel echoed.

Pavano felt a chill. "What do you mean? What's going on here?" He avoided Samuel's red eyes. Maybe if he ignored them . . . "Listen. Your mom is waiting for you outside. I need you to come with me now. I need you to trust me. Will you come with me?"

No one budged. Daniel narrowed his eyes at Pavano. "I don't think we can be trusting you, sir."

"Why not?"

"We trust ourselves now. We rule the school."

"I heard that. But it doesn't explain what's going on here."

"We don't have to explain." Daniel nodded to his twin.

Samuel stood taller, then aimed his eyes at Pavano.

"Hey, what the hell. What the hell are you doing?"

Samuel aimed a glowing scarlet beam of light. And Pavano felt a burst of pain, just above his eyes, like a searing hot knife blade in the middle of his forehead. Then he heard a tearing sound—like fabric ripping—and felt hot blood spurt down his face.

With a cry of pain, he ducked his head, tried to elude the scorching beam from the kid's eyes. He cried out again as another beam seared his hair.

Too dizzy to stand, he dropped to the floor and rolled between the desks. Ira and Elena, still pinned against the wall, cried out.

A red beam shot over Pavano, made a sizzling sound as it slanted over the floor behind him.

I'm not going to fail this time. I'm not going to die. I'm not going to fail.

Head reeling, blood trickling into his eyes, Pavano tightened his muscles, readied himself. With an animal roar, he leaped to his feet, tried to dodge the blast of light, but the roar turned into a scream of pain as his shoulder exploded.

The blast knocked him back to the floor. He writhed on his back, unable to shake away the scorching waves of pain, tasting the hot blood flowing from the gash that split his head.

With an agonized moan, he managed to pull himself onto his side. Through the wash of blood, he glimpsed the classroom doorway. Saw the figure move quickly into the room. And gasped: "What are *you* doing here?"

71

Mark didn't answer as he burst into the room at full speed. He saw Ira and Elena huddled in terror in the middle of the room and he knew he had to move fast. He knew he had surprise on his side.

A jumbled text message from Lea had made him think the kids were being held in the school. It read: *Kids school help.* Her second text was just as frantic: *Twins evil dangruss.*

When Mark sneaked in through the basement entrance, he nearly fell over the charred body of Mrs. Maloney. The sight of her corpse, burned black and tossed on the basement floor near the furnace room, sent him into a breathless panic. *Ira? Elena? Are the kids being burned, too?*

Now he tore into the classroom, intent on saving his children. He had seen the cop go down. Saw the tear in the cop's scalp and the blood flowing down both sides of his face. Saw the cop thrashing on his back in pain.

Mark roared down the aisle and heaved himself over the teacher's desk. Eggs and potatoes went flying, and the plates crashed to the floor.

Startled, the twins froze.

Sliding over the desk on his stomach, Mark shot out both arms in a desperate grab for the two boys. He tightened his fingers in their hair and *smacked* their heads together as hard as he could.

The collision made a *clonnnk* sound like wood smashing against wood.

Samuel grunted in pain, as the fire in his eyes dimmed like a car cigarette lighter dying.

Cursing, Daniel squirmed and tried to spin away.

Hold on. Hold on. You can do it.

Mark squeezed his fingers into their hair, and with a grunt of effort, smashed their heads together again with all his strength.

Without even a groan, their jaws went slack and their eyes rolled up. Mark loosened his grip on their heads, and they slumped to the floor behind the desk.

Gasping for breath, he lowered himself to the floor, then turned and motioned frantically to Elena and Ira, frozen in the aisle, gaping at him in shock. "Dad! How did you get in here?" Ira cried.

"Hurry! Out of here!" He hurried over to them and wrapped them in a tight hug. "You're okay? You're not hurt?" They nodded. Mark glanced at the twins, still unconscious, piled on top of each other on the floor. He knew they wouldn't be out for long.

"No time! No time! I have to get everyone out." He guided them urgently toward the open window and watched as they eased their legs over the ledge and disappeared over the side.

"I'll be back!" he called to the cop thrashing in pain on the floor. "I'll come back for you."

He sucked in a deep breath, coughing from the smoke-filled air, and took off running down the long hall to the front doors, shoes skidding on the tiles. He grabbed the door handles, fumbled with the bolt that held them locked, shoved it aside, and flung the doors open wide.

Then he turned and tore back down the hall—all a blur of shadows, the walls, the rows of dark lockers, the classroom doors.

You can do this. Keep going. You can do this.

"Out! Everybody out!" His hoarse screams rang off the walls. "Everybody outside!"

Flinging open doors, he shouted at the kids sitting at the tables, on the floor, on window ledges. "Out the front door! Your parents are waiting! Out! Get moving!"

The halls were suddenly alive with jubilant shouts and excited kids stampeding to the doors. Whatever hold the twins had over these kids had ended, and they rushed to celebrate their freedom.

Heart pounding, Mark remembered the wounded cop. He dove into a classroom, careened off a wooden table, bounced to the window, and threw it open. Through billowing curtains of black smoke, he saw cops and feds in several windows down the row.

"Cop down!" he screamed. "There's a cop down inside! He needs help."

FBI agents and uniform cops swarmed to the window, and then black jackets were everywhere, in his window and at the door. They didn't seem to recognize him or remember that he was a fugitive.

"It's the twins! I knocked them out. But the cop was hurt. The twins did it. You have to take them." Mark realized he must sound crazy.

A stern-faced cop grabbed Mark's arm. "Just take us to the cop, okay?"

He led them into the hall, nearly silent and empty now. Trotted toward the classroom. Was this the right room? Yes. He saw the poster of the president with the blue arrow on his cheek. Black smoke billowed into the room from outside.

Pavano had pulled himself to a sitting position and was gripping his head with both hands to stanch the flow of blood. Two cops rushed to his side, one of them shouting into a radio-phone for help.

Mark waved the FBI agents to the front of the room. "The twins. It's the twins. They're the killers! I'll explain later. Just grab the twins!"

He saw their skeptical looks. They hesitated, then moved toward him, suspicious. "Who are you, mister? How'd you get in here?"

Mark shook his head. "I'll explain everything. But you've got to get these twins. I knocked them out. Get them. Behind the desk. Watch out . . . Watch out for the eyes."

The agents drew their weapons and he stood back. He watched them go into a stalking stance as they approached the desk.

"The twins. They're on the floor. I . . . I knocked them out. We got them. We *got* them!"

Two agents lurched behind the desk. They appeared to freeze, as if someone had pushed a pause button. Slowly, one of them raised his gaze to Mark. "No one here. No one." He glanced at the open window. "We're too late, I think. They got away."

72

Mark saw Lea walking determinedly down the middle of the Sag
Harbor pier, eyes searching for him among the two rows of parked
cars. He could see her distress from her body language, arms tensed
at her sides, hands balled into fists, shoulders slumped, strides
clipped and rapid.

He waited at the far end of the pier, the meeting place he had
suggested that morning. Behind him, the water of the bay lapped
darkly against the pilings below. The white yachts lining both sides
of the pier stood as still as if on land, too big to be rocked by the
gentle waves. One enormous yacht had a red Porsche parked on its
wide stern and white-uniformed staff carrying breakfast trays to
the main cabin.

Mark stepped out from behind a black Mercedes SUV, watching
the pier behind Lea, making sure she hadn't been followed.

The morning had started out cloudless and bright, but now the
sky was leaden with acrid smoke. Mark glanced at his watch. Not
quite eleven o'clock, and the pier was pretty empty. In an hour or
so, as lunchtime approached, the parking spaces would all be filled.
He watched men unload shrimp and lobsters from the back of a
white panel truck and carry them across the pier into the small
shingled Dock House clam bar.

He took a deep breath, expecting to smell salt water. But sour smoke burned his nose. *That fire must still be out of control.*

A man and a teenage boy walked past carrying fishing rods. The boy pointed to a spot on the side of the pier, but the man waved him off, and they kept walking. No one else in sight. Mark slid out from the SUV and called to Lea.

She stopped short, as if surprised to see him there. Then she came running, dark hair bobbing at the sides of her face, no smile for him.

"Lea—"

"Oh, Mark, here you are."

He wrapped his arms around her and pulled her against him. He wanted to squeeze her tight, hold her there for a long time. She was his old life, his good life, and he desperately wanted to hold on to her. He kissed her, then pressed his stubbly cheek against her face.

"Mark." She pulled away, out of his arms. "I got your text. You're okay? How did you get away from the school?"

"The FBI agents didn't recognize me. I slipped out while they were searching the classrooms." He held onto her. "Thank God the kids are okay."

He felt her shudder. "I saw Ira and Elena. I talked with them. They're fine. Roz took them home. It's so wonderful, Mark. You got them all out."

She raised her face to him. "The twins? Did you see them? Are they—?"

"They got away. I knocked them out, Lea. I . . . I slammed their heads together. I think it broke their spell over the kids. But they escaped. I don't know where—"

"Oh, Mark . . . you were so brave, sweetheart. But . . ."

But?

He waited for her to continue, but she didn't. When she raised her eyes to him, he could tell she was holding something back. She changed the subject. "Where did you stay all weekend?"

"At Nestor's. In his poolhouse. The police came to the house, but they didn't search the poolhouse. I hid in a tiny closet. But they never searched back there."

Her dark eyes locked on his. "Thank God you're safe. You look horrible."

"I . . . haven't slept much. I've been worried—"

She pressed a finger to his lips. "So much to tell you." More tears welled in her eyes. "The twins. I'm so sorry. I should have listened to you. I didn't know—"

A green BMW pulled in beside the Mercedes. Mark guided Lea away toward the Dock House.

"It's our last morning, Mark."

Her words sent a chill to the back of his neck. He squinted at her, unable to respond.

"Maybe we could try to have a normal morning, okay? Wouldn't that be nice? A last normal morning?"

"Lea, what are you saying? You're talking in puzzles. Tell me about the twins. What do you know about them? What did you find out?"

She ran a finger down his cheek. It made his skin tingle. He had rescued the children. They were safe. Why were her eyes so sad? What was she hiding from him?

"A normal hour or two," Lea said. "Look how pretty it is. The white yachts, the pier stretching into the bay, the seagulls against the sky. This is one of my favorite spots in the Hamptons. It always reminds me of Sausalito. Remember that weekend in Sausalito? That restaurant down by the water? We were so young."

He grabbed her shoulder. "Lea, you need to tell me what's going on. Why are you talking about Sausalito? Why are you acting like this? You are really frightening me."

She forced a tense smile and turned away. "I think the waffle cone place is open. Let's get waffle cones, Mark, and maybe walk through town. You know. Like a normal couple. Just stroll aimlessly up and down Main Street and people-watch, the way we used to. We can do it, Mark. The police won't be looking for you anymore."

"No. Not till you explain to me." He grabbed her by the arms and locked his eyes on hers, trying to see her thoughts.

She turned away, as if his stare was too much to bear. "I . . . I'm so sorry, Mark. It's all my fault, don't you see. That's why I feel so bad. I feel so bad for you, Mark. Especially for you. Because you've been so wonderful and loving and trusting. Yes, trusting. And I . . . I've ruined everything."

"But—how? What are you *saying*?"

A sob burst from deep inside her. "Don't you understand, darling? This is the last hour? It's our last hour. Don't you *see*, sweetheart?"

"No. It can't be. Come here." He tried to hug her but she stood rigid, her dark eyes finally coming to rest on his face.

"Don't you see, Mark? I guess you can't. I guess I have to say it. Okay. Okay. I'll tell you. I died on Cape Le Chat Noir. I died there, honey. I'm so sorry. I died in the hurricane."

73

Mark felt a tingle of fear run down his back. Overhead, a seagull screamed as if reacting to Lea's words. A burst of wind off the bay ruffled Lea's hair.

He held onto the sleeve of her sweater. "Lea, you're not making any sense. We need to get you home. The stress—"

"No. It's true, Mark. I . . . didn't want to tell you, darling. I suspected it all along. Didn't you notice how different I was when I returned from the island? I suspected it. I fought it. I fought it every day. I hoped against hope. But I knew. I knew. And then Martha emailed me . . ."

"Lea, you're not dead. You're standing here with me. You're just very distraught, and we need to find you help. I know several good doctors—"

Another seagull cry rang in Mark's ears. He glanced up and saw two fat gulls circling them low overhead.

"I didn't want to leave you. I didn't want to leave Ira and Elena." Tears glistened in her dark eyes and rolled down her cheeks.

"You don't have to leave. I'll take care of you."

"No." Her voice turned sharp. "No. You can't. I have proof, Mark. I have proof right here. I know you don't want to see it, honey. Telling you this . . . doing this to you . . . it's like I'm dying again."

"Stop saying that!" He didn't mean to sound frantic. How had she become so delusional? Did she see something unspeakable on the island? *Is that why her mind has snapped?*

Lea fumbled with her small black leather bag. Some makeup tubes and a mirror fell out. The mirror shattered on the asphalt.

Seven years bad luck, Mark thought. But he immediately scolded himself for having such a superficial thought when his wife was in such distress.

She pulled out some folded-up papers and uncreased them with trembling hands. She made no attempt to wipe away the tears that glistened on her face.

"Here. Oh, here. I'm so sorry. Martha sent these. I'm so sorry, Mark." She pushed the papers at him. Photographs, he saw.

"This is proof?"

She nodded.

He raised the first photo to his face. Black-and-white, very grainy. His eyes focused on a scene of destruction. Fallen houses. Debris everywhere. And then his eyes settled on the two blond boys standing forlornly in the foreground.

"The twins?" He gazed over the photo at her. "Samuel and Daniel? Taken after the hurricane?"

"Oh, Mark." A long sigh escaped her throat. "Yes. The twins. Taken after the hurricane . . . but a different storm, Mark. A different storm. The hurricane of 1935."

The papers nearly flew from his hand. "Lea, please. You're not making sense."

"The second photo, too. I *am* making sense." She struggled to pull out the second sheet for him. "Martha is a photo researcher. I told you that. She found these photos from 1935. Then she emailed me, Mark. Yesterday. She emailed me all the details. She found the truth, Mark. You won't like it, sweetheart. It's all so sad and horrible. You won't like it but you have to hear it now."

Mark took the photo and gazed at the twins standing bare-chested in the midst of the rubble. "I don't believe it," he said softly, "but let's say it's true. What does it mean, Lea? Tell me."

She nodded, tangles of hair, wet from tears, falling down the sides of her face. "There's a ritual on Le Chat Noir. It's called *Reve-nir*. It means *return*. It's performed by a priest." She stopped and pushed his hand away. "Don't look at me like that. I'm not crazy, Mark. I *wish* I was crazy but I'm not. Just let me finish."

He took a step back, the photos fluttering in his hand. "Okay. Sorry."

"The priest who performs the *Revenir* rite can bring back the dead. It sounds insane but I saw it. I saw it done. I didn't believe it when I was there. But it's true. He brings back the dead, Mark. And in that hurricane of 1935, the priest brought back the twins. The twins died in the hurricane, and the priest brought them back. But—"

He grasped her shoulders gently. "Take a breath. I'm listening. I won't interrupt you. But you're forgetting to breathe."

She swallowed. Her chin trembled. More tears glistened in her eyes. "The priest brought the boys back, but he did it all wrong. There were so many deaths to deal with. He messed it up, Mark. He . . . he waited too long. The boys were dead too long. And when they came back, they had all of death's evil in them. They looked the same. They seemed the same. They were alive again, but they were alive with evil."

What am I going to do? I've got to get her to a hospital. I know some doctors who can treat this. I can make some calls.

"The twins came back to life with evil powers, Mark. Hypnotic powers and powers to kill. The priest brought them back from the world of the dead. But he made mistakes. He told Martha he made mistakes. The boys have been the same age since 1935. Martha says they lived by themselves all these years, waiting . . . waiting for someone to take them off the island so they could work their evil. And I . . . I was the one. I brought them both here. I brought them into our family, our lives, and, and . . . I'm the only one who can take them back."

"Lea, stop. Please. Please stop. Let's not talk about it anymore. How about that waffle cone? Would that make you feel better?"

Anything to make her stop talking this insane nonsense. Why didn't I see that she was having a breakdown? How could I not have seen?

"No. It's too late for ice cream now, honey. Look at the third photo. Martha sent a third photo. I knew what it would show. I mean, I had a strong feeling. But there it is. There's my proof, Mark. I . . . I didn't want to show it to you. I don't want to leave. But I don't have a choice."

"You're not leaving. You're not going anywhere. Stop saying that. I love you. The kids love you. They need you. We won't let you go anywhere."

She pushed the papers. "Just look."

The third photo was in color. It showed a strange-looking man in a red robe. He had a large blue tattoo on the top of his bald head. He had one long-fingered hand raised . . . raised over Lea. Yes. He was leaning over Lea, who sat in a chair with her eyes closed, head tilted back.

Mark raised his eyes to her. "What does this prove?"

"I died in Martha Swann's house. Part of the roof came down in the hurricane. It landed on me, and I died. Martha and James— they knew where to find the priest. They risked their lives out in the storm. They brought him and he performed the *Revenir* rite on me. I came back, Mark. He brought me back. But I wasn't the same. Much as I tried, I wasn't the same. I've been obsessed . . . obsessed with death. I . . . don't really feel as if I belong here."

Her shoulders trembled. A sob racked her entire body. "If only I hadn't brought the twins home, maybe we could have gotten along for a while. Maybe I could have pretended. But . . . I ruined our lives. If only . . ." Her voice trailed off and she grabbed him and pulled his arms around her and pressed her tear-drenched face against his chest.

He held her tight. The photos fluttered across the pier. He wanted to wrap her up and keep her safe. He knew she could be okay again. Of course she could. The island hurricane had been a terrible trauma. So much horror—it could affect *anyone,* especially someone as sensitive as Lea.

Her head pressed against him, he saw the twins over her shoulder. He saw them walk past the old colonial windmill near the street and come toward them, down the center of the pier.

Lea turned, as if sensing they were approaching.

The boys strode rapidly side by side, past the Dock House, past the rows of parked cars on both sides, their eyes straight ahead on Mark and Lea. Mark felt Lea shudder.

As the twins drew close, he called to them. "How did you get here? What are you doing here?"

Daniel's answer came back in his high little-boy's voice. "We came to hurt you."

74

Mark studied their faces. Hard, jaws set tight, eyes like frozen blue ponds.

If they were twelve in 1935, they'd be nearly ninety years old. Ridiculous.

"Come here, boys." Lea stepped in front of Mark and stretched out her arms. "Come here. How did you find us?"

They hung back. "We saw you at the school, Mum. We followed you here. Pa tried to hurt us. Now we need to hurt Pa."

Both boys had dark bruises on the sides of their faces.

"Pa did a bad thing," Samuel said.

"Now, wait—" Mark's breath caught in his throat. "Let's put a stop to this right now. Answer me. What did you think you were doing in that school?"

They ignored him, eyes on Lea. "Pa did a bad thing," Daniel said.

"A bad thing," Samuel repeated. "Pa hurt us. We were ruling the school. But Pa ruined everything."

Mark felt his face grow hot. "Stop saying that. I . . . had to stop you."

"Mark had no choice," Lea told them. She stretched out her arms again. "Come here. I know how hard it's been for you boys.

I know the whole story. Please—come to me. Let me give you a big hug."

"We can't have a hug, Mum," Daniel replied, almost sadly. "We have to hurt Pa now." He turned to Samuel. "Are you ready, Sammy lad?"

Mark uttered a sharp cry when he saw Samuel's eyes blaze.

"Move away, Mum," Daniel warned.

"No. Stop," Lea protested. "Listen to me, boys. We need to talk. The three of us have to stick together now."

"Move away, Mum. We don't want to put the burn on you, too."

The fiery glow of the boy's eyes was so bright, it brought tears to Mark's eyes. Samuel swung his head around, and a blast of heat grazed Mark's chest.

In that second, Mark's questions were answered, and he knew that Lea was telling the truth. He understood how the murders had been done. He understood that the twins had murdered, scorched and murdered. And now he felt the searing heat from Samuel's eyes burn his chest.

They're going to kill me now.

He lowered his head and took off.

"Samuel—stop it!"

He heard Lea's frightened plea over the pounding thuds of his shoes on the asphalt pier. He didn't turn around.

A blazing burst of pain exploded on his back. He heard his shirt sizzle and felt his skin erupt in a circle of fire. Mark dropped to his knees and rolled toward the row of parked cars across the pier. Slid between two cars as another scorching beam cut the air. The blue Honda beside him burst into flames.

With a cry, Mark jumped to his feet. Gasping from the pain that radiated over his back, he stumbled toward the tiny shingled Dock House. When he ducked under another red ray of fire, it sailed over his head and died in the water beyond the pier.

Lea's shrill screams . . . Daniel's shouted instructions to Samuel . . . the boys' pattering footsteps as they pursued him—all became a blur of sound beneath the bass-drum pounding in his chest.

Where am I running? How can I escape them?

He couldn't think straight. No time to make a plan. The terrifying beam from Samuel's eyes could barbecue him in seconds. And as that thought raced through his mind, he also realized that Lea was probably telling the truth about herself. And that he could lose her.

Lose her. Oh no. Oh no. Lose her.

A hoarse cry escaped his throat as he started to heave himself through the open door of the food shack. He thought better of it. Wheeled around and ran crazily, off-balance, in a wild stagger, and stumbled to the far side of the little building—just as it burst into flames.

He heard shrieks of horror, turned, and saw three or four workers run out, pushing each other as they fell through the doorway, crying and shouting their shock and horror. The long apron on a young red-headed woman was on fire. She struggled with the straps, then dropped to the ground on her belly, trying to smother the flames.

A second explosion sent flames shooting off the low, flat roof. Mark glanced back. The twins were ambling toward him, not even bothering to hurry. So relaxed and confident. And why not? Mark was helpless against the boy's unnatural weapon. Helpless against the evil magic Lea had warned him about. Sure, he could run. But where? He couldn't escape. And he couldn't turn and face them down.

Over the crackle of the flames, he heard shouts. People came running out of the waffle cone shop and from the restaurant at the end of the pier. He didn't have long to watch them. Another scorching stab of pain caught him in the back of the leg, hobbling him. Forcing him to his knees.

This is it. It's over.

A sharp stab in his right shoulder and the skin split open. He felt the burn run down his arm. With a scream of horror and pain, his leg throbbing and aching, he lurched to the edge of the pier. Swung his body around—and glanced to the water.

Will I be safe in the water?

He gripped the low, white metal railing at the edge of the pier.

His right arm throbbed. He could barely hold on, but he started to lower his body toward the rolling water. Glancing back, he saw Daniel's intense stare and the pulsing red eyes of his twin as they made their steady way toward him.

A powerful heat blast bounced off the metal railing, shook the rail, and made a *craack* like a lightning bolt. Another shot sent an explosion of heat over the top of Mark's head.

He glimpsed the dark water below. He took a deep breath and prepared to loosen his hold on the rail.

And then stopped.

He gripped the rail tight and stared across the pier as Lea caught up to the boys. They had all their attention on Mark. Daniel was pushing his brother forward, moving them in for the final burn. They didn't see Lea come up behind them.

Ignoring his pain, Mark hung on the rail and watched Lea move up behind the boys. She stretched out her arms as if to tackle them both. Instead, she wrapped her arms around them, pulled them into a tight hug from behind.

They struggled to free themselves. The three of them moved in an awkward dance, held together in Lea's tight embrace.

As she wrestled with them, she called to him. "Good-bye, Mark. Good-bye, darling. It's the only way. I have to take them back."

"Lea, no!"

Gripping the rail, he watched helplessly as Lea spread her hand over Samuel's blond hair—and turned his face to her. Turned his burning eyes on her.

Took the beam of fire. Turned it on herself.

Mark couldn't stop the howl of horror that burst from his throat. Working his legs against the pier wall, he struggled to pull himself up. To get to her. To reach her in time.

But no.

Lea burst into flames that consumed her instantly, rising like candlefire, straight, without a flicker. She didn't move or struggle or make a sound. The boys squirmed and thrashed. But even as she burned, Lea held them close, pressed them to her. And the fire swallowed them, too.

Unable to breathe or cry out, Mark watched all three of them in the fire, statues in a dark embrace, then ash, crumbling ash, a sinking pile of ash inside the single tall flame.

Then gone.

Gone, and the fire vanished with them, leaving the asphalt unmarked.

Mark felt hands grip his arms. Saw faces above him. People tugging him up from the pier side. He heard screams and cries. Sirens approaching. Smoke swept over him from the still-flaming Dock House. People came running onto the pier, faces tight with alarm. Seagulls screamed in the sky.

He let it all fade to the back of his mind. He pictured Lea. Her smile. Her bright, dark eyes.

Gone. Lea was gone.

As he stared, the fire that had consumed her went out with an almost-silent *hussssh*.

Mark found Roz in the flower bed at the side of the guesthouse. She was on the grass, digging with a trowel in a square of black dirt. Axl, in red shorts and a sleeveless red T-shirt, sat nearby in a clump of freshly planted petunias, stabbing at the ground with a plastic shovel in imitation of his mother.

Roz looked up and brushed a bee away from her shoulder. "Who was that on the phone?"

Mark hunkered down beside her. He liked the smell of the fresh dirt. Like rich coffee. "Sergeant Pavano. You remember. The cop."

Roz nodded. "Of course I remember him. What did he want? To arrest you for some other murder you didn't do?"

Mark snickered. "Don't be bitter. He had no choice really."

"Of course he did. And I'll be as bitter as I want. He was a total idiot."

"Not total," Mark said. "Don't forget. He was brave. He tried to rescue Ira and Elena and the other kids. He went in before anyone."

She shoved the trowel into the dirt. "So what did the big hero want?"

"Actually, I think he called to apologize for the way the police treated me. But he never got around to it. He just asked how everyone is doing. You know. With Lea gone."

"What did you tell him?"

"I said Ira and Elena hadn't really accepted it yet. But they were doing the best they could. What else could I say?"

Roz sighed in reply.

Mark twisted his face in a frown. "Pavano says he's going back to New York City. He said the city is a lot safer than out here."

Roz concentrated on the trowel. "Maybe he's right."

"Look this. Look this." Axl called to them, holding up his yellow shovel.

They turned to see what the little guy was staring down at. Mark saw two fat brown insects in the scoop of the shovel. "Those are called beetles," he said.

Axl held the shovel close to his face. His dark eyes studied the two bugs. "Look what Sammy teached me. Sammy teached me this."

Roz's mouth dropped open. "What? What about Sammy?"

"Sammy teached Monkey Boy."

Mark felt his heart skip a beat as Axl's eyes flared. In a few seconds, they were fiery red. Axl lowered his glowing gaze to the shovel, and all three of them watched as the beetles sizzled and burned.

Acknowledgments

First, I need to thank Stacy Creamer, whose excitement and enthusiasm for this novel gave me the courage to venture through the red rain and complete what was a very ambitious project for me. I'm so appreciative of her support.

Andrew Gulli of the *Strand Magazine* must be thanked for coercing me from my day job of scaring children into the world of scaring adults.

My friend and longtime (and long-suffering) *Goosebumps* editor, Susan Lurie, was an enormous help, as was my wife, Jane Stine, who is painfully insightful and always right about my books.

Finally, I need to mention three old horror movies: *Village of the Damned, Children of the Damned,* and *Island of the Damned.* While this book is not a reimagining of those films, the horrifying children in all three of them gave me the inspiration that disgustingly evil children might be a fitting subject for me.

Thanks, all.

The Three Day Rule

The Three Day Rule

Josie Lloyd & Emlyn Rees

WILLIAM HEINEMANN : LONDON

First published in the United Kingdom in 2005 by William Heinemann

1 3 5 7 9 10 8 6 4 2

William Heinemann
The Random House Group Limited
20 Vauxhall Bridge Road, London, SW1V 2SA

Random House Australia (Pty) Limited
20 Alfred Street, Milsons Point, Sydney,
New South Wales 2061, Australia

Random House New Zealand Limited
18 Poland Road, Glenfield,
Auckland 10, New Zealand

Random House (Pty) Limited
Isle of Houghton, Corner Boundary Road & Carse O'Gowrie, Houghton, 2198,
South Africa

The Random House Group Limited Reg. No. 954009

www.randomhouse.co.uk

A CIP catalogue record for this book
is available from the British Library

Papers used by Random House
are natural, recyclable products made from wood grown in
sustainable forests. The manufacturing processes conform to
the environmental regulations of the country of origin

ISBN 0 434 01147 9

Typeset by SX Composing DTP, Rayleigh, Essex
Printed and bound in Great Britain by
Mackays of Chatham plc, Chatham, Kent

For our three godsons, Oliver, Jack and Paddy.
(You can always spend Christmas with us!)

Acknowledgements

With many thanks to our fabulous editor, Susan Sandon, and everyone at Random House, especially Georgina Hawtrey-Woore and Cassie Chadderton. Also, as always, many thanks to our brilliant agents, Vivienne Schuster and Jonny Geller, at Curtis Brown, for their support, as well as to the lovely Carol Jackson, Stephanie Thwaites and Doug Kean. Thanks to Andrea for being such a star with Roxie, and, of course, to our families and friends and our wonderful daughters, for keeping us sane throughout.

DAY 1

Christmas Eve

Chapter 1

Kellie Vaughan pulled back the thick drapes and shivered, tying the white hotel robe around her. From where she was standing in the bay window of the penthouse suite, she could see down over the grey slate roofs of the houses to the harbour where small fishing boats littered the shallow inlet. At the far end, beyond the quayside with its old stone harbour wall, the headland was covered in purple and yellow heather and, beyond that, the Channel – this morning a deep navy-blue – glistened beneath the powdery sky, where a high wisp of cloud hung like a question mark.

In the far distance, she thought she could just about make out the small island where Elliot would be spending Christmas with his family, but maybe it was wishful thinking on her part.

Kellie turned away and sighed, looking round at the neutral creams and beiges of the hotel room and at the upside-down champagne bottle in the ice bucket on the table next to the plush sofas. She was in Fleet Town, the capital of St John's, which was the largest island of the group off the south Cornish coast. The islands themselves had a reputation as a great holiday destination, but now, in the depths of winter, they seemed bleak and uninspiring. Even though she couldn't complain about the five-star luxury surrounding her, three days stretched ahead and, for most of that time, she'd be here on her own.

Perhaps it was something she should have considered when Elliot had first suggested her coming – but she hadn't. She'd done what she'd always done: made out that she was the fun, impulsive chancer she always was, happy to be swept up in Elliot's romantic proposal, flying in a Sikorsky helicopter from Penzance and staying in the best, most exclusive spa hotel on the island. He'd made it sound so simple and plausible, but now she could see that she was going to have to fill hours of her time.

But surely it was a small price to pay? Every moment they could be together counted, even snatched ones. That was what being in love was all about.

Besides, she should be used to it by now. In the summer, when Elliot had been forced into spending a two-week holiday with his family in Italy, he'd ensured that Kellie was in the hotel in the next bay and he had taken up one-man sailing as a hobby so that he could be with her every afternoon.

Once again, here she was, on the same clandestine terms, but this time twenty-eight miles off the coast of Cornwall, and Kellie couldn't help fearing that Elliot's certainty that he'd be able to sneak away and spend at least one night and the majority of each day with her wasn't as realistic as he was making out. After all, his father's house was on Brayner, one of the smaller islands. Elliot had made it sound as if it was next door, but Kellie could see for herself that it was a lot further than that. Sneaking back and forth would require a boat, the same as in Italy, but even assuming Elliot got hold of one, could sloping off in the middle of a family Christmas really be as simple as he'd led her to believe?

Behind her Elliot stirred in the dishevelled bed.

'What are you doing over there?' he said, his voice husky with a hangover after all the brandy they'd drunk together in the hotel bar last night as well as the champagne back in the room. 'Come back.' He closed his eyes, smiled and slumped his head on the pillow, patting the Kellie-shaped dent on the bed beside him.

Kellie smiled and walked over, kneeling down and

4

ruffling his hair. She loved him the most when he was like this, his hair all messed up from sleep, his sexy smell of sweat and expensive aftershave. He squinted up at her through blue-grey eyes.

'You've got too many clothes on,' he said.

She laughed. 'I thought you had a hangover.'

'So cure me.'

'But it's nearly time,' Kellie said, wriggling out of her robe and lying in his arms. She knew that his family were all expecting him to arrive on St John's today, after a big work function in London last night. They had no idea that Elliot was already here.

'I know. Oh, Christ, Kel. I'm so jealous of you being here. I wish I was having a break,' he said, turning to her, 'but I suppose you do deserve one.'

Kellie felt a flush of pleasure that he'd finally acknowledged how hard she'd been working. Elliot was the most driven man she'd met in her career and he pushed her hard in hers too – so much so, that lately it seemed as if she'd given up her whole life to WDG & Partners, the law firm where they both worked. The pressure had never seemed to stop. She'd been promoted at the beginning of the year, which had been hard enough, and then, when a reshuffle had happened a few months ago, she'd been promoted again. She knew that Elliot had been involved with the decision-making process, but that had only made her even more determined to prove herself on her own terms. When everyone at the office stopped speculating and found out after Christmas that she and Elliot were together, she didn't want anyone accusing her of sleeping her way to the top.

She was glad, however, that he was jealous of her having a break. The more he imagined her to be having a wonderful time, chilling out, the harder he would try to get to be with her.

5

'Yes . . . well you deserve one, too,' she said.

Elliot groaned. 'I just can't bear it,' he said, scrunching up his face so that he looked like a little boy. 'I don't want to go.'

Kellie was used to this. Elliot was far worse than her every time they had to part. She knew he felt guilty about spending time with his family, away from her, and, ironic though this was, more often than not she was the one who ended up being strong about it. It was almost as if there were two Elliots: the one at work who was powerful, masterly and strong, and this Elliot, the one she loved the most, but also the one who made it almost impossible to believe he had a child of his own.

Usually, Kellie laughed at him, but now, as she lay her chin on his chest and walked her fingertips through the thick ruffle of dark hair between his nipples, her usual composure was replaced by suffocating jealousy.

'Then don't go. Stay here with me. Don't go at all,' she said. 'We can stay in bed for days and live off room service. No one would ever know . . .'

'I'd love to, believe me,' he said, stretching.

'But you can't,' she said, finishing his sentence for him. Or won't, she wanted to add, but stopped herself.

'Hey, look on the bright side,' he said, gently. 'I was supposed to be going for a whole week, but I absolutely refused. The three-day rule must be obeyed.'

'What's that?'

'You know, the saying . . . families are like fish. Three days and they go off.'

'If it's going to be so terrible, why don't you just bin it? Think about it. This could be the perfect opportunity. Call Isabelle. Tell her it's over.'

Elliot sighed. 'Bloody hell, it's tempting, believe me, but we've been through this. There's Taylor . . . and my father . . . it's Christmas . . .'

6

There it was again: Christmas. Kellie knew it was fatal to sound as if she was whining, or harassing him (she knew these were the most loathed traits of Elliot's daughter and wife), but she didn't understand this big deal about Christmas. She wasn't religious and Elliot wasn't either. Sure, she liked to celebrate it along with everyone else, but that whole family togetherness thing was so archaic. Her own family would never dream of deeming Christmas enough of a reason to get together. Her brother was on a ship somewhere off Canada, her mother lived and worked in Paris, and her father had remarried back home in Australia a few years ago and had another family to worry about now.

'Christmas. Christmas. I hate bloody Christmas,' she said, rolling away from him and folding her arms. She thought about the iPod play list she'd put together entitled Shite Christmas which included Big Boss Man's 'Christmas Boogaloo', Grandaddy's 'Alan Parsons in a Winter Wonderland' and, Kellie's personal favourite, Robin Laing's 'The Man Who Slits the Turkeys' Throats at Christmas'. She was going to have a long bath and play it as soon as Elliot had gone.

'Bah humbug,' Elliot said.

'I do. It's such bollocks. We just get suckered in to all this consumerism and nobody really gives a shit. The only people who benefit are the shops. It's like being hit by a tsunami of tackiness. I went to Oxford Street last week and it was hell on a stick.'

Elliot laughed.

'And Christmas cards?' she continued on her rant. 'What's all *that* about? It's such a waste of trees. Half the time people don't even sign them. Oh, and those round robin letters –' She paused, a thought occurring to her. She turned over, leaning on her elbows, and looked at Elliot. 'Does Isabelle send one? I bet she does.'

7

Elliot groaned and covered his face.

'Ha! I knew it. Tell me all about it. Go on. Is it –'

'Excruciating? Yes, it is,' Elliot said, cutting her off, as he looked through the gaps between his fingers. He clearly wasn't going to relent and give her all the details, but she knew this already. Elliot was a diplomat and he only liked bitching about Isabelle on his own terms (usually when he was drunk) but not like this, not when Kellie tried to instigate conversations that would force him to say unkind things. 'Fortunately for me,' he continued, pressing the end of Kellie's nose and smiling, 'I have you to get me out of all that stuff. Thank God.'

'You could just get out of it now, if you wanted to . . .'

'Oh darling. Please don't make this harder than it already is. I have to do what's right, and I have to do this. Just this one time, OK?'

'But you are still going to tell them in the new year like you promised?' she asked.

'Yes.'

'*By* New Year?' she specified.

'I've told you: I'm going to fix it.'

She knew it was pointless pressing him any further. She had to trust him. She did. She loved him. He'd broken down a few months ago and told her that he'd fallen in love with her and that she'd shown him that all that he had in his life meant nothing without her. Since then, their future together had become certain.

'It's going to be far worse for me,' he said, smoothing a strand of her long wavy brown hair away from her face. 'How do you think I'm going to feel, knowing you're here? I need to be able to think about where you are every second. What are you going to do when I go?'

Now that he'd asked her such an obvious question, it occurred to Kellie that she'd given it almost no thought. She supposed she could amuse herself. She'd take spa treatments and indulge herself with some quality time doing nothing. Suddenly she felt less brave at the prospect.

'I bet you'll be in heaven with all those movies to watch without me to interrupt,' he said.

She didn't have the heart to tell him that she'd already checked out the hotel room's DVD collection and had seen every one, just the same as she'd seen nearly every film in her local video store. She'd inadvertently turned into an amateur movie buff – an unexpected benefit of all those late nights she'd spent on her own, waiting for Elliot to call.

'I suppose . . . or I can explore a bit. Catch up on some sleep . . . read . . .' She rubbed her eyes, last night's mascara crunching beneath the heel of her hand. 'Take off my make-up,' she continued, showing the black smudge to Elliot. 'Attractive, huh?'

'Very. You're beautiful, Kel. Even when you're impersonating a panda. Now, how about you bring that perfect, sexy body of yours over here?' he said, pulling her on top of him.

Then slowly, sensuously, they began to make love.

Kellie had never intended to become Elliot's mistress, but a year into their relationship, the facts were simple: Elliot made her happy and she made him happy too. Happier than he'd ever been in his life, so he said, and she believed him. Despite their ten-year age difference, they had a sexual connection and an emotional compatibility that they both talked about as being fated – and even though being a mistress came with its harder moments, there wasn't even a glimmer of suspicion in her mind that Elliot was 'fucking his cake and eating it', as Jane, her oldest but now extremely distant friend, had so bluntly summed it up. Kellie was impervious to such accusations. The reality was Elliot had been unhappy for years, long before he'd met Kellie.

9

In fact, his reputation as a miserable ogre had somewhat preceded him when she'd started working on her first corporate law case with him at WDG & Partners. Apparently, Elliot Thorne was the big, ferocious, uncom-promising boss, reportedly so demanding that he'd made plenty of other minions in Kellie's position cry. But Kellie had taken a different approach, answering him back and making him apologise for being rude. She'd fought fire with fire, and playing Elliot at his own game had seemed to do the trick. Within days she'd made him laugh. Within weeks they'd become friends.

It wasn't long before he'd tentatively opened up to her and she'd discovered that he was just about the loneliest man she'd ever met. Soon Kellie knew all about his control freak, business-obsessed wife, Isabelle, and his surly, withdrawn daughter, Taylor. Kellie knew she shouldn't get involved, but she'd found herself wanting to make Elliot's life a better place.

Then, last Christmas, they'd spent every night in the run-up to Christmas working on a case until the small hours. When they'd finally said goodbye, Kellie had fought back tears of an altogether different sort to those of her predecessors. She'd known that she was going to miss him, and it wasn't the kind of missing that was healthy to feel about one's boss.

Which is why, when a soaking wet, distraught-looking Elliot had run up the road after her and had flattened her against the railings, apologising and kissing her in quick succession, she'd known that she wasn't the only one in the grip of something bigger than she'd ever experienced.

They'd barely spent more than a day apart since, and when Elliot had rented the flat up the road from the Chancery Lane office, it had seemed like the most natural and convenient thing in the world for Kellie to move in. He might have been keeping her a secret from his family until the time was right, and it certainly wasn't right to let anyone at work know, but Elliot's commitment to her never wavered.

And now, afterwards, as she lay in his arms, silently stroking his smooth skin, she felt more in love with him than ever. Eventually, Elliot stretched before getting up and heading into the en-suite bathroom.

Kellie admired the view of his naked backside, as he looked at himself in the mirror.

'So what's this Brayner island like, then?' she asked, getting out of bed.

'It's a nice place to come in the summer, but why Dad has moved here permanently is a mystery. No one expected him to retire here full time.'

'I quite like the idea of retiring to a small island,' Kellie said, joining him in the bathroom. 'It's romantic.'

'And totally impractical, but he's so stubborn there was no telling him.'

'I'd like to see it one day. It's beautiful, right?'

'If you like that kind of thing, but to be honest, at this time of year it's just barren and bleak and windswept, and there's absolutely nothing to do. For city people like us, it's just . . . I don't know . . . you'd find it much too low level. Boring.'

Kellie put her arms around his waist and pressed her cheek against his back, as he started to brush his teeth. She didn't want to argue with him. He always seemed to forget that she'd grown up in Australia and was used to wilderness. It didn't matter. She liked him referring to them as an 'us'.

'You never talk about your family much, apart from what happened to Stephanie. How is she?' Kellie felt for Elliot's elder sister. She wished she could reach out to her, but she knew that even thinking this was overstepping the boundaries of her current relationship with Elliot. It was

11

so frustrating to be so central to his life in some ways and entirely excluded in others.

'Coping, I guess. I suppose that's one good thing about Christmas at Dad's. It'll take her mind off things. It might cheer her up a bit.'

'You can cheer her up, I'm sure.' Kellie let go of him and looked at him in the mirror, trying to memorise the details of his face, knowing that very soon she'd once again be aching to see him. 'What about her husband? How's he?'

Elliot sighed and turned to her. 'Do we have to talk about them? It's bad enough that I've got to see them all in a little while.'

She picked up her toothbrush, noticing that the contents of her washbag were strewn all over the side, whilst Elliot's were neatly stashed in his leather bag, which he now zipped closed. Why didn't he understand that of course she wanted to talk about them? After all, one day they'd be her family too. But she knew it was still too soon to discuss that particular issue.

'Darling,' Elliot said, looking at her in the mirror. 'They're just family. It's not important.'

'Isn't it?' Suddenly, she felt like crying.

'Don't be like that. Don't you know I'm going to miss you every second?'

He pulled her into his arms and kissed her. Perhaps she was being unfair, she thought, as she felt him sigh into her hair. Perhaps it really was going to be worse for him.

'At least there's Taylor,' she said, as he rubbed her back. She pulled away and looked up at him, trying to be brave.

'I know. I just hope it's not too late to get through to her before she grows up completely. She's changed so much since she's been away at school. She'll probably go out of her mind without Sky Plus on Brayner, but at least it'll mean I get to spend some time with her.'

Kellie wondered what Taylor looked like. Elliot hadn't

12

shown Kellie a recent picture of his daughter, but she'd memorised the details of the cute little toddler framed in silver on Elliot's desk. She tried to transpose those baby features on to a young girl. She imagined Taylor in braids and braces shyly staring through an overgrown fringe.

'You've just got to be kind to her – and don't patronise her. Don't come over the big lawyer. She'll have to let you in eventually,' she said.

'I hope so, I really do. I need to make things right with her. I need her to know that when things change in the new year she'll still be a part of my life. That she always will be.'

'She'll know that. We'll make her see. I promise.'

We . . . she'd said it without even thinking about it. And he hadn't even flinched. We . . . that's what they were: Kel and El. A team.

Elliot hugged her again. She was glad that he trusted her intuition about his daughter. She was looking forward to meeting Taylor and nervous too. Kellie was under no illusion that it might be hard for Taylor to come to terms with her father being with a new partner. She could still remember how angry she'd been at her own parents for splitting up – and she'd been nearly out of school, five years older than Taylor was now. Nevertheless, Kellie hoped she could provide some of the stability and attention that seemed to be missing from Taylor's life. The girl was only a young teenager. Perhaps they might even be friends, once Taylor could see for herself how much Kellie loved her father. For a moment, Kellie spun off into a mini fantasy, picturing herself and Taylor laughing and linking arms as they walked down the King's Road, laden with shopping bags.

'Hey, I've got something for you,' Elliot whispered.

Kellie glanced down between them and felt him press against her. 'Again?'

13

She laughed as he lifted her up and carried her back towards the bed.

'But don't you have to meet your sister –'

'You're more important,' he silenced her with a kiss, 'and I've got something else for you too,' he said, as he put her on the bed. She watched him scramble across the room and reach into the pocket of his coat.

She looked up at Elliot, wide-eyed as he returned. He grinned back as she took the small Tiffany box from his hand.

'Go on,' he said.

Inside was a beautiful twisted platinum chain, with a heart-shaped diamond pendant on it. It looked incredibly expensive and it couldn't have been more perfect if she'd chosen it herself.

'What's this?' she asked, unsure of what it meant.

'I want you to think of it as an anniversary present, just in case you thought I'd forgotten,' he said.

She flung her arms around his neck. 'I love it.'

'And I love you, baby,' he whispered, 'and I promise you, we'll be together every Christmas after this.'

Chapter 2

It seemed to have got much colder, as the boat finally reached Brayner and moored next to the barnacle-covered jetty in Green Bay harbour. Stephanie could hardly wait to get off. She realised that for most of the twenty-five-minute journey from Fleet Town, she'd been holding her breath. She truly hated being on the water, especially in a boat with all her family on board. She took a deep breath now to steady her nerves. The air was so fresh and cold it hurt the inside of her nose.

She shaded her eyes and looked up at the typical postcard shot of Green Bay village, which consisted of around forty houses and cottages, a tea shop, the Wind-cheater public house, the post office and a youth hostel, which was open in the summer. The only other buildings of significance were the lighthouse behind her, the old school house, with its corrugated iron roof adorned with Christmas lights, and the pretty Norman church. The tourist board couldn't have designed it any better if they'd tried, but for Stephanie, arriving in Green Bay was always tinged with a certain disappointment. It never matched the rather romantic sun-drenched image she held of it in her memory, especially on a day like today.

'Be careful!' Stephanie called, as her son Simon barged past her to be first out of the boat. In a second he was off, running up the steep, cobbled slipway towards the road, where a Santa decoration flapped in the breeze on the iron lamppost.

She could tell, as she watched him ignore her warning

and spread out his arms to zoom away, that he was thrilled to be back on the island. Like his grandfather, Simon found the sheer expanse of sky a taste of freedom. It was certainly a different world from the one he was used to in their traffic-clogged, graffiti-adorned suburb of Bristol.

But at least in Bristol, Simon could be contained. She felt her heart lurch as he reached the road.

'David, can you just leave Nat and watch him,' she said, irritated that her husband was unsteadily lifting up Nat, their five-year-old daughter, as well as two of the bags and the rucksack, out of the boat. 'Just give her to me,' she snapped. 'Come to Mummy,' she said, holding out her arms.

'Simon's fine, OK? Let him go,' David said, as Stephanie took Nat from him.

David was tall and still as slim as he was when Stephanie married him ten years ago, but he looked bulky in the black North Face puffer jacket. His cheeks were pink from the cold boat ride and his face was creased with laughter lines, but he looked deadly serious as his brown eyes now flashed a warning at her.

Stephanie ignored it. She knew he didn't want her to draw attention publicly to Simon, but that was because David refused to recognise that there was a problem.

The truth was that Simon *was* a problem. Or rather, he wasn't. He was perfect; he was her son – but he *did* need watching. He *did* need more attention than other eight-year-olds. He just had so much energy, so many thoughts, that sometimes he had difficulty channelling them all productively. That's what the child psychiatrist had told Stephanie. He'd outlined a plan for her and David to help Simon focus more on what was going on around him, and to take each thought at a time and work it through. It infuriated her that David didn't take this as seriously as

16

she did. He was distrustful of psychiatrists. He didn't think Simon needed one. He thought that if they all stuck their heads in the sand, then the problem would simply go away.

David brushed roughly past her with the bags, as he climbed out of the boat.

'Does Uncle Elliot have any more treats?' Nat whispered to Stephanie, giggling conspiratorially. The fake fur trim on her pink suede coat tickled Stephanie's face and she put her hand out to flatten it down. As she did, she could see that Nat's tongue was blue with food dye.

Elliot had been slipping both children handfuls of M&Ms the whole way over behind Stephanie's back, as they'd bumped through the spray. She'd wanted to stop him, but she also knew how pleased the kids were to see their favourite uncle.

'I thought you were feeling seasick?' Stephanie said.

'I'm not now, Mummy. Please,' Nat begged.

'No. You've had enough.'

Stephanie unloaded the rest of the bags, before helping Nat off the boat. She felt relieved when they were safely on dry land. She turned back and looked at Elliot, who was still talking to the guy in the boat who'd brought them over from St John's.

Her brother, oblivious to all the stress she felt, seemed happy and relaxed. He looked surprisingly well, Stephanie noticed, feeling envious and affectionate, at the same time. But then, Elliot had always had a charmed life. Still, she was so relieved he'd met up with them all in Fleet Town. Without him to lift their spirits, Stephanie would almost certainly have lost her temper with David.

'And you can come and take us back whenever we want? I just give you a call?' Elliot checked with the ferryman. She watched Elliot reach under his buttoned up navy coat into the back pocket of his jeans, bringing out a silver money clip and peeling off a note.

'Just get on the radiotelephone if you need me,' the man said. He stood patiently on the boat, as the waves slapped against the slipway. 'Just ask for Ben. That's me. Your father will have the number.'

'Come on,' Stephanie said to Elliot. 'It's freezing.'

He handed over some cash and stepped reluctantly on to the slipway with his expensive-looking leather Gladstone bag. Ben unhooked the rope, and revved the motor, obviously anxious to get going. A cloud of blue smoke sped across the water.

Stephanie rolled her eyes at her brother before grabbing his arm. 'It's not going to be that bad,' she said, before calling out to Ben, 'Don't worry. He won't need to escape, I promise. Thanks for the lift. Happy Christmas.'

Ben waved and the boat turned away.

Ahead of them, Stephanie heard the beep of a car. Her father was pulling up on the small road in front of the cottages in his dark green Land-Rover. He stepped out and waved. Stephanie felt her heart lift as she waved back, undergoing the familiar cocktail of emotions she always went through when she arrived to see him: nostalgic homecoming mixed with anxiety and that slightly shaken feeling, as if she'd wrong-footed herself in a no-man's-land between her adult life and her childhood self.

From down here, he looked older, his white hair blowing upright in the wind, but he was alive and smiling and that was all that mattered. He opened the double door at the back of the Land-Rover and Rufus, the last remaining offspring of Samson, Elliot's childhood Springer, leapt out and started racing around in circles of excitement. Stephanie watched her father being almost bowled over by Simon, who became swiftly enveloped in her father's green padded jacket. Then, before Stephanie

18

could protest, Nat was running towards Stephanie's father, too.

She watched Nat go, listening to her shriek of delight. She could see in her children's faces how much they needed a holiday, how desperately they needed a break from her. It made her so sad; she felt the urge to grab them back and hug them both. Their dysfunctional and yet familiar family dynamic was about to be diluted into the greater whole of the Thorne clan. How would she cope, left alone with David without the protection of her children, who were bound to get sucked into the vortex of the Christmas jamboree?

Christmas. She'd been dreading it for so long and now it was finally here, but seeing her father and hearing his laughter borne up on the breeze made her realise that she *had* to make an effort. She didn't have to let the old family hierarchy slot back into place. Living under her father's roof, by his and Elliot's rules – whose turn it was to lay the table, who was best at being in charge of asking the Trivial Pursuit questions, who got to walk the dog in the morning and who decided what to watch on the box – she didn't have to let *any* of this slowly drive her nuts. And she *wouldn't*. She'd float through it all serenely, like a perfect, private cloud. She'd resist the temptation to revert to type and start acting like the argumentative teenager she'd once been. She wouldn't squabble with Elliot about his cigars, or leaving the newspaper on the floor in the downstairs loo, she'd rise above it all. They all could. They could all act like adults. Just for three days. Could it really be that hard?

'Here, let me help,' Elliot said, as Stephanie loaded up with all the carrier bags by her feet.

'Thanks,' she said. 'I don't know how we've managed to bring so much junk for three days.'

She glanced up at him. He had a mole high up on his cheekbone, a genetic legacy from their mother's side of the family which Simon had inherited, too. It had been the mark of her mother's beauty and now, in his prime, the small blemish made Elliot more handsome than ever. She noticed the wrinkles around his eyes and the flecks of grey in his hair, but she could still see the boy inside him, the boy who had broken the hearts of all her friends, even though they'd been older than him.

'You OK, Steph?' he asked. He had a way of engaging anyone he spoke to with full eye contact, almost as if he wanted to look right inside them. It was a clever trick for getting people to like him – and to tell the truth. So, for a second, she was tempted to tell him how she felt. She wondered whether her perfect brother with his perfect career and perfect family would ever begin to understand how difficult the prospect of this Christmas was for her, but she'd never burdened him with her problems and now was not the time to start.

She nodded and smiled quickly.

'Come on,' she said. 'Let's not keep Dad waiting.'

At the top of the slipway, Gerald reached out and plucked a piece of loose cotton from Stephanie's coat, before hugging her. The gesture reminded her of school photo days, long long ago, and suddenly all his little foibles came flooding back.

'I'm so glad you've made it,' he said, kissing her on the side of her head, next to her ear, as he always did.

It had been three months since she'd last seen her father, when he'd gone to London to a concert and had stayed with Elliot and Isabelle. Stephanie had driven up from Bristol the next day and they'd all gone out for Sunday lunch in some grim Fulham gastro pub near Elliot's house, where her father had grumbled about the over-familiar service and the quality of the steak.

He seemed so much more relaxed on his home turf and he looked hearty and well. As he hugged her, Stephanie breathed in his scent – a comforting concoction of musty jumpers, dog hair and the aftershave he'd used for years. As usual, the strength of the embrace took her by surprise, leaving her feeling vulnerable and childlike, as if all her achievements, her own family, her position in the surgery, her abilities as an adult, had been suddenly erased.

'Hello, Daddy,' she said.

They all squeezed into the cramped Land-Rover, Rufus protesting loudly from behind the bars in the boot as Stephanie corralled Simon on to her lap, losing her argument about seatbelts, when her father reminded her there weren't any. David sat in the back next to her with Nat on his lap, tickling her so that she kept jerking about, as they bumped along the road.

Elliot sat in the front next to her father. Now she had a chance to observe them like this together, Stephanie remembered how similar they were in their mannerisms, how their heads seemed to tilt towards each other and how naturally a smile came to her father's lips when Elliot spoke. She fought down her childish jealousy at being left out of their friendship.

As they chatted and Nat squealed with laughter, Stephanie stared out of the mud-splattered window as they drove north, past the churchyard, which was strewn with forgotten gravestones tilting left and right like a flotilla of dinghies flexing their sails before the wind. She remembered walking round there at the end of the summer holidays, the last time she'd been here. The salt air had left the stones' inscriptions as illegible as smudged pencil marks. Rumour was that some of the graves were of sailors whose ships had been dashed into matchsticks on the other side of the island, on the treacherously rocky shores of Hell Bay.

She thought of her mother's neat memorial, unremarkable in a row of square-cut polished granite stones at the crematorium in Exeter. She wondered whether she'd ever visit it again. Even now, three years after the sudden, unexpected stroke had killed Emma Thorne in the garden of their old family home, Stephanie missed her dreadfully. Her absence seemed more profound than ever now that they were all together. Stephanie was determined that her mother would be remembered on Christmas Day.

'Is there going to be a service in the church this year, Dad?' she asked her father.

Gerald looked at her in the rear-view mirror. His eyes were still a clear blue-grey beneath white bushy eyebrows.

'There was talk of the vicar coming over from Fleet Town on Christmas morning, but I don't think there's enough interest.' He turned his attention back to the road. 'She's a woman you know. I don't hear great things about her.'

'What's wrong with her?'

'She's a bit stuffy. Puts people's backs up.'

'No chance of you running off with her then?' Elliot teased.

'Er, no,' her father replied, adding to Elliot, 'not with that moustache.'

Elliot guffawed. How could he even joke about their father being with another woman? Stephanie wondered. But her father didn't seem to mind. On the contrary, the good-humoured banter continued, as the car continued further north, past the row of cutesy cottages which tailed out of the village.

Suddenly, beyond the twee, low-walled cottage gardens, the land became rocky and boulder-strewn, rank with heather and gorse, suitable for sheep farming and not much else. The road snaked ahead of them, up and around the mighty domed shape of Solace Hill that protruded from the centre of the island, 'like a great fat tit' as Elliot had always loved to say. A couple of horses were at the top. They stared down impassively at the Land-Rover as it drove past.

Then came the row of stone houses, facing the sea, incongruous in their isolation.

'All empty again,' her father commented, as if it were some kind of mistake.

Stephanie knew that inside they were all done up for rent, with Welsh quilts on their beds and decorated with tourist-friendly brass fixtures and sepia photographs. Weekends and summertime, lights glowed in their windows at night and smoke curled up from their chimneys into the sky, but now, at Christmas time the windows were dark.

'Don't sound so surprised, Dad,' Elliot said, laughing. 'Who would be mad enough to come here at this time of year?'

'You lot, for starters,' her father replied. 'I think it's wonderful in the winter. A real adventure. Perfect for the kids.'

In spite of his optimism, Stephanie felt herself shiver with a sense of foreboding. Instinctively, she held Simon a little tighter.

'Ow,' he said, 'Mum, let go. You're hurting me.'

As they pulled up at her father's house, five minutes later, Stephanie could see Isabelle putting the finishing touches to a Christmas wreath on the knocker of the white wooden front door. She had arrived yesterday and must have brought the wreath with her, Stephanie concluded, knowing that her father wasn't big on Christmas and that there was no way such an unpractical item could have been purchased in any of the island's limited stores. Then another thought occurred to her: Isabelle had probably made the wreath herself. Perhaps she majored in arts and crafts, the same as she seemed to in everything else she turned her hand to.

Isabelle turned and waved, flashing them an ortho-dontically perfect, professionally whitened American smile. As the kids waved back, Stephanie could see that her sister-in-law was looking as groomed as ever, her blonde hair perfectly sculpted to fall behind her ears. Today, she was wearing a pink cashmere jumper, a rabbit fur gilet which ruffled in the wind like the poor thing was still alive, and designer jeans tucked into furry boots. She stamped her feet, excitedly, waiting for everyone to join her at the front door, waving and shrieking with delight as Simon and Nat piled out of the car and ran over to hug her.

Inside, after all the hellos, Stephanie noticed that the house felt different. It was warm and the soft tones of unobtrusive hotel-lobby-style jazz played in the back-ground, rather than the usual dull rumble of Radio Four. It smelt different, too: of cinnamon and baking and furniture polish, rather than fishing tackle and sandy wellies.

Stephanie had come in the summer when her father had first moved in permanently to this, their old family holiday home, after having sold the house in Exeter, but she was surprised to see everything now fully unpacked: the grandfather clock, the rocking chair, the old black and white photograph of her father in his university gown. His sailing ship prints had all found places on the hallway walls.

Stephanie held Nat's hand as they moved through to the dining room off the hall, where the mahogany table had been polished until it shone. In the corner by the fire, a brand new synthetic tree was laden with bows, lights and decorations. It could have been in a window display at Harrods, it was so beautifully done.

Stephanie felt her heart sink with disappointment. This was her job. She'd been hoping to find the old Christmas box, which was stuffed full of a tangled collection of

Christmas essentials. Just the smell of it and its contents – a few strings of dog-eared tinsel, a child's shoe-box full of baubles, tarnished angel chimes, old red candles, a nativity scene which had lost most of its characters years ago – and the battered box containing the synthetic tree that her family had had since the Woolworth's special offer in 1981, took her straight back to a time when Christmas meant something. And this year, more than ever, she needed a glimpse of that feeling.

She'd been looking forward to sharing her Christmas tree decorating ritual with Nat, as she once had with her mother. She'd hoped that her daughter would also enjoy finding the box, assembling the tree and hanging up the chipped red and gold baubles. It was one of the things that reminded Stephanie most of being a child herself.

'Oh,' Nat said, clearly disappointed. 'Mummy, you said *we* could do the tree.'

'Oh, God,' Isabelle said, clasping her hands together. Stephanie could see that the skin on them was perfect, her large square-cut diamond engagement ring as showy as ever. 'We were just desperate for something to do last night when we were waiting for you all to arrive.' Isabelle put her hand out and touched Stephanie's arm. Her nails were French manicured and Stephanie wondered where she found the time to be so indulgent. She was a captain of industry, wasn't she? Wasn't that meant to involve some actual *work*?

'And I thought we'd agreed we'd do the tree before Christmas Eve?' Isabelle said, her southern American accent as soft and seductive as ever.

Stephanie often wondered whether it was Isabelle's accent alone that had made her so successful in business as well as in securing her brother's heart. Because if you took away her voice and went on looks alone and the steel-hard don't-mess-with-me eyes, Isabelle was truly terrifying.

25

Stephanie had no grounds to argue with her now, remembering Isabelle's call a few weeks ago. Stephanie had been in a supermarket queue, trying to deal with Simon and Nat fighting, and she hadn't had a chance to listen properly, before Isabelle had closed her into agreeing with whatever it was she was proposing.

So now Stephanie assumed that this was the first fall-out from Isabelle's planned timetable. It was her own fault she'd missed out on the tree or rather, it was David's. They should have been here last night with Isabelle and Taylor, but David, who'd been tied up on a deadline at the computer magazine where he was an editor, had changed the plans at the last minute. There was no point in being childish, Stephanie told herself. It was only a tree.

'Yes, of course we did. Did you find any of Dad's decorations?' Stephanie asked.

'I found a box full of stuff, but I threw most of it away. Oh my God, Gerry has been keeping such a collection of old junk!'

Stephanie bit her lip. 'Well, it looks lovely,' she forced herself to say.

'Doesn't it?' Isabelle said, pleased with the compliment.

'There's plenty of other things to do,' Stephanie said to Nat. 'I think it's rather lovely that Aunty Isabelle has made the house so Christmassy.'

Nat pointed towards the mass of presents perfectly wrapped under the tree. 'Look at all those. Are they for us?' she asked.

Isabelle smiled and leant down so that her face was level with Nat's. 'Some of them, Natascha.' Suddenly, Isabelle gasped. '*Sweetheart*! What on earth have you done to your head?'

'I slipped on the door step at home,' Nat said, as Isabelle pushed up Nat's dark fringe to reveal the bruise on her forehead. Isabelle looked up at Stephanie.

'It's just a bump,' Stephanie said, angry at the shame and guilt that instantly rose up in her. It wouldn't go away. She felt Isabelle was judging her now, the same as she'd felt as if everyone had been judging her since what had happened last summer. It was like everything she'd been before – a respected GP, a strong and successful mother, and a caring daughter and a loving wife – had been wiped away by the events of a single second. That day had changed everything, for ever. Even though everyone knew it hadn't been her fault, Stephanie wondered how many conversations Isabelle had had with Elliot behind her back. How many times had they laid the blame at her feet? Could it even be as many times as she had done herself?

'You were very brave, weren't you, darling?' Stephanie told Nat, giving the bruise a gentle kiss. 'Now why don't you go and see how Grandpa is getting on?'

When they'd arrived at the house, her father had announced that he was going to be busy chopping up logs in the back garden whilst they all settled in. She looked out of the dining room window but could only see Rufus digging a hole in the lawn. Her father must be hiding in the shed.

Stephanie and Isabelle both watched Nat running off back to the hall. Neither of them spoke. Stephanie had been about to elaborate on the accident that had resulted in Nat's injury, but instead, she let the moment pass. She didn't have to justify herself, not to anyone.

'So how have you been?' she asked, steering the conversation on to fresh ground, as they moved through towards the kitchen.

'Just so hectic,' Isabelle said. 'You know how it is. Work . . . family . . . Christmas.'

Stephanie nodded, but the truth was that she didn't know. Isabelle was one of the top directors of a big mobile phone

27

company. She dealt with marketing slogans and product launches, Stephanie with broken femurs and weeping old men. Their worlds couldn't have been further apart.

'But what the heck. It's the holidays now. You know, I can't remember the last time I had more than two days when I didn't have to do something for work,' Isabelle continued, 'and it's *so great* not to be travelling. Those red-eye flights. Man, they're a killer.'

'And there's no chance of it all slowing down in the new year?'

'Forget it. The industry moves so fast, it's a full-time job just staying on top of developments, and we're restructuring which doesn't help. I had to make a hundred and five people redundant last week.'

'A hundred and five?' Stephanie repeated, shocked. She knew from her experience in the doctor's surgery the devastating effects on people's health that redundancy could make. 'Those poor people. Right before Christmas . . .'

'I know. But the way I figure it, at least they'll be with their families and have time to reflect. Firing them in January would be so much worse. Bad news to start off the year, and broke after Christmas. Just awful. This way, they can make a fresh start.' Isabelle nodded, as if her justification closed the topic. She always did that, Stephanie now remembered. She had an unshakeable belief that everyone should see the world the way she did.

Their path was blocked by David, who appeared in the kitchen doorway, wrestling Simon. Isabelle stepped out of the way quickly. 'Oh my,' she said, slipping into her shocked Southern belle accent again.

Simon crashed on to the floor, laughing.

'You two,' Stephanie said, glancing at Isabelle. Isabelle's expression hadn't changed, but Stephanie momentarily wondered whether she was thinking that children should be seen and not heard. That would go some way to explaining why Isabelle and Elliot had packed off their only child to boarding school. Elliot had said that it was because of their work commitments, but Stephanie couldn't imagine sending Simon or Nat away from her. Not for a day.

But then Isabelle had never been very maternal. She'd fallen pregnant with Taylor within a year of meeting Elliot, when she was just finishing her masters and he'd been on a sabbatical with a law firm in New York. At first, Isabelle had freaked out about ruining her career chances, but Elliot, besotted with his blonde, beautiful prom queen and intent on doing the right thing, had proposed and brought her back to England. Isabelle had checked into an expensive private maternity hospital, before employing a full-time nanny and a personal fitness coach whilst recovering from her elective Caesarean, much to the bemusement of Stephanie and her parents. A giant traditional wedding had followed, during which Stephanie had held Taylor all day, as if Taylor had been her baby and not connected to the bride and groom at all. Within a month, Isabelle had taken a running jump at her career ladder and hadn't looked back since.

'Be careful,' Stephanie told David, flicking her eyes towards Isabelle.

'We're only playing,' David said, as Stephanie helped Simon back on to his feet.

'Yes and you're four stone heavier than him. Just watch it OK? Let him calm down.'

'Oh, let them play,' Isabelle said, smiling at David. 'Simon's turned into a real tiger, hasn't he?'

So much for Isabelle believing in kids being seen but not heard. Or maybe it was just her own kid who Isabelle didn't like mucking around, Stephanie thought.

'Ladies,' Elliot said, stepping forward and joining the

29

bulging family portrait which the kitchen doorway now framed. 'Can I interest you in a drink? There's some wonderful mulled wine on the go.' He buried his nose into a steaming glass in his hand. 'Ah, fruity,' he said. 'Might as well start as we mean to go on.'

'In a minute. Do you mind if I go and unpack first?' Stephanie said.

'I've put you and David in the green room,' Isabelle said. 'I thought it would be more comfortable, and nearer the kids. Now then, where has Taylor got to? I know she's so looking forward to seeing Simon.'

Upstairs, Stephanie pushed open the bedroom door, feeling unduly annoyed. David joined her, carrying the rest of the bags.

'What is it?' David asked, as Stephanie groaned.

She pointed to the twin beds which had been pushed together. The corners of the quilt had been pulled down and a little box of chocolates had been set on each of the plumped up pillows.

'So what?' David asked. 'It's just a bit of fun.'

'It's not a bloody hotel.'

'She's just trying to help.'

'She's not my mother. I wish she'd stop acting like she owned the place.'

Stephanie went over to pick up the two hot water bottles which had each been positioned on a graded set of folded green towels. She wanted to throw them out of the window – or through it. This was her father's house, her only surviving parental home. Surely it wasn't too much to expect not to be treated like a guest? Especially by Isabelle.

She wished again that they'd arrived first. At least then Stephanie could have organised the sleeping arrangements herself. At home, she and David slept in separate rooms. It had been that way for nine months, ever since Nat had begun having nightmares and wetting her bed at least twice a week, waking up and screaming, gasping for air. Stephanie slept on the playroom sofa-bed, next to Nat's room, so that she could get to her before she woke up Simon. Stephanie couldn't remember the last time she'd been naked in front of David, let alone been in bed next to him, but it was too late to make a fuss now.

There was a long pause. She braced herself, expecting David to have a go at her for all their grievances on the journey, but, to her surprise, he checked the door was closed and then moved towards her. He nodded to the bed and the hot water bottles in Stephanie's hands.

'It should be quite cosy. We might not need those.' His tone sounded placatory, friendly even.

Stephanie was so taken off guard that it took her a moment to realise his real motive. Then she tensed, appalled by his insinuation.

'David, I really don't think –' she began, stepping away from him and hugging both empty hot water bottles to her chest. She felt queasy, as if he were a stranger making an unwelcome pass at her.

David ran his hand over his hair. 'Can't we just . . .'

'What?'

'It's Christmas, Steph,' he said. A pleading tone had crept into his voice. 'I don't know. I don't want it to be like this. These past few weeks have been worse than ever. You've been behaving as if you hate me.'

He looked at her hopefully, as if she was going to deny it. Stephanie looked quickly away from him at the floor, fear gripping her chest as she glimpsed, in the shadows of her mind, words she never dreamed she'd say. They weren't fully formed yet, but she knew what they were. Once they were out, everything would change.

David stepped towards her and laid his hand on her

arm. His fingers were long and tanned. She used to call them piano player's hands and tease him that he could be a hand model. She used to love them. But now . . .

She was so tired, she thought. Tired of waiting for it all to get better. Tired of hating the fact that they didn't talk any more, tired of being scared of what would happen if they did.

'What is it?' David persisted. Her whole body seemed to cringe away from him. These were the hands that had failed Paul, and no amount of counselling could change the fact that she couldn't bear for them to touch her.

'I'm going down to have a drink. They'll be waiting,' Stephanie said.

'Stephanie?'

'Please, let's just get through this Christmas, OK?'

Stephanie walked out of the bedroom on to the landing, her eyes blurring with unwanted tears. Over the banister, she looked down into the hallway below.

'I can't find Dad. He's disappeared,' Elliot was saying, coming through the front door.

'Hey, hey, hey,' she heard Isabelle say. Then Stephanie saw her, walking towards Elliot with a cheeky grin.

'Just relax, baby. He'll show up soon enough.' She pulled him by the lapels of his coat, steering him under the huge bunch of mistletoe which hung from the light in the hall. Stephanie hadn't even noticed it was there.

'Izzy, what are you doing?' Elliot said, but there was a smile in his voice.

'You don't think you're going to get away with it that easily, do you?' Isabelle said, putting her arms up around his neck. 'I want a proper Christmas hello from you, Mister.'

Stephanie looked away, as Isabelle leant in to kiss Elliot. She stepped silently into the bathroom, her heart beating fast. That was all she'd wanted when she'd got married: to be in love with David, just like Elliot and Isabelle were with each other.

She turned on the tap and washed her face. She watched the water swirling down the plug hole. She'd never considered that love could simply drain away through the cracks in a marriage, but that's what had happened, and the fact that David wanted to carry on as normal, as if nothing had changed – especially at Christmas – made her want to punish him more than ever.

She looked at herself in the bathroom mirror. Next to Isabelle, she looked old and worn out, she thought. She reached into the pocket of her fleece, pulling out her purse, where she was sure she had a lipstick in amongst the change. As she opened the wallet, she saw the picture in the clear pouch. It was a miniature print of the photograph on the mantelpiece at home. She carried it everywhere with her.

It was a traditional portrait of her and David with their three children, taken at a photographer's studio two years ago, and there was Paul, their second son, sitting on Stephanie's lap, smiling without his front teeth, his expression so innocent and happy, his hair soft and dark, like hers. Her Paul, she thought. Her poor, poor Paul.

She turned away from the photo, its image etched on her memory. It was almost too painful to look at, because in none of their faces was a single trace of all the ruined Christmases stretching into the future.

Chapter 3

Michael grabbed the iron crowbar from where he'd stashed it under his bed, next to the old back issues of *Playboy*, which he'd nicked off his dad and now kept hidden from his mum. He took his grey Gortex jacket from his bed and pulled it on, then he zipped the crowbar in underneath and stuffed his black woollen balaclava into his pocket.

Rock, sport and film stars stared down at him from the walls he'd painted red himself: Brando, Rooney, Morrison, Lennon, Crowe, System of a Down, Muse, De Niro, Kasabian and Jack Johnson. There were photos of Michael and his school mates pinned up on the darts board and a shot of a surfer riding a tube.

Michael had never been to America or surfed a wave. One day, though, he was determined to do both. He was going to stick out school and then he'd travel. After that, he'd come back home and move to London and do something cool for a living, like maybe run a bar, or work for a radio station, or be a chef. He was going to retire early and kick back somewhere hot, like Thailand, or India, or even Californ-I-A.

He jogged down the grubby green-carpeted stairs and through to the kitchen, which smelt of Marmite and Mr Muscle. His stepfather, Roddy, who was wearing a jumper the colour of a wet teabag, glanced up at Michael from his TV show, before staring disinterestedly back at the screen and continuing to pick his teeth with a broken match.

'Another important consideration when deciding where to relocate,' the TV show's host was saying, 'is local amenities. Where will you shop? And where, if you have them, will you be able to send the kids to school?'

As Michael started pulling his mud-caked boots on by the back door, smoke curled up into his eyes from a half-extinguished cigarette in a fish-shaped ashtray on the blond pine kitchen table. Through the brown bead curtain which divided the kitchen from the living room came the whine of a hairdryer. Michael could see his mum through the beads, like a prisoner behind bars, crouched down by the radiator, teasing her corn-yellow hair up into a frizz on the top of her head.

Michael's mum had first met Roddy at a friend's birthday party on St John's. That was a year ago, just after her divorce from Michael's dad had come through. Roddy had only been over on a visit, seeing his cousin, but within three months he'd quit his job as a taxi driver in Truro and had moved in with Michael's mum.

Which was fine by Michael, at least most of the time, anyway, because he wanted his mother to be happy, but then, six weeks ago, his mother and Roddy had announced that they'd decided to put the Windcheater up for sale. As soon as someone bought it, they'd informed him, they'd all move to the mainland. The idea was to run a tea shop there. In Truro. In Roddy's home town. Even now, the thought made Michael want to spit.

Stepping outside was like stepping out of a sauna. Michael sucked in the cold air with relief as the back door banged shut. Roddy shouted out something in complaint, but the words came out muffled and Michael didn't bother to reply.

The back half of the building, where Michael now stood, was where Michael, his mum and Roddy lived. The front half was the pub which they ran, the only pub on Brayner island. Michael had no memory of any other home.

He hurried now down the thin alleyway which ran

along the side of the pub, past the broken flower pots and cracked slates stacked against the mildewed wall.

Wind whistled down the deserted road at the front of the house, whipping a hissing black plastic bag along the potholed tarmac. The dark wet plunge of Green Bay harbour was dead ahead, its unmanned lighthouse pointing up at the sky like a great fat forefinger.

To the right, the road led south, out through the village, then on, zigzagging down the east side of the island, connecting the village to the few scattered houses and hamlets beyond. There weren't many cars on the island, on account of them having to be specially brought out from the mainland and then winched ashore, and the road was empty of them now.

Michael turned left and headed along the road to the north. There was no one else in sight this way either. He pulled his balaclava on, wearing it rolled up so that it looked like an ordinary woollen hat. He was fourteen, but could have passed for seventeen. He was fair-skinned and fair-haired, tall and thin. There was a fragility about him, and a vulnerability to his brown eyes, but he was stronger than he looked.

He'd watched *The Deer Hunter* for the first time the week before and hadn't been able to get it out of his mind. Next to the characters in the film, he'd felt like no kind of a man at all. His life this year had been about exams and timetables, about thinking, not doing. The film had left him frustrated. He was sick of being a kid.

Michael wasn't much good at drawing, what with History and English and Music being more his thing, but he still could have sketched out Green Bay harbour with his eyes shut, right down to the very last stone. The same went for much of the rest of Brayner, which was only three miles long and two miles wide. He'd been brought up here since he was three.

Green Bay harbour was so named on account of the emerald green seaweed which grew on its rocks and which exuded an alien subaqua gleam in the summertime. Michael had grown up slinging the slimy stuff around with his ex-best friend Greg, taking turns at playing Superman and Lex Luther, pretending the seaweed was kryptonite, or writing swear words with it on the pavement outside the post office, to get a rise out of Mrs Carling, who ran the shop there and thought that swearing, along with spitting and running in the street, was a mortal sin.

Michael missed Greg. He'd been the only other kid on the island Michael's age and he'd moved away three years ago, up to Manchester, where his parents had inherited a big house after Greg's grannie had died. Michael's mum had promised Greg's mum that they'd visit, but they never had.

Michael passed the school house, which had closed down in 1971, long before he'd been born. The school Michael attended was on St John's. He had to catch a taxi boat, paid for by the government, there and back every day during termtime. His mates on St John's thought this was the coolest thing in the world, but the fact was that, most times, the sea was like wallpaper to Michael, just something that had always been there. The journey to St John's and back chewed up an hour of free time each day.

He carried on north out of the village, along the empty road which cut through the wild scrubland, for almost a mile. He undid his coat and took out the iron crowbar, swinging it back and forth in time with his steps.

Then he saw them – Taylor and Simon – two stick figures up ahead, silhouetted against the sky on the slope of Solace Hill. Simon was Taylor's eight-year-old cousin. He hadn't been here yesterday when Michael and Taylor had arranged to hook up, and Michael was surprised to see him here now. Taylor shouted something, but all Michael caught of it was the word 'fuck'. She was probably narked at him for being late. He broke into a run.

'Sorry,' he said as he reached her. He hated the way you couldn't text here on Brayner, because phone signals were so unreliable. Most of the islands fell into a communications black spot, so that their inhabitants had to rely on radio-telephones for their day to day calls. Taylor always joked that it made socialising like living in the past.

'So you should be, you unreliable git. Didn't you know it was rude to keep a lady waiting?'

'Is that what you are now?' he asked. 'A lady?'

'That's what I've always been, Michael,' she said.

She was right and he knew it. The way she spoke, the way she dressed, Christ, even the way she walked, she was the poshest girl he'd ever met.

'I had to help Mum peel potatoes,' he said. 'We've run out of frozen chips.'

Michael avoided Taylor's eyes when he spoke. He was worried, the same as always, what might happen if he stared for too long into her eyes. He might blush and end up looking like a jerk. The times he did look at her were the times when she was looking at something else, and when he did, he never blinked, as if he was a camera, as if he was burning her image into his brain.

Simon screamed out, 'Hello!' and Michael turned to watch him racing, forging his way through the thick heather. He was making machine-gun noises, playing at being a soldier. His curly dark hair ruffled in the wind, as he leapt sideways with a great roar, pretending that he'd trodden on a mine. 'What do you think?' he demanded of Michael, getting up and running towards him.

'Nine out of ten for style,' Michael said, 'but ten for effort.'

'Ha!' Simon said delighted, before holding up his right

palm, which Michael dutifully high-fived.

'How've you been?' Michael asked. He hadn't seen Simon since the summer.

Simon shifted his weight back and forth from one foot to the other. 'OK. Yes, good. I got into the football team at school for a match and we beat Rainsford High one-nil, but it wasn't me who scored the goal. It was Garry Egan and he's really fast. And I came last in Maths and Science, as well. And Mum still makes me go to see the doctor about what happened to Paul. And it's not fair, because she doesn't make Nat go, because she says she's too young . . . which is rubbish, right, because Nat says she has nightmares about it all the time, and she wakes me up crying sometimes . . . And Mum and Dad have made me have a tutor at home in the evenings for Maths, but they're not making me do piano lessons any more, because I called Miss Perkins, my piano teacher, a fat, ugly witch and she said I made her cry, but that was only because she wouldn't listen to me, no matter what I said, and she kept pushing my hands on to the keys and hurting my fingers –'

'Sounds like you've been busy, then,' Michael said, cutting Simon off as he took a breath, knowing that if you didn't he was likely to carry on talking for ever.

'Watch this!' Simon shouted, turning and taking a running jump back into the heather.

Taylor and Michael watched him go.

'Do you remember that time that you and me and Simon and Paul camped out in Granddad's back garden and we convinced them that we were surrounded by zombies?' Taylor asked.

'Yeah.'

'That was so funny,' she said. 'We kept them wound up for hours.'

That was three years ago, when both Michael and

Taylor had been eleven. It was the last time they'd slept in a bed together, and therefore the last time, he guessed, that they'd really been kids.

Taylor was now five foot seven, a couple of inches shorter than Michael. Last year, her hair had been blonde. When she'd worn it loose it had hung as low as her waist. Now it was cropped close above the collar, low-lit, with streaks of black and pink mixed in ('Just till I go back to school,' she'd said, 'because then the tossers will make me take it out'). She was wearing a green combat puffer jacket, a tatty denim skirt, stripy tights and tough black boots. She'd lost weight, too, since the summer – or 'skinned down', as she'd said. She looked hard, streetwise, like a character from a video game who'd been designed to fight.

She'd changed shape in the last year, and even more so since the summer holidays. She'd elongated, stretched, switched from angles into curves. She didn't look like a kid any more, not to him. And he didn't feel like a kid either, not when he looked at her.

Michael fancied her rotten. He'd thought about doing it with her ever since he'd had his first wet dream a little over a year ago – and even that had been about her. He'd imagined them in his bedroom, together under the duvet, kissing and exploring each other's bodies with their hands. Then he'd imagined them getting bolder, trying out all the different kinds of positions he'd read about in mags and seen on the web: missionary, doggy, sixty-nines, her on top, or spooning side by side.

In reality they'd never done anything. They hadn't even kissed. His biggest fear was that they never would. He hadn't told her yet that he'd soon be moving away from the island. Whenever he was with her, he felt like it would last for ever. He didn't want to ruin that feeling. Not yet.

'What are you looking so intense about?' she asked.

As he thought of something to say, he glanced across at

40

her and watched her pulling her metallic-looking green G-STAR baseball cap down low on her brow.

'Cool hat,' he told her, guessing that she wouldn't have been wearing it if it wasn't.

Her expression softened. 'Thanks,' she said, 'but it's a knock-off. I got it down Portobello market on the cheap.'

'Even cooler,' he said, though in truth he didn't even know if 'knock-off' meant the hat was stolen or merely a fake.

It was an ignorance he kept to himself. Taylor came from London and Michael sometimes worried that she might think he was backwards and completely out of touch, for having been brought up the way that he had, here on a tiny island in the 'arsehole of nowhere', or the 'edge of the world' – depending on whether you subscribed to Roddy's or his mother's point of view.

Michael compensated for his isolation by keeping up with things on the web and through magazines and TV shows. He knew what was in and what was out, what bands were cool and which were over, and he'd run all this past Taylor in the first ten minutes that they'd met, when she'd arrived on the island the day before, just so she wouldn't think he wasn't her equal, just to make sure that she'd know he was still pretty cool to be around.

A lick of hair hung down below the brow of her cap, trailing over her eye, flapping in the wind. He wished he had the confidence to reach out and brush it away, but his hands stayed by his sides.

'You got the crowbar, then,' she said, glancing down at his hands. 'Good. Let's go.'

He fell into step beside her and they walked on quickly, in silence. Up ahead of them, Simon became an aeroplane, as if he was running reconnaissance for them, scouting the ground over which they must travel. Arms outstretched, he set about shooting down imaginary MiGs, dogfighting across the brow of the hill.

The crowbar felt cold in Michael's hand. The wind picked up and he shivered, remembering why they were here.

'Do you really think it's a good idea,' he asked, 'bringing Simon along . . .'

'Why not?'

'Well, look at him,' Michael said, as Simon tore through a clump of heather with a roar. 'He's like a cyclone.'

'What do you expect? He's just arrived,' she said. 'I've decided it's time he had some fun, away from his mum. She'd keep him locked up all day, given half a chance. She made me swear not to let him out of my sight.'

Taylor was an only child and she'd always treated Simon like her own kid brother. She said it was because she thought he was sweet, but Michael knew it was because she liked having him there to boss around too. Taylor was good at bossing people. She was the one who'd invented all the good games they'd played over the years as they'd grown up. It was she who'd always made the rules. Like today. Like where they were going. Today was her idea as well.

'It could turn out to be dangerous in there,' Michael reminded her.

'Isn't that the point?' she asked.

In there . . . the old Wilson tin mine. That was where they were going. That's what the crowbar was for. They were going to break into the mine and explore.

Sticking to the thin old track which generations of sheep had worn into the hillside, Taylor didn't break her stride as they arced away from Simon and he disappeared from sight.

'But what if he starts mucking about?' Michael went on. 'Or flips out. He could really hurt himself. Or one of us . . .'

Simon had a track record of doing that, of freaking out when things didn't go his way.

'So we'll leave him by the entrance,' Taylor said. 'Then, if anything goes wrong, he can run and get help.'

'He won't want to be left on his own.'

Taylor shot Michael a glance. 'He'll do as he's told, OK? And stop talking about him like he's a loony, because he's not. He's not even on pills and I know a hell of a lot of kids more crazy than him. He's just had a shit year and his Mum's making it worse. I just want to give him a break.'

Michael wouldn't have let anyone else his age talk to him like this, but Taylor was different. He took it on the chin. He didn't answer back. She always said what she thought, even to adults, and he admired her for it. She was also fiercely loyal to the people she liked, and protective of the people she knew, and he admired her for that too.

'Forget I even spoke,' he said.

'I will,' she answered, and out of the corner of his eye he watched her smile.

He smiled too as the last of his anger left him. Conflict was like sport to her. She always got the last word, no matter what.

Michael had first met her eight years ago, when he'd been invited over to her grandfather's house to play. Her family, the Thornes, had been coming to the island for their holidays for years, from long before Michael's mum and dad had bought the Windcheater.

Michael loved having Taylor here. The school holidays got so boring whenever she wasn't around, especially since Greg had split. Sure, Michael sometimes went to St John's, to hang out and crash over with his school mates, with Dougie and Gaz, but that still left a lot of lonely days. It wasn't that he didn't like the island. He did. He loved it. It was his home. It's just that he liked it even more when he got to share it with her.

She stopped now as they approached the brow of Solace Hill. She sniffed the air, like an animal out hunting, he

43

thought, scenting out prey. She took off her cap and ran her hand through her hair.

The island stretched away from them in every direction. Its coast was uneven and scattered with bays, leaving it looking from here as it did on the maps, like a jigsaw piece, or a chunk of cheese that had been gnawed at by rats.

Apart from the three of them, there wasn't another soul in sight. This was how it always was in the winter. Summertime, it was different. June to October, you'd get European school parties visiting on geography field trips. They'd wander the island, filling out questionnaires, eating crisps and cheese and salad sandwiches, coolly smoking cigarettes in hidden places, or sneaking round first and second bases behind their teachers' backs. You'd see them from up here, dotted amongst the gorse in their brightly coloured windproof jackets, like so many downed, abandoned kites flapping in the breeze.

'God, I love it here,' she said. 'Once you're away from the house and there's no one to tell you what to do. I've been looking forward to this for months. School's so fucking tedious it makes me sick.'

Taylor went to boarding school, seven days a week, ten weeks a term. She said it was like a prison. She said they had a million rules. She hated her parents for making her go.

She smiled at him, then cartwheeled, once, twice, ahead along the edge of the path. She rubbed her muddy hands together before wiping them carelessly on her skirt.

'Impressed?' she asked.

'Amazed.'

'Simon!' she called out. 'Where the fuck –'

They watched him surface twenty yards away, like a diver emerging from a green sea and coming up for air.

Michael's eyes returned to Taylor, as Simon came sprinting back. Then they walked on together, past the gnarled black stump of a lightning-scorched silver birch. They were already a mile and a half away from the village. They'd soon be at the mine.

Chapter 4

Ben stood steady on the boat as the waves rocked it back and forth against the stone wall of the Old Quay in Fleet Town harbour. He clicked the built-in bow locker shut and lashed the steel beer barrel against the back of the cockpit with two lengths of fluorescent yellow rope.

A Gorillaz track, 'Feel Good Inc.', was being played on a radio in one of the nearby boat-building sheds, and it drifted out towards Ben in snatches on the cold breeze. Ben knew the song well. It was from an album he'd bought at the start of the summer, when he'd still been getting used to being single. He'd bought it to cheer himself up, but now it only served to remind him of how desperate and miserable he'd been.

As he wiped the back of his hand across his burning brow, the familiar stink of engine oil filled his nostrils. It was a smell he'd grown up around. It had always been there on his father, as pungent as an aftershave, and on his grandfather, too. Time was when Ben had thought it was a smell he'd scrubbed off for the last time, but he'd been wrong.

Ben's sandy blond hair was matted and still tangled from when he'd got out of the shower that morning. Snagged woollen threads trailed from the back of his black crewneck jumper. His once pristine Nike trainers and CK jeans were spattered with paint and smeared with oil. Only his hands were well-groomed, manicured and trimmed.

He gazed at the copper band which he wore on his right wrist. It countered rheumatism, he'd been told one summer, well over a decade ago now, when he'd still been a teenager. He'd worn it as a kind of talisman since, though the fact was that his luck of late had been dire – and it had stained his skin a dirty green beneath. On his left wrist was an expensive TAG Heuer watch. A crack like a bolt of lightning ran across its face. Ben had smashed it on a door handle ten minutes before, but not even that had managed to sabotage his good mood.

'Thanks, Mick,' he called up to the thickset, beer-bellied, older man, who was standing on the quayside, zipping up his worn black leather jacket over his Ry Cooder sweatshirt.

Mick spat and lit a cigarette. A bead of sweat ran down his cheek and hung from his jaw like a pearl. His face still bore the patina of ancient adolescent acne and his thinning, pony-tailed black hair had started to turn grey. Mick was forty, nearly ten years older than Ben, and his father owned the Fleet Town general store. A long time ago, when Ben had been no more than a skinny little boy, Mick had taught him how to swim by throwing him into the deep end of the local lido and shouting at him to kick.

The boat Ben stood on belonged to Ben's father, George Stone. It was a red RIB, a rigid inflatable boat, twelve feet long, and it was capable of carrying eight people.

Ben and Mick would sometimes use it for water-skiing in the summer, always going out near twilight, when the sun cast the sea into a silver block. They'd take turns at the wheel, charging across the shimmering waves, leaving a widening V of rippling foam churning in their wake. Ben was athletic and could mono like a pro and stay up for an hour, whereas Mick had the grace of a hippo on ice skates, and would hit the water like a whale dropped from space whenever he wiped out.

Today, however, the boat was about work, not play, and the two of them had just finished loading her up with provisions that Ben would now take out to Brayner island on his own.

Ben sucked cold air deep into his lungs and smiled. His back and his arms ached from the recent exertion, but a sense of satisfaction underpinned the fatigue. This was the last trip the boat would be making this side of Christmas and Ben was glad that it would be with him at the wheel. It was good to be here, with a sense of purpose, taking charge of himself and his future once more.

'Smoke?' Mick asked, waggling a red and white Marlboro packet at Ben.

'I quit.'

'When?'

'This morning.'

Because of a dream, Ben thought, a dream he'd had last night, a dream where he'd been sitting in a damp armchair in a gloomy earthen burrow – the kind which an animal might carve out of the ground to hibernate in – with a cigarette in his hand and a full ashtray on the arm of the chair, and a TV on in front of him, showing a black and white show of him doing exactly the same thing, like the TV screen was a mirror, reflecting how his whole life had ground to a halt.

'Why not wait until New Year?' Mick asked.

'Because then I'd have a hangover and would need all the comfort I could get.'

Ben had woken sweating from his dream. Was that really all his life had left to offer him? Depression and decline? The first thing he'd done had been to reach for the packet of cigarettes lying by his bed. He'd crushed it in his fist and thrown it in the bin.

Mick stared at the smoking tip of his cigarette, as if he too were contemplating throwing it away and quitting, but instead, he took a long drag and smiled.

'Good for you,' was all he said.

Ben had actually only taken up smoking again a year ago. Before that, he hadn't touched a cigarette for over a decade. He hadn't needed to. He'd been self-disciplined and driven. He'd built a secure life which hadn't needed props of any kind. Then it had all turned sour. He'd taken an emotional beating, at the hands of his ex, Marie, which had left him reeling. He'd turned to cigarettes. And booze. And boozy friends. His last six months had been a cycle of late nights and hungover days. It had got so bad that four weeks ago he'd stopped going out in the evenings, just to give himself a break, and then, today, had come this dream, an affirmation of what he already knew.

What his dream had been telling him, he'd decided, was this: it was time to get *involved* again, not to return to his bad old friends and his bad old ways, but instead to start picking up the broken pieces of his life and stick them back together again. It was time to get back to who he was before it had all gone wrong. That's what the quitting represented to him: a step forward, a step out of the gloom and into the light.

His father had been moaning that morning about his back and so Ben had told him to take the day off. Ben had been dressed and out of the house and here on the quay with a list of things to do by eight. He'd already taken a couple of Canadian tourists out round Skeen island and had taxied a family over to Brayner for their Christmas break.

'No more trips, then?' Mick asked.

'That's the plan.'

Unless, of course, Ben thought, the father of the family he'd just dropped off on Brayner – Elliot something – really meant what he'd said about perhaps coming back here to Fleet Town some time over the next few days.

Ben doubted it. People stayed put over Christmas. TV,

comfort food, red wine, and sleep . . . everyone was a sucker for the same, and no doubt that guy would be no different. But not Ben. Not this year. He was going to set up his laptop, which he hadn't even switched on for weeks. He was going to get online and check out his business mail and start making plans for next year. No more stasis, he told himself. It was time he started making things happen for himself.

'Did you hear the forecast?' Mick asked. He glanced up at the sky, which was as white and smoky as breath on glass.

Ben reached for his coat, a navy-blue donkey jacket he'd borrowed off his Dad, which was hanging over the boat's wheel. Now that the physical work of loading up the boat was over, the cold wind had begun to bite.

'Let me guess,' he joked. 'They're expecting a heat wave.'

Mick grinned. 'Snow, actually. Tonight. Several inches of it.'

'They think it's going to stick?'

'So they say. Storms too. Saw it on the webcast this morning. If the temperature stays low long enough, they reckon there's even a chance there'll be sea ice by tomorrow or the day after.'

Snow settling here on the islands . . . Ben had seen it before, but not often. As for sea ice . . . well, the only time he'd ever seen that had been in the old sepia photographs, hanging up in the Atlantic Arms on Rupert Street, which had been taken during the Big Freeze of 1962, and then, more recently, in 1976, when Ben had been alive, but too young to remember. Ben's grandpa had told him about the ice, though, about how it spread like crazy paving off the coasts, confining all but the biggest ships to their harbours. Ben's grandpa had said it looked like magic, like an enchantress had cast a spell across the sea.

50

'The sooner I get this lot out to Brayner, the better, then, eh?' Ben said.

Mick laughed. 'Too right. And say hi from me to Sally and Roddy at the Windcheater, when you drop off that beer. Tell them I'll be out in the new year for a couple of pints.'

The Windcheater did a brisk business in the summer, when the bigger ferries shuttled tourists back and forth, but the ferries didn't run during the winter months, on account of there not being enough customers to make it worth their while. That's where boats like Ben's father's came into their own, cashing in on the remaining titbits of trade that the bigger boats had spurned, like starlings by a pond of well-fed ducks.

'Right, well that's me done,' Mick said, flicking his cigarette into the choppy harbour waters. 'The old man's shutting up the shop early, so I'm going to slope off down the pub.'

Ben climbed out of the boat and joined him up on the quay. He shook Mick's hand.

'Thanks for the help,' he said.

Mick opened his mouth to reply, but then they both fell silent, because that's when they saw her, walking down the quayside towards them.

The woman was wrapped up tightly in a shiny-looking jacket. She was in her mid to late twenties, Ben guessed, a few years younger than him. Her hair was brown and curly and held up on top of her head with a tortoiseshell clip.

He wouldn't have described her as beautiful – at least, not in a conventional sense, anyway. Hers wasn't the kind of face he could imagine gracing the cover of a glossy magazine, it was too unusual for that, but there was an intensity to her features, he saw, as she came closer, an intelligence, which drew the eye.

Something else compelled the two men to stare. The

51

woman was incongruous, here among the chipped paintwork of the weathered boatsheds, with their grimy, cobwebbed windows and rusted gutters.

As she drew level with them and stepped over an oily puddle in her spotless chunky black leather boots, she didn't so much as spare them a glance. She was concentrating on her phone instead. She looked frustrated, but instead of finding this unattractive, Ben wondered what she'd look like if she smiled. She slipped her phone into her pocket and pulled the hood of her jacket up.

'Well, she's not from round here, and that's for sure,' Mick said once she was out of earshot. 'And trust me,' he added, 'I never forget a pair of legs.'

Ben stared after her. His friend was right. She wasn't the kind of girl you'd forget. He felt a sudden and intense sense of pique that he'd noticed her but she'd failed to notice him, and this surprised him, because the fact was that, since Marie, he'd not been paying much attention to women at all, whether they looked at him or not.

'She must be a tourist,' he said.

'Here today, gone tomorrow,' Mick said, as if that was an end of it. Because that's what they'd grown up thinking, that tourist women were only worth pursuing for a fling or a one-night stand, and this woman hardly seemed a likely candidate for either. Mick slapped Ben's back with his fat paw of a hand. 'I'll be in the Mermaid's Rest,' he said. 'Pop in for a jar when you get back.'

'Sure,' Ben said, 'I'll see you there.'

But Ben wasn't really paying attention. His eyes were still fixed on the woman. She'd reached the end of the Old Quay and was gazing back at the town, across Town Beach, the lifeboat station, and Torthmellon Beach. She then stared out past Hench Island, to where the churning sea met the sky in a blur of grey.

Ben was still standing by the RIB, waiting, when the

woman returned. He'd expected her to be meeting someone, but no one had come to join her. It must have been ten
minutes that she'd waited alone out there on the point.
Had she been stood up? Had she gone there to be on her
own, or to get away from someone else?

As she reached Ben now, he racked his brains for
something to say. It suddenly struck him as vital that he
did speak. It felt like a compulsion. Like his usual urge to
take a cigarette when it was offered to him and thread it
between his lips, it was simply something that he knew he
had to do. Why *not* talk to her? he thought. Why not see if
he still had it in him to make someone stay and talk to
him? It's what his female friends had been urging him to
do since he and Marie had split. 'You get back only what
you put out,' one of them had said. He was in a chipper
mood and he liked the look of this stranger, so now felt as
good a time as any to find out if his friend had been right.

'You should get a cloak,' he told the woman, half-
stepping into her path.

'What?' She stopped and dropped her hood, so that he
could again see her face.

'You know, a cloak, with a hood like your jacket, only
long and black, as well. Then you'd look the part.'

'What part?'

'*The French Lieutenant's Woman* . . .'

Her expression remained blank.

'What you were doing just then,' he explained.
'Staring out to sea, brooding . . . waiting for your lover to
return . . .'

Finally she got it. And there: he got the smile he'd wondered about. It changed her face completely, like a ripple
running across a pond of clear water, bringing it to life.

'You're talking about that film,' she said. Her accent, he
realised, was Australian.

'With Meryl Streep in it . . .'

'Based on that book . . .'

'By John Fowles.'

'That's a kind of obscure film reference to fire at a total stranger, isn't it?' she asked.

'Well, you got it, didn't you?'

'I guess I did.'

He suddenly wished he'd had a shave, but he hadn't, not for a week. He wondered how he must look through her eyes. Like a wild man, he guessed, someone who'd come down from the hills, scavenging for food. He pushed his hair back from his face.

'So *were* you waiting for someone?' he asked.

'I was trying to see Brayner island.'

'You'd have a job managing that . . .' he said, pointing in the opposite direction from the one she'd been looking in, '. . . when it's actually over there.'

The woman blushed, embarrassed at her mistake. Her eyelashes were long, her eyes green, as crystal-like as seawater in a rock pool on a summer's day. She pulled a folded piece of paper out of her jacket pocket and weighed it in her hand. 'I never was much good at map reading,' she said, turning to face the direction he'd shown her. 'Brayner's meant to be beautiful.'

'It is, but it's too far to see . . . today, anyway . . . in this visibility . . .'

'That's a shame.'

A thought occurred to him. 'I could show you,' he said, 'if you like.' He indicated the boat. 'I've got to deliver some stuff out there now.'

He was as taken aback as she was by what he'd just said, but far from regretting it. All it did was spur him on. He could hardly believe he was doing it, actually chatting someone up, stone cold sober, in broad daylight. It had been so long that the sheer nervousness of the moment was giving him a buzz. It felt like a game, trying

54

to detain her like this, trying to keep her attention hooked.

'You could come along for the ride,' he said. 'It won't take long.'

She looked him over, as if seeing him for the first time. 'But I don't even know you,' she said.

He couldn't tell whether she was flattered or annoyed. 'It's all right,' he said. 'I'm the ferryman. Everyone knows me round here.'

'Benjie!'

A woman in jeans, a red waterproof jacket and a blue woollen bobble hat came hurrying towards them down the quay.

'See,' Ben said. 'What more proof do you need?'

'You forgot your sandwiches, love,' Ben's mother told him, as she handed him a rectangular tin-foil packet. 'Marmite. His favourite,' she added for the younger woman's benefit.

'Thanks,' Ben said, feeling himself starting to blush.

His mother then handed him an orange thermos flask as well. 'Hot drinking chocolate,' she said. 'Nice and sweet. Why aren't you wearing your scarf?' she asked. 'The one I gave you for your birthday.'

Ben smiled. 'I don't know, Mum. I suppose I just wasn't in a green and purple paisley kind of a mood.'

He noticed the trace of a smile crossing the younger woman's lips.

'Well, don't blame me if you catch your death of cold,' his mother chided him. She looked the other woman up and down approvingly. 'Aren't you going to introduce us, then?' she asked Ben.

'Mum, meet . . .' Ben shrugged, '. . . Meryl Streep. Meryl, my mum.'

The comment left Ben's mother confused and the younger woman rolling her eyes.

'Actually, it's Kellie,' she said. She turned to Ben. 'And you're . . . Benjie, right?'

'Most people just call me Ben,' he said, as he felt himself blush again.

'Oh,' his mother said, 'so you two have only just met.'

'Yes,' Kellie said, 'and I really should get going. Back to my hotel. I'm staying at the Excelsior.'

'I was just saying to her,' Ben interrupted, 'to Kellie, Mum, that I could take her out to Brayner with me. She's never been.'

'Oh, you really should visit, dear,' Ben's mother said. She was an amateur historian and her enthusiasm for the islands knew no bounds. 'Are you here with friends? Perhaps Ben could take them too?'

Ben looked at her expectantly. *Was* she here with someone? Well, thanks to his mother, he was about to find out.

Kellie shifted on her feet. 'No,' she said, 'I'm here on my own.'

'It would only take a couple of hours,' Ben said.

It felt odd, trying to coax this woman he'd only just met into making a decision, especially in front of his mother, but his intrigue kept building. What *was* someone like Kellie doing here alone on Christmas Eve? And what was there to lose by asking her to take a trip? The worst that could happen was that she'd turn him down and she'd be back out of his life, exactly the same as she had been five minutes before.

Kellie looked back at the town, at the bus station and taxi ranks which could take her to the heliport, and the hotels and bars where she could while away the hours, keeping warm by the fire. The windows and rooftops of the seafront buildings looked as dull and dark as mud.

She was wavering, Ben could tell. He held up the tin-foil package his mother had given him.

56

'What if I throw in lunch as well?' he asked.

'That's very kind,' she told him, 'but no, I think I'm going to head back.'

Their eyes met and suddenly Ben felt foolish, like he'd been rejected, like he'd asked her out on a date and she'd told him no. Which in a way, he supposed, was exactly what *had* happened.

'Maybe some other time,' he said.

'Maybe. Goodbye. And happy Christmas,' Kellie added, 'to you both.'

Ben and his mother watched her walk towards the town.

'A pretty girl,' Ben's mother said.

'Yep.'

'But there's something sad about her, as well,' she added. She squeezed his hand. 'It might have done you both good to spend some time together.'

Back on the boat, Ben started the engine and left it idling as he pulled on his lifejacket. He tried putting the girl out of his mind, but he kept picturing her, standing next to him, gazing out across the bay. He wondered again what she was doing here alone. St John's wasn't like Blackpool or Brighton. You didn't just hop on a train and come here on a day trip. It took planning and effort, trains and taxis to get you to the coast, and then a ferry, a helicopter, or a plane to bring you out from the English mainland to here.

'I've changed my mind,' a voice above him said.

He looked up to see Kellie smiling awkwardly down at him, as if she wasn't quite sure whether she actually meant what she'd said.

He didn't give her a chance to change her mind. He couldn't believe she'd come back.

'Great,' he said, and reached out his arm to help her down into the boat.

'I should warn you: I haven't got any cash.'

'You won't need any,' he said.

'But I should pay you. For taking me.'

'It was my idea.'

'But still. I'd like to. When we get back.'

'Call it an early Christmas present,' he said. 'Islanders' hospitality,' he added. 'We're famous for it, didn't you know?'

He handed her a lifejacket, and she put it on before he could tell her how.

'Looks like you know a bit about boats already, then?' he said.

She sat on the stern seat, beside the beer barrel. 'Enough not to get in your way.'

He didn't want silence to fall between them. He said the first thing that came into his mind: 'Favourite nautical movie?'

'What? You're checking to see whether my getting *The French Lieutenant's Woman* thing was a fluke?' She smiled.

'Maybe. Or maybe I just like talking about films.' Which he did. Almost as much as he liked watching them, because lately life had seemed so much less complicated to him, so much more ordered, when it was being acted out by other people on the screen.

'Let me think,' she reflected, gazing out at the horizon, as if the answers she was looking for might roll down off it like the credits at the end of a film. 'Most recent: *Pirates of the Caribbean* or *Master and Commander*. Most charming: Tom Hanks and Daryl Hannah in *Splash*. Most cheesy: *Voyage to the Bottom of the Sea*. But best of all time, that would have to be either *Das Boot* or *The Crimson Pirate*.' Her eyes were a challenge and there was a triumphant twinkle in them.

'Very impressive,' he said. The last film she'd mentioned, a Burt Lancaster swashbuckler, was one of *his* favourites of all time. He reached into the port locker and pulled out a couple of hats. 'And now for an easier question,' he said. 'Baseball, or woolly?'

'I'm OK as I am. As you've already observed, this jacket's got a hood.'

'I'm serious,' he said, holding up the hats, 'take one. It gets bloody cold out there. You'll be grateful for the extra layer, I swear.'

'Baseball, then,' she finally agreed.

'It suits you,' he told her, once she'd put it on.

'Thanks.' She didn't look convinced. She pushed her hands into her jacket pockets. 'So what exactly is it you run here?' she asked. 'A ferry service?'

He started the motor and cast off the lines. The boat drifted away from the quayside.

'It's more like a taxi,' he said. 'We run people out to Brayner and the other small islands, tourists on day trips, then pick them up later. Seal watching, too, and we take supplies out for the people who live on the islands full-time.'

'We?'

'My family. Or my dad, anyway.'

Ben nudged the boat's throttle forward and began chugging out towards the open water of the bay. A cold wind whipped across them as they left the lee of the Old Quay.

Kellie joined him at the wheel, as Ben began taking the boat north-west, out past the headland on the left of the bay. He increased the boat's speed and the engine's noise rose to a growl. The RIB's PVC hull began thudding against the waves. Ben looked across at Kellie, but she kept staring straight ahead, completely focused, almost as if she were willing Brayner into existence.

They rounded the headland and, within five minutes, there, in the distance, sandwiched between two closer islands, Brayner came into view, a craggy hump rising up against the horizon, a mountain growing out of the sea.

'Hold on tight,' Ben said as he pushed the throttle up towards full speed. 'We're in for a rough ride.'

He felt suddenly disarmed by her standing here with him on the boat, as the distance widened between them and solid ground. A tightness grew in his chest. This no longer felt like the game it had been when he'd first started chatting her up. What this suddenly felt, as they raced on towards Brayner, was very real.

Chapter 5

Michael, Simon and Taylor rounded a copse of hawthorn trees and the Wilson shaft engine house loomed into view. Set on the cliffs overlooking the Atlantic rollers which raced across Hell Bay, it was a grey stone building, over eighty feet tall.

Michael had grown up with this sight, but today it looked different, unpredictable, and packed with possibilities. It was as if a stone statue had suddenly sprung to life.

They joined the ancient, grass-bearded road which ran along the west side of the island and terminated here at the mine. Simon raced ahead once more, wailing wolfishly and howling at the thickening sky.

On a flat half moon of land to the right of the engine house were the remnants of the deserted mining cottages, plundered of their brickwork over the years by the inhabitants of Green Bay harbour. All that remained was a ghost village. No one had lived here for a hundred years. The land was inhospitable, exposed to the elements, and raked by the icy Atlantic gales which raced in like Valkyries from Hell Bay. Broken slates glinted on the ground. The air stank of brine and Michael shivered as he felt the damp settling on to his skin like a claw.

He knew the history of this place well. He'd done a project on the Wilson tin mine for school. There'd been workings on the site for thousands of years. First Ancients, then Romans, and even Phoenician traders, had dug down into the ground like rabbits, carving out a warren of tunnels, scratching and sniffing out lodes of tin and wolfram, nickel and arsenic and lead. Then, in 1849, a London company, the Wilson Mining Corporation, had come along and made the mistake of thinking they could turn the site into a modern commercial venture. They'd been advised – falsely, as it was to turn out – that it would be possible to take the mine down to two hundred fathoms, maybe more, and even tunnel out beneath the sea.

They'd built their tower and started to sink their shaft. It was meant to have turned out like the bigger mines on the mainland, such as Geevor, and if the Wilson Corporation had got its way, the same as on the mainland, a mining community would have sprung up here where the few broken cottages now stood. There'd have been hundreds of men, and children as young as eight, working down the shaft and tunnels, six days a week, ten hours a day.

But it never happened. The deeper they sank their exploratory shaft, the less the Corporation found. Soon, they reached the only conclusion they could – that they'd been ripped off, scammed, stitched up.

The Wilson Mine Corporation folded in 1854. The mine was shut down, its entrances sealed up, and its engine house and the fledgling village abandoned. In 1919, an attempt had been made to convert the engine house to domestic accommodation, but that too had failed. It was now derelict and roofless, with its great doorway and windows bricked up.

'Do you think it's true what they say about it?' Simon asked as they caught up to where he was waiting for them by the rusted barbed wire perimeter fence.

'About the ghosts?' Michael guessed.

'Of the Romans . . .'

Folklore had it that the ghosts of the ancient miners who'd died here remained. If you visited Hell Bay at night, it was said you could still hear the sounds of their distant, muffled cries, and the knock and scrape of their tools as they attempted to dig themselves out from their rocky tomb inside the cliffs.

'And the pirates . . . and their gold . . .' Simon said.

That was another of the myths associated with the mine. Prince Rupert had operated a pirate fleet out of the islands during the reign of Queen Elizabeth the First, harrying Spanish treasure ships, with the Virgin Queen's unofficial support and consent. He'd hidden his plunder in the islands' caves, it was thought, before taking it back to the mainland, but some of it had got lost. Some of it was still waiting to be found.

'That's all bullshit,' Taylor said, delivering a well-aimed kick at the rotten wooden gate set into the fence. 'There's no such thing as ghosts. Or hidden treasure.'

'Then why are we here?' Simon asked.

'Just because. Because no one's been inside for years. Because it's been locked up and that's a good enough reason to break in.'

In spite of his growing apprehension, Michael was glad that they were doing this, together. Sometimes, hanging out here on the island on his own, it felt like nothing he did was real, because no one was here to witness it. That's what Taylor did: she brought the island to life.

Tufts of snagged sheep's wool fluttered on the fence in the breeze. Taylor kicked the gate again. The weather-blistered sign which had been hanging from it fell and landed in a brackish puddle. All that was legible of what it had once said was a zigzag of lightning, which, as they all knew, meant danger. Taylor stamped on the sign, cracking it in half.

She kicked the gate a third time and this time its rusted hinges gave up. It toppled backwards and landed with a soggy splat in the mud. Taylor stepped through and stood with her hands on her hips.

'I wonder who owns this place,' she said.

'Government, probably,' Michael said.

That was what his mother reckoned, anyway. Michael had asked around himself and had found out from Mr and Mrs Whelan, who prepared herbal remedies in a workshop outside the village, that the British Army had briefly commandeered the place during the Second World War. They'd shipped supplies here and guarded them inside the tunnels, but then they'd deserted the place as well, and left it locked up behind them.

Michael stared through the gateway, wary of the land beyond. The danger sign had been put there for a reason. A network of tunnels ran off the mine shaft like the roots of a tree. People said there were sink holes around here that could swallow a man whole. A few tourists' dogs, and several of the hardy Jacob sheep which grazed freely across the island, had gone missing since Michael had been born. None of their bodies had been found.

'What about the next person who comes along?' he asked Taylor, leaning down and picking up the two parts of the broken sign. He propped them up against a fence post, and wedged two rocks up against them to pin them there. 'They might not know how risky it is.'

'Sometimes,' Taylor told him, 'you can be such a fucking square.'

Simon picked up a rock and threw it hard against a slate leant up against what was left of an old work hut on the other side of the fence. The resulting crack echoed like a bullwhip through the village. A rabbit, startled by the noise, ran from a nearby oak tree with its white tail flashing, and disappeared down a nearby hole.

When Taylor and Michael had come here last, back at the end of the summer, they'd climbed over this fence and wandered through the ghost village. They'd sat on the warm bricks of a collapsed wall, drinking cans of Coke in the sun, and had then decided to try and find a way down to the beach. They'd not been looking for danger then. They'd just wanted to hang out. He remembered how he'd felt as if he could have walked with her all day. He'd wanted to tell her not to go back to London, but he hadn't known how.

'This place gives me the creeps,' Simon said. He was looking at the remains of the cottages, stretched out in a jagged row, like the remains of a castle destroyed in a siege. 'I've seen places like this in films and in comics and there's always monsters and vampires and things hiding in the buildings . . . and what they do is wait for you to come past, and then they jump out at you and grab you and suck out your brains, or drink your blood . . . and no one ever finds your body, because they eat that too, or turn you into zombies, which is when you, like, become one of them and then go and suck other people's brains out as well . . . and I don't want that and I want to go home.'

'Not until we do what we came here to do,' Taylor told him. 'Not until we get inside and have a look.'

'Michael, you know about zombies and things, don't you? We don't want them to get us, do we?' Simon asked.

Michael knew Simon had always looked up to him, and treated him like an adult, and Michael liked that, especially in front of Taylor, but Taylor didn't give him a chance to answer Simon now.

'Come on, Si,' she said, resting her hands on her little cousin's shoulders and squeezing them tight. 'If we go back, we'll only end up getting bored with the grown-ups. This is going to be much more fun. I promise. And you know I'm always right.'

Simon dug his hands into his pockets and made a *brrrrr*-ing noise with his lips. He nodded his head.

Michael knew it was useless to try and change Taylor's

mind. Back in the summer, Taylor had told her father that they'd found a way into the mine, but instead of being excited as Taylor had hoped, Elliot had expressly forbidden them to set foot near this place ever again – and it had been then, by telling Taylor *not* to do it, that Elliot had virtually guaranteed that she *would*. Michael knew that if he turned back now, Taylor would only go on alone.

They followed the track towards the engine house, then stopped. If the cottages were like the remains of a castle's walls, then this was its keep. It had been built to house a steam-powered pumping engine which would have allowed the proposed undersea tunnelling at the bottom of the shaft to be carried out in safety. Solid and square, the tower stretched up above them and Michael felt sick with vertigo as he stared up and watched the clouds scud past above.

'I thought we were going down the mine,' Simon said, kicking the damp but solid brickwork with which the front entrance of the engine house had been sealed. 'I can't see how. What are we meant to do? Should we try and climb up? Can we climb up and then, if we do, can we climb down the inside and get in that way? Because it's a long way and we don't have a rope, do we? And even if we did it would have to be incredibly long and we'd probably have to throw it like a lasso, just to get it over the wall. Maybe we could tie a rock to the end of it, because that way –'

'It's OK,' Taylor said, smoothing his hair. 'We don't have a rope, but that doesn't matter. The front door's not the only way in. Come on,' she said. 'We'll show you – but remember,' she warned him, 'this is our secret. You're never to tell anyone we've been here.'

That day last summer, when Michael and Taylor had gone looking for a way down to the beach – that was when they'd first discovered it, the path leading down from the back of the mine. However, it hadn't been a path to the beach, as they'd then hoped. It had led instead to an escape tunnel, half a mile away from the main shaft.

They hurried along the side of the engine house now and joined a muddy sheep track at the back that led off into a thicket.

'I'm freezing,' Simon grumbled, as he and Michael followed Taylor like soldiers into the camouflage of the brambles and trees. 'I mean, really, really, cold. Like I might freeze to death and –'

'We'll get you home soon,' Michael promised, glancing up at the sky, which was darker than even a few minutes ago.

The bushes seemed to close in around them as they walked on. He didn't like it here. They were too far from other people. They were too alone. The air became chilled, musty and sickly sweet. From everywhere came the sound of running water, dripping off plants, trickling in rivulets around the pebbles on the path, and deeper, too, underground, running through unseen channels, out towards the sea. The further they walked, the more it felt to Michael that the whole island was nothing but a giant sponge.

The path wound downwards, away from the mine. The ground grew soft, a rotting mattress of pine needles and decaying beech leaves, each one coloured like a bruise – but still, it was easier to follow than the first time Michael and Taylor had come down here. Much of the summer flora had died away, and it wasn't long before Taylor stopped in front of an ancient oak tree which blocked their way.

Michael could hear the sea – the percussion of waves – but could no longer see it. They were in a steep valley, a fold in the hillside. Rocky ground rose up sharply on either side. Above them, somewhere to the right, perhaps a hundred and fifty feet up now, but obscured from view by the trees and the folds in the hill, was the Wilson shaft engine house.

'I think it's here,' Taylor said, forcing her way through some brambles at the left of the path, to where the hill rose up steeply, back towards the mine. 'Fuck,' she called back. 'Watch out for the thorns.'

Protecting himself with his jacket sleeves, Michael drew back a curtain of brambles and ushered Simon through.

Then, there it was: the entrance to the escape tunnel which led out of the mine.

It was like a giant had punched his fist clean into the side of the hill. Just as Michael remembered it, the tunnel entrance was roughly oval in shape, reaching up ten foot high from the ground. It was covered by a rusted metal grille, the wires of which crisscrossed like the strings of a tennis racket.

Even on second inspection, it looked like a cave, but as Michael stepped in close and peered into the gloom, he saw once more how it stretched back into the darkness, like a throat.

'Do it,' Taylor said.

He'd rather they left right then, but he wanted to please her too.

The grille had been bolted to the rock on its left side by several hinged metal brackets. To the right, it was attached to a further central bracket, and bound to it by a padlock. Michael tried ramming the crowbar in under this bracket, to allow him to prise it free.

'Again,' she told him, as he failed to dig it in.

She was standing so close now that he could smell the conditioner she used in her hair, sweet, like flowers in the summertime. His cock twitched involuntarily in his pants and he focused back on the lock. He tried again, but again the tip of the crowbar slipped, skidding across the bracket. A third attempt brought the same result, only this time, when the bar slipped, it hit with such force that the padlock, rusted and ancient as it was, snapped clean in half and fell with a clatter to the stony ground.

'Brilliant!' Taylor exclaimed.

She scratched at her knee where she'd snagged her tights on the brambles. A line of pale skin showed through like a scar. She put her arm around him and squeezed his shoulder.

'Ready?' she asked.

He could have stayed standing there with her for ever, but he saw a defiance in her eyes which he knew could easily turn to scorn.

'Don't tell me you're chickening out,' she said.

'I'm not.' He was scared, but he wasn't going to tell her that. The truth was that he wished they'd never found this way in. Whenever he'd thought of him and Taylor together, he pictured them on beaches, laughing, lying next to each other in the sun – never in there, in the dark and the cold.

'You're positive?'

He knew it was too late to turn back now. 'Yes,' he said.

'Oh, fuck,' she said.

'What?'

'The torches.'

'What about them?'

'We didn't bring any.'

It was all he could do not to sigh out loud with relief. 'You mean you forgot.'

'No. Yes. I had the bag with them in over my shoulder, but then Dad asked me to give him a hand moving the Christmas tree. I must have left the bag in the hall.'

'I guess we'll just have to turn back then,' Michael said.

'No way,' she said. 'Let's go in as far as we can. To check it's not just a cave.'

Michael's mind raced, searching for a response that would get him out of here with his honour intact. Now that he was standing in front of this gaping black hole again, he remembered why it had scared him the first time. This was an escape tunnel. It had been built to provide a way out in case the main tunnels inside the mine caved in. It was here to lead people *out* of danger, not to lead them *in*. He didn't want to go in there, and certainly not without a torch.

However, Taylor wasn't waiting for an answer. She slid her fingers through the grille, and pulled at the door. It shuddered open, inch by inch, dragging on the ground. Then there was a gap, less than a foot wide, and Simon slipped through.

'Wait,' Michael said.

It was too late. Simon was already inside.

Michael and Taylor yanked the door open wider and they followed Simon into the crepuscular light. There was something otherworldly about it. It made Michael think of the cinema, of that moment between when the lights go down and the screen bursts into life, that moment of hushed and awed anticipation of what is to come.

'Boo,' Simon shouted.

His normally high-pitched voice boomed out at them like a cannon, then echoed into silence. He cackled at the effect. Michael peered through the gloom. The tunnel was wide enough for the three of them to stand side by side. Water dripped *plipliplip* from its roof. A drop landed on the nape of Michael's neck and trickled down his spine. Ahead of them the light faded into inky darkness. Fear spiked Michael, as if he was five or six years old again and had just woken from a nightmare in a blackened bedroom, alone. But here there was no bedside light, and no adult to call out to in the room next door.

Taylor took a step forward. 'I'm so pissed off at myself about the torches,' she said.

'We should be careful,' Michael said. 'There could be holes in the ground.'

Taylor took another two steps, then stopped, and toed the dark ground before her like a horse.

Michael would have run if he'd been on his own. He'd seen too many horror films not to get freaked out. He thought of *The Ring*, *The Grudge*, *My Little Eye* – all those sick moments of victims being stalked . . .

He listened to the sound of their breathing. His eyes strained to filter sense out of the blackness, but all he got was the peripheral light coming from behind. Someone . . . something . . . could be here, now, only feet in front of him, and he wouldn't know, until . . . The breathing he heard might be someone . . . something else's, and he wouldn't realise until it was too late.

He wanted out. Now.

'We should go,' he said.

'You're right,' Taylor agreed. 'I can't see a fucking thing.'

'Taylor!' Simon sniggered behind them. 'Stop saying fuck.'

'Go fuck yourself,' she told him, making him shriek with laughter. 'I can do anything I fucking want.'

'Fuck!' Simon shouted. 'Fuck! Fuck! Fuck! Fuck! Fuck! Fuck! Fuck!'

Michael took Simon by the shoulder and steered him back into the light. He heard Taylor's footsteps behind him. She was following, thank God. They could go home now. He could walk back home with Taylor and she'd still think he was as brave and as fearless as she was.

They reached the exit, stepped outside, and stood there blinking in the light. Simon ran off up the path which led back to the mine and Taylor watched him go. Michael was crushed by what she said next.

'We'll come back tomorrow. With the torches. Then we'll see how far we can get.'

She laughed and that's when he felt it – there, on his neck, another tiny pin prick, but this time different from the creepy sensation he'd felt inside the tunnel. This was more like an electrostatic shock. Then came another and another.

Michael looked up. A snowflake landed on his lips. He saw another, and another. Then he saw them all, hundreds, thousands, drifting down through the treetops. Simon laughed and Taylor started spinning with her arms outstretched, catching the snowflakes in her hands.

He smiled at her. He couldn't help himself.

'Isn't it amazing?' she shouted.

And it was. Amazing that it had started to snow and amazing that he was standing here with her. Watching her spin, he knew she was the most beautiful thing he'd ever seen.

She stopped and stared up at the swirling white sky. She opened her mouth.

'Got one,' she shouted, laughing and sticking her tongue out at him. 'And another. And another. I love it here,' she told him. 'It's all ours. There's no one here to tell us what to do. You *will* come back with me tomorrow, won't you, Michael? Promise me that you will.'

'But it'll be Christmas Day. Don't you think we should just –'

'Just promise,' she said.

He thought again of *The Deer Hunter* and pictured the moment when the wild deer was plumb in the middle of the gun's telescopic sights. All the books Michael had studied and all the films he'd watched were full of such life-defining moments. Would the hunter pull the trigger or not? To which course would you commit? What kind of man would you become?

'All right,' he told Taylor. 'You can count me in.'

Chapter 6

The journey from Fleet Town had been a bumpy but exhilarating ride. What with the noise of the wind and the engine it had been impossible to speak, but now the boat was slowing and Ben turned to Kellie.

'Can you believe it?' he asked.

She couldn't. Snow had started to fall. It came in soft flakes from the light grey blanket of sky above them. There was something calming about it, as it threw a soft focus filter on to the view.

'We should probably drop these supplies off sharpish, then get you back to St John's, but there's somewhere I want to show you first.' Ben glanced up at the snow. 'Shall we risk it?'

'Will it be worth it?'

'Definitely.'

Kellie smiled. 'OK. You're the boss,' she said, clearing the damp strands of hair away from her face and looking out at the island.

It was odd knowing that Elliot was somewhere on it. She wondered whether he was thinking of her and what he'd say if he could see her now. Would he be cross, she wondered, or just laugh, as he always did, about the fact she couldn't help being so curious? So much for her sauna and massage back at the hotel.

Despite what Elliot might or might not think, she was glad now that she'd made the decision to come and wasn't sitting in the hotel driving herself crazy. Anyway, she could do with the company and Ben seemed like a decent guy. Ought she to feel guilty, she wondered, for being alone like this with a man? She glanced over at him. He was taller than he'd appeared at first, his chin was covered in stubble, but Elliot was much more her type. No, it was fine, she concluded. Ben seemed completely safe.

'So what can I tell you about Brayner, ladies and gentlemen?' he said, impersonating a tour guide. 'The island has 101 inhabitants, one of whom is Timothy Lee, the local artist, who's more famous for his flatulence than anything else. Another is Jim Peters, who likes dressing up as a woman, but then don't we all?' Kellie laughed. 'Brayner is home to Savages flower farm, exporting quality flora to Covent Garden, although Richard, the elder brother also has a sideline in *very* exotic plants shall we say . . .'

Up on the headland sheep huddled together at the top of the fields. It was so beautiful and rugged and remote. Seagulls circled ahead of the boat, as it cut though the dark water.

'What about that? What is it?' she asked, pointing at a forbidding tower perched precariously on the cliffs up ahead. There was something prison-like about it, with its lack of windows. Far below it, spumes of white spray launched into the air as the waves hit the rocks.

'It's part of the old tin mine. They wanted to tunnel down through the cliffs, right under the sea, but they never did. It's been deserted for years.'

Even the thought of being that far underground made her shiver.

Ben drove the boat slowly round the rocks which guarded the north shore of the island. Ahead of them white sandy coves stretched into the distance. As they drove in closer, Kellie saw that the nearby rocks were covered in a colony of seals.

'Wow!' she shouted out as the boat slowed again. 'They're amazing.'

Ben drove in closer and she reached into her coat pocket

for her camera. Above the salt of the sea, the air had a tinny, cold taste to it, but Kellie didn't care. It was so long since she'd been somewhere so remote. They couldn't be more than ten feet from the seals now, watching them slide over the rocks and slip into the water. Here, they were sheltered by the cliff and the snow seemed even softer.

'Look at that one,' she laughed, pointing to a huge seal who was peering at them down his whiskery nose. 'I don't think he approves of me taking photographs.'

'How do you know it's a he?' Ben asked.

'Because of its beer belly, of course.'

'And that one over there,' Ben said, pointing to another seal perched on the edge of a rock, which seemed to be staring at its reflection in the waves, 'that must be a she, right, because she's doing her make-up . . .'

'No, that's a teenager,' Kellie said, 'picking zits.'

They came in closer still, Ben standing next to Kellie. It was sweet that he seemed so amazed by these creatures too, even though he must get to see them all the time.

Suddenly, Kellie lurched forward, as the boat hit something. She grabbed on to the black handle on the side, and managed to regain her balance.

'Shit,' said Ben, scrambling from the wheel to the back of the boat. The outboard motor was screeching. Black smoke poured out.

'What's happened?' she asked, trying to keep her balance.

The engine suddenly died. Ben tipped it up so that the propeller was out of the water and leant over to inspect it. 'I wasn't concentrating. I must have hit something in the water,' he said. 'A piece of wire, or something.'

'Can you see what's wrong?' she asked.

'Yep.'

'And?'

75

He didn't say anything, inspecting the propeller blades. Kellie buried her hands in her pockets and shivered. It was freezing out here. Thank God for her thick coat. She'd bought the Spiewak fleece from a designer shop in Notting Hill last year. The sales assistant said it had been imported from New York and was designed to be wearable in temperatures of minus thirty degrees. Kellie had bought it especially for a weekend trip to Reykjavik that Elliot had planned, but he'd called it off at the last moment when Isabelle had suddenly cancelled one of her business trips. So the coldest place the coat had been so far was the freezer aisle in Kellie's local Marks & Spencer. Until now.

'Hmmm,' Ben said.

'What does that mean?'

'Well, I think the technical marine engineering term for it is that it's totallyfuckedup.'

Kellie smiled. 'Totallyfuckedup?'

'Totally. Although,' he said, glancing back over his shoulder, 'it's also possible that it could be utterly-fuckedup.'

'Utterly? Is that worse or better?'

'It's hard to tell. Then again,' he reflected, pulling a tool kit out from under one of the seats, 'I could be wrong altogether and it might turn out that it's only partially fucked up.'

'In which case we've got nothing to worry about,' she guessed.

'See,' he said, 'I knew you knew more about boats than you were letting on.'

It wasn't long before Kellie realised that Ben really wasn't joking, despite being so calm about it. She looked on anxiously, passing him tools as he tried to repair the propeller, but after what seemed like ages, the engine still wouldn't work. They were slowly drifting as the tide began to suck them out.

76

Finally, he turned round to face her. He grimaced apologetically.

'It's even worse than I feared,' he said. 'It's totally-utterlyfuckedup. Or utterlytotally. I can never remember which.'

'You mean you can't fix it?' Kellie asked. Despite his attempt to humour her, she was worried now. She wrapped her arms around herself.

'Probably, but not here. We'll have to go ashore.' She hadn't noticed before how green his eyes were.

Ben turned the keys in the ignition one last time, but the engine still wouldn't start. Kellie shivered, holding out her hand as fatter snowflakes started to fall. The wind was picking up, too.

'Oh,' she said. 'It's getting worse.'

'*And* a blizzard? Great!' Ben said. He stared up at the sky. 'How about a plague of locusts, too?' he asked. 'Or maybe a localised typhoon, just for us, to keep us on our toes? I'm turning out to be a fabulous tour guide, aren't I?'

Kellie laughed. 'It's OK. What shall I do to help?'

'Grab an oar. We'll have to row in. Let's head for that cove over there.'

Kellie had worked up a real sweat by the time they reached the shore. She was used to the rowing machine in the high tech gym in the basement of their office building, but the real thing was much more difficult in these weather conditions. It was hard keeping in time with Ben and she kept getting it wrong. It didn't help that every time she made a mistake, he made her laugh. The whole situation seemed so bizarre. It was surreal to be in a boat in the snow.

By the time the bottom of the RIB crunched against the sandy shore, the snow was settling.

'I'm going out, Captain Scott,' Ben said, 'and I may be some time.'

He jumped down into the shallow water.

'Wait for me,' she said, leaning forward and letting him lift her out.

She could see now that the cove was bigger than it had looked from the water. Kellie imagined that the small beach here must be incredible in the summer, but on a bleak winter's day, Ben was right, it did seem like they were Arctic explorers. At the back an old ramp led up to a fisherman's wooden shed. Set high in the cliffs above, the great black eye of a cave looked down upon them.

Ben lifted the beer barrel out of the boat. He winked at her. 'Just off for a quick pint,' he said, before trotting up the beach, rolling the barrel before him as he went.

He was back in a moment and she hauled on the plastic handle at the front left side of the boat, as Ben went to the other side, and they began to drag the RIB up the slope of the beach towards the fisherman's ramp.

By the time they got there, Kellie was exhausted.

'Well done,' Ben said, clapping her on the back. 'Nothing like a nice afternoon workout.'

'Maybe you should consider a career change,' she suggested. 'Personal trainer instead of tour guide. Move down to London and you could make a fortune.'

'Maybe I will,' he laughed, dragging the boat the last few metres on his own, right to the top of the ramp. 'We're safe here,' he said. 'The tide doesn't come up this high.' He tried to beat off snowflakes which swarmed around them like bees. 'Not that the tide's exactly our number one worry right now,' he added.

He reached in and pulled a tarpaulin out of the boat.

'I'm so sorry about this,' he said. 'I normally leave the old kidnapping the maiden and taking her to my icy hideaway routine to the other guys . . .'

78

'Like Frankenstein . . .'

'Hey,' he said, feigning offence, 'just because I haven't shaved . . .'

'I meant the film . . .'

'With Robert De Niro . . .'

'Of the book . . .' she said.

'By Mary Shelley . . .'

She found herself staring into his eyes, remembering the similar conversation they'd had about Meryl Streep back in Fleet Town. For a guy who worked boats in a remote corner of England, he was surprisingly easy to talk to, and he sure knew a hell of a lot about books and films. Why was it so easy to share banter like this with him? Elliot hardly ever got any of her cultural references. He was much more interested in fancy restaurants and fine wine.

'We must stop doing this,' she said, half meaning it.

He smiled. 'You're right. We should confine ourselves to statements of fact instead.'

She waved her hand at the snowflakes spiralling from the sky. 'Like remarking on the weather,' she joked.

'Exactly.' He paused. 'Fucking freezing.'

'I'd say that was a fairly accurate statement of fact.'

'I mean it. You should get in the hut, or you'll get frozen.'

But Kellie stayed to help him. She felt they were in this together. Just before they covered the final part of the boat, Ben reached inside for the thermos flask his mother had given him.

'I thought it's always supposed to be sunny here?' she said, as Ben joined her at the door of the fisherman's hut.

He said, 'Looks like the rules just changed,' and with that they stepped inside.

It was a plain wooden shelter, with a tiny window, and a couple of old nets rolled up and attached to the ceiling. The floor was just the rock on which the hut had been built. It didn't look like anyone had been here for years, but at least there was a bench. Kellie sat down and rubbed her hands together, before pressing them between her knees. She was freezing. She looked at her feet; her new leather boots were sodden with salty water. She stretched out her legs and flexed her toes.

'Looks like that'll be two hundred quid's worth of Russell and Bromley boots ruined,' he said. 'Who didn't get the protective spray from the assistant, then?'

She laughed, surprised that he even knew the name, let alone that he'd rumbled her about the leather spray. 'How on earth do you know that?'

'I knew a woman once who was into that kind of thing.' There was something disparaging in his voice, but she wasn't sure if it was because he was thinking about the woman, or the cost of the boots. 'And you've still got the label on the bottom,' he added.

She smiled, feeling herself blush. She hadn't met someone who could tease her like this for years.

'So. What now?' she asked.

'We wait, for the snow shower to pass. I thought it wouldn't settle until later,' Ben said, pulling the door closed.

'You mean you *knew* it was going to snow?'

'Sure, but I thought we'd be back by the time it started.'

Kellie suddenly felt unsure about this whole situation. It seemed to have got much more out of hand than she'd realised. Her decision to come with Ben had been impulsive, but she'd assumed that she was going to see the island from the boat and then go back to the hotel, before there was any chance that she'd cross Elliot's path. Now that they were land-bound by the snow, suddenly things looked a bit more serious.

'And then what? After the snow passes. Assuming it actually does. How are we going to get back to St John's?'

'I'll sort out the boat, and if I can't, then there are other people here on Brayner who can help. It'll be fine.'

Here on Brayner. Other people. The phrase rang like an alarm bell in her head. Here on Brayner was exactly where she wasn't meant to be, and there was a chance that those 'other people' were exactly the people she couldn't risk meeting.

'Aren't you worried?' she asked, sounding more stern than she meant to. 'I mean, this is quite serious, isn't it?'

'Hey! There's no point in getting uptight.' He smiled at her and there was something infectious about it that made her relax a little. Kellie wondered whether he was always so confident and calm in a crisis. He crouched down on his haunches, unscrewed the lid of the thermos flask and poured a cupful of hot chocolate.

'This will warm you up,' he said, handing it to her.

'Thanks.'

She took a sip, feeling awkward. She hadn't been alone like this with a man other than Elliot for as long as she could remember.

'So,' Ben asked. 'What made you change your mind?'

Kellie shivered, taking another sip of the sweet warm chocolate. 'About what?'

'About coming out here to Brayner with me? Don't tell me it was the offer of Marmite sandwiches that swung it?' Ben set about unwrapping the tin-foil package.

'No way, I hate the stuff.'

'Of course. You're an Aussie and if you're like all the Aussies I met over there, then Vegemite's probably more your thing? Brand loyalty right. You wouldn't be seen dead eating any of this Pommie excrement.'

'You've been to Australia?' she asked, laughing at the dreadful Aussie accent he'd just attempted.

'Yeah. I went there on my honeymoon. On a diving holiday. Cairns.'

81

So he was married. Kellie felt a momentary and quite ridiculous flicker of disappointment. She looked at Ben, imagining him in a wet suit and how graceful he would probably be below the waves. She couldn't imagine what his wife must look like. Was it she, she wondered, who was into the shoes? She noticed, as he offered her the mound of unwrapped sandwiches, that he wasn't wearing a wedding ring. He obviously wasn't the type.

'Seriously. No thanks.'

Ben smiled. 'Do you dive?'

'Of course. I used to love it. I was brought up near Manly beach in Sydney. I'm a typical Cancerian. I love the water. I was a swimmer for ages. I got on to the Sydney junior team.' She wanted to tell him more, to relive her sun-filled days back at home, but she was too intrigued about his wife. 'Do you and your wife still go diving?'

'I'm afraid we don't do much of anything any more.'

'Oh?'

'We're divorced.'

'I'm sorry.'

'Yeah, well, shit happens.'

Kellie didn't push more for details. She didn't want to pry, but she couldn't help wondering how it must be for Ben living on an island like St John's. She wondered whether his wife was still nearby, whether they still saw each other around, and how he felt about getting divorced when he so clearly had all the rest of his life ahead of him. Looking at him now, she found it hard to believe that he was the one who had done anything wrong. Somehow, he seemed too honest and straightforward.

But what was she thinking? She couldn't judge him on a situation she knew nothing about. In fact, she shouldn't really judge him at all. After all, very soon she'd be officially with a divorced man herself. Suddenly, she had an inkling of all the prejudice that Elliot being divorced might bring. Would people automatically assume that she and Elliot had loads of baggage, that their relationship was more complicated and therefore somehow less likely to succeed?

Elliot. She reached into her pocket and pulled out her mobile phone, handing the chocolate back to Ben, so that he could have his turn with the cup. If she could only get through to him on his mobile, maybe he'd be able to come and rescue them.

'Why don't I just see if I can call someone –' she started to say.

'Forget it. You'll never get a signal in this,' Ben said. Brayner's got terrible coverage, even in good conditions. Anyway, who would you call? Thunderbirds?'

She didn't have the courage to admit that she wanted to contact Elliot. 'What about air sea rescue?'

'Believe me, they'll have more important things to do than worry about us.' Ben nodded in the direction of the sea. 'We're not out there. That's the main thing. And I don't think the helicopters can even fly in this, particularly if the wind keeps picking up.'

Kellie's cheeks burned as she put her phone back in her pocket. If there was no coverage, that would explain why she hadn't heard from Elliot, and it didn't seem likely now that she would. But even if she had been able to get a signal, it was a crazy idea to even attempt to contact him. Elliot would be furious if he discovered that she was here, and he'd be right. She'd been stupid. She should never have come.

'Do you go home much?' Ben asked, unaware of her racing mind. 'To Australia?'

She had to focus. She must put Elliot out of her mind and trust that Ben would get her back to safety, without Elliot even suspecting that she'd been here.

'No. I live in London now. What about you? Were you born on St John's?'

'Born there, grew up there, same with my parents and grandparents. We even lived here for a bit on Brayner when I was younger. My dad used to run the boatyard, but then he took over the boat taxi business on St John's. I think my mum still misses being here.'

Kellie thought back to the friendly woman she'd met on the quayside and how drawn to her she'd felt. It was the same with Ben – as if she had connected with him straight away. Did this happen to other people, she wondered. Was it normal to meet a complete stranger and banter with them, as if they were an old friend?

'She's lovely. Your mum.'

'Yeah? You think so?'

'I wish my mum would bring me sandwiches to work every day.'

Ben looked embarrassed. 'She doesn't . . . not every day –'

'I'm just teasing.'

'OK,' he said, smiling. 'So what about you? What do you do?'

'I'm a lawyer.'

'That's cool.'

'Most of the time. But I don't know . . . being here . . .'

She paused. What the hell, she thought. She might as well tell him a little bit about herself. She had nothing to lose. After all, Ben had nothing to do with her life and in a few hours' time, once they'd sorted out the boat and returned to St John's, she probably wouldn't ever see him again.

'I haven't really stopped work for months,' she admitted. 'To tell you the truth, I haven't even really been *outside* for months. When you get away from it all, from London, the rat race . . . you realise . . . well, sometimes I wish my life could be more simple.'

84

'In what way?'

'I don't know. You seem to have a good life. I mean, people like you . . .' She didn't want to sound patronising, but she couldn't help admiring Ben's uncomplicated way of life, even though he had got them into this scrape. 'You get to do all the simple things, like go and hang out with seals for the hell of it. I wish I could be more – '

'Engaged with nature?' he asked, and she knew that she'd sounded patronising after all. There was a trace of annoyance in his voice. 'Living a yokel's life, like me?'

'I didn't mean to offend you,' she said, meaning it. Actually, she was rather shocked that she'd been so honest. She wouldn't dare admit to Elliot that her career wasn't the most important thing to her. Maybe it was seeing Ben with his mother, their close family bond, that had made her suddenly homesick, as well as worried for her own future. What kind of mother would she make? she wondered. Then it occurred to her once more, would she ever get to be a mother at all?

He grinned and raised his eyebrows at her.

'Oh,' she said, 'you're teasing me.'

'What you said about hanging out with seals . . . you could always get a season ticket to London Zoo.'

'Thanks. I'll bear that in mind.'

'So,' he then said, 'what *is* a girl like you doing out here on her own on the islands at Christmas?'

'Mostly thinking.'

'I see.' She wondered whether he was going to press her for details, but instead he seemed to respect the fact that maybe the time wasn't right. 'More hot chocolate?' he asked.

She watched as he poured some into the cup for her. What would he think about her, she wondered, if he knew the real reason she'd come to the islands for Christmas?

85

Why had she chickened out of telling him about Elliot when she'd had the chance?

Ben stood up. 'I think I'll try and sort us out with a fire. Then I'll have another crack at the engine,' he said.

Kellie nodded, but didn't look at him as he left the hut.

Chapter 7

Michael was lying sprawled on a seat in the bay window of the Thornes' sitting room when he heard the front door slam. Outside, the snow danced thick and fast, so that each of the square lead-beaded panes of glass in the windows looked like a TV with the aerial pulled out.

Looking up from the Nintendo DS's split-screen, Michael listened to the footsteps in the hall and fleetingly wondered if it was his mother, come to pick him up and take him back home, but almost as quickly dismissed the thought from his mind.

His mother hated the cold. She kept the pub as hot as a snake house all year round and nothing short of mortal danger would convince her to come out in this. And she knew Michael was safe. Taylor's grandfather had already called her on the radiotelephone, which the islanders used to communicate with one another, to let her know that he was here.

Taylor was lying a few feet away from Michael, stretched out like a cat on the red Indian rug in front of the crackling, flickering fire. She was silent, listening to her iPod, and idly flicking through a back issue of *heat*.

She'd taken off her jacket and jumper when they'd got back here from the mine. She was wearing a tight, V-neck white top and a grey coral necklace at her throat. Her bra showed through the top's thin material, clearly outlining the shape of her breasts.

Michael thought her tits were pretty much perfect. Not too small, but not too big either. Not too round, but not too pointy. There were some girls at his school whose tits all the boys covertly, and sometimes overtly, discussed and admired. If Taylor had been at Michael's school, he figured that she'd have been one of those girls. People would have pointed her out as she'd run round the athletics track, or nudged each other discreetly in the ribs as she'd hung out in the schoolyard at break, or simply gazed as she'd queued up alongside them in the refectory for pizza and chips.

Michael looked away now as she rolled on to her side, not wanting her to catch him sneaking a peek.

Simon sat at the antique roll top writing desk in the corner of the room, drumming his fingers on its green leather surface, watching a moth twitch spasmodically in a cobweb on the ceiling above his head.

The Thorne house was like a second home to Michael and normally he felt completely relaxed here, but he'd never been here at Christmas before, and everything about it felt stagy and fake.

The enforced tidiness was part of the problem. Old Mr Thorne liked his clutter and usually there'd be sailing boots and waterproofs drying by the fire, half-finished crosswords and Su Doku puzzles scattered alongside dirty coffee mugs across the tables, and sketches pinned to the back of the door.

But Taylor's mum had whisked through here ten minutes ago like someone off one of those TV make-over shows that Michael's mum and Roddy liked watching while they were eating their tea. She'd swept the place clean, even lifted Michael's elbow up to pull out one of Nat's creased crayon drawings, as he'd played his game.

You could take a photo of the room now, Michael reckoned, and use it as a Christmas card, it was that perfect, but there was something lifeless about it as well, something *posed*. It felt like being trapped inside the photograph.

The clock ticked on the wall and the TV was off. The wind thumped sporadically at the window frames. It looked wild and dangerous out there, and like so much fun that it made Michael's legs itch to sit here so still.

Michael preferred it here in the summer. Then the windows were open and a breeze blew through, bringing with it the sweet scent of honeysuckle and jasmine, and you could hear birdsong outside, competing with the crash of waves on the rocks below.

There was a rustle of clothing and Taylor's dad came in, taking off his wet bright red waterproof coat and laying it down on the swept square paving slabs in front of the fire. His blue jeans were tucked into thick woollen socks and his plain blue cardigan was zipped up tight to his neck. He picked up a poker and stirred the fire which hissed as the sparks flew.

'It's bloody freezing out there,' he said. 'The wind's so strong you can actually lean into it and not fall down. Talk about intense.'

'Who were you trying to call?' Isabelle asked as she walked in.

'When?' Elliot asked.

Isabelle looked around, as if she was searching for something, but picked nothing up.

'Just now,' she said, nodding towards the window. 'Out there against the wall. On your mobile. I saw you from the kitchen.'

Michael followed Elliot's gaze to the dark wall of the garage extension, beneath a row of firs, which could just be seen through the swirl of snow.

Elliot replaced the poker in its stand. 'Oh,' he said. 'There. The office, actually. To see if there were any messages.'

'And were there?'

'I don't know. I couldn't get a signal.'

Michael couldn't understand why Elliot had even tried.

Cell phones hardly ever worked here on the island. That's why everyone, including Elliot's father, had radio-telephones in their homes.

'I'm amazed there'd be anyone there to answer, even if you could,' Isabelle said. 'Anyway, I thought we had a pact not to use the cell phones outside office hours. I switched mine off the moment I left work. This is family time, remember?'

Elliot smiled. 'You really should go outside, darling,' he said. 'Just to see. I don't think I've ever been out in something that extreme in this country before.' He turned his attention to Michael, Taylor and Simon. 'What about you lot?' he asked. 'You should give it a go for a few minutes. Try it out. It's amazing.'

Taylor's gaze stayed fixed on the iPod's screen.

'Mum won't let us,' Simon said. 'Won't let *me*. She says it's dangerous and that it's too cold. Which isn't fair and we'd be fine and we all think we should be allowed to go, but we're not.'

'Aunty Stephanie's being a cow,' Taylor said. Her earphones were now in her hand.

'Taylor,' Elliot warned

'It's true.'

'I still won't have you talking about her like that. Not in front of Simon. And not in front of me.'

'I'm going to talk to her,' Taylor said. 'I'm sick of sitting in here and getting bored.'

She marched past Elliot, and Michael and Simon followed.

In the kitchen, David was standing by the kettle, waiting for it to boil. Stephanie was sitting at the table with Nat, cutting out star shapes from a sheet of marzipan.

'Dad says we should be able to go outside,' Taylor said. '*All* of us.'

'Now hang on a minute,' Elliot intervened, appearing in

90

the doorway behind her, 'that's not actually what I –'

'Yes, it is. You've just been out and you said we should try it, too.' Taylor sat down on the table next to Stephanie and folded her arms. 'So why don't you let Simon go?'

Stephanie looked up sharply. 'I've already told you. Because it's too dangerous. It's freezing out there, the wind's getting worse all the time, and you know how near to the cliffs we are.'

'But Simon can wrap up, and the garden's got a wall around it. It's not as if we're going to get blown off.'

'Leave it,' Elliot said.

'I don't want to.'

'This isn't up for debate, Taylor,' Stephanie said. 'Simon's staying here until the snow stops, and that's final.'

'But it'll be dark by then,' Simon said, 'and it'll be even more dangerous then and we won't be able to see the snow, so it wouldn't be any fun at all, because it would be like going out to play with a blind-fold on, and that way we wouldn't be able to throw snowballs, because we'd miss every time.'

'I said final,' Stephanie told him.

'So make it un-final,' Taylor said.

Michael watched Stephanie's features tense and crease, but this time she didn't rise to the bait. Michael noticed a glint in Taylor's eye. She was enjoying every second of this.

David coughed. 'It'll still be there tomorrow,' he said. 'I'll take you out in the morning, Simon. I promise.'

'But how do you know it won't melt? *How*?'

'That's enough, Simon,' Stephanie said.

'It's not fair. Dad. Tell her. Tell her that I *should* be allowed to, and that –'

'Come on, Si,' David said. 'There are plenty of other things you can be doing inside.'

'Like what? Nat's broken the Sony and the TV signal's

rubbish and I've watched all the DVDs at least a gazillion times before.'

'Use your imagination,' said Stephanie. 'You've got the run of the whole house and lunch will be ready in less than an hour.'

'I'll play with you,' Nat said, but it was too late; Simon was already running out.

David stared at Stephanie and Stephanie stared at the empty doorway. She handed Nat a shiny metal cutter shaped like a Christmas tree.

'Here,' she said, 'let's try this one next.'

'Unbelievable,' Taylor said to Michael.

'Go on, you two,' Elliot said. 'Go after him and find something else to do.'

This was all turning too nasty for Michael. The last thing he wanted was to be stuck here in the middle of someone else's family row.

'Your dad's right,' he said. 'We could all play table tennis.'

Taylor flashed Michael a look of contempt, then she marched out of the kitchen. Michael stared stupidly after her for a second, uncertain what he'd done.

'I'll come too,' David said.

Taylor was waiting for Michael in the corridor. She hung back while David walked ahead.

'What was all that about?' she hissed, as soon as David disappeared around the corner.

'All *what*?'

'Suckbutting my dad like that. Backing him up about us going to hang with Simon . . .'

'But I thought you felt sorry for Simon.'

'So what if I do? I make my own decisions, OK? I don't need to be forced into one by him or Aunty Steph or anyone else. So next time, keep your big nose out of it.'

She didn't wait for a reply, which was lucky, because

Michael hadn't one to give. He stared after her, stunned. He'd only been trying to help.

Simon came running back to fetch him. 'Can I be on your side?' he asked. 'Only Dad's rubbish and if I play with him then I'll lose, and I want to win. Like we did in football at school against Rainsford High.'

Michael hardly spoke over the next half hour as they played doubles at the table in the garage. Taylor barely looked at him. He wanted to apologise to her and let her know that he hadn't meant to upset her. Then, ten minutes before lunch, he thought of a way to make it up to her. Shooting her a meaningful look, he excused himself from the room, saying he needed to go to the loo.

Taylor caught up with him in the hallway by the front door.

'What do you want?' she asked.

'I thought you might like one of these.'

He pulled a packet of cigarettes from his jeans pocket.

'I didn't know you smoked.'

'Oh, yeah.'

She'd told him last holiday that she learned to smoke at boarding school. He'd learned since. He'd chucked his guts up the first time he'd tried, but he'd got over that. Now he smoked like a seasoned pro, sometimes as many as five a day.

He'd brought cigarettes with him that morning, a pack which he'd pinched off his mum, hoping he and Taylor might get to share one together, but Simon had come along with them to the mine and Michael had kept his stash secret, unsure whether Simon might have snitched if he'd sparked one up.

'How many have you got?' Taylor asked.

Michael opened the lid of the pack and counted. 'Eighteen left. What do you reckon?' he asked. 'Outside?'

'No. My room. Upstairs.'

93

'But won't your granddad –'

Michael liked Taylor's grandfather and he didn't want him to get upset. Since old Mr Thorne had come to live here full-time, Michael had fallen into the habit of calling in on him now and then when Taylor was away. He'd run errands for Mr Thorne in St John's during his daily visits there for school, and bring him back whatever items of shopping he might need. Sometimes they'd drink tea together and chat. Michael would always ask him about Taylor and how she was getting on. Mr Thorne was always happy to talk about her. Talking about her made her seem closer to them both.

'He never goes into my room,' Taylor said, 'only his studio – and even if he did catch us, I don't think he'd really care.'

Taylor's room occupied a third of the attic, the remainder being taken up by her grandfather's painting studio next door. A thick brick wall containing the chimney breast lay in between.

Inside her room, the floorboards were bare and unvarnished. A set of cupboards ran the length of it and led into the eaves. Against one wall was a wooden bed, with its duvet turned back, and a long pink striped shirt on its pillow. Was that what she wore in bed? Michael wondered. In the corner was a wash basin and a copy of *The Bell Jar* lay on the bedside table, next to a half-eaten Snickers.

The small window overlooked the back garden. The snow was falling so thickly, it was like looking out on fog. Michael had been up here before, but it felt different this time, probably because they'd argued, he guessed. Maybe that was why he felt so nervous now.

On the windowsill were two cans of lager, one unopened and one with its rim flecked with cigarette ash. Next to it was a can of aerosol deodorant, a green

Clipper lighter and a crumpled-up ten-pack of Marlboros.

Taylor cracked the fresh beer can and took a swig. They each lit one of Michael's cigarettes and he watched her as she leant forward to open the window. His stomach twitched as her top rode up her back, momentarily showing a strip of pale and flawless skin.

The wind hissed in from outside, so cold, it felt almost solid. It made Michael think of digging frozen meals out of the pub chest freezer. After his dad had left two years ago, Michael had had to learn to help out around the pub kitchen. In high season, with ferries shuttling back and forth, he'd end up cooking as many as thirty meals a day.

'I'm sorry,' Taylor said, pushing the can into Michael's hand, 'about snapping at you before.'

'It's OK. I'd forgotten about it already.'

'I get angry sometimes.'

'Doesn't everybody?'

'I mean really angry. I know I shouldn't, but I do. Sometimes Mum and Dad . . . and sometimes my teachers . . . sometimes people just really piss me off.'

'It's the same with me,' he said.

'It is?'

'Yeah.' He had a temper too. Everybody did. He tried not to show it, though. He'd seen enough fights between his mum and dad, before his dad had left. He didn't want to end up the way they had.

'Grown-ups, you know,' Taylor said. 'They can be so fucking selfish. The way they just expect you to do what you're told, and lump it, no matter what. Like whatever it is you think just isn't important enough to take into consideration.'

'It's like my mum and Roddy,' he said. 'All their decisions . . . they never ask me about them. They just happen. They just tell me how it's going to be.'

Michael meant their decision to leave the islands and

move to Truro. He didn't want to go. He didn't want to leave his friends from Fleet Town behind, and he didn't want to change school. Most of all, he didn't want to go because he knew that leaving here would mean that he might never see Taylor again.

'Like what?' she asked. 'What pisses you off the most?'

Michael noticed a cut on the back of her hand, scabbed from where it had been picked. It was thin and straight, like it had been made with a knife.

'Just everything.' Michael wanted to be specific. He wanted to tell her the truth: that the next time she came to the island, he'd be gone. But he didn't. He couldn't. Telling her would be asking her for a reaction. Telling her would be asking her how much it would upset her too, and he couldn't face her not being upset, or handle the rejection of her simply taking it in her stride. It meant so much more than that to him. 'It's like my opinion doesn't count,' he said instead.

'It's like me and school,' Taylor said, 'and them sending me there. They said that if I didn't like it, I could come home, but that was a load of crap. They'd piled on so much pressure about their work commitments, and what a great school it was, and how good it would be for me, that there was no way I ever could . . .'

'Maybe they really did think it was best for you.'

'Fuck that. Do you know whose idea it was to send me away?'

'Your dad?'

'No. Just my mother. And do you know why she wanted me out of there? So that she could spend more time alone with my dad.'

'But how do you –'

'Because I heard her. I fucking heard her telling her friend on the phone. She said that her and Dad didn't get enough quality time together, and that she was really

96

worried about them drifting apart, and that he was always staying late at work, and that having me away in termtime would at least mean they got their weekends together.'

'What a cow.'

'No. You don't get it. I thought that at first, and I fucking hated her for it, but then I got thinking about it and I realised that it's actually the other way round. He's the shit. Not her. He's the one fucking up their marriage by working late and not giving her enough of his time. It's because of *him* that she had to send me away.'

Taylor blew smoke at the window. 'That's why I'm mean to them sometimes. Her, but especially him. That's why I like to piss them off . . . just to let them know that they haven't got away with it, just so they know that just because they sent me away doesn't mean I've disappeared . . .'

Michael didn't know what to say, and he got the feeling she didn't want him to say anything, anyway. All she'd wanted was for him to listen. He took a final drag and another swig of beer. He stubbed out the cigarette and gave the can back to Taylor, who finished it off. He was too cold by the window and was feeling a little light-headed, so he sat down on the edge of the bed.

Taylor's black and white Adidas bag lay unzipped by his feet. Her clothes were scattered across the floor, her jeans and jumpers, knickers and bra. There were a couple of guys in Michael's year at school who'd fucked girls. They said it was the best thing in the world. Michael wondered what Taylor would look like, in just her bra and pants. He wondered if he'd ever find out for real.

What if he asked? That was the question. *What if he told her how he really felt? That he wanted her. That he wanted to be with her and sleep with her. What if he suggested that they both just take off their clothes and climb in under the sheets?* But there was another question which stopped him dead in his tracks. *What if he did ask her and she told him no?*

She walked over and picked the bra up.

'Sorry,' she said, watching him closely as she weighed it in her hands, 'I suppose I should be more tidy, shouldn't I?'

He looked down at his socks, embarrassed that he'd been caught out. 'My room's a mess as well,' he said.

She put the bra away in a drawer in the bedside table. Back at the window, she lit a second cigarette. She stared first at its glowing tip and then at Michael.

'So what other secrets have you got?' she asked.

'I don't know.'

'Did you ever smoke weed?'

Michael thought about the kids in his year at school, who bragged about necking e's at the weekend and shagging their girlfriends in bathrooms at other people's house parties. Michael reckoned most of them were bull-shitters, the same as he reckoned that if he lied to Taylor now, she'd know.

'Nope.'

'Nope dope,' she laughed. 'It sounds like one of those rubbish slogans the government come up with. Just say nope to dope. I haven't tried it either,' she admitted, 'but I would. I will. The first chance I get. The way I see it, you should try everything at least once, don't you think?'

'Sure.'

'How about drink?' she asked. 'Have you ever got seriously drunk?'

'I live in a pub.'

'Yeah, but how many times have you got smashed? I mean, totally . . . so you can't even hardly stand up?'

'Lots.' He was lying. The truth was, he'd only ever been drunk a few times, and only been completely hammered the once, and that had been when his father had finally left

98

home for good. Michael had taken a bottle of Cinzano from the cellar and had drunk it sitting on the rocks down on Hell Bay. He'd hurled the empty bottle spinning into the sea, and had then cried himself stupid and been as sick as a dog.

'I've got drunk on vodka,' she said. 'Misha, she's this girl I'm at school with, she snuck a whole litre bottle in from home, and me and her and this other girl, Louise, drank it all with lemonade. I couldn't even see straight by the end.'

'Did you get caught?'

'We stayed out in the park until we felt better, then went back after and said we'd got lost. They believed us. They're so fucking dumb. So long as you look like you really mean it, people will believe anything you say.'

'Do you still hate it? School, I mean?'

'Doesn't everyone?'

'What about your parents? Do you still miss them?'

'Not really. Not any more. They obviously thought I was grown-up enough to handle it. So that's what I did – I grew up. Or grew away from them, at least. Anyway,' she reflected, 'it's not all shit. There are some pluses to being away from home.'

'Like what?'

'Like smoking – and getting wrecked. There's no way I'd get away with that at home. Not with Mum. You've seen how much she nags my dad about his cigars. And then there are the boys, of course . . .'

'What boys?' He'd thought her school was all girls.

'Oh, I don't know. Different ones. We have these dances with the local boys' school.'

He didn't want to hear about other boys. He tried to change the subject.

'I don't like dancing too much,' he said.

'Have you ever kissed a girl?'

99

He nearly started to tell her about a girl called Elaine who he'd kissed at the September Fete in Fleet Town, only a few months ago, a girl from Sunderland, a year older than him, with a stipple of acne across her brow, who'd been pissed up on snakebite and black. He'd gone up to her and asked for a kiss for a dare, and she'd got off with him in the sunshine in the car park at the back of the Tourist Information Centre on Porthcressa Beach, while he'd fumbled unsuccessfully underneath her Radio 1 T-shirt to unclip her bra.

But he didn't tell Taylor a thing. He didn't tell her, because he didn't want her to think he gave a shit about any other girl but her.

Instead, he answered: 'No.'

And in return for his lie, she left him crushed.

'I've kissed boys,' she said, watching him closely to see how he'd react, 'and more. This one guy, I even let him –'

A creak on the stairs cut the conversation dead. Taylor tossed her cigarette butt out of the window and pulled the window shut. She grabbed the deodorant and squirted it round the room. By the time the bedroom door squeaked open, they were both sitting on the floor, examining Taylor's iPod.

'Lunch is up, fellahs,' Elliot said, sticking his head round the door. 'What's that smell?'

Both Taylor and Michael shrugged.

'I'm starving,' Michael said, 'let's go and eat.'

Although the plain truth was, he didn't think he'd be able to hold down a thing. The door swung shut and Taylor slipped a strip of chewing gum into her mouth. As she bit down on it, she whispered into Michael's ear: 'Talk about a close call . . .'

The smell of mint would stay with him for the rest of the day.

Chapter 8

In the kitchen, Stephanie remembered what it was she most hated about Christmas: that it was always a huge anticlimax. As she let out the dirty water from the sink and shook out the metal sink sieve in the bin, she felt like a fool for ever hoping it could be anything other than intensely irritating. Being cooped up together like this for three days just wasn't natural. She was only a couple of hours into it and already she felt like running away.

Finished with the washing up at last (Isabelle had issued firm instructions on not overloading the dishwasher), Stephanie opened the fridge to inspect the contents. As she unscrewed a jar of cranberry jelly, recoiling at the thick crust of mould inside, it struck her as typical that Isabelle had failed to clean out the fridge. Just as she'd suspected from the start, her sister-in-law's role as a domestic goddess was all for show. It was clear that Stephanie was expected to do all the dirty work.

For example, over brunch it had been 'decided' that Stephanie would be stuffing the turkey for tomorrow's lunch. Isabelle had even printed out the recipe she wanted Stephanie to use. Stephanie didn't mind taking on this task, except that once again Isabelle had avoided anything that might compromise the perfection of her nails. Instead, Isabelle would be the one who would be serving up the turkey on her perfectly laid table and, of course, taking all the credit.

Stop it, Stephanie told herself. It didn't matter. She shouldn't feel like this about her family – but the forced *bonhomie* and cheerful togetherness that Isabelle had tried to instil since they'd arrived was grating on Stephanie's nerves more and more. Enforced fun was never fun. Fun was meant to be spontaneous, not planned. Wasn't that the point?

Added to which, she was still smarting from her row with Taylor. Was the child stupid? There were snowstorms raging outside, and she wanted to go out into them! What did she want to do? Give Simon hypothermia?

Stephanie used to get on so well with her niece, but now? Well now, Taylor was just arrogant and rude. She was so much tougher than she'd been before Isabelle had sent her away to school, and there was something else, too. Apart from her ridiculously contrived punky image (which, rather than provoking anyone, just made David and Elliot laugh at her behind her back), there was something mean about Taylor, even potentially dangerous. As if Taylor wanted to push any authority as far as she possibly could. Just to see what would happen. Elliot was going to have his hands full with her and no mistake.

Worse than Stephanie's row with Taylor, however, was that she'd received virtually no back-up from David, Elliot or Isabelle. Nobody had mentioned that Stephanie was absolutely right and that the conditions outside were potentially lethal. Instead, she'd been labelled a kill-joy. Everyone else seemed entranced by the snow, as if it had some magical quality that it might lend to this so far awful Christmas – and, as if to rub in Stephanie's failure to get on with Taylor, Isabelle was going on an all-out charm offensive with Simon and Nat.

'I never expected that we'd get a white Christmas,' Isabelle was saying, moving away from the window back towards the children at the large wooden table. 'When we went skiing in Colorado last year, it was just amazing.'

'It's all because of global warming,' Simon said. 'The weather. We did it in school.'

'Did you?' Isabelle asked, as if it was the most interesting thing she'd ever heard.

'It's to do with the North Atlantic currents.'

Stephanie glanced over at Simon, who was feeding a month's worth of chocolates from the advent calendar to the dog. 'Not too many now, darling, or he'll be sick.'

'Don't listen to your mother, Si, give him as many as you want,' Elliot said, coming in from the hall. 'Poor old Rufus. Dad's got him on that horrible dry food. Where is the bloody sellotope?' he asked, opening and shutting all the kitchen cupboards and getting in Stephanie's way. Irritated, Stephanie remembered now how Elliot could make something small seem like the most time-pressured important task in the world.

She knew what he was looking for: the clunky ancient tape machine that her parents had owned since the dawn of time. In the age of throw-away plastic tape dispensers, Stephanie (and apparently Elliot) retained a unique affection for the object which was so heavy that it had once killed a mouse when Elliot had knocked it off the mahogany dresser.

'And did you know that there's a big chunk of ice about to drop off which will wipe out all of California?' Simon continued.

'Oh my, Simon, don't scare me,' Isabelle said. 'I've got relatives there. By the way, El, did I show you that letter in the card from Bob and Mary Jo in San Diego?'

'Er, yes,' Elliot said, glancing at Stephanie. 'This year, Mary Jo's got new boobs,' he whispered, 'and Bob has a new station wagon.'

Stephanie smiled. She still couldn't believe that her brother actually knew such people, let alone mixed with them.

'Lucky them,' Stephanie said. 'You know this place is a total health hazard. You should have seen what I found in this fridge. Do you think Dad's coping?'

'He's fine. Stop worrying,' Elliot said.

'What do you think Father Christmas will bring you tonight, then, Natascha?' Isabelle said in her wide-eyed children's television presenter mode.

Nat, who was sitting at the end of the table, drawing, was clearly terrified of Isabelle. She glanced at Stephanie for support.

'Go on, darling. Tell Aunty Isabelle.'

'A bike.'

'A bike?' Isabelle gave Stephanie a knowing smile. 'What kind of bike?'

'Well, no, we discussed this,' Stephanie began, closing the fridge, 'Father Christmas might not be able to get a bike out here to the island, because –'

'A pink one. A Barbie one,' Nat went on.

'Oh, Father Christmas brings excellent bikes,' Elliot said. 'Do you remember the one he brought Taylor that year in London?'

'Oh yes,' Isabelle said, smiling fondly at Elliot. 'It was so gorgeous. Covered in bows and glitter balloons. Maybe you'll get one like that, Nat.'

'Well, don't get your hopes up too high, darling,' Stephanie said, running her hand over Nat's head, 'and think of all the other nice things he might bring you.' She joined Elliot by the door. 'Thanks a bunch,' she told him, under her breath.

'What did I say?'

'Perhaps you could explain to Nat the difference between the Father Christmas that comes to Chelsea in a Harrods delivery van and the one that comes across the water to a remote island with hand luggage. There are no bloody Barbie bikes.'

104

'Oh. Sorry,' Elliot said, but he didn't sound sorry to Stephanie. He was looking behind her, over her shoulder. 'Uh oh.'

'What?'

'That'll be the Yuletide log, then.'

Stephanie turned to see that Rufus had relieved himself in the middle of the floor.

'Very funny,' Stephanie said, but she couldn't help herself grinning at his joke. 'Perhaps you should put a sprig of holly on it,' she suggested.

'And some berries.'

'Oh my God! Oh my God! Rufus!' Isabelle screeched, jumping up from her seat, as the dog straightened up from his squat. 'That's gross! Oh. I'm gonna be sick. Kids, stay back. Stay back.'

'You encouraged the chocolate eating . . .' Stephanie said to Elliot, raising her eyebrows at him.

'No, Steph, no,' he said, backing away. 'I can't. You'll have to –'

'No way,' she said. 'He's your dog.'

'No he's not. He's *related* to my old dog. That doesn't mean –'

'You know the rules. You clean up your own shit. See ya,' she said.

'I'll give you twenty quid,' he called after her, 'Fifty?'

But Stephanie ducked out of sight, a wry smile on her face. It would be good for her brother to have to deal with some shit for once in his over-privileged life.

Stephanie was on her way to see her father, when she found David unloading the holdall full of presents on to the dining room table, turning each gift over, as if utterly perplexed. The cheap slippery paper Stephanie had picked up at the twenty-four-hour garage the night before last looked embarrassingly shabby next to the tasteful gold embossed thick cream paper which Isabelle had used for her presents.

'I was going to do that,' Stephanie said. She wanted to check that all the presents had arrived intact.

'What are all these?' David asked, looking in a plastic bag full of little presents.

Stephanie snatched the bag and hid it back in the holdall. 'They're for the kids' stockings.'

'Well, I wasn't supposed to know, was I?'

No, she thought. You wouldn't have a bloody clue.

'Nat wants a bike from Santa,' Stephanie informed him, determined not to have a row. 'How are we going to get around that one?'

'She won't care. You know what kids are like on Christmas Day. There are so many presents lying around that they don't even know which ones are theirs, let alone have time to worry about what they didn't get.'

'She *will* care,' Stephanie said, feeling cross that she felt so inadequate. They'd already argued about presents before they'd left home, when David had suddenly announced that he'd been shopping for the kids. Stephanie had already bought the children's presents, but David had told her to stop being so controlling. That if he wanted to buy extra presents, then he could. Now, after all of that, he was making out that the kids wouldn't care in any case.

There was a short pause, as she zipped up the bag.

'So have you got a present for Isabelle and Elliot?' David asked.

'Of I course I have.'

'What is it?'

Why did he need to know right now? she thought, irritated that he expected her to randomly access a section of the vast quantity of information that had been occupying her brain during the whole run-up to Christmas.

She let out a frustrated sigh.

106

'It's that one,' she said, pointing to the box on the end of the table. She watched David go towards it, but somehow, just as he picked it up, it slipped out of his hand. The box fell on to the hearth.

'David! For God's sake!'

'Calm down,' he said, picking up the box. 'It's no big deal.'

'Er . . . yes, David, it is,' Stephanie said, snatching it off him and shaking the box. The unmistakable sound of shattered glass came from inside.

She saw his cheeks flush, but he didn't apologise.

'What the hell was in there?' he asked.

'Cut glass brandy tumblers.'

'Cut glass? Well what do you expect?' he said, as if the breakage was her fault. 'After the boat ride, they were probably already broken. Way before I dropped it.'

How typical that his immediate response was to wriggle out of any responsibility, Stephanie thought.

'It was rather a stupid present, if you ask me,' he said.

She wanted to tell him that it wasn't a rather stupid present. She wanted to tell him that she'd bought the glasses because they would actually make a rather *nice* present, considering that Elliot had a penchant for brandy and Isabelle collected that exact design of cut glass and would be delighted with the gift. But looking at David now, Stephanie didn't bother. Instead, she threw the box down on the table and gripped her fringe in her hand. She must not lose control, she thought, even though she felt her chest tightening with anxiety. She must not allow this to escalate into a full-blown argument, because if it did, she didn't know where it would end.

David planted his hands on his hips.

'So? What do we do now?' he asked. 'Was that all you got them?'

'What do you mean *all I got them*? They cost a fortune.'

107

'But two glasses . . . it's not very big, is it? It doesn't look like much.'

Stephanie stared at him. Was their worthiness now to be measured by the proportion of space under the tree their Christmas present occupied? What exactly did he think was big enough? A set of golf clubs? Monogrammed luggage?

'We'll just have to give them the present that I bought for the kids to give them,' Stephanie said.

'What did you get?'

'I don't know. Pot pourri, or something. It's there.' She pointed to the pile under the Christmas tree, as she ripped off the label from the box of smashed glass.

'*Pot pourri*?' There was an edge of horror to his voice.

'It's in a nice designer glass dish thing. It'll match their lounge.'

David searched through the pile and picked it up.

'We can't give them just that,' he said. 'It's miserly.'

Stephanie stared at him. They wouldn't have to if David hadn't smashed the glasses. This was all his fault in the first place.

'And anyway,' he continued. 'You always used to laugh about stuff like that and how pointless it is. I mean, come on . . . pot pourri? It's not a very nice gift. Not for close relatives.'

Stephanie clicked her tongue, wondering where to start. Had *he* ever tried buying presents for the entire family on a budget, dragging himself around the shops after a hard day at work, sweating in the bad-tempered crowds, racking his brains for something appropriate to buy from the children? Had *he* suffered the intense migraine brought on by deep resentment and time-pressured indecision? And when he'd stood in the giant queue and paid for the god-damned thing with the money earmarked for his own haircut, had *he* then carted the said bowl of pot pourri through the freezing drizzle to the car where its

108

sickly scent had permeated all of the other shopping?

No, actually, she didn't think he had.

And whilst she was on the subject, had it been *David* who stayed up to midnight, trying to rub off the price label's super-sticky glue residue before wrapping the bloody thing?

Er . . . No.

And had *he* written the loving message and signed it from his children, as if the gift were a flippant whimsical token of their affection?

No he bloody well hadn't. So how *dare* he accuse her of buying a horrible gift?

'I'm sorry you feel that way, David,' she said, her voice measured, 'but I think under the circumstances, we have no other choice.'

David let out a sigh, that was more like a grunt. 'Are you going to do this all of Christmas?' he asked.

'Do what?'

'Take that tone? Argue with everything I say?'

'You started it.'

'No. I simply asked you whether you'd got a present for Isabelle and Elliot.'

Stephanie glared at him. 'Yes. And I did have. A very nice one.'

'Fine, have it your own way,' David said, throwing up his hands. 'You're always complaining that I don't help, but I guess it's just easier to leave you to it. I'm going to play with the kids.'

Upstairs, Stephanie knocked on her father's studio door in the attic and entered. Gerald was sitting on a low wooden stool in front of an easel by a large square double-glazed window, which looked out of the back of the house. In spite of the snowstorm outside, it was quiet. She remembered that they'd used to play in here when her parents had first bought the house. In those days it had been dusty and full of boxes and the windows had been boarded up, but now bright lights shone on a wall of photographs, all of the same subject – the headland and the old tin mine which overlooked Hell Bay.

'So. This is where you're hiding,' she said, finding a path towards him through the piled-up canvases and towers of books, which had yet to be put in the bookcases on the walls.

A few of the low purple velvet chairs which used to be in the hall in the house she'd grown up in in Exeter were balanced precariously on top of one another. An ornate mahogany table, which she also recognised, was covered in newspaper, bottles of paint and old mugs of tea. She was relieved to see that, judging from the junk and dust, Isabelle had yet to get her Swiffered mitts up here.

'I'm glad we're all safe inside,' her father said, not looking around. She noticed his toes protruding through his holey socks, wriggling up against the fan heater. 'Look at it out there. I've never seen anything like it.'

He was right. From up here, all she could see was the whiteout. Snowflakes butted the window, piling up in the corners.

'How's everyone settling in down there?' he asked.

'Fine. Rufus disgraced himself, but Elliot's on the case.'

Stephanie stood behind her father and gently massaged his shoulders through his green woollen jumper. It was nice to be away from them all, finally to have a moment of peace. She watched the snowflakes tumble and twist, as fast and furious as TV static. She'd read somewhere that no two snowflakes ever looked the same under a magnifying glass. The structure of each was unique. When they melted, they were lost to the world for ever.

'It's not very good, is it?' her father said after a while, casting a critical eye over the painting through the glasses

110

on the end of his nose. Then he looked at the photos, pointing his paintbrush at the view. 'I wanted to have this finished in time to give to Elliot and Isabelle for Christmas, but I still can't get the proportions of that damn headland.'

'It's an improvement on the last one,' she said, looking at the painting and its shaky water-coloured lines. She was very familiar with this scene, but her father never seemed to tire of painting the same view over and over again. It was where he and her mother had always picnicked and walked.

Gerald extended his brush and added a small green blob to the paper.

'Hey, I got those pills for you,' Stephanie said, stepping forward and placing the small bottle which she'd brought from the surgery on to her father's easel. She'd been worried about his arthritis for a while now.

'Thank you. I hope you didn't break the rules?'

'Bent them. But just for you. Is it getting worse?'

'It's not too bad. Uncomfortable in this weather, but I'm managing.'

'You know, I do worry about you being by yourself, Dad. It's strange being here for Christmas.' Stephanie looked outside and shivered. 'It seems more remote than ever.'

Her father sighed, reaching up and placing his hand over hers on his shoulder. His skin was still remarkably unwrinkled for a seventy-year-old, but she could see that his knuckles were swollen, where the arthritis threatened to gnarl up his joints like a decaying tree. 'Well don't. I don't need you to worry, I'm fine.'

Stephanie knew it was true. He *was* fine. More than fine. He seemed to have an inner strength and peace that she had never come near to finding herself. He also seemed perfectly relaxed about doing whatever he wanted, when he wanted, even with a house full of his own family. She realised now that it was the first time in months she'd had a chance to talk to him on his own.

'I just thought that after Mum died, you'd come nearer to us,' she said. She was still not willing to give up on the same old argument she had with him time and again on the phone.

'And have you rushing about taking care of me?'

'Yes!' she said. 'Exactly.'

'I don't want that,' he said, 'not whilst I'm fit and healthy. You've got your own life to lead. Your own family.'

'But you're so isolated here.'

'I like the solitude. I've spent a lifetime surrounded by people.'

'But it's so far away from us.' Stephanie couldn't help sounding petulant. She wondered if she'd feel so alone if he lived nearer to her. Being with her father always gave her a sense of connection to herself as the person she was before her life became so complicated.

'I know, but you're here now.'

Stephanie didn't argue. She knew that he knew that she loved him and would always come here to see him, even if it did mean crossing the water, which he knew she hated.

'Your mother always joked that we started our lives together in London and every ten years we moved a couple of hundred miles further away, but this is my last outpost. When I'm gone, you can scatter my ashes over Hell's Bay.' He nodded out of the window at the view.

'Oh, Dad.' Stephanie squeezed his shoulders. 'Please don't get morbid.'

Her father chuckled. 'I'm not on my way out yet. You'd be surprised. There's life in the old dog yet.'

'I'm glad to hear it,' she said, busying herself by collecting the mugs up from the table. 'Anyway, you'd better get a move on up here. Isabelle says lunch will be ready by three.'

'What were all those sausages and eggs supposed to be two hours ago? Can't we have an early supper later on?'

'No, Gerry,' Stephanie said, impersonating Isabelle's American accent. 'It's not in the Christmas schedule.'

'Now, now.'

'Well, honestly,' Stephanie said.

Her father took off his glasses and turned on the stool to face her. 'I know she winds you up, but she's doing her best.'

'But –'

'I don't want any fighting, OK? You're all welcome here for Christmas and I want it to be a happy time.'

'But she's so bossy.' Even as the words left her mouth, Stephanie knew that they made her sound like a child.

'That's as maybe, but Isabelle loves Elliot and he loves her, and that's all that's important. She's good for him and for this family. She broke her back last night to get it all ready here for you all.'

'I know, I know.'

Her father took off his glasses.

'Sweetheart, are you all right?' he asked. 'You seem a bit low to me. Is everything OK between you and David?'

Stephanie nodded, hating herself for lying, but there was no way she could tell her father how she felt. She smiled briskly, avoiding his earnest stare. She wasn't going to ruin his Christmas by sharing her misery with him.

'We're fine. We just had a long journey today. That's all. I don't feel very Christmassy yet.'

'And you're missing Paul.'

She turned away with the mugs. 'Yes,' she said, suddenly feeling incredibly tired, as she walked towards the door.

Chapter 9

Ben wiped away the snow that had settled on his bare neck, between his hat and his upturned jacket collar. The gusting, icy wind scratched at his face, dragging tears from his eyes. The noise made by the wind was incredible. It was like being trapped inside a car with the sound system tuned into static and switched up to the max.

He was crouched down at the bottom of the worn concrete ramp outside the fisherman's hut, trying to fix the RIB's outboard engine. The boat's small tool kit lay by his side, but none of its ratchets, spanners or screwdrivers had done any good.

The engine was trashed and would need someone with a lot more mechanical knowledge than Ben to fix it. The hull looked damaged as well, from when they'd dragged it up the beach, but he couldn't tell if it was actually holed, because he didn't have the strength to lift up the boat and look.

He stood up and kicked it in frustration.

'Piece of shit,' he said, as if that would do any good.

The markings on the boat's sides were faded like a T-shirt that had been washed too many times over too many summers. Another season and she'd probably need replacing, Ben guessed, taking comfort from the fact that at least this wasn't a brand new vessel that he'd potentially wrecked. It was, however, still an expense his father could do without, but that was OK, too, Ben supposed, because at least he'd now be in a position to insist on paying for a new RIB without insulting his father's pride.

Ben had enough money put aside to manage this and

more. He had no siblings or dependants to spend his savings on, no one but himself and his parents, not like so many of his friends and contemporaries, people he'd worked with, or had studied with at art college, who now talked about their birthing plans and complications, and the cute things their kids did and said.

Sometimes these people would invite Ben out for drinks, or to dinner parties, where they'd sit him down next to their equally mortified single female friends, before observing them like two items left on eBay, with the time ticking down towards zero and still no bids being made. Or he'd find himself inexpertly asking their older kids at the weekends what they'd been learning at school, lamely inquiring what band they considered the most *phat* or *def*, or awkwardly holding babies at arm's length, whilst simultaneously trying not to groan as they barfed up organic parsnip and carrot mush all over his new DKNY jacket.

Ben had always imagined that he might be a parent himself by this age, and that he'd be busy on cold Christmas Eves, buying presents for his own children, before staying up late to set up a new Scalextric track, or to bolt a trampoline together, so that it would be ready for them to discover with wide-eyed wonder in the morning.

Somehow it hadn't turned out that way and, instead, he'd be spending this Christmas Eve with his own mum and dad, exactly the same as he had done when he'd been a little kid himself.

So long as he managed to get him and Kellie off this beach, that was, he reminded himself, as he glanced up at the frantic white sky.

His fingers were numb and his temples had started to ache. If he stayed out here much longer, he knew, it would only get worse. He looked down the beach, which had now turned almost completely white with snow, and then

115

out to sea. The wind had picked up. Seals lay slumped, like great black water balloons, against the grey rocks. Waves tore across the bay. Even if he did fix the engine, he wouldn't risk taking the boat out into that. She'd be flipped by the wind for sure.

He tucked the boat's ship-to-shore radio back under the red tarpaulin. That had turned out to be a piece of shit, too, and he'd addressed it as such only minutes before. Reception was zero and all he'd managed to squeeze out of it had been a few sentences from a BBC documentary broadcast about the plight of indigenous Fenland wildlife – facts he could easily have lived without.

He looked around, taking stock. This was a weird one, all right, suddenly finding himself stuck here when, only a couple of hours ago, the day had promised little other than a return to Fleet Town and a quick drink in the pub with Mick, and then maybe some TV and a spot of dinner with his mum and his dad.

Ben knew he should be angry, with himself, with his luck; he should be focusing on getting them out of here and nothing else; but as the wind cracked across the tarpaulin once more, his frown became softened by the trace of a smile. It was because of her: Kellie, sitting inside the hut only feet away.

Instead of feeling cursed to have been washed up here, he was glad he'd been given this time with her. He didn't believe in fate, he wasn't even religious, but he was starting to believe again in the kind of chemistry that could happen between two people, the kind of attraction that could occur in the blink of an eye. He already knew that if he'd met Kellie anywhere else, in a bar, or on a train, even on a street corner, in the kind of optimistic mood he'd been in this morning, he would have spoken to her, he would have asked her out.

'Jesus, it looks like *The Day After Tomorrow* out there,'

she told him, as he came in and heaved the door closed behind him.

The hut was thinly veiled with smoke and Kellie was sitting on the rickety bench in front of the fire Ben had managed to build on the rocky floor in the corner. A thin snake of smoke curled upwards from the remains of the fire and out through a ventilation hole in the hut's ceiling, which Ben had punched through earlier with the end of one of the oars.

'It's worse,' he said. 'It's more like the start of the Apocalypse. I kept expecting to see the Four Horsemen galloping across the beach to take us away.'

'They're welcome to try. Anywhere's probably more hospitable than here,' she said.

'Speak for yourself. I can't stand horses. Too many teeth. Haven't you noticed? They look like they're wearing dentures. And have you ever seen a horse take a piss? Astonishing. It goes on for hours. It's like they've got a tap strapped on under there, connected to the mains . . .'

'Nice image,' she said, screwing up her face. 'Thanks for that.'

'Anyway,' he went on, 'I doubt the Four Horsemen even ride horses now. They've probably modernised, the same as everyone else.'

'What, like they're the Four Vespa Riders of the Apocalypse?'

'Yeah, exactly, or maybe even something a little more sensible, because – let's face it – they're not exactly youngsters any more.'

'How about the Four Volvo Estate Drivers of the Apocalypse?' she suggested.

'Spot on – but it would probably be the Four Volvo Estate *Diesel* Drivers of the Apocalypse, because they'd have a hell of a lot of mileage to cover, what which *apocalypting* being a pretty much global affair.'

'They might even have mellowed with age,' she said. 'They might not want to *apocalyse* anything any more.'

'True. They probably only use their Volvo for visiting spa hotels, or going to the GP for their prescriptions, or for driving to their secluded gîte in Provence.'

Kellie opened her mouth to speak, then closed it again. 'No,' she then said, smiling, 'I think we've probably taken that one as far as we can – or indeed should.'

He grinned back at her. 'I think we probably have,' he agreed.

'Meanwhile, back in the real world,' she said, 'how did it go with *our* motor? Any luck?'

'Nada.'

'So it is totallyutterlyfuckedup?'

'Indubitably.'

She smiled at him expectantly and, for a moment, the sight of her, sitting here by the fire, threw him. She might have been an old friend, or even a lover. She might have been someone he'd rented a pretty country cottage with for the weekend, to relax with, far away from the worries of the world. She might have been looking at him now, waiting for him to suggest which nice little nearby pub they should visit for lunch.

Then the moment vanished, and with it came a pang of loss which took Ben by surprise. He and Kellie weren't friends or lovers. They barely knew each other. And they weren't here to relax. They were here because he'd cocked up.

The fire, which hadn't been much of a fire to begin with, was nearly out. The driftwood they'd salvaged from outside had been damp and had smouldered and died. The only dry wood they'd found had been an old wooden crate and a vertical beam, which Ben had torn off the inside wall at the back of the hut. All that remained were embers and ash.

'So what *are* we going to do?' she asked.

She was staring at him with absolute confidence, as if it was only a matter of time before, like a magician with a rabbit up his sleeve, he would produce an appropriate solution. He breathed in the warming smell of wood smoke and gazed at their lifejackets, which lay useless beside the fire.

'Here,' he said, digging into his pockets, glad that he did at least have something to produce.

Clasped in his fist was a bunch of chocolate bars, which he'd taken from one of the boxes of provisions intended for delivery to Green Bay harbour. He pushed them into Kellie's hands.

'You'd better eat one of these,' he said. He stared down at his fingers. 'And can you open one for me too? Only my fingers have kind of seized up.'

He went to rub his hands together, but she grabbed his right wrist.

'Don't,' she told him, turning his palm upwards to face him.

He stared down at his hands again.

'See how white your skin's gone,' she said. 'That's frostnip.'

His hands did look odd, pale and waxy, and they still felt numb, throbbing in a dull kind of a way, even here inside.

'Frostnip?' he said. ' Let me guess, would I be correct in assuming that this would be frostbite's younger, and not quite so famous, brother?'

'I'm serious,' she explained. 'That's exactly what it is – a mild form of frostbite. It'll be OK if you leave it be, but rubbing it will only make it worse. So don't. That white colour . . . those are the frost crystals trapped in your skin and they'll damage the tissue, unless you take good care and don't rub your hands until they're gone.'

'And how would an Aussie know something like that?' he asked. 'Let me guess: you're a Google-holic, a cybercondriac . . . Your idea of a good night in is trying to match any symptoms you have with a variety of potentially fatal diseases . . .'

'For your information,' she said, 'I don't even use the net outside the office, but do feel free to look up Australia and snow on Google, because then you'll see that we *do* get snow there. So much, in fact, that I used to ski a lot as a kid; and as a teen as well, both there and in France. I even took a job as a chalet girl during my year out after school.'

'Which is why you know what's wrong with my hands . . .'

'Yes.'

'Well, you've certainly been busy,' he said. 'What with all that and the diving, as well . . . it sounds as if there are a lot of things you used to do . . .'

He hadn't meant for the comment to be barbed – after all, it was none of his business – but he saw immediately, from the look on her face, that he'd somehow managed to offend her.

She let go of his hand. 'It was a long time ago,' she said.

'Thanks for the advice,' he hurriedly told her. 'I'll be careful not to rub.'

Outside, the wind howled, suddenly picking up. The roof creaked, as if the hut might disintegrate at any second and shoot spiralling upwards, like Dorothy's house in *The Wizard of Oz*.

'That doesn't sound good,' she said.

'No.'

He walked to the door and took it off the latch. The force of the wind nearly threw him back. Snow rushed in and he forced the door shut.

'So what's with the chocolate?' she asked, tearing the tops off the wrappers with her teeth. 'Let me guess: they're so that if we freeze to death, then at least we'll be found with smiles on our faces.'

'It was for just in case,' he said, finding himself staring at his hands once more. If he had frostnip already, he was thinking, then what next?'

'For just in case of what?'

'For just in case the storm got worse.'

'Which it just has.'

'Right.'

She stared at the chocolate bars. 'Let me guess,' she said, 'these are magic chocolate bars, which are going to turn into a helicopter and lift us out?'

'No.'

'That was meant to be a joke,' she said, handing him a bar and snapping another one in half, before taking a bite.

'I know,' he said, 'but it's kind of not.'

'What do you mean?'

'Just that I think we *will* need to get out of here.'

A snowflake drifted down through the makeshift chimney above their heads and spiralled to the ground.

'But surely the snow's going to stop soon?' she said.

'The forecast said that once it started, it was going to keep going . . .'

'Yeah, well, they got their timing wrong on that already,' she reminded him. 'So maybe they got the length of the storm wrong, too.'

He could tell just from looking at her that she didn't realise the seriousness of their circumstances. And why would she? He was only just waking up to it himself. After all, it wasn't that long ago that she was busy playing tourist, snapping photos of seals, off a group of islands famous for their unusually temperate climate.

But when he'd said Apocalypse earlier, he'd meant it, because he'd never witnessed weather like this before. Now it had got even worse, and weather like this didn't just blow over. This was a storm and they were stuck in its heart.

'If the forecast *is* right,' he said, 'and we decide to stick it out here in this hut and the snow doesn't stop . . . well, we're already out of firewood, so we're only going to get colder . . . and then it'll get dark. I don't know about you, but I don't fancy our chances if we get stuck here overnight.'

The back wall of the hut flexed like a sail as another gust of wind hit it hard. He couldn't believe he'd been stupid enough to bring her out to Brayner, even if the snow hadn't been due until later on, and he'd been mad to bring her to see the seals. This side of the island was unin-habited, what with all of the decent building land above the bay having been used up for the old mine. Even if Ben's parents had become concerned and raised the alarm, they'd never think of looking here. Not until it was too late.

'So what are you saying?' she asked.

He touched his pocket absentmindedly, searching for the cigarette packet that wasn't there. He could have done with a smoke to ease his nerves, to give him pause for thought before doing what he knew he had to do.

'We're going to have to walk out of here,' he said, making the decision he'd hoped to avoid, 'And the sooner, the better. That's what the chocolate's for, to give us the energy to make it up the cliffs and then across to the other side of the island.'

She stared at his hands. For the first time, he saw a flash of fear in her face. 'To Green Bay harbour?' she asked.

'Yeah. That's where the nearest houses are.'

She fell silent for a moment, then asked, 'Is that where the people you brought here this morning live?'

Had he mentioned the earlier trip to her? He couldn't remember.

'No, they're nearly a mile from the village. Why?' he

asked, as a possibility suddenly occurred to him. 'Do you know them?'

'No. I . . .' she seemed to falter. 'I was just thinking that, if they didn't live in the village, their house might be nearer.'

'It is,' Ben said, 'but it's on its own and this storm's working up to a whiteout. Green Bay harbour's a much bigger target. I think we should head there.'

'Then I agree.'

She seemed suddenly relieved, probably, he guessed, that a decision had been made. He was glad she was being positive. The more they worked together, the easier this would be.

'I suppose we'd better not waste any more time, then,' she said, standing up and pulling the baseball cap down tightly on her head. She pulled up her hood.

He bit into the chocolate bar, which was already so cold that he could hardly taste it at all. He forced himself to eat, biting down on the waxy chunks.

'How long will it take us to get there?' she asked.

'In normal conditions? Half an hour tops. But in what's out there . . . who knows? There's a pathway at the back of the shed which leads up to the cliffs. From there, we head round Solace Hill. Or over it, depending on how the weather breaks. It's rough ground, so we'll need to take care, but we should be able to manage it.'

'Only *should*?'

'*Will*,' he told her. He could and he would get them through this. He forced what he hoped was a breezy smile on to his face, but it felt all wrong and lopsided and fake. 'I can go on my own, if you like,' he said, 'and get help and come back.'

'No,' she said. 'That would just put more people in danger. I'm coming with you. You're right. There's no point in staying put and waiting to freeze. Here,' she said, just as he was about to open the door. 'Let me. I'm worried about your hands.'

Before he could stop her, she'd unwound her scarf, snagged it on a nail on the wall, and started tearing it into strips.

'What about you?' he asked.

'I'll manage OK.'

Again, he found himself wondering what a woman like this could be doing alone here at Christmas. His thoughts wandered to that country cottage which had never been, the one he'd imagined when he'd stepped back into the hut just now. In spite of their circumstances, in spite of the fact that he knew Kellie would probably rather be anywhere else, he was glad she was here with him now.

'You're being very brave about this,' he said.

She tied some strips round his hands and then set about wrapping her own hands with what was left of her scarf. 'It's not like I've got much choice. Come on,' she said. 'Let's go.'

In spite of the threat of danger, a childish part of Ben thrilled to the challenge as he reached to open the door, but immediately it became clear that they might not be able to make it to the village at all.

The wind slammed into them, throwing the door wide open as he took it off the latch, cracking it hard against the inside wall of the hut. Kellie cried out in surprise and Ben felt fear rise up inside him.

This wasn't a game. They were stepping into a storm. Bent almost double, he forced his way outside and pulled Kellie after him.

'Jesus Christ, Ben!' she shouted.

He pulled her close to him. 'Are you sure you want to come?' he yelled.

She looked terrified, but still she called back, 'Yes.'

Ben looked to the beach, but the visibility was even worse than when he'd been out here trying to fix the engine. The snow was now falling so thickly and so fast that he could no longer see the sea. He shielded his eyes, but when he looked up, he couldn't see the top of the cliff which enclosed the bay, even though it couldn't have been more than a hundred feet above. Snow danced dizzyingly before his eyes.

He dipped his head against the wind. He'd been here before as a child. The path was a good one, a solid one, and he knew the way. He *would* get them out.

The path zigzagged steeply upwards from the back of the hut, cutting through the gorse and the rock. After five yards, however, it petered out in a swirl of snow.

Kellie grabbed on to Ben and shouted into his ear, 'Are you serious?'

He pulled her into a huddle.

'Go first,' he told her. 'I'll catch you if you slip.'

'What if *you* slip?' she shouted back at him. Her eyes were wide with terror, her nose brushed across his.

'I won't. Make sure you stay as low as you can. Keep below the wind.'

They broke apart and Kellie set off. Ben followed. With every yard of altitude they gained, the wind grew more fierce. Soon it was pounding at them like fists, threatening to knock them sideways, or tear them backwards, and send them tumbling, spinning back down on to the rocks below.

Ben made the mistake of glancing behind him only once. Even though the snow blurred the extent of the drop, the view back down made his stomach lurch. He imagined them both falling, and pictured blood on rocks. No one would find them for days.

He fixed his eyes on Kellie, who was swaying as she stumbled onwards, step by arduous step, over wet stone and sliding mud and snow. He half-expected her to fall with each step, or that her expensive boots would give out, but they didn't. She kept on moving. They were approaching the top of the cliff now. Another two minutes and they'd be clear.

That's when she slipped. Her jacket billowed and swelled like a sail in a gale as a yowling gust of wind rushed upwards, raising her like driftwood on a wave. She cried out as she fell back on to Ben and, for an instant, he thought she was gone.

He heard her scream.

Somehow he managed to get hold of her jacket and keep hold. He rocked backwards as if he might keel over himself. Then, momentarily, the wind dropped, and in that tiny pocket of calm, Ben managed to pull Kellie in tight. She clung on to him as if he was a tree, as if he was rooted to this mountainside and couldn't possibly fall. And suddenly that was how he felt. He wouldn't fall, not with her in his arms. He tried to remember the last time he'd held on to someone else this tightly, but it was like chasing a drunken memory. Slowly, they sank to their knees and crouched there together, steady once more.

She pressed her face to his. He stared into her eyes. 'Are you OK?' she shouted.

'We need to keep going,' he said.

She nodded and let go. They stood again and they trudged on, upwards, into the wind.

It was only when they reached the top of the path and the land began to flatten out that Ben noticed his racing heartbeat. He became aware of his breath, too, coming fast and short, fast and short, like a piston on a steam train, racing down the track. Kellie stumbled on, away from the edge of the cliff, inland, towards a thick group of firs. He put his arm around her and they knelt again.

'Thanks,' she yelled into his ear, once she'd got her breath back. 'For saving my life.' Her face was red like a burn.

'You wouldn't be in danger in the first place,' he told her, 'if it wasn't for me.'

She glanced back over her shoulder. 'I'm so cold – but we did it!' Inside her hood he could see her eyes shining with elation, and with pride.

He shouted, 'Let's go.'

Instinctively linking their arms together, they stood, and began the walk inland.

Five minutes went past, then ten, then fifteen, and more – and still the snow swirled all around. The visibility had become so poor now that bushes and trees lurched out at them from the snowstorm without warning. The world was a churning mass of white and grey.

Ben couldn't tell where the ground ended and the sky began. His eyes were sore and streaming, but whenever he went to wipe at them with the back of his bound hands, he remembered Kellie's warning about frostnip and made himself hold back. His forehead ached from the cold, like he'd been punched. His skin felt stretched and his limbs had hardened like marble. His knuckles had locked.

The ground was rugged and treacherous. He hoped Kellie felt better than he did. Her strength had amazed him. She'd said nothing since they'd set off again, but she hadn't slowed down once. She'd fallen twice in the last few minutes and he'd fallen once himself, but they'd picked themselves up without protest each time.

Ben's legs ached and his breathing was shallow. He thought of all the cigarettes he'd smoked, and wished he'd quit before today. He remembered his dream about being in a burrow, about watching that TV, and he remembered his interpretation of it, that he was wasting his life, and his resolution to remedy the situation, by getting more

127

involved. Well, he was involved now, wasn't he? Right up to his neck.

It was like somebody was playing a great big joke on him. It seemed ludicrous to him that they were battling through the countryside, huddled against the wind, like a scene from an old Christmas card. But where was Bing Crosby? Where was the welcoming Disney stranger, opening the cottage doorway and inviting them in to sit by the fire?

This wasn't supposed to happen. Not in the modern world. Never in the UK. Kellie had been right: it *was* like *The Day After Tomorrow* out here. It did look like the global climate system had gone into meltdown. Fucking global warming, Ben thought. Fucking shitty governments and multinationals. Right about now, he was meant to be sitting in the pub with Mick, sinking a pint and flicking up dry roast peanuts and catching them in his mouth. If he came out of this alive, he was going to sign up to the Green Party for life.

What made matters even worse was that he'd lost his bearings. By his reckoning, they should have reached Green Bay harbour by now, but they hadn't. The snow had devoured the landscape. There was a little boy in Ben that wanted to cry out and break down, but he couldn't. What would Kellie think? How would he be able to look at himself in the mirror again? Or ever look at her?

She stumbled and fell for a third time.

'Come on,' he shouted, helping her up.

'I'm tired,' she called out. 'How much further?'

'I don't know.'

'But –'

He pulled her up against an upturned oak tree which loomed out at them from the whiteout. The depression in the earth made by its exposed, snow-covered roots formed a natural windbreak and they crouched together inside.

'What do you mean, you *don't know*?' she demanded.

He pulled her in close. 'I don't know how to tell you this . . .'

'What?'

'We're lost.'

The wind hissed so loud, they might as well have been in a snake pit.

'*Lost*? You're joking, right?'

'No.' He felt sick, ashamed. He'd done the one thing he'd not wanted to: he'd let Kellie down.

'But we can't be,' she said. 'You come here all the time.'

'No. I haven't been, not for years.'

'*For years*? But – but it's your job.'

'No,' he told her, 'you've got it all wrong. I don't even live on the islands. Not any more.'

She stared at him, horrified. 'What do you mean?'

'I live in London. In Kentish Town.'

'Kentish Town!'

She pulled back from him. 'You told me you were the ferryman.'

'And I am – but only this week. My father's got a bad back. He's the real ferryman. I've just been helping him out. I work in Soho. In the media.'

'You're a fucking liar!' she shouted.

And he was. He was a fraud and now he'd been caught out. He'd never meant it to come to this. When he'd taken her out on the boat and she'd assumed that running a boat taxi was what he did full time, he'd let her go on believing it, because it had been fun. She'd seen what she'd wanted to. A man of the sea. A master of the elements. And it had only been a white lie, after all. His father *did* run the boat taxi, and it *was* a trade Ben had grown up around. He'd been going to set her straight about who he really was, about what he really did. He just hadn't got round to it yet.

But this joke wasn't funny any more.

'I'm sorry,' he said. 'For everything.'

'It's too fucking late!' she screamed and, for a second, he thought she was going to lash out.

Then she seemed to deflate right there in front of him.

He gripped her shoulders. He couldn't handle seeing her like this. He had to make this right.

'I will get us out of here,' he promised her.

He stared into the tunnel of her hood. Her eyes were slits. She looked nothing like the woman he'd seen walking along the Old Quay only hours before.

'Then do it,' she told him.

Five more minutes. That's what he gave them. Then they'd have to stop, and find somewhere – anywhere, a cave or another fallen tree – to dig in and try and sit this out. He forced himself not to panic. He prayed that it wouldn't come to that.

They set off once more across the white landscape. Keep straight, he told himself. If you keep straight, then you might just find a landmark.

But the further he walked, the more he felt like he was still at sea. The land rose one moment, only to fall the next. It was like riding over waves in the boat. His boots felt so heavy. It would be nice to sit down, he thought, just for a minute, just to give himself a chance to catch his breath. The snow looked soft and welcoming beneath his feet. If he lay down now, it would probably feel just like a bed.

He heard what sounded like a growl.

And again.

'There.'

He realised it was Kellie.

'There!' she shouted a second time. 'Look! There!'

Her outstretched arm flapped in the wind. He looked to where she was pointing, but saw nothing. She must have been confused, he thought, imagining things where there were none. He saw nothing but snow.

Then he saw it, too: high up above them, a dark vertical shape. Then came a flash of light, just for a second, at the top of the shape. Then it was gone. He watched, confused. Then the light flashed on again.

It hit him what it was.

'The lighthouse!' he yelled.

The wind swept away her answer, but he didn't care. He felt a burst of energy and his drowsiness vanished.

'Come on!' He pulled her onwards. Strength rushed through him. 'That's the lighthouse. It's Green Bay harbour. We've nearly made it. We're nearly there.'

Chapter 10

Lunch had been a long, drawn out affair, with the Thorne family and Michael all sitting down together. Outside the wind howled like a wounded beast and the snow fell ceaselessly, but inside, all was still.

Michael, Simon, old Mr Thorne and Taylor and her parents were all in the sitting room. Elliot was reading a newspaper, and Mr Thorne a book, both of them in armchairs in front of the fire. Isabelle was cross-legged on the floor, painting her fingernails with long careful licks of a bright red brush. David could be heard in the kitchen, sharpening knives.

Michael was at the table, leafing desultorily through the pile of newspaper supplements and magazines that Elliot had dumped there fifteen minutes ago for his and Taylor's benefit. Taylor was sitting opposite him, twisting her hair and humming the tune from *The Great Escape* over and over again, whilst watching her father out of the corner of her eye.

She'd said nothing for over ten minutes, not even to Michael. She was still annoyed with Stephanie for not caving in to her demands and letting Simon go outside, and she wasn't going to let Elliot forget it. Chances were she didn't even want to go outside herself any more. Michael certainly didn't. It was the principle of the matter than kept her going, he supposed, the principle being that someone had told her no.

Michael felt trapped, oppressed, as if he was in the middle of a double maths lesson at school, looking out

132

across the empty sports fields on a hot summer's day. He was ready to go home. At least he could play on his computer there. Maybe Taylor would even go with him. And if she did – he let his mind wander and momentarily pictured the two of them there, up in his bedroom, perched on the edge of his bed, at a sudden, awkward loss for words . . .

He sighed. Even thinking of this potentially awesome alternative was torture. They weren't going anywhere, not until the snow stopped.

'How about another game of table tennis?' he suggested, but all Taylor did was yawn loudly. She wasn't going to let her father off the hook that easily. She started humming again.

Elliot laid his newspaper out on his lap. 'I don't think I can take much more of this,' he said.

Isabelle cleared her throat. 'I'm going for a bath,' she announced.

She stood up and stretched, staring out through the window, towards the same line of fir trees beneath which Elliot had earlier attempted to make his phone call. It was growing dark now and even the falling snow was fading from view. Michael thought how pale Isabelle looked, and how tired, but then she shot Elliot a brilliant smile, and the years seemed to fall from her. She went over to him and pulled him up out of his chair, slipping her arms round his waist, and pulling him in tight.

'Maybe you should have a lie-down, too,' she said. She trailed her fingers across the back of Elliot's thigh, before finally setting off towards the door.

'Why not play a game?' Elliot suggested to Taylor. 'Trivial Pursuit?'

'I hate it.'

'Scattergories?'

'That's pants, as well. All board games are. That's why

they're called board games,' she added flatly, 'because that's how they make you feel.'

'So play a different kind of game. I know. How about hide and seek?'

'How about over my dead body?' she asked back.

Michael hid his smile behind his hand.

'Hide and seek is a game for babies,' she declared.

'Even I know that,' Simon agreed. 'Only the little kids at school play that and nobody else does, because it's too easy and not much fun, not when you think of all the other games there are and how much better they are, and –'

'Sardines, then,' Elliot said.

'What's that?' Simon asked.

'You remember, don't you, Taylor? We played it in America a few years ago.'

Michael knew the game, too. The rules were easy. One person went and hid somewhere big enough for other people to hide too. Everyone else went to look for them. The first person to find the person hiding then hid with them. And so on. The loser was the person to find the others last.

'Six years ago,' Taylor corrected her father. 'When I was eight.'

'My point exactly,' Elliot said. 'When you were the same age as Simon is now.'

'Forget it,' she said.

Elliot looked to Michael for support, but Michael had already learnt his lesson about siding against Taylor, and this time he looked away.

'I'll tell you what,' Elliot continued. 'Why don't I make it worth your while by offering up a fiver for whoever hides the longest?'

'Make it twenty and you've got yourself a deal,' Taylor said.

Elliot smiled, either pleased to have got his way, or out

of respect for his daughter's decision to negotiate. Michael waited impatiently to hear what Elliot said next. Twenty pounds was a lot of money. Michael's mother paid him two pounds an hour for washing up and cooking meals in the pub. This was a chance, then, of earning in an instant what would otherwise take him ten hours' hard work. All Elliot had to do was agree.

Old Mr Thorne stirred in his armchair, and turned round to watch.

'Fifteen,' Elliot said, taking a clipped fold of cash from his pocket and licking the tip of his finger, preparing to count the notes off.

'Seventeen-fifty,' Taylor said.

Elliot considered this for a moment, then said, 'Done.'

'Excellent,' Simon said, punching his hand in the air. 'That's loads. You can buy stacks of stuff with that. Toys and comics and sweets and crisps and you'd still have some money left to save up for something else like a game, or –'

'Michael?' Taylor asked him.

'Count me in,' he said without hesitating. So what if sardines was a kids' game? Cash was still cash. It was as simple as that.

They agreed they'd play the game three times in order that they could find a winner. They'd each take turns to hide and the person who hid the longest without the other two people finding them would get the money. They drew straws to decide who went first and Michael got the shortest so Taylor and Simon stayed in the kitchen and Simon began counting to a hundred.

Not wanting to look too uncool, even though he was determined to win the cash, Michael walked slowly out of the kitchen and then padded up the stairs, trying not to make them creak and give away the fact that this was the way he'd chosen to go.

He knew his way round the Thorne house pretty well,

he'd been here so much. There were three bedrooms on each of the corridors which led off the landing at the top of the stairs. Another flight led up to the attic. Michael went down the corridor to the left, passing a gallery of framed black and white photos on the pale yellowed walls.

A part of him had always wanted to live here, even before his dad had left home and Roddy had moved in. There was none of the acrid stink of spilt beer, or the guff of stale smoke that he was used to at home. The hubbub of pub chatter that Michael had grown up with was thankfully absent too. It felt private here, not public like his own home did so much of the time.

Michael stopped at the second bedroom door he came to. If he remembered right, this was where Simon's parents usually slept, and seeing as they were downstairs (David in the kitchen; Stephanie and Nat in the TV room), he guessed they wouldn't mind him hiding in here. Away from Taylor and Simon, he felt even more ridiculous creeping around, but he told himself to think of the money, and didn't look back.

The moment he stepped inside and closed the door behind him, he could tell the room was definitely an adult one. It was spotless. There were no clothes littering the floor, or sound system or games. Michael scanned around for possible hiding places, quickly dismissing under the double bed, inside the antique wardrobe and behind the cream curtains, each of them being too obvious.

There was a second door on the opposite side of the room, which led, he guessed, to an en-suite bathroom. He was about to go in and check it out, when he spotted a pine blanket box pushed up against the flaking whitewashed stone wall. It was three feet deep, three feet wide, and five feet long.

He opened it up and saw it was empty. There wasn't

much room, but enough for two, and that was the most the game would require. Climbing inside – feeling a bit of tit, but not enough to make him forsake the possibility of making some easy cash – he wondered what would happen if Taylor found him first. Would she climb in here beside him? And what then? What would happen if they ended up lying here together in the dark? How much of a kids' game would it feel like then?

The light faded as he pulled the lid down on top of him, but complete darkness never came. There was a row of small round ventilation holes in the front of the box, just beneath the lip of the lid. Repositioning himself, he propped himself up on his elbow and peered through one of the holes into the empty room.

The scent of lavender filled his nostrils. He could hear his own breathing, and remembered standing in the escape tunnel earlier that day. He shivered. That place gave him the creeps and he hoped Taylor would change her mind about bothering to go back.

Footsteps thudded down the corridor. The bedroom door flew open and smacked hard against the wardrobe.

'Oh, Miiii-chaellll,' Simon called in a ghostly voice as he walked into the bedroom. 'Are you iiiiiinnn here?'

Michael watched through the holes as Simon walked over to the bed and got down on his knees and peered beneath. Then he straightened up and surveyed the room. Then Michael froze, not because Simon had spotted him, but because Michael had spotted something else. Behind Simon, the bathroom door was opening and Isabelle stepped out.

She was wearing a white towel dressing gown, tied off at the waist with a neat bow. Her blonde hair was wet and combed back, and looked darker than before. Steam hung in the bathroom doorway. *Oh, shit*, Michael thought, *I'm in the wrong room. She's been in there all along, having a bath.*

'What are you doing?' she asked Simon, taking him by surprise and making him jump.

'Looking for Michael,' Simon said, springing to attention.

'Michael?'

'We were playing sardines,' he explained.

'Well, he's not in here, honey.'

'No, Aunty Izzy. Sorry, Aunty Izzy.' Simon backed towards the door. 'I'm going to go and check the other rooms. I'll see you later.'

'You do that, sweetie,' she called after him.

She closed the door.

Michael moved to lift the lid up, thinking that the sooner he said he was hiding here, the better. But at that exact moment, Isabelle unfastened the bow at her waist, and let her dressing gown fall to the floor.

She stood there naked.

Shit, he thought. *Shit, shit, shit, shit, shit . . .*

What the hell was he meant to do now? He tried not to breathe, tried not to panic, but that only made him breathe deeper, that only made him panic more. What if she heard him? What was he going to do? He should do the decent thing and climb out. He should cover his eyes. If she caught him in here now, he'd be dead. He should apologise to her. But he didn't. He *couldn't*. He could hardly even contemplate the embarrassment that he knew would ensue, let alone bring it down on himself.

So instead, he just stared.

He'd never see a naked woman before, not in the flesh, anyway – and Isabelle looked nothing like the photos of the airbrushed strippers he'd accessed on the internet, or the girls from the seventies, with their huge hairy snatches and bouffed-up hair-do's, who featured in the old copies of *Playboy* he kept beneath his bed.

There was something almost shocking about Isabelle's

138

normalness, as if she was almost *too* real, but there was something beautiful about her too and he hated himself for the way she made him feel, for finding himself now fancying Taylor's mother as well as her.

He wasn't the only one who was taking a good hard look, either. He now saw that she was examining herself in the full-length mirror on the wardrobe door. She traced her face with her fingers, touching the faint wrinkles at the corners of her eyes. She then turned side-on to the mirror, unknowingly facing him, and he watched her stomach tense. She cupped her breasts in her hands, pushing them together, so that their cleavage grew deeper and dark. Her skin was still pink from the bath. He stared at the neat, cropped vertical line of dark blonde hair between her legs.

Then came footsteps. The bedroom door opened with a click.

Isabelle reached for her dressing gown, but then relaxed. Michael didn't; he only felt worse. It wasn't Simon again, or Taylor, as he'd half-expected. It was Elliot who now entered the bedroom and shut the door behind him.

'I hoped you'd come up,' Isabelle said.

'I thought you were having a bath.'

'I was, but Simon disturbed me. He was mucking around in here.'

'*Mea culpa.* I gave them some money to play. Naughty, I know, but I'd have done anything to stop Taylor from humming that bloody annoying tune.'

'She's a determined girl.'

'Just like her mum, eh?' Elliot said.

He started round to the other side of the bed, where Michael could see an open bag on the floor, but Isabelle stepped neatly in front of him, blocking his path.

'Guess what I'm determined to have now?' she asked.

He stared at her blankly.

She told him, 'You.'

'What about the kids?' Elliot asked. 'One of them might come in again.'

'They won't,' she said, 'but if you're worried about them, why not lock the door?'

Michael couldn't believe what was happening, let alone deal with what might happen next. If they found him here now, he'd never live it down. He'd never be able to speak to them or Taylor again, or even look them in the face.

Isabelle stepped up close to Elliot and pressed herself against him, but Elliot stepped quickly back.

'I can't right now,' he said. 'Where's my jumper? I promised David I'd help him get some wood in from the shed.'

'But Elliot . . .'

He had already knelt down in front of his bag. He unfurled a faded checked green and white jumper. 'It's freezing out there. I'd feel awful if I left him to do it on his own.'

Isabelle picked up her dressing gown from the floor.

'Well, come up afterwards,' she said. 'It won't take long, will it? I can wait.'

Elliot grimaced. 'I think Stephanie wants to get dinner going pretty soon, darling.' He kissed Isabelle on the forehead. 'I'll see you downstairs, OK?'

Isabelle nodded and watched him leave. The bedroom door clicked shut. She stood staring after him for so long that Michael actually wondered whether she'd fallen asleep.

When she did move, it was as if she was shaking herself from a trance. She sat down on the bed, lifted the dressing gown to her mouth and bit down into it. Her whole body tensed, and then began to shake.

As she lowered her hands, he saw her face. It was creased with pain and tears streamed down her cheeks.

140

She screwed her eyes up tight, then opened them and walked into the bathroom, closing the door behind her.

Michael's legs and arms felt cramped, but he had to move. This was his chance. Now. He raised the blanket box lid. He checked the bathroom doorknob and prayed it wouldn't turn. Then he stepped out of the box and lowered its lid. Softly, slowly, he made his way to the bedroom door. Caution vanished the instant he reached it. In a second, he was out.

No sooner had he shut the door, than Taylor rounded the corner of the corridor. She stopped dead in her tracks, folded her arms and stared.

'Where the fuck have you been?' she asked. 'I've been looking for you everywhere.' She noticed he was still holding the door handle. 'Is that where you were?' she asked. 'In Mum and Dad's room?'

'No. I just stuck my head round the door to see if you two were in there but no one was. I thought you might have given up and played a trick and started hiding from me.'

She looked him up and down. 'Why are you blushing?' she asked.

'I'm not. I'm just hot.'

'Let's go find Simon,' she said, 'there's still that money to be won.'

She dipped her head towards him as they walked along side by side.

'You stink of flowers,' she said. 'Of lavender, or something. What are you? Some kind of a queer?'

Chapter 11

Kellie slipped inside the door to the Windcheater bar, being careful not to make a sound with the latch. Breathing in, she hid behind the thick velvet curtain, pulling it aside just a fraction so that she could check out what was going on. She couldn't take any chances. She had to make sure that the coast was clear and that Elliot, or any of his family, had not turned up at the pub. Not that she'd recognise them anyway, it occurred to her, even if they had.

Everything seemed safe. The walls were festooned with red and gold decorations and an electronic reindeer and sleigh leapt across the two front windows. Reams of thick tinsel adorned the low beams. A lino floor dotted with round wooden tables led to a roaring fire, beside which two locals were playing darts.

She knew she was being paranoid, but then, she was less than a mile away from where Elliot was staying. It was still snowing outside, so at least he wouldn't be on his way here now, she hoped. Would he freak out, she wondered, if he knew she was here? Part of her longed to bump into him, to fall into his arms, to explain what had happened and how frightened she'd felt, but she also knew he'd be furious with her and that he wouldn't be sympathetic at all.

And he'd have every right to be cross. She should have stayed on St John's. She should never have climbed into that boat. She remembered Ben's words to her as they'd accelerated away into the open sea. 'Hold on tight,' he'd said. 'We're in for a rough ride.' She hadn't known then quite what an accurate prediction that would turn out to be.

Sally, the pub landlady, was wearing a black poloneck jumper with a flashing Santa badge on her ample bosom, and was polishing glasses behind the bar. A cigarette burned in a plastic ashtray on the bar in front of her. Smoke curled up towards a row of pewter tankards hanging from a row of hooks above her head. The sound of the radio playing the Christmas number one with its *a cappella* rip-off of a sixties Motown classic, which Kellie had so loathed yesterday, filtered through from the open kitchen door behind her. Today, she found it kind of comforting.

Ben was standing at the radiotelephone at the far end of the bar. He smiled at Kellie tentatively as she came in, but she didn't smile back. Despite what they'd been through, they were still strangers. Worse than that, she thought. He'd lied to her, about who he was, about what he did. She knew less than nothing about him and that made it seem ridiculous, them being here together. Ben confused her. She didn't know whether to be angry with him, or grateful. He'd nearly got them killed, but he'd saved their lives as well.

Sally smiled at her too, and stepped out from behind the bar. 'Everything OK next door?' she asked. 'Feeling better? Clothes OK?'

'Yes, thank you,' she said, wondering how she could ever repay Sally's kindness. Even if the velour sweatshirt top and elasticated jeans were possibly the worst fashion items Kellie had ever worn, they were warm and dry – and anyway, who did she have to impress with her appearance? She realised now that it was the first time she'd ever been to a pub without her make-up on.

She smiled back at Sally, instinctively reaching out to kiss her cheek. The landlady smelled of cigarettes and cheap perfume. She reminded Kellie of her mother.

Spending Christmas with her mum in Paris suddenly no

longer seemed like such a bad idea, Kellie thought. At least she knew people there. Even if she and her mother didn't always get on, she still loved her, and, just as important, Kellie could be herself with her. Which she couldn't be here.

'Roddy has made some tomato soup,' Sally said, ushering Kellie to a small table by the fire. 'It's tinned, but it'll soon warm you up. I'll just get it.'

Kellie wondered whether anyone in her local pub in the city would have been so charitable.

'You're a life saver,' she said, taking a seat as Sally returned to the bar.

Kellie felt so weird. The storm outside had been insane, but here everything was normal and eerily still, like a vacuum. It was as if the storm had never happened. Only, of course, it had – and now she was stranded here.

Kellie and Ben had arrived freezing and sodden a few hours ago, falling in through the pub door, numb with cold. Sally had taken them in, rushing to get them in front of the fire. Kellie had been so angry with Ben, furious that he'd brought them to Brayner in the first place, furious that he'd got them lost and furious with herself for being such a fool.

She'd tried to comfort herself that at least she wasn't still outside, that they'd made it back without getting injured or needing medical help, but she'd been close to tears as Ben had explained to Sally and Roddy what had happened. Ben had still been intent on trying to get back to the boat to fix it, but Roddy had told him to forget it. It would be dark soon, he'd said. They'd try again in the morning. Ben had been upset, saying that he couldn't encroach on their hospitality at Christmas and that he had to get Kellie back, but Sally had taken one look at Kellie and insisted. They could have the annexe, she'd said. Roddy had told Ben she was right: they had no choice but to stay on Brayner for the night. There was no way a boat was going to come out and fetch them in weather like this.

Kellie had reluctantly agreed, not being able to face the prospect of going outside again and only wanting to warm up. The annexe had turned out to be a row of one-bedroom cottages, each with a tiny bathroom and kitchen. Sally rented them out during the summer, but there was no one here now and Roddy was in the middle of doing roof repairs. She had let them into the nearest one and switched on the plug-in radiator. Then she'd lent Kellie the clothes as well as thermal walking socks and old trainers.

'Did you get through to your parents?' Kellie asked Ben now, when he hung up the radiophone and joined her at the table. Here in the warm, it seemed incredible that they'd ever been in real danger, but they had, and he'd got them through it. They'd got through it together.

'Yes,' he said, 'and your hotel. To let them know you're safe.'

She wondered whether Elliot would get through and find that she was missing. Would he find out that she was on the island? Would he be worried about her? She supposed it didn't matter. Even if he did know she was here, he wouldn't risk seeing her. He might as well be hundreds of miles away.

'Thanks. How are your hands?'

'They're OK now,' he said, holding them up to her. 'How about you?'

'So much better,' she said.

She felt suddenly embarrassed. She wondered whether he was cross with her for having shouted at him when they'd got lost, and whether she should still be cross with him for having lied. She certainly had been after they'd arrived here. She'd barely been able to look him in the face as they'd been shown by Sally to the annexe.

Ben was wearing what could only be one of Roddy's

145

acrylic jumpers with a multicoloured moose head on it. She felt selfish for taking the shower first and for not checking sooner that he was comfortable too.

'Nice look,' she said.

'Oh, the jumper. Yes, well, it's part of a new fashion range I've got planned out, called Yesterday's Threads, or *Vêtements d'Hier*, as I've decided to title it in French.'

Her lips parted into a smile.

'I've already spoken to Jean Paul Gaultier about it,' he went on, 'and he's considering featuring it in his winter collection, or *Collection d'Hiver*, as he likes to say. Come to think of it,' he added, 'in that get-up, you might be able to head up the women's range.'

So he wasn't angry with her, then. Well, that was something, anyway.

'Here we are,' said Sally, coming towards them with two large steaming bowls of red soup. 'This should sort you out.'

She set them down and left Kellie and Ben alone. There was an awkward moment of silence.

'Ben, look I'm sorry,' Kellie said, 'about being so cross with you out there.'

He shook his head. 'It was my fault. Everything. Bringing you here . . .'

'No one forced me to get on that boat. I shouldn't have been rude. And thanks for getting us here safely.'

She watched him eat, but her own appetite had deserted her. She still felt churned up.

Ben noticed her toying with her spoon.

'Not hungry?' he asked.

She might as well tell him what was on her mind. There was no point in pretending it didn't bother her.

'Why didn't you tell me that you were from London?' she asked.

'Does it make a difference?'

146

'No, not really. I was wondering why you didn't say anything, that's all.'

'I thought you were one of those London-centric people and I didn't want to ruin your tourist experience. That's why people come here, isn't it? For a bit of local colour?'

'I suppose . . .'

'And, of course,' he added, 'what with you being so enigmatic, too . . . about what you were doing here on your own . . . well, it felt like a bit of a game, so I thought I'd create some mystery about myself, just to even up the score . . .'

She could see that he was watching her for a reaction, that he wanted some answers from her as well, but she wasn't being drawn.

'But I'm sorry,' he went on. 'I shouldn't have deceived you. Not now I know a little bit more about you.'

'And what exactly is it that you think you know?'

'That you're an Aussie with loads of pluck.'

'Pluck?'

'Something my mum says. You were very brave today. It was horrible out there, and I definitely believe what they say about you getting to see who people really are in a crisis . . . Have you forgiven me?'

She shivered, remembering again how he'd risked his life for her, back there on the cliff.

'I don't know. How do I know that everything else you've told me isn't a lie?'

'It's not. None of it.' He smiled. 'Although, of course, I could be lying now.'

She flicked a bar mat at him in frustration. 'I'm serious,' she said.

'And so am I. Everything else I told you is true.'

'Everything?'

'Sure.'

'Like, for example . . .' – she said the first thing that came into her head – 'I don't know . . . like what you told me in the hut, about being divorced . . . is that really true?'

But he didn't have a chance to reply before a huge man burst in through the outside door, bringing a blast of cold air with him. He shook the snow off his hair and shoulders.

'Fuck me,' Ben shouted. 'Someone get a camera. I've just spotted a yeti!'

'Ben,' the man shouted back, raising up his giant hands. His cheeks were ruddy and he was wearing an anorak and a fake Father Christmas hat. 'Look out,' he went on, 'the unemployed millionaire's back in town. Drinks are on you are they, rich boy?'

Kellie stared on, uncertain whether she must have just misheard. Unemployed *what*?

Ben rolled his eyes at her. 'Hello, Jack,' he said, standing up and allowing himself to be hugged.

Kellie let the information sink in for a moment. Everything she'd thought about Ben – assumed about him – was completely wrong.

'And who is this?' Jack said, smiling at Kellie.

'Kellie. A friend,' Ben said.

She was strangely flattered by his description.

'And a very pretty one, too. Maybe there are some advantages to getting divorced, eh?'

'See!' Ben said to Kellie. 'I told you I was telling the truth.' He turned back to Jack. 'Why don't you let me finish this, OK?' gesturing to the soup, 'and then we'll catch up.'

'OK,' Jack nodded, before extending his arms towards the bar. 'Sally, my angel. Happy Christmas.'

'Jack! I was getting worried that no one was going to come out. How is it going out there. Is it still snowing?'

'It's easing up and the wind has dropped. Everyone will

148

be in soon. Now come here and give your best customer a kiss.'

Kellie watched him for a moment more, then took a sip of soup

'You kind of get known around here,' Ben said. He was blushing.

'The unemployed millionaire?'

'Ah, yes. That . . .'

'More truth?'

'Sort of.'

'Sort of . . . ?'

'My wife – ex-wife – Marie . . . we used to run a business. Anyway, we were quite successful and made some money, but to cut a very long story short, I wasn't happy, and so she's just bought me out. I only got the money through recently. Millions, though, is a bit of a lie, unless you convert it into rupees. It's not enough to retire on, but it is enough to set up something else. Although I have no idea what to do. Anyway, I don't know how Jack got to hear about it.'

Marie. It was the first time Kellie had heard her name. It was like discovering a piece of a puzzle and it made her suddenly want to find out more. She couldn't have got this guy more wrong if she'd tried.

'What was the business? You said media, didn't you? When we were out in the storm . . .'

'It was just a little thing – taking people's home videos and editing them into proper films, with music and stuff, but using the right equipment to make it all look professional.'

'Sounds like a great idea to me.'

'It was, except that Marie got bored with making movies of people's kids. She got seduced by the whole business thing. She wanted to go down the corporate route. Make training videos. Dull stuff. I thought the idea was to keep it

149

simple. I wanted to make people happy, put a smile on their faces.'

'And she didn't?'

'No. Not on my face anyway.'

'I see.'

'It's complicated,' Ben said.

'Don't you feel sad about it? About walking away from it all?'

'Not really. It was never about the money. It was about me and Marie. Once we were over, so was it.'

He drained the last of his pint.

'Another one?' she asked.

At the bar, as Kellie waited for Sally to come and serve her, she glanced back at Ben, who was now being greeted by some more new arrivals. The weather must be slackening off outside, she thought. The village was finally waking up, and so was she – to what and who Ben really was.

Everything about Marie and the business perplexed her. He'd made it sound so black and white, but Kellie didn't buy it. She knew from bitter experience how complicated life really was. Was he really as over Marie as he was making out? Had it been that easy for him to walk away? She wondered how old Marie was and what she looked like. It alarmed her that she suddenly cared.

Sally was on the radiotelephone. She smiled and held up her finger to Kellie to ask her to wait.

'And Michael's been OK?' Kellie overheard her saying. 'Good. Good . . .'

Sally cupped her hand over the receiver and whispered to Roddy, 'Gerry Thorne says Michael's still there with Taylor, but he'll be back soon.'

Roddy smiled. 'Him and that Taylor! Well, as long as he's safe.'

150

Sally returned her attention to the phone. 'Thanks,' she said.

Kellie had tensed at the mention of the Thornes' name. It was obvious that Sally and Roddy knew the Thorne family, and that their son was friends with Elliot's daughter. Close friends by the sound of it.

Kellie had always imagined Taylor in isolation, a solitary, meek little kid, but finding out that she had friends here unsettled her. Somehow it seemed to strengthen the Thorne family, to lock them to the island and to each other.

For a fleeting and irrational moment, she wanted to blurt out her own link with the Thornes, but she quashed the urge. How would they treat her, she wondered, if they knew about her connection to Elliot? And what would Elliot's family think if she was discovered here? How would they react if they found out who she really was?

Worse, how would Ben take it, if she told him? Would he feel used or duped? He thought she was a hapless tourist, but how would he feel if he knew she'd come to the island because of Elliot? Just because she'd selfishly wanted to catch a glimpse of where her lover was staying?

Kellie ordered two more drinks from Roddy.

'Now, you are going to sing for Roddy aren't you?' Sally said, coming over. 'He's getting out the karaoke machine, since it's Christmas Eve. There'll be a few more in here any moment, now the weather's eased, and you've to join in.'

'Oh no. I really can't sing.'

'No one can. That's the point. It's just a bit of fun.'

Despite the weather conditions, Jack was right. It seemed as if everyone in the village had battled through the snow to come and have a good time, and before long, the pub was filled with the sound of laughter and

Christmas music. There must have been thirty or more people in the small bar. The room glowed with twinkling Christmas lights.

Again, Kellie worried about Elliot turning up, but again she told herself that it wouldn't happen. He'd come to be with his family. That was the whole point of his visit. The last place he'd be on Christmas Eve was in the pub, especially one that apparently specialised in karaoke. Elliot couldn't stand anything like that.

Kellie and Ben soon moved to a bigger table where a whole crowd of islanders were drinking. The conversation flowed in a steady stream of banter, and a while later, as Kellie queued at the bar for more drinks, she realised her cheeks were hurting from laughing so much.

It all seemed so laid-back and non-judgemental, she thought, like parties in a pub should be, but rarely were. It reminded her of being a student in Sydney. People had just accepted each other for who they were back then. None of them had had anything to prove.

She realised that she hadn't felt this included by people her own age, let alone older people, for as long as she could remember. There'd been a time when she'd used to go out drinking with her peers after work, but since she'd been seeing Elliot, she'd stopped going out in groups. Things between her and Elliot had always been more intimate, not free-flowing and fast like this, and not – dare she say it? – nearly so spontaneous and fun.

They were all talking about Christmas when she got back to the table with a full tray of drinks.

'I like the presents and stuff and getting excited,' Ben said, smiling up at Kellie before shuffling along to make room for her on the bench seat. She sat down next to him. 'I can't wait until I've got my own kids to spoil.'

Kellie looked at Ben feeling a pang of jealousy, or was it regret? It was so refreshing to meet a man who wanted to have children. He made it sound so simple and so inevitable. If only it was the same for her. She hadn't even discussed having her own kids with Elliot.

She found herself looking over at Toni, who had her baby, Oliver, cuddled into her chest, his face buried snugly into her neck. What if Kellie never had the chance to do that herself?

'Oh come on. Don't you just think it's commercialism out of control? Everyone else does,' said Jed, one of the guys Ben had been at school with. At least she thought he was called Jed. It was hard to keep track of all the new names.

'No, I like the fact that everyone has to get off their arse and go to the shops and think about each other. That's what it's all about. Being together,' Ben said. 'Don't you agree, Kellie? You love Christmas, don't you?'

Kellie thought about her iPod Christmas play list. Christmas here was certainly a different kind of experience from everything that made her so cynical about it in London. She felt her anti-Christmas stance wavering in the face of Ben's enthusiasm.

'I suppose,' she said.

'You always were a big old softie, Ben. So what about you? Why are you here for Christmas?' Jed asked Kellie.

'It's a long story,' she said, not wanting to elaborate.

'We like long stories,' Toni said, moving her neck and checking Oliver's sleeping face, before picking up her pint.

'It's just . . .' Kellie looked around at the assembled faces, liking them all for being interested, liking them for making her feel as if she was a part of their crowd. She wished that she could be honest, but instead she said, 'I've got a sort of boyfriend.' She avoided looking at Ben. 'But he's away and . . . I don't know . . . it seemed stupid to arrange anything without him, so I came to St John's on a whim, just for a break, and now I've ended up here.'

A sort of boyfriend! Why had she said that? she wondered. Why had she edited the truth so heavily it was tantamount to a lie? She glanced up at Ben to try and see what he was thinking. She couldn't tell.

'What sort of boyfriend is that?' Toni said, addressing the others. 'Fancy leaving this one alone at Christmas.'

Kellie smiled. 'Yes, it seems to have got me into all sorts of trouble.'

'What about your family?' Ben asked. 'Won't they be missing you?'

'My parents are both abroad, so I was going to be on my own anyway.'

'Well, don't worry, love, this will be a Christmas to remember, by the looks of things,' Erin, one of the older women, said, smiling at her and flicking her eyes towards Ben.

Kellie looked at Ben, as she took a sip of her pint, embarrassed by the insinuation. Why hadn't she explained properly? Why hadn't she told him that she was in love? Why had she made her relationship sound so flippant and disposable, when it was quite the opposite. She looked down at the table, wishing she'd said more, but the moment had passed.

'Aha!' said Jed, as Roddy, standing next to the karaoke machine, began to address the pub.

Sally hadn't been joking when she'd said that no one could sing, but it didn't matter. As the beer slipped down, everyone felt more confident, and eventually Kellie surrendered to the inevitable herself, agreeing to sing, 'Last Christmas' by Wham!

Perhaps it was the pints of beer and that glass of Roddy's mulled wine, or maybe it was just that Ben was making her laugh, but as she got into her stride, singing into the microphone, Kellie realised she couldn't stop smiling.

She grinned at Ben, before looking out at the rest of the crowd. She couldn't believe she was doing this. What would her friends think if they could see her now? Singing Wham! In elasticated jeans? It was hardly the coolest thing she'd ever done, but suddenly Kellie didn't give a damn. All the schmaltz of Christmas that she'd always detested suddenly overcame her in a wave of goodwill as everyone sang along with her. She was loving this.

'Special, special,' she sang, impersonating George Michael, camping up the echo and singing along with the instrumental break.

And then her grin froze on her face as she saw Elliot Thorne staring back at her. He had his hand on the shoulder of a tall, fair-haired teenaged boy, ushering him in through the door, but his eyes didn't waver from Kellie's for an instant.

She could feel her cheeks burning, as she stumbled through the final chorus. She replaced the microphone and walked back to her seat, ignoring the applause. She had goosepimples all over her, as if someone had poured cold water down her spine.

People were speaking to her. Ben was congratulating her, saying something about the Eurovision song contest, but none of the words she heard made any sense.

She watched Elliot go to the bar and greet Sally, who gave the boy a hug. It must be Michael, she thought, Sally's son.

Then Elliot turned to face Kellie and walked over. She held her breath, her heart pounding.

'Hi again,' he said, holding his black leather gloves in his hand and staring down at Ben, who was sitting on the edge of the bench. Elliot was wearing his navy-blue cashmere coat and he loosened a smart grey-checked scarf. His smooth cheeks were pink from the cold outside. Snowflakes were still in his dark hair. In amongst all the locals, he looked out of place and formal, like an undertaker at a wedding.

As he glanced briefly at Kellie and then back at Ben, she recognised his expression. It was the one he used to interrogate anyone who opposed his clients.

'Oh, hello again,' Ben said, not paying much attention to Elliot, but smiling as Erin took to the stage and a roar went up, as the sleigh bells at the start of 'Merry Christmas Everybody', by Slade pumped out from the karaoke machine.

'I thought you were going back to Fleet Town?' Elliot said, feigning confusion.

'I did, but then we came back and now we're stranded,' Ben said, distracted.

'Because of the weather?'

'Yeah. Hey, Kellie, check out Erin,' Ben laughed. 'She's even worse than you!'

Elliot nodded and backed away, clearly stumped. Kellie knew that he wasn't used to people dismissing him like Ben just had. She could tell that he was furious.

'I'll be getting back then, Sally,' Elliot shouted over the music, waving towards the bar. His eyes flicked towards Kellie's.

Kellie could hardly breathe as she watched Elliot leave the pub.

'I'm just going to the loo,' she said, getting up. 'Back in a minute.'

Outside, the moon was as a bright as a searchlight over Gotham City. The snow had stopped falling, but it had settled all around and bounced the light back. The sky was twinkling and violet. Black footprints patterned the ground.

Elliot leant against the brick wall in the alleyway between the pub and the block of outside loos. It looked as

156

if he was dissolving into shadow. The red eye of a cigarette glowed as it tumbled through the air.

It was freezing. Kellie shivered, the cold hurting her throat. She hadn't brought her coat and after the warmth of the pub, the icy air cut through Sally's jumper in an instant.

'What are you doing here?' Elliot asked, gripping her arm. Through the cloud of steam his breath made in the cold air, she couldn't tell whether he was furious or delighted. He smelled of smoked. She knew he only smoked cigarettes when he got very agitated.

'It's been a nightmare. I came on a sight-seeing tour and we got stranded. Then we had to come here through the snow –'

'Sight-seeing?' he interrupted. 'What the hell did you think you were playing at?'

Kellie shook her arm free. After everything she'd been through, she was astonished at his reaction.

'I'm fine, by the way,' she said. 'The whole country is at a standstill with Arctic weather conditions, and I got caught out in the worst blizzard they've had here for fifty years, oh and I nearly fell down a cliff, but hey, I survived.'

'Obviously. Well don't let me ruin your fun in there.'

'Elliot,' she said. 'You got me into this by bringing me here . . .'

'I didn't bring you here. Not *here*.'

They both froze for moment, as a man came out of the loo block behind Elliot and walked back into the pub.

'What's the matter with you?' she asked, when it was safe to talk again. 'Aren't you even vaguely pleased to see me?'

'Yes, but . . .'

'But what?'

'I didn't expect to see you cavorting with the locals.'

'Ben?'

'Yes. Him. In there.'

Now she saw what this was all about. Elliot was jealous. Unflappable, unshockable Elliot Thorne was jealous of Ben. She stared at him amazed, never having seen him like this before.

'Well it's thanks to "him in there" that I'm alive, and that's the only reason – the *only* reason – that I'm talking to him at all.'

Elliot looked away.

'El?' she asked, searching out his eyes. 'You're being ridiculous.'

'Am I?'

'Yes! Of course you are! This is *me*, remember?' she said, punching him gently on the chest, as if to remind him. 'How about a hello?'

Elliot exhaled suddenly and pulled her into a hug. 'I was just frantic with worry. About the weather. About not being able to talk to you tonight.'

'Were you?'

'Of course, but then you were there. You gave me such a shock.'

'I'm sorry.'

'Especially in those clothes. God, you look awful.'

She hit him, playfully. 'Thanks a bunch.'

'Oh, darling, I'm so glad you're safe.'

She let him hug her and she put her arms around him, feeling his cold coat against her cheek.

'You haven't told him, have you? About us?' Elliot said, pulling away.

'Who?'

'What's-his-name? The ferry boy?'

'No. No of course I haven't.' She felt a sudden sense of indignation. 'And for your information, Ben isn't a boy or a ferryman. He runs a business in London. He's only here to see his parents.'

'I don't care about him. Only you.'

Elliot looked furtively around, before pulling her up against the wall and kissing her hard on the lips. 'I've missed you,' he whispered. 'Like crazy.'

Eventually, she struggled away from him, worried that they were going to get caught.

'Are you going back tonight to the hotel? On the boat?' he asked.

'No. We can't. The boat's broken, so I'm stuck here. It's too dangerous to go back. Anyway, I'm not going anywhere in the dark. I hate the bloody dark.'

'So where are you staying?'

'Sally's letting us use the annexe next door.'

'Us?'

'Yes, me and Ben.'

'You're staying the night together?'

'Elliot, for God's sake! Stop behaving like this. I don't like it any more than you do.' It had seemed to escape his notice that he was spending the night with his wife.

'Meet me tomorrow then.'

'Where?'

'In the morning, by the boatsheds at the quay. The green one. You can't miss it.'

'When?'

The pub door opened and Jack stepped out. 'Hello there,' he said, nodding at Kellie and Elliot. They sprang apart pretending to be strangers.

'Half past ten,' Elliot said, as if he had been telling her the time.

'OK,' she mumbled. 'Happy Christmas.'

She nodded briefly at Elliot, before putting her head down, her heart pounding as she walked back to the warmth of the pub.

Chapter 12

It was nearly midnight and Stephanie's head was heavy with exhaustion and red wine. She stood alone by the fireplace in the dining room, looking at the picture on the mantelpiece of her mother.

When she and Elliot had been kids, they'd always had stockings at the end of their beds. She remembered the sensation of waking up with one of her mother's nylons stuffed full of presents over the blankets and sheets weighing down her feet. She'd done the same for her own children every year, wanting them to feel the same way too.

But over dinner, Isabelle had insisted that the stockings should be left by the chimney, working Nat up into a frenzy about chimneys and reindeer and whether Father Christmas would get stuck, and how would he get the soot off his snowy white beard. Stephanie was annoyed that her father had allowed this break in tradition to happen, but David had accused her of being pernickety.

Now Stephanie's heart filled with a dull emptiness as she stuffed chocolate money into Nat and Simon's stocking, noticing that Isabelle had even marked the hearth with sooty 'reindeer footprints'.

She knew she should be rejoicing in the fact that Simon and Nat were still here. She should be filled with antici-pation, looking forward to seeing their faces tomorrow morning. However, she could only seem to look back instead of forwards – and every time she looked back, the truth hit her like a punch: she should be filling up three stockings. Not two. And the longer they went on without

Paul, rather than it becoming less painful, all she did was miss him more. Especially now. Especially as he'd always loved Christmas so much.

Tears started oozing out of the corners of her eyes. What was wrong with her? Why couldn't she just switch it off the way everyone else seemed to have done? Why couldn't she find a way to cope like David had, and like her father had about her mum?

Because Paul should be here too. That was why. That was the hideous fact she kept returning to. Over and over again. David could have stopped it happening. She felt cold resentment harden inside her as his laughter spilled out of the kitchen, where he was sharing a nightcap with Elliot and her father.

She mustn't do this, she thought. She must get on with Christmas. She mustn't fall into that black hole and ruin it for everyone else. She stuffed more presents into the stockings, trying to make herself believe in the magic of Christmas, trying to make herself believe that this was all worthwhile, but the memory of Paul, of what had happened to him, came back and back. She squeezed her eyes shut, and saw it all once more . . .

It had been sixteen months ago, at the start of the second week of the first family summer holiday they'd had abroad in ages. The first week had been wonderful. Stephanie remembered the heat – and she remembered how happy she and David had been. They'd stayed up in the French campsite every night and had made love in the woods behind the tents under the stars.

Then everything went wrong.

They all got up early, because the bright heat radiating through the tent had made it impossible to stay inside. It was a glorious morning. They sang songs as they drove down to the local lake where Simon wanted to hire a boat.

161

'I'll stay with Nat and set up the picnic,' Stephanie said to David, as they parked the car. 'You take the boys and go and have fun.'

David kissed her quickly, rolling his eyes at Nat, who had started screaming and swiping her tiny fingers at her mosquito bites. Good luck, he mouthed, as he set off with Simon and her beautiful Paul. Stephanie called out good-bye to them but Paul was already chasing Simon through the trees on the dry mud path, as they ran to the boat hut. She shaded her eyes against the sun, laughing at five-year-old Paul in his little khaki shorts and red hat, trying to keep up.

It took ages to get Nat off to sleep in the buggy. Stephanie pushed her down to the picnic tables by the lakeside, adjusting the umbrella on the buggy to shade her face. She stood by the shore, looking out at the boats on the lake, trying to see David and the boys. She watched a rouge cloud pass over the sun, its shadow running across the pebbles. The waves rippled in at a sharp angle. Everything was perfect. She was happy to be alive.

And then, just as she turned to set out the picnic on one of the tables, she heard yelling. She saw David, rowing back to shore. Too fast. He was rowing too fast. And then she realised it was Simon who was yelling, shouting and shouting for her.

She dropped the glass she was holding and ran into the water. Her thin cotton skirt plastered to her legs, as she half waded, half fell towards the boat. She could see Simon screaming at the prow. And David, drenched. But where was Paul? She couldn't see Paul. She couldn't see her little boy. She lunged for the boat as it reached her and looked inside. Paul wasn't there.

And David's face. Pale horror. As she looked into his eyes, she knew.

Everything happened so quickly after that.

They ran to the boatshed to raise the alarm. The life guard ran with David to the rescue boat and she watched them race out on to the lake.

But it was too late. She sensed it inside her as fact.

Stephanie felt nothing as the rescue boat returned. She held her sobbing family, but it was as if she wasn't there.

She saw Paul's body a few hours later, swollen and blue. They'd found it tangled in the reeds fifty metres from where he'd fallen in. She hugged him to her. She didn't want to let him go. She wanted to fall asleep with him and never wake up.

When they finally took him away from her, she pressed her lips against his. She remembered the perfect little baby he'd been. She remembered the first time she'd held him. It struck her as the happiest moment of her life.

Then came silence. She looked around her and saw Simon wrapped in a blanket with his eyes tight shut. She felt David clinging desperately on to her arm. She watched Nat's mouth locked wide open in a continuous scream.

She watched the men in the yellow jackets carry Paul's body away from her into the back of an ambulance. She watched the crowd that had gathered, simultaneously cowering away and staring on, their hands held over their mouths in shock.

Then the sound came back and she fell to her knees.

It was only afterwards that she found out the details of what had happened. It was only later that David attempted to explain the inexplicable horror of it all.

The boys had been fighting over the fishing rod and whose turn it was, he said, and Paul had been fiddling with his lifejacket. He hadn't been able to cast the rod with it on. So he'd taken the jacket off.

David had let her son, who couldn't swim, take his lifejacket off.

He'd only turned his back on Paul for a moment.

For *that* moment, *the only moment that mattered.*

He'd been helping Simon untangle the landing net, but when he'd turned around, Paul had gone.

They hadn't heard him fall in. Neither Simon nor David had heard even a splash. David had dived in straight away, groping through the water to find Paul, but the current had been too strong.

The rest: the coroner, the police, the hospital, the mortuary, all passed in a blur. The aeroplane home. Even the funeral.

And then everything slowed down. Slower than before. Each day became interminably long, black and heavy with truth. Her baby was gone. Paul was gone. Her baby boy was dead.

'Hey there.'

Stephanie was jogged out of her thoughts by Isabelle, who was hovering in the dining room doorway, nursing a mug of hot chocolate. She was wearing matching cream silk pyjamas and an open silk robe. Her hair was brushed back and she didn't have any make-up on, but she still looked perfect. Stephanie quickly turned away, so that Isabelle wouldn't see her tears.

'They're going to be so excited,' Isabelle said.

'Who?'

'Nat and Simon of course, and I hope Taylor and Elliot are too. Especially El. I've got him a very special surprise this year.'

Stephanie didn't say anything. She simply didn't have the energy to buy into Isabelle's excitement or enthusiasm.

'Stephanie? You know, I'm glad I've got you on your own . . .'

Stephanie knew what was coming, but she couldn't stomach any sympathy. Not from Isabelle. Not from anyone.

'Well. That's me done. I'm off to bed,' she said, cutting her off.

'I really want to talk to you about –' Isabelle said, but Stephanie was already dashing past.

'I'll be more useful in the morning. Honestly, Isabelle. It's very late. Night night,' she said, and ran up the stairs.

DAY 2

Christmas Day

Chapter 13

'This place is a dump,' Roddy said.

Roddy, Michael and his mum were in the public bar of the Windcheater. It was ten in the morning, but it felt like night. The snow was piled up so thick against the window that only the palest of light showed through, as if someone was holding up a candle behind cloth. Michael was sweating. The radiators were blasting out heat, but still he shivered, thinking about the tin mine, wondering if Taylor would still want to go there, and hoping that she would not.

'Useless thing,' Roddy said, slapping the side of the wall-mounted TV, which was hissing like a cat, picking up nothing but static.

It was Christmas Day, but it was like any other day. As with every morning after the night before, the bar felt as if it had had the life sucked out of it. There were patches of spilt red wine on the carpet. It looked like a murder scene through which a bloodied body had been dragged. The jukebox was silent. The fruit machine lights were off. It was hard to believe that only a few hours ago, the room had been full of drunk people, merrily singing carols and old Christmas pop standards.

The pub would be open again in a couple of hours, just to catch anyone who felt like briefly ducking out of their family commitments for a swift pint. It was important to squeeze as much business out of the place as possible, Roddy reckoned, while they still could.

Time was, when Michael's dad had still been here, that Michael wouldn't have set foot in the bar on Christmas

Day. His dad had always been a sucker for Christmas and all its festive tat. He'd been a drunk, and sentimental with it.

Michael smiled now, as he remembered how it had been. They'd always left clearing up the pub till Boxing Day. They'd stayed in bed late instead, and had then opened their presents and gone out to play. Michael's dad had taught him how to fly a kite one Christmas and had snagged it in a tree. Another year, he'd fallen flat on his arse and twisted his ankle whilst trying to show Michael how to jump a pavement kerb on his first skateboard. Michael would help his dad and mum cook a lunch visible from space in the afternoon, then they'd curl up on the sofa in front of the fire and watch repeats of the shows Michael's dad had loved when he'd been a kid himself: *The Two Ronnies* and *Monty Python*. Or they'd settle down in front of a movie, one of the classics, like *The Bridge on the River Kwai*, or *Gone with the Wind*.

That had all stopped, a year or two before Michael's dad had gone. Christmas had become about empty wine and whisky bottles and silent meals. It had been about Michael, his mum and his dad staring out through the windows as if they'd had bars.

And now Christmas had gone altogether. All his Dad's old seasonal favourites – the dancing snowman, the Christmas tree ice lolly moulds, and the hairy fairy for the top of the tree – were tied up in bin bags up in the attic, along with the now moth-eaten clothes he'd never come back to pick up.

Michael had listened to the national news on the radio earlier that morning with his mother as they'd eaten their breakfast. It was official: there was a white Christmas across the UK. The usual warnings had gone out: don't drive unless you absolutely have to; keep the kids away from canals and frozen ponds; wrap up warm and check on your elderly neighbours if you can.

A ship had gone missing off Newquay. The red and white coast guard helicopter had scoured the shores for wreckage, but nothing had been found. The whole country had practically come to a standstill. Roads were blocked and people had been stranded in their cars on the motorways all night. There'd been no mention of St John's or Brayner, though. All the news had centred around London and Cardiff and Edinburgh and the dense populations there. It was as if the world had turned its back on Michael and his family. It was as if they'd been forgotten or had ceased to exist.

'At least this is the last Christmas we'll be having to do this,' Roddy said, pushing a grey-haired mop across the red lino floor near the bar, leaving it shining like ice in his wake.

He had a hangover. He sniffed hard and made a show of clearing his throat, in protest at the guff of chemical stench thrown off as he plunged the mop head into the bucket of foaming brown water. He'd been grumbling for what seemed like an age and Michael glowered at him from the corner of the room, where he was wiping down a table with a wet cloth.

Cleaning up the pub wasn't something Michael relished, but it wasn't something he hated either. It was just part of the mechanics of the day, like brushing his teeth, and he hated Roddy for making such a big deal of it. Michael had grown up here. This was his home. Roddy hating it the way he did made Michael feel as if Roddy was hating a part of him too.

Fuck him, Michael thought, and fuck his rancid fucking tea shop in rancid fucking Truro. What did Roddy think? That it would be different there? That there'd be no clearing up to be done?

Michael wanted to scream at both Roddy and his mum,

to *tell* them he wasn't going to go with them, but he couldn't. He didn't want to hurt his mum – and telling her what he really thought about moving to Truro *would* hurt her, because Roddy had convinced her that leaving Brayner behind was what *she* wanted to do. Everything Roddy had told her, she'd passed on to Michael as Gospel truth: that they'd have a better quality of life in Truro, and a bigger home; that Michael would soon make new friends; that they'd all have more money and would be able to go to the Caribbean on holiday next Christmas.

But Michael knew the truth. They weren't going to Truro for any of these reasons. They were going there because that was what Roddy wanted. He was going to take the cash from the pub and buy what he hadn't been able to afford in Truro when he lived there on his own.

'It's a pigsty in here,' Roddy said.

Only because you got shitfaced last night and kept it open till gone one, Michael thought.

'Only because nobody bothered to tidy up last night,' he said.

'Nobody like you,' Roddy said.

'Because I was in bed. Because I'm a kid, remember?'

'Yeah, a kid with an attitude problem.'

Michael opened his mouth to tell him to fuck off. He'd done it once before, when his mother hadn't been there to hear, and it had led to a god-damned almighty row, which had terminated in Michael screaming at Roddy that he wasn't his dad, and Roddy shouting back at him that at least he could thank his lucky fucking stars for that.

'Will you two stop bickering?' Michael's mother intervened. She was busy behind the bar, stacking up the glass washing machine, nursing a hangover (the same as Roddy). She was wrapped up in a white towel dressing gown with brown coffee stains patterned across its

172

sleeves. Her face was smudged with last night's make-up. Michael had fixed her an Alka-Seltzer as soon as she'd got up, but it didn't seem to have worked.

'He started it,' Michael said.

Roddy leant down by the fireplace and lit a cigarette off last night's still-smouldering embers. His eyes were bloodshot and the bags beneath them were the colour of dough.

'All I'm saying is that the sooner someone buys this place off us, the better.'

'It's not even yours to sell,' Michael said.

Michael's mother looked up sharply and immediately Michael wished he hadn't spoken.

'Sorry,' he said.

'Don't apologise to me,' she said.

'I'm going out to fetch some wood,' Roddy announced.

'No,' Michael said. 'Let me.'

He hurried out, before Roddy could object, angry with himself for having spoken out. It had been pointless, childish. Roddy made his mother happy, he reminded himself, the same as he did at least ten times a day. That was all that should matter. So what if the pub wasn't Roddy's to sell? They were selling it, anyway, and nothing Michael could say, he told himself again, would make a blind bit of difference to that.

He shoved through the heavy white fire door, which separated the public bar from the rest of the house. Red carpet replaced the linoleum on the other side and, as the door hissed shut behind him, the smell of this morning's bacon and eggs, which he'd cooked for himself and his mum, and which she'd turned over with her fork as if they'd been covered in mould, took over from the reek of dead hedonism in the bar next door.

Christmas terminated here too. In front of the punters, Roddy had more seasonal spirits than a herd of reindeer, but only because it loosened up their wallets and made them spend their cash. In the family side of the building, neither Roddy nor Michael's mum had made much of an effort this year.

Inside the kitchen, the only concession to December the 25th was a tiny Poinsettia in a red plastic tub at the centre of the table and a few cards parading across the top of the microwave. Michael breathed in and sighed, scrunching up his nose. There was a plug-in pine air freshener in the electric socket by the door. The sticker on its front advertised the fresh smell of a forest glade, but Michael thought it smelt more like a toilet.

There was cat food on the white tiled floor, next to the cat bowl and ginger hairs floated on the surface of the half inch of murky water inside plastic ice-cream tub. Michael's mum and Roddy were always too busy keeping the public side of the building looking good for the customers to take much care of in here. Michael gave the place a once-over every evening, while they were working at the bar, but most mornings after, when he came downstairs, it was as if it had never been done. He pictured the Thorne house, the carefully prepared lunch he'd been party to yesterday, the shining cutlery and gleaming glassware, and the clean, sweet smell of the air.

He sat down on the kitchen mat beside the three-bar electric fire and started to pull on his boots.

His mother came in and stood over him, reaching down to ruffle his hair.

'Come on,' she said, 'everything's going to be all right.'

He yanked his laces tight. 'I know.'

'It'll be easier, once we've moved . . . I promise.'

Michael made a show of focusing on his laces, tying them in perfect double knots. Every time his mother talked to him about this – about her and him and Roddy, about where their lives were going next – it made him feel like a baby, as if he was about to cry. It made him want to shout at her that it just wasn't fair.

'I know you don't want to leave here,' she went on, 'but it's just something we've got to do. It's not right for us to stay. It's not fair on Roddy. This place is too full of memories, and none of them are his.'

Michael undid the lace he'd just fastened. He didn't want to look up, didn't want her to know that he was upset. How could he ever explain to her that he wanted to stay here for the exact memories that she wanted to leave? Sometimes, walking round here, it was as if his dad had never left, as if he'd just gone over to St John's on the boat and would be back home soon. Michael still hated his dad for leaving, but he loved him enough to want him back as well.

'Me and your dad made this place what it is,' his mother said, 'but that's over now. It's time to move on. You'll understand when you're older.'

Michael turned his jeans up above the tops of his boots. He'd rung his father six weeks ago and told him they were moving back to the mainland. He'd asked if he could move in with him and Carol, the young teacher his dad had left his mum for, but his dad had told him they hardly had enough room in their flat as it was, and that money was tight. He'd told Michael he'd be much better off sticking with his mum.

'Thanks for helping Roddy,' Michael's mother said.

I'm not, Michael thought. I just want to get away from him.

He looked up guiltily and watched a smile light up her face. The smile broadened.

'What?' he asked.

'Just you. Getting older.' She briefly cupped his chin in her hand. 'I should have got you an electric razor for Christmas, eh?'

175

He stood, embarrassed, and felt himself blush. Nothing made him feel less of a man than her commenting on his appearance like that.

'I'm making Roddy a cup of tea,' she said. 'Do you want one?'

'No, I'll be fine.'

She picked up a bag of sprouts off the vegetable rack and laid it on the kitchen table.

'After you've done the wood,' she said, 'can you sort out that chicken for me? A big one, mind. So there's enough for tomorrow as well.'

'Sure.' Michael pulled on his coat.

He stepped outside and shut the door behind him. The kitchen overlooked a long rectangular yard, which sloped upwards away from the back of the pub, bordered by a high red brick wall. At the end of the yard, the wood shed and chicken hut stood side by side. His dad had built the chicken shed. Michael reckoned his mum only kept it there at all, because she knew that it would upset him if she had it ripped down. She found plucking the birds for the table a bore and used frozen chicken portions with pre-packed gravy sachets for the customers. The only reason she was cooking a fresh chicken at all today was because they'd run out of frozen last night.

It was normally grotty out here, the brickwork damp and mossy, with chicken shit spattered like punctuation marks across the cracked concrete, but now everything was pristine, as if the whole world had received a fresh coat of white paint. The snow lay inches deep and uniform on the ground, patterned by the tiny footprints of birds.

Pulling his woollen balaclava from his pocket and tugging it down on his head, rolled up like a hat, Michael took the shovel from beside the back door and set about clearing a path round the side of the pub and then up to the top of the yard.

176

He stood there, catching his breath, and stared out across the village. Snow lay in waves across the roofs of the nearby cottages. Looking back, he could see it slumped in drifts against the back of the pub and the yard walls. A collar of slate showed on the roof at the base of the chimney, where the heat from the fire had melted the snow overnight. Ice teeth grinned down from the gutter.

From inside the chicken shed behind him came the inquisitive clucking of hens. He'd feed them and get them fresh water, but first he'd fetch the wood. He wheeled the barrow out from inside the wood shed and stacked it high, then began pushing it down towards the house.

A movement snared his attention and he froze. His mother and Roddy were standing there, framed by the kitchen window from their waists up, like they'd been caught in a photo. As Michael watched them kiss, he felt ashamed: for being angry with them, for hating them for wanting to build a new life for themselves.

They weren't the problem, he suddenly understood. It was him. He was the one who no longer fitted in.

He looked away, again remembering what he'd seen at the Thorne house the day before. Again he saw Elliot turning away from Isabelle, and again he saw Isabelle's features crumple as she started to cry and buried her face in her dressing gown.

A diamond of ice glinted on Michael's knuckle, like a ring. He looked up at the sky and hoped that Taylor hadn't forgotten about coming to see him later on. It was funny how much he missed her, when it was hardly twelve hours since he'd seen her last. He thought of himself in Truro, with his mother and Roddy in their new home. He was going to miss Taylor Thorne so much more then.

He kept warm by working, taking three wheelbarrow loads of logs round to the front of the pub and emptying them outside the front door. He then took them inside and stacked them neatly either side of the fire. Then he trundled the wheelbarrow back round to the shed.

That's when he noticed the chicken. Its gnarled feet were sticking out from the ventilation gap beneath the hut. It was stone dead, and Michael picked it up as its frozen feathers snapped off in his hands like twigs.

'Happy Christmas.'

Michael started and turned round to see Taylor. She was grinning at him, her eyes as bright and twinkling as the snow. He felt his stomach twist and realised again how much he wanted her, but then she noticed the dead bird.

A smile, half horror, half intrigue, flickered across her face. 'I hope that's not my present,' she said.

He laughed. 'Of course not.'

She looked at him curiously. 'You didn't just . . .'

'What?'

'Kill it . . .'

'No. It died of cold. It must have got locked out last night.'

Roddy, Michael thought. Roddy must have put the chickens away last night while Michael had been over at the Thornes'. This chicken was dead because of him.

He dropped the dead bird into the black bin by the side of the shed. Taylor stared at his empty hands, then clasped her own together. She was wearing a bright green O'Neill skiing jacket, a silver hat with a pink bobble, and what looked like new jeans.

'I thought you and Simon weren't coming till later,' he said.

'We still are, but Dad needed to come into the village now and I fancied the walk.'

'Where is he?'

'Over at the yacht chandler's.'

'But they'll be shut . . .'

178

'That's what I thought, but he says they're expecting him. He's picking up a present for Granddad. I'm meeting him round the front of the pub in half an hour.' She scuffed her boot in the snow. 'So did you get anything good for Christmas?' she asked.

Taylor's cheeks were rosy. She looked wide awake. He imagined how Christmas must have been at her house this morning. So different from his. As cuddly and cute as a Disney DVD, he guessed. Stockings and wrapping paper littering the carpets, everybody swapping presents in front of the fire. He wanted that when he grew up. If he ever had a family of his own, that's how he'd want it to be: perfect, like hers.

'Binoculars,' he said. 'From my dad. How about you?'

'We're not opening our presents till later. Did you get the torches?' she asked.

The great, dark entrance of the mine yawned open inside his mind.

'Two,' he answered, 'but I can get more. Mum keeps a stack of them behind the bar for guests. I put them upstairs in my room. But don't you think we should forget it? At least until the snow's gone . . .'

'Why? I managed to make it from Granddad's to here, didn't I? So long as it doesn't start up again, we'll be fine. I think we should still go after lunch. Can you get to ours by two-thirty?'

He'd lain in bed the night before, flicking through a copy of *Kerrang!*, whilst listening to Good Charlotte's latest through his earphones to drown out the noise of the pub below. He'd pictured Taylor standing by that gaping hole which led into the earth, and he'd seen a gnarled claw scythe out of the darkness and drag her screaming down into the depths. He'd woken soaked in sweat.

'Won't you still be eating?' he asked.

'They will, but we'll slip away. You know how these

179

things are. They'll all be too legless to notice. I'll nick some booze and bring it for us, too, if you like, but we'll have to drink it on the sly so that Simon doesn't see.'

'Cool,' he said, even though he felt anything but.

'Do you fancy a quick . . .' She mimed smoking a cigarette, by tapping her fingers against her lips.

'I've got to . . .' He faltered, unsure how to phrase it.

'What?' Taylor asked.

Michael nodded at the chicken shed. 'You know . . . for lunch . . .'

'You're having eggs for lunch?'

'No . . .'

'You mean you *are* going to kill one?'

'Well, it's not exactly going to commit suicide,' he said.

She looked over at the bin. 'What about that one? Can't you?'

'Best not. Anything might have been at it during the night.'

She stared back at the shed. You could just about make out the silhouettes of the chickens' heads bobbing back and forth inside, behind the wire mesh.

'How will you do it?' she asked. 'With a knife?'

He pulled his top lip back over his teeth. 'Or wit a lee-tle bite,' he told her in his best Transylvanian accent.

'Ha-ha. No, really. How? Do you wring their necks?'

'You can. It's quickest . . . kindest . . . that way – so long as you know what you're doing.'

This was the way he normally did it. His father had taught him how, tucking the body in tight under his arm, before twisting and pulling the neck up sharp and hard. He'd never given it much thought, really, until today. It had never occurred to him that it might be a source of fascination, especially not to someone as worldly as Taylor. To Michael, killing chickens was no different from digging up spuds from the veggie patch his dad had used

180

to keep outside the village. The birds were food, nothing else. None of them even had names.

But Taylor wasn't worried anyhow. 'It's only a chicken,' she said.

Michael took his Leatherman knife from his pocket. He unfolded its honed blade and watched her stare at it, enraptured. 'Or you can do it with a knife,' he said, thriving on her fascination now, enjoying the sense of power his esoteric knowledge gave him.

'And you've done that, too?' she asked.

'Sure.'

She glanced between Michael and the shed, seeming to weigh something up in her mind. Then she fixed her eyes on him.

'Let me do it,' she said. 'Let me do it with the knife.'

'But aren't you . . .'

'What?'

'I don't know . . . most girls I know . . . they're, they'd be . . .' He was fumbling for words. *Squeamish*, he wanted to say, or *freaked out*, or *grossed out*, but none of these words fitted Taylor, because she wasn't that kind of girl.

'I want to know what it feels like,' she said. 'I want you to teach me.'

Something in her eyes, something he'd never noticed there before, made his heart race. The way she was looking at him, with admiration, with respect, made him feel older, and stronger too. He felt like someone she might want.

'Are you sure?'

'Well, why not?' She laughed nervously. 'I'm happy enough to buy it shrink-wrapped in the supermarket when someone else has done the dirty work for me, right? So what's the big deal about doing it myself?'

'Fine,' he told her and opened the chicken shed door. 'Then be my guest.'

The chickens scrabbled around as Michael reached inside and fished one out. The selected bird then sat motionless in the crook of his arm, blinking stupidly between him and Taylor in turn.

Michael talked Taylor through it. He explained to her about the positioning of the knife, there, just behind and above the lower jaw. He demonstrated with his fingers how then to roll the bird's head a little to the left and apply upwards pressure with the blade of the knife, before pulling it sharply across the bird's jugular.

He half-expected her to balk at this point, to tell him that she'd just been kidding and didn't even want to watch him kill it, let alone perform the deed herself.

But she didn't waver. She didn't even ask him to explain twice. She already had the knife in her hand and now she took the chicken from him and gripped it tight.

'Here?' she checked, placing the knife blade where he'd told her.

She had it exactly right. 'Yeah,' he half-whispered, shocked by how quickly she'd turned the tables, amazed by how it was that it was suddenly *him* staring at *her* in awe, rather than the other way round.

Her brow creased in concentration as she rolled the chicken's head. Then she sliced the blade sideways with the grace and exactitude of a violinist working a bow.

Taylor's eyes blazed as the chicken bled. She knelt down and let the bird go, then watched it jerk spasmodically on the ground by her feet. There was blood on her fingertips and blood on the snow.

'Why isn't it dead yet?' she asked.

'It can take as long as three minutes,' he told her.

As the bird approached death, its wings began beating frantically.

'It's like it's trying to take off . . .' Taylor said. 'Like it's trying to fly away from here, before it's too late . . .'

The bird died and slumped sideways on to the snow.

'That was amazing,' Taylor told him. 'I think that's the most beautiful thing I've ever seen.'

Afterwards, after he'd handed the newly killed chicken over to his mother to scald and pluck, and he nicked – at Taylor's insistence – a couple of Bacardi Breezers from behind the bar, Michael told his mother they were going to go outside to try out his new binoculars. He took Taylor round to the front of the pub and checked that no one was around, before ducking behind a sprawling holly bush with her and lighting them both a smoke. They twisted open the Barcardi bottles.

'I don't think I've ever got drunk this early before,' Taylor said, 'but what the fuck,' she added, taking a swig, 'it's Christmas . . .'

Michael followed suit.

Then they clinked their bottlenecks together and each took another swig. He glimpsed her momentarily through the bottle, distorted and trapped, like a genie locked behind green glass. They both tipped back their heads until the bottles were empty. Taylor chucked hers casually over her shoulder and Michael did the same.

He took a long drag of his cigarette, and raised the binoculars to his eyes. He tried tracking a seagull high up in the sky, then he scanned along the empty road. The snow made the village look like something from another planet, as if his ordinary world had switched to science fiction and anything might happen today.

'Give us a go,' Taylor said.

She checked out the village for a while, then turned to face the harbour.

'Wow,' she said. 'They're good. Hey, and look . . . It's my Dad . . .'

She was right. Michael saw a figure in a bright red

waterproof, which he guessed was the same one Elliot had been wearing the day before when he'd come in out of the snow. He was walking along the row of boatsheds, where the island people kept their sailing dinghies and fishing equipment. He stopped at one with a green door, opened it and stepped inside. Then the door shut and the harbour side was deserted again, as if he'd never been there.

'What's he doing in Grandpa's shed?' Taylor pondered aloud. 'He's meant to be at the chandler's. He can't be thinking about taking the boat out . . .'

'Even if he wanted to, he couldn't. Look . . .' Michael said.

Taylor lowered the binoculars and he pointed out to sea.

'No one's going anywhere,' Michael said. 'Not today.'

Something was clearly wrong with the grey expanse of water. Its border, where the sea reached the land, was flat, immobile, covered with cracks. Sparks of light appeared and died on it, in it, ephemeral as flaws inside a jewel.

'Sea ice,' Michael explained.

It had gathered there overnight, as incongruous and solid as a stone terrace. His mother had pointed it out to him earlier that morning.

'Look how far out it goes,' Taylor said. She turned to him with a smile. 'It's incredible. Is it thick enough to walk on?'

He thought about kissing her, right there and then.

'Hey, guys!' a voice called out.

It was Ben, walking towards them from the annexe, from where the holly bush failed to shield them. His footsteps crunched across the snow.

Taylor flicked her cigarette away.

'Don't worry about me,' Ben said, eyeing the cigarette butt as it melted the snow by her feet and then disappeared.

Michael dropped his cigarette anyway, and crunched it beneath his boot.

184

'Those look pretty smart,' Ben commented, checking out the binoculars.

'They're his,' Taylor said.

'I got them for Christmas,' Michael explained.

'So who are you spying on?' Ben asked.

'No one,' Taylor told him. 'We were just looking at the ice.'

Ben was a few inches taller than Michael and dressed in an old black greatcoat which had once belonged to Michael's dad. Michael's mum had lent it to Ben that morning, after Ben had turned up on the scrounge for some teabags and milk to take back to the cottage where he and the posh woman were staying.

Michael knew Ben's parents well enough, but had only met Ben a couple of times. He had a kind face and made Michael's mother laugh, and Michael thought he was probably OK.

'How come you're not back on St John's?' Taylor asked. 'I thought that's where you lived.'

For a moment, Michael wondered how they knew each other, then realised that it must have been Ben who'd ferried Taylor and her mother over the day before.

'It's a long story,' Ben said. 'I knackered my boat and I was hoping someone might be able to fix it, but it looks like nothing's doing, not with that ice.'

'You poor thing,' Taylor said.

'Oh, I don't know,' Ben said cryptically. 'Things could be worse.'

They waited for him to explain, but he didn't.

Instead, he said to Taylor, 'Can I have a go with them?'

She handed him the binoculars and he scanned the sea, then the harbour.

'Oh, look,' he said. 'There's Kellie.'

185

Michael watched another figure, slighter this time, dressed in black walking around the harbour towards the boatsheds where Elliot Thorne had gone before.

'Who's Kellie?' Taylor asked.

'My friend. The one I'm staying in the annexe with. She's a tourist. I was showing her round the island yesterday when the boat broke. Wow,' he said. 'She looks great, even from here.'

Ben winked at Michael and passed the binoculars to Taylor. Then he turned his back on Kellie and the harbour.

'I've just been talking to your mum,' he told Michael. 'She's agreed to do me a favour, but I'm going to need some help from you.'

'Like what?' Michael asked.

'I want to make it up to Kellie. She's meant to be back in her hotel in Fleet Town, but now she's stuck here because of me, and so I want to make her Christmas as good as I can. Your mum's asked us over for lunch, but I don't want to intrude, and so I've come up with a plan of my own . . .'

'Go on,' Michael said, but even as he listened to Ben's request, he became aware of Taylor staring through the binoculars once more. She seemed frozen, her attention locked on the harbour. Then Michael saw why. The tiny figure of Kellie had stopped outside the green door of Taylor's Granddad's boatshed. Something seemed wrong. Then Michael saw what it was. Kellie was opening the door and stepping inside.

'Is that OK?' Ben asked.

'Sorry?' Michael said.

Ben smiled, realising he hadn't been listening. 'Do you want me to run that by you again?' he asked.

'Er . . . yes . . .'

Again, Michael found himself staring at the quayside. This time, Ben turned to look, too, but there was no one there. Like Elliot Thorne before her, Kellie had stepped inside the shed and disappeared.

Taylor lowered the binoculars. Her skin was pale, her expression blank. She stepped between Michael and Ben.

'Your friend Kellie . . .' she said. 'What did you say she'd come here for?'

Chapter 14

Elliot tasted strange, an unfamiliar mixture of mints and coffee, and his hair had the lingering scent of a cigar, but as he held Kellie to him, she sighed with relief. In his arms, she suddenly felt safe. He was hers and she was his. Holding him made her feel solid again, as if he'd reconnected her to everything she knew and understood.

She made to pull away from him, to talk to him, but he stopped her, kissing her as if they'd been apart for years, not just hours, and he couldn't get enough from her. Taking her hands, he pinned them with his against the wall behind her, pressing himself against her. She kissed him back, and he circled his arms around her, pulling her into a tight hug. As she surrendered to him, she felt as if she was recommitting herself to him.

'Hey, happy Christmas,' he said eventually. He pressed his forehead against hers.

The boatshed was lit by one bare bulb. The air shimmered with dust.

'Happy Christmas.' She smiled at him, scanning the features of his face. Held by his eyes like this, it felt as if nothing else existed in the world and nothing else mattered.

'Fancy seeing you here.'

'Yes,' she said. 'Fancy that. I didn't expect to be here, believe me.'

'Well, I'm glad you are,' he said, pulling back and tenderly smoothing a strand of hair behind her ear.

'Are you? I thought you were furious.'

'Don't be silly. I was just a little thrown last night. You've made my Christmas. I was so afraid you'd have to be on your own and I wouldn't see you.'

He kissed her again. Everything was all right between them after all.

Their whole encounter last night had left her reeling. It had been so dangerous. What if Elliot had been with anyone else from his family? What would have happened then? And what about Ben? She'd felt so wretched in front of him after Elliot had left. He'd been lovely to her all evening, and all she'd done in return was lie.

She'd stayed for one more drink, before making her excuses, pleading exhaustion, insisting that Ben stay on with his friends. She'd retreated to the annexe, dithering for ages about the sleeping arrangements. She'd been unnerved by Elliot's jealous reaction to seeing her and Ben together. Had Elliot really thought that she could ever have flirted with someone else? Was he really as cross with her as he'd seemed at first? And if Elliot, who knew her so well, could have jumped to such a conclusion, then might Ben have done the same? She liked him, but not like that, and she didn't want to give him the impression that she did.

In the end, she'd made a bed for Ben downstairs and had taken the room upstairs for herself, but despite her tiredness, sleep had proved elusive. She'd lain awake, looking at the shadows on the ceiling, listening to the faint music from the pub, wishing she was free to join in.

She'd heard Ben come in some time after one. He'd tripped over something, giggling and shushing himself, and she'd smiled to herself, picturing his face. For a moment, she'd been tempted to go down and talk to him. There'd been so much she still wanted to ask him: how he felt about the break-up with his wife, what their marriage had been like, how he'd known it was coming to an end, who had eventually called it off, and how he felt about his

189

future now. But she'd stopped herself. Her curiosity had landed her in enough trouble for one day. Besides, she'd reasoned with herself, she hardly knew Ben. What would be the point in asking him anything? It was none of her business.

She'd listened intently in the darkness, waiting for him to fall asleep, but Ben had wriggled around on the small creaky sofa downstairs and she'd known he was awake too. She'd felt scared of moving in case he'd have interpreted it as some sort of invitation from her, and scared of the conversation she didn't want to have with him, scared of the answers she'd have to give to all the questions she knew he had.

Now, as she kissed Elliot again, she was glad that she'd trusted her instinct. In the cold light of day, she was very glad she hadn't had a late night truth session with Ben. She shivered and Elliot rubbed her arms.

'I wish we could stay here all day,' Elliot said. He didn't add it, but Kellie knew he meant *but we can't*. She looked down at their hands and how their fingers had instinctively intertwined.

'I do too, but it's a bit draughty in here, isn't it?'

Elliot laughed. 'I know. What *are* we going to do?'

His eyes were tender. He stroked her cheek again.

'It's so bloody freezing out there. There's no way to get between here and St John's. It looks I'm staying for Christmas.'

'Will you be OK?'

'I suppose so, but I'm so worried. This is such a tiny island, isn't it? I mean, what if someone sees me? What if I bump into your dad, or you and Isabelle together? What am I supposed to say then?'

'Say nothing. They don't know you. Nobody has the faintest idea about us. Nobody has even seen us together.'

'But –'

'Everything will be fine, darling. We're having a big Christmas lunch, so everyone will be inside. All you have to do is keep a low profile. Just sit it out and get on a boat first thing in the morning. I'll be with you by lunchtime tomorrow. Nobody in the family will ever know that you were here.'

Kellie knew he was right, but she didn't like it. 'This is so bloody ridiculous, isn't it? All this skulking about? I wish it could be different.'

And it could, she thought. If you'd told Isabelle about us before Christmas, then we wouldn't even be here.

'So do I,' he said.

'I hate having to lie to people. Sally and Roddy, they've been so kind. I feel like a fraud.'

'Forget about them. Why do you even care about what they think?'

She didn't answer. She did care. She pictured herself coming back here a year from now, with Elliot, to visit his father. All the people she'd met last night would recognise her, know her for the liar she was and treat her accordingly. And what about Elliot's father? What would he think of her for having deceived his neighbours and friends?

But perhaps Elliot was right. Perhaps she shouldn't give a damn who judged her. What would it matter what anyone else thought, once she and Elliot were together?

She stepped away from him.

'So what is this place, anyway?' she asked.

'Dad's boatshed.'

It was the first time she'd ever been somewhere directly connected to Elliot's family. A set of wooden doors at the end were in bad repair and thin strips of white winter light crept through. On the wall, there were various hooks, housing an odd assortment of coats, as well as worn-looking lifejackets. There were adult sizes and child

191

sizes too. The boom of a windsurfer and a board were strapped to the ceiling with bungee straps.

In the middle of the shed was a white sailing dingy, its mast collapsed and the sails rolled up.

She walked towards it. 'So is this where you come in the summer?' She looked again at the small lifejackets. One of them must have been worn by Taylor. She was suddenly aware of all the history that the Thorne family shared, all of Elliot's memories that she'd never be a part of.

Elliot nodded. 'We used to. I bought Dad this boat when he retired, but I don't think he uses it that much any more.'

Kellie ran her hand along the fibreglass side of the boat, walking away from Elliot.

And then she saw it. She stopped, her hand moving away from the boat as if she'd been scorched. In looping blue letters was the name: *Isabelle*.

Elliot had bought his father a boat and it was called Isabelle?

'What is it?' Elliot asked.

She turned round, forcing a smile, forcing herself to hide the jealousy she felt. Had Elliot named it, or his father? She didn't know which was worse. Or – the thought made her feel so sick that she instantly dismissed it – or had Elliot not bought it for his father, but for Isabelle? Could he be lying to her?

'Nothing,' she said.

She would have to be strong. She remembered how ridiculous Elliot had seemed last night when he'd become jealous and she was determined not to make the same mistake herself. Besides, she reminded herself, if she was going to be with Elliot, then there would be hundreds of reminders of Isabelle. She couldn't react like this to each one. Once Elliot was hers, there'd be nothing to be jealous of.

'I just wish we were back home,' she said, meaning it

192

more than ever. She could hardly compute in her head that they'd moved from their flat in London, to the comfort of a double bed in a hotel, to whispering in a cold boatshed like fugitives, all in less than forty-eight hours.

How could she tell him that this place gave her the creeps? That all of this stuff, clearly so familiar to him, was totally alien to her. Perhaps if she'd come here, as she'd always imagined she would, as a guest of his father's, once Elliot had made her official, then she'd have felt differently. Then she would have been able to explore the boatshed and ask about Elliot's memories without feeling so horribly insecure. Instead, she was here in secret and it just made the life she shared with him in London further away than ever.

'Come here,' he said, his familiar wicked grin on his face. 'I know a good way to make you feel better.'

'Elliot,' she said, not moving, 'it's freezing.'

'That's never stopped you before. What about that time on the Moors?'

They'd been for a weekend away when they'd had a case up in Yorkshire only a few months ago.

'You really want to do it here? Now?'

'Why not? It's Christmas.'

Elliot tried to kiss her, but this wasn't a game to her and she wasn't in the mood to play.

'What's wrong?' he asked.

She wiped her mouth on the back of her hand. 'I can't.'

'Why not?' He looked at her, his expression confused and hurt.

'Because . . . because this is your father's boatshed. It just feels all wrong.'

'Nobody's going to catch us,' Elliot said.

'It's not about being caught.'

She looked at him, willing him to understand, willing him to make it all better. She knew that rejecting him like this was breaking some sort of unspoken code in their relationship, but she couldn't take it back now

'I want it all to be . . . proper,' she said. 'I want to be with you properly. Not like this.'

'We will be. You know we will be.'

'Because you ought to know that this is not my ideal Christmas Day,' she said, feeling close to tears. 'In fact it's a complete and utter fuck-up.'

Utterlyfuckedup, she suddenly thought, remembering Ben making her laugh on the RIB. She thought of the sky and the sea and all that light – but now she was in a dingy boatshed. It was nothing less than *totallyutterlyfuckedup*, in fact.

Elliot sighed a heavy sigh, then pulled her into a gentle hug. 'Don't get upset. Come on . . .'

'You're going to have to go back,' she said. 'They'll be missing you, won't they?'

She waited for him to protest, to come up with an ingenious excuse that would mean they could spend more time together, but instead Elliot kissed the top of her head.

'OK,' he said, before putting his finger under her chin, so that she was looking up at him. 'I suppose you're right, but just give me one last smile for me to remember.'

She did manage a smile of a sort, but it wasn't the kind she'd ever felt herself give him before.

'That's my girl,' he said.

It was a phrase she kept coming back to, long after he'd gone and left her behind on her own in the gloom.

As Kellie walked from the boatsheds back up to the main road, she stuffed her hands in her pockets. There was a cold wind blowing and the snow still lay thick on the ground. The sky was a pale mauve and yet the sun was shining. The red and green doors of the stone houses stood out against the whiteness.

194

She thought she'd be happy after seeing Elliot, but now she was more anxious than ever. Only a few days ago, their secret had made her feel buoyant, as if the knowledge that they loved each other was a light shining inside her. Now it felt more like a worm chewing her up.

As she reached the road, she looked down at the harbour, where the boats were covered with a dusting of snow. She took a deep breath, looking out across the flat water. Grey ice made the harbour look like a village pond. It was so beautiful, it made her feel as if she'd stepped into a Dickens novel. She wasn't a fan herself, but no doubt Ben, who seemed to have read every book that had ever been made into a movie would have something to say about it.

'Hey. How's your head?' Ben asked, suddenly appearing from around the corner and making her jump. Now she wondered whether he'd seen her coming from the boatshed. She felt herself blushing, but he was smiling at her. 'Fresh air helped?'

She'd exaggerated her hangover this morning, in order to get out of the house so that she could meet Elliot.

'I'm OK,' she said, starting to walk along the road with him.

'You and I must stop bumping into each other,' he said. 'People will talk . . .'

She wasn't in the mood for banter, much less mild flirtation. 'Any joy with the boat?'

'I'm not even thinking about it while that ice is out there.' He held her up as she slipped on the compacted snow on the road. 'Steady there.'

Ben saw a couple coming out of one of the houses further up the road and called a greeting to them, swapping Happy Christmases.

'It doesn't feel like Christmas Day. It's so strange being here,' Kellie said.

195

'No stranger than being in a hotel on your own, surely?'
They slowed to a halt.

She could tell that he thought she was weird. It hit her now how odd she must appear to Ben, despite her half-hearted attempt at an explanation in the pub last night. She didn't blame him for being curious. After all, if their situations had been reversed, she'd have had a million and one questions. Just for a second she longed to tell him the truth. To make him understand that she had proper reasons for being here. That she was a rational human being with a very real explanation, and that her motives were the most honourable motives of all, because they were motives of love – but she knew she couldn't. Instead, she tried to laugh it off.

'At least I might have got a Christmas lunch at the hotel,' she said.

'But you'd have had no one to pull your Christmas cracker with . . .'

'I could have used both hands to pull it by myself.'

Ben held out his arms, testing out the physical possibility of this claim. 'But you might have hit a waiter with your elbow.'

'No, I'm too co-ordinated for that.'

'You'd still have had no one to read the crap joke to,' he pointed out.

'That's true,' she conceded.

'Well, you needn't worry,' he told her, 'about missing out on Christmas lunch, because we're not going to starve. I managed to scrounge a few bits and pieces from the pub.'

It was typical of him, to have thought of her like this. 'I'm not a bad cook,' she offered. 'I'll give you a hand.'

'No, no. Leave it to me. I'll fix it. It's only beans on toast. We can go to the pub afterwards and have crisps for pudding.'

Beans on toast . . . she tried to keep the disappointment from her face. What did it matter, she quickly reminded herself. Christmas was irrelevant, wasn't it? It was just a label given to a certain day by a faith she didn't believe in.

'Beans on toast sounds mighty fine,' she told Ben. 'What are we going to do in the meantime?'

'Well, I've got to pop over to Jack's for a bit. I promised him I'd take a look at his dad's computer, which is knackered. I'd ask you to come along, but it's not going to be much fun. His dad's a bit of a nut, to tell the truth.'

'So I'll see you at lunchtime?'

'Yep. I'll come and find you.'

'OK, see you then.' She smiled briefly at him and headed away, but just as she turned her back, she felt something hit her squarely between the shoulder blades.

She gasped and turned to see Ben grinning at her, already gathering up another snowball.

'You swine!' Kellie said.

'Oh, come on,' Ben said. 'You're a perfect target. Irresistible, in fact.'

With that, he threw another snowball at her. She ducked at the last moment, so that it hit the wall beside her.

'Hey!' She scrambled away from him, racing to gather up snow to defend herself, but Ben was too fast for her and it wasn't long before Kellie's hood was down and her hair was a mess. She was sweating and laughing, as she ran after Ben and, grabbing his arm, held him long enough to jump up and squish a snowball down the back of his neck.

He collapsed, shouting and pawing at his collar. 'I surrender, I surrender, no more,' he begged.

Kellie laughed and stood back, slapping her gloves together. She was breathless with exertion. It was as she extended her hand to help Ben up from the road that she saw Elliot, standing outside the pub. He stared at her for a moment, his expression stony, and then he turned away.

'You got me,' Ben said, jumping to his feet and flicking the snow out of his hair. He smiled at her, his cheeks red, his eyes sparkling in the sun.

'You started it,' she said, but her heart wasn't in their game any more and she didn't smile back.

'Are you OK?' he asked.

She forced a smile. He mustn't know that she'd just seen Elliot, or even hint at the significance of it. She had to pretend that everything was fine. 'I'm suddenly cold, that's all. I'm going back to warm up.'

'See you in a while,' he called after her as she walked off. He waved to her and she half-waved back.

As Kellie hurried back to the pub annexe, her head was crowded with Elliot. She felt so ashamed that he'd seen her snowball fight with Ben. From the look on his face, he was obviously still jealous and now she felt guilty, as if he'd caught her out. She couldn't bear it. His last image of her was of her holding on to Ben. He'd get it all wrong. Her mind raced with panic. How could she reach him now to reassure him?

Then again, why should she have to reassure him? He should trust her, just as she trusted him. After all, the onus of trust always fell on her. He was the one who was with his family. He was the one with a boat named after his wife, for God's sake. What was she supposed to do when he was with Isabelle, anyway? Never laugh? Never have any fun?

She looked around her. Everything seemed so white and innocent, yet she felt more guilty than she'd ever felt – but she had nothing to feel guilty about, she told herself. Certainly not Ben.

She thought back to her meeting with Elliot, just ten minutes ago and any residual reassurance from his kiss now vanished. The boat had been such a physical

198

reminder of Isabelle. Kellie had always imagined that Isabelle would just quietly disappear once she and Elliot were together, but now she realised it would never be that easy. Would Elliot's family blame her for splitting up his marriage? Of course they would. Would they accept her enough so that one day they could share a family Christmas all together? Only time would tell.

She suddenly realised that she was about to walk into some people on the street. She stopped, recognising the teenaged boy immediately. He stared at her. It was Sally's son, the teenager Elliot had brought to the pub last night.

'You must be Michael,' Kellie said.

'Yes.' His eyes shifted away from hers. She noticed his bum-fluff moustache and his gangling awkward limbs and remembered the acute embarrassment of being his age.

'I thought so. Your mum's been very kind to me. I'm staying in the annexe.'

'I know.'

She smiled at him, but he didn't smile back. Kellie turned to the young woman standing next to him, her stomach lurching as eyes frighteningly similar to Elliot's stared back at her.

'Come on, Taylor,' Michael said, 'let's get going.'

Kellie felt her mouth grow dry as Taylor's gaze never faltered. She looked so much older than Kellie had ever imagined her to be. She must be the same age as Michael, but she already looked like an adult. Her posture was almost regal and her gaze was so self-assured, it was arrogant.

Kellie hurried past, out of their way, almost running for the cottage door. She felt sick as she opened it and went inside, flattening herself against it as she slammed it shut.

Her cheeks burned as she looked around the cottage: at

the bedraggled duvet by the fire where Ben had spent the night. All she wanted to do was to get as far away as possible.

This was disastrous. She wasn't supposed to meet Taylor like that: not without Elliot, not before Elliot and Isabelle had broken up. She felt as if everything she'd planned had just shifted further out of her reach.

Worse than this, she felt something else. Impossible as it seemed, she was sure that Taylor *knew*.

Chapter 15

In Gerald Thorne's dining room, the frenzy of present opening was in full swing. Isabelle's *Christmas with the Rat Pack* CD was playing and Frank Sinatra was crooning 'Have Yourself a Merry Little Christmas' as the fire hissed and crackled. Despite the cold weather outside, the room was stiflingly hot. The smell of cooking turkey and boiling potatoes wafted in from the kitchen, clashing with the sickly smell of the 'Christmas-scented' tea-light candles that Isabelle had distributed around the room.

By the piano in the corner, Elliot popped a champagne cork, before filling up the glasses on the silver tray. Stephanie, who was kneeling on the floor by the Christmas tree, wished he would hurry up. If they didn't get the rest of the presents opened soon, she wouldn't be able to get back to the kitchen in time and lunch would be ruined.

Perhaps she was turning into Isabelle, she thought grimly, annoyed with herself for being annoyed, but she couldn't help it. Thanks to Elliot and his trip out this morning with Taylor, present opening had been thrown off schedule and Stephanie had better things to do than wait around for her brother, especially since Gerald had insisted that lunch should be on the table at one o'clock so that everyone would have the chance to go out after lunch if they wanted to. Where exactly he thought they would go was a mystery to Stephanie, and after the snow yesterday it was far too cold anyway.

Elliot didn't seem to be in any kind of a hurry. She watched him handing out the champagne. Uninterested in fashion as she'd become this last year but informed none the less from her coffee-time browsing of the glossy magazines in the surgery's waiting room, Stephanie recognised how tragically preppie and establishment Elliot's combination of blue blazer and slacks was. She supposed it was inevitable after all these years, but he really had morphed into Isabelle's perfect cardboard cut-out Chelsea husband. Today, for example, he'd clearly dressed up for Christmas in a way she'd never seen before. He'd even had a shower and shave.

He was only thirty-nine old, for God's sake, younger than she was. Just where had this middle-aged, middle-class wannabe patriarch come from? What had happened to the rebellious teenager who'd used to extol to her the virtues of the Buzzcocks and the Sex Pistols? The same kid who'd been suspended from school for having a copy of *Men Only* in his desk, the kid she'd taught how to smoke and to swear, and who'd sat in the bath in his jeans until they'd clung to his skinny little legs like bark round two trees?

Was it just age? She knew she'd changed, but Elliot had changed more in the past few years. Perhaps if she'd been more attentive she could have stopped them drifting so far apart; she didn't seem able to access him any more on a level where he would acknowledge that they had once been so close. Now it made her sad to think that she didn't really know him, or have the first clue what was going on in his head.

As if sensing her thinking about him, Elliot looked over at her. He smiled and raised his eyebrows, trying to be friendly. Perhaps he was still the old Elliot after all, she thought, but she couldn't be sure.

What did he feel when he looked at her? she wondered, suddenly self-conscious. Was it pity? She didn't know. She rarely even looked in the mirror these days, let alone took time to change her clothes in order to impress somebody else. She'd used to love clothes for their own sake. It had felt like magic, the way the simple act of putting on a short skirt and a pair of high boots had once been capable of making her feel confident and glamorous, even after a day spent examining unidentified rashes and handing out prescriptions. She half-smiled now, remembering her guilty shopping trips with her best friend, Tessa.

Then her smile faded. The time had come when clothes had made no difference to the way she'd felt. Her feelings had locked like the hands of a broken clock and nothing had been able to make them turn.

She'd give anything to make them work again, only she didn't know how.

She pinched herself hard on the back of the hand, pushing the thoughts from her mind. They did no one any good she told herself. Instead, she surveyed the wreckage from earlier this morning, when Nat and Simon had opened their stockings. Wrapping paper and empty boxes were strewn all over the floor, despite her attempts to keep things tidy.

She looked at them together by the fire, head to head, as David prised open the battery compartment of Simon's mini remote controlled car. Nat was busily peeling off hologram stickers from a sheet and sticking them on the carpet. Then Stephanie noticed Gerald standing beside her, inspecting his feet in the green Shrek slippers Simon had given him.

He handed Stephanie a glass of champagne. 'I rather like being an ogre,' he said. 'Any chance of getting me the rest of the outfit for my birthday?'

Stephanie squeezed his hand. 'I'll do my best, Dad,' she said, knowing he was only trying to cheer her up.

'Oh! Canapés!' Isabelle said, rushing off to the kitchen as if it was on fire.

As soon as she opened the living room door, the dog bounded into the room, knocking into Elliot's legs.

'Come on, Rufe. Time out in the conservatory, until the pressies are done,' he said, glancing at Stephanie as he led the dog by the collar to the door and ushered him through. 'We're not having a repeat performance from you.'

As soon as Elliot's back was turned, Taylor shot up out of the leather armchair she'd been sitting in, and quickly swiped a glass from the tray and downed the champagne in one, before flopping back on to the chair and kicking her legs over the side.

'Steady on there,' Gerald said to her. 'Are you allowed champagne, darling?'

'I drink it all the time,' Taylor informed him.

Gerald chuckled. 'Do you now? Well, I think that was David's.' He walked over and refilled the champagne glass, handing it to David. 'You've got to be quick off the mark around here,' Stephanie heard him say quietly.

'Well, cheers everyone,' Elliot said, as Isabelle came back in and put down a china plate on the table.

Stephanie looked at the piles of smoked salmon blinis, stacked with crème fraiche and chives. They were guaranteed to take away everyone's appetite. In the background the dog whined loudly on the other side of the door.

'Happy Christmas all,' Gerald said.

'Happy Christmas,' Isabelle echoed dutifully, accepting a glass from Elliot and sighing with satisfaction, as if the huge effort she'd just made had been absolutely one hundred per cent, from tip to toe and top to bottom worth it.

Isabelle was radiant this morning. Her make-up was perfect, her eyes glistening. She was wearing tailored cream trousers and a beige mohair jumper, which made her look fuzzy around the edges, as if she was in soft focus.

She looked relaxed and happy, but that was probably due to the two-hour bath she'd had this morning, whilst Stephanie had been stuffing the turkey. Timing was everything and Isabelle had it down to an art.

Next to her, Stephanie felt utterly bedraggled, realising that she was still wearing her flour-spattered apron. She'd hardly slept at all. David, who'd come to bed late, had snored all night, and then she'd been up at the crack of dawn when Nat and Simon had wanted to go and open their presents. Stephanie had quickly dressed in what she'd been wearing yesterday and had made a half-hearted attempt to wake David, but he'd grunted and rolled over and she'd hurried downstairs. By the time he'd surfaced, the kids had already opened most of their presents. Stephanie could tell he'd been disappointed, but she'd ignored him. Why should he claim all the glory? He certainly wasn't the Father Christmas in their family – and if he wasn't that, then what was he? She wasn't sure she knew any more.

'Maybe we should toast absent loved ones?' Isabelle said, looking expectantly at first Stephanie and then Gerald.

'Let's save the toasts until lunch, shall we?' Gerald said, glancing at Stephanie, as if to remind her of her promise not to get wound up.

It was so hard not to. It wasn't Isabelle's place to propose such a toast – Emma Thorne hadn't been her mother and Paul hadn't been her son. She didn't have the faintest idea what Stephanie or her father felt.

'Taylor, don't, darling,' Isabelle said, reverting back to normal, 'that's very annoying.'

Taylor ignored her and continued to test ring tones on her new mobile phone, whilst absentmindedly kicking the huge pile of expensive presents stacked up against the side of her chair.

'Can I have some bubbles?' Nat asked, shoving her fingers into Stephanie's glass and licking the liquid from them.

'No. Not too much now,' Stephanie said, trying to lift the glass out of the way. 'Why don't you offer the canapés around to the grown-ups?'

'Keep the presents coming then, Stepho,' Elliot said.

'This one's for you and Isabelle from us,' Stephanie said, holding up the badly wrapped box containing the glass dish filled with pot pourri.

Isabelle, swallowing a mouthful of champagne, flapped her hand and sidestepped through all the wrapping paper towards Stephanie, who put the present on the carpet.

'Let's do them at the same time. Ours are there for you and David. Here, this one's yours,' she said, stepping over Stephanie to lifting a heavy-looking present and hand it to her. 'David, here's yours,' Isabelle continued, pretending to lose her balance as she gave him an oversized parcel.

David shot Stephanie a glance and she knew what it meant: he was embarrassed about the present. They both knew he was right. It was too measly. Stephanie had been planning on telling Isabelle what had happened to the glasses, but now, aware of David staring at her, she chickened out. She didn't want to risk Isabelle thinking she was stupid for buying glasses too. She would just have to try and find a way to tell Elliot what had happened later.

'Go on, you first,' Isabelle said, her face alight with expectation, as she knelt down next to Stephanie.

Stephanie unwrapped the large package. Inside was a bottle of perfume and matching body cream, which together must have cost a fortune. There was also a fashionable make-over book that Stephanie had wanted to buy for herself, but had thought too frivolous. Embarrassment of another kind now hit her. Did she look so awful that people were compelled to buy her books to improve herself?

'Oh . . . goodness . . .' Stephanie said.

'My friend says it's fantastic,' Isabelle said. 'Totally changed her life. I mean, it's so difficult to know what to wear as you get older, isn't it? You stick to the same style . . .'

Stephanie was gratified that Isabelle was digging herself a hole.

In the background, Simon's remote control car burst into life. Next to her, Taylor started throwing peanuts up into the air, trying to catch them in her open mouth. There was a peal of laughter as Elliot, David and her father shared a joke.

'. . . I mean, I've been so lucky, you know, having Lucy. She's been my personal shopper at Selfridges for years and knows exactly what I like . . . but for other people . . .' Isabelle continued.

'I'm sure it'll be useful,' Stephanie said, letting her off the hook and leaning over to kiss her cheek.

Isabelle smiled. 'Well, let's see what we have here,' she said, picking up Stephanie's present from the floor, childishly lifting and balancing it as if to guess the contents.

Stephanie folded up the expensive wrapping paper from Isabelle's present, feeling sick. Once again, she tried desperately to formulate the right sentence to tell Isabelle that this was just the secondary, reserve present, but again, she couldn't find the right way to say it, without sounding as if she was making excuses. What was more agonising was that Isabelle was deliberately eking it out, carefully pulling Stephanie's cheap wrapping apart, until, finally, the bowl of pot pourri was revealed.

'Oh, my!' Isabelle said, kneeling up and leaning over to kiss Stephanie. Either she was an exceptionally good liar, or she really did like it. 'It'll go perfectly in our lounge room.'

'That's what I thought,' Stephanie said, feeling like an utter heel.

She smiled briefly at Isabelle who smiled back and there was a small pause. That was it. All of Isabelle's excitement and anticipation had gone in a moment, popped like a bubble with a pin. Just like that. Neither of them could pretend that it was anything other than a huge anticlimax.

It was all so pointless, Stephanie thought. Everyone was making out that Christmas was wonderful and that it all meant something, but none of them had gone to church. Even though there hadn't been a service, Stephanie regretted not simply going into the building to say a prayer. It would have been good to take the kids. There was no context at all for the frenzy of fluffy consumerism going on around her. She glanced over at Simon, who was stuffing his face with crisps, whilst pounding the control for the small car. He didn't have a clue what it all meant. And why should he? What had she done to advance his spiritual well-being? As the car sped under the table, she felt like a complete failure.

'What about you, Dad?' Taylor was saying. 'Shouldn't you give Grandpa his present. That *is* why we went into town this morning, after all.' There was an edge to her voice, a deliberate nastiness that none of them missed.

Isabelle tutted and laughed as she stood up to walk over to David who was opening his present. 'Honestly, Gerry, talk about last-minute shopping.'

Elliot smiled at Isabelle and Taylor. 'You two. Will you stop grassing on me. Happy Christmas, Dad,' he said, handing over a small box. 'Sorry it's not wrapped properly.'

'It's the compass I wanted for the boat,' Gerald said, opening the box. He was clearly delighted. 'Thank you, son.'

208

'He got it from the chandler's,' Taylor said. 'Didn't you, Dad? That's where you went this morning.'

'Er . . .' Elliot began.

'Phil?' Gerald said. 'I didn't think he'd be open on Christmas Day.'

'Oh yes,' Taylor said. 'You'd be surprised what people do on Christmas Day. Isn't that right, Dad?'

Elliot half smiled at her. 'Shall we make a start on those blinis?' he said.

'Wow! This is great!' David said, unfolding the soft brown leather jacket Isabelle had given him.

'Do you like it?' Isabelle said. 'I thought the colour would really suit you.'

Stephanie had bought David a jacket, too. He'd unwrapped it earlier and she'd been able to tell in an instant that he didn't like it. She didn't particularly like it either, but it had been reduced in the sale.

'Here's one for you, Nat,' Stephanie said, diverting attention away from David, who was trying on the jacket whilst Isabelle fussed around him, brushing the shoulders.

'My, you look handsome,' Isabelle said, laughing as David kissed her cheek.

Stephanie turned her attention back to Nat, who was ripping open her package and pulling out a full length fancy dress princess outfit with matching sparkly shoes. Nat held the dress up against her, gasping with delight.

'Aunty Isabelle, it's my best present *ever*,' she said.

Stephanie felt her reaction like a stab in the stomach. Yesterday, Nat had been petrified of Isabelle, now she was acting as if she was her favourite person in the world.

'A princess dress for a real princess,' Isabelle said, smiling at Stephanie and coming over to see Nat. 'I just couldn't resist.'

'Is this mine too?' Nat asked, pulling a small sparkly

doll out of the mound of crisp pink tissue paper. Her eyes widened with incredulity as she looked at Stephanie.

'I couldn't leave her in the shop now, could I?' Isabelle said.

'What do you say?' Stephanie prompted.

'Thank you,' Nat said, throwing her arms around Isabelle's neck.

'Really Isabelle, that's far too generous of you,' Stephanie said, meaning it.

Isabelle started to help Nat into the dress. 'Oh go on! They're only children once. It's so important to spoil them.'

Elliot came over to admire Nat in her dress. 'How are we doing? Is there a present under there for Isabelle?' he asked.

Isabelle clapped her hands together like an excited toddler. 'Oh, goodie, is it my turn?' she asked.

Stephanie rummaged through the debris of the presents, but couldn't find anything.

Elliot made a show of getting down on his hands and knees, finally locating a tiny package right under the tree.

'Ta da!' he said, with a flourish, handing it to Isabelle.

It was jewellery, Stephanie concluded, spotting the Tiffany logo on the small box. She quashed the jealousy she felt and the annoyance that her brother flashed his money around as he did. David had never bought Stephanie anything extravagant. This year he hadn't bought her anything at all.

'Oh my!' Isabelle exclaimed, looking at the box, and then she opened it. She shrieked with delight before lifting out the contents.

Stephanie hated herself for her curiosity. Why was she even bothering to rubber-neck Isabelle's present? Why did it matter? But she couldn't help herself. She stared at Isabelle as she took out the beautiful necklace. It was a heart-shaped diamond pendant on a twisted platinum chain.

Isabelle twirled to the fireplace and admired herself in the tinsel-adorned mirror over the mantel, smoothing the diamonds against her flawless skin with her fingertips.

'Oh darling. It's wonderful,' she said, turning to fling her arms around Elliot. He looked suitably pleased with her reaction, patting her on her back as he smiled at everyone over her shoulder, rocking his head and rolling his eyes in a self-deprecating way.

Stephanie couldn't watch any longer. Isabelle was so unbearably smug. She had no idea how tough life was for everyone else. How dare she show off so blatantly, as if they all lived life the whole time in a De Beers advert.

'Can somebody clear all this up and lay the table?' she asked, standing up, her legs stiff and full of pins and needles from where she'd been kneeling too long. 'I'm going to crack on with lunch.'

'Wait! Aren't you going to open this?' David said, flapping a badly wrapped thin red package towards her. In the leather jacket Isabelle had given him he looked like a stranger, as if he belonged in a seventies TV detective show.

'What is it?' She couldn't help feeling suspicious. She'd been annoyed that David hadn't bothered buying her a present, but she realised now that that was preferable to being put on the spot like this.

'Well, open it and see.'

She took the small package from him.

'Sorry about the wrapping,' he said.

Inside was a thin wallet envelope with the logo of a travel agent on it. 'What's this?'

'It's tickets to the opera. In Vienna,' he said, blushing.

She stared at the envelope in her hand, not opening it. She couldn't believe it. Suddenly, the room seemed to go

211

very quiet. She noticed that the CD had stuck on 'White Christmas', so that Dean Martin was singing, 'Why – why – why – why – why' over and over again. As she looked at the shiny white wallet, she could feel everyone's eyes on her.

Tickets to the opera in Vienna. It had always been one of their dreams to go there, a dream they'd both discussed, but a dream she'd entirely forgotten about because it didn't mean anything any more. It belonged to the person she'd been before Paul had died. It belonged to the person who'd loved her husband, who'd thought their future would be happy, not filled with pain.

'Darling?' David asked.

She felt a flash of anger. She wasn't his darling. How could David do this? In public. Like a coward. Because he knew full well what she'd have said if he'd handed her this in private.

What did he want? To pretend it was still Christmas two years ago? To skip back in time? Pretend that Paul's death had never happened? Or that Paul had never existed at all? Pretend that they were still a couple who might swan off to the opera for the weekend?

'Aren't you pleased?' he asked. 'Say something.'

'I don't think we can go,' Stephanie said, rubbing her eyebrows and handing the tickets back to him. She couldn't tell him how she really felt. Not here. Not now, in front of everyone. She didn't trust herself not to completely lose it.

'Why not?' David wouldn't accept them.

'You know we can't. We can't leave the children.'

'Why – why – why – why – why –' Dean Martin continued to sing.

'But of course you can,' Isabelle said, extricating herself from Elliot's arms and grinning at David. 'We've worked it all out. Nat and Simon can come and stay with us. Taylor will be back from school, so she can help out with them.'

'But –'

'You're flying from Heathrow, so it's easy,' Isabelle hurried on, excitedly. 'It's all settled. David and I have discussed it.'

'Why – why – why – why –' Dean Martin screamed in Stephanie's ear. She marched over to the CD player and stabbed the stop button.

'Easy, Steph,' Elliot said.

'Why can't I come with you?' Simon asked David.

'I told you before. It's supposed to be a romantic trip for two, kiddo, that's why,' David said, pretending to punch him on the shoulder.

'We'll discuss it later,' Stephanie said, icily.

Suddenly there was a crash, as Taylor toppled her pile of presents. They all looked around.

'Are you OK, Muffin?' Elliot asked, crouching down next to her. He reached out as if to stroke her hair, but she jerked away from him and gathered up her presents in her arms.

'I'm bored,' she said, getting up. 'I'm going to lie down.'

'Don't go just yet,' Isabelle said.

Taylor turned around to face her. 'Why?'

'Well, darling,' Isabelle said, covering her mouth with her hands. 'I want you to be here for this. I wasn't going to do it like this, but as everyone is here, and in *such* a good mood, I might as well . . .'

'What?' Elliot asked.

'I've got a confession to make,' Isabelle said, lacing her fingers together. 'I've been keeping something secret from you.'

'Oh, darling,' Elliot joked, 'I told you not to buy me that Porsche.'

'I'm serious,' Isabelle said. 'I've got some news, darling, and I wanted to save it for now. I only found out a few days ago, and, well, I wanted to tell you all at the same time. Because it's Christmas, and Christmas is all about family. And so is this . . .'

She grinned manically and reached out for Taylor, to take her hand.

'Elliot . . . Taylor . . . everyone. We're going to have a new member of the family. I'm going to have a baby.'

Chapter 16

'Kellie!' Ben called up the stairs. 'Are you there?'

It was just gone one o'clock and Ben was sweating as if he was on a Caribbean beach, even though he'd just stepped into the cottage from the freezing cold outside.

He had a cut on his forefinger, which he'd bandaged with a piece of kitchen roll wrapped round with a strip of electrical tape he'd found in a drawer. He glanced into the oval wooden mirror on the wall and saw that he was smiling nervously like a school kid, which actually came as no surprise, because that was exactly how he felt. He'd shaved. His hair was wet from where he'd brushed it back from his face. He stared up the cheap, scuffed pine staircase which led to the small bedroom in which Kellie had slept last night.

Would what he was about to show her be enough to make her think of him differently? he wondered. Would it make her like him any more?

He almost laughed at himself. Because these weren't the thoughts of a grown-up but, again, of a kid. He was a company director – or *ex* company director, at least – a manager. He hired – *had* hired – and had occasionally even fired people for a living. He'd also just nose-dived out of a messy divorce and the last thing he needed was to become emotionally involved with someone else, especially someone he hardly knew, and who was already involved, albeit only 'sort of', with another man.

Or perhaps Kellie was *exactly* what he needed, because, from the moment she'd left him, he'd missed her. He'd felt

215

her absence like a slap. Just when he'd thought he'd been getting to know her, she'd slipped through his fingers like sand.

One step forward, two steps back – that was how it felt, being with her. Like the snowball fight this morning: in the very moment he'd got her to relax, he'd watched her shut back down.

Well, he wasn't going to be put off that easily. He'd smiled more, felt more, and feared more for somebody else's life in the last twenty-four hours than since he'd first met and fallen in love with his ex-wife, but not even with Marie had he ever felt the need to impress as he did with Kellie today. Maybe it was being ignored that did it. Perhaps the very fact that Kellie *had* been able to walk away from him – because she had someone else waiting for her at home – was what was galvanising him now. Was it this competition, with a man he'd never met who'd left Kellie alone at Christmas, that had made Ben so determined to catch her eye, to make her stop and stare? But it felt deeper than that. Whatever was driving him on felt less to do with pride and more to do with hope.

'Kellie!' he called up again.

He heard a creak on the landing, then she was there, rubbing at her eyes with the heel of her hand, pushing her fingers back through her wavy brown hair. She was dressed in a baggy white V-neck jumper, a long grey cardigan, faded blue jeans and thick woollen socks, all of them borrowed from Sally. A necklace glinted at her throat in the glare of the bright ceiling light.

'Don't tell me,' she half-said, half-yawned, 'because I already know . . .'

'What?'

'That I look like a tramp . . . or a member of a vaudeville act.'

216

'I was thinking more Robin Williams in *The Fisher King*, or a kids' TV presenter – maybe from Sesame Street, circa nineteen seventy-nine.'

She smiled sleepily and warned him, 'Spare me the theme tune, Ben. Did you have any luck?' she then asked, as she walked down the stairs, the tail of her cardigan trailing behind her like a wedding train.

He stared at her blankly.

'With Jack's dad's computer.'

'Oh,' he said, 'that. Yep, all fixed.'

She stood against the radiator and looked through the small arched doorway beneath the stairs which led into the tiny kitchen. There was a loaf of bread and a can of beans on the worktop.

'Lunch?' she asked.

'It was all I could get.'

'It's better than nothing, and I make a mean beans on toast.'

'What if you could have something else?' he asked.

'Like what?'

'Anything. If you could click your fingers, right now, like a genie, and summon it up . . . What would be your ideal Christmas lunch?'

'In this weather? A roast. Definitely. Beef, or chicken, or turkey. Anything.'

'With potatoes,' he said, 'and gravy . . .'

'Green beans . . .'

'And carrots and peas . . .'

She laughed. 'Stop it. You're making me drool.' She pushed away from the radiator and walked through to the kitchen, where she picked up the can. 'Beans on toast for two,' she said. 'Coming right up.'

'Wait.'

'What?'

'The cooker . . . it needs a new gas bottle. Sally said we

should take the full one from the empty cottage next door, but it's heavy, so I'm going to need a hand.'

'No worries.' She put the can back down, and donned a tatty Harris tweed overcoat and a pair of oversized, paint-spattered trainers.

The wind whipped at them as they stepped outside, but the door to the next cottage along in the pub annexe was already unlocked and Ben quickly ushered her in.

This cottage was identical in dimension and design to the one they'd slept in, but far from looking unoccupied, its lights and radiators were on. It was much warmer than the other cottage, on account of the fire which was blazing in the grate. He closed the door behind them and they stood in silence, side by side.

Ben waited for her to speak, but she still didn't open her mouth. He felt itchy with nerves. Why had he picked now, of all times, to quit smoking?

'Please don't tell me you're like that girl in *Gremlins*,' he said, 'the one who hated Christmas because when she was a child her father tried climbing down the chimney in a Santa outfit and slipped and broke his neck?'

'Er . . .'

'Or, that you're a sworn disciple of the Grinch, or a member of a fundamental Christian sect which believes that Christmas lunch is an heretical celebration of greed set before us by the very devil himself?'

'Well . . . no, but . . .'

'In which case,' he said, 'I can only conclude that the absence of a smile on your face is simply indicative of the fact that you're a lawyer, and as such have an instinctive and overwhelming aversion to surprises of any kind . . .'

She wrapped her arms around him in a huge hug.

The gesture took him by surprise, so much so that his arms hung uselessly. By the time he thought to move them and hug her back, the moment was gone.

Letting him go, she turned to face the room. Stuck along the black wooden beam which bisected the low ceiling were pieces of A4 paper, each with a letter scrawled on it in blue biro. Together, they made up the message:

HAPPY CHRISTMAS!

Coal glowed in the fireplace, beneath the shimmering flames. The smell of roasting meat filled the air, drifting through from the kitchen where the table had been laid with two chipped tea mugs, some mismatching plates and an opened bottle of white wine.

'Roast chicken,' Ben announced, with a theatrical flourish of his arm. 'Potatoes, carrots, cauliflower cheese and peas. It should all be ready in about ten minutes. I'd like to apologise in advance for the stuffing, which is out of a packet – and the cutlery, which is two bent forks and one knife between us, because that's all they had in the drawer . . .'

This time, her silence delighted him. It was exactly the reaction he'd hoped for as he'd beavered away in here these last few hours.

'But how?' she finally asked.

'Would you expect David Blaine to reveal how he lasted so long in that glass box above the Thames without food?'

'No . . .'

'Or Houdini how he made an elephant vanish?'

'No.'

'Exactly. A good magician never reveals his secrets. Let's just say that I'm a better scavenger than I am a sailor.'

'Like Tom Hanks in *Cast Away*,' she suggested.

He smiled, remembering the film, and remembering, too, that she'd yesterday listed Hanks as one of her favourites.

'Exactly,' he agreed. Then he remembered the volley-ball, which Hanks's character in *Cast Away* had used to

219

chat with as if it had been a real person, to stop himself from going insane. 'Only I do hope you're going to provide me with better conversation than . . .'

'That ball,' she said, obviously thinking the same thing, 'that he decided to call –'

'Wilson,' he said.

'That's right, Wilson.'

She picked up a sprig of holly from the corner table and turned it over in her hands.

'This is *amazing*,' she said. '*You*'re –' But she never finished the sentence. Instead, she turned away. 'Thanks, Ben,' she told him. 'It's such a lovely thing to have done.'

He followed her through to the kitchen. She trailed her fingers along the edge of the table. She looked at the cheap, dented steaming pans on the flickering blue gas burners, and the old plastic chopping board and broken potato peeler on the stained white Formica worktop. The cheaply veneered cupboard doors were all open, as if they'd been ransacked by a thief, but all they had inside were assorted odd teacups and dusty saucers and plates. By the back door was a gently buzzing, yellowed fridge, which looked as if it had been liberated from a scrap yard, and on top of it was a small clock radio, which looked like the timer for a primitive bomb. Through the crackle of static came the intermittent sound of carols being sung. There were cobwebs at the windows and an open orange flip-top bin stood in the corner of the room, piled high with potato peelings. On the wall above was a faded calendar, with a photo of Fleet Town. The date above it read June 1986.

'It's a bit of a time warp, I'm afraid,' Ben said. 'Like something out of an episode of *Doctor Who*.'

Kellie pressed her palm against the wall. 'Only the scenery's a lot less wobbly . . .' She stared up at the beige pinstriped pelmets above the window. 'Some of this stuff is so far out of fashion, it's come back in,' she said, 'but

220

who cares, eh?' Breathing in deeply, she knelt down and gazed through the darkened, greasy glass oven door at the chicken roasting inside. 'And the chuck smells great. But how the hell did you manage to –'

'Michael,' Ben explained, 'the kid at the pub. He got it for me. Sally and Roddy had offered to have us over for lunch, but I told them I'd rather cook for you myself.'

'But why?'

'Because I wanted to. As a way to say sorry for having messed up your Christmas.'

'No more apologies,' she told him. 'OK?' She held out her hand for him to shake. 'Let's just draw a line under it.'

'For a lawyer, you sure are letting me off the hook lightly.'

'And for a businessman, you sure don't seem to know much about quitting while you're ahead.'

He took her hand and shook it.

'You're cold,' he told her as he let go.

She rubbed her hands together, then something on the table caught her attention and she leant forward and picked up the name card he'd made for her out of a rectangle cut off the box of stuffing. She stared at it in silence. It read, *KELLIE ???*

'My mystery guest,' he said. 'An enigma, wrapped in a riddle, wrapped in pair of borrowed trainers and a moth-eaten tweed coat. Talking of which,' he said.

She turned her back on him and shrugged it off into his hands.

'God,' she said, 'it's nice to be warm at last. I can't believe how hot you've got it in here.'

As she turned round to face him, Ben took a closer look at her necklace, which was impossible not to stare it, presented the way it was in the V of her jumper. He knew a little about jewellery, just from the pieces he'd bought for Marie over the years. Even beneath the harsh fluorescent tube the diamonds shone like ice in sunlight against her throat as she looked up into his eyes.

'That's a stunning necklace,' he said.

She brushed her fingers against it self-consciously, as if she'd forgotten it was there.

'It was a gift. From a friend.'

She didn't elaborate, but then, she didn't have to. He could tell from the way she'd said it, from the wistfulness in her voice, that it was from him: her 'sort of' boyfriend. And she was thinking about him now. Ben hung her coat over the back of a chair.

'It seems crazy,' she said, staring down at the name card which she still held in her hand, 'that even the people who send me my gas and electricity bills know my surname, but you don't.'

'So tell me,' he said. 'Then the next time your boiler breaks I can come around and fix it.'

'It's Vaughan. And what about you? Let me guess: Dover.'

'You're wasted as a lawyer. You should have been a satirist,' he said with a smile. 'Or, then again, maybe the Christmas cracker joke industry might have been more your thing.'

'Thanks a bunch.'

'My name's actually Stone. Ben Stone.'

'It suits you,' she said.

'It does?'

'Yeah. It's solid. Like a rock. Like you had to be to get us through yesterday. To get us safely back here.'

'Even though I got us lost.'

'Sure, because then you got us found again.'

He looked away, embarrassed, and turned up the volume on the radio. 'The Little Drummer Boy', by Rolf Harris drifted out at them.

She laughed. 'Wow, you've even come up with some Aussie music. What more could a girl want?'

'How about a Christmas drink?' he said. 'I can't vouch for the year, but it's the only one the pub had.'

He poured them both a mug of wine and they sat down on opposite sides of the table.

'A toast,' she said. 'To you. For all the effort you've put in. For making today fun and for putting a smile on a girl's face.'

'The smile's worth it.'

It was. It was addictive. Kellie had made him remember how much fun flirting could be. The more he made her smile, the more he wanted to make her smile again – and the more it fired the spark he felt between them. He wanted to know how it would be, the two of them together as a proper couple. He imagined it as perfect. As to whether he'd ever find out, well, Kellie was like a guessing game to which he had no answers. He could only try his best and wait and see.

She rolled her wine around the rim of her mug, as if she were in a restaurant and gazing at him through a fine crystal glass.

'It's funny, isn't it?' she said.

'What?'

'How quickly we – you know, people – can adapt and adjust. Like being with you now, here, in this cottage, sitting down for lunch . . . it almost seems normal.'

'Maybe that's what normal is: being able to relax.'

'But I don't normally relax with people I don't know.'

'Perhaps,' he said, 'you know me better than you think.'

'We only met yesterday.'

'But surely getting to know someone isn't only about how much time you've spent with them. I mean, you can spend a lifetime with some people and not know the first thing about them. But then you can also become close friends with someone else' – he clicked his fingers – 'just like that.'

'Is that what we are now then?' she asked. 'Friends?'

'I'd like to think so.'

'I normally don't make new friends either,' she said.

He pictured her again, the ice maiden walking past him on the quay in Fleet Town, but he sensed that something about her had changed. Even here, in the past five minutes, it was as if she'd finally begun to thaw.

'Why not?' he asked.

'Because normally I don't need to, because I'm already with old friends.'

'Like your *sort of* boyfriend?'

'Yes,' she reflected. He was surprised she'd answered. He'd half-expected her to move the conversation on. 'That *was* how I described him, wasn't it? Last night . . . in the pub . . .'

'Yes . . .'

The buzzer on the cooker sounded and she smiled.

'Saved by the bell,' she said, pushing back her chair and getting up. She stood by the oven and rubbed her hands together. 'Right,' she said, 'what do you need me to do?'

Chapter 17

Stephanie looked up at the clock on the mantelpiece and calculated that it had taken just thirty-three minutes for them to eat Christmas dinner. Thirty-three minutes. She looked at the wreckage on the table: the turkey carcass, the last remaining roast potato, the dribble of gravy on the white cloth, the bread sauce that nobody apart from her father had touched, the burnt devils on horseback, the wilted cabbage and the congealed glazed carrots. It had all been such an effort and now it had taken thirty-three minutes to devour it all. What an incredible waste.

She looked at her family, red faced and bloated, each wearing a lopsided paper hat from the crackers they'd opened. At the other end of the table, Elliot was making everyone laugh with an anecdote about one of his cases. Nearer to her, Simon was scratching a groove in the leg of the table with his set of mini screwdrivers that he'd got from his cracker. Nat, who was equally bored, was trying to stuff the sparkly doll Isabelle had given her into one of her grandfather's best wine glasses.

Stephanie had never felt so un-festive in all her life. She downed the rest of her red wine and refilled her glass. She'd already drunk far too much, but David's surprise holiday offer and Isabelle's shocking announcement earlier had left her with too many mixed-up emotions to process. She'd felt humiliated, resentful, guilty and upset all at once and hadn't been able to show anything. Instead, she'd had to bite it all back and congratulate Isabelle and Elliot. Afterwards, she'd quickly escaped to slug back a large glass of cooking wine in the kitchen to steady her nerves. She hadn't stopped since.

She leant down to retrieve her napkin from the floor. Under the table, Rufus was licking a roast potato and Taylor was fiddling with the iPod in her lap. As Stephanie sat back up, she could see now that Taylor had one earphone in place, the white wire cleverly hidden by her hair. No wonder she'd been so quiet.

Simon was increasing the pressure on the screwdriver and Stephanie could hear a nasty scraping sound, as he leant back in his chair.

'Simon, stop it,' she said.

David tore his attention away from Elliot. 'Don't keep having a go at him,' he said under his breath. 'What's the matter now?'

She hated him for not backing her up. Why did she always have to be the bad parent with Simon? Why wouldn't David give him any discipline at all? All she was doing was trying to bring up her kids to be decent human beings and yet, at every step along the way, he undermined her.

'Fine,' she said. 'Simon, your father thinks it's absolutely fine for you to scratch a hole in Grandpa's antique table. You go right ahead.'

'For God's sake,' David said.

Simon put the screwdrivers back on the table and sat on his hands. 'Sorry, Mum,' he mumbled.

David ruffled Simon's hair and then turned back to his conversation with Elliot. Stephanie took another slug of wine.

'Can I leave the table?' Simon asked.

'No.'

'Mummy, do you think Father Christmas goes to McDonald's for lunch?' Nat asked.

Stephanie was so tempted to tell Nat the truth, to tell her

226

that Father Christmas didn't exist, that Stephanie herself was Father Christmas, to explain that it was all just a giant hoax in order to exploit people into spending more money on presents that nobody wanted – and that the reason everyone hoodwinked their kids was to divert their attention away from the inevitable truth that they were going to discover as adults: that Christmas was shit, a horror show of forced smiles and unhealthy food. She wanted to tell Nat that, if she had any sense, she would start saving all her pocket money now, so that she could spend future Christmases on a beach with her friends, because Christmas was never going to get any better for her from this moment on.

'I don't think there's a McDonald's at the North Pole,' Stephanie said instead.

'There is everywhere else,' Simon said.

'I think he has lunch with all his helpers,' Nat said, 'and maybe Snow White and Tinkerbell come too.'

'No, they don't, durr brain.'

Nat yelped. 'He kicked me.'

'Did not,' Simon said.

'Did.'

'I'm going to the bathroom,' Stephanie said, leaving the table.

Once there, she sat on the side of the bath and buried her head in her hands. What was wrong with her? Why couldn't she handle this? It was all David's fault. If he hadn't presented her with the tickets, then she could have soldiered through this Christmas until they were safely back home. Instead he'd deliberately piled on the pressure. He'd deliberately brought things to a head. And now he'd left her with no choice – she knew, with absolute certainty, that they didn't have a future. They couldn't go to Vienna for the weekend. They'd couldn't even spend five minutes in the same room with each other without arguing. No, the future was for couples like Elliot and Isabelle who were having another baby. Not for her and David. She couldn't even look at his face without hating him.

She took a deep breath. She had to hold it together, just for a few more hours. Then Christmas would be more or less over. She could plead exhaustion and go to bed. She could knock herself out with some sleeping pills and when she woke up it would nearly be time to go home. And then?

And then, she'd give it to David straight. She'd break whatever delusion he was under. But until then, she must not lose control. This was her dad's Christmas. Simon's Christmas. Nat's Christmas. Even Stephanie and Elliot and Taylor's Christmas. This wasn't just about her and her marital crisis. She had to remember that.

She went back downstairs, holding on to the banister for support. She felt flushed and drunk and unsteady on her feet. She was about to go back into the dining room, when she saw through the crack in the study door that Isabelle and Elliot were loading the dishwasher in the kitchen.

'It cost a fortune from Lidgates,' Isabelle was saying. 'I had to order it six weeks ago.'

'She totally over-cooked it,' Elliot said.

'I told her she'd had it in the oven for too long, but she wouldn't listen. I gave most of mine to Rufus. At least he appreciated it.'

Stephanie's face began to burn. Her heart raced.

'I would have said something, but she's so bloody oversensitive,' Elliot said.

'Tell me about it. I couldn't believe how she reacted about the Vienna trip. Poor David went to all that effort. I mean, I know I booked it for him, but it was his idea. You know, he's such a great guy and she's vile to him . . .'

'It's none of our business,' Elliot said. 'She's still so upset about Paul. Perhaps you shouldn't have mentioned the baby.'

'I did try and talk to her last night, but it would have made no difference anyway. She's just locked in this horrible negative space. She's got to move on. For herself. For all of them. She's just terrible to those kids. She won't let Simon so much as breathe, and she practically ignores poor Natascha who's just desperate for attention. Even your father agrees.'

'When did you talk to him about it?'

'I haven't yet, but I can tell how he feels. The way he looks at her when she snaps at David, or the kids. We all feel it, don't we?'

'We mustn't go jumping to conclusions. We should just stay out of it.'

'You know, when I see how unhappy they are and how dreadful she looks, I just thank God we've got each other.'

'You know, Izzy, I wish you'd told me before. About being pregnant.'

'I wanted it to be the perfect Christmas surprise.'

'Well it was certainly that.'

'Good.'

'You still should have told me. And Taylor. Did you see the look on her face?'

'She'll get used to it. She's always wanted a sibling.'

'But she didn't think she was ever really going to have one,' he said. '*I* didn't think we could any more. I thought that's why you said it was safe to come off the pill.'

'Yes, but I was wrong, honey, and isn't it such exciting news? Imagine. You and me together as parents again. We were so young the first time, and now we know so much more. Just think about it. A little baby. It's going to be so much fun . . .'

Stephanie walked back to the dining room and took her seat. She was so shocked, she felt entirely numb, as if she was seeing herself from the corner of the room. She refilled her glass yet again.

Elliot was carrying the Christmas pudding when he came back in. He hurried over and put it on the place mat in front of Stephanie.

'Why don't you divvy up?' he said, smiling at her.

He took a pile of china bowls that Isabelle handed him and put them down next to Stephanie. It took all her effort not to hurl them at his head. Instead, she rose to her feet, grabbing the table for support. She picked up her wine glass and took a gulp.

'Steph. Haven't you had enough? Maybe you should have a glass of water,' Isabelle said, laughing to try and make light of it.

Stephanie banged her glass down, hitting the side of the pudding dish by accident. The stem snapped, and the wine seeped into the tablecloth, like blood on snow. Everyone went quiet.

'Don't you dare tell me what to do,' Stephanie said, measuring each word. She knew that she was breaking a sacred and unspoken family code. No one ever rowed at Christmas. It had been her mother's golden rule. But after what she'd overheard in the kitchen, Stephanie felt as if war had been declared. Suddenly, the whole atmosphere of the room had changed.

Isabelle ran her tongue over her teeth. She made a big show of taking a controlled breath. 'You know, Stephanie, I have just about had it with you being rude to me today. You're sitting down there at the end of the table in some kind of black cloud. Whatever it is that's bugging you . . . how about you just keep it to yourself, OK?'

'Why don't we all calm down?' David said. 'I think –'

'Shut up! Just shut up!'

It came from Stephanie's mouth before she'd even thought about it. As an out of control shout.

There was a horrible silence.

Gerald scraped his chair back. 'Stephanie, I won't have you behaving like that at the table. Not in front of the children.'

'You don't understand,' she said. 'None of you do.'

'Mummy, stop it!' Nat said. There were tears in her voice. Stephanie couldn't look at her. She stared down at the Christmas pudding, her vision blurring.

'Don't worry, darling,' David said to Nat. 'Everything's fine.'

The doorbell rang.

'That'll be Michael,' Taylor said, jumping to her feet and throwing her napkin down on the chair. 'I'll go.'

'Come on kids. Why don't we all go and answer the door together?' Gerald said, standing up and taking Nat's hand. He flicked his head at the door and then at Simon. His expression was icy as he looked at Stephanie. 'And then why don't we go and see if there's any brandy to put on the Christmas pudding?' he went on. 'And by the time we come back, hopefully the grown-ups will have started to behave themselves.'

Stephanie stared after him. She'd broken her promise and let him down, but she hadn't been able to stop herself. She knew she should apologise and sit down and shut up, but she couldn't make herself.

'Well done, Steph,' Elliot said, slow clapping. 'Ruin Christmas lunch, why don't you?'

'You really can be a sanctimonious bastard,' she said. 'So what if I've ruined Christmas lunch? It was already ruined. I know what you two think. I heard you in the kitchen just now.'

Elliot looked panic-stricken at Isabelle. But Isabelle looked defiant.

231

'Well . . . it should do you good to hear a few home truths,' she said.

'Stephanie,' David began, 'leave Elliot and Isabelle out of this. I know you're feeling emotional –'

'You don't know how I feel.'

'I do.'

'No, you don't. You don't know what feelings are. You don't have any.'

'What's that supposed to mean?'

Did he really not get it?

'If you did have any feelings, or any modicum of intuition, you wouldn't be sitting here, laughing away when . . .'

'When what?'

'When Paul isn't here,' Stephanie shouted. Then she turned on Isabelle. 'Oh yes, that's right, you think I should be over it, don't you? I should move on?' she said, quoting her from the kitchen. 'Or did I mishear you?'

'Don't try making this about me,' Isabelle said. 'It's not.'

Stephanie had had enough. 'Why don't you just butt out, you smug, meddling bitch. I'm sick of you lording it over me, with your perfect fucking marriage and your perfect fucking life. Well, you know what? You can stick it all, right up your perfect fucking arse!'

Isabelle sucked in her cheeks. 'I can see that you're not being rational,' she said. 'So rather than focusing your anger on me, maybe you and David should take some time to sort this out. Come on, Elliot.' She stood to leave. Elliot stood up too.

'Please,' David said. 'Can't we just –'

'And for your information, Isabelle . . .' Stephanie continued, ignoring him. She was shaking. '. . . I do love my kids. Very much. And I'm a damn good mother. At least I don't shove them off to boarding school and pay someone

232

else to look after them. You should look at your own mothering skills before you start judging mine.'

Isabelle had gone red. 'You leave Taylor out of this. You're just jealous.'

'Of what? Of the fact you can't control your own daughter? At least I'm there for my kids. What are you going to do with this baby, Isabelle? Use it as a designer accessory? Palm it off on a nanny, like you did with Taylor? That's not being a mother –'

'You –' Isabelle began, but Elliot was holding her arm and steering her quickly out of the room.

'Come on,' he said, throwing a dark, angry look at Stephanie.

Left alone with David, she felt indignant tears well up as she waited for David to speak. She was ready to fight anything he said. She wanted to fight him. She'd tell him the truth. About what she thought about Isabelle and Elliot. And him.

David walked over to her. For a moment, she thought he was going to slap her face – not that he ever had before – but when he spoke, his voice was soft.

'I find it hard, too.'

She let out a suppressed sob. 'No you don't.'

'I miss him as much as you, but that won't bring him back.'

Stephanie had wanted to talk about Paul's death for so long with David, but now that they had actually reached this moment, she realised that it would serve no purpose. She'd gone beyond the point where she could try and make sense of it all with him. She found the sympathy in his voice too much to bear. The tears she'd felt so close vanished again, replaced by a stony determination.

'I can't move on,' she said.

'He was my son, too. But we can't change what happened.'

'*You* could have.'

Her statement hung between them, like a bullet. She knew that they were words that could never be taken back. David stared at her, his mouth open.

She turned away from him, terrified by what she'd just said. Her stomach felt strange, as if she'd just stepped off the top of a building and was falling.

David jerked her around to face him.

'Have you any idea of what you've just said? Have you?' he shouted.

She stared at him, falling still . . .

A tear ran down his face. 'Take it back.'

But she couldn't. 'It's the truth.'

'You don't mean it. You can't. I know you –'

'No you don't. You don't know how I feel. About anything.'

'But –'

'I can't look at you any more.'

'Because you think I'm responsible,' he said.

Her eyes slowly rose to meet his.

'You think I'm responsible?' he repeated.

David stepped towards her and held both her arms.

'Please don't do this, Stephanie. Please. I love you.'

'You don't get it, do you?' she said, shaking free.

'Get what?'

'It's over, David. I want a divorce.'

He shrank away from her as if she'd punched him. Then he turned, and left the dining room, slamming the door behind him. Under the table, the dog began to retch.

Chapter 18

'I'll go first,' Michael said, staring into the gloom of the escape tunnel.

'No.'

Taylor brushed past him. She took a swig from one of the miniature bottles of spirits she'd stolen from her granddad's house, then threw it hard against the tunnel wall and watched it smash. She switched on her torch. The shards of glass glinted up at them like cats' eyes.

So much for not letting Simon know that they had any booze, Michael thought.

Taylor had hardly said a word to either Michael or Simon since the three of them had set out from her granddad's house twenty minutes before.

Michael had gone there after lunch to collect them, as agreed. Taylor and Simon had answered the door with their grandfather and he'd told them it was fine for them to go outside for a walk. It was only when they'd moved away from the house that Michael had noticed that Simon's eyes had been puffy with tears and Taylor's had been like steel.

'What's been going on?' Michael had asked, as Taylor had set off towards Solace Hill without even saying hello.

Simon had told him, 'My parents are fighting and Aunty Izzy's going to have a baby. I don't know why Aunty Izzy wants –'

'They're arseholes,' Taylor had shouted back at them. 'All of them. But the biggest arsehole of all is my dad.' She'd turned and yelled down the hill at the house: 'Elliot Thorne is the biggest arsehole of all!'

Now Taylor was still acting like she couldn't give a shit He marched on without looking back. She was drunk. That last miniature, a whisky, had been her fourth. She'd already downed a vodka, a Drambuie and a Baileys on the way here.

But Michael was hardly in a position to criticise. His own stomach was on fire. He'd had a vodka and a schnapps, downing them both in front of Taylor only minutes before. He imagined his mum and Roddy, who'd be opening the pub around now. He wished he was with them. He wished he was anywhere but here.

He shook his head and tried to sober himself up. A baby? Isabelle was going to have a baby. He pictured her in her bedroom the day before, studying her stomach in the mirror. But why had she been crying? Why hadn't she been pleased?

'Stick with me,' he told Simon, 'and if you get scared, or if it gets too dangerous, we're turning back, all of us.' He looked for Taylor, but she had passed him and the darkness had already swallowed her up. All he could hear was her wet footsteps, fading up ahead. Michael switched on his torch and carved out a passage through the dark, a tunnel within a tunnel, through which he and Simon swiftly walked.

The tunnel floor was sticky. It felt and sounded like they were walking on chewing gum. Their breath came back at them so fast and so loud that they could have been marching in a crowd. The tunnel smelt wrong, not of nothing, as he'd imagined it would, but alien, and alive.

'I'm not scared,' Simon started whispering. 'I'm not scared. I'm not, I'm not, I'm not . . .'

Michael's eyes and ears picked out details: cracks and overhangs; echoes and drips. There was a gloss to the smooth, water-polished stone which surrounded them, as if it had been licked by a giant tongue, and again Michael remembered how he'd first thought the entrance to the tunnel looked like a throat. Well, now they'd stepped into it, now they were letting themselves be swallowed alive.

'Wait up,' Michael shouted after Taylor, as the tunnel began curving round to the left, but the only answer he got was a mocking echo as his own words bounced back at him. Then he heard scratching sounds ahead, as if someone was shaking a box full of sand. The ground grew uneven. His torch beam lurched from side to side, as if it was swinging on a rope.

Then it settled on Taylor. She was featureless, her back to them, nothing but a silhouette. She'd stopped and, as they drew level with her, it was easy to see why. The tunnel was wider here than before, but low, so that Michael had to stoop. He shone his torch alongside Taylor's, illuminating the ground in front of them. There was a gash in the tunnel floor ahead, four or five feet wide, as if the ground had been torn apart. The gap was too wide to jump, because of how low the tunnel roof was. Michael leant forward and peered down inside.

The first thing he thought of was death. If they'd walked along here without a torch yesterday, then the first one to have reached this hole would have fallen in and died. The hole dropped away, like the shaft of a well, into nothing.

Michael could see twenty, maybe thirty feet, and then blackness, as if it might have no bottom at all. Taylor shone her torch across to the other side, to where the tunnel continued to veer off upwards and to the left. Then she fixed the beam steady on the right of the hole, where a one-foot-wide ledge connected this side of the tunnel with the other.

'No fucking way,' Michael said, reading what was in her mind.

'Why the fuck not?' Taylor laughed. 'Mum's got another kid on the way. I'm replaceable now.'

She walked straight for it. Michael would have called out *Stop*, but it was too late. She'd already gone. She pressed her hands, one still holding her torch, against the tunnel wall. She sidled across the ledge. He shone his own torch on the ground ahead of her, to guide her way. It was glistening, wet. Her trainers flashed bright white, like snow against coal. One wrong move and she'd drop like a stone.

'Easy,' she then said, as she stepped down on the other side. Michael's torch beam crossed her grinning face. 'OK,' she said, 'so who's next?'

'Wow!' Simon gasped. 'Wow-eee, wow-wow!'

Michael wanted Taylor back by his side. Was this what it would be like, he wondered, when they said goodbye in a few days' time, with him staring after her and her looking mockingly back? He had to tell her soon that he was leaving Brayner. He had to find out how she felt.

'Come back,' he told her.

'No.'

Michael silently cursed. He should have just lied to her, told her that the torches were broken, even secretly broken them himself and then demonstrated the fact to her. Then they couldn't have come today. They'd be back at her house now, or his, maybe together alone, with Simon somewhere else. And then . . .

But there was no then. Wasn't that the point? Wasn't that why he'd really come? Because there was no next week for them, or next year, not now that his mother and Roddy were taking him away. If he didn't explore the tunnel together with Taylor today, she'd only come back and explore it without him the next time she came to the island. And he didn't want this place to be *hers*. He wanted her to remember him whenever she came here, or thought of here. He wanted to make this place *theirs*.

'We can't take Simon,' he said.

238

'Why not?' Simon asked.

There was anger in his voice and a defiance which Michael recognised from other times when Simon had lost his temper. Michael waited for Taylor to intervene, because she must have spotted the danger sign, too, but she said nothing.

'Because if you fall down there, you'll break your neck,' Michael told Simon, 'and because you shouldn't even be here with us, because you're –'

'Don't tell me I'm too young,' Simon interrupted, 'because I'm not. I'm not a baby, and you shouldn't tell me that – anyway, just you watch!'

Simon ran for the ledge, and before Michael could stop him, he too had started across.

'Come on, Simon, you can do it,' Taylor called out from the other side.

There was a scratch, like a claw being dragged across rock, as Simon's foot slipped, but Taylor was there, reaching out, gripping him by the shoulder and setting him right. Michael breathed out in relief. Another two side steps and Simon was safe.

'Ha!' Simon shouted. 'I did it. I did it. Did you see that, Michael? I did it on my own. And you said I couldn't, but look at me: I did!'

'Are you coming, or not?' Taylor asked.

Michael walked to the ledge and looked down at its glistening, burnished surface. Would it hold him? He was heavier than Simon, heavier than Taylor, too. He stared into the hole. It was only here, he reasoned, because the ground beneath had given way. Which meant the whole tunnel was unsafe.

No one knew they were here. If anything happened, they were on their own.

But stronger than the fear he felt, stronger than his desire to be outside, was his desire to be with Taylor – and to protect her. If he didn't follow, then there'd be no one there to take care of her if something did go wrong.

He placed one foot on the ledge, then another. He leant against the tunnel wall for support, as he'd seen the others do. His torch beam flickered across the tunnel roof. The rock was cold and slick. He slowly moved to the other side.

'See,' Taylor said. 'It's a piece of piss.'

They continued along the tunnel. Taylor led, Simon went next, and Michael was last. He turned round at one point and swept his torch beam back. The tunnel was no longer straight, and all he saw was rock. The ground sloped upwards in the direction from which they'd come. He wondered how far under the ground they were. It was impossible to tell. How long was it since someone had walked this way? Decades? Years?

Then Taylor said, 'Oh, my God!'

Michael walked into the back of Simon, who'd stopped dead in his tracks.

'What?' he asked, but then he saw exactly what. 'Switch off your torches,' he said.

The moment they did, they gasped. There were a thousand shining pin points in streaks and patches all around, phosphorescent and bright as stars, like a miniature Milky Way. They might have been looking up at the night sky through a telescope, only it was close enough to touch.

'What are they?' Simon asked.

'I don't know,' Michael said. 'Some sort of moss, I suppose . . .'

'They're incredible,' Taylor said.

'Amazing,' Simon agreed.

Taylor stepped up close to Michael. 'Astonishing,' she whispered in his ear.

Then he felt her cold fingers on his face and smelt the alcohol fumes on her breath. Her lips brushed briefly against his.

'Beautiful, isn't it?' she said, then stepped quickly back. 'What was that?' she asked.

What was *what*? Michael hadn't heard a thing. But then he did. He heard a moan – soft, mournful and distant.

'I'm frightened,' said Simon. 'Now I'm scared. Now I'm scared. Now I'm scared.'

His voice made Michael start; he'd entirely forgotten Taylor's little cousin was there.

'It's nothing,' Michael said. 'It's probably just the wind.'

'But how do you know? It could be any—'

'Michael's right,' Taylor said. 'Let's just keep moving.'

Michael's mind was still reeling as they set off again, not from the noise they'd just heard, but from what had happened before. Thoughts whirred through his head like the lights on the pub fruit machine, all of them a blur, moving too fast to allow his brain to turn them into sense.

What did it mean, what she'd just done? That kiss. Had it been a kiss? Had Taylor really just kissed him on the lips? The darkness had cloaked whatever expression she'd worn. Had it been an accident? Had their lips only touched because it had been dark, and she hadn't known where he was? Then he remembered her fingers, stroking across his face, mapping it out. Could it still have been an accident, even after that? His heart pounded loud in his ears, so loud he wondered if Taylor and Simon could hear.

Then ahead of them, the tunnel split into two.

'Which way now?' Simon asked. 'We're lost, aren't we? Are we? Are we lost?'

Michael answered, 'I don't know.'

'Here,' said Taylor, 'stepping into the left branch of the tunnel. She aimed her torch along it. It curved upwards,

241

then to the right. 'Can you feel it?' she asked them. 'It feels like . . .'

They heard another moan, louder this time, as if it was closer, as if it had come from one of their mouths. Simon whimpered and grabbed Michael's jacket, but this time Michael was certain they had nothing to fear.

'It's definitely the wind,' he said, 'coming from the sea. I can smell the salt.'

It was only now that he had something to compare it with that he realised how stifling and stale the air they'd been breathing had been. He wiped his hand across his brow. He was drenched with sweat.

He took the lead and felt the breeze growing stronger with each step he took, funnelling down the tunnel towards him until it felt like a cold tap running on his face. Then the quality of the darkness began to shift. The blackness through which his torch beam cut began to get less solid. It was becoming more grey, more transparent. Then Michael's heart soared as he realised why.

'It's a way out!' he shouted back to the others. 'Look. There. There's daylight up ahead.'

It turned out that he was both right and wrong. The tunnel did lead out into daylight, but it wasn't a way out, not unless you had a 200-foot-piece of rope, or could fly.

The tunnel terminated in a deep, wide cave set into the side of the cliff. It must have been at least ten times the width of the tunnel and the wind howled through it like an angry pack of wolves. Keeping low, Michael crawled to the front, to where it opened on to an enormous sky. He lay flat on his stomach and stared out, breathing in the icy air, happy to be free from those cramped tunnel walls.

Relief swelled inside him as he recognised the view. Hell Bay stretched away below, to the left and to the right. The sea ice hugged the land here as well, running alongside it like a cobbled street thrown down from space. Further out,

242

angry white waves rushed across the sea. The beach was no longer visible, buried beneath the ice and the snow.

Taylor crawled up beside him. 'I can't believe how high up we are,' she shouted above the roar of the wind.

It was the first time he'd seen her face since she'd kissed him but, looking at her now, it was impossible to tell whether or not he'd imagined the whole episode.

'There's no way down,' he shouted back, 'not from here.'

'How much longer do you think we've got before it starts to get dark?'

He checked his watch and then the steely afternoon sky. 'We should probably start heading –'

'Look, what's that?'

She was pointing down to the old fisherman's hut on the rocks at the back of the beach. In the snow beside it were splashes of red.

'It looks like blood,' she shouted. 'Like someone jumped off here and died.'

'Or some*thing*,' Simon called out, squeezing in between them.

Their jacket collars and sleeves whip-cracked in the wind.

'What?' Taylor teased. 'Like a ghost?'

Simon shook his head furiously. 'Ghosts can't bleed,' he yelled. 'They're already dead. It must be a sheep, or a dog . . . Ha! Or even a sheepdog!'

'I think –'

But Michael never heard Taylor's answer, because it was torn from her lips by the wind. He signalled to the others that he was moving back and they shuffled after him into the centre of the cave, a safe distance from the edge, before standing up, then he led them over to the black hole at the back which marked the beginning of the tunnel from which they'd emerged. He crouched down on

243

the ground and they huddled down next to him. The wind was less strong here. They could hear one another speak.

'It's not blood,' he told them. 'That red stuff in the snow. It's a boat. It must be Ben's, the one he brought Kellie over in.'

'That bitch,' Taylor said. She spat on the ground. 'That vile fucking bitch . . .'

'Who's Kellie?' Simon started to ask. 'Why's she a –'

'Mind your own business,' Taylor warned him.

A rush of wind hissed through the cave and Taylor got up and walked across the back of the cave to a flat outcrop of rock in its far corner. Simon looked inquisitively at Michael, but all Michael did was shrug. It wasn't his place to tell Simon what he and Taylor had seen down at the harbour that morning – and besides, what was there to tell? Kellie and Elliot had walked into the same boatshed and closed the door behind them. That was all Michael knew. What had gone on in there between them was anyone's guess.

'Stay here,' Michael told Simon. He picked up a sharp piece of rock from the floor between his boots. 'Take this stone and see if you can scratch your name, or even better, all of our names, into the rock.'

Simon took the stone. 'What for?' he asked.

'I don't know,' Michael said, unsure himself. 'Then because I suppose it makes this place ours, and anyone who comes here afterwards will know that we got here first.'

'Like we're the winners,' Simon said.

'Exactly. Just like when your football team won at school.'

Simon weighed the stone in his hand, then looked up shyly. 'You just want to talk to her, don't you?' he said. 'And you'd rather I wasn't there . . . so that it's just the two of you, so that –'

'No,' Michael said, 'it's not like –'

244

'It's OK,' Simon told him. 'I don't mind.'

He turned his back on Michael and began scraping the stone across the rocky wall.

'Just like a real cave man, eh?' Michael told Taylor a few seconds later, as he sat down beside her.

'Cave boy,' she told him.

Even back here the wind was still strong enough to ruffle her hair like the feathers of a bird. Michael's throat was dry, from the booze and the exertion.

'I'm so fucking angry,' she said.

'You mean your mum, the baby . . .'

'No, I mean *her*. I mean, what the fuck is she doing here?'

'Kellie . . .' he guessed.

'I mean, who *is* she? Why's she here? And don't tell me it's because Ben brought her. I already know that.'

'I don't know her any better than you do. Just because she's staying in the annexe doesn't mean I –'

'*You* might not know her, but my father does . . .'

'You can't be sure.'

'Oh, get real, Michael. You saw. Both of them. In there. What? You think it was a coincidence? The two of them going into that boatshed, less than a minute apart?'

No, he didn't think that – but he couldn't explain it, either.

'They *know* each other,' Taylor told him. 'They have to. And he lied to us all. To me. To Mum. To Granddad. He lied about why he wanted to go to the village this morning. He said he was going to the chandler's. And he wasn't. He had Granddad's present all along. I saw him put the package – the one with Granddad's present in it – I saw him put it in his coat pocket before we left. They must have arranged to meet there. Him and that bitch. I just don't know how.'

Then it hit Michael. 'The pub,' he said. 'They could have

met in the pub last night. She was there and so was your dad, after he brought me home.'

Her eyes flashed with understanding. 'That's it, then.'

'But that still doesn't explain *why* they were going to meet.'

It did to her. 'There's only one reason you go to meet someone else in secret,' she said.

Was she also talking about herself and Michael when she said this? He knew the question was a selfish one and that, right now, he was probably the last thing on her mind, but he couldn't stop himself wondering, all the same.

Taylor stared into Michael's eyes. 'It would kill her, you know. My mum. She loves him so much . . . I mean, she even sent me away to school, so that she could be with him more . . . and now that she's going to have another fucking kid – and, Christ, you should have seen Dad's face when she told him about that – it would kill her, I know it would, if what I'm thinking is true . . . that somehow Dad and Kellie . . .'

'You don't *know* anything,' Michael reminded her. 'Only that they met. It *could* have been coincidence. It's possible. She could have followed him in there to see what he was doing.'

'Then why did he lie about the present?'

Michael had no answer for that.

'She cries, you know. My mum. I've seen her. When she doesn't think I'm looking. And do you know when she cries?'

'When?'

'At night. In the school holidays, when I'm at home, but he's not. And at the weekends, too. When he's had to go into work . . .'

Michael had seen her cry as well, when she'd thought that she'd been on her own. He remembered the way his

246

father had been, towards the end. He'd left his mother on her own. He'd left her alone to cry.

Michael just said it: 'So you think he's having an affair . . .'

'Yes.'

'With Kellie . . .'

'Yes.'

'But she came here with Ben. It was an accident. It doesn't make sense.'

'I know. But she *is* from London. And Dad got here after us. I know it sounds crazy, but he could have –'

She was suddenly looking away from him and he followed her stare. In foot-high lettering across the cave wall, Simon had scrawled the words:

SIMON AND TAYLOR AND MIKEL
4 EVER

Simon was staring at Michael and Taylor and tears were streaming down his face.

Michael jumped up as Simon ran to the front of the cave. In his hand was the stone he'd been scratching their names with. He threw it as hard as he could, out of the cave and down towards the boat. Michael grabbed hold of him and pulled him down out of the wind.

'Don't be crazy,' he yelled at him, dragging him back. 'You could have fallen!'

Simon tried shaking him off. 'Let go!' he shouted.

Michael wrestled Simon backwards, hauling him towards the darkness of the tunnel, where he half-dragged, half-carried him into the gloom. Here the wind dropped and all Michael could hear was Simon, hissing like a cat.

'What is it? What's the matter?'

'Nothing,' Simon shouted, tearing one hand free and rubbing angrily, ashamedly, at his eyes.

247

'Do you want to go home?'

Tears ran down Simon's face. 'They hate me. They don't want me there.'

'That's not true,' Michael said.

'It *is*. I wish I was dead. I wish it had been me instead.'

Paul. He was talking about his dead brother.

Taylor prised Simon away from Michael and wrapped her arms around him. Michael watched helplessly as Simon shuddered against her.

'They think it was my fault,' he said.

'No, they don't. No one does.'

'They do! They always will.'

'No, Simon. I promise you.'

'They *will*! It's always going to be my fault. The doctor they send me to says it isn't, but it is. She says everything will change, but it doesn't. And she asks me the same questions over and over and I tell her the same things, and nothing ever gets better and it won't ever get better, and now my mum hates my dad as much as she hates me . . .'

'No,' Taylor told him again. 'They love you, Simon. They love you with all their hearts.'

'All I wanted to do was save him,' Simon sobbed. 'That's all I wanted to do.' A thread of spit stretched between his lips, then snapped. He screwed his eyes shut. 'I'd do anything to save his life. I'd do anything to make it all better.'

'I promise you,' Taylor told him. 'Everything *will* be all right.'

'I don't want them to get divorced.'

'No one said –'

'I don't want them to,' Simon shouted, pulling back.

Taylor held him by the wrists and stared into his eyes. 'Look at me, Simon,' she said. 'No one's getting divorced. Do you hear me? No one.'

There must have been something, a spark of determination, a diamond of such strength inside her eyes that the tension dropped from Simon's limbs and he fell against her, burying his head in her chest.

And then, as she looked at Michael – and he saw that spark, that diamond, now aimed at him – he could do nothing but believe her too.

'That's right,' she whispered into Simon's ear. 'You let it all out. You let it all out and then we'll go home together, before it gets dark.'

Chapter 19

'That's the end of it,' Ben said, twisting the bottle and watching the last few drops of wine runnel into Kellie's mug.

They were in the tiny sitting room of the annexe cottage, on the tatty two-seat sofa which they'd pulled up in front of the fire. Pans and plates protruded from the sink, waiting to be washed. The remains of the chicken carcass stood on the kitchen table, next to a hexagonal glass vase which Kellie and Ben had used as a gravy jug, and a tarnished ice-cream scoop which had served as a ladle.

Normally, Ben thought, as he gazed into the fire, on the back of a good meal and in good company like this, he'd be sparking up a cigarette, just to seal the moment's perfection in his mind. But the nicotine cravings which had been dogging him all day had dwindled. It was because of her, he knew, because of Kellie, because she didn't smoke, and his being able to resist sitting here and blowing smoke in her face made him feel glad – and strong.

'God, I feel great,' Kellie sighed, taking a final swig from her mug. She set it down on the border of black and white tiles which separated the fire from the worn and faded blue carpet. 'It's so weird to think of what we were doing this time yesterday.'

'Nearly dying, you mean.'

'Exactly, and yet here we are now, rested and sheltered and fed.'

'It's not exactly the Dorchester . . .'

'No, but we're hardly slumming it either, and in a way it's even better than a posh hotel.'

'How so?'

'Well,' she said, 'if you were at the Dorchester, you'd expect it to be amazing, wouldn't you? You'd want the best food, the best wine, an astonishing room, with an out-of-this-world bathroom, piled high with incredible lotions and potions. You'd expect it to be perfect, right? Because that's what you'd be paying for.'

'Yes . . .'

'And you'd be pissed off if it wasn't, wouldn't you? Because your expectations would be sky high. But here. Today. When I woke up and you fooled me into coming round here, well, my expectations were virtually nil. All I thought the day had in store for me was a can of beans and some toast, followed by an afternoon spent shivering up against that crappy little oil radiator in my room.' She stared up at the banner which Ben had taped to the beam. 'But I was wrong. It's turned out to be a million times better than anything I expected. So, yeah,' she told him, 'they can keep the Dorchester – because today, right now, there's nowhere else I'd rather be than here.'

'I get the feeling,' he said, 'that if you were a cat, you'd be purring pretty loudly right now.'

'I get the feeling you're right.'

She combed her fingers slowly back through her hair. If he could have made this day last for ever, then he would. He felt every passing second like a heartbeat. But today *would* end. Kellie *would* leave – tomorrow, or the next day. The moment the sea ice was gone, she would be, too.

Ben should have been happy, happy for the time he'd had with her, happy to have dug himself out of the introspection he'd been bogged down in these last few months, happy to have got on well with a stranger, even happy for the same reason she was, because they were safe and fed and here in the warm.

251

But he now wanted so much more. Their lives would never have collided this way in London. They'd never have achieved this current intimacy so soon. He wanted this day to turn into a tomorrow, and then another day, and then a future for them both. He wanted to make the most of the series of chances which had led them here.

'No regrets, then?' he asked.

'None.'

She stood and took off her cardigan, then, as an after-thought, her jumper, too. She was wearing a tatty black singlet underneath, and it rode up her back as she pulled the jumper over her head. He caught a glimpse of a flat black mole just above the line of her left hip, a tiny imperfection against her skin. She tossed her jumper on to an armchair, and sat back down. The singlet showed off the curve of her breasts. As she looked at him, he turned away and stared into the fire.

'Do you know what I'm going to do now?' she asked.

'What?'

She rolled up her jeans and peeled off her socks. Then she stretched out her legs towards the fire and wriggled her toes.

She lay back and closed her eyes. 'Pretend I'm lying on a beach . . . being fanned by a warm Caribbean breeze . . .'

'Hey,' he complained, 'I thought you said there was nowhere else you'd rather be.'

Her eyes stayed shut. 'I meant in reality,' she said. 'This is just fantasy. Anyway,' she added, 'you can come too. It's a free flight and all you need to pack is your imagination.'

'Do we go business class?'

'No, it's a dream, we go first.'

His eyes ran the smooth length of her calves to her ankles. Then he, too, closed his eyes.

'Do you know what my favourite thing is?' she asked. 'My favourite thing in the whole world?'

252

'Well,' he said, 'judging from your freakishly broad knowledge of the cinema, I'd have to guess that it was curling up on the sofa in front of a really good film. And at this time of year, I suppose you'd probably go for either *It's a Wonderful Life*, or *Merry Christmas Mr Lawrence.*'

'Nope. Not my favourite thing. Though you're right about both films being the ones I'd watch if I could right now.'

'So what *is* your favourite thing, then?'

'Watching nothing. Just being. Just lying on the sand, running my fingers through it, listening to the waves breaking gently on the shore . . .'

He pictured them there on this imaginary beach, the two of them, side by side. He was in shorts and she was wearing a green bikini. She had a necklace of dark beads around her neck and he could smell the coconut oil in her hair. The beach stretched for miles in either direction and was deserted apart from them. Palm trees arched above. Their shadows stretched across the white sand to the azure shallows beyond.

'I'd go swimming,' he said. 'I'd walk slowly into the sea, deeper and deeper, until the swell of a wave lifted me off my feet.'

'And leave me alone on the beach?' she protested.

He smiled. So she could see him there as well . . .

'I'd come back,' he said, 'after a while . . . I might even have caught some fish.'

'With your bare hands?'

'Why not? This is a fantasy, isn't it? I'd be the fastest swimmer and have the fastest hands in the world.'

She giggled. 'Kind of like *The Man From Atlantis* and Bruce Lee combined . . .'

'Bruce Atlantis. Now there's an idea for a TV series . . . Or how about *Fighting Nemo*?'

'And, meanwhile, back on the beach . . .' she reminded him. 'What would we do next?' she asked.

'Next? We'd –'

He pictured himself lying down on the towel beside her, and reaching out to take her hand, then rolling over on top of her. Drops of sparkling water fell from his face on to hers . . .

'We'd wait until sunset and then I'd build a fire,' he said.

He wondered what the touch of her lips would be like on his, and how she'd feel as she moved against him. What might she whisper into his ear?

'And then we'd –'

She sat up abruptly beside him on the sofa.

'This is a silly game,' she said, rolling down her trouser legs. She picked up her socks and began pulling them on.

'Sorry,' he said, 'was it something –'

'No.' She seemed flustered. 'It's me. Look, can we just talk about something else?'

'Sure.' But for the first time since he'd met her, he found himself stumped for something to say. 'Like what?' he finally asked.

'Anything,' she said. 'Food?' She started to tell him about the best meal she'd ever had, at a restaurant called the Bather's Pavilion in Sydney.

And then there they both were: back on safe ground. Just like they'd been during the meal, when they'd chatted about theatre and music and travel, the places they'd been and the things they'd seen. How they both lived in flats in different parts of London, him in Kentish Town and her in Chancery Lane. What their flats were like; how they'd never found the time or will to plant their window boxes, or make their kitchens as funky as those of their friends. Neutral subjects, in other words, the kind of conversation you could strike up with a complete stranger at a party, just for sociability's sake.

254

'. . . and I tell you,' she said, 'that chef should be given a knighthood. Hey!' She suddenly reached out and poked him in the ribs. 'You're not listening. Let me guess,' she said, 'it's professional jealousy, right?'

'What?'

'Because you're not such a bad cook yourself. You certainly took me by surprise, rustling up that lunch out of nowhere like that. You're obviously a man of hidden talents.'

'I'm not hiding anything,' he said. 'I've got no secrets. Not from you.'

He hadn't meant to bring the conversation so abruptly back to the personal, but now that he had, he was glad. He didn't want to do small talk. Not with her. Not today.

She looked him over curiously. 'Why me?' she then asked.

'I don't know. Because I trust you. I know I've got no reason to, but I do.' He smiled. 'And besides,' he added, 'you don't know anyone I do. You're safe. I could tell you all my hopes and fears and it wouldn't matter, because we've got no friends in common, so you've got no one to tell.'

'Like confiding in someone on a desert island.'

'Exactly,' he said. 'Which is kind of fitting. Because I suppose we have been shipwrecked, in a way.'

'Like Crusoe and Man Friday, hey? Or Hanks and his volleyball . . .'

'Wilson.'

'Like Hanks and Wilson . . .'

'Two perfect strangers who get along just fine . . .'

'I guess it is sometimes easier to talk to someone you don't know,' she said, 'and sometimes more interesting, too.' She stared at him. 'But seriously, you've really got no secrets you'd keep from me? Because I should warn you, I can be a pretty nosy girl . . .'

'You can ask me whatever you want.'

She folded her arms and contemplated him. 'I'm not sure I know where to start. About your wife perhaps? Your ex-wife. About Marie. About why you're not together any more . . .'

He opened his mouth to speak, but she raised her forefinger to her lips.

'How about continuing this conversation outside?' she suggested. 'Only, if I stay here by the fire much longer, I'm going to fall asleep.' As if to prove it, she let out a terrific yawn. 'And I wouldn't want you to think you're boring me,' she told him, 'because you're not.'

They walked down to the brightly coloured boatsheds, with the snow creaking like polystyrene beneath their feet. It was still freezing. Within a couple of seconds, Ben felt wide awake. They stopped by a wooden bench and looked out across the harbour. The few fishing boats moored there were gripped by ice, locked in unnatural angles, as if they'd run aground.

'It looks like a scene out of *Whisky Galore!*,' she said, 'or *Scott of the Antarctic*.'

'We've both got far too much movie trivia cramming up our heads, you know. It can't be healthy.'

'Maybe we've both just had far too much time on our hands.'

She wasn't wrong, not as far as he was concerned, anyway, because the truth was that the main reason he'd ended up watching so many films on his own was because he'd had so much time on his own to spend. He wondered if the same were true for her.

'Maybe there's a link between loneliness and watching movies,' he said.

'Maybe there is.'

A dog barked in the distance and Ben turned up his coat

collar, remembering yesterday again, remembering how he and Kellie had huddled together for warmth, during their yomp to the village from Hell Bay.

He could have put his arm around her now. It would have felt, to him, like the most natural gesture in the world. But to touch her now would be different, intimate, not practical – and he remembered how quickly she'd sat up on the sofa inside, how abruptly she'd terminated their game.

'So Marie and me,' he said, returning their conversation to where they'd left it in the cottage. 'The reason we're no longer together is because . . . because she's with someone else. Someone I used to know.'

'A friend?'

'An ex-friend.'

Danny. The ex-friend's name was Danny. Ben had found out from Danny's wife. She'd suspected Danny of having an affair and had hired a detective to discover who with. She'd shown Ben photographs of Marie and Danny kissing by the statue of Peter Pan in Regent's Park. The image still sickened Ben. They looked as if they'd been together for years.

'I'm surprised,' Kellie said.

'At what?'

'I thought it would have been the other way round. I thought it would have been you who left her.'

'Why?' he joked. 'Have I got the look of a wild adulterer about me, or something?'

'Actually, the opposite.'

'You mean I look safe?' he asked, unsure how to react.

'No. You look confident and composed. I suppose it's just that I find it difficult to imagine you in a situation you're not in control of, that's all.'

Ben laughed.

'What?' she asked.

'Just, if you could have seen me this time last year . . .'

'It's been tough?'

'Yeah, and I've been a mess. Totally *out* of control, as a matter of fact.'

'Well, you look as if you've come out the other side to me.'

'Thanks,' Ben said. 'And, yeah, I'm starting to agree.' As they continued to walk, he told her, 'It was never meant to be about control, Marie and me. It was meant to be about partnership, and equality, right from the start.'

'Isn't that what everyone strives for?'

'Yes, but we really made it happen. At least, we did for a while. When we came home from our honeymoon, we both quit our jobs, me at a film company, her in advertising. We set up our own company and called it Roundabout. The idea was to make enough money from doing something we liked, so that it would then enable us to enjoy the rest of our lives. So that we'd never have to be wage slaves. Or work weekends. Or do any of that stuff that our original careers had entailed.' He smiled. 'Marie got this logo done of a circle of people holding hands. That was what it was meant to be about, cohesiveness, harmony, cooperation . . . It was meant to be fun. We were going to make people happy by turning their memories into films, and in the process we were going to end up happy ourselves.'

'But you didn't?'

'No. The way it all turned out, we'd have been better off calling the company Seesaw. Because that's how it ended up, with Marie and me fighting like cat and dog over every company decision we made.'

'And let me guess,' Kellie said. 'It eventually spilt over into your home life.'

'Work has a habit of doing that, especially when you work together, don't you think?'

She shrugged. 'I don't know. I suppose it's different for

258

different people. I imagine that sometimes working together can make for a fantastic relationship.'

'Perhaps.'

They watched as a gull landed on the ice and slid across it, before coming to a confused standstill.

'What happened . . . between Danny and Marie . . .' Ben said. 'It really hurt. The fact that I knew him made it twice as hard.'

'I'm sure.'

'It made me ask myself a lot of questions – about who my friends were, but about myself as well. About who I was and what I wanted.'

'And what conclusions did you reach?'

'That I'd actually been unhappy for a long time. Even though it was Marie who left, to be with Danny, she wasn't the one who ended it. It was over – *we* were over – long before Marie and Danny did what they did. And you know what?'

'What?'

'I'm never going to let that happen again. I'm never going to just sit back and watch something that could have been wonderful die. That's what I did. And I've finally figured it out – that's what has been getting me down ever since. I became a quitter. I became something I thought I'd never be.'

'I don't see you like that.'

'Good,' he said, 'because I'm not any more. I'm leaving all that behind. I'm moving onwards, and up – and whoever I end up with next, I'm going to give them everything I've got.'

They reached the other side of the harbour and stood with their backs to the harbour wall, looking towards the village.

'You seem remarkably sorted about it,' she said. 'Considering . . .'

He smiled. 'I've had a lot of time to think things through. It's been a long divorce. You know how you lawyers like to string these things out,' he joked.

'Hey.' She punched his arm. 'It's only a job. And anyway, divorce isn't my thing.' She peered into his eyes. 'Has there been anyone since?' she asked. 'I mean since you and Marie split up?'

The last time he'd had sex had been nearly three months ago now. It had been the second person he'd slept with since breaking up with Marie and it had been a clumsy awkward disaster. He'd woken the next day in an ex-work colleague's bed, with a hangover and her hand holding his. He'd unlinked their fingers and, by the time she'd woken up, he'd already been dressed.

'A couple,' he said. 'Flings. An old girlfriend from way back and a woman I used to work with. Neither of them serious, though. I've been stumbling around, I suppose, trying to find my feet.'

'Have you got a photo?' Kellie asked. 'Of Marie?'

He was surprised by the directness of the question. 'What, like in my wallet? Why?'

'Well, it's always a good way to tell . . .'

'To tell what?'

'Whether someone really is over someone else, or whether they're still holding up a flame to them, after all.'

Ben took his wallet out of his jeans pocket and slid out a passport-sized photo of Marie from behind a stack of credit cards. She was blonde, smiling in that contrived kind of way that people always did for photos they knew they'd have to have around for years to come.

'Exhibit A,' he said, handing it over.

'She looks very young,' Kellie observed.

'She was. So was I. It was taken years ago, in Australia. She had to get a new passport after her bag got stolen on the beach.'

'She's beautiful,' Kellie said, 'but that doesn't surprise me. You're a good-looking guy.'

It was the first compliment she'd given him and it made her frown. She handed him back the photograph.

'Thanks,' he said, and held out his arm, letting the wind whip the photo away.

Kellie gasped, watching it spin over and over through the air. It landed on the icy harbour surface. 'What did you do that for?'

'Because it was only you asking me that made me remember that I still carried a photo of her at all. And because there's probably nothing better to douse an old flame with than a few hundred tonnes of frozen seawater.'

They watched as the photo flipped over a couple of times in the breeze, and then seemed to stick to the ice. Ben blinked and then could no longer see where it was. He felt glad about that.

'And here my tale of *Kramer versus Kramer*-style divorce woe comes to an end,' he said. 'Leaving me young-ish, free and single. With one ex-wife, one ex-best friend, too big a movie collection, and no real girlfriend to speak of. Not even,' he added, choosing his words carefully, 'a *sort of* one. . . .'

She rolled her eyes, as if he'd just told her a very bad joke. 'Which brings us neatly back to me . . . to my sort of boyfriend,' she said. 'I can't exactly compliment you on your subtlety.'

'It never exactly was my strongest skill.'

She wrapped her arms around herself and stared out across the translucent mosaic of water and ice.

'The man I'm seeing,' she said. 'He's married.'

Ben nodded his head as everything slotted into place: her being here alone . . . because her 'sort of' boyfriend was with his wife; Kellie wanting to get away from Christmas . . . because her lover had chosen to spend it with somebody

261

else. Ben had already guessed that there were complications with whoever it was she'd got herself involved with, but he'd assumed it would be to do with *where* the other man worked or lived – not *who* he was living with.

'So that's why he's "sort of",' she said. 'Because he's not completely mine. Not yet.'

'But he will be soon?'

'He'd better be. He loves me, and I've waited long enough.'

'How long?'

'A year.'

Ben said, 'If he loves you so much, then why hasn't he already left his wife?' But as soon as he'd asked, he knew the answer. 'Let me guess,' he said. 'Kids.'

'One. A daughter.'

'Who he doesn't want to mess up, right? Which is why he's had to put off leaving his wife for so long . . .' There was a sarcasm to Ben's voice which he hadn't intended, but he meant it, every word. He suddenly felt angry, not at her, at *him* – at this man he'd never met who'd left Kellie dangling like a puppet from its strings.

She told him, 'I don't feel good about this, you know, so please don't moralise.'

'But isn't the whole point about being with someone that you *do* feel good?'

'What I mean is that I don't feel good about the circumstances. I wish he wasn't a father and I wish he wasn't married. I wish he'd been single when we met, the same as me. But he and his wife were breaking up anyway. They would have separated, whether I came along or not.'

Was this how it had been for Marie and Danny? Ben suddenly wondered. Had they talked about him then, in the same way that Kellie was now talking about her lover's wife: as an inconvenience, as somebody better off out of the way?

'So how come they *hadn't* already separated? How come they *still* haven't? How come he's just keeping you hanging on?'

'You've got no right,' she told him, suddenly angry. 'You don't know how any of this really is. He loves me, Ben. We're in love.'

It didn't sound like love to Ben.

'I know it sounds bad,' she said, 'but . . .'

Words formed in his mind and he found himself speaking them, before he'd a chance to consider their effect.

'If you were mine,' he said, 'I wouldn't keep you hanging on, not even for a second.'

She stared at him in silence.

'But I'm not yours, Ben,' she said.

'No,' he said, 'but if I were to . . .'

'What?'

And what exactly *was* he going to say? he thought, as the wind picked up and he stared into her eyes. Because what exactly was there *to* say? Because she'd already said it all. *We're in love*; that's what she'd said. She'd told him that she was in love with another man.

And this was why the words, *But if I were to kiss you now, then I know you'd kiss me back* had died, unwanted, on Ben's lips.

He stared across the water, and the village beyond became a blur. What did he know about love? He, who was already divorced. He, who'd only ended up spending any time with this woman at all because of a quirk of fate.

But I'm not yours, Ben.

It felt as if he'd been kicked in the stomach.

'It doesn't matter,' he said. 'We should get back. It's cold.'

They started walking, side by side, back past the boatsheds towards the Windcheater's annexe. Cold thin rain began to fall. Ben opened the bright red umbrella he'd brought with him and held it up above their heads. They huddled beneath it, like commuters in a lift.

He remembered how he'd watched her in the pub last night. He'd felt proud of her, and proud to be associated with her, and to be assumed by the others to be her friend. He remembered how charming she'd been to Jack and Toni and the others, and how smoothly and easily she'd fitted in. Maybe that's what had got him confused. Maybe she'd just been charming to him as well, and maybe it had been so long since someone new had taken a shine to him like this, that he'd mistaken it for something more.

He could feel her looking at him now. He knew it was wrong to allow this sudden awkwardness between them to last. It had been a wonderful afternoon. He mustn't let it end on a sour note. He forced a smile.

'Did you ever hear the joke,' he asked, 'about what the inflatable teacher in the inflatable school said to the inflatable boy who had a pin in his hand?'

'No?'

He put on a school-matronly voice: 'You're going to let me down, and yourself down, and the whole school down.'

But as she laughed at the punch line, he knew that the biggest joke of all was him.

Chapter 20

Kellie stood alone in the cottage kitchen, washing the dishes from lunchtime with tepid water and shampoo, her mind occupied with Ben. Everything had gone wrong between them. Ever since she'd admitted to her affair, everything had changed. A barrier had gone up, and the easy banter they'd shared earlier had disappeared.

She felt embarrassed now that she'd opened up about Elliot, because it was obvious that Ben disapproved – and no wonder. After his wife had left him for a friend of his, to hear about *any* affair must be tough. Still, she thought, he'd been wrong to judge her the way he had, and she was glad she'd stood up for herself. He'd had no right to make all this about himself.

Yet she still couldn't help thinking that, perhaps, if she'd only explained more about her relationship with Elliot, Ben might have understood. She should have done more to convince Ben that she and Elliot really *were* in love. She should've explained Elliot's home-life situation and stopped Ben thinking that she was just some kind of selfish home-wrecker.

It was too late now, and maybe it was safer this way, having this barrier up between herself and Ben, preventing them becoming any closer than they already had. Because she had to admit, today had been amazing. Nobody had ever done anything so . . . so romantic for her.

But there. That was the problem. The word romantic. Involuntarily, instinctively, she'd thought it herself – and if she was thinking it, then maybe Ben was too.

Was that what he'd been about to say, when she'd told

him that she wasn't his? Was he going to say something about their relationship? Was he going to admit that he had feelings for her? She didn't know, and now she never would.

She shook her head, annoyed that she was even thinking about it., annoyed that she felt so confused. Why did it matter what Ben thought of her? She was with Elliot; whether Ben found her attractive or not shouldn't have any relevance to her whatsoever.

'Who are you talking to?'

She jumped, turning around to see Ben in the doorway. She felt herself blushing.

'Was I talking out loud?'

'More muttering incoherently.'

She shrugged, embarrassed but relieved as well. He'd be horrified if he really knew what was going on inside her head. 'I must be going mad.'

'You're sure you don't need a hand?'

'There's not really enough room for us both,' she said, 'and you've done so much already. I'm fine.'

He nodded, putting his hands in his back pockets. 'Then I'll leave you to it. I'm off to the pub.'

'Oh, OK,' she said, biting her lip. He wasn't staying to keep her company, then.

He turned to go.

'Ben,' she began.

He turned back. 'What?'

His eyes were hard. Not unfriendly. Just hard.

'Nothing,' she said.

The moment he left, she felt more lonely than alone. But it was better like this, she reminded herself, better that they re-establish their own space. She finished the washing up and tidied everything away. Then she took down the Happy Christmas sign and bunched it up, before throwing it on the fire. She watched it burn. It shouldn't mean anything – and she'd make sure that it didn't.

As she stood by the door in her coat, she looked at the empty cottage, trying to remember lounging by the fire with Ben, feeling content and happy just a few hours ago. It seemed like a dream.

Back in their cottage next door, she flicked through an ancient *Country Life* magazine, bored and irritated. But what else was there to do? She couldn't go to the pub, because Ben was there, and even if she did now want to join him – which she didn't – he'd made it pretty clear that he wanted to go alone. For the first time since she'd arrived on the island, she now felt truly stranded.

She thought about Elliot and his precious family Christmas. She tried to picture him at home, imagining everyone laughing by a warm fire. They were probably all drinking sherry and playing games. She wished now, more than ever, that she could just march in there and tell everyone about her and Elliot and end this ridiculous charade. But Elliot had promised her that he'd do it on his own terms and she had to trust him.

She stood up, putting her hand on the back of the sofa. The duvet Ben had used was scrunched in a heap, the jumper he'd worn yesterday was on the floor. It mirrored the way Kellie had left her room upstairs. She remembered a comment he'd made at lunchtime about life being too short to floss. She'd laughed at the time, agreeing with him, liking him for being so spontaneous, admiring him for thinking that the way he looked was much less important than the way he felt. And that was the whole point about Ben, she mused. He did feel. Lots of things. And he wasn't afraid to articulate those feelings. He had no side, no way of hiding from who he really was.

Suddenly, she found herself remembering the way Elliot trimmed his nose hairs with nail scissors and the trouser press in the corridor of the flat in London, and the way his shirts were delivered in their plastic wrappers every week. She thought about the hairs on the back of his shoulders which she tried to ignore. She thought about the way he danced, and the fact that it made him look as if he was trying too hard to be young.

Stop it, she told herself, feeling panicked. She mustn't start thinking negatively about Elliot. She loved him. But still Ben's words came back to her: *If you were mine, I wouldn't keep you hanging on, not even for a second.* It wouldn't go away. She fingered the heart pendant around her neck and stood by the window, looking out into the dark, willing Elliot to come and find her. Willing him to prove Ben wrong. Willing him to make everything OK again. Willing him to stop her feeling this confused.

But there was no point in hoping for the impossible. Elliot was probably assuming she was with Ben – and from his face earlier on, was assuming much more besides. There was no way he was going to come and find her. She'd have to wait until they were both back in Fleet Town, where she could explain everything.

But Fleet Town and their penthouse suite seemed a million miles away. What on earth had she been thinking? Kellie now wondered. Why had she ever agreed to come to the islands with Elliot in the first place? She pictured their empty hotel room. Had she been mad? How could she ever have spent three days alone there?

Suddenly the light started flickering and she went to the door and took a torch off the shelf. Just as she did, the power cut out completely. She gasped, shocked by the dark.

She told herself not to be stupid. That it was crazy to be frightened, but still, her hands were shaking as she put the torch on, banging it to make the beam stay steady.

In the dark, the cottage felt creepy. She would have to go

to the pub, she concluded, and brazen things out with Ben. After all, there was no reason to work herself up into a state. It wasn't like she was backing down on her decision to cool things off with him, because it wasn't like she had a choice.

The front door was wrenched out of her hand by the wind. Kellie held on to the hood of her coat, her hair underneath whipping around her face. Ahead of her, the path to the pub looked treacherous in the weak torch beam. It was ridiculous, but without Ben by her side, she felt vulnerable and alone.

Inside the pub, Sally was lighting candles. There was a warm glow from the huge fire. The wind roared in the chimney. Without the jukebox, the pub was strangely quiet. In the corner, a man was tuning up a guitar.

'It's looking serious,' Sally explained. 'When the power goes down like this, it's always a while before it's back on again. Roddy has gone to have a look at the generator, but if it's still on the blink, I doubt if the power's going to be back on tonight.'

Kellie spotted Ben over in the corner at a table by the fire. He waved to her.

'There you are. I was just coming to see whether you were OK. We were just having a chat,' Ben said, pointing to the man opposite him.

He must be another friend of Ben's from the island. Kellie walked over and stood awkwardly next to the table.

'Hi,' the stranger said. He was handsome, in his early forties, but there was something sad about his face as he half-smiled at her.

'Do you mind if I join you?' she asked Ben. 'The electricity's out next door, too.'

'Fine by me,' Ben said.

The man drained his tumbler of whisky as Kellie sat down and took off her coat. There was a long pause. Ben was watching her re-tie her hair behind her head in a pony-tail, his pint glass poised mid-way to his lips.

'Maybe you two want to be –' she began, worried that she'd interrupted something.

'No, no, stay,' Ben said. 'Maybe you can help out. A female perspective could be just what our friend here needs.'

'You've been great, listening to me. I must be boring you rigid.'

Kellie could see now that Ben didn't know the man either.

'Not at all. Another one?' Ben asked, standing up and picking up the man's glass. He widened his eyes at Kellie and she could tell that Ben had been held captive, listening to the man. 'What are you having, Kellie?'

She should have come to the pub before, she now realised. Whatever bad vibes there'd been between her and Ben now seemed to have vanished. He'd obviously got over it, whatever it was that had been bothering him, and moved on.

'Rum and coke, I think,' she said.

'Might as well,' Ben said. He leant down towards her and whispered, 'I've got a feeling it's going to be a long night.'

Kellie smiled at Ben and he winked. What a fool she'd been to work herself up into such a state about nothing. She and Ben were friends and that was just fine. There was no reason why they shouldn't have a nice time together. Now she was here, she felt as if they were a team again and she was supporting him.

'Perhaps you've got some words of wisdom for our friend. You see, she told him today. His wife,' he said, pointing at the man to fill Kellie in on the situation.

There was a long pause as Ben left the table and went to the bar with their glasses.

'Your wife told you . . . ?' She was unsure whether

270

she should be asking a complete stranger something so intimate.

'That she wants a divorce,' the man said. In the flickering candle light she could see now that his eyes were bloodshot with emotion and whisky.

'Oh God. I'm sorry,' Kellie said, realising she'd accidentally stumbled on a crisis far bigger than she'd imagined.

'Yep. Kind of put a downer on Christmas dinner, let me tell you.'

She'd thought at first that the man was a local, but now something about the way he spoke and the way he was dressed made her think otherwise. He leant his elbows on the table and put his head in his hands. His shoulders began to shake.

Kellie looked on helplessly. She almost patted his shoulder, but she didn't.

'I'm sorry,' he said, wiping his eyes. 'It's just it's been such a fucking shock.'

'It's OK,' she said, feeling for him. Whatever the story was for this poor guy, it certainly put her own problems in perspective.

'I'm a good listener,' she said, smiling gently at him. 'If you want to talk about it.'

'She thinks it's my fault,' he said.

'Thinks what's your fault?'

'We lost our son, eighteen months ago. He drowned. Stephanie thinks it's . . . it's my fault. But I tried. God, I tried . . .'

Kellie couldn't believe that this was happening. She felt her cheeks flush. She could hardly breathe. This man was David. *The* David. Stephanie's husband. Elliot's brother-in-law, and her potentially future brother-in-law too. Her mouth had gone completely dry.

'Everything that's been going wrong for the past year between us all makes sense now. She hates me, because

271

she thinks I should have saved him. But how can she think that?' David appealed to her. 'I loved him, too.'

Kellie thought quickly. She had to appear like a concerned stranger – and she *did* care. This poor man was in so much pain. But she mustn't betray who she was.

'It was probably just the pressure of Christmas,' she said, shifting on her seat. Her mind raced with the implications of what David was telling her. How had everyone reacted? No wonder Elliot hadn't ventured out to try and find her. Her image of a cosy Thorne family Christmas with them all playing charades shattered. 'People always go a bit loopy, don't they? You know, being around their families. What did she say exactly?'

As David started to tell her about the row and about what had happened to Paul, the guitarist in the corner starting to sing quietly, gently strumming his guitar. Kellie thought about the raucous karaoke last night. It seemed like a year ago.

'I'm so sorry,' she said, reaching out to touch David's hand. 'How awful for you. Especially at Christmas. How was everyone else?' she asked. 'I mean, did you have any other family there?' She tried to make it sound like a logical question.

'Just my brother-in-law and his wife. Stephanie was so furious with them as well. For interfering, she said. She called my sister-in-law a meddling bitch. She told her to stick her perfect fucking marriage up her perfect fucking arse, when all Isabelle was doing was trying to help.'

'Oh?' Kellie said. She could barely compute the mag-nitude of what he was telling her.

'But Isabelle will survive. She survives everything.'

'Here's some more drinks,' Ben said, putting them down on the table. He smiled at Kellie and briefly clasped David's shoulder.

'Come on, mate, it'll be OK.'

Kellie took a large glug of her drink, trying to curb her beating heart. She felt unsure of herself, as if each step she took forward into the future was into quicksand. She felt as if she was sinking in all the lies she'd told. She didn't know which way to turn.

Selfishly, she couldn't help wondering what David and Stephanie's row would mean for her and Elliot. How would Elliot be able to make his own announcement now, when Stephanie and David were on the verge of their own divorce? The whole house must be in uproar. And Isabelle had got it in the neck too, according to David, for sticking up for him. She hardly sounded like Elliot had always made her out to be. Worst of all, David had described Isabelle's marriage to Elliot as perfect – and what had he meant when he said that Isabelle would survive – that Isabelle survived everything? What did that mean?

While Kellie wanted nothing more than to quiz David, she knew that there was no way she could say anything which would arouse his suspicion. Especially not in front of Ben.

'What do you think he should do, Kellie?' Ben asked.

What she thought was that she was in way out of her depth.

'I'm not sure. Maybe your wife is blaming you because she feels guilty herself,' she said to David, her conversations with Elliot all coming back to her. 'You know what doctors are like.'

'How did you know that Stephanie was a doctor, did I say?' David asked.

Kellie took a hasty sip of her drink. She looked at Ben and David over the top of it. 'You must have done. Earlier on.'

David looked tired. 'You must be right.'

'Everyone gets a bit emotional at Christmas time,' Ben reassured him, before turning to Kellie. 'Everyone says

273

stupid things and makes fools out of themselves.'

Kellie wondered whether he was referring to their walk this afternoon, to what he'd said to her.

'I don't know why I'm telling you all this,' David said.

'It's easier to tell strangers,' Ben said, repeating what Kellie had said earlier.

She glanced at him.

'The thing is, I really do love Steph,' David said. 'I always have. Not in a flashy way. I'm not the type of guy who's going to give her a diamond necklace, but that doesn't mean I love her any less.'

Kellie's hand automatically went to the neck of her buttoned-up shirt, feeling the necklace Elliot had given her underneath it.

'Then you should tell her how you feel,' Ben said.

David shook his head. 'She's shut me out. It's like something inside us died when Paul did. It's too late. If she really doesn't love me, then what's the point in staying together?'

'But what about your other kids?' Ben asked.

David rubbed his face. Then he shook his head. 'I don't know. I really don't know. I thought everything was fine. That we'd get through this. But now? I don't know what I'm going to do. I wouldn't even know how to start being single again. I look at you two together and – '

'We're not together,' Kellie corrected him, feeling Ben's eyes on her.

'We're just friends,' Ben said.

'But I could have sworn . . . you look . . .' David said, then stopped. 'Stephanie's right. I don't have any intuition. I can't get anything right.'

274

Chapter 21

Stephanie lay wide awake in the dark in the bedroom in her father's house, listening to the howl of the wind outside. Every muscle in her body was tense. Her head ached with the hangover from all the wine she'd drunk. Her throat was dry and her skin felt uncomfortable, as if the shame of what she'd done had brought her out in some kind of rash.

Exhausted, she sat up in bed and turned her head towards the door. For hours now her senses had been on red alert as she strained to hear the front door opening, or anything that would mean David had come back. It wasn't even as if she wanted him to come back – but not knowing whether he would or not, or even where he was, was driving her mad.

She'd lost track of time in the dark, trying to count the minutes between shadows passing under the crack of the door. Now she was sure that everyone had gone to bed. It must be very late. She knew it would be simpler to turn on the light and look at the bedside clock, rather than to torment herself like this, but if she turned the light on, someone might realise she was awake and attempt to talk to her, and that was the last thing she wanted.

She held her head in her hands, wondering what the hell she was going to do. Everything was such a mess. Earlier on, when she'd put Nat to bed, Nat had been inconsolable, sobbing and sobbing for David, until Stephanie had become cross. Now she regretted that too. She wondered what the impact of today would be on Nat's future. Would she remember crying alone in the dark for David? Would

275

she turn out to be horribly insecure because she thought Stephanie didn't love her? Would she hate Christmas now for the rest of her life?

And Simon? Well, Simon wasn't talking to her, punishing her with his silence and his wounded eyes. She didn't know where he'd been this afternoon, and he'd refused to tell her. He'd never been this rebellious before. He was only eight years old, and already she'd lost his respect for good.

Taylor had only made her feel worse by being overprotective, not allowing Stephanie a moment to talk to him alone. She had been left in no doubt as to what Taylor thought of the situation. She'd been tempted to say something, to make Taylor back off, even something along the lines of how it was a good thing that her days as a spoilt only child were numbered, but Gerald had been watching like a hawk and she had had no choice but to put up with it.

At least the kids were showing their emotions, she thought. That was far preferable to the way everyone else had reacted.

When she'd finally left the dining room, reeling from her conversation with David, she'd been expecting a showdown with Isabelle, or with her father. She'd been prepared for someone to say something to her, to call her to account, to make her apologise. Or even to ask her how she was. The house had thin walls. Surely they must have heard what she'd said to David? Surely they must all have wondered how she was feeling?

In the way that her family always had, however, Stephanie's momentary blip into emotional irresponsibility had been immediately covered with the familiar veneer of civility. The 'unpleasantness' that had occurred at lunchtime had been firmly swept under the carpet.

Nobody had mentioned that David had left the house.

Nobody had questioned where he'd gone, although it was obvious that no one knew. Isabelle had disappeared for a lie-down, Gerald had taken the dog for a long walk, Nat had done a jigsaw puzzle with Elliot by the fire, whilst Stephanie had scrubbed the kitchen, her mind in a frenzy.

Then, a few hours ago, when Taylor and Simon had come back and Isabelle had got up, they'd all sat down together to watch the DVD of *The Wizard of Oz*, as if nothing out of the ordinary had happened. Everyone had been perfectly polite to each other, as they all had a cup of tea and a slice of Christmas cake. Even Stephanie had found herself playing along, attempting to mend bridges by pretending to be interested in the book Isabelle had given her. There had even been a few jokes made.

However, David's absence had filled the silences in between with unspoken accusations. The hours had dragged on. Finally Stephanie hadn't been able to stand the pretence any longer and had busied herself with getting the kids off to bed. Then she'd excused herself, claiming a headache. Now, in the dark, she had a long night ahead in which she could analyse what had happened.

She realised, of course, that she'd been building up to saying what she'd said to David today ever since the accident, and over that time, she'd only focused on the words – words that had gathered momentum, becoming so destructive, that she knew that once she said them, they'd become the wrecking ball that brought down their marriage.

But now, sitting in the rubble of what she'd just done, instead of feeling vindicated, or relieved that the words were finally out, she just felt that she'd created more of a mess than ever. She'd had no satisfaction from hurting David. On the contrary, his reaction had rather startled her. She'd almost made herself believe that when she

277

confronted him, he'd agree that their marriage was over. She hadn't expected him to tell her that he loved her, right up until the end.

She shivered in the dark. She felt more scared than she'd ever felt. She hadn't thought about the consequences of actually getting divorced. She hadn't thought about what it would mean for the children and how it would affect them all. She didn't even know how she would go about it. There'd be lawyers involved. And estate agents. Strangers would enter their lives.

David barged into her thoughts, images of him flicking through her head like a never-ending Rolodex of memories. Would their lives really be that easy to separate?

She held her breath as she saw a shadow fill the light under the door.

'Steph. Are you in there?'

The door opened and Stephanie sat bolt upright in bed. Her father was silhouetted by the corridor light. She didn't know whether to be relieved or disappointed that he wasn't David.

'Can I come in?'

Gerald didn't wait for an answer. Instead he shut the door and came towards the bed, as Stephanie shuffled up and turned on the bedside light. He sat down next to her on the duvet. She felt ashamed that she was still fully clothed.

'It's blowing a fair old gale out there,' he said.

She felt like a little girl. She knew she'd detonated Christmas Day and hurt everyone's feelings. She wondered whether her father was going to deliver a lecture. She didn't have the energy to be contrite.

'I heard from Sally at the pub,' he said. 'David's going to stay the night there.'

Stephanie nodded. 'Oh,' she said.

'He's a bit drunk, apparently. I'll check that he's OK in the morning.'

Her father pressed his palms down on his knees. She was expecting him to leave, but he didn't.

'What exactly happened today?' he asked.

'I don't want to talk about it, Dad.'

'Oh, I think you do. I think talking about it would help you very much.'

From the tone of his voice, she realised she had no choice.

'We argued about Paul.'

'Paul?'

'I told David that I think Paul's death was . . .' She stopped, remembering David's face.

'Was . . .?' her father prompted.

'Was his fault.'

The words, uttered for a second time, seemed irrationally cruel. Her eyes suddenly welled up.

'Oh. Oh, I see,' he said. He put his hand over hers. It was warm and steady.

Stephanie felt tears coming now as if a tap had been turned on. Uncontrollable, grief-laden, angry tears.

'All I know is that I can't get past it. Whenever I think about Paul, I can't get past thinking about them in the boat.' She looked at her father, imploring him to understand. 'How could David not have seen him fall into the water? How could it have been that difficult to save him?'

'You weren't there. It was an accident.'

'But . . .'

All she could see was Paul's body, as she'd held him in her arms, and the tears she had not shed then overwhelmed her now.

Her father's voice was calm and gentle. 'Don't you think David's punished himself enough over this? Don't you think he cares?'

'No, he's moved on. He's done what I never could.'

'I think it's very brave of David to deal with it the way

279

he has. Lots of weaker men would have crumbled, but David has picked himself and dedicated himself to being the best father he can to Nat and Simon.'

'It's like Paul was never with us. You know . . .' she paused, tears making it almost impossible to speak. 'We've never really talked about it. I was so numb for so long, and now . . .'

'Now?'

She took a deep, shuddering breath. 'Now, it's too late.'

Her father searched out her eyes. 'Too late?'

'I could have stopped them. I could have stopped them going out on the boat.'

'Steph, darling, you can't blame David, or yourself. It was a whole combination of circumstances, most of which were out of your control.'

'But it shouldn't have happened,' she cried.

'But it did, and that doesn't mean it's anyone's fault.'

And now it came. A wail, unstoppable and loud. Right from somewhere deep down inside her. Like a demon leaving her body. Her tears burst out of her as she grieved for her little boy. Her father rocked her in his arms, gently stroking her hair.

She wept for the wonderful little person Paul had been and the adult he'd never become, she wept for the big brother and little brother he'd never be, and for the girl he'd never marry. She wept for all the smiles he'd never smile and the tears he'd never cry.

'I'm sorry,' she said eventually, her voice no more than a hoarse whisper.

'Don't be. You know, it should be David here, not me. You should tell him how you feel.'

'I told him I want a divorce.'

'Divorce?'

The way he said it made it sound so drastic. Stephanie shook her head, wrung out.

280

'I can't go on like we have been,' she said.

'And you think splitting up will solve it?'

'Everything's such a mess, Dad. If I'm alone with the kids, I –'

'If you take those kids away from him, you'll destroy him. You can't really want that?'

'No. But –'

'Whatever happened today doesn't mean you have to end your marriage.'

'It's over anyway. All we do is argue. I look at Elliot and Isabelle and how perfect they are, how much of a future they're building. I don't know . . . seeing them this Christmas has only reinforced how far David and I have grown apart. We don't even like each other, let alone love each other like they do.'

'Their marriage has nothing to do with yours. What you need to do is sit down with David and talk.'

'It's too late.'

'Sleep on it. Please. Promise me that at least you'll do that.'

Stephanie hunkered down under the covers, as her father left the room. The house was quiet, except for the wind outside. She thought about David in the pub. What a terrible way to end Christmas. She turned over, knowing she wasn't going to sleep. Then, next door, she heard the muffled rhythmic thump of the bed against the wall. It was coming from Isabelle and Elliot's room.

They were having sex. She was falling apart and they were having sex.

Chapter 22

He couldn't see a thing. The night was as black as the bottom of a well. The wind roared, rushing past the pub like a river, nearly sweeping Ben and Kellie off their feet. It was like stepping out on to the deck of a boat in a storm, Ben thought.

'Jesus Christ!' Kellie shouted, grabbing Ben to steady herself.

Ben hardly felt rock steady himself. His recent abstemious lifestyle hadn't done him any favours in preparing him for the evening he'd just spent. He'd lost count of how many drinks he and Kellie and David must have put away between them. Over the course of several hours, David had veered from depression, to euphoria, to fatalism and back to euphoria again, and Kellie and Ben had joined him for the ride. They'd now called it a night with a final round of tequilas, which was just as well, because they'd all been slurring for the last hour at least, none of them making much sense.

A shaft of wavering candle light shone weakly out from the pub door behind them, casting their black shadows across the snow-covered street, like paper-chain people cut from a white sheet of card. David lurched out on to the pavement beside them, drunkenly clawing at Ben. Then the shaft of light vanished and darkness returned.

'Are you sure it's OK that I stay with you?' David asked, for what must have been the tenth time in so many minutes. His words came out in a drunken bellow, hacking through the noise of the wind.

'Positive,' Ben bawled back. 'You can crash in the living room with me.'

'But maybe I should walk back?' David said.

'Forget it.'

Ben doubted David would make it even if he tried, not in this weather and not in his condition. Besides, what David really needed to do was sleep himself into sobriety. Ben had only met David's wife briefly when he'd ferried her over, but he guessed that if David were to turn up in this state – stinking of whisky and cheese and onion crisps, with bloodshot eyes and a Guinness stain on his shirt – it would only make their problems worse. He took a torch from his pocket and shone it down the street towards the annexe. Memories of the day he'd spent with Kellie were cast in footprints in the snow ahead of him.

Ben linked arms with David and Kellie and they set off together, driving into the wind, like a rugby scrum front row. He pictured his flat back in London: his retro B&O sound system, the Smith Brothers armchair and sofa, and his Fuegotech steel-shuttered gas fire. He'd only moved into the apartment three months before, after his share of the house he'd lived in with Marie had finally been deposited in his bank, but he'd splashed out quickly on making it feel – or at least *look* – like a home. He'd compensated for the lack of connection he'd truly felt for his new and alien living space by filling it with luxuries and gadgets. He'd surrounded himself with them like crutches, just to keep himself propped up, and when his friends had called round and looked over his funky little bachelor pad, they'd all smiled with relief and had commented on how well and how quickly he'd managed to adjust.

Leaving the pub last night, a little hazy, a little drunk (a lot less drunk than they were now), Ben had hoped that one day he might get to show it to and share it all with Kellie.

He'd hoped she would smile, too, and maybe even want to stay.

But now he knew she never would. He'd got ahead of himself, dreaming up a future for the two of them. It had been a fantasy which she'd stamped all over that afternoon down by the harbour wall. He'd been left reeling as if he'd been dumped. Which made her huddling up against him now, using his body to protect herself from the wind, all the more difficult to handle.

Idiot, he told himself. *Sucker, loser, jerk, fool* . . .

He hated himself for not flinching and moving away. He hated the way he still wanted her. He knew this physical contact was nothing but pragmatic, at best the result of her being too tipsy to stand alone, and yet still he couldn't help wishing it was something more.

She should be old news by now. He should have rejected her when she'd walked into the pub earlier this evening, for the sake of his ego if nothing else. He should have clawed back some of his lost pride by giving her the cold shoulder and leaving her to sit at the bar by herself.

But he hadn't. He'd crumbled. Like some lovesick troubadour, trapped inside his own private *Groundhog Day*, he'd found himself warming to her all over again.

Why? That's what he wanted to know. Why was he torturing himself? Why couldn't he accept what she'd told him down by the harbour? Why couldn't he throw her, and the possibility of them together, out of his mind? Why did he still feel hope?

When they reached the cottage doorway, they broke apart. The tarpaulin on the roof whipped and cracked in the wind, then suddenly shrieked, rearing upwards like a great winged creature. Ben fumbled for the door handle.

Sheet lightning switched the sky on like a lamp and he turned from the door to look up. Again the sky flashed white, like a mirrored reflection of the snow-locked land. He turned to see Kellie lurching towards him.

'I feel really unwell,' she told him. 'Really pissed . . . everything's starting to spin . . .'

'It's OK –' he began to tell her, but then, before he could catch her, she was suddenly no longer upright. Her legs had shot out from underneath her, sending her crashing flat on to her back.

She didn't cry out and she didn't move. He dropped to his knees and shone the torch down on her face. One of her eyes was closed, the other was a half-open slit, registering nothing. Her lips were moving as if she was speaking, but he could hear no words.

Adrenaline punched through him, shocking him into sobriety. From being woozy himself, he now felt as if he'd just dived into a plunge pool of freezing water. His mind cleared and his whole body shifted into overdrive. He squeezed her hand hard.

'You're going to be OK,' he said.

Then he noticed the trickle of blood on her neck, just behind her left ear, and he saw that she was lying on what looked like a metal sign. Wind hissed through his hair. Her head lolled to one side, then her eyes snapped open and she looked around, disoriented.

'It's me,' he said. 'Ben.'

He held the torch close and searched her scalp above the trickle of blood. There was the wound. A swelling, angry and raw, bloomed beneath her hairline at the base of her skull. He pressed his fingertips to it. It felt sickeningly soft, and fragile as an egg yolk, as if it might burst.

'My head . . .' she said. She reached up to touch the cut. 'Don't.'

He scanned her face again. She was staring up at him, confused. He should get her to a doctor, he thought, and soon. Chances were that she'd passed out from too much drink, but he didn't know how hard she'd hit her head, and he hadn't enough first-aid to know whether or not she was actually concussed. Her eyelids drooped. For all he knew, her skull could be fractured and she might be slipping into shock. It wasn't a risk he was going to take.

'Help me get her inside,' he told David.

David knelt down beside Ben and the two of them got Kellie to her feet. It was only then that Ben saw what was written on the sign she'd slipped over on. It read 'DANGER'. No fucking kidding, he thought. He shone the torch up at the annexe roof. That's where the sign must have blown down from, he guessed.

They got Kellie quickly inside.

'What happened?' she asked.

'You slipped,' Ben told her. 'Or passed out. It's hard to tell.'

'Oh, shit,' she mumbled. 'I'm such a jerk.'

Her eyes drooped, again, then closed. Her whole face seemed to relax, and in that moment, Ben realised he'd never seen anyone so serene, so beautiful before. Nothing had happened between them, not even a kiss, and yet everything had. Her life felt as precious to him as his own.

'She's gone again,' David said.

'We need to get her checked out by someone,' Ben told him. 'I don't know how hard she hit her head and I'd rather be safe than sorry.'

'I agree.'

'Can you get back to the pub and tell Sally and Roddy what's happened? Tell them to bring their car.'

'And then what?' David asked.

'We need to get her to a doctor,' Ben said. 'Or a nurse. And we need to do it fast.'

DAY 3

Boxing Day

Chapter 23

Where the hell was she? Kellie rubbed her eyes. She was lying in a narrow bed. There was a blackout blind over the window, but she could see daylight creeping around the edges, illuminating the small single bedroom. Her eyes ached with an intense pain, as did her head. As she tried to sit up, she felt queasy.

Squinting through the slits of her eyes, wincing, she saw Ben dozing in the armchair pulled up next to the bed. He was fully dressed. Where was she? What was he doing here? She felt as if her mind was swimming through cloudy water.

And then her heart lurched, as she stared at his face. Last night . . .

Suddenly, disjointed images flashed into her mind, like a strobe. The pub . . . David . . . drinking . . . the wind. Then nothing.

She groped backwards in her mind, trying to remember what had happened. She'd been outside with Ben. She remembered being drunk. Through her pain, she felt a deep flush start creeping up her until her cheeks burned.

Had anything happened? Had she and Ben . . . ?

'Oh God,' she said, aloud. Her voice was no more than a croak.

Ben snapped out of his sleep and leant forward. He looked tired, his forehead creased into a worried frown.

'How are you feeling?' he asked.

Embarrassed, ashamed, frightened, nervous, were all too difficult to articulate.

Ben stood over her, making her lie back. His touch made her feel even more worried. It felt familiar.

'Hey, don't move too fast.'

'My head hurts,' she said.

'Hang on one second.'

He settled her back on the pillow and walked quickly to the door, lifting the old-fashioned latch.

'One second,' he repeated, before disappearing.

Kellie lay back and looked at the ceiling before tentatively touching her head. There was something bulky and soft just by her ear. She explored the dressing and it crackled like sellotape. She twisted her wrists, and saw that her hands were filthy, her nails caked with blood.

What had happened? She started to panic. This must be more serious than she thought.

Then Ben was back in the room with a woman. She was tall, with brown hair and a strong, intelligent face. She walked towards Kellie.

'You're awake, that's good,' she said. She stood next to the bed and put her hand on Kellie's forehead. 'How are you feeling? Rotten, I should imagine?'

'You can say that again,' Kellie said. This had to be the worst hangover she'd ever experienced. 'I'm not sure what's going on.'

'Didn't Ben tell you?' the woman said, glancing at him.

'She's just woken up,' Ben said.

'You fell over in the storm last night.'

'It was a sign,' Ben said.

Kellie stared at him, confused. 'A sign? That I should do what?'

Ben smiled. 'No, I didn't mean that kind of sign. Not a sign sent from God. Just a regular sign. You tripped over it and banged your head. Don't you remember?'

'No.' She didn't remember it at all. Now that he was

290

telling her about it though, she felt like an utter fool. How could this have happened?

'May I?' The woman lifted up Kellie's wrist and squeezed it, taking her pulse.

'You fainted. You needed a doctor,' Ben explained, 'and a couple of stitches. Stephanie here did the honours.'

Stephanie? This woman next to her was Stephanie? Suddenly, the sleep-inducing fog that had threatened to overtake her disappeared in Kellie's head.

'But . . . but you're Elliot's sister,' Kellie blurted out, before she had time to censor herself.

Stephanie frowned and looked at Ben and then back at Kellie as if she couldn't see the relevance at all.

'I didn't know you knew my brother.'

'I . . . I don't . . . I –'

'David talked to us last night,' Ben explained.

Kellie could feel herself blushing furiously. She remembered the pub, her and Ben and David . . .

'I just remembered David talking and . . . I hope everything . . .' She trailed off, not trusting herself to speak. Ben must have got Stephanie to come to the pub. This must be Michael's room. She couldn't believe she was meeting Stephanie like this. She was supposed to be meeting Stephanie as an equal. She was supposed to be impressing Stephanie as someone who was going to make her brother's future happy. She wasn't supposed to be caked in blood, lying in a bed.

'All you need now is some rest. I think David's got a lot to answer for, getting you so drunk, but I suppose it could have been so much worse. You're very lucky,' Stephanie said.

Was she? Kellie thought. From where she was lying, this was disastrous. She couldn't help staring at Stephanie. She was so different from how Kellie had pictured her. In her mind's eye, Stephanie had been much older than Elliot, maybe with her hair in a bun. Somebody serious and frumpy and old. Kellie remembered what David had said last night about his argument with Stephanie, but none of the inner turmoil Stephanie must be feeling showed at all. Instead, she seemed steady and efficient and strong, and very, very sober.

'I'm fine, honestly,' Kellie said, throwing back the covers. 'I really shouldn't bother you any more.'

'No,' Stephanie said. 'You're not going anywhere just yet.'

'Please, I –'

'No. Doctor's orders. I don't want you to go rushing off.'

'I'm so glad you're OK,' Ben said, before stifling a yawn. 'Sorry.'

'You should go and get some rest too,' Stephanie said to him. 'We'll all keep an eye on Kellie. You look shattered.'

'OK. If you're sure, I'll pop back to the village.'

'The village? What do you mean?' Kellie said.

'It's not far. I'm just going back to the pub. Remember?' Ben said.

'But we're in the pub.'

'No, no,' Stephanie said. 'Ben and David brought you here last night. This is my father's house.'

Kellie thought she was going to throw up.

'Mum? Can I come in yet?'

Kellie looked up to see a young boy pushing open the door.

'This is my son, Simon,' Stephanie said.

Simon didn't smile. He stared at Kellie. 'When can I have my room back?' he said pointedly.

'I'm sorry,' Kellie said. 'Ben, wait. I'll come with you.'

'How are we doing in here?' A small, pretty blonde woman was pushing open the door with her foot and entering with a tray. 'Hey! You're awake. That's great.'

She had an American accent.

She had an American accent.

Kellie stared at her, already knowing exactly who she was as Stephanie said, 'This is Isabelle, my sister-in-law.'

'Hi,' Isabelle said.

She was gorgeous. More than that. She was perfect. Everything about her. She was wearing tightly fitting designer jeans and had a baby-blue cashmere jumper casually knotted around her shoulders, like an airbrushed Tommy Hilfiger model.

'It's getting a bit crowded in here, isn't it,' Stephanie said. 'Come on Simon.'

'Thanks,' Kellie managed, unable to take her eyes off Isabelle, as she put the tray down on the empty chair by the bed.

'I've brought you some breakfast, if you fancy it,' Isabelle said.

'Well, I'll leave you to it,' Stephanie said.

'I'll stay with you, if you like.' Ben had clearly sensed Kellie's panic.

'No, you get some rest,' Stephanie said. 'Come on. Let's give Kellie some space. You take your time,' she said to Kellie. 'I'm sure Isabelle won't mind running you a bath.'

'I'll see you later,' Ben said as Stephanie ushered him out with Simon. Kellie wanted to yell out at him to stop, to beg him to take her with him, for him to do anything but leave her alone with Isabelle, but she was mute with shock.

She felt her heart racing as the bedroom door closed with a soft click.

'He's a real find, isn't he? You lucky girl,' Isabelle said. 'David's told me all about him. Ben's sat by your side all night. Said he wouldn't forgive himself if you weren't OK.'

Kellie couldn't say anything. If she did, she might cry.

'Why don't you sit up and you can have some of this?'

Isabelle picked up the tray and slid it on to the bed. There were a few slices of toast, a glass of orange juice and a cup of tea.

Where was the nightmare bitch-from-hell who made Elliot's life a misery? Where was the stuck-up captain of industry who was too busy to be civil to anybody. Certainly not here. Kellie could only think how *normal* Isabelle was.

'You are being so nice to me.' She wanted to crawl out of her skin, like the snake she was.

'You've done us all a favour. At least David is back now.' Isabelle looked at Kellie and flapped her hand. 'It doesn't matter. You're not interested in all that. It's just family stuff.'

'Oh.'

'So you're having quite a Christmas, I gather?'

Kellie felt her throat close up. Her nose tingled with tears.

'You could say that.' What did she know? What had Ben told her? About the fact that she'd come to the island on her own?

'Hey, I brought you some clothes. We're probably about the same size. I guess you could do with changing,' Isabelle said, pointing to a pile of clothes on the chest of drawers. They'd been folded so neatly, they looked like new.

'Thanks. You're very kind.'

Isabelle leant over Kellie to get the glass of water on the bedside table, and there, right in front of her face, Kellie saw the heart-shaped pendant dangling around Isabelle's flawless neck.

'Your necklace . . . ?'

'Isn't it lovely?' Isabelle smiled and fondled the pendant as she stood up straight. 'My husband gave it to me for Christmas. He's so romantic. I'm so lucky. You know, Ben mentioned that you're a lawyer. I know law circles are very small in London. My husband is Elliot Thorne. He's a partner at WDG & Partners. You must know him. Or at least know *of* him. Anyway, you'll meet him when you come downstairs.'

Chapter 24

Taylor was like a cobra watching a mouse, waiting for the optimum moment to strike.

Proof. That's what she wanted. She wanted proof of her suspicion that something was going on between her father and Kellie. Michael wanted proof, too: proof that she was wrong, because the more Taylor obsessed about this idea of hers, the less she focused on him. He wanted her attention back. All of it.

Taylor had called round for Michael at the pub at eight that morning. 'That bitch,' had been the first two words out of her mouth. 'That bitch is staying at our house.'

Nothing Michael had been able to say had convinced her that Kellie's transferral to the Thorne house had been anything other than deliberate and insidious. Taylor didn't care about the storm or the injury. She only knew that Kellie had taken yet another intrusive step, deeper into her life.

'It makes me sick,' Taylor had said, 'knowing that she's there. In our house. Near my mum. Near my family and me. He's nearly old enough to be her dad.'

Now Michael and Taylor were in the Thornes' sitting room, feigning playing poker at the table, though the truth was that neither of them had so much as glanced at the cards which Taylor had steadily and monotonously dealt.

Kellie was sitting side-on to them, next to old Mr Thorne in front of the fire. She had a small square white dressing taped to the back of her neck. Stephanie had come in ten minutes before to give her a painkiller and to check that she was OK. Kellie had said she wanted to go back to the village, but Stephanie had been insistent: she wanted to keep her here under observation, just for a few hours longer, just to be safe.

Observation: it was an idea to which Taylor had subscribed as well. Although, in her case, surveillance, or even spying, might have been a more accurate description. She hadn't taken her eyes off Kellie, not since the interloper had first appeared, dressed in 'my *mother*'s fucking clothes', and had joined Stephanie and Gerald for coffee in the kitchen.

Using Michael as her stooge, Taylor had trailed Kellie from kitchen to hallway to TV room, and finally into here, the sitting room. Throughout this whole time, she had barely acknowledged Kellie's existence. Even when Stephanie had attempted to introduce Taylor and Michael to Kellie, all Taylor had said was, 'We've already met.'

It felt odd in here to Michael, as if it was simultaneously hot and cold. The snow-frosted window lent the room a cold, pale light, as if they were in the middle of the Arctic wastes.

'I've never understood why anyone born in Australia would ever want to visit here, let alone stay,' Gerald was saying. 'I once went to the Opera House in Sydney. With Emma. My wife. It was one of the best evenings out I ever had.'

Elliot came in and walked up to the bookcase. He made a show of looking for something to read.

'Yes, a fantastic country,' Gerald went on. 'Did you know, Elliot, that your mother and I once considered emigrating to Australia? It was before you and Stephanie were born. Back when the Australian government were so desperate for new citizens that they'd pay your boat fare over.'

'Imagine that,' Elliot said, turning to Kellie with a smile. 'You and I might have grown up as neighbours, Kellie. But

297

then, I suppose we already are, in a way, what with us both now being Londoners.'

'Yes,' she said. She stared straight ahead of her as she spoke.

'And both lawyers too . . .' Gerald said. 'What did you say your firm was called, Kellie?'

'I didn't,' she answered. 'That is,' she said more mildly, 'they're very small. I doubt your son will have heard of them.'

'Oh, he knows everyone. Don't you, Elliot?'

'Absolutely.' Elliot smiled at her again. 'No doubt we'll bump into each other some time. It's such a small world. We'll probably find out that we've got absolutely stacks in common.'

He left the bookcase without choosing a book and walked casually in front of his father and Kellie to look out of the window, across the white landscape.

Taylor gripped Michael's wrist, but there was no need. He'd seen it, too, even if old Mr Thorne had not. There, on the carpet by the fire, was a piece of paper, screwed up, tossed there so casually by Elliot only two seconds before, as if he'd meant it to land on the fire and disappear in smoke. Which he might have, Michael thought, because Taylor might still be wrong.

'I'm taking Rufus out for a walk,' Elliot announced to no one in particular.

He left and Kellie and Mr Thorne continued to talk.

Michael and Taylor's eyes were fixed on the paper. Michael had to admit it: now that they were teetering on the verge of discovering just how right Taylor was, he was starting to get a sick kind of kick out of all this.

It had been like when he'd used to go hunting with his father. There were goats on the island, domestic ones which had long since escaped their fetters and bred and turned wild. They'd trash back gardens and vegetable patches, and from time to time Michael's dad and the other islanders with guns used to organise a cull, and go out and decimate the goat population in a matter of days. Michael remembered the thrill of it all, of following tracks up through the woods, crossing over streams, until . . .

Well, that was where he and Taylor were now: at the moment of truth. Was their prey just around the corner? Had Kellie seen the piece of paper? Was it meant for her and was she really going to pick it up? They were about to find out.

Michael watched and waited. He counted his heartbeats . . . one . . . two . . . three . . . four . . . five . . .

And then Kellie pointed out a photograph on the mantelpiece.

'Who's that?' she asked. 'The woman in that photo . . .'

'My wife,' Gerald said, getting up to retrieve it. 'Emma . . .'

There, in that moment, any doubt that Michael still had vanished because there and then, as Mr Thorne stood with his back to Kellie, she ducked quickly down and furtively snatched up the crumpled paper, before enfolding it in her fist.

A few moments later, she stood and bent over the fire, as if warming her hands. Michael saw her drop the paper on to the flames. It curled over on itself, like an autumnal leaf, then crumbled into ash.

Michael only half-caught the excuse Kellie made to Mr Thorne about having to fetch something from her room. Michael rose to follow her, but Taylor only gripped his wrist again. They listened to Kellie's footsteps echoing in the hall outside, and then they both heard what they'd expected: the sound of the back door open, then close.

'What did I tell you?' Taylor hissed as they rushed down the hall after her. '*And* she's a bloody lawyer. I bloody knew it.'

299

Taylor threw Michael his coat from the hall stand, then rifled through the other coats hanging there for her own. Putting it on, she pulled the door ajar and peered through the gap, before stepping outside.

At first, as Michael joined her and silently shut the door behind them, it looked to him as though, even now, Taylor might still be wrong. Kellie was twenty yards away from them, tramping along the south side of the house, crunching over half-buried flowerbeds and beneath the row of cast iron arches where roses blossomed in the spring. She continued on towards the driveway which would lead her up to the road and, from there, back to the village – whereas Elliot was at the top of the garden with the dog and his back to them all, as if unaware of either their or Kellie's existence. He was stationary, making a show of examining a beech tree which fanned out like a cobweb against the still white sky. The panes of glass in the long low greenhouse beside him sweated like so many car windscreens in a winter traffic jam.

Then Elliot moved. He reached the wooden fence at the top of the garden which, thanks to the snow which had drifted and settled there, now looked as if a great white wave had lapped up against it. He knelt down, letting Rufus off his lead, and the dog rushed on ahead, out of sight, barking, into the trees beyond. Three wood pigeons applauded themselves into flight. A buzzard wheeled across the sky in a perfect arc, like a paper kite taut on the end of a string.

'This way,' Taylor said, hurrying after Kellie the moment that Elliot disappeared into the trees. 'We need to keep as far away from Rufus as possible, or he'll sniff us out.'

She didn't seem to care if Michael followed her or not, but he was committed now, whichever she wanted. The thrill of the hunt flowed through him. All he could hear

300

was the *crump-crump-crump* of his boots in the snow. To him, it sounded out as loud as a drum.

'The further back we stay, the better,' he told her. 'I promise I won't let her give us the slip.'

Kellie stopped when she reached the end of the driveway and the beginning of the road. Michael and Taylor came to a halt, too, ducking in close beneath the low branches of a spruce. Snow showered them, slithering down Michael's spine through the gap between his collar and his neck. Taylor didn't even flinch.

They watched Kellie looking around, as if taking her bearings. Their prey then turned and stared. For a second Michael recoiled with horror as he thought she might have seen them, or might be about to turn back, in which case they'd be busted. Then she trudged on another ten yards along the road towards the village. And stopped. And waited.

One minute went past.

And then two.

And then Kellie confirmed why they were here. She doubled back on herself, walking swiftly past the end of the drive and on, up the footpath which wound towards the same woods into which Elliot had walked the dog only five minutes before.

Michael and Taylor followed.

The ground around them grew thick with hellebores and ferns. Thick knots of brambles and thickets of holly thrust up through the snow. Icicles hung from branches high up the trees. There was a scent in the air which Michael didn't recognise. It was heavy, pungent like a mushroom, but there was something bitter about it too which caught in his throat and made him want to gag.

They weren't hard to find: Kellie, Elliot and the dog. They were in the woods, halfway up the slope, guarded by a clump of oaks. Rufus was tied to a tree.

301

The dog's barks and whines, combined with the gentle breeze which rustled through the bushes and trees, provided Michael and Taylor with sporadic cover as they approached, but still they trod carefully, and slowly, too. The frozen leaves crunched beneath Michael's boots like spilt crisps on the pub floor. His muscles grew tight. He felt like he had the day before, when he'd been staring down from the cave at the beach below. It was adrenaline, the possibility of freefall. It was the scent of danger, sharpening his mind.

Twenty yards away from Taylor's dad and Kellie, Michael and Taylor switched from a crouch to a crawl, moving slowly forward on their hands and knees. Michael was the first to stop. The palms of his hands were livid from being pressed against the snow. His knees and ankles throbbed from the stabbing of sticks and stones.

Taylor must have been hurting, too, because she hunkered down beside him, in a jagged patch of ferns, the leaves rigid and webbed with translucent ice, like the fins of some exotic fish.

It was as if Michael and Taylor were frozen too, as they squatted there, listening. The dog barked, and snatches of conversation were relayed to them by the wind.

'I never wanted it to –' It was a woman's voice, Kellie's voice, raised, emotional, '– this wasn't the way –'

Then Taylor's dad was talking over her, they were talking over each other, and none of it made any sense.

Taylor began crawling forward, further into the ice sculpture of fern. Michael reached out to hold her back, but she pushed him away. She slithered away from him like a serpent, leaving an icy green tunnel in her wake.

'– you're not listening to what I'm saying –' It was Kellie again, louder than before.

The dog started its whining again and Elliot shouted at it to shut up. There was a yelp and the dog fell silent. Elliot was talking, softer now, more urgently, but Michael couldn't make out what it was he had to say. He edged to his right, pressing up against a fallen, rotting log. A trumpet of fungus rested against his face. Through the crisscross of foliage ahead of him, he saw Elliot and Kellie, as if through bars.

'– love –'

The word was unmistakable, but Michael wasn't sure who'd said it. Rufus barked, jumping now, jerking against the lead. He'd sensed something in the air. He knew something lay hidden nearby. If Elliot were to unleash him, he'd be on to them in a flash.

But Elliot and Kellie ignored the dog. Their faces were only inches apart. Both of them were talking again. Elliot was gesticulating with his hand, cutting her off, driving home whatever it was he had to say, like a lawyer in a court room movie, Michael thought. Elliot's words, shouted and impassioned, now hit Michael in rush.

'– and last summer, all those days, across that bay and back. Because I wanted to be with you. Because we love each other –' His voice faded momentarily, like the signal of Michael's radio in his room back home. Then it came back strong. 'Tomorrow. On the mainland. I'm telling Isabelle, her and Taylor . . . that I'm leaving them . . . that –'

A twig snapped. Rufus barked, suddenly rigid, his snout jutting out towards Michael and Taylor. Michael ducked down flat. Had they seen him? Or Taylor? Footsteps approached. Michael rolled so slowly on to his side that he felt his body creak like a branch. He rolled over again, deeper into the foliage, inch by inch.

A shaft of sunlight lanced down between the treetops, smiting his face. He saw Taylor's trainer, there in the bushes ahead of him and to his left, then his forearm, a knot of sinew and tendons. It was streaked with mud.

Michael kept dead still as a final footstep fell beside him. His back flexed rigid as he held his face off the ground and a glistening tongue of ivy lapped at his brow. He pictured steam rising off him as if from a hard-ridden horse. He refused to breathe out. He could feel Elliot behind him, so close that Michael knew that if he were to kick out now, he'd surely connect.

Michael closed his eyes.

Elliot and Kellie had been having an affair. This thought loomed even larger in Michael's mind than his fear of imminent discovery. *Elliot* was going to walk out on Isabelle and Taylor, so he could be with Kellie instead. Taylor's dad was planning on leaving her for good.

A gust of wind blew. The dog began to howl.

'There's nothing here,' Elliot called out.

His footsteps retreated. Michael breathed out. He let his head fall to the ground.

Then came a crackle of ice beside him and he saw Taylor. Her face was red all over, as if she'd swum through boiling water. She was slithering backwards, away from him. She didn't even look at him. He followed her back, away from Elliot . . . two yards . . . five . . .

And then ten.

She got to her feet behind the wide trunk of a sycamore, and then she ran, back towards the Thorne house. She ran like she didn't ever want to stop.

Michael caught up with her by the back door. She was panting, her face as pink as a stick of gum.

'I'm so sorry –' he began to say.

She kissed him, hard, pushing him up against the door. This time there was no mistaking what she meant, not like in the mine.

She spoke against his face. 'You'll help me,' she told him. 'You will. You're going to help me make this right.'

She kissed him harder still. Her lips were freezing

against his, her tongue wet and strong inside his mouth. He closed his eyes and felt her whole body flex against him, as if it was a single muscle. She ground her hips hard on his.

The door rattled behind them. Someone shouted. They moved aside and the door sprang open. Simon was standing there. Michael needed to sit. He slumped against the wall by the door.

'Where've you been?' Simon asked. 'I've been looking every—'

Michael and Taylor ignored him. They were staring at each other

'What's going on?' Simon asked again. 'What have you been doing? What's going on?'

'That woman,' Taylor said. 'She's been sleeping with my Dad. *Fucking* him. She's been fucking him behind my mother's back.'

'But –'

'Shut up, Simon,' Taylor said.

Simon looked wildly between them.

'I'm going to tell Mum,' he said. 'Right now. You'll see. And I'm going to –'

Taylor grabbed hold of him by both arms. 'You tell anyone,' she told him, 'and you're dead.'

Simon looked terrified, but he didn't move.

'What then?' Michael asked.

Taylor let go of Simon and pulled Michael to his feet. She gripped him so tightly he nearly cried out.

'We're going to deal with this ourselves,' she said.

As he looked into her eyes again, and again saw that burning fire, he knew he would do anything for her, anything at all.

Chapter 25

Kellie couldn't believe she was standing in a wood, in the freezing cold, having nearly died twice in the past three days. Well, perhaps it had taken a whack on her head to bring her to her senses. Kellie felt as if she was seeing Elliot Thorne for the first time – and to think that she had thought that, by today, she'd be about to spend every day of the rest of her life with him. It seemed almost laughable now. Her dream of being with Elliot had been like a house of cards – and from the second she'd agreed to take the trip with Ben, she'd started to put one too many cards on the stack. She'd believed that she and Elliot would work, that their love for each other would be triumphant, but when she'd met David last night, she'd felt the whole stack start to wobble. Then, when she'd woken up in Simon's bed this morning, they'd started to topple. And once she'd met Isabelle, her dream had collapsed spectacularly. Now, any vestige of hope that her relationship with Elliot could work had vanished.

She'd found out something that she'd never suspected. That Elliot Thorne was a lying, cheating bastard.

'No, Elliot,' she said.

'But –'

'I said no. I can't do this.'

'What? Kellie . . . darling . . .'

'This is just a game to you, isn't it?'

He looked flustered, panicked even. The dog started to howl. 'Fucking shut up!' Elliot yelled at it.

She stared at him. What was worse? That she'd fallen out of love with Elliot, or that she'd let herself down so badly? How had she been suckered in so readily? How had she allowed herself to fall for Elliot's charm? She'd managed to get herself from the other side of the world, into a top corporate job, and made herself a life in London. How had she then made such a whopping mistake? She thought back to what her friend Jane had said about Elliot fucking his cake and eating it. She'd denied it so furiously, ditching all her friends to be with Elliot, but Jane had been right. That was exactly what Elliot had done.

She shook her head. 'Elliot, I'm standing here in your wife's clothes.'

'I know. They suit you.'

Kellie stared at him. He was pathetic.

'No,' he said, misreading her, 'that's not what I meant. I meant that they look even *better* on you than they do on her.'

She let out a yelp of frustration. 'You don't get it do you? It's not about who looks best. Or maybe that's exactly what it *is* about to you. To me it's about being humiliated, Elliot. Because that's how I feel. Your family took me in, and all I've done is lie to them. And what was all that shit you pulled in front of your father?' She bitterly quoted his own words back at him: '*We'll probably find out that we've got absolutely stacks in common.* Did you think that was funny? Did it amuse you, having a good old snigger at your father behind his back? Do you have any idea how excruciating that was for *me*?'

She thought back to Gerald, to how kind he'd been, to the fact that she'd looked in his face and only been able to think how like her dream father-in-law he was, and what a lying fraud she was in return.

'He'd hate me so much if he knew why I was here,' she said. 'And Stephanie? Your *sister* tucked me up in bed like a child, for fuck's sake. Don't you see what position that puts me in?'

'They're just family. They don't matter.'

307

'They do. Don't you get it? I hate being the liar you've turned me into.'

'Darling, you're just getting upset, because you hit your head.'

He put his hands on her arms. She shook him off.

'Don't touch me.'

'Kellie, stop this. It's you I want. We've got something so special –'

'How can you say that? You lied. You can't stop yourself. You're even lying now. I've met your wife.'

'I'm not lying. I swear it. Isabelle. She . . . you don't know how hard it is. You think you're seeing her how she is, but she's not like that . . .'

'The joke is that I've been faithful to you,' she continued. 'All this time that you've been leading a double life. What kind of man gives his wife and his mistress the same necklace for Christmas? What did you do, Elliot? Get two for the price of one?'

Elliot stepped back from her. 'Oh, oh, I see. I know why you're doing this. It's because of him, isn't it? That Ben guy.'

'Don't you dare turn this around on me. There's nothing going on with me and Ben, you idiot.'

'So why is he behaving like there is?'

'I don't have to justify myself, or Ben, to you.'

But Elliot looked at her suspiciously. He suddenly tried a different tack. 'So I bet this was all some kind of plan of yours, to catch me out,' he said, nodding slowly, as if he'd cannily uncovered the truth.

'What?'

'Well, isn't it a bit odd that you got so drunk, you fell over, and the only doctor around was Stephanie? Did you make David and Ben bring you here in the middle of the night, when you knew I couldn't object?'

'You are not seriously suggesting that I did this

deliberately? Have you gone out of your fucking mind?'

Elliot stared at her. Then, to her amazement, he exhaled, as if she'd passed some kind of test.

'Then there's no reason for us not to be together. Come on,' he said, before untying the dog and starting to march down the hill towards the house. 'Christmas is over, and you're here now. Let's just sort this out. I'm going to tell Isabelle.'

Was he serious? She stared at him aghast, as he walked away from her. Did he really think . . .

He did.

'No, Elliot!' she shouted. Then she ran after him. 'I don't want you to.'

She pulled his arm and turned him around to face her.

'You're not listening to me,' she said. 'It's over.'

'But this is what you want,' he said.

'No. It's not. What I want is for you to stay with your wife.'

He looked at her, aghast. 'But what about us?'

'I'm not in love with you, Elliot. I'm not. Not any more.'

There. She'd said it. And now that she had, she realised how true it was. The man she'd been in love with was gone. The more she'd learnt about him this Christmas, the more she'd come to understand that he'd never really existed at all.

She shivered and folded her arms. Elliot stared at her for a long time. His arguments had all run out. He cleared his throat.

'Well, it seems that you've made up your mind,' he said. His face was hard. He stared at her like the subordinate she was. Had he been bluffing, she wondered, when he'd threatened to tell Isabelle just now? It didn't matter whether he had been or not. She'd had enough of Elliot keeping her guessing. She'd had enough of his games.

309

'I would appreciate it if you could leave my father's property now,' he said.

'Don't worry. I intend to.'

And she did. She wanted to get as far away as possible. She'd had a rollercoaster of a Christmas, but now, finally, she could get off this crazy ride. It was over. It was time to get out of these clothes, get off this island, and get back to who she was. Back to who she was before she'd got involved with Elliot bloody Thorne.

'Perhaps, as one final courtesy, you would agree not to tell Isabelle about us?'

'Just go back to them, Elliot.'

There was no goodbye. He glanced at her briefly then, calling the dog, strolled away, as if she was no more than a stranger he'd just met whilst walking in the woods.

She watched him go. She wondered whether he'd turn back, but he didn't. She realised that she had no idea how he was feeling. Would he have regrets? Or would he do what she suspected he'd do and pretend it had never happened at all?

A moment later, he'd disappeared through the trees. She waited for the onslaught of emotions she should feel after such an ignominious end to their affair, but all she felt was relief. She'd finished with Elliot, and she was safe. Nobody had found out about them. The whole, horrible, sordid affair was over.

She waited a moment more. Waiting to feel sad, but instead she was smiling. Suddenly, she was running as fast as she could back to the village.

Chapter 26

Ben was naked, wet and shivering from the shower he'd just taken, which had been cold, thanks to the power still being off. At least it had woken him up and washed his sleepless night out of his head. He was in the tiny bathroom next to the bedroom at the top of the stairs in the annexe. He wiped the steam from the bathroom mirror and stared at his reflection, which was split in two by a grubby, jagged crack running from top to bottom down the centre of the glass. It reminded him of the symbol used for theatre, the shield-shaped mask, divided in two, with one half happy and the other half sad.

One face, two people . . . was that what Ben now was, as well? That's certainly how it felt, because he didn't know whether to laugh or to frown from one minute to the next. Kellie had turned his head into a washing machine where his thoughts now spun round like clothes, tied up and knotted, overlapping and confused.

He was simultaneously happy and sad. He was happy she was still near, but sad that she'd soon be gone. He was happy that she liked him, but sad that she didn't like him enough. And he was happy that he'd found her, but sad that he'd lost her as well.

He knew, of course – not least from the counsellor he'd visited a few times in the wake of his discovery of Marie's affair with Danny – that happiness wasn't something you found in other people, but in yourself. He also knew, however, that it was Kellie who'd helped him rediscover his capacity for joy. She'd woken up feelings inside him which before had lain dormant, buried like seeds in the dirt. She'd been his springtime, his catalyst for growth. It was because of her that he now felt so alive.

He started humming 'Keep on Moving', as he shaved, because that's what he was going to do. He wasn't going back to the deadbeat, scruff-bag persona he'd adopted in the run-up to Christmas. Not ever again.

Kellie's rejection of him hurt, but he was determined to keep positive, no matter what, because what had happened these last few, insane days *was* positive. If he'd never made that decision to quit smoking and get *involved* with his life again, he'd never have asked Kellie to take a ride with him on the boat. And if he'd never done that, then he'd never have discovered what he now knew: that he still *did* have the wondrous ability to fall in love with someone who wasn't Marie – and to fall in love harder than he ever had done before.

He could still do it. He still had it in him. Life could still be an incredible place. This knowledge, this certainty, had given him a strength he'd previously lost. Kellie had ended his winter. Even without her, he'd go back to London and continue to grow.

He finished shaving and washed the stubble down the plug hole. He checked out his reflection and this time the whole of him smiled back. He was still a young man. He still had so much to give. He was grateful he'd realised it before it was no longer true.

Then he started. He'd heard the cottage front door open downstairs. Now it slammed shut.

'Ben?' Kellie shouted. 'Ben! Are you here?'

He grabbed his towel and wrapped it hurriedly round his waist.

'What?' he shouted, stepping out of the bathroom and on to the small landing.

His first thought was that something bad must have happened, another accident perhaps, but as Kellie stepped into view from under the stairs, from where she must have been looking for him in the kitchen, it immediately struck him that nothing looked wrong. Quite the opposite, she looked radiant, as if she'd just got back from a workout at the gym. The clothes she had on were fashionable and clean and made him stare. She was smiling, too, staring up the stairs at him. Then the smile faltered and faded, and was gone.

'What is it?' he asked. 'What's the matter?'

She advanced uncertainly up the stairs and stopped.

'You know that moment that always happens in romantic movies . . .' she said, '. . . when one person decides that they want to be with another person . . . only they don't know if that other person is interested in them, or how that other person is going to react when they find out . . .'

'Like in *As Good As It Gets*,' he said automatically, 'or *An Officer and a Gentleman*, or –'

She pushed her forefinger against his open mouth to silence him. 'Or any one of a thousand other movies,' she said. 'Well, this is that moment. This is that moment for me. I don't know if this is what you want,' she said, 'but I hope it is, because I know it's what *I* want.'

Then she stretched up on tiptoe and pushed her face close to his and kissed him softly on the lips.

He froze, eyes wide open. His lips refused to respond to the movement of hers. His arms and back seemed rigid. He stood there, passionless, unblinking, like a guard outside Buckingham Palace until, finally, Kellie pulled away.

'I think I've been wanting to do that since the moment I met you,' she said. 'It's just taken me this long to realise how much.'

He didn't know what he'd been expecting her to say, but it hadn't been this. How could he ever hope to work this

313

woman out, when each time he guessed heads she came up tails?

She closed her eyes and tried kissing him again, but again, he failed to respond. All he could do was stare. He might as well have been a bank clerk with a robber's gun pressed tight to his head. She stepped back.

'What is it?' she asked.

'I –'

She looked down at her shoes. 'It's OK,' she said, 'if you don't feel the same way. I thought you did, but I understand . . .'

'You . . .' No sooner had the word left his mouth, than he forgot what it was he'd been going to say.

'I've got no right to expect anything from you,' she told him, but even as she spoke she took his right hand between hers and squeezed it tight. 'I've messed you around and I'm so sorry, and now all I want to do is to let you know that –'

Finally, a logical question entered his head. 'What about him? The man, the man you said you were in love with . . .'

'I've told him it's over.'

'Over?' Ben wondered if he was dreaming. That's certainly how it was beginning to feel.

'I told him I didn't love him,' she told him, 'and I don't. Not any more. Because of you.'

Because of *me*? Ben thought. What did she mean? Did the fact that she'd fallen out of love with this other man mean she'd fallen for him instead?

'Where is he?' Ben asked. 'Did you call him at home?' He trailed off. What did it matter where he was, or how she'd managed to get hold of him? It only mattered that she'd broken it off. Her being here, wanting Ben the same way he wanted her, that was all he needed to know.

'There are things I've got to tell you, Ben. I've been such an idiot and I can't even begin to –'

314

'Don't,' he said. 'Not now.'

'But I need to. I want to.'

He kissed her and then they were twisting and turning, moving through to the bedroom. She pulled off her coat and jumper, and unbuttoned her shirt. Then she backed up against him and unfastened her bra. He pushed the straps down along her arms, cupping her breasts in his hands, slowly, instinctively, caressing them, as he gently kissed her neck. She pushed back hard against him, then twisted round to face him, continuing to kiss him as she ran her hands across his chest.

'You have no idea how much I want you,' she hissed into his ear.

As she kicked off her shoes, they both somehow lost their balance. They stumbled backwards, laughing, and collapsed on top of one another on the bed.

He stared down at her and smiled. 'So I guess this is my new technique for getting a girl, right?'

'What?'

'I strand her on an island, nearly kill her in a storm, and then hang about with her until she gets concussed in the middle of the night. Then, hey presto, look, she finally throws herself into my arms.'

'Maybe you should write a book about it,' she said, 'or even a film. You could call it –'

'Or I could just kiss you again.'

She swept her hair back from her face and grinned up at him. 'And make all my Christmases come at once . . .'

Pulling him gently down on her, she closed her eyes. They kissed again, lingeringly. The awkwardness, which had led them to stumble only a second before, now melted away. Their movements seemed to mesh. He savoured it all, from the touch of her lips and the rolling movement of her tongue, to the slow sensual patterns her fingertips and nails were tracing across his back.

315

He then began moving slowly down her body, brushing his lips across her neck and across the ridge of her collarbone. She arched her back as she pressed herself against him, and gripped his shoulders as he continued to kiss his way along the faint undulation of her ribs and the soft skin of her stomach. He slid slowly backwards off the bed and stood. She giggled as he dropped his towel and she shuffled half out of her jeans and knickers and he pulled them off and threw them behind him.

Then he knelt before her on the bed, stroking his hands across her thighs. Her fingers clawed through his hair, as she pulled him down. She began to gyrate herself slowly and rhythmically against him, then she began to moan.

As she shuddered against him and gripped him like a vice, he felt as if a great wave was washing over him, sweeping away all the old stress and the misery and the uncertainties from his life. None of that mattered any more. None of it. Only this. Only her. Only now, and what might happen next.

Chapter 27

Down at Green Bay harbour, the wind was cold, but the sky was clear. Kellie held on to Ben's arm as they walked with Jack towards the icy slipway. Jack had agreed to take Ben around the island to retrieve the broken boat. By tonight, Ben had promised Kellie, they'd be safely away from the island. She couldn't wait. She wanted to get away right now, but she knew she only had to be patient for a few more hours.

'Are you sure it's going to be safe?' Kellie checked again.

'I told you. The ice is melting. Nothing can go wrong.'

'He's rubbish with boats,' Jack said, nudging Ben and leaning forward to look at Kellie. 'There probably isn't anything wrong with it at all. It was all a ruse to spend Christmas with you.'

'Oh really?' Kellie said, knowing he was teasing her. She liked it. She liked feeling included like this. She liked the feeling that other people accepted her and Ben together.

Ben rolled his eyes. 'We'll have it fixed and back here in no time.'

Kellie smiled. 'OK, but don't be long.'

They'd all come to a stop at the top of the slipway.

'Can I have a few seconds?' Ben said to Jack. 'In private.'

'Sure,' Jack said with a smirk, slipping his arm around Ben and winking at Kellie, 'but won't Kellie get lonely?'

'Very funny.'

'You don't know what you're missing,' Jack said, feigning rejection. 'I'm a great kisser and an even better cook. See you later, love,' he told Kellie, before hauling his tool kit over his shoulder and treading carefully down to his dinghy which was bobbing in the murky harbour water below.

'My guess is you're a much better kisser,' she told Ben and, as if to prove it, she kissed him gently on the lips.

Had she meant things to go so far with Ben so fast? She didn't know, but it didn't matter. It had felt wonderful. It still did.

'You know what I said earlier . . . about needing to tell you something . . . about –'

'There's no rush,' he interrupted her. 'There's a time and place for everything.' He looked around them at the empty windswept village. 'And this is neither.'

'But –'

'Maybe later. Once we're back in Fleet Town.'

'That'll be the last thing on my mind when you get me back there . . .'

'Come on,' Jack shouted.

'Seriously,' she said. 'We *will* be able to talk about all this, won't we?'

'There's nothing we won't be able to talk about,' he said and he kissed her again.

She knew she had to tell him about Elliot. She knew more than ever that she had to come clean. There was no way she could continue even knowing Ben, let alone have any kind of relationship with him, let alone the one she hardly dared hope she might have, if he didn't know the truth. She had to tell him why she'd come to the island in the first place, and admit the dreadful mistake she'd made in trusting Elliot.

Would Ben hate her for deceiving him? Would he be horrified that she'd got tangled up with Elliot? Not if she could explain properly, surely? Not if this afternoon meant as much to Ben as it did to her. And not if, as she

318

planned to, she could tell him more about how she felt about him.

She wanted to tell Ben that he was wonderful. That he was more than wonderful. That this felt right. And that most of all, it felt deliciously, excitingly, fabulously *real*.

'Look, take this torch,' Ben said, pulling one out from his pocket, 'and get some batteries from the pub. It'll be dark in a bit, and if the power's still out and I'm not back, you might need it.'

'Just hurry back. Are you sure I can't come with you?'

'No. You've had enough excitement for one day.' He raised his eyebrows at her and she blushed and then laughed. 'Seriously. Just stay here and don't go anywhere until I get back.'

'But I'm going to drop these clothes off for Isabelle,' she said, nodding to the carrier bag at her feet. 'Then I promise, I'll wait for you back at the pub.'

She didn't know how to leave it. She wanted to hold on to him and kiss him.

'OK. See you,' he said.

'See you.'

Ben walked away from her down the slipway. Then suddenly, he stopped and turned and leapt back up the ramp to kiss her again.

'Be good,' he said, holding her as if he couldn't bear to rip himself away.

'I will.'

Kellie squeezed her lips together as he walked down towards the boat, a smile spilling on to her face. She wanted to patter her feet like an excited little girl.

No wonder it was called Boxing Day, she thought, waving to Ben as the boat chugged out into the harbour. She felt as if she'd had several rounds in the ring already, but after this afternoon with Ben it was as if she'd won the championship.

319

She wanted to put everything on pause and pinch herself, just to make sure she wasn't dreaming this. It seemed almost impossible that she'd finished with Elliot and committed herself to Ben, all within an hour. But then, if she was being honest, she'd fancied the pants off Ben since he'd brought her here.

She watched as the dinghy rounded the harbour wall and disappeared out of sight. Then she sighed happily to herself and yawned.

She set off up the road. Her plan was to leave the bag containing Isabelle's clothes by the front door of Gerald's house. She'd already written a short note thanking Isabelle and Stephanie, which she'd left inside. If she ran up to the door and back to the road, she wouldn't see anyone and wouldn't have to answer any questions. It would be the last time she'd ever need go near the Thornes' again.

The bag seemed heavy in her hand, as if it was laden with her guilt, along with her ex-lover's wife's clothes. The sooner they were returned, the better she'd feel. The sooner she'd start to feel like herself again, like the honest, caring, decent person she knew she was. At least all the ridiculous subterfuge with Elliot was over for good, she comforted herself, and it was over without anyone getting hurt. All she wanted to do was put the whole, sordid episode behind her and move on. She already knew that the first thing she was going to do when she got back to London was to quit her job, and then move out of the flat. There was no way she could go back to working with Elliot, or have anything to do with him.

She knew it was going to be tough. She would have to find somewhere else to live and she'd have to think of a plausible enough excuse to leave WDG & Partners, without jeopardising her references. Would Elliot stand in her way, she wondered?

She couldn't imagine where she could possibly be this

time next year. Would she be working for another law firm, maybe the one who'd head-hunted her a few months ago? Or would she be doing something else entirely? For so long, her career had been mapped out that it made her feel strangely light and buoyant to have no plans.

Who knew what the future held? She certainly couldn't have predicted a week ago that she'd be in this situation, or feeling the way she did. Now she'd seen for herself how unpredictable things could be, and she was just going to let the future happen. All this time, she'd been waiting and waiting for Elliot to make a decision – she'd given him all the power over her life and in doing so had lost sight of what she really wanted – but meeting Ben had blasted open a world full of possibilities.

And what about Ben? Would he want to make plans with her? It seemed to her that they were suddenly in the same situation. Could this be an opportunity to build a future together in London? Would he let her stay with him, was it crazy to assume so much, so soon? Perhaps it would be better to see if she could patch things up with Jane, and ask if she could stay with her for a couple of weeks, just until she'd found her own place.

She was nearing the house now. She could see the lights on in the windows and her heart started beating fast. She imagined Elliot inside with Isabelle, and felt so glad that nobody was any the wiser about what had happened between them. She liked Elliot's family. She respected them. How dare Elliot be so dismissive about them? He had no idea how lucky he was. He had no idea about anything at all, she reminded herself. Thank God she was out of it. And thank God for Ben. She sprinted for the front door, careful not to slip on the ice.

Twenty minutes later, Kellie allowed herself to draw breath. She'd made it. She'd delivered the clothes without

321

anyone seeing her, and now the house was far behind her. Smiling to herself, she turned down the road going back towards the annexe.

It was only then that she heard someone calling her name. She turned to see Michael running down from the brow of the hill.

At first, she couldn't think why he could possibly want her, but as he ran up to her, she started to worry.

He was panting, trying to catch his breath. 'Quickly! There's been an accident,' he said.

Kellie's heart jolted. Despite herself, her first thought was of Elliot. He hadn't done something stupid had he? Her mind started racing.

'What? What's happened?'

'In the mine,' Michael said. 'Simon. He's stuck.'

'What mine? Simon? I . . . I don't understand,' she said. She looked around for help, but they were the only people on the road.

'Come on,' Michael said, starting to run back.

Did he really expect her to follow, Kellie wondered. 'Michael? Michael?' She called after him. 'Stop. Wait. We should get your parents. Or Simon's parents.'

'Now!' he shouted back over his shoulder. 'There's no time. It's just over here.'

This was ridiculous. And crazy. What could she possibly do to help? But the genuine panic in Michael's face frightened her. What if something really bad had happened? She thought of Stephanie this morning and how kind she'd been and pictured her quiet little boy.

She looked back at the harbour, remembering her promise to Ben that she would be good. She mustn't get involved again with the Thorne family. It was too dangerous. She had other priorities now.

'Come on!' Michael shouted.

'OK, OK, I'm coming,' she said, promising herself that

322

she would see if she could help and then come straight back.

By the time they reached the mine ten minutes later, Kellie was feeling sick. She stopped and flopped forward, trying to catch her breath. She was splattered in mud from trailing after him through the dank, slushy puddles where the ice had already started to thaw. She was furious that Michael hadn't stopped when she'd repeatedly asked him to, but by now she was convinced that whatever had happened to Simon must be very serious. She was terrified that they'd be too late, which was why she'd run after him until her pulse was pounding in her throat. As he scrambled down a slope ahead of her, fear gripped her racing heart.

They were in a small canyon. The wind howled through it.

'This way,' Michael said. Where the hell was he going? She could only see the top half of him now, as he traced his way through sodden scrub.

'Michael. Stop. Wait!'

She followed him, pushing through the bushes, flinching as soaking wet lumps of slushy snow soaked her jeans. Then, out of nowhere, a tunnel entrance appeared. Michael ran on and disappeared inside. She followed.

As she stepped into the darkness, adrenaline coursed through her body. In here the sound of the wind vanished, as if the outside world had been switched off. The air was freezing. She felt as if she'd been swallowed by the cliff. Her mouth filled with saliva in the stagnant air.

This place was horrible.

There was something else, too. Something wrong about all this. She felt goosebumps prickle all over her body.

'Michael,' she said. 'Where are you?' Her voice sounded strange. She couldn't see where he'd gone as her eyes tried to adjust to the gloom.

Then Michael was back with Simon, holding Simon's arm.

'But you're OK!' Kellie said to the boy. He didn't look at her. She didn't understand.

'What the hell is going on?' Even as she said it, she already knew that her instincts had been right. Something was very wrong indeed. Then Michael pushed her hard and she fell. He ran for the tunnel entrance, dragging Simon after him.

'Wait,' Kellie shouted, scrambling to her feet, but it was too late. They were too fast for her.

She heard something clank shut up ahead, and she arrived just in time to see Taylor snapping the padlock shut on a closed gate.

'What the hell are you doing?' Kellie shouted, shaking the grille, like a caged animal, but Taylor, Michael and Simon were already backing away from her.

Simon looked terrified.

'Taylor?' Kellie yelled. 'Stop!'

Taylor stared back, calm and cold.

'You need to be taught a lesson,' she said.

'What? I don't understand.'

'Don't lie.'

Kellie was terrified by the look on Taylor's face.

'I'm not lying. Why are you doing this? Let me out. Now. Please. This isn't funny.'

'It's not meant to be funny. The same as you having an affair with my dad isn't funny.'

Kellie felt as if cold blood was plummeting down to her feet. She couldn't believe what she was hearing. How could Taylor possibly know? A thought hit her: had Elliot gone through with his original threat, after all? Had he gone back to the house and confessed all? To everyone? Was that why Taylor and Michael had lured her here?

'What?' Taylor said. 'You thought no one else knew?

You're not as clever as you think. We saw you . . . meeting him . . . down on the quayside yesterday . . .'

Taylor's expression, there by the harbour, burst back into Kellie's mind. The concentrated hatred in her eyes . . .

'And today . . . up in the woods . . . meeting him again . . . talking about last summer in Italy . . . and how much you're both in love, you dirty fucking whore.'

'But you're wrong. If you were there,' Kellie said, her heart racing, 'then you'd have heard that –'

'I've heard enough!' Taylor shouted. 'You've fucking said enough!'

'But I told him it was over. I told him –'

'You're a liar! You're a fucking liar! You've lied to everyone. You even lied to my grandpa, about the name of the law firm where you work. Oh, yes, I've worked that out as well. Because you work with him, don't you? You work with my fucking dad.'

'Yes, but –'

'Well let me tell you something. You may think you're something special, but you're not. He's never going to leave us for you. Not now my mum is having a baby.'

Kellie felt as if she'd been hit. Isabelle was having a baby? Elliot's baby? And he'd known all along? Had he ever intended to tell her? Not that it mattered now.

'Taylor. Listen to me. You've got it all wrong . . .'

'Let her go, Taylor.'

It was Simon. He was crying.

'No. Not until she's learnt her lesson.'

'But she has, Taylor. She has,' Simon implored. 'Mum and dad are going to kill us.'

'No, they're not. Because no one's going to tell them.'

'But *she* will,' Simon wailed.

'No, she won't. Because then she'll have to tell them why we did it. Isn't that right, you stupid bitch?'

'Just let me out. I can explain everything. I won't say a

325

word. I promise. I'll get right away from here and never come back.'

'I'll let you out when I'm ready. *If* I'm ready. And until then,' Taylor said, gripping Simon by the coat collar and turning him away, 'you can stay there and rot.'

'Taylor! Taylor!' Kellie shouted, as Taylor, Michael and Simon scrambled away. 'Jesus Christ! Taylor!' she shrieked, 'Ben will be back. He'll know I'm missing.'

But they'd gone and Kellie's pleas were lost on the wind. She took a deep breath. They'll come back, she thought. They were just kids, trying to scare her. They wouldn't really leave her here, would they? Would they?

But she already knew the answer. She knew how determined Taylor was and exactly where that determination came from.

'Shit. Shit. Shit!' she shouted, shaking the grille as hard as she could. Then she noticed it, through the branches of the trees and bushes which surrounded the entrance to the cave: it had started to snow again.

Chapter 28

Nat's tiny finger squeaked on the glass, as she drew lines on the steamed-up kitchen window. They looked like bars. How appropriate, Stephanie thought, because since the snow had started, the house had felt more like a prison than ever. And worse, there was no way she'd be able to leave today in this.

She hated Boxing Day. She had ever since she was a kid. It was the day when everyone felt hungover and stuffed full of too-rich food, when the best television had already been shown. And this year was setting a new standard in terrible Boxing Days. Stephanie knew she was responsible for causing most of the bad atmosphere, but she didn't know what to do to make it better. She'd considered trying to smooth things over with Isabelle, but the moment hadn't presented itself and she'd lost heart. She should be happy about the baby, that Isabelle and Elliot were having another chance after all this time, but she knew that anything she said now would just sound like a false platitude.

And she ought to be glad that David was back, but he was in the worst mood that she'd ever seen him in, and she wished he'd stayed at the pub. He'd hardly said two words to her since he'd arrived in the middle of the night and had slurringly asked her to help Kellie. It had been tense and awkward, not helped by the fact that David was trying to pretend that he wasn't drunk and by the fact that she was only half sober herself.

At first, she'd been annoyed that he'd brought home random strangers, but then she'd recognised Ben and had busied herself dressing Kellie's head. Her father had insisted that Kellie should stay and that Stephanie should keep an eye on her. And so, when Simon had got up to see what all the fuss was about, Stephanie had suggested that Kellie sleep in his room, and had later taken Simon to bed with her. She had no idea where David had slept, but she assumed it must have been on the sofa.

'Ah, that should do it,' Gerald said, moving away from the stove, where a huge vat of liquid was bubbling on the hob. He wiped his hands on his apron, which had the torso of a voluptuous woman in a bikini pictured on it. A blob of tomato puree adorned her belly, like a stab wound.

Stephanie looked at the debris all over the table and units. It was the same every year, this ridiculous Boxing Day ritual he went through: in an uncharacteristic flurry of culinary activity, her father boiled up the turkey carcass to make turkey broth, which he then froze in little Tupperware pots. It smelt disgusting.

The effort involved was by no means commensurate with the taste of the rather salty weak soup, but her father insisted on its nutritional and healing qualities, serving it up whenever anyone in the family felt ill.

It had taken a great deal of will power on Stephanie's behalf not to point out to him that if he'd only spread out the effort he made in the kitchen over the whole year, instead of exhausting himself on Boxing Day, he might have a much better diet.

He tapped the top of the new bread-baking machine and looked at his watch, satisfied. Apparently, there was sun-dried-tomato focaccia in the offing too. Stephanie didn't have the heart to tell him the fancy loaves he'd made so far with the machine had been almost inedible. After yesterday, she'd forfeited the right to make any kind of negative comments to anyone. Her father was still upset by what had happened and was trying his best to chivvy her along, but Stephanie knew that this was all too much for him, that he wasn't used to dealing with emotional situations. She felt duty-bound not to stamp on his fragile efforts, or comment on the fact that the longer she spent in his company, the more odd and eccentric he seemed

She smiled weakly. 'Smells great, Dad,' she said.

'I thought I might clean this lot up and then make a start on unpacking those boxes in the studio. What do you say? Why don't you give me a hand? Nat, why don't you come too?'

'OK,' Stephanie said, too exhausted to argue.

'Hello, Uncle Elliot,' Nat said, as Elliot came into the kitchen, carrying a folded newspaper. He looked dishevelled and angry as he opened and shut all the cupboards.

'Hi, sweetie-pie,' he said, but the usual affection in his voice was missing. Stephanie supposed that he must be feeling tired too.

She saw Elliot tuck a bottle of whisky under the newspaper. He caught Stephanie's eye.

'What?' he said.

'Nothing,' she replied. 'Aren't you starting rather early?'

'What's it to you?'

Stephanie realised her father was watching her. She knew she couldn't start another argument with Elliot.

'I'll be in the dining room, if anyone wants me,' Elliot said.

'Would you like a bowl of turkey broth?' her father asked.

'You know I hate that bloody awful stuff, Dad.'

'Well, you don't have to be so rude. I'm going up to give some to Kellie. I'm sure she'll like it.'

'She's not here,' Elliot said, bluntly. 'She's gone back to the village. She went ages ago.'

'Well, no one told me,' Stephanie said. She was rather offended that Kellie hadn't said goodbye. It had been a couple of hours, she realised, since she'd last seen her. She'd assumed that she was upstairs having a bath and relaxing, but apparently, she'd sneaked off – but then she must be embarrassed, Stephanie thought. It must be horrible waking up in a strange house with a hangover. Still, it was odd that she had slipped out without even thanking Gerald for putting her up for the night.

'Oh, dear,' her father said, clearly disappointed. 'I suppose she wanted to get back to Ben.'

They both watched Elliot walk out without saying anything more.

Stephanie bit her lip. 'He's not in a great mood, is he?'

'I don't think anyone is,' her father replied. 'Now, give me a hand, would you?'

I'm sorry, she wanted to say, but she didn't. She couldn't. She didn't know quite what she should apologise for. For bringing her misery into her father's Christmas, perhaps? Or for causing a scene? His tone made it perfectly clear that the only way she could make amends was by not causing any more trouble. As she cleared up the kitchen, she felt like a teenager again.

Upstairs in her father's studio, it was cold, so Nat went downstairs to find a jumper to wear over the sparkly Barbie princess dress she had yet to take off.

'Might as well start with this box,' her father said to Stephanie, after he'd turned on the lights. 'Just see if there's anything you want to keep. I'm on for doing a big clear-out. It's mostly old photos.'

Stephanie opened the box. It was full of pictures of her wedding and of the kids when they were little. She sighed. 'I know what you're trying to do, Dad,'

He shrugged and tried to look innocent. 'I just thought you'd want to look. If you want to just throw them all away . . .'

330

She put her hand on the box. 'I told you last night, my mind is made up.'

'I know, but I just thought . . . well, . . . the thing is . . .' he paused and stepped towards her. 'I want to tell you something.'

'What?' She felt exhausted. Was he going to launch into a lecture about the sanctity of marriage?

'You see, I've been waiting for the right moment. And I wanted to say something yesterday, but . . .' He looked at her and looked away again quickly.

Here it comes, thought Stephanie, folding her arms like a child receiving a talking to.

'It's just that I've been seeing someone. Here.'

Stephanie didn't move. She stared at him open-mouthed. These were just about the last words she'd ever imagined him saying.

'What do you mean? Seeing someone?' she managed, eventually.

Gerald took a deep breath. 'I haven't told the others yet. I wanted to tell you first.'

Stephanie felt her knee trembling. She wished it would stop. How could this be happening? How could he be telling her this now?

'Is it serious?' she asked.

'Fairly serious. She's called Tina Belling. She moved into the Steadmans' old cottage last year, and . . . well, she likes the same things that I do and . . .'

Stephanie hardly heard what he was saying. There was a woman here that her father had been seeing? What did that mean? She had no idea how to process the information he was telling her.

'Her family is here for Christmas. Her daughter Toni and her grandson Oliver. I haven't met them yet, but I thought that I'd invite Tina over tomorrow for a drink. If it's OK with you. Only now that David is back, I thought –'

331

At the mention of David's name, Stephanie snapped back into focus with what he was saying. So this big confession was all so that her father could present a loving, happy family? He thought that Stephanie and David and Elliot and Isabelle would make him look good. The doctor and the lawyer. Happily married. That's what he thought. She could see it in his eyes.

Had he no idea what she'd just been through?

She wiped her hands over her mouth. She felt like such a fool. Now that he said it, it was so bloody obvious. All the clues had been there and she'd missed them. She thought about how well he looked, how he'd disappeared with the dog – when they'd first arrived and again after lunch yesterday. She hadn't given it a second thought, but now she wondered whether he'd been keeping secret assignations behind everyone's back. Had he gone to meet this Tina person, to let off steam about his own family? Is that why he'd been so rational and understanding towards her last night? Had he consulted Tina about it?

And this morning – he had stuck by her side. She could tell now that he'd been on tenterhooks wanting to tell her this.

'Well, Dad, um . . .'

She ran out of words. She'd thought he was her rock. But he wasn't. He belonged to someone else.

'You'll like her,' Gerald appealed to her.

She thought back to how he'd been this Christmas. How content he seemed. How strong. Had Tina done that? Is that why he'd moved here permanently? To be near her? And all this time she'd been worrying about him . . .

Stephanie suddenly felt as if the world had turned up-side down without her noticing. Everything was different. Everything she'd assumed about the way her family would always be had just been ripped away from her.

She tried to conjure up a memory of her mother to help her, but she could only see her father standing in front of her like a nervous teenager. He was wringing his hands.

'I want you to be happy for me, Steph.'

Stephanie didn't know whether to cry, or slap his face, or both, but she forced herself to do neither. For the first time in her life, she recognised that her father needed to stop being a parent for a moment and for her to be an adult. Against every instinct inside her to run away, she took a step towards him and hugged him.

'I guess Mum would have wanted this,' she whispered, a tear spilling down her cheek. 'She wouldn't have wanted you to be lonely.'

'You can meet Tina. You can see for yourself,' he said. She felt his body relax in her embrace. Stephanie forced herself to swallow her tears as she stepped away.

Then behind her, the door opened.

'Ah, David. Come in, come in,' Gerald said, as if he hadn't just dropped a bombshell, as if everything was completely normal – and Stephanie saw now that it was for him. This was *his* world. 'We were just talking . . .'

David cleared his throat. He didn't move. Stephanie wondered for a second whether her father had stage-managed this in order to get them to talk.

'Ben's downstairs,' he said, immediately dispelling any doubts in Stephanie's mind about her father's involvement. His tone was hard. Detached. As if he didn't want to be anywhere near Stephanie or her father. 'He says Kellie went to see him this afternoon, then he went to get his boat, but when he got back, she wasn't there. He's worried about her and thinks she might have called back here.'

'No, we haven't seen her,' Gerald said.

Stephanie walked past David into the corridor and he jerked away so that she wouldn't touch him. It felt unbearable being this close to him. It was as if they both repelled each other like the opposite ends of magnets.

Stephanie went down the stairs ahead of him.

'I was merely asking you whether you'd seen her. I'm capable of sorting this out myself, Stephanie,' he said.

She thought about the photographs she'd held in her hands only a few moments ago. Could those really be pictures of her and David? How could two people so happy and together end up like this?

'I should look for her, or at least find out what's happened,' Stephanie said. 'She's my patient. If anyone needs to find her, it's me. She's had a nasty bump on her head. She could have fainted or fallen down.'

'Well, perhaps you shouldn't have let her leave so soon.'

'And perhaps *you* should be taking care of your new friends, David. Since you obviously enjoyed such a heart to heart with them last night, I'm surprised you haven't been with them asking for more advice.' It still annoyed her that he'd so obviously told Kellie and Ben all about their problems. How else would Kellie know so much about her and her family?

She regretted it the moment she'd said it – not because it wasn't true, but because all the comment would do was further fuel David's resentment, and thereby lengthen this conversation. She had no more words left to give him. She'd said all she could say to him yesterday. Before he could answer, she hurried down the stairs.

Isabelle was talking to Ben in the hallway.

'I found this carrier bag by the front door with my clothes in it,' Isabelle was saying. 'She left a note, thanking us.' She looked up at Stephanie.

'Well, I wish she'd listened to me,' Stephanie said. 'She should be resting. Hello, Ben.'

'Hi, Stephanie,' Ben said. 'I've looked everywhere else.

334

She said she was going to bring Isabelle's clothes, then she'd wait at the pub, but she hasn't been back there. I really thought she'd be here.'

'I have no idea where she could be,' Stephanie said. There was something odd about this. She could feel it.

'But she can't have just disappeared. People don't just vanish.'

'Don't worry,' David said, coming down the stairs. 'She'll turn up.'

'I don't understand it. We're meant to be going back tonight. That's why I went to get the boat.'

'I thought you might. I was going to ask you whether you'd take me with you,' David said.

He didn't look at Stephanie. She'd been planning on asking Ben to take her and the kids back to the mainland, but if David was prepared to bail out first, then so much the better. This was, after all, her family home and not his. She thought about what her father had just told her. She couldn't leave now, even if she'd wanted to.

'I'm not going anywhere on the boat in this,' Ben said. 'It's horrible out there. That's why I'm so worried about Kellie.'

In the dining room, Stephanie saw that Elliot was reading a newspaper, alone by the fire. He seemed unaware of the commotion.

'Have you seen Kellie anywhere?' Stephanie called through the door.

'Not since I went to walk the dog,' he said, from behind the paper, rustling it to signal his displeasure at being disturbed.

In the television room, Michael and Taylor were watching a film. Taylor didn't look at her, but stared straight ahead at the screen. Stephanie recognised that it was *Finding Nemo*, the bit where Nemo was trying to escape the fish tank in the dentist's waiting room.

335

'Have you seen Kellie?' Stephanie asked.

'No,' Taylor said, not even glancing at her. 'Why would we have?'

'Michael?' Stephanie asked.

He shrugged, his eyes darting away from hers back to the screen.

She walked back into the hall. 'No luck, I'm afraid. You're welcome to look around, but I really don't think she's here.'

'Why don't you stay?' Isabelle suggested to Ben. 'Wait until the snow has stopped.'

'No, I should keep looking.'

'Simon?' Stephanie called. 'Nat?'

Nat appeared at the top of the stairs with Gerald.

'Where's Simon?' Stephanie asked.

'I don't know,' Gerald said. 'I thought he was down there.'

Stephanie realised she hadn't seen him for a few hours.

'I'll go and look upstairs,' David said, throwing Stephanie a look which clearly meant that he thought she should have been keeping an eye on Simon, too.

She opened the door of the television room again, feeling flushed and guilty. Michael sat down suddenly on the sofa and folded his arms. His cheeks were red. Taylor continued to stare at the screen and ignore Stephanie.

'Where's Simon?' she asked them both.

They were up to something. She knew it.

'What? Lost him too, have you?' Taylor said.

Stephanie had had enough. She marched over and switched off the television.

'What's going on?' she demanded. 'Where's Simon?'

'We don't know,' Michael said. His voice sounded strange.

'Well bloody well find him,' Stephanie said.

Suddenly, she felt her heart start to race. Where could

Simon be? Why was everyone behaving so strangely? Was she the only one who was worried?

Back in the hall, Stephanie met David at the bottom of the stairs.

'He's not here,' David said.

It was the first time that Stephanie had held eye contact with him since their fight yesterday. Now as their eyes connected, her heart jolted with fear.

Chapter 29

'There *has* to be a way,' Kellie said, out loud, yet again, but she knew that she was starting to sound hysterical.

It had been an hour since Taylor, Michael and Simon had left and the storm had got worse and worse. Now it was dark.

She held the torch that Ben had given her with one hand and tried to use a small rock she'd found to smash the gate near where the padlock had it bracketed to the wall. It still wasn't budging, however, and she was getting weaker with the cold. She staggered backwards, away from the flurry of snow which blasted through the grille and sat against the wall, near to some shattered glass.

Think, she told herself. She had to think.

She'd worked out by now that Taylor and Michael weren't coming back. Even if they'd wanted to, the snow-storm was probably too bad.

What were they doing? she wondered. Were they sitting in Mr Thorne's house pretending that nothing was wrong?

The thought made her want to scream. How dare they behave so irresponsibly. Didn't they realise that she could die of exposure out here? She thanked God for her hooded Spiewak jacket, for being back in her own clothes, not Sally's or Isabelle's.

Then Kellie thought back to the way Taylor had looked at her. She wasn't going to crack. She wasn't going to tell anyone what she'd done, because she believed she was right. She believed that Kellie should be punished.

How bloody ironic, Kellie thought. Just when she'd realised that she didn't want Elliot after all, and that she didn't want to mess up his family and that neither, probably, did he, his psycho daughter decided to take matters into her own hands. To think that Kellie had actually believed, only a few days ago, that she and Taylor would one day be friends.

'Aaagh!' she said out loud. Why, oh why had she been such a bloody fool? How could this have happened?

There had to be a way through this. Somebody had to come and rescue her. Ben must have realised she was missing by now.

Or would he? Another thought had occurred to her. What if Taylor had got to Ben and told him a pack of lies? What then? What if she'd managed to convince him that Kellie was safe? Because she might have, mightn't she? In just the same way she'd made a complete fool of Kellie and tricked her into coming here.

Kellie wished now that it had all been different. She wished she'd followed her gut instinct and had insisted on telling Ben about Elliot before anything had happened between them. Because now, if Taylor had miraculously told the truth and confessed what she'd done and why, then Ben would hate Kellie anyway. He would have found out that she'd lied about Elliot, and surely that would invalidate everything that had happened between them?

That was the worst case scenario, surely? But then something else occurred to her too. What if Ben had got stuck in the snowstorm in the boat? What if he was in trouble himself? What if something had happened to him?

Genuine fear gripped her again, but she forced the bad thoughts away. She was going to survive this, she told herself, and the only way to do that was to escape. She had to get out. And soon. She knew now for certain that she couldn't spend the night here. If she did, she'd be lucky to survive. She took a look around her.

This place must be a mine of some sort, because that's

what Michael had called out to her when he'd first raised the false alarm. He'd said that Simon was stuck in the mine – but this didn't look like a mine shaft to her. Didn't they go down vertically? Not that she'd ever been in one, and the only ones she'd ever studied at school had been opal, not tin. Well, one thing was for sure, she thought, shining the torch inside, it had to lead somewhere, and anywhere was better than here.

She remembered what Ben had said about men tunnelling deep beneath the island. What if she fell? What if she tumbled down a shaft so deep nobody would ever find her? She looked into the darkness and felt terrified.

On the other hand, she thought, forcing herself to take the opposite perspective, what if there was an exit just around the corner? What if there was an easy way out? What if she was helplessly panicking, and froze to death here just because she was too afraid to move?

She shone the weak torch beam into the tunnel. It was swallowed up in the darkness. If she was to go down there, would she be swallowed up too?

She looked back through the grille. No one was coming. She knew that for sure. She would just have to be brave. She had to think about the positives. She had her big coat to keep her warm, she had a torch and she had music. Warmth, light, music. What was there to be scared of, then?

She felt into her pocket pulled out her iPod and put in the earpieces. Music. That was going to help the most – but her hands were shaking as she selected her play list. How typical that she'd deleted the Batman movie soundtrack. She felt like a bat, rustling around on her own in the dark. If only there was a red emergency phone on the wall and a Batmobile.

'It Must be Love' was the first track. It gave her confidence. It brought back all that was normal in the world, as she set off into the darkness. Where there's a will, there's a way out, she told herself.

She was determined. She was going to get out of here and back to Ben.

Ben. It was all she wanted. To see Ben again. To make everything right between them.

Ahead of her the tunnel became narrower. She held the torch in her mouth, and it wavered around as she felt her way with both hands. The walls were slippery and freezing cold.

For a second, she closed her eyes and said a silent prayer. Are you listening, God? she thought. *Because I just want to get out of here alive.* How odd, she thought, that she'd finally got religious at Christmas time.

Where was this tunnel going to lead her to? She had to find out. She shuffled forwards into the darkness, her heart pounding with fear.

And then her foot slipped.

Chapter 30

Michael's throat was parched. His skin itched from where his sweat had dried all over his body.

'What are we going to do?' he asked Taylor.

'Shut up.'

'But –'

'Don't say a fucking word.' She spoke through gritted teeth. 'Not a fucking word, or they'll hear.'

The sound of footsteps hurried down the hallway towards them. 'Simon?' a man's voice shouted.

Outside the Thorne house, the storm raged. The TV room's windows were like portholes on a ship tossed at sea: the light they threw off showed up flashes of movement and snow in an otherwise dark and dangerous world. Michael thought of Kellie, out there alone, trapped behind that metal grille. What had happened – what they'd *done* to her – he wanted to undo it all. He wanted to make it not so. It was all too real, too grown-up. He didn't want to be a grown-up, not any more.

'Move.'

Taylor pushed him backwards, away from her, towards the door.

'Hi, Uncle David,' she then said with an innocent smile, as David appeared in the doorway.

'Have either of you seen –'

'Simon?' Taylor interrupted. 'No. Aunty Stephanie just asked us. Not for a while, but we're coming to help you look.'

'I'm going to check the garage,' David said.

'Good idea. We'll search upstairs. We were playing

sardines up there yesterday. Simon's probably just hiding, you know.'

'I know,' David said. There was a forced calmness to his voice, which his eyes betrayed. 'But let's just find him quickly, eh?'

Taylor trotted up the stairs ahead of Michael.

'We need to talk,' Michael hissed at her, as they reached the landing.

'Find Simon first. If he's hiding, then he's doing it because he's freaked out – and if he's freaking out, then he's probably going to blow it for us all. We need to get hold of him, before he starts blubbing and grasses us up. You go that way,' she said, pointing down the corridor to the right, 'and I'll go this. Check all the wardrobes and under the beds.'

They separated and searched the rooms. Michael didn't think he had the energy for it – not after the cold sweat and silence of the last two hours, since they'd abandoned Kellie in the mine – and yet here it was again: panic, building up inside him like an electrical charge. It made him want to shout, to scream. He felt as if his head would burst.

He kept seeing Kellie's face, etched with fear and anger and disbelief at what they'd done. He'd hardly been able to believe it himself. Up until then, up until the moment the padlock had clicked shut, it had all been such a rush, like a dare. Taylor had just said it and they'd gone ahead and done it. Other than Taylor getting the padlock from her granddad's garage, they hadn't even needed to plan. It had been a game, just like any other that he and Taylor and Simon had played. Only it had been better than make believe, because Kellie *had* done wrong. She'd hurt Taylor and, therefore, Michael as well. Kellie had had it coming.

But Michael now realised something else. What they'd

343

done to Kellie as pay-back was worse, *so* much worse than what she'd done, and every fresh second that passed by was making it even worse still.

'Any luck?' Taylor asked him, as they met back on the landing.

'No.'

David appeared at the bottom of the stairs. 'Is Simon there?' he called up.

'No,' Taylor said.

Stephanie almost ran into David. Her skin was livid, like a bruise. 'Well, don't just stand there, keep looking,' she shouted up.

Michael and Taylor stepped back from her line of sight.

They heard Ben now, talking in the hall.

'I'm going to go back to the village,' he said, 'and see if Kellie's turned up there.'

'Please, Ben.' It was old Mr Thorne. 'Give it another five minutes. Just to see if the storm eases.'

'There's only my room left,' Taylor told Michael. 'The little shit must be hiding up there.'

She turned and ran up the stairs into the attic. Michael chased after her. She threw the door open and called out Simon's name. There was no answer. Taylor got down on her hands and knees and opened one of the deep recessed cupboards which ran the length of the room and led into the eaves.

'Come on, Simon,' she called into the dusty dark space, 'we know you're in here somewhere . . .'

'This has all gone too far,' Michael said. He wanted to have never woken up this morning. 'We need to own up.'

'Are you fucking insane?' Taylor said. 'Have you any idea what they'll do to us? Have you any idea of what it'll do to my mother when she finds out why? Don't you dare go turning chicken shit on me now,' she told him.

'But you heard what Ben was saying. He *knows*

344

something's not right. We're going to get caught.' And they were. Michael knew it in his bones.

'No, we're not. Not if we stick to our plan. Not if we leave her there till the storm dies down and then go and let her out. Ben's an idiot,' Taylor said. 'He thinks Kellie likes him, which makes him as much of a sucker as my dad. He won't work out what's happened. No one will. Come on, Simon!' she shouted, pulling open another cupboard door.

Michael flung the bedroom window open. Icy wind raced in, blowing ash off the beer cans on the windowsill and sending one toppling, clanking on to the floor. The sky was black and angry. Like the ocean after dark, it seemed to heave with a limitless force. It looked like something alive.

'Look,' he told her. 'Look how fucking cold it is out there.'

'So what?'

'So what do you fucking think? Kellie will freeze. We need to let her out. She'll get frostbite or hypothermia, or whatever it's fucking called.'

'She hasn't been there long enough.'

'Yeah?' Anger flared up inside him. 'You know that for sure, do you? You're a doctor now, right? And what about that huge fucking hole in the tunnel? Where Simon nearly fell off the ledge ... What if Kellie goes in? What if she falls down it and fucking dies?'

'It's pitch black in there and she hasn't got a torch. She'll stay exactly where she is. She'll wait for us to come back.'

'You don't know that. You –'

'I do,' she told him. 'You're the one who hasn't got a fucking clue.'

Michael wanted to scream. She always had an answer. She always had an answer, no matter what. She turned her back on him and opened another cupboard door and peered inside.

345

'You're starting to really piss me off now, Simon . . .' she called.

'Let me finish it,' Michael begged her. 'Now. Let me go back and get Kellie. She won't say anything. Just like you said when we locked her in. She won't say anything because she can't. You don't even have to come. Give me the key to the padlock and I'll go and get her and take her back to the village.'

'You'd never make it through the storm. Even if I wanted you to go, you'd have to wait for it to end.'

She moved along to the final cupboard and looked inside.

'You wanted to scare her, right?' Michael said. 'Well, you've done it. Do you really think she'll ever go near your dad again? Not a fucking chance. You've got what you wanted, now let her go.'

Taylor glared at him over her shoulder. 'I didn't just want to scare her. I wanted to punish her.'

'What's that meant to mean?'

Taylor got to her feet and rubbed the dust from her jeans. 'It means I'll say when it's time to let her out,' she said.

'But what if we're wrong?' This was it. This was what had been really freaking him out. What if even the idea which had driven them to do what they did had been wrong, right from the start? 'What if she *was* telling the truth? What if she's not seeing your dad, not any more?'

What, in other words, was the point in trying to teach Kellie a lesson that she'd already learnt?

Taylor didn't care. 'That doesn't make any fucking difference,' she said. 'She did it. That's what matters. Don't you fucking see? Everything. *Everything* is because of her. My mum and dad were never drifting apart. That's not why they sent me away. My dad was never working late at the office. He was fucking her. That's what he was

346

doing. He was fucking Kellie all the time. He packed me off because of her, and now he wants to get rid of my mum as well.'

Taylor marched up to Michael. 'We need to stick together,' she whispered. 'You and me, Michael.' She pressed her lips to his. 'So long as we stick together, then everything's going to work out.'

He pushed her away.

'I don't want any more to do with this,' he said.

She laughed at him, actually *laughed*, and he remembered her downstairs, there in the TV room, after they'd got back from locking Kellie inside the mine. They'd sat in silence, watching *Finding Nemo*. Just acting like nothing had happened, just letting the seconds tick by into minutes, the minutes towards hours, giving Kellie plenty of time to think about what she'd done.

Taylor had laughed, actually *laughed* at the jokes in the film, as if she hadn't given a shit about Kellie. The laughter had been mechanical, switched on, then off. How could she have done that? That's what Michael wanted to know, and how could she still be doing it now? How could she be laughing at him, like *he* was the one who'd got himself all confused? How could she be laughing at him when this was the most serious moment of his life?

'It's too late for that,' she told him. 'You were there. With me. Even worse, you actually *led* her there. If it wasn't for you, she wouldn't be missing in the first place. You're in this up to your neck, exactly the same as me, and exactly the same as Simon too.'

He stared at her in horror, into her eyes, trying to find the same girl he'd grown up with, the same girl who'd kissed him for the first time yesterday, the same girl he'd fallen so hard for that it had felt like dropping off a cliff. But he couldn't find her. She was no longer there.

In that moment, everything he'd ever felt for her died.

347

'Yeah,' he said, 'well, that's the fucking problem, isn't it? Were not *all* here, are we?'

Taylor turned and kicked the final cupboard door shut. 'No,' she conceded, 'the little shit must be somewhere else . . .'

Then it hit him.

'Oh, my God,' he said.

'What?'

'That's where he is. He's gone there. To the mine. He's gone to let her out.'

'Don't be ridiculous. Look at what it's like out there. He's only a little kid. He wouldn't dare. He knows he's not allowed out.'

But Michael's mind was already reeling backwards. To the mine. To the cave they'd found the day before. What was it Simon had said? About his brother Paul? About how all he'd wanted to do was save him . . . about how all he'd wanted to do was save his life and make it all better . . .

He hadn't been able to do that for Paul, but what if he'd decided to do it for Kellie instead?

'The key,' Michael said. 'The key to the padlock. Where is it?'

'If you think I'm going to tell you –' But then he saw it in her eyes, too, that flicker of doubt, that flash of fear. She was frightened he was right.

'Just tell me,' he shouted, 'or I'll go down there and tell them everything. I swear to God I will. Now where –'

'In my coat pocket. In my coat, hanging by the front door . . .'

Michael pushed past her and ran for the door. She called something after him, but he didn't hear what it was and he no longer cared. He thundered down the first flight of stairs, nearly knocking Isabelle over, before racing down the next flight and on into the hall. He rifled through the coats on the stand by the door until he found Taylor's. He turned out the pockets and, instantly, he knew that he'd been right.

Taylor caught up with him.

'It's gone,' he said. 'Now what about the torches? Where were they?'

'In that bag,' she said, pointing at the Peter Jones bag by his feet.

He picked it up. It was empty.

'I'm going,' he said.

'No.' She grabbed him by the shoulders. 'You can't.'

'Get your fucking hands off me!' he shouted, shoving her away from him, as hard as he could. She fell back on to the floor, just as Isabelle rounded the corner.

'What's going on?' she demanded.

'I'm leaving,' Michael said.

'Not in this you're not.' Isabelle lunged for him 'Not until you tell me –'

'Let go of me,' Michael tried to shake himself free. 'Now.'

But she wouldn't let go. 'Don't you dare speak to me like that,' she snapped, 'and how dare you push my daughter, you little thug?'

Elliot came running down the corridor towards them now.

'What the hell is going on?'

Taylor was back up on her feet. 'Let him go,' she told her mother.

'No, not until –'

'Let him go!' Taylor screamed.

More footsteps rushed towards them. The shouting was acting like smoke drawing people to a fire. Suddenly, everyone was there, jamming up the hallway like a school corridor after the last bell had been rung. Faces flooded Michael's vision. Elliot and Isabelle, Ben and David, and now Stephanie and old Mr Thorne. It was Stephanie's voice that finally rose above the rest. She pushed Isabelle aside and stared into Michael's eyes.

'You know where he is, don't you? You know where Simon is.'

No sooner did Michael open his mouth, than Taylor screamed: 'Shut up! Shut up, you fucking traitor!' Spittle flew from her mouth and landed on his cheek.

Stephanie rounded on her. '*You* shut up.'

'Taylor?' Elliot asked.

'Fuck off! I hate you,' she told him, starting to sob. 'I hate you, you fucking shit.'

As Isabelle wrapped her arms around her daughter, Elliot turned to Michael with a look of sudden fear, but it was Stephanie whose desperate, hungry eyes Michael was staring into now.

'Tell me,' she begged. 'Tell me where he is.'

Chapter 31

'He's gone to the mine,' Michael said.

Stephanie gripped him by the shoulders. He looked straight at her. He was terrified.

'What have you done?'

'Simon's gone to the mine,' he repeated.

'How do you know?'

'Because the padlock's gone, and the torches.'

Stephanie couldn't believe what she was hearing. 'But he can't have gone out in this? Why would he do that? Why would he go there? Are you *sure*?'

'He wants to make everything better,' Michael said. He was starting to cry.

'Better?'

'He wants to save a life. Because of Paul.'

David was suddenly by Stephanie's side. She recoiled from Michael, covering her mouth with her hands. She felt David's hand on her shoulder.

'Michael,' he said, 'what's going on?'

Taylor shrieked something behind them.

'Shut up!' Stephanie shouted at her. 'Let him speak.'

'Michael. What have you done?' David demanded.

'We locked Kellie in the mine.'

'*You did what?*' Ben said.

'We only meant to frighten her, and then the storm started.'

'You stupid little shit,' Elliot said suddenly, lurching towards Michael. 'This is all your fault –'

'But why?' Ben asked, cutting Elliot off, holding out his arm to stop him advancing any further.

Taylor turned and ran, pushing through her family. Her footsteps echoed down the hall and thundered up the stairs. Michael looked wretchedly at the floor. 'Because Elliot and Kellie have been having an affair,' he said. 'We saw them together. We heard them making plans.'

Suddenly Elliot was lunging towards Michael again, but Isabelle got in the way just in time and slapped him so hard that he staggered backwards.

'How could you?' she shouted.

Elliot held his cheek. He looked horrified. 'Darling. I never meant this to happen. The kids have got it all wrong. Kellie and I are over. It's you I love.'

'I don't believe you,' Isabelle screamed, storming past him. 'I *knew* it was her!'

Elliot stumbled after her, shouting.

Stephanie was no longer listening. A red roar had risen inside her ears. She didn't give a fuck about her brother or his sordid affair.

David must have been thinking the same, because he already had their coats in his hands. Without speaking, she took hers from him and quickly pulled it on. Ben silently followed suit as Elliot and Isabelle continued to shout behind them.

'You're coming with us,' David told Michael. 'To show us where.'

Michael said nothing, but reached for his coat.

'What torches have you got, Gerald?' David asked. 'And rope. Get them now.'

Outside it was freezing. The snow was easing off, but the wind was still strong.

'This way,' Michael said. They leant forward into the wind and marched in single file, first Michael, then Ben, then David, then Stephanie, up the driveway to the road.

352

Had Simon come this way too? How long ago? How could he have made it by himself?

They followed the road for a hundred yards, then stopped for a moment as Michael and Ben shouted with David over the shrieking of the wind. David took the lead and in that very instant, in that tiny movement of his, from third place to first, Stephanie remembered his strength.

He would get her there. He would get her to their son.

David led them eastwards, upwards, over the brow of Solace Hill. It was the short cut to the cliffs overlooking Hell Bay, and to the mine. Her feet grew heavy with snow. Her muscles hurt, but she wouldn't stop. She'd never stop.

When Ben had grilled Michael outside the door, Michael had told them it shouldn't take more than twenty minutes. Twenty minutes? In this? How the hell was her little boy meant to have managed that?

But he *would* have managed it. Stephanie willed it to be so. He would have made it through the snow. Just as they now *would* find him. Hope. She held it inside her like a flame. She would protect it from the wind no matter what. She would not allow it to die.

But still Michael's words resonated in her head. *He wants to save a life. Because of Paul.*

As she stumbled in the snow, the horrible truth hit her. This was her fault. It wasn't David's fault. It wasn't Simon's fault. It was *all* her fault, because Simon must have felt the weight of her blaming everyone else fall on his shoulders.

How could she let her little boy feel that he needed to be a hero? He couldn't bring back Paul. Nobody could. She saw that now. All this time she'd been so wrapped up in the past, but now she was suddenly terrified about the future. Because if anything happened to her family . . .

353

Oh God. What had she done?

She felt sick with fear. Her son had gone to save Kellie, because Taylor had left Kellie in the mine alone. Stephanie couldn't believe what Taylor had done or why. Kellie and Elliot. It all seemed impossibly ridiculous. All the lies. Affairs. Revenge. Anger. None of it meant a thing when compared to life. Her little boy's precious, precious life.

Stephanie stumbled on in the dark. It seemed like a nightmare, as if she were in space, the snowflakes zooming towards her like meteors. She thought about her father's paintings of Hell Bay. She tried to imagine where she was going. She tried to push the thoughts of sink holes out of her mind.

Could Simon really have made this journey on his own? she asked herself again. And if she was this scared, how must he be feeling?

They came to a halt.

'How far now?' David shouted back.

'It's just up ahead,' Michael said, and took the lead again.

Stephanie walked over to David and slid her hand into his. He squeezed it. They would face this together. Whatever was ahead.

'We're here,' Michael shouted, a few moments later, pushing branches aside.

David looked at her and they both raced up to him.

'Simon,' she shouted. 'Simon?' But her voice got lost on the wind.

Then they were by some metal gates. What was this place? How the hell had the kids ever found it? She thought they'd just been playing outside. How had they discovered this? It was terrifying.

'Oh my God, where are they?' Stephanie asked, as Ben pulled at the gate and it swung open.

David and Ben ran through, shouting out for Simon and

354

Kellie, sweeping the tunnel entrance with the flashlight. The wind howled all around.

Stephanie started to panic.

'He should be here,' Michael said. 'They both should be.'

'Keep calm,' Ben told him. 'It'll be OK.'

Then Stephanie heard a weak voice, coming from the darkness. 'Mummy?'

'David! He's here,' she shouted, as she ran towards the sound of the voice.

Then she was on her knees, scooping Simon up from where he was huddled in the dark. He was so small and fragile. He felt tiny in her arms.

She sobbed as she held him. He was crying, clinging on to her. He was shivering violently.

'You're safe, you're safe,' she said, kissing his face and his hair. 'We're here now.'

Then David was running towards them both and they hugged Simon between them.

'My darling, darling boy,' Stephanie said, pulling back to stroke Simon's face.

'Kellie's not here, and I was too frightened to go any further. We shouldn't have left her. I told Taylor –'

'Shh,' Stephanie said, trying to soothe his fright away. 'We're here now. Everything is going to be OK.'

'But Kellie? What if something's happened to her?' Simon sobbed.

Stephanie squeezed him tight. David stroked the back of his head.

'It's thanks to you that we're here at all,' David said. 'You've been very brave.' He looked over Simon's head into Stephanie's eyes, and she felt something hard shift inside her.

'I'm going on,' Ben said, hurrying into the tunnel.

'Don't forget what I told you about the hole. You have

355

to go along the ledge. Do you want me to come?' Michael called after him.

'Stay where you are,' Ben shouted back.

'Are we in trouble?' Simon asked, after Ben had gone.

'No, darling, no,' Stephanie said, holding him to her.

'I'm so sorry,' Simon cried. 'I'm so sorry about everything. I wanted to save Kellie. I wanted to make everything better –'

'Shh,' David said.

'Oh Simon, it's all my fault,' Stephanie said. 'All that matters is that you're safe. All that matters is this.'

Then she held him tight and reached her arm out to David and held him tight too. She never wanted to let them go. David's eyes seemed bright with tears as they locked with hers, and Stephanie realised what she hadn't considered possible for so long: that she loved him. That it was David who was her rock, and nobody else. That she didn't want to lose him. That she *couldn't* lose him. That if he'd only let her back in, then she'd do whatever it took to make them all happy.

'Are we going home together?' Simon asked. 'All of us?'

He looked up between Stephanie and David. They were still staring at each other.

'Can we?' she asked.

Chapter 32

Kellie was all out of courage. It was as if she was in a computer game where, at each level, everything became more of a nightmare.

She'd never imagined that going through the tunnel would involve such a gruelling journey. Retrospectively, it was almost more terrifying than it had been at the time. When she'd hung on, on the ledge, looking down into that black, black hole, behind her, knowing that one false move and she'd be dead, she'd forced her feet to move inch by inch. Forced herself not to be paralysed with fear. She'd kept repeating in her head, over and over again that she *would* find a way out. She'd forced herself to believe that the tunnel had to have an end.

And it did.

And here it was.

Except that it wasn't an exit. It was a cruel joke. She was in the mouth of the cave, high up in the cliffs, that she'd seen with Ben when they'd pulled the boat ashore only two days ago. And it was hundreds of feet up. And there was no way down.

The snow had stopped and a waning moon had broken through the clouds, illuminating the cave and the water far below. It looked black and terrifying, the swell making waves crash over the rocks. Had Ben made it back in the boat? Was he safe?

As she leant over the edge, Kellie could pick out the fisherman's hut where she'd been with Ben. The boat was gone.

If she hadn't spent an hour trying to break open the padlock, then she could have got here in time to see Ben leaving with Jack. Then maybe they'd have seen her, and maybe she'd be out of here by now.

Instead she was trapped.

She hurried back, out of the wind, and sank down against the wall of the cave. On the wall opposite her torch picked out SIMON AND TAYLOR AND MIKEL 4 EVER. Whichever one of them had written it couldn't even spell Michael's name. She'd been fooled by a bunch of stupid kids. She put out the torch.

But now she realised, if they'd got in here, they'd also got back out. The moon disappeared behind the clouds again and she switched on the torch once more. It flickered for a moment and then went out. Her fingers trembled so violently that the torch fell and clattered away over the floor of the cave. And to think that only a few hours ago she'd thought she'd been safe, away from the tangle of the Thornes, about to leave the island for good.

Instead, she was trapped here, in a place that must be as close to hell as she could possibly imagine. Was she being punished by some malevolent God for her heathen ways? Was this all because she didn't believe in Christmas? Or was this happening to her because of Elliot bloody Thorne? Deceitful, arrogant, faithless, lying cheating bastard that he was.

She ripped the necklace Elliot had given her from around her neck and hurled it out into the night. She didn't hear it land, and she didn't care. She never wanted to so much as set eyes on Elliot ever again. She couldn't be responsible for what she might do to him. Then, as an afterthought, she pulled out her purse and felt for the photo of Elliot she kept there. She remembered Ben casting his photo of Marie to the wind and she did the same now, but instead of flying way, she saw photo flutter to her feet. Growling with anger and frustration, she stamped her heel on it repeatedly until it disintegrated.

Kellie reached forward and retrieved the torch. Feeling in the dark, she opened it up and licked the end of the batteries, then put them back inside. Wasn't that supposed to elongate their lives? She wished now she'd paid more attention to watching survival programmes on the television. She felt ridiculously under-equipped with knowledge for the predicament she was in. It was no good. The torch was definitely dead.

She pulled the hood of her coat right over her head and crouched in the darkness out of the wind. She didn't know what else to do. She couldn't go back through the mine again. She couldn't go back to the yawning hole in the ground that had nearly swallowed her. If she tried to negotiate the ledge in the dark, without a torch, she would almost certainly die.

So, she would have to wait until morning, and hope that enough light would filter into the tunnel to allow her to get back to the entrance.

But what if she got so cold in the night she died? What if she fell asleep and didn't wake up?

The darkness seemed to crowd in all around her. She shut her eyes, but the fear wouldn't go away. If no one found her, then she'd die without experiencing true lasting love, without seeing half the places in the world she wanted to, without being brave and taking the future into her own hands, without having any faith, without having her own children, without growing old . . .

She forced herself to concentrate on relaxing, because if she carried on shivering so violently, it would exhaust her even more. She had to think about something good. Something positive.

Ben.

She rested her forehead on her knees. In her ears, the forgotten iPod suddenly burst into life with what must be a hidden track on an album. It was a sad acoustic guitar number that she'd never heard before.

Suddenly, a movie was playing in her head and she saw herself photographing the seals with Ben; she saw their snowball fight, and her singing karaoke in the pub; she saw his silly banner and the Christmas lunch he'd made for her. And in every shot she was smiling.

Then she saw them this afternoon in bed, and she remembered how she'd felt, how *he'd* made her feel – he'd made her feel as if she was being absolutely herself. He'd made her feel as if he'd wanted all of her. And she'd wanted to give all of herself in return. Everything. Her thoughts, her feelings, her hopes, her future. All the things she'd never given Elliot.

She put her face in her hands and accepted the truth.

She'd blown it.

She let herself go, her tears turning into pitiful, heart-wrenching sobs.

Then suddenly she became aware of something grabbing her.

She screamed. Terrified.

There was light.

Then the earplugs fell out of her ears.

There, as if he was an angel, was Ben crouching down in front of her, holding her arms. The flashlight was on the floor beside him.

'Oh Jesus, you're OK. I thought you'd gone further into the mine. I thought you were dead.'

He was real. He wasn't a dream. She cried out with relief and shock, leaning into his arms.

'Are you OK? Are you hurt?' he asked.

She nodded her head, then shook her head, hardly able to speak. 'How did you find me?'

'Simon came to rescue you. Didn't you hear him calling out for you?'

Simon. She thought back to the way he'd begged Taylor to let Kellie go.

'He came *here*?' she asked. 'Is he OK?'

'He's fine. He's with his mum and dad.'

'How did you find me? I don't understand. I thought nobody was going to find me, ever. I thought . . .'

She shuddered, too upset and relieved all at once to speak.

'Michael confessed all,' Ben said.

Kellie took a deep breath. It had happened then. One of them had cracked.

'He told you why they locked me in?'

'Yes.'

'All of it?'

'Yes.'

'Oh. Oh God.' She covered her face with her hands. 'Oh Ben. I'm so sorry. I'm so ashamed.'

'Yes, well . . . I guess it was just as well you weren't there. Elliot's wife had a few choice words to say on the subject . . .'

'You must hate me. For lying to you. I wanted to explain. I wanted to tell you.'

Ben didn't say anything. He helped her to her feet. Her legs shook.

'Come on. Let's get you out of here,' he said.

But she didn't want to go. Not yet. Not until she'd had a chance to explain. This was too important.

'No Ben, listen, you've got to listen. I've got to explain. You see, when I met you, I started to realise that I'd made a terrible mistake with Elliot, and I told him today that it was over for ever, but the kids, they got it all wrong. Because they didn't hear me telling him it was over. But it is. This afternoon . . . I . . .'

She looked at him, her eyes still brimming with tears. She couldn't bear it that she'd lost him. But if she had blown it, as she knew she had, then she had nothing to lose. She had to try and make him understand.

'The thing is, I know I've only known you for a little while, but today I thought I was going to die, and all I could think about was you and how you make me feel,' she paused. 'And I know I've totallyutterlyfucked it up between us, but –' .

Ben stopped her, putting his finger gently on her lips. 'Shhh,' he said. 'I think totallyutterlyfucked up would be going a little far.'

She stopped. Staring at his face. Could he really mean that? Could he really have forgiven her?

'What?' she asked.

'I was thinking about it on the way here, too. You haven't lied to me. You just didn't tell me the truth. And yes, that's something you need to work on. I had no idea you were hiding something so big. God, you're good at subterfuge. You must be one hell of a lawyer.'

'No, I'm not. Look at where it's got me. The whole thing. Oh Ben,' she sniffed and wiped her face on the cuff of her coat. 'I'm so, so sorry.'

'Hey, you know what? I think you might have been punished enough.'

He pushed her hair out of her face and smiled at her. She felt her heart leap.

'So I haven't totallyutterlyfucked up then? Or utterlytotally? I can't remember which it is.'

'On this occasion, I'd say, only partially.'

She flung her arms around his neck. 'Oh Ben, oh Ben, thank you,' she cried.

She lifted her face and kissed him, and then he held her tight and kissed her back. She felt as if he was kissing her soul, warming her right from within, and she knew that she would never let him down again.

Finally, he took her hands from his neck and warmed them in his.

'You know, all I wish is that we'd just stayed in that hut,' she said.

'I don't. I wouldn't have got to see you naked,' he teased.

'You don't regret that now, do you?'

'Hell, no.'

'Good. Because I don't. Not at all. It's the best thing that's happened to me. Apart from you being here right now.'

She kissed him again.

'So what's going to happen now?' he asked.

'I want to get out of here and then get as far away as possible.'

'Where?'

'I want to go home. To Australia. And then . . . then to everywhere else.'

He laughed. 'Sounds good to me.'

'You mean you'll come with me?'

'You don't think I'd rescue the girl, only to miss out on flying off into the sunset, do you? Isn't that how all good movies end?'

'Believe me. This is much, much better than a movie.'

'Hello?'

They both turned at the sound. It was David.

'Thank God. Is everything OK?' he asked, stepping out of the dark into the mouth of the cave. He was shining a bright flashlight at them.

'Oh yes. I found her at last,' said Ben.

'Yes you did,' Kellie said.

363

A New Day

Chapter 33

Michael stared down through his bedroom window. The sea ice had melted. The icicles had dropped from the gutters, and only patches of snow now remained on the land, translucent against the tarmac, grubby with mud on the flowerbeds. The sky was clear and blue, and sunlight twinkled on the choppy brown harbour waves.

His room was as hot as a beach in summertime. The heating had been on full blast since the morning before, when Roddy, with the help of an engineer from St John's, had finally managed to fix the generator which supplied the pub's power.

The final seconds of 'New Born', by Muse thumped out from the speakers behind him, before 'Yesterday' by the Beatles began. The room was transformed into a cradle of comfort and it now seemed impossible to imagine the night before last, when Michael had led Ben and the others to the mine's escape tunnel. He already found himself unable to grasp the series of events as a whole. He could only face up to it as fragments, as flashes.

Flash: he remembered the walk to the mine through the snow, with Ben, David and Stephanie, never slackening, never letting up. Flash, flash: over the hill top; through the ghost village; on past the engine house and down the hill. And then Simon: a bundle of brightness, slumped up against the wall of the tunnel entrance like jumble outside a charity-shop door. Then another flash: going deeper into the mine. The death of the wind. The echoes of Ben's voice, calling out Kellie's name. Torch beams plunging down into the pitch-black nothingness of the gaping crack in the tunnel floor . . . Then later . . . Kellie . . . back here at the pub. Ben telling Roddy and his mother the news.

What had been distilled from the whole night was this: Simon was alive. Simon was alive. Simon had lived. Simon and Kellie and all of them had lived.

Even now, butterflies stretched their wings in Michael's stomach at these thoughts. His heart clenched around them, as if holding on to hope. Simon and Kellie had lived. Neither of them had even been injured. All yesterday, all today, Michael had kept catching himself thinking of how it could so easily not have turned out right. Simon could have fallen on his way to the mine, or he could have gone further in and been devoured by the mine itself. He could have plunged down into its gullet, never to be seen again. Kellie could have gone the same way, and Ben as well, when he'd gone in to bring her back.

And then what? Where would Michael's own life have been then? Over. Truly. Over and out. Because he'd been a coward. Because he hadn't stood up to Taylor. Because he'd helped her to do the things that she'd done.

But the fact remained – thank God! – that *no one* had died. They'd lived. And, ultimately, that *had* been thanks to him. He'd led Ben and the others to the mine in time. He'd made amends for his earlier weakness and cowardice. He had, hadn't he? He'd made up for helping Taylor to lure Kellie into the mine. And he'd made up for being too scared of losing Taylor to stand up to her. And he'd made up for not being brave like Simon, who'd gone out into the storm on his own to set things right. Michael couldn't change these things, and would have to live with them, but at least he'd wiped clean a slate that would otherwise have been covered in blood. At least he'd finally done the right thing, by confessing to Stephanie before it had become too late.

He'd made amends for Kellie, but a different guilt

368

altogether haunted him still, because he knew that Taylor had been right as well, when she'd called him a traitor. She'd asked him to choose, between her and them. And he hadn't chosen her.

Michael's mother and Roddy blamed Taylor. Roddy said Taylor was crazy. He said she needed help. Taylor blamed Kellie. Isabelle blamed Elliot. Elliot blamed Michael.

They'd reacted like a pack of circling dogs, each one of them snapping after the other's tail. No one had wanted the responsibility for what had happened. Each had accused the other instead.

Stephanie and David, however, had kept their silence. There'd been no accusations from them, no recriminations, and no threats. In the moment they'd got their son back, it had been as if he'd never been gone.

Of all of them, Michael supposed, it was Ben and Kellie who should have wanted justice the most – Ben as a victim of deceit, Kellie as one of revenge – but they'd chosen not to press charges. No one had been hurt, Kellie had told Ben, and Michael's mum. She'd not wanted the police involved. She'd wanted this part of her life left here. And Ben had agreed, because Ben was now part of the new life she'd started to build.

Michael had watched their faces as they'd emerged from the mine. He'd seen their fingers intertwined. Kellie was leaving all this behind her for the simple reason that she *could* leave all of this behind her, because she had somewhere else to go, and someone else to go there with.

Michael and Taylor had been wrong about Kellie as much as they'd been right. They'd been right to suspect her of conducting an affair with Elliot Thorne, but wrong to think she hadn't finished it. She had and, in the same breath, she'd started another. They'd been right to think

369

she'd fallen in love with someone on the island, but they'd got the wrong man.

Kellie and Ben had re-emerged from the depths of the mine together. Stephanie had checked Kellie over, but had waved away her attempts at apology. In turn, Ben and Kellie had declined Stephanie's invitation to return to the Thorne house. The snow, by then, had stopped falling. Kellie and Ben had elected to return to the village with Michael instead. Michael had known even then that none of them would ever set foot in the Thorne house again.

He had tried making his own apology to Kellie, not then, but later, outside the Windcheater, before they'd gone in to confront his parents. He hadn't done it for forgiveness. He hadn't even done it to ease the anger which he'd known would soon rise up inside the pub like a typhoon. He'd done it because he'd known that what he'd done had been wrong.

'We all do stupid things,' was all Kellie had told him, 'but the only truly stupid thing is not to try and put them right.'

He hoped he had. He hoped he'd continue to do the same. He'd set out with Taylor to teach Kellie a lesson, but he'd ended up learning one himself. He'd watched Ben and Kellie leave in Ben's boat yesterday. Kellie had turned and waved at him. He thought he'd seen her smile.

He opened the window now and looked out. He could see them there, the remains of the Thorne family, grouped together by the harbour slipway, waiting for the boat to arrive to pick them up. Old Mr Thorne was leaning against his green Land-Rover. Stephanie and David and Simon and Nat were standing at the top of the cobbled slipway, facing the sea.

Simon looked so suddenly young, standing beside his father. David lifted him high into the air, as if he was made of polystyrene. Simon's laughter reached up to Michael

370

like the cry of a gull as David spun him round. Then Stephanie picked up Nat and took a step towards her husband. The gap between them shortened, then vanished. They leant into each other, with their children in their arms.

The only people missing from this outdoor family portrait were Elliot, Isabelle and Taylor. Two silhouettes were hunched in the back of the Land-Rover: Taylor and Isabelle, Michael guessed. Elliot had gone back to the mainland the day before. He'd travelled on the rival boat-taxi service to the one owned by Ben's dad, and he'd travelled alone.

Another high-pitched shout rose from Simon, and Michael looked out to sea. There was an approaching red RIB, bouncing across the waves. Michael took his binoculars . . . a fat guy with greying hair, who Michael didn't recognise, was at the wheel. He panned the binoculars back round to the harbour, in time to see David and Simon unpacking bags from the Land-Rover, while Isabelle stepped out.

Michael thought of Isabelle and the baby inside her. Once more, he pictured her naked, up in her room, as she'd studied herself in front of the mirror. He saw now what he hadn't seen then, that she already knew that she was pregnant, that she was observing herself with the knowledge that she was about to change. Had she been crying because of the child? Or because she'd already suspected she was losing Elliot – because she'd been frightened the child, rather than calling him back to her, might drive him further, and faster, away?

Then Michael forgot about Isabelle. He only had eyes for Taylor. He zoomed the binoculars in on her as she emerged from the car and walked to the slipway. He wondered if she'd turn, and if the sunlight might flash on the binoculars and give him away. But she didn't turn back to look at where she knew he must be.

371

She was still beautiful. He could see that, as she stood side-on to him now, but she was no longer *his* Taylor, the perfect girl with whom he'd hoped to end up one day. The whine of the RIB's engine rose as it nosed in through the harbour entrance.

Michael knew he should stay where he was. He'd been forbidden to go near the Thornes by his mother – not that he would have, even if he could, not in a million years. But at the same time, he felt the urge to get closer. Something was happening. He could feel it in his blood. It was the same feeling he'd had the day his father had left, the same feeling he'd had the day Roddy had moved in, and the same feeling that had hijacked him when he'd walked out of his primary school gates for the last time. It was the feeling of the present becoming the past, right in front of his eyes.

He hurried downstairs and out through the back door. He stopped at the front of the house, near where he and Taylor had hidden on Christmas morning, drinking their stolen alcopops and cigarettes. He stepped back under the branches of the holly tree, so that he couldn't be seen.

Everything would have been so different if they'd smoked their cigarettes somewhere else, and had never seen Elliot and Kellie walk into that shed. Everything, that was, apart from now, because Taylor would still have been leaving today, and Michael would still have been left. The world would have kept on turning. He suddenly saw that. No matter what they'd done, the two of them would still have been torn apart.

He had never got round to telling Taylor about his mum and Roddy putting the pub up for sale, about how he'd soon be leaving the island himself. And now he never would, because he knew that once he was gone, he'd never come back. Now he'd lost her, there was nothing else for him to come back to.

He stayed there, as the branches of holly swayed around him in the wind, trailing their spiked leaves across his ears and clothes and through his hair, like the fingernails of tiny hands. He remained motionless until the boat carrying the Thornes left the harbour and set out across the open sea.

Only then did he break cover, and run, skidding and sliding, past the cobbled slipway, past old Mr Thorne's Land-Rover, careless now whether he was seen or not. He rushed on past the boatsheds and clambered up on to the harbour wall, clawing and scrambling, startling a cormorant and sending it shrieking and wheeling into the air.

He stood and watched the boat begin to speed across the waves. His whole body tensed, as if he was an athlete, loading up energy, preparing to run, preparing to leap into the air and join them.

He wiped away the single tear which ran down his cheek. He wouldn't cry for Taylor. There'd be other girls. It might not feel like it now, but there would. He thought of Kellie and Ben – but mostly he thought of Kellie, how she'd come to this island to see one man, only to leave with another, how she'd stumbled out of a mine one night, only to disappear over the horizon the following day.

'People can fall in love more than once,' Michael's dad had once told him, as part of his own apology, on the day that he'd left.

Michael had despised him for his selfishness at the time, but he now hoped his dad had been right. He hoped his dad was still in love and he hoped his mum was, too – even if they were both now in love with different people. Hope, that's all he had, but maybe that's all there was – hope that things would work out for the best.

That kiss, the *real* kiss, the one that Taylor had given him inside the mine, under the shimmering lights of their own private sky, *that* was what Michael would remember her for. He still hoped that kiss really had come from her heart. Not like the other kiss, hot with anger, embittered by the poison of vengeance, outside the door of the Thorne house, after he and Taylor had spied on Elliot and Kellie up in the woods.

Michael would keep that first kiss with him instead, because everything else that had happened, and that he'd *wanted* to happen between himself and Taylor, all their flirting, all their banter, all his hopes of her and him being and staying together, in love and in bed – he no longer knew how much of that had been real, and how much he'd exaggerated to fit with his fantasies. She'd become dream-like to him already, just like the events of the three days of Christmas.

The further the boat motored out to sea, the smaller it became, and the less real. It soon looked like a plasticine model, set upon a plasticine sea. Michael felt like a giant in comparison, as if he could reach out and pluck the boat and everyone in it from the ocean between his forefinger and thumb. As he stood there, face to the wind, he felt the island shrink around him, like something he'd outgrown. With one step, he thought, he could set foot on St John's. With another, he'd reach the mainland. He'd overtake the boat and its passengers. He'd leave behind the places he'd grown up. He'd set out on his own. The world was a big place. He could see that now. He was going to fit into it just fine.